The Lovels of Arden

M. E. Braddon

THE

LOVELS OF ARDEN

BY THE AUTHOR OF

"LADY AUDLEY'S SECRET, " "AURORA FLOYD, " "VIXEN, "
"ISHMAEL, " ETC., ETC., ETC.

MISS BRADDON'S NOVELS

INCLUDING

"LADY AUDLEY'S SECRET, " "VIXEN, " "ISHMAEL, " ETC.

"No one can be dull who has a novel by Miss Braddon in hand. The most tiresome journey is beguiled, and the most wearisome illness is brightened, by any one of her books. "

"Miss Braddon is the Queen of the circulating libraries. " —
The World.

CONTENTS

CHAP.

CHAPTER I.

COMING HOME.

The lamps of the Great Northern Terminus at King's Cross had not long been lighted, when a cab deposited a young lady and her luggage at the departure platform. It was an October twilight, cold and gray, and the place had a cheerless and dismal aspect to that solitary young traveller, to whom English life and an English atmosphere were somewhat strange.

She had been seven years abroad, in a school near Paris; rather an expensive seminary, where the number of pupils was limited, the masters and mistresses, learned in divers modern accomplishments, numerous, and the dietary of foreign slops and messes without stint.

Dull and gray as the English sky seemed to her, and dreary as was the aspect of London in October, this girl was glad to return to her native land. She had felt herself very lonely in the French school, forgotten and deserted by her own kindred, a creature to be pitied; and hers was a nature to which pity was a torture. Other girls had gone home to England for their holidays; but vacation after vacation went by, and every occasion brought Clarissa Lovel the same coldly worded letter from her father, telling her that it was not convenient for him to receive her at home, that he had heard with pleasure of her progress, and that experienced people with whom he had conferred, had agreed with him that any interruption to the regular course of her studies could not fail to be a disadvantage to her in the future.

"They are all going home except me, papa, " she wrote piteously on one occasion, "and I feel as if I were different from them, somehow. Do let me come home to Arden for this one year. I don't think my schoolfellows believe me when I talk of home, and the gardens, and the dear old park. I have seen it in their faces, and you cannot think how hard it is to bear. And I want to see you, papa. You must not fancy that, because I speak of these things, I am not anxious for that. I do want to see you very much. By-and-by, when I am grown up, I shall seem a stranger to you. "

To this letter, and to many such, letters, Mr. Lovel's reply was always the same. It did not suit his convenience that his only daughter should return to England until her education was completed. Perhaps it would have suited him better could she have remained away altogether; but he did not say as much as that; he only let her see very clearly that there was no pleasure for him in the prospect of her return.

And yet she was glad to go back. At the worst it was going home. She told herself again and again, in those meditations upon her future life which were not so happy as a girl's reveries should be, — she told herself that her father must come to love her in time. She was ready to love him so much on her part; to be so devoted, faithful, and obedient, to bear so much from him if need were, only to be rewarded with his affection in the end.

So at eighteen years of age Clarissa Lovel's education was finished, and she came home alone from a quiet little suburban village just outside Paris, and having arrived to-night at the Great Northern Station, King's Cross, had still a long journey before her.

Mr. Lovel lived near a small town called Holborough, in the depths of Yorkshire; a dreary little town enough, but boasting several estates of considerable importance in its neighbourhood. In days gone by, the Lovels had been people of high standing in this northern region, and Clarissa had yet to learn how far that standing was diminished.

She had been seated about five minutes in a comfortable corner of a first-class carriage, with a thick shawl over her knees, and all her little girlish trifles of books and travelling, bags gathered about her, and she had begun to flatter herself with the pleasing fancy that she was to have the compartment to herself for the first stage of the journey, perhaps for the whole of the journey, when a porter flung open the door with a bustling air, and a gentleman came in, with more travelling-rugs, canes, and umbrellas, russia leather bags, and despatch boxes, than Clarissa had ever before beheld a traveller encumbered with. He came into the carriage very quietly, however, in spite of these impedimenta, arranged his belongings in a methodical manner, and without the slightest inconvenience to Miss Lovel, and then seated himself next the door, upon the farther side of the carriage.

Clarissa looked at him rather anxiously, wondering whether they two were to be solitary companions throughout the whole of that long night journey. She had no prudish horror of such a position, only a natural girlish shyness in the presence of a stranger.

The traveller was a man of about thirty, tall, broad-shouldered, with long arms, and powerful-looking hands, ungloved, and bronzed a little by sun and wind. There was the same healthy bronze upon his face, Clarissa perceived, when he took off his hat, and hung it up above him; rather a handsome face, with a long straight nose, dark blue eyes with thick brown eyebrows, a well cut mouth and chin, and a thick thatch of crisp dark brown hair waving round a broad, intelligent-looking forehead. The firm, full upper lip was half-hidden by a carefully trained moustache; and in his dress and bearing the stranger had altogether a military air: one could fancy him a cavalry soldier. That bare muscular hand seemed made to grasp the massive hilt of a sabre.

His expression was grave—grave and a little proud, Clarissa thought; and, unused as she was to lonely wanderings in this outer world, she felt somehow that this man was a gentleman, and that she need be troubled by no fear that he would make is presence in any way unpleasant to her, let their journey together last as long as it would.

She sank back into her corner with a feeling of relief. It would have been more agreeable for her to have had the carriage to herself; but if she must needs have a companion, there was nothing obnoxious in this one.

For about an hour they sped on in silence. This evening train was not exactly an express, but it was a tolerably quick train, and the stoppages were not frequent. The dull gray twilight melted into a fair tranquil night. The moon rose early; and the quiet English landscape seemed very fair to Clarissa Lovel in that serene light. She watched the shadowy fields flitting past; here and there a still pool, or a glimpse of running water; beyond, the sombre darkness of wooded hills; and above that dark background a calm starry sky. Who shall say what dim poetic thoughts were in her mind that night, as she looked at these things? Life was so new to her, the future such an unknown country—a paradise perhaps, or a drear gloomy waste, across which she must travel with bare bleeding feet. How should she know? She only knew that she was going home to a father who had never loved her, who had deferred the day of her coming as long as it was possible for him decently to do so.

The traveller in the opposite corner of the carriage glanced at Miss Lovel now and then as she looked out of the window. He could just contrive to see her profile, dimly lighted by the flickering oil lamp; a very perfect profile, he thought; a forehead that was neither too high nor too low, a small aquiline nose, a short upper lip, and the prettiest mouth and chin in the world. It was just a shade too pensive now, the poor little mouth, he thought pityingly; and be wondered what it was like when it smiled. And then he began to arrange his lines for winning the smile he wanted so much to see from those thoughtful lips. It was, of course, for the gratification of the idlest, most vagabond curiosity that he was eager to settle this question: but then on such a long dreary journey, a man may be forgiven for a good deal of idle curiosity.

He wondered who his companion was, and how she came to be travelling alone, so young, so pretty, so much in need of an escort. There was nothing in her costume to hint at poverty, nor does poverty usually travel in first-class carriages. She might have her maid lurking somewhere in the second-class, he said to himself. In any case, she was a lady. He had no shadow of doubt about that.

She was tall, above the ordinary height of women. There was a grace in the long flowing lines of her figure more striking than the beauty of her face. The long slim throat, the sloping shoulder, not to be disguised even by the clumsy folds of a thick shawl—these the traveller noted, in a lazy contemplative mood, as he lolled in his corner, meditating an easy opening for a conversation with his fair fellow-voyager.

He let some little time slip by in this way, being a man to whom haste was almost unknown. This idle artistic consideration of Miss Level's beauty was a quiet kind of enjoyment for him. She, for her part, seemed absorbed in watching the landscape—a very commonplace English landscape in the gentleman's eyes—and was in no way disturbed by his placid admiration.

He had a heap of newspapers and magazines thrown pell-mell into the empty seat next him; and arousing himself with a faint show of effort presently, he began to turn these over with a careless hand.

The noise of his movements startled Clarissa; she looked across at him, and their eyes met. This was just what he wanted. He had been curious to see her eyes. They were hazel, and very beautiful, completing the charm of her face.

"May I offer you some of these things? " he said. "I have a reading lamp in one of my bags, which I will light for you in a moment. I won't pledge myself for your finding the magazines very amusing, but anything is better than the blankness of a long dreary journey. "

"Thank you, you are very kind; but I don't care about reading to-night; I could not give you so much trouble. "

"Pray don't consider that. It is not a question of a moments trouble. I'll light the lamp, and then you can do as you like about the magazines. "

He stood up, unlocked one of his travelling-bags, the interior of which glittered like a miniature arsenal, and took out a lamp, which he lighted in a rapid dexterous manner, though without the faintest appearance of haste, and fixed with a brass apparatus of screws and bolts to the arm of Clarissa's seat. Then he brought her a pile of magazines, which she received in her lap, not a little embarrassed by this unexpected attention. He had called her suddenly from strange vague dreams of the future, and it was not easy to come altogether back to the trivial commonplace present.

She thanked him graciously for his politeness, but she had not smiled yet.

"Never mind, " the traveller said to himself; "that will come in good time. "

He had the easiest way of taking all things in life, this gentleman; and having established Clarissa with her lamp and books, sank lazily back into his corner, and gave himself up to a continued contemplation of the fair young face, almost as calmly as if it had been some masterpiece of the painter's art in a picture gallery.

The magazines were amusing to Miss Lovel. They beguiled her away from those shapeless visions of days to come. She began to read, at first with very little thought of the page before her, but, becoming interested by degrees, read on until her companion grew tired of the silence.

He looked at his watch—the prettiest little toy in gold and enamel, with elaborate monogram and coat of arms—a watch that looked like a woman's gift. They had been nearly three hours on their journey.

"I do not mean to let you read any longer, " he said, changing his seat to one opposite Clarissa. "That lamp is very well for an hour or so, but after that time the effect upon one's eyesight is the reverse of beneficial. I hope your book is not very interesting. "

"If you will allow me to finish this story, " Clarissa pleaded, scarcely lifting her eyes from the page. It was not particularly polite, perhaps, but it gave the stranger an admirable opportunity for remarking the dark thick lashes, tinged with the faintest gleam of gold, and the perfect curve of the full white eyelids.

"Upon my soul, she is the loveliest creature I ever saw, " he said to himself; and then asked persistently, "Is the story a long one? "

"Only about half-dozen pages more; O, do please let me finish it! "

"You want to know what becomes of some one, or whom the heroine marries, of course. Well, to that extent I will be a party to the possible injury of your sight. "

He still sat opposite to her, watching her in the old lazy way, while she read the last few pages of the magazine story. When she came to the end, a fact of which he seemed immediately aware, he rose and extinguished the little reading lamp, with an air of friendly tyranny.

"Merciless, you see, " he said, laughing. "O, *la jeunesse,* what a delicious thing it is! Here have I been tossing and tumbling those unfortunate books about for a couple of hours at a stretch, without being able to fix my attention upon a single page; and here are you so profoundly absorbed in some trivial story, that I daresay you have scarcely been conscious of the outer world for the last two hours. O, youth and freshness, what pleasant things they are while we can keep them! "

"We were not allowed to read fiction at Madame Marot's, " Miss Lovel answered simply. "Anything in the way of an English story is a treat when one has had nothing to read but Racine and Télémaque for about six years of one's life. "

"The Inimical Brothers, and Iphigenia; Athalie, as performed before Louis Quatorze, by the young ladies of St. Cyr, and so on. Well, I confess there are circumstances under which even Racine might become a bore; and Télémaque has long been a synonym for dreariness and dejection of mind. You have not seen Rachel? No, I suppose not. She was a great creature, and conjured the dry bones into living breathing flesh. And Madame Marot's establishment, where you were so hardly treated, is a school, I conclude? "

"Yes, it is a school at Belforêt, near Paris. I have been there a long time, and am going home now to keep house for papa. "

"Indeed! And is your journey a long one? Are we to be travelling companions for some time to come? "

"I am going rather a long way—to Holborough. "

"I am very glad to hear that, for I am going farther myself, to the outer edge of Yorkshire, where I believe I am to do wonderful execution upon the birds. A fellow I know has taken a shooting-box yonder, and writes me most flourishing accounts of the sport. I know Holborough a little, by the way. Does your father live in the town? "

"O, no; papa could never endure to live in a small country town. Our house is a couple of miles away—Arden Court; perhaps you know it? "

"Yes, I have been to Arden Court, " the traveller answered, with rather a puzzled air. "And your papa lives at Arden? —I did not know he had any other daughter, " he added in a lower key, to himself rather than to his companion. "Then I suppose I have the pleasure of speaking to Miss—"

"My name is Lovel My father is Marmaduke Level, of Arden Court. "

The traveller looked at her with a still more puzzled air, as if singularly embarrassed by this simple announcement. He recovered himself quickly, however, with a slight effort.

"I am proud and happy to have made your acquaintance, Miss Lovel, " he said; "your father's family is one of the best and oldest in the North Riding. "

After this, they talked of many things; of Clarissa's girlish experiences at Belforêt; of the traveller's wanderings, which seemed to have extended all over the world.

He had been a good deal in India, in the Artillery, and was likely to return thither before long.

"I had rather an alarming touch of sunstroke a year ago, " he said, "and was altogether such a shattered broken-up creature when I came home on sick leave, that my mother tried her hardest to induce me to leave the service; but though I would do almost anything in the world to please her, I could not bring myself to do that; a man without a profession is such a lost wretch. It is rather hard upon her, poor soul; for my elder brother died not very long ago, and she has only my vagabond self left. 'He was the only son of his mother, and she was a widow. '"

"I have no mother, " Clarissa said mournfully; "mine died when I was quite a little thing. I always envy people who can speak of a mother. "

"But, on the other hand, I am fatherless, you see, " the gentleman said, smiling. But Clarissa's face did not reflect his smile.

"Ah, that is a different thing, " she said softly.

They went on talking for a long while, talking about the widest range of subjects; and their flight across the moonlit country, which grew darker by-and-by, as that tender light waned, seemed swifter than. Clarissa could have imagined possible, had the train been the most desperate thing in the way of an express. She had no vulgar commonplace shyness, mere school-girl as she was, and she had, above all, a most delightful unconsciousness of her own beauty; so she was quickly at home with the stranger, listening to him, and talking to him with a perfect ease, which seemed to him a natural attribute of high breeding.

"A Lovel, " he said to himself once, in a brief interval of silence; "and so she comes of that unlucky race. It is scarcely strange that she should be beautiful and gifted. I wonder what my mother would say if she knew that my northern journey had brought me for half-a-dozen hours *tête-à-tête* with a Lovel? There would be actual terror for her in the notion of such an accident. What a noble look this girl has! —an air that only comes after generations of blue blood untainted by vulgar admixture. The last of such a race is a kind of crystallisation, dangerously, fatally brilliant, the concentration of all the forces that have gone before. "

At one of their halting-places, Miss Lovel's companion insisted upon bringing her a cup of coffee and a sponge-cake, and waited upon her with a most brotherly attention. At Normanton they changed to a branch line, and had to wait an hour and a half in that coldest dreariest period of the night that comes before daybreak. Here the stranger established Clarissa in a shabby little waiting-room, where he made up the fire with his own hands, and poked it into a blaze with his walking-stick; having done which, he went out into the bleak night and paced the platform briskly for nearly an hour, smoking a couple of those cigars which would have beguiled his night journey, had he been alone.

He had some thoughts of a third cigar, but put it back into his case, and returned to the waiting-room.

"I'll go and have a little more talk with the prettiest woman I ever met in my life, " he said to himself. "It is not very likely that we two shall ever see each other again. Let me carry away the memory of her face, at any rate. And she is a Lovel! Will she be as unfortunate as the rest of her race, I wonder? God forbid! "

Clarissa was sitting by the fire in the dingy little waiting-room, with one elbow resting on the arm of her chair, her chin leaning on her hand, and her eyes fixed thoughtfully upon a dull red chasm in the coals. She had taken off her gray felt hat, and she looked older without it, the traveller thought, in spite of her wealth of waving dark brown hair, gathered into a great coil of plaits at the back of the graceful head. Perhaps it was that thoughtful expression which made her look older than she had seemed to him in the railway carriage, the gentleman argued with himself; a very grave anxious expression for a girl's face. She had indeed altogether the aspect of a woman, rather than of a girl who had just escaped from boarding-school, and to whom the cares of life must needs be unknown.

She was thinking so deeply, that she did not hear the opening of the door, or her fellow-traveller's light footstep as he crossed the room. He was standing on the opposite side of the fireplace, looking down at her, before she was aware of his presence. Then she raised her head with a start; and he saw her blush for the first time. "You must have been absorbed in some profound meditation, Miss Lovel, " he said lightly.

"I was thinking of the future. "

"Meaning your own future. Why, at your age the future ought to be a most radiant vision. "

"Indeed it is not that. It is all clouds and darkness. I do not see that one must needs be happy because one is young. There has been very little happiness in my life yet awhile, only the dreary monotonous routine of boarding-school. "

"But all that is over now, and life is just beginning for you. I wish I were eighteen instead of eight-and-twenty. "

"Would you live your life over again? "

The traveller laughed.

"That's putting a home question, " he said. "Well, perhaps not exactly the same life, though it has not been a bad one. But I should like the feeling of perfect youth, the sense of having one's full inheritance of life lying at one's banker's, as it were, and being able to draw upon the account a little recklessly, indifferent as to the waste of a year or two. You see I have come to a period of existence in which a man has to calculate his resources. If I do not find happiness within the next five years, I am never likely to find it at all. At three-and-thirty a man has done with a heart, in a moral and poetic sense, and begins to entertain vague alarms on the subject of fatty degeneration. "

Clarissa smiled faintly, as if the stranger's idle talk scarcely beguiled her from her own thoughts.

"You said you had been at Arden, " she began rather abruptly; "then you must know papa. "

"No, I have not the honour to know Mr. Lovel, " with the same embarrassed air which he had exhibited before in speaking of Arden Court. "But I am acquainted—or I was acquainted, rather, for he and I have not met for some time—with one member of your family, a Mr. Austin Lovel. "

"My brother, " Clarissa said quickly, and with a sudden shadow upon her face.

"Your brother; yes, I supposed as much. "

"Poor Austin! It is very sad. Papa and he are ill friends. There was some desperate quarrel between them a few years ago; I do not even know what about; and Austin was turned out of doors, never to come back any more. Papa told me nothing about it, though it was the common talk at Holborough. It was only from a letter of my aunt's that I learnt what had happened; and I am never to speak of Austin when I go home, my aunt told me. "

"Very hard lines, " said the stranger, with a sympathetic air. "He was wild, I suppose, in the usual way. Your brother was in a line regiment when I knew him; but I think I heard afterwards that he had sold out, and had dropped away from his old set, had emigrated, I believe, or something of that kind exactly the thing I should do, if I found myself in difficulties; turn backwoodsman, and wed some savage woman, who should rear my dusky race, and whose kindred could put me in the way to make my fortune by cattle-dealing; having done which, I should, of course, discover that fifty years of Europe are worth more than a cycle of Cathay, and should turn my steps homeward with a convenient obliviousness upon the subject of the savage woman. "

He spoke lightly, trying to win Clarissa from her sad thoughts, and with the common masculine idea, that a little superficial liveliness of this kind can lighten the load of a great sorrow.

"Come, Miss Lovel, I would give the world to see you smile. Do you know that I have been watching for a smile ever since I first saw your face, and have not surprised one yet? Be sure your brother is taking life pleasantly enough in some quarter of the globe. We worthless young fellows always contrive to fall upon our feet. "

"If I could believe that he was happy, if I could think that he was leading an honourable life anywhere, I should not feel our separation so much, " the girl said mournfully; "but to be quite ignorant of his fate, and not to be allowed to mention his name, that is hard to bear. I cannot tell you how fond I was of him when we were children. He was seven years older than I, and so clever. He wanted to be a painter, but papa would not hear of that. Yet I think he might have been happier if he had been allowed to have his own way. He had a real genius for art. "

"And you too are fond of art, I suppose? " hazarded the traveller, more interested in the young lady herself than in this reprobate brother of hers.

"Yes, I am very fond of it. It is the only thing I really care for. Of course, I like music to a certain extent; but I love painting with my whole heart. "

"Happy art, to be loved by so fair a votary! And you dabble with brushes and colours, of course? "

"A little. "

"A true young lady's answer. If you were a Raffaelle in glacé silk and crinoline, you would tell me no more than that. I can only hope that some happy accident will one day give me an opportunity of judging for myself. And now, I think, you had better put on your hat. Our train will be in almost immediately. "

She obeyed him; and they went out together to the windy platform, where the train rumbled in presently. They took their places in a carriage, the gentleman bundling in his rugs and travelling-bags and despatch boxes with very little ceremony; but this time they were not alone. A plethoric gentleman, of the commercial persuasion, was sleeping laboriously in one corner.

The journey to Holborough lasted a little less than an hour. Miss Lovel and her companion did not talk much during that time. She was tired and thoughtful, and he respected her silence. As she drew nearer home, the happiness she had felt in her return seemed to melt away somehow, leaving vague anxieties and morbid forebodings in its stead. To go home to a father who would only be bored by her coming. It was not a lively prospect for a girl of eighteen.

The dull cold gray dawn was on the housetops of Holborough, as the train stopped at the little station. The traveller alighted, and assisted Clarissa's descent to the platform.

"Can I see about your luggage, Miss Lovel? " he asked; but looking up at that moment, the girl caught sight of a burly gentleman in a white neckcloth, who was staring in every direction but the right one.

"Thank you very much, no; I need not trouble you. My uncle Oliver is here to meet me—that stout gentleman over there. "

"Then I can only say good-bye. That tiresome engine is snorting with a fiendish impatience to bear me away. Good-bye, Miss Lovel, and a thousand thanks for the companionship that has made this journey so pleasant to me. "

He lifted his hat and went back to the carriage, as the stout gentleman approached Clarissa. He would fain have shaken hands with her, but refrained from that unjustifiable familiarity. And so, in the bleak early autumnal dawn, they parted.

* * * * *

CHAPTER II.

BEGINNING THE WORLD.

"Who on earth was that man you were talking to, Clary? " asked the Reverend Mathew Oliver, when he had seen his niece's luggage carried off to a fly, and was conducting her to that vehicle. "Is it any one you know? "

"O, no, uncle; only a gentleman who travelled in the same carriage with me from London. He was very kind. "

"You seemed unaccountably familiar with him, " said Mr. Oliver with an aggrieved air; "you ought to be more reserved, my dear, at your age. A young lady travelling alone cannot be too careful. Indeed, it was very wrong of your father to allow you to make this long journey alone. Your aunt has been quite distressed about it. "

Clarissa sighed faintly; but was not deeply concerned by the idea of her aunt's distress. Distress of mind, on account of some outrage of propriety on the part of her relatives, was indeed almost the normal condition of that lady.

"I travelled very comfortably, I assure you, uncle Oliver, " Clarissa replied. "No one was in the least rude or unpleasant. And I am so glad to come home—I can scarcely tell you how glad—though, as I came nearer and nearer, I began to have all kinds of fanciful anxieties. I hope that all is well—that papa is quite himself. "

"O, yes, my dear; your papa is—himself, " answered the parson, in a tone that implied that he did not say very much for Mr. Lovel in admitting that fact. "Your papa is well enough in health, or as well as he will ever acknowledge himself to be. Of course, a man who neither hunts nor shoots, and seldom gets out of bed before ten o'clock in the day, can't expect to be remarkably robust. But your father will live to a good old age, child, rely upon it, in spite of everything. "

"Am I going straight home, uncle? "

"Well, yes. Your aunt wished you to breakfast at the Rectory; but there are your trunks, you see, and altogether I think it's better for you to go home at once. You can come and see us as often as you like. "

"Thank you, uncle. It was very kind of you to meet me at the station. Yes, I think it will be best for me to go straight home. I'm a little knocked up with the journey. I haven't slept five minutes since I left Madame Marot's at daybreak yesterday. "

"You're looking rather pale; but you look remarkably well in spite of that—remarkably well. These six years have changed you from a child into a woman. I hope they gave you a good education yonder; a solid practical education, that will stand by you. "

"I think so, uncle. We were almost always at our studies. It was very hard work. "

"So much the better. Life is meant to be hard work. You may have occasion to make use of your education some day, Clary. "

"Yes, " the girl answered with a sigh; "I know that we are poor. "

"I suppose so; but perhaps you hardly know how poor. "

"Whenever the time comes, I shall be quite ready to work for papa, " said Clarissa; yet she could not help wondering how the master of Arden Court could ever bring himself to send out his daughter as a governess; and then she had a vague childish recollection that not tens of pounds, but hundreds, and even thousands, had been wanted to stop the gaps in her father's exchequer.

They drove through Holborough High Street, where there was the faint stir and bustle of early morning, windows opening, a housemaid kneeling on a doorstep here and there, an occasional tradesman taking down his shutters. They drove past the fringe of prim little villas on the outskirts of the town, and away along a country road towards Arden; and once more Clarissa saw the things that she had dreamed of so often in her narrow white bed in the bleak dormitory at Belforêt. Every hedge-row and clump of trees from which the withered leaves were drifting in the autumn wind, every white-walled cottage with moss-grown thatch and rustic garden, woke a faint rapture in her breast. It was home. She remembered her old friends the cottagers, and wondered whether goody Mason were still alive, and whether Widow Green's fair-haired children would remember her. She had taught them at the Sunday-school; but they too must have grown from childhood to womanhood, like herself, and were out at service, most likely, leaving Mrs. Green's cottage lonely.

She thought of these simple things, poor child, having so little else to think about, on this, her coming home. She was not so foolish as to expect any warm welcome from her father. If he had brought himself just to tolerate her coming, she had sufficient reason to be grateful. It was only a drive of two miles from Holborough to Arden. They stopped at a lodge-gate presently; a little gothic lodge, which was gay with scarlet geraniums and chrysanthemums, and made splendid by railings of bronzed ironwork. Everything had a bright new look which surprised Miss Lovel, who was not accustomed to see such, perfect order or such fresh paint about her father's domain.

"How nice everything looks! " she said.

"Yes, " answered her uncle, with a sigh; "the place is kept well enough nowadays. "

A woman came out to open the gates—a brisk young person, who was a stranger to Clarissa, not the feeble old lodge-keeper she remembered in her childhood. The change, slight as it was, gave her a strange chill feeling.

"I wonder how many people that I knew are dead? " she thought.

They drove into the park, and here too, even in this autumn season, Clarissa perceived traces of care and order that were strange to her. The carriage road was newly gravelled, the chaos of underwood among the old trees had disappeared, the broad sweeps of grass were smooth and level as a lawn, and there were men at work in the early morning, planting rare specimens of the fir tribe in a new enclosure, which filled a space that had been bared twenty years before by Mr. Lovel's depredations upon the timber.

All this bewildered Clarissa; but she was still more puzzled, when, instead of approaching the Court the fly turned sharply into a road leading across a thickly wooded portion of the park, through which there was a public right of way leading to the village of Arden.

"The man is going wrong, uncle! " she exclaimed.

"No, no, my dear; the man is right enough. "

"But indeed, uncle Oliver, he is driving to the village. "

"And he has been told to drive to the village. "

"Not to the Court? "

"To the Court! Why, of course not. What should we have to do at the Court at half-past seven in the morning? "

"But I am going straight home to papa, am I not? "

"Certainly. "

And then, after staring at his niece's bewildered countenance for a few moments, Mr. Oliver exclaimed, — —

"Why, surely, Clary, your father told you — —"

"Told me what, uncle? "

"That he had sold Arden. "

"Sold Arden! O, uncle, uncle! "

She burst into tears. Of all things upon this earth she had loved the grand old mansion where her childhood had been spent. She had so little else to love, poor lonely child, that it was scarcely strange she should attach herself to lifeless things. How fondly she had remembered the old place in all those dreary years of exile, dreaming of it as we dream of some lost friend. And it was gone from her for ever! Her father had bartered away that most precious birthright.

"O, how could he do it! how could he do it! " she cried piteously.

"Why, my dear Clary, you can't suppose it was a matter of choice with him. 'Needs must when'—I daresay you know the vulgar proverb. Necessity has no law. Come, come, my dear, don't cry; your father won't like to see you with red eyes. It was very wrong of him not to tell you about the sale of Arden—excessively wrong. But that's just like Marmaduke Lovel; always ready to shirk anything unpleasant, even to the writing of a disagreeable letter. "

17

"Poor dear papa! I don't wonder he found it hard to write about such a thing; but it would have been better for me to have known. It is such a bitter disappointment to come home and find the dear old place gone from us. Has it been sold very long? "

"About two years. A rich manufacturer bought it—something in the cloth way, I believe. He has retired from business, however, and is said to be overwhelmingly rich. He has spent a great deal of money upon the Court already, and means to spend more I hear. "

"Has he spoiled it—modernised it, or anything of that kind? "

"No; I am glad to say that he—or his architect perhaps—has had the good taste to preserve the mediaeval character of the place. He has restored the stonework, renewing all the delicate external tracery where it was lost or decayed, and has treated the interior in the same manner. I have dined with Mr. Granger once or twice since the work was finished, and I must say the place is now one of the finest in Yorkshire—perhaps the finest, in its peculiar way. I doubt if there is so perfect a specimen of gothic domestic architecture in the county. "

"And it is gone from us for ever! " said Clarissa, with a profound sigh.

"Well, my dear Clary, it is a blow, certainly; I don't deny that. But there is a bright side to everything; and really your father could not afford to live in the place. It was going to decay in the most disgraceful manner. He is better out of it; upon my word he is. "

Clarissa could not see this. To lose Arden Court seemed to her unmitigated woe. She would rather have lived the dreariest, loneliest life in one corner of the grand old house, than have occupied a modern palace. It was as if all the pleasant memories of her childhood had been swept away from her with the loss of her early home. This was indeed beginning the world; and a blank dismal world it appeared to Clarissa Lovel, on this melancholy October morning.

They stopped presently before a low wooden gate, and looking out of the window of the fly, Miss Lovel saw a cottage which she remembered as a dreary uninhabited place, always to let; a cottage with a weedy garden, and a luxuriant growth of monthly roses and honeysuckle covering it from basement to roof; not a bad sort of place for a person of small means and pretensions, but O, what a descent from the ancient splendour of Arden Court! —that Arden which had belonged to the Lovels ever since the land on which it stood was given to Sir Warren Wyndham Lovel, knight, by his gracious master King Edward IV., in acknowledgment of that warrior's services in the great struggle between Lancaster and York.

There were old-fashioned casement windows on the upper story, and queer little dormers in the roof. Below, roomy bows had been added at a much later date than the building of the cottage. The principal doorway was sheltered by a rustic porch, spacious and picturesque, with a bench on each side of the entrance. The garden was tolerably large, and in decent order, and beyond the garden was a fine old orchard, divided from lawn and flower-beds only by a low hedge, full of bush-roses and sweet brier. It was a very pretty place in summer, not unpicturesque even at this bleak season; but Clarissa was thinking of lost Arden, and she looked at Mill Cottage with mournful unadmiring eyes. There had been a mill attached to the place once. The old building was there still, indeed, converted into a primitive kind of stable; hence its name of Mill Cottage. The stream still ran noisily a little way behind the house, and made the boundary which divided the orchard from the lands of the lord of Arden. Mill Cottage was on the very edge of Arden Court. Clarissa wondered that her father could have pitched his tent on the borders of his lost heritage.

"I think I would have gone to the other end of the world, had I been in his place, " she said to herself.

An elderly woman-servant came out, in answer to the flyman's summons; and at her call, a rough-looking young man emerged from the wooden gate opening into a rustic-looking stable-yard, where the lower half of the old mill stood, half-hidden by ivy and other greenery, and where there were dovecotes and a dog-kennel.

Mr. Oliver superintended the removal of his niece's trunks, and then stepped back into the fly.

"There's not the slightest use in my stopping to see your father, Clary, " he said; "he won't show for a couple of hours at least. Good-bye, my dear; make yourself as comfortable as you can. And come and see your aunt as soon as you've recovered from your long journey, and keep up your spirits, my dear. —Martha, be sure you give Miss Lovel a good breakfast. —Drive back to the Rectory, coachman. —Good-bye, Clarissa; " and feeling that he had shown his niece every kindness that the occasion required, Mr. Oliver bowled merrily homewards. He was a gentleman who took life easily—a pastor of the broad church—tolerably generous and good to his poor; not given to abnormal services or daily morning prayer; content to do duty at Holborough parish church twice on a Sunday, and twice more in the week; hunting a little every season, in a black coat, for the benefit of his health, as he told his parishioners; and shooting a good deal; fond of a good horse, a good cellar, a good dinner, and well-filled conservatories and glass-houses; altogether a gentleman for whom life was a pleasant journey through a prosperous country. He had, some twenty years before, married Frances Lovel; a very handsome woman—just a little faded at the time of her marriage—without fortune. There were no children at Holborough Rectory, and everything about the house and gardens bore that aspect of perfect order only possible to a domain in which there are none of those juvenile destroyers.

"Poor girl, " Mr. Oliver muttered to himself, as he jogged comfortably homewards, wondering whether his people would have the good sense to cook 'those grouse' for breakfast. "Poor Clary, it was very hard upon her; and just Like Marmaduke not to tell her. "

* * * * *

CHAPTER III.

FATHER AND DAUGHTER.

While Mr. Oliver went back to the Rectory, cheered by the prospect of possible grouse, Clarissa entered her new home, so utterly strange to her in its insignificance. The servant, Martha, who was a stranger to her, but who had a comfortable friendly face, she thought, led her into a room at the back of the cottage, with a broad window opening on to a lawn, beyond which Clarissa saw the blue mill-stream. It was not a bad room at all: countrified-looking and old-fashioned, with a low ceiling and wainscoted walls. Miss Level recognised the ponderous old furniture from the breakfast-room at Arden—high-backed mahogany chairs of the early Georgian era, with broad cushioned seats covered with faded needlework; a curious old oval dining-table, capable of accommodating about six; and some slim Chippendale coffee-tables and cheffoniers, upon which there were a few chipped treasures of old Battersea and Bow china. The walls were half-lined with her father's books—rare old books in handsome bindings. His easy-chair, a most luxurious one, stood in a sheltered corner of the hearth, with a crimson silk banner-screen hanging from the mantelpiece beside it, and a tiny table close at hand, on which there were a noble silver-mounted meerschaum, and a curious old china jar for tobacco. The oval table was neatly laid for breakfast, and a handsome brown setter lay basking in the light of the fire. Altogether, the apartment had a very comfortable and home-like look.

"The tea's made, miss, " said the servant; "and I've a savoury omelette ready to set upon the table. Perhaps you'd Like to step upstairs and take off your things before you have your breakfast? Your papa begged you wouldn't wait for him. He won't be down for two hours to come. "

"He's quite well, I hope? "

"As well as he ever is, miss. He's a bit of an invalid at the best of times. "

Remembering what Mr. Oliver had said, Clarissa was not much disturbed by this intelligence. She was stooping to caress the brown setter, who had been sniffing at her dress, and seemed anxious to inaugurate a friendship with her.

"This is a favourite of papa's, I suppose? " she said.

"O Lord, yes, miss. Our master do make a tremenjous fust about Ponto. I think he's fonder of that dumb beast than any human creature. Eliza shall show you your room, miss, while I bring in the teapot and such-like. There's only me and Eliza, who is but a bit of a girl; and John Thomas, the groom, that brought your boxes in just now. It's a change for your pa from the Court, and all the servants he had there; but he do bear it like a true Christian, if ever there was one. "

Clarissa Lovel might have wondered a little to hear this— Christianity not being the dominant note in her father's character; but it was only like her father to refrain from complaint in the hearing of such a person as honest Martha. A rosy-faced girl of about fifteen conducted Miss Lovel to a pleasant bedroom, with three small windows; one curiously placed in an angle of the room, and from which—above a sweep of golden-tinted woodland—Clarissa could see the gothic chimneys of Arden Court. She stood at this window for nearly ten minutes, gazing out across those autumnal woods, and wondering how her father had nerved himself for the sacrifice.

She turned away from the little casement at last with a heavy sigh, and began to take off her things. She bathed her face and head in cold water, brushed out her long dark hair, and changed her thick merino travelling-dress for a fresher costume. While she was doing these things, her thoughts went back to her companion of last night's journey; and, with a sudden flush of shame, she remembered his embarrassed look when she had spoken of her father as the owner of Arden Court. He had been to Arden, he had told her, yet had not seen her father. She had not been particularly surprised by this, supposing that he had gone to the Court as an ordinary sight-seer. Her father had never opened the place to the public, but he had seldom refused any tourist's request to explore it.

But now she understood that curious puzzled look of the stranger's, and felt bitterly ashamed of her error. Had he thought her some barefaced impostor, she wondered? She was disturbed in these reflections by the trim rosy-cheeked house-maid, who came to tell her that breakfast had been on the table nearly a quarter of an hour.

But in the comfortable parlour downstairs, all the time she was trying to do some poor justice to Martha's omelette, her thoughts dwelt persistently upon the unknown of the railway-carriage, and upon the unlucky mistake which she had made as to her father's position.

"He could never guess the truth, " she said to herself. "He could never imagine that I was going home, and yet did not know that my birthplace had been sold. "

He was so complete a stranger to her—she did not even know his name—so it could surely matter very little whether he thought well or ill of her. And yet she could not refrain from torturing herself with all manner of annoying suppositions as to what he might think. Miss Lovel's character was by no means faultless, and pride was one of the strongest ingredients in it. A generous and somewhat lofty nature, perhaps, but unschooled and unchastened as yet.

After a very feeble attempt at breakfast, Clarissa went out into the garden, closely attended by Ponto, who seemed to have taken a wonderful fancy to her. She was very glad to be loved by something on her return home, even a dog. She went out through the broad window, and explored garden and orchard, and wandered up and down by the grassy bank of the stream. She was fain to own that the place was pretty: and she fancied how well she might have loved it, if she had been born here, and had never been familiar with the broad terraces and verdant slopes of Arden Court. She walked in the garden till the village-church clock struck ten, and then went hastily in, half-afraid lest her father should have come down to the parlour in her absence, and should be offended at not finding her ready to receive him.

She need not have feared this. Mr. Lovel was rarely offended by anything that did not cause him physical discomfort.

"How do you do, my dear? " he said, as she came into the room, in very much the same tone he might have employed had they seen each other every day for the last twelve months. "Be sure you never do that again, if you have the faintest regard for me. "

"Do what, papa? "

"Leave that window open when you go out. I found the room a perfect ice-house just now. It was very neglectful of Martha to allow it. You'd better use the door at the end of the passage in future, when you go into the garden. It's only a little more trouble, and I can't stand open windows at this time of year. "

"I will be sure to do so, papa, " Clarissa answered meekly. She went up to her father and kissed him, the warmth and spontaneity of their greeting a little diminished by this reproof about the window; but Clarissa had not expected a very affectionate reception, and was hardly disappointed. She had only a blank hopeless kind of feeling; a settled conviction that there was no love for her here, and that there had never been any.

"My dear father, " she began tenderly, "my uncle told me about the sale of Arden. I was so shocked by the news—so sorry—for your sake. "

"And for your own sake too, I suppose, " her father answered bitterly. "The less this subject is spoken of between us in future, the better we shall get on together, Clarissa. "

"I will keep silence, papa. "

"Be sure you do so, " Mr. Lovel said sternly; and then, with a sudden passion and inconsistency that startled his daughter, he went on: "Yes, I have sold Arden—every acre. Not a rood of the land that has belonged to my race from generation to generation since Edward IV. was king, is left to me. And I have planted myself here—here at the very gates of my lost home—so that I may drain the bitter cup of humiliation to the dregs. The fools who call themselves my friends think, that because I can endure to live here, I am indifferent to all I have lost; that I am an eccentric bookworm—an easy-going philosophical recluse, content to dawdle away the remnant of my days amongst old books. It pleases me to let them think so. Why, there is never a day that yonder trader's carriage, passing my windows, does not seem to drive over my body; not a sound of a woodman's axe or a carpenter's hammer in the place that was mine, that does not go straight home to my heart! "

"O, papa, papa! "

"Hush, girl! I can accept pity from no one—from you least of all. "

"Not from me, papa—your own child? "

"Not from you; because your mother's reckless extravagance was the beginning of my ruin. I might have been a different man but for her. My marriage was fatal, and in the end, as you see, has wrecked me. "

"But even if my mother was to blame, papa—as she may have been—I cannot pretend to deny the truth of what you say, being so completely ignorant of our past history—you cannot be so cruel as to hold *me* guilty? "

"You are too like her, Clarissa, " Mr. Lovel answered, in a strange tone. "But I do not want to speak of these things. It is your fault; you had no right to talk of Arden. *That* subject always raises a devil in me. "

He paced the room backwards and forwards for a few minutes in an agitated way, as if trying to stifle some passion raging inwardly.

He was a man of about fifty, tall and slim, with a distinguished air, and a face that must once have been very handsome, but perhaps, at its best, a little effeminate. The face was careworn now, and the delicate features had a pinched and drawn look, the thin lips a half-cynical, half-peevish expression. It was not a pleasant countenance, in spite of its look of high birth; nor was there any likeness between Marmaduke Lovel and his daughter. His eyes were light blue, large and bright, but with a cold look in them—a coldness which, on very slight provocation, intensified into cruelty; his hair pale auburn, crisp and curling closely round a high but somewhat narrow forehead.

He came back to the breakfast-table presently, and seated himself in his easy-chair. He sipped a cup of coffee, and trifled listlessly with a morsel of dried salmon.

"I have no appetite this morning, " he said at last, pushing his plate away with an impatient gesture; "nor is that kind of talk calculated to improve the flavour of a man's breakfast. How tall you have grown, Clarissa, a perfect woman; remarkably handsome too! Of course you know that, and there is no fear of your being made vain by anything I may say to you. All young women learn their value soon enough. You ought to make a good match, a brilliant match—if there were any chance for a girl in such a hole as this. Marriage is your only hope, remember, Clarissa. Your future lies between that and the drudgery of a governess's life. You have received an expensive education—an education that will serve you in either case; and that is all the fortune I can give you. "

"I hope I may marry well, papa, for your sake; but—"

"Never mind me. You have only yourself to think about. "

"But I never could marry any one I did not esteem, if the match were ever such a brilliant one. "

"Of course not. All schoolgirls talk like that; and in due course discover how very little esteem has to do with matrimony. If you mean that you would like to marry some penniless wretch of a curate, or some insolvent ensign, for love, I can only say that the day of your marriage will witness our final parting. I should not make any outrageous fuss or useless opposition, rely upon it. I should only wish you good-bye. "

Clarissa smiled faintly at this speech. She expected so little from her father, that his hardest words did not wound her very deeply, nor did they extinguish that latent hope, "He will love me some day. "

"I trust I may never be so imprudent as to lose you for ever, like that, papa.. I must shut my heart resolutely against curates. "

"If bad reading is an abomination to you, you have only to open your ears. I have some confidence in you, Clary, " Mr. Lovel went on, with a smile that was almost affectionate. "You look like a sensible girl; a little impulsive, I daresay; but knowledge of the world—which is an uncommonly hard world for you and me—will tone that down in good time. You are accomplished, I hope. Madame Marot wrote me a most flourishing account of your attainments; but one never knows how much to believe of a schoolmistress's analysis. "

"I worked very hard, papa; all the harder because I was so anxious to come home; and I fancied I might shorten my exile a little by being very industrious. "

"Humph! You give yourself a good character. You sing and play, I suppose? "

"Yes, papa. But I am fonder of art than of music. "

"Ah, art is very well as a profession; but amateur art—French plumbox art—is worse than worthless. However, I am glad you can amuse yourself somehow; and I daresay, if you have to turn governess by-and-by, that sort of thing will be useful. You have the usual smattering of languages, of course? "

"Yes, papa. We read German and Italian on alternate days at Madame Marot's. "

"I *promessi Sposi*, and so on, no doubt. There is a noble Tasso in the bookcase yonder, and a fine old Petrarch, with which you may keep up your Italian. You might read a little to me of an evening sometimes. I should not mind it much. "

"And I should like it very much, papa, " Clarissa answered eagerly.

She was anxious for anything that could bring her father and herself together—that might lessen the gulf between them, if by ever so little.

And in this manner Miss Lovel's life began in her new home. No warmth of welcome, no word of fatherly affection, attended this meeting between a father and daughter who had not met for six years. Mr. Lovel went back to his books as calmly as if there had been no ardent impetuous girl of eighteen under his roof, leaving Clarissa to find occupation and amusement as best she might. He was not a profound student; a literary trifler rather, caring for only a limited number of books, and reading those again and again. Burton's *Anatomy of Melancholy*, Southey's *Doctor*. Montaigne, and Swift, he read continually. He was a collector of rare editions of the Classics, and would dawdle over a Greek play, edited by some learned German, for a week at a time, losing himself in the profundity of elaborate foot-notes. He was an ardent admirer of the lighter Roman poets, and believed the Horatian philosophy the only true creed by which a man should shape his existence. But it must not be supposed that books brought repose to the mind and heart of Marmaduke Lovel. He was a disappointed man, a discontented man, a man given to brooding over the failure of his life, inclined to cherish vengeful feelings against his fellow-men on account of that failure. Books to him were very much what they might have been to some fiery-tempered ambitious soldier of fortune buried alive in a prison, without hope of release, —some slight alleviation of his anguish, some occasional respite from his dull perpetual pain; nothing more.

Clarissa's first day at Mill Cottage was a very fair sample of the rest of her life. She found that she must manage to spend existence almost entirely by herself—that she must expect the smallest amount of companionship from her father.

"This is the room in which I generally sit, " her father said to her that first morning after breakfast; "my books are here, you see, and the aspect suits me. The drawing-room will be almost entirely at your disposal. We have occasional callers, of course; I have not been able to make these impervious country people comprehend that I don't want society. They sometimes pester me with invitations to dinner, which no doubt they consider an amazing kindness to a man in my position; invitations which I make a point of declining. It will be different with you, of course; and if any eligible people—Lady Laura Armstrong or Mrs. Renthorpe for instance—should like to take you up, I shall not object to your seeing a little society. You will never find a rich husband at Mill Cottage. "

"Please do not speak of husbands, papa. I don't want to be married, and I shouldn't care to go into society without you. "

"Nonsense, child; you will have to do what is best for your future welfare. Remember that my death will leave you utterly unprovided for—absolutely penniless. "

"I hope you may live till I am almost an old woman, papa. "

"Not much chance of that; and even if I did, I should not care to have you on my hands all that time. A good marriage is the natural prospect of a good-looking young woman, and I shall be much disappointed if you do not marry well, Clarissa. "

The pale cold blue eyes looked at her with so severe a glance, as Mr. Lovel said this, that the girl felt she must expect little mercy from her father if her career in life did not realise his hopes.

"In short, " he continued, "I look to you to redeem our fallen fortunes. I don't want the name of Lovel to die out in poverty and obscurity. I look to you to prevent that, Clarissa. "

"Papa, " said Clarissa, almost trembling as she spoke, "it is not to me you should look for that. What can a girl do to restore a name that has fallen into obscurity? Even if I were to marry a rich man, as you say, it would be only to take another name, and lose my own identity in that of my husband. It is only a son who can redeem his father's name. There is some one else to whom you must look— —"

"What! " cried her father vehemently, "have you not been forbidden to mention that name in my hearing? Unlucky girl, you seem to have been born on purpose to outrage and pain me. "

"Forgive me, papa; it shall be the last time. But O, is there no hope that you will ever pardon— —"

"Pardon, " echoed Mr. Lovel, with a bitter laugh; "it is no question of pardon. I have erased that person's image from my mind. So far as I am concerned, there is no such man in the world. Pardon! You must induce me to reinstate him in my memory again, before you ask me to pardon. "

"And that can never be, papa? "

"Never! "

The tone of that one word annihilated hope in Clarissa's mind. She had pushed the question to its utmost limit, at all hazards of offending her father. What was it that her brother Austin had done to bring upon himself this bitter sentence of condemnation? She remembered him in his early manhood, handsome, accomplished, brilliant; the delight and admiration of every one who knew him, except her father. Recalling those days, she remembered that between her father and Austin there had never been any show of affection. The talents and brilliant attributes that had won admiration from others seemed to have no charm in the father's eye. Clarissa could remember many a sneering speech of Mr. Lovel's, in which he had made light of his son's cleverness, denouncing his varied accomplishments as trivial and effeminate, and asking if any Englishman ever attained an honourable distinction by playing the piano, or modelling in clay.

"I would rather have my son the dullest plodder that ever toiled at the bar, or droned bald platitudes from a pulpit, than the most brilliant drawing-room idler, whose amateur art and amateur music ever made him the fashion of a single season, to leave him forgotten in the next. I utterly despise an accomplished man. "

Austin Lovel had let such speeches as this go by him with a languid indifference, that testified at once to his easy temper and his comfortable disregard of his father's opinion. He was fond of his little sister Clary, in rather a careless way, and would suffer her companionship, juvenile as she was at that time, with perfect good nature, allowing her to spoil his drawing paper with her untutored efforts, and even to explore the sacred mysteries of his colour-box. In return for this indulgence, the girl loved him with intense devotion, and believed in Him as the most brilliant of mankind.

Clarissa Lovel recalled those departed days now with painful tenderness. How kind and gracious Austin had been to her! How happy they had been together! sometimes wandering for a whole day in the park and woods of Arden, he with his sketching apparatus, she with a volume of Sir Walter Scott, to read aloud to him while he sketched, or to read him to sleep with very often. And then what delight it had been to sit by his side while he lay at full length upon the mossy turf, or half-buried in fern—to sit by him supremely happy, reading or drawing, and looking up from her occupation every now and then to glance at the sleeper's handsome face in loving admiration.

Those days had been the happiest of her life. When Austin left Arden, he seemed always to carry away the brightness of her existence with him; for without him her life was very lonely—a singularly joyless life for one so young. Then, in an evil hour, as she thought, there came their final parting. How well she remembered her brother loitering on the broad terrace in front of Arden Court, in the dewy summer morning, waiting to bid her good-bye! How passionately she had clung to him in that farewell embrace, unable to tear herself away, until her father's stern voice summoned her to the carriage that was to take her on the first stage of her journey!

"Won't you come to the station with us, Austin? " she pleaded.

"No, Clary, " her brother answered, with a glance at her father. "*He* does not want me. "

And so they had parted; never to meet any more upon this earth perhaps, Clarissa said to herself, in her dismal reveries to-day. "That stranger in the railway-carriage spoke of his having emigrated. He will live and die far away, perhaps on the other side of the earth, and I shall never see his bright face again. O, Austin, Austin, is this the end of all our summer days in Arden woods long ago! "

* * * * *

CHAPTER IV.

CLARISSA IS "TAKEN UP. "

For some time there was neither change nor stir in Clarissa Lovel's new life. It was not altogether an unpleasant kind of existence, perhaps, and Miss Lovel was inclined to make the best of it. She was very much her own mistress, free to spend the long hours of her monotonous days according to her own pleasure. Her father exacted very little from her, and received her dutiful attentions with an air of endurance which was not particularly encouraging. But Clarissa was not easily disheartened. She wanted to win her father's affection; and again and again, after every new discouragement, she told herself that there was no reason why she should not ultimately succeed in making herself as dear to him as an only daughter should be. It was only a question of time and patience. There was no reason that he should not love her, no possible ground for his coldness. It was his nature to be cold, perhaps; but those cold natures have often proved capable of a single strong attachment. What happiness it would be to win this victory of love!

"We stand almost alone in the world, " she said to herself. "We had need be very dear to each other. "

So, though the time went by, and she made no perceptible progress towards this happy result, Clarissa did not despair. Her father tolerated her, and even this was something; it seemed a great deal when she remembered her childhood at Arden, in which she had never known what it was to be in her father's society for an hour at a time, and when, but for chance meetings in corridors and on staircases, she would very often have lived for weeks under the same roof with him without seeing his face or hearing his voice.

Now it was all different; she was a woman now, and Mill Cottage was scarcely large enough to accommodate two separate existences, even had Mr. Lovel been minded to keep himself aloof from his daughter. This being so, he tolerated her, treating her with a kind of cold politeness, which might have been tolerably natural in some guardian burdened with the charge of a ward he did not care for. They rarely met until dinner-time, Clarissa taking her breakfast about three hours before her father left his room. But at seven they dined together, and spent the long winter evenings in each other's company, Clarissa being sometimes permitted to read aloud in German or Italian, while her father lay back in his easy-chair, smoking his meerschaum, and taking the amber mouthpiece from his lips now and then to correct an accent or murmur a criticism on the text. Sometimes, too, Mr. Lovel would graciously expound a page or two of a Greek play, or dilate on the subtilty of some learned foot-note, for his daughter's benefit, but rather with the air of one gentleman at his club inviting the sympathy of another gentleman than with the tone of a father instructing his child.

Sometimes, but very rarely, they had company. Mr. Oliver and his wife would dine with them occasionally, or the Vicar of Arden, a grave bachelor of five-and-thirty, would drop in to spend an hour or two of an evening. But besides these they saw scarcely any one. The small professional men of Holborough Mr. Lovel held in supreme contempt, a contempt of which those gentlemen themselves were thoroughly aware; the country people whom he had been accustomed to receive at Arden Court he shrank from with a secret sense of shame, in these days of his fallen fortunes. He had therefore made for himself a kind of hermit life at Mill Cottage; and his acquaintance had come, little by little, to accept this as his established manner of existence. They still called upon the recluse occasionally, and sent him cards for their state dinners, averse from any neglect of a man who had once occupied a great position among them; but they were no longer surprised when Mr. Lovel pleaded his feeble health as a reason for declining their hospitality. A very dull life for a girl, perhaps; but for Clarissa it was not altogether an unhappy life. She was at an age when a girl can make an existence for herself out of bright young fancies and vague deep thoughts. There was that in her life just now which fades and perishes with the passing of years; a subtle indescribable charm, a sense of things beyond the common things of daily life. If there had been a closer bond of union between her father and herself, if there had not been that dark cloud upon her brother's life, she might have made herself entirely happy; she might almost have forgotten that Arden was sold, and a vulgar mercantile stranger lord of those green slopes and broad ancient terraces she loved so well.

As it was, the loneliness of her existence troubled her very little. She had none of that eager longing for "society" or "fashion" wherewith young ladies who live in towns are apt to inoculate one another. She had no desire to shine, no consciousness of her own beauty; for the French girls at Madame Marot's had been careful not to tell her that her pale patrician face was beautiful. She wished for nothing but to win her father's love, and to bring about some kind of reconciliation between him and Austin. So the autumn deepened into winter, and the winter brightened into early spring, without bringing any change to her life. She had her colour-box and her easel, her books and piano, for her best companions; and if she did not make any obvious progress towards gaining her father's affection, she contrived, at any rate, to avoid rendering her presence in any way obnoxious to him.

Two or three times in the course of the winter Mrs. Oliver gave a little musical party, at which Clarissa met the small gentry of Holborough, who pronounced her a very lovely girl, and pitied her because of her father's ruined fortunes. To her inexperience these modest assemblies seemed the perfection of gaiety; and she would fain have accepted the invitations that followed them, from the wives of Holborough bankers and lawyers and medical men to whom she had been introduced. Against this degradation, however, Mr. Lovel resolutely opposed himself.

"No, Clarissa, " he said, sternly; "you must enter society under such auspices as I should wish, or you must be content to remain at home. I can't have a daughter of mine hawked about in that petty Holborough set. Lady Laura will be at Hale Castle by-and-by, I daresay. If she chooses to take you up, she can do so. Pretty girls are always at par in a country house, and at the Castle you would meet people worth knowing. "

Clarissa sighed. Those cordial Holborough gentry had been so kind to her, and this exclusiveness of her father's chilled her, somehow. It seemed to add a new bitterness to their poverty—to that poverty, by the way, of which she had scarcely felt the sharp edges yet awhile. Things went very smoothly at Mill Cottage. Her father lived luxuriously, after his quiet fashion. One of the best wine-merchants at the West-end of London supplied his claret, Fortnum and Mason furnished the condiments and foreign rarities which were essential for his breakfast-table. There seemed never any lack of money, or only when Clarissa ventured to hint at the scantiness of her school-wardrobe, on which occasion Mr. Lovel looked very grave, and put her off with two or three pounds to spend at the Holborough draper's.

"I should want so many new clothes if I went to the Castle, papa, " she said, rather sadly one day, when her father was talking of Lady Laura Armstrong; but Mr. Lovel only shrugged his shoulders.

"A young woman is always well dressed in a white muslin gown, " he said, carelessly. "I daresay a few pounds would get you all you want. "

The Castle was a noble old place at Hale, a village about six miles from Holborough. It had been the family seat of the Earl of Roxham ever since the reign of Edward VI. ; but, on the Roxham race dying out, some fifty years before this, had become the property of a certain Mr. Armstrong, a civilian who had made a great fortune in the East, in an age when great fortunes were commonly made by East-Indian traders. His only son had been captain in a crack regiment, and had sold out of the army after his father's death, in order to marry Lady Laura Challoner, second daughter of the Earl of Calderwood, a nobleman of ancient lineage and decayed fortunes, and to begin life as a country gentleman under her wise governance. The Armstrongs were said to be a very happy couple; and if the master of Hale Castle was apt to seem something of a cipher in his own house, the house was an eminently agreeable one, and Lady Laura popular with all classes. Her husband adored her, and had surrendered his judgment to her guidance with a most supreme faith in her infallibility. Happily, she exercised her power with that subtle tact which is the finest gift of woman, and his worst enemies could scarcely call Frederick Armstrong a henpecked husband.

The spring and early summer brought no change to Clarissa's life. She had been at home for the greater part of a year, and in all that time one day had resembled another almost us closely as in the scholastic monotony of existence at Madame Marot's. And yet the girl had shaped no complaint about the dulness of this tranquil routine, even in her inmost unspoken thoughts. She was happy, after a quiet fashion. She had a vague sense that there was a broader, grander kind of life possible to womanhood; a life as different from her own as the broad river that lost itself in the sea was different from the placid mill-stream that bounded her father's orchard. But she had no sick fretful yearning for that wider life. To win her father's affection, to see her brother restored to his abandoned home — these were her girlish dreams and simple unselfish hopes.

In all the months Clarissa Lovel had spent at Mill Cottage she had never crossed the boundary of that lost domain she loved so well. There was a rustic bridge across the mill-stream, and a wooden gate opening into Arden woods. Clarissa very often stood by this gate, leaning with folded arms upon the topmost bar, and looking into the shadowy labyrinth of beech and pine with sad dreamy eyes, but she never went beyond the barrier. Honest Martha asked her more than once why she never walked in the wood, which was so much pleasanter than the dusty high-road, or even Arden common, an undulating expanse of heathy waste beyond the village, where Clarissa would roam for hours on the fine spring days, with a sketch-book under her arm. The friendly peasant woman could not understand that obstinate avoidance of a beloved scene—that sentiment which made her lost home seem to Clarissa a thing to shrink from, as she might have shrunk from beholding the face of the beloved dead.

It was bright midsummer weather, a glorious prolific season, with the thermometer ranging between seventy and eighty, when Lady Laura Armstrong did at last make her appearance at Mill Cottage. The simple old-fashioned garden was all aglow with roses; the house half-hidden beneath the luxuriance of foliage and flowers, a great magnolia on one side climbing up to the dormer windows, on the other pale monthly roses, and odorous golden and crimson tinted honeysuckle. Lady Laura was in raptures with the place. She found Clarissa sitting in a natural arbour made by a group of old hawthorns and a wild plum-tree, and placed herself at once upon a footing of perfect friendliness and familiarity with the girl. Mr. Lovel was out—a rare occurrence. He had gone for a stroll through the village with Ponto.

"And why are you not with him? " asked Lady Laura, who, like most of these clever managing women, had a knack of asking questions. "You must be a better companion than Ponto. "

"Papa does not think so. He likes walking alone. He likes to be quite free to dream about his books, I fancy, and it bores him rather to have to talk. "

"Not a very lively companion for you, I fear. Why, child, how dismal your life must be! "

"O, no; not dismal. It is very quiet, of course; but I like a quiet life. "

"But you go to a good many parties, I suppose, in Holborough and the neighbourhood? I know the Holborough people are fond of giving parties, and are quite famous for Croquet. "

"No, Lady Laura; papa won't let me visit any one at Holborough, except my uncle and aunt, the Olivers. "

"Yes; I know the Olivers very well indeed. Remarkably pleasant people. "

"And I don't even know how to play croquet. "

"Why, my poor benighted child, in what a state of barbarism this father of yours is bringing you up! How are you ever to marry and take your place in the world? And with your advantages, too! What can the man be dreaming about? I shall talk to him very seriously. We are quite old friends, you know, my dear, and I can venture to say what I like to him. You must come to me immediately. I shall have a houseful of people in a week or two, and you shall have a peep at the gay world. Poor little prison flower! no wonder you look thoughtful and pale. And now show me your garden, please, Miss Lovel. We can stroll about till your father comes home; I mean to talk to him *at once.* "

Energy was one of the qualities of her own character for which Laura Armstrong especially valued herself. She was always doing something or other which she was not actually called upon by her own duty or by the desire of other people to do, and she was always eager to do it "at once. " She had come to Mill Cottage intending to show some kindness to Clarissa Lovel, whose father and her own father, the Earl of Calderwood, had been firm friends in the days when the master of Arden entertained the county; and Clarissa's manner and appearance having impressed her most favourably, she was eager to do her immediate service, to have her at the Castle, and show her to the world, and get her a rich husband if possible.

In honest truth, this Lady Laura Armstrong was a kindly disposed, sympathetic woman, anxious to make the best of the opportunities which Providence had given her with so lavish a hand, and to do her duty towards her less fortunate neighbours. The office of Lady Bountiful, the position of patroness, suited her humour. Her active frivolous nature, which spurned repose, and yet never rose above trifles, found an agreeable occupation in the exercise of this kind of benign influence upon other people's lives. Whether she would have put herself seriously out of the way for the benefit of any of these people to whom she was so unfailingly beneficent, was a question which circumstances had never yet put to the test. Her benevolence had so far been of a light, airy kind, which did not heavily tax her bodily or mental powers, or even the ample resources of her purse.

She was a handsome woman, after a fair, florid, rather redundant style of beauty, and was profoundly skilled in all those arts of costume and decoration by which such beauty is improved. A woman of middle height, with a fine figure, a wealth of fair hair, and an aquiline nose of the true patrician type, her admirers said. The mouth was rather large, but redeemed by a set of flashing teeth and a winning smile; the chin inclined to be of that order called "double; " and indeed a tendency to increasing stoutness was one of the few cares which shadowed Lady Laura's path. She was five-and-thirty, and had only just begun to tell herself that she was no longer a girl. She got on admirably with Clarissa, as she informed her husband afterwards when she described the visit.

The girl was fascinated at once by that frank cordial manner, and was quite ready to accept Lady Laura for her friend, ready to be patronised by her even, with no sense of humiliation, no lurking desire to revolt against the kind of sovereignty with which her new friend took possession of her.

Mr. Lovel came strolling in by-and-by, with his favourite tan setter, looking as cool as if there were no such thing as blazing midsummer sunshine, and found the two ladies sauntering up and down the grassy walk by the mill-stream, under the shadow of gnarled old pear and quince trees. He was charmed to see his dear Lady Laura. Clarissa had never known him so enthusiastic or so agreeable. It was quite a new manner which he put on—the manner of a man who is still interested in life. Lady Laura began almost at once with her reproaches. How could he be so cruel to this dear child? How could he be so absurd as to bury her alive in this way?

"She visits no one, I hear, " cried the lady; "positively no one. "

"Humph! she has been complaining, has she? " said Mr. Lovel, with a sharp glance at his daughter.

"Complaining! O no, papa! I have told Lady Laura that I do not care about gaiety, and that you do not allow me to visit. "

"*Aut Caesar aut nullus*—the best or nothing. I don't want Clarissa to be gadding about to all the tea-drinkings in Holborough; and if I let her go to one house, I must let her go to all"

"But you will let her come to me? "

"That is the best, my dear Lady Laura. Yes, of course she may come to you, whenever you may please to be troubled with her. "

"Then I please to be troubled with her immediately. I should like to carry her away with me this afternoon, if it were possible; but I suppose that can't be—there will be a trunk to be packed, and so on. When will you come to me, Miss Lovel? Do you know, I am strongly tempted to call you Clarissa? "

"I should like it so much better, " the girl answered, blushing.

"What! may I? Then I'm sure I will. It's such a pretty name, reminding one of that old novel of Richardson's, which everybody quotes and no one ever seems to have read. When will you come, Clarissa? "

"Give her a week, " said her father; "she'll want a new white muslin gown, I daresay; young women always do when they are going visiting. "

"Now, pray don't let her trouble herself about anything of that kind; my maid shall see to all that sort of thing. We will make her look her best, depend upon it. I mean this visit to be a great event in her life, Mr. Lovel, if possible. "

"Don't let there be any fuss or trouble about her. Every one knows that I am poor, and that she will be penniless when I am gone. Let her wear her white muslin gown, and give her a corner to sit in. People may take her for one of your children's governesses, if they choose; but if she is to see society, I am glad for her to see the best. "

"People shall not take her for one of my governesses; they shall take her for nothing less than Miss Lovel of Arden. Yes, of Arden, my dear sir; don't frown, I entreat you. The glory of an old house like that clings to those who bear the old name, even though lands and house are gone—Miss Lovel, of Arden, By the way, how do you get on with your neighbour, Mr. Granger? "

"I do not get on with him at all. He used to call upon me now and then, but I suppose he fancied, or saw somehow or other—though I am sure I was laboriously civil to him—that I did not care much for his visits; at any rate, he dropped them. But he is still rather obtrusively polite in sending me game and hot-house fruit and flowers at odd times, in return for which favours I can send him nothing but a note of thanks—'Mr. Level presents his compliments to Mr. Granger, and begs to acknowledge, with best thanks, &c. "—the usual formula. "

"I am so sorry you have not permitted him to know you, " replied Lady Laura. "We saw a good deal of him last year—such a charming man! what one may really call a typical man—the sort of person the French describe as solid—-*Carré par la base*—a perfect block of granite; and then, so *enormously* rich! "

Lady Laura glanced at Clarissa, as if she were inspired with some sudden idea. She was subject to a sudden influx of ideas, and always fancied her ideas inspirations. She looked at Clarissa, and repeated, with a meditative air, "So *enormously* rich! "

"There is a grown-up daughter, too, " said Mr. Lovel; "rather a stiff-looking young person. I suppose she is solid, too. "

"She is not so charming as her father, " replied Lady Laura, with whom that favourite adjective served for everything in the way of praise. To her the Pyramids and Niagara, a tropical thunderstorm, a mazourka by Chopin, and a Parisian bonnet, were all alike charming. "I suppose solidity isn't so nice in a girl, " she went on, laughing; "but certainly Sophia Granger is not such a favourite with me as her father is. I suppose she will make a brilliant marriage, however, sooner or later, unattractive as she may be; for she'll have a superb fortune, —unless, indeed, her father should take it into his head to marry again. "

"Scarcely likely that, I should think, after seventeen years of widowhood. Why, Granger must be at least fifty. " "My dear Mr. Lovel, I hope you are not going to call that a great age. "

"My dear Lady Laura, am I likely to do so, when my own fiftieth birthday is an event of the past? But I shouldn't suppose Granger to be a marrying man, " he added meditatively; "such an idea has never occurred to me in conjunction with him. " And here he glanced ever so slightly at his daughter. "That sort of granite man must take a great deal of thawing. "

"There are suns that will melt the deepest snows, " answered the lady, laughing. "Seriously, I am sorry you will not suffer him to know you. But I must run away this instant; my unfortunate ponies will be wondering what has become of me. You see this dear girl and I have got on so well together, that I have been quite unconscious of time; and I had ever so many more calls to make, but those must be put off to another day. Let me see; this is Tuesday, I shall send a carriage for you, this day week, Clarissa, soon after breakfast, so that I may have you with me at luncheon. Good-bye. "

Lady Laura kissed her new *protégée* at parting. She was really fond of everything young and bright and pretty; and having come to Mr. Lovel's house intending to perform a social duty, was delighted to find that the duty was so easy and pleasant to her. She was always pleased with new acquaintances, and was apt to give her friendship on the smallest provocation. On the other hand, there came a time when she grew just a little weary of these dear sweet friends, and began to find them less charming than of old; but she was never uncivil to them; they always remained on her list, and received stray gleams from the sunlight of her patronage.

"Well, " said Mr. Lovel interrogatively, when the mistress of Hale Castle had driven off, in the lightest and daintiest of phaetons, with a model groom and a pair of chestnut cobs, which seemed perfection, even in Yorkshire, where every man is a connoisseur in horseflesh. "Well, child, I told you that you might go into society if Lady Laura Armstrong took you up, but I scarcely expected her to be as cordial as she has been to-day. Nothing could have been better than the result of her visit; she seemed quite taken with you, Clary. "

It was almost the first time her father had ever called her Clary. It was only a small endearment, but she blushed and sparkled into smiles at the welcome sound. He saw the smile and blush, but only thought she was delighted with the idea of this visit to the Castle. He had no notion that the placid state of indifference which he maintained towards her was otherwise than agreeable to her feelings. He was perfectly civil to her, and he never interfered with her pursuits or inclinations. What more could she want from a father?

Perhaps she assumed a new value in his eyes from the time of that visit of Lady Laura's. He was certainly kinder to her than usual, the girl thought, as they sat on the lawn in the balmy June evening, sipping their after-dinner coffee, while the moon rose fair and pale above the woods of Arden Court. He contemplated her with a meditative air now and then, when she was not looking his way. He had always known that she was beautiful, but her beauty had acquired a new emphasis from Lady Laura Armstrong's praises. A woman of the world of that class was not likely to be deceived, or to mistake the kind of beauty, likely to influence mankind; and in the dim recesses of his mind there grew up a new hope—very vague and shadowy; he despised himself for dwelling upon it so weakly—a hope that made him kinder to his daughter than he had ever been yet—a hope which rendered her precious to him all at once. Not that he loved her any better than of old; it was only that he saw how, if fortune favoured him, this girl might render him the greatest service that could be done for him by any human creature.

She might marry Daniel Granger, and win back the heritage he had lost. It was a foolish thought, of course; Mr. Lovel was quite aware of the supremity of folly involved in it. This Granger might be the last man in the world to fall in love with a girl younger than his daughter; he might be as impervious to beauty as the granite to which Laura Armstrong had likened him. It was a foolish fancy, a vain hope; but it served to brighten the meditations of Marmaduke Lovel—who had really very few pleasant subjects to think about— with a faint rosy glow.

"It is the idlest dream, " he said to himself. "When did good luck ever come my way? But O, to hold Arden Court again—by any tie— to die knowing that my race would inherit the old gray walls! "

* * * * *

CHAPTER V.

AT HALE CASTLE.

Mr. Lovel gave his daughter twenty pounds; a stretch of liberality which did not a little astonish her. She was very grateful for this unexpected kindness; and her father was fain to submit to be kissed and praised for his goodness more than was entirely agreeable to him. But he had been kinder to her ever since Lady Laura's visit, and her heart was very light under that genial influence. She thought he was beginning to love her, and that belief made her happy.

Nor was there anything but unqualified pleasure for her in the possession of twenty pounds—the largest sum she had ever had at her disposal. Although the solitude of her life and the troubles that overshadowed it had made her thoughtful beyond her years, she was still young enough to be able to put aside all thought, and to live in the present. It was very pleasant to go into Holborough, with those four crisp new five-pound notes in her purse, to ask her aunt's advice about her purchases. Mrs. Oliver was enraptured to hear of the visit to the Castle, but naturally a little despondent about the circumstances under which the visit was to be paid. That Clarissa should go to Lady Laura's without a maid was eminently distressing to her aunt.

"I really think you ought to take Peters, " Mrs. Oliver said meditatively. "She is a most reliable person; and of course nobody need know that she is not your own maid. I can fully rely upon her discretion for not breathing a word upon the subject to any of the Castle servants. "

Peters was a prim middle-aged spinster, with a small waist and a painfully erect figure, who combined the office of parlour-maid at the Rectory with that of personal attendant upon the Rector's wife— a person whom Clarissa had always regarded with a kind of awe—a lynx-eyed woman, who could see at a glance the merest hint of a stray hair-pin in a massive coil of plaits, or the minutest edge of a muslin petticoat, visible below the hem of a dress.

"O no, aunt; please don't think of such a thing! " the girl cried eagerly. "I could not go with a borrowed servant; and I don't want a maid at all; I am used to do everything for myself Besides, Lady Laura did not ask me to bring a maid. "

"She would take that for granted. She would never expect Mr. Lovel's daughter to travel without a maid. "

"But papa told her how poor he was. "

"Very unnecessary, and very bad taste on his part, I think. But of course she would not suppose him to be too poor to maintain a proper establishment in a small way. People of that kind only understand poverty in the broadest sense. "

Mrs. Oliver consented to forego the idea of sending Peters to the Castle, with a regretful sigh; and then the two ladies went out shopping—Clarissa in high spirits; her aunt depressed by a conviction, that she would not make her first entrance into society with the surroundings that befitted a Lovel of Arden Court.

There seemed so many things indispensable for this all-important visit. The twenty pounds were nearly gone by the time Miss Lovel's shopping was finished. A white muslin dress for ordinary occasions, some white gauzy fabric for a more important toilette, a golden-brown silk walking or dinner dress, a white areophane bonnet, a gray straw hat and feather, gloves, boots, slippers, and a heap of feminine trifles. Considerable management and discretion were required to make the twenty pounds go far enough: but Mrs. Oliver finished her list triumphantly, leaving one bright golden sovereign in Clarissa's purse. She gave the girl two more sovereigns at parting with her.

"You will want as much as that for the servants when you are coming away, Clary, " she said imperatively, as Clarissa protested against this gift. "I don't suppose you will be called upon to spend a shilling for anything else during your visit, unless there should happen to be a charity sermon while you are at Hale. In that case, pray don't put less than half-a-crown in the plate. Those things are noticed so much. And now, good-bye, my dear. I don't suppose I shall see you again between this, and Tuesday. Miss Mallow will come to you to try-on the day after to-morrow at one o'clock, remember; be sure you are at home. She will have hard work to get your things ready in time; but I shall look in upon her once or twice, to keep her up to the mark. Pray do your best to secure Lady Laura's friendship. Such an acquaintance as that is all-important to a girl in your position. "

Tuesday came very quickly, as it seemed to Clarissa, who grew a little nervous about this visit among strangers, in a great strange house, as it came nearer. She had seen the outside of the Castle very often: a vast feudal pile it seemed, seen across the bright river that flowed beneath its outward wall—a little darksome and gloomy at the best, Clarissa had thought, and something too grand to make a pleasant habitation. She had never seen the inner quadrangle, in all its splendour of modern restoration—sparkling freestone, fresh from the mason's chisel; gothic windows, glowing with rare stained glass; and the broad fertile gardens, with their terraces and banks of flowers, crowded together to make a feast of colour, sloping down to the setting sun.

It was still the same bright midsummer weather—a blue sky without a cloud, a look upon earth and heaven as if there would never be rain again, or anything but this glow and glory of summer. At eleven o'clock the carriage came from the Castle; Clarissa's trunks and travelling-bag were accommodated somehow; and the girl bade her father good-bye.

"I daresay I shall be asked to dinner while you are there, " he said, as they were parting, "and I may possibly come; I shall be curious to see how you get on. "

"O, pray do come, papa; I'm sure it will do you good. "

And then she kissed him affectionately, emboldened by that softer manner which he had shown towards her lately; and the carriage drove off. A beautiful drive past fertile fields, far stretching towards that bright river, which wound its sinuous way through all this part of the country; past woods that shut in both sides of the road with a solemn gloom even at midday—woods athwart which one caught here and there a distant glimpse of some noble old mansion lying remote within the green girdle of a park.

It was something less than an hour's drive from Arden to Hale: the village-church clock and a great clock in the Castle stables were both striking twelve as the carriage drove under a massive stone arch, above which the portcullis still hung grimly. It was something like going into a prison, Clarissa thought; but she had scarcely time for the reflection, when the carriage swept round a curve in the smooth gravel road, and she saw the sunny western front of the Castle, glorious in all its brightness of summer flowers, and with a tall fountain leaping and sparkling up towards the blue sky.

She gave a little cry of rapture at sight of so much brightness and beauty, coming upon her all at once with a glad surprise. There were no human creatures visible; only the glory of fountain and flowers. It might have been the palace of the Sleeping Beauty, deep in the heart of the woodlands, for any evidence to the contrary, perceptible to Clarissa in this drowsy noontide; but presently, as the carriage drove up to the hall door, a dog barked, and then a sumptuous lackey appeared, and anon another, who, between them, took Miss Lovel's travelling-bag and parasol, prior to escorting her to some apartment, leaving the heavier luggage to meaner hands.

"The saloon, or my lady's own room, miss? " one of the grandiose creatures demanded languidly.

"I would rather see Lady Laura alone at first, if you please. "

The man bowed, and conducted her up a broad staircase, lined with darksome pictures of battles by land and sea, along a crimson-carpeted corridor where there were many doors, to one particular portal at the southern end.

He opened this with a lofty air, and announced "Miss Lovel. "

It was a very large room—all the rooms in this newly-restored part of the Castle were large and lofty (a great deal of the so-called "restoration" had indeed been building, and many of these splendid rooms were new, newer even than the wealth of Frederick Armstrong)—a large room, furnished with chairs and tables and cabinets of satin wood, with oval medallions of pale blue Wedgwood let into the panelled doors of the cabinets, and a narrow beading of lustreless gold here and there; a room with pale blue silken hangings, and a carpet of white wood-anemones scattered on a turquoise-coloured ground. There were no pictures; art was represented only by a few choice bronzes and a pair of Venetian mirrors.

Lady Laura was busy at a writing-table, filling in the blanks in some notes of invitation. She was always busy. On one table there were an easel and the appliances of illumination; a rare old parchment Missal lying open, and my lady's copy of a florid initial close beside it. On a small reading-desk there was an open Tasso with a couple of Italian dictionaries near at hand. Lady Laura had a taste for languages, and was fond of reviving her acquaintance with foreign classics. She was really the most indefatigable of women. It was a pity, perhaps, that her numerous accomplishments and her multifarious duties towards society at large left her so very little leisure to bestow upon her own children; but then, they had their foreign governesses, and maids— there was one poor English drudge, by the way, who seemed like a stranger in a far land—gifted in many tongues, and began to imbibe knowledge from their cradles. To their young imaginations the nursery wing of Hale Castle must have seemed remarkably like the Tower of Babel.

The lady of the Castle laid down her pen, and received Clarissa with warm affection. She really liked the girl. It was only a light airy kind of liking, perhaps, in unison with her character; but, so far as it went, it was perfectly sincere.

"My dear child, I am so glad to have you here, " she said, placing Miss Lovel beside her on a low sofa. "You will find me dreadfully busy sometimes, I daresay; but you must not think me neglectful if I cannot be very much with you downstairs. You are to come in and out of this room whenever you please. It is not open to the world at large, you know, and I am supposed to be quite inaccessible here; but it is open to my favourites, and I mean you to be one of them, Clarissa. "

"You are very good, dear Lady Laura. "

"No, I am not good; I daresay I am the most selfish creature in Christendom; but when I like people, I like them with all my heart. And now tell me what you think of Hale. "

"It is lovely—it is like fairyland. "

"Yes, it is pretty, isn't it, this new side? It has all been done in my time—it has all been my doing, indeed, I may venture to say; for Fred would have gone on living contentedly in the old rooms till his dying day. You can't imagine the trouble I took. I read no end of books upon the domestic architecture of the middle ages, went all over England hunting for model houses, and led the poor architect a fine life. But I think, between us, we succeeded in carrying out a very fine idea at last. The crenellated roof, with its machicolations, is considered a great success. There was a time when one was obliged to get a license from the sovereign to build that kind of thing; but it is all changed now. The sovereign is not afraid of rebellion, and the machicolations are only for ornament. You have not seen the old hall yet. That is splendid—a real original bit of the Castle, you know, which has never been tampered with, as old as Edward III., with a raised platform at the upper end, where the lord of the castle used to sit while his vassals ate below him; and with a stone hearth in the centre, where they used to make their wood fires, all the smoke going through an opening in the roof—rather pleasant for my lord and his vassals, I should think! Take off your hat, Clarissa; or perhaps you would rather go to your room at once. Yes, you shall, dear; and I'll finish my letters, and we can meet at luncheon. "

Lady Laura rang a bell twice; which particular summons produced a very smart-looking maid, into whose charge my lady confided Clarissa, with a pretty little wave of her hand, and "*à bient't*, dear child. "

The maid conducted Miss Lovel to a charming chintz-curtained bedroom on the second floor, looking westward over those gorgeous flower-banks; a bedroom with a bright-looking brass bedstead, and the daintiest chintz-patterned carpet, and nothing medieval about it except the stone-framed gothic window.

"I will send a person to unpack your trunks, miss, " the maid said, when she had listened with a deferential air to Clarissa's praise of the room. "I am very glad you like your rooms; my lady was most anxious you should be pleased. I'll send Fosset miss; she is a very handy young person, and will be always at your service to render you any assistance you may require. "

"Thank you—I am not likely to trouble her often; there is so very little assistance I ever want. Sometimes, when I am putting on an evening dress, I may ask for a little help perhaps—that is all. "

"She will be quite at your service, miss: I hope you will not scruple to ring for her, " the chief of the maids replied, and then made a dignified exit.

The maid of inferior degree, Fosset, speedily appeared; a pale-complexioned, meek-looking young woman, who set about unpacking Clarissa's trunks with great skill and quickness, and arranged their contents in the capacious maple wardrobe, while their owner washed her face and hands and brushed the dust of her brief journey out of her dark brown hair. A clamorous bell rang out the summons to the midday meal presently, and Clarissa went down to the hall, where a watchful footman took her in charge.

"Luncheon is served in the octagon room, miss, " he said, and straightway led her away to an apartment in an angle of the Castle: a room with a heavily-carved oak ceiling, and four mullioned windows overlooking the river; a room hung with gilt and brown stamped leather, and furnished in the most approved mediaeval style. There was an octagon table, bright with fruit and flowers, and a good many ladies seated round it, with only here and there a gentleman.

There was one of these gentlemen standing near Lady Laura's chair as Clarissa went into the room, tall and stout, with a very fair good-natured countenance, light blue eyes, and large light whiskers, whom, by reason of some careless remarks of her father's, she guessed at once to be Mr. Armstrong; a gentleman of whom people were apt to say, after the shortest acquaintance, that there was not much in him, but that he was the best fellow in the world—an excellent kind of person to be intrusted with the disposal of a large fortune, a man by whom his neighbours could profit without a too painful sense of obligation, and who was never so happy as when a crowd of people were enjoying life at his expense. Friends who meant to say something very generous of Frederick Armstrong were wont to observe, that he was not such a fool as he looked. Nor, in the ordinary attributes of a country gentleman, was the master of Hale Castle behind his compeers. He rode like Assheton Smith, never missed his bird in the open, and had a manly scorn of battues; was great in agriculture, and as good a judge of a horse as any man in Yorkshire. His literary attainments were, perhaps, limited to a comprehensive knowledge of the science of farriery, a profound study of *Buff's Guide*, and a familiar acquaintance with *Bell's Life* and two or three weekly newspapers devoted to the agricultural interest; but as he had the happiness to live amongst a race which rather cultivates the divine gift of ignorance, his shortcomings awakened no scorn.

When he was known to have made a bad book for the Leger or the Great Ebor, his friends openly expressed their contempt for his mental powers; but no one despised him because an expensive university training had made him nothing more than a first-rate oarsman, a fair billiard-player, and a distinguished thrower of the hammer. He was just what a country gentleman should be in the popular idea—handsome, broad-shouldered, long-limbed, with the fist and biceps of a gladiator, and a brain totally unburdened by the scholiast's dry-as-dust rubbish: sharp and keen enough where the things that interested him were in question, and never caring to look beyond them.

To this gentleman Lady Laura introduced Clarissa.

"Fred, this is Miss Lovel—Clarissa Lovel—and you and she are to like each other very much, if you please. This is my husband, Clarissa, who cares more for the cultivation of short-horns—whatever kind of creatures those brutes may be—and ugly little shaggy black Highland cattle, than for my society, a great deal; so you will see very little of him, I daresay, while you are at the Castle. In London he is obliged to be shut-up with me now and then; though, as he attends nearly all the race-meetings, I don't see very much of him even there; but here he escapes me altogether. "

"Upon my word, Laura—upon my word, you know, Miss Lovel, there's not a syllable of truth in it, " exclaimed the gentleman with the light whiskers. "My wife's always illuminating old Missals, or rending Italian, or practising the harmonium, or writing out lists of things for her Dorcas club, or something of that sort; and a fellow only feels himself in the way if he's hanging about her. She's the busiest woman in the world. I don't believe the prime minister gets through more work or receives more letters than she does. And she answers 'em all too, by Jove; she's like the great Duke of Wellington. "

"Do you happen to take a lively interest in steam-ploughs and threshing-machines, and that kind of thing, Clarissa? " asked Lady Laura.

"I'm afraid not. I never even saw a steam-plough; and I believe if I were to see one, I should think it a most unpicturesque object. "

"I am sorry to hear that. Fred would have been so delighted with you, if you'd shown agricultural proclivities. We had a young lady from Westmoreland here last year who knew an immense deal about farming. She was especially great upon pigs, I believe, and quite fascinated Fred by tramping about the home farm with him in thick boots. I was almost jealous. But now let me introduce you to some of my friends, Clarissa. "

Hereupon Miss Lovel had to bow and simper in response to the polite bows and simpers of half a dozen ladies. Mrs. Weldon Dacre and three Miss Dacres, Rose, Grace, and Amy, tall and bony damsels, with pale reddish hair, and paler eyebrows and eyelashes, and altogether more "style" than beauty; Mrs. Wilmot, a handsome widow, whom Frederick Armstrong and his masculine friends were wont to call "a dasher; " Miss Fermor, a rather pretty girl, with a piquant nose and sparkling hazel eyes; and Miss Barbara Fermor, tall and slim and dark, with a romantic air. The gentlemen were a couple of officers—Major Mason, stout, dark, hook-nosed, and close-shaven; Captain Westleigh, fair, auburn-moustached and whiskered— and a meek-looking gentleman, of that inoffensive curate race, against which Clarissa had been warned by her father.

She found herself very quickly at home among these people. The Miss Fermors were especially gifted in the art of making themselves delightful to strangers; they had, indeed, undergone such training in a perpetual career of country-house visiting, that it would have gone hard with them had they not acquired this grace. The three tall pale Dacres, Rose, Grace, and Amy, were more conventional, and less ready to swear alliance with the stranger; but they were not disagreeable girls, and improved considerably after a few days' acquaintance, showing themselves willing to take the bass in pianoforte duets, sing a decent second, exhibit their sketch-books and photographic collections in a friendly manner, and communicate new stitches and patterns in *point de Russe* or *point d'Alençon*.

After luncheon Miss Lovel went off with Captain Westleigh and Miss Fermor—Lizzie, the elder and livelier of the two sisters—to take her first lesson in croquet. The croquet-ground was a raised plateau to the left of the Italian garden, bounded on one side by a grassy slope and the reedy bank of the river, and on the other by a plantation of young firs; a perfect croquet-ground, smooth as an ancient bowling-green, and unbroken by invading shrub or flower-bed. There were some light iron seats on the outskirts of the ground here and there, and that was all.

Clarissa received her lesson, and (having been lucky enough to send her ball through the hoop now and then) was pronounced to have a natural genius for croquet. It was a pleasant, idle afternoon, passed amidst so bright and fair a scene, that the beauty of her surroundings alone was enough to give Clarissa's life a new zest—a day which the mind recalls in the stormier periods of after-life, wondering at its gracious peace, its utter freedom from care or thought. Too soon came the time when there could be no more of such girlish happiness for Clarissa, such perfect respite from thought of to-morrow, or regret for yesterday.

By-and-by came dressing for dinner, and then an assemblage of visitors in the drawing-room—county people from neighbouring parks and halls and courts—mingling pleasantly with the Castle guests, and then dinner in the great dining-room; a splendid chamber, with a music-gallery at one end, and with the earliest crystal chandeliers ever used in England, and given by Queen Elizabeth to the Lord of Hale, for its chief decorations. At eight o'clock these crystal chandeliers glittered with the light of many wax-candles, though there was still the soft glow of sunset in the gardens beyond the great gothic windows.

That first visit to a great country house was like a new page in life to Clarissa. She had not wearied of her quiet existence at Mill Cottage, her books, her art, her freedom from the monotonous tasks and dull restraints of school; but she felt that if life could always be like this, it would be something very sweet and joyous. Captain Westleigh had contrived to take her in to dinner.

"I was determined to do it, " he told her confidentially, as they sat down; "so I made a rush across to you when I saw Lady Laura's eye upon you, with a malicious intention of billeting you upon young Halkin, the great cloth-manufacturer's son. I know Lady Laura so well; she will be trying to plant all those rich manufacturing fellows upon you; she has quite a mania for that sort of people. "

The Captain made himself very pleasant all through that long ceremonial of dinner. If the brilliant things which he said were not quite the newest in the world, they were at least new to Clarissa, who rewarded his efforts to please her by seeming very much amused, and flattered, and stimulated him to new flights by her appreciation. He told her all about the people round her, making her feel less like a stranger in a foreign country; and that pageant-like dinner, long as it was, did not seem at all too long to be pleasant.

After dinner there was a little music and singing at one end of the drawing-room, to which people listened or not, as they pleased; a friendly whist-table established at the other end, at which four elderly, grey-whiskered, and bald-headed country gentlemen played gravely for an hour or so; and a good deal of desultory strolling out through the open windows to the terrace for the contemplation of the moonlit gardens, with perhaps a spice of flirtation. Lady Laura was never quite happy unless she saw something like flirtation going on among her younger visitors. She was pleased to see Captain Westleigh's attention to Clarissa, though she would rather that James Halkin had occupied the ground. But, alas! Mr. Halkin, stiff and solemn as a policeman on duty, was standing by the chair of the very palest and least beautiful of the Miss Dacres, mildly discussing a collection of photographs of Alpine scenery. They had both been over the same country, and were quite enthusiastic when they came to peaks and mountain gorges that they remembered.

"I was there with another fellow, and he nearly slipped just on that edge there. It was as near as a— —" Mr. Halkin was going to say "a toucher, " but it occurred to him that that vague expression was scarcely permissible in conversation with a lady—"the nearest thing you ever saw in your life, in fact. If it hadn't been for his alpen-stock, it would have been all over with him; and the guides told us there'd been a fellow killed there the year before. We stopped at Rigot's—I think the dearest hotel I was ever at; but they gave us some very fair still champagne—very fair indeed. "

Lady Laura took occasion to warn Clarissa against the Captain when they separated for the night, in the corridor upon which my lady's rooms opened.

"Very nice, isn't he, dear? Come into my dressing-room for a few minutes' talk; " and my lady led Clarissa into another charming chamber, all blue silk and satin-wood, like the morning room. "Yes, he is very nice, and he really seemed quite *épris*. Poor Herbert Westleigh! I've known him for years. He belongs to one of the oldest families in Somersetshire, and is a capital fellow, as my husband says; but a person not to be thought of by you, Clarissa. There are a crowd of brothers, and I doubt if Herbert has a hundred a year beyond his pay. Did you notice that Mr. Halkin, a rather sandy-haired young man with a long nose? That young fellow will come into thirty thousand a year by-and-by. "

"Yes, Lady Laura, I did notice him a little when he was talking to one of the Miss Dacres. He seemed very stupid. "

"Stupid, my dear Clarissa! Why, I have been told that young man made a good deal of character at Oxford. But I daresay you are taken by Herbert Westleigh's rattling way. Now remember, my dear, I have warned you. "

"There is no occasion for any warning, Lady Laura. Believe me, I am in no danger. I thought Captain Westleigh was very kind, and I liked him because he told me all about the other people; that is all. "

"Very well, dear. You will see a good many people here; there is an advantage in that—one influence neutralises another. But I should really like you to take some notice of that Mr. Halkin. He will be a good deal here, I daresay. His family live at Selbrook Hall, only four miles off. The father and mother are the plainest, homeliest people, but very sensible; live in a quiet unpretending style, and can't spend a quarter of their income. When I speak of thirty thousand a year, I don't reckon the accumulations that young man will inherit. He is the only son. There is a sister; but she is lame and a confirmed invalid—not likely to live many years, I think. "

Clarissa smiled at Lady Laura's earnestness.

"One would think you were in league with papa, dear Lady Laura. He says I am bound to marry a rich man. "

"Of course; it is a solemn duty when a girl is handsome and not rich. Look at me: what would my life have been without Fred, Clarissa? There were five of us, child: five daughters to be married, only think of that; and there are still three unmarried. One of my sisters is coming here to-morrow. I do so hope you will get on with her; but she is rather peculiar. I am glad to say she is engaged at last—quite an old affair, and I think an attachment on both sides for some time past; but it has only lately come to a definite engagement. The gentleman's prospects were so uncertain; but that is all over now. The death of an elder brother quite alters his position, and he will have a very fine estate by-and-by. He is coming here, too, in a few days, and I'm sure I hope the marriage will take place soon. But I must not keep you here chattering, at the risk of spoiling your fresh looks. "

And with a gracious good-night Lady Laura dismissed her new *protégée*.

Yes, it was a pleasant life, certainly; a life that drifted smoothly onward with the tide, and to all seeming unshadowed by one sorrowful thought or care. And yet, no doubt, with but a few youthful exceptions, every guest at Hale Castle had his or her particular burden to carry, and black Care sat behind the gentlemen as they rode to small country meetings or primitive cattle-fairs. To Clarissa Lovel the state of existence was so new, that it was scarcely strange she should be deluded by the brightness and glitter of it, and believe that these people could have known no sorrow.

She found herself looking forward with unwonted interest to the arrival of Lady Laura's sister, Lady Geraldine Challoner. To a girl who has never had a lover—to whom the whole science of love is yet a profound inscrutable mystery—there is apt to be something especially interesting in the idea of an engagement. To her the thought of betrothal is wondrously solemn. A love-match too, and an attachment of long standing—there were the materials for a romance in these brief hints of Lady Laura's. And then, again, her sister described this Lady Geraldine as a peculiar person, with whom it was rather doubtful whether Clarissa would be able to get on. All this made her so much the more anxious to see the expected guest; and in the morning's drive, and the afternoon's croquet, she thought more of Lady Geraldine than of the landscape or the game.

Croquet was over—Clarissa had taken part in a regular game this afternoon—and the players were strolling about the gardens in couples, in an idle half-hour before the first dinner-bell, when Miss Lovel met Lady Laura with another lady. They were sauntering slowly along one of the sunny gravel walks—there was every charm in this Italian garden except shade—and stopped on seeing Clarissa.

"Now, Geraldine, I shall be able to introduce you to my favourite, Clarissa Lovel, " said Lady Laura; "Captain Westleigh you know of old. "

The Captain and Lady Geraldine shook hands, declaring that they were quite old friends—had known each other for ages, and so on;

and Clarissa had a few moments' pause, in which to observe the young lady.

She was tall and slim, her sister's junior by perhaps five years, but not more; very fair, with bright auburn hair—that golden-tinted hair, of which there seems to be so much more nowadays than was to be seen twenty years ago. She was handsome—very handsome—Clarissa decided at once; but it seemed to her rather a cold, hard style of beauty; the straight nose, the mouth, and chin chiselled with a clearness and distinctness that was almost sharpness; the large luminous blue eyes, which did not seem to possess much capacity for tenderness.

Lady Laura was very proud of this sister, and perhaps just a little afraid of her; but of course that latter fact was not obvious to strangers; she was only a shade less volatile than usual in Geraldine's presence. Geraldine was the beauty of the Challoner family, and her career had been a failure hitherto; so that there was much rejoicing, in a quiet way, now that Lady Geraldine's destiny was apparently decided, and in an advantageous manner.

She was sufficiently gracious to Clarissa, but displayed none of that warmth which distinguished Lady Laura's manner to her new friend; and when the sisters had turned aside into another path, and were out of hearing, Geraldine asked rather sharply why "that girl" was here?

"My dear Geraldine, she is perfectly charming. I have taken the greatest fancy to her. "

"My dear Laura, when will you leave off those absurd fancies for strangers? "

"Clarissa Lovel is not a stranger; you must remember how intimate papa used to be with her father. "

"I only remember that Mr. Lovel was a very selfish person, and that he has lost his estate and gone down in the world. Why should you trouble yourself about his daughter? You can only do the girl harm by bringing her here; she will have to go out as a governess, I daresay, and will be writing to you whenever she is out of a situation to ask some favour or other, and boring you to death. I cannot think how you can be so inconsiderate as to entangle yourself with that kind of acquaintance. "

"I don't mean Clarissa to be a governess; I mean her to make a good marriage. "

"O, of course it is very easy to say that, " exclaimed Lady Geraldine scornfully; "but you have not been so fortunate as a match-maker hitherto. Look at Emily and Louisa. "

"Emily and Louisa were so intractable and difficult to please, that I could do nothing for them; and now I look upon them as confirmed old maids. But it is a different thing with Clarissa. She is very sensible; and I do not think she would stand in her own light if I could bring about what I wish. And then she is so lovely. Emily and Louisa were good-looking enough half a dozen years ago, but this girl is simply perfect. Come, Geraldine, you can afford to praise her. Is she not lovely? "

"Yes, I suppose she is handsome, " the other answered icily.

"You suppose she is handsome! It is really too bad of you to be prejudiced against a girl I wanted you to like. As if this poor little Clarissa could do anybody any harm! But never mind, she must do without your liking. And now tell me all about George Fairfax. I was so glad to hear your news, dear, so thoroughly rejoiced. "

"There is no occasion for such profound gladness. I could have gone on existing very well as Geraldine Challoner. "

"Of course; but I had much rather see you well married, and your own mistress; and this is such a good match. "

"Yes; from a worldly point of view, I suppose, the affair is unexceptionable, " Geraldine Challoner answered, with persistent indifference; simulated indifference, no doubt, but not the less provoking to her sister. "George will be rich by-and-by, and he is well enough off now. We shall be able to afford a house in one of the streets out of Park Lane—I have a rooted detestation for both Belgravia and Tyburnia—and a carriage, and so on; and I shall not be worried as I have been about my milliner's bills. "

"And then you are very fond of him, Geraldine, " Lady Laura said, softly.

There were still little romantic impulses in the matron's heart, and this studied coldness of her sister's tone wounded her.

"Yes, of course that is the beginning of the business. We like each other very well, " Lady Geraldine replied, still with the same unenthusiastic air. "I think there has always been some kind of liking between us. We suit each other very well, you see; have the same way of thinking about most things, take the same view of life, and so on. "

Lady Laura gave a faint sigh of assent. She was disappointed by her sister's tone; for in the time past she had more than once suspected that Geraldine Challoner loved George Fairfax with a passionate half-despairing love, which, if unrequited, might make the bane of her life. And, lo! here was the same Geraldine discussing her engagement as coolly as if the match had been the veriest marriage of convenience ever planned by a designing dowager. She did not understand how much pride had to do with this reticence, or what volcanic depths may sometimes lie beneath the Alpine snows of such a nature as Geraldine Challoner's.

In the evening Lady Geraldine was the centre of a circle of old friends and admirers; and Clarissa could only observe her from a distance, and wonder at her brilliancy, her power to talk of anything and everything with an air of unlimited wisdom and experience, and the perfect ease with which she received the homage offered to her beauty and wit. The cold proud face lighted up wonderfully at night, and under the softening influence of so much adulation; and Lady Geraldine's smiles, though wanting in warmth at the best, were very fascinating. Clarissa wondered that so radiant a creature could have been so long unmarried, that it could be matter for rejoicing that she was at last engaged. It must have been her own fault, of course; such a woman as this could have been a duchess if she pleased, Clarissa thought.

Lizzy Fermor came up to her while she was admiring the high-bred beauty.

"Well, Miss Lovel, what do you think of her? "

"Lady Geraldine? I think she is wonderfully handsome—and fascinating. "

"Do you? Then I don't think you can know the meaning of the word 'fascination. ' If I were a man, that woman would be precisely the last in the world to touch my heart. O yes, I admit that she is very handsome—classic profile, bright blue eyes, complexion of lilies and roses, real golden hair—not dyed, you know—and so on; but I should as soon think of falling in love with a statue of snow as with Lady Geraldine Challoner. I think she has just about as much heart as the statue would have. "

"Those people with cold manners have sometimes very warm hearts, " Clarissa, remonstrated, feeling that gratitude to Lady Laura made it incumbent on her to defend Lady Laura's sister.

"Perhaps; but that is not the case with her. She would trample upon a hecatomb of hearts to arrive at the object of her ambition. I think she might have made more than one brilliant marriage since she has been out—something like ten years, you know—only she was too cold, too obviously mercenary. I am very sorry for George Fairfax. "

"Do you know him? "

"Yes, and he is a very noble fellow. He has been rather wild, I believe; but of course we are not supposed to know anything about that; and I have heard that he is the most generous-hearted of men. I know Lady Geraldine has contrived to keep him dangling about her whenever he was in England for the last six or eight years; but I thought it was one of those old established flirtations that would never come to anything—a kind of institution. I was quite surprised to hear of their engagement—and very sorry. "

"But Lady Geraldine is very much attached to him, is she not? "

"O yes, I daresay she likes him; it would be almost difficult for any one to avoid liking him. She used to do her utmost to keep him about her always, I know; and I believe the flirtation has cost her more than one chance of a good marriage. But I doubt if we should have ever heard of this engagement if Reginald Fairfax had not died, and left his brother the heir of Lyvedon. "

"Is Lyvedon a very grand place? "

"It is a fine estate, I believe; a noble old house in Kent, with considerable extent of land attached to it. The place belongs now to Sir Spencer Lyvedon, an old bachelor, whose only sister is George Fairfax's mother. The property is sure to come to Mr. Fairfax in a few years. He is to be here to-morrow, they say; and you will see him, and be able to judge for yourself whether Lady Geraldine is worthy of him. "

There was a little excursion proposed and planned that evening for the next day—a drive to Marley Wood, a delicious bit of forest about seven miles from the Castle, and a luncheon in the open air. The party was made up on the spot. There were ladies enough to fill two carriages; a couple of servants were to go first with the luncheon in a waggonette, and the gentlemen were to ride. Everybody was delighted with the idea. It was one of those unpremeditated affairs which are sure to be a success.

"I am glad to have something to do with myself, " said Lady Geraldine. "It is better than dawdling away one's existence at croquet. "

"I hope you are not going to be dull here, Geraldine, " replied Lady Laura. "There are the Helston races next week, and a flower-show at Holborough. "

"I hate small country race-meetings and country flower-shows; but of course I am not going to be dull, Laura. The Castle is very nice; and I shall hear all about your last new *protégées,* and your Dorcas societies, and your model cottages, and your architect, and your hundred-and-one schemes for the benefit of your fellow-man. It is not possible to be dull in the presence of so much energy. "

* * * * *

CHAPTER VI.

AND THIS IS GEORGE FAIRFAX.

The next day was lovely. There seemed, indeed, no possibility of variation in the perfection of this summer weather; and Clarissa Lovel felt her spirits as light as if the unknown life before her had been all brightness, unshadowed by one dread or care. The party for Marley Wood started about an hour after breakfast—Lady Laura, Mrs. Dacre, Barbara Fermor, and Clarissa, in one carriage; two Miss Dacres, Lady Geraldine, and Mrs. Wilmot in the other; Lizzy Fermor and Rose Dacre on horseback; with a small detachment of gentlemen in attendance upon them. There were wide grassy waste lands on each side of the road almost all the way to the wood, on which the equestrian party could disport themselves, without much inconvenience from the dust of the two carriages. Once arrived at the wood, there were botanising, fern-hunting, sketching, and flirtation without limit. Lady Laura was quite happy, discussing her Dorcas societies and the ingratitude of her model cottagers, with Mrs. Dacre; Lady Geraldine sat at the foot of a great shining beech, with her white dress set off by a background of scarlet shawl, and her hat lying on the grass beside her. She seemed too listless to ramble about with the rest of the party, or to take the faintest interest in the conversation of any of the gentlemen who tried to talk to her. She amused herself in a desultory way with a drawing-book and a volume of a novel, and did not appear to consider it incumbent on her to take notice of any one.

Clarissa and Barbara Fermor wandered away into the heart of the wood, attended by the indefatigable Captain Westleigh, and sketched little bits of fern and undergrowth in their miniature sketch-books, much to the admiration of the Captain, who declared that Clarissa had a genius for landscape. "As you have for croquet and for everything else, I think, " he said; "only you are so quiet about your resources. But I am very glad you have not that grand sultana manner of Lady Geraldine Challoner's. I really can't think how any man can stand it, especially such a man as George Fairfax. "

"Why 'especially'? " asked Miss Fermor, curiously.

"Well, I don't know exactly how to explain my meaning to a lady— because he has knocked about the world a good deal—seen a great deal of life, in short. *Il a vecu*, as the French say. He is not the kind of man to be any woman's slave, I should think; he knows too much of the sex for that. He would take matters with rather a high hand, I should fancy. And then Lady Geraldine, though she is remarkably handsome, and all that kind of thing, is not in the first freshness of her youth. She is nearly as old as George, I should say; and when a woman is the same age as a man, it is her misfortune to seem much older. No, Miss Fermor, upon my word, I don't consider them fairly matched. "

"The lady has rank, " said Barbara Fermor.

"Yes, of course. It will be Mr. and Lady Geraldine Fairfax. There are some men who care for that kind of thing; but I don't suppose George is one of them. The Fairfaxes are of a noble old Scotch family, you know, and hold themselves equal to any of our nobility. "

"When is Mr. Fairfax expected at the Castle? "

"Not till to-night. He is to come by the last train, I believe. You may depend Lady Geraldine would not be here if there were any chance of his arriving in the middle of the day. She will keep him up to collar, you maybe sure. I shouldn't like to be engaged to a woman armed with the experience of a decade of London seasons. It must be tight work! "

A shrill bell, pealing gaily through the wood, summoned them to luncheon; a fairy banquet spread upon the grass under a charmed circle of beeches; chicken-pies and lobster-salads, mayonaise of salmon and daintily-glazed cutlets in paper frills, inexhaustible treasure of pound-cake and strawberries and cream, with a pyramid of hothouse pines and peaches in the centre of the turf-spread banquet. And for the wines, there were no effervescent compounds from the laboratory of the wine-chemist—Lady Laura's guests were not thirsty cockneys, requiring to be refreshed by "fizz"—but delicate amber-tinted vintages of the Rhineland, which seemed too ethereal to intoxicate, and yet were dangerous. And for the more thirsty souls there were curiously compounded "cups: " hock and seltzer; claret and soda-water, fortified with curaçoa and flavoured artistically with burrage or sliced pine-apple.

The banquet was a merry one; and it was nearly four o'clock when the ladies had done trifling with strawberries and cream, and the gentlemen had suspended their homage to the Rhineland. Then came a still more desultory wandering of couples to and fro among the shadowy intricacies of the wood; and Clarissa having for once contrived to get rid of the inevitable Captain, who had been beguiled away to inspect some remote grotto under convoy of Barbara Fermor, was free to wander alone whither she pleased. She was rather glad to be alone for a little. Marley Wood was not new to her. It had been a favourite spot of her brother Austin's, and the two had spent many a pleasant day beneath the umbrage of those old forest-trees; she, sitting and reading, neither of them talking very much, only in a spasmodic way, when Austin was suddenly moved by some caprice to pour out his thoughts into the ear of his little sister—strange bitter thoughts they were sometimes; but the girl listened as to the inspirations of genius. Here he had taught her almost all that she had ever learned of landscape art. She had only improved by long practice upon those early simple lessons. She was glad to be alone, for these old memories were sad ones. She wandered quite away from the rest, and, sitting down upon a bank that sloped towards a narrow streamlet, began to sketch stray tufts and clusters of weedy undergrowth—a straggling blackberry-branch, a bit of ivy creeping sinuously along the uneven ground—in an absent desultory way, thinking of her brother and the days gone by. She had been alone like this about half an hour, when the crackling of the brambles near her warned her of an approaching footstep. She looked up, and saw a stranger approaching her through the sunlight and shadows of the wood—a tall man, in a loose, gray overcoat.

A stranger? No. As he came nearer to her, the face seemed very familiar; and yet in that first moment she could not imagine where she had seen him. A little nearer, and she remembered all at once. This was her companion of the long railway journey from London to Holborough. She blushed at the recollection, not altogether displeased to see him again, and yet remembering bitterly that cruel mistake she had made about Arden Court. She might be able to explain her error now, if he should recognise her and stop to speak; but that was scarcely likely. He had forgotten her utterly, no doubt, by this time.

She went on with her sketching—a trailing spray of Irish ivy, winding away and losing itself in a confusion of bramble and fern, every leaf sharply defined by the light pencil touches, with loving pre-Raphaelite care—she went on, trying to think that it was not the slightest consequence to her whether this man remembered their brief acquaintance of the railway-carriage. And yet she would have been wounded, ever so little, if he had forgotten her. She knew so few people, that this accidental acquaintance seemed almost a friend. He had known her brother, too; and there had been something in his manner that implied an interest in her fate.

She bent a little lower over the sketch-book, doing her uttermost not to be seen, perhaps all the more because she really did wish for the opportunity of explaining that mistake about Arden Court. Her face was almost hidden under the coquettish gray hat, as she bent over her drawing; but the gentleman came on towards her with evident purpose. It was only to make an inquiry, however.

"I am looking for a picnic party, " he said. "I discovered the *débris* of a luncheon yonder, but no human creature visible. Perhaps you can kindly tell me where the strayed revellers are to be found; you are one of them, perhaps? "

Clarissa looked up at him, blushing furiously, and very much ashamed of herself for the weakness, and then went on with her drawing in a nervous way, as she answered him, —

Yes, I am with Lady Laura Armstrong's party; but I really cannot tell you where to look for them all. They are roaming about in every direction, I believe. "

"Good gracious me! " cried the gentleman, coming a good deal nearer—stepping hastily across the streamlet, in fact, which had divided him from Clarissa hitherto. "Have I really the pleasure of speaking to Miss Lovel? This is indeed a surprise. I scarcely expected ever to see you again. "

"Nor I to see you, " Clarissa answered, recovering herself a little by this time, and speaking with her accustomed frankness. "And I have been very anxious to see you again. "

"Indeed! " cried the gentleman eagerly.

"In order to explain a mistake I made that night in the railway-carriage, in speaking of Arden Court. I talked of the place as if it had still belonged to papa; I did not know that he had sold it, and fancied I was going home there. It was only when I saw my uncle that I learnt the truth. You must have thought it very strange. "

"I was just a little mystified, I confess, for I had dined at the Court with Mr. Granger. "

"Papa had sold the dear old place, and, disliking the idea of writing such unpleasant news, had told me nothing about the sale. It was not wise, of course; but he felt the loss of Arden so keenly, I can scarcely wonder that he could not bring himself to write about it. "

"It would have been better to have spared you, though, " the unknown answered gravely. "I daresay you were as fond of the old home as ever your father could have been? "

"I don't think it would be possible for any one to love Arden better than I. But then, of course, a man is always prouder than a woman—"

"I am not so sure of that, " the stranger muttered parenthetically.

" —And papa felt the degradation involved in the loss. "

"I won't admit of any degradation in the case. A gentleman is none the less a gentleman for having spent his fortune rather recklessly, and the old blood is no less pure without the old acres. If your father were a wise man, he might be happier now than he has ever been. The loss of a great estate is the loss of a bundle of cares. "

"I daresay that is very good philosophy, " Clarissa answered, smiling, beguiled from painful thoughts by the lightness of his tone; "but I doubt if it applies to all cases—not to papa's, certainly. "

"You were sketching, I see, when I interrupted you. I remember you told me that night of your fondness for art. May I see what you were doing? "

"It is hardly worth showing you. I was only amusing myself, sketching at random—that ivy straggling along there, or anything that caught my eye. "

"But that sort of thing indicates so much. I see you have a masterly touch for so young an artist. I won't say anything hackneyed about so fair a one; for women are showing us nowadays that there are no regions of art closed against them. Well, it is a divine amusement, and a glorious profession. "

There was a little pause after this, during which Clarissa looked at her watch, and finding it nearly five o'clock, began to put up her pencils and drawing-book.

"I did not think that you knew Lady Laura Armstrong, " she said; and then blushed for the speech, remembering that, as she knew absolutely nothing about himself or his belongings, the circumstance of her ignorance on this one point was by no means surprising.

"No; nor did I expect to meet you here, " replied the gentleman. "And yet I might almost have done so, knowing that you lived at Arden. But, you see, it is so long since we met, and I——"

"Had naturally forgotten me. "

"No, I had not forgotten you, Miss Lovel, nor would it have been natural for me to forget you. I am very glad to meet you again under such agreeable auspices. You are going to stay at the Castle a long time, I hope. I am booked for an indefinite visit. "

"O no, I don't suppose I shall stay very long. Lady Laura is extremely kind; but this is my first visit, and she must have many friends who have a greater claim upon her hospitality. "

"Hale Castle is a large place, and I am sure Lady Laura has always room for agreeable guests. "

"She is very, very kind. You have known her a long time, perhaps? "

"Yes. I have been intimate with the Challoners ever since I was a boy. Lady Laura was always charming; but I think her marriage with Fred Armstrong—who worships the ground she walks on—and the possession of Hale Castle have made her absolutely perfect. "

"And you know her sister, Lady Geraldine, of course? "

"O yes, I know Geraldine. "

"Do you know Mr. Fairfax, the gentleman to whom she is engaged? "

"Well, yes; I am supposed to have some knowledge of that individual. "

Something in his smile, and a certain significance in his tone, let in a sudden light upon Clarissa's mind.

"I am afraid I am asking very foolish questions, " she said. "You are Mr. Fairfax? "

"Yes, I am George Fairfax. I forgot that I had omitted to you my name that night. "

"And I had no idea that I was speaking to Mr. Fairfax. You were not expected till quite late this evening. "

"No; but I found my business in London easier to manage than I had supposed it would be; so, as in duty bound, I came down here directly I found myself free. When I arrived at the Castle, I was told of this picnic, and rode off at once to join the party. "

"And I am keeping you here, when you ought to be looking for your friends. "

"There is no hurry. I have done my duty, and am here; that is the grand point. Shall we go and look for them together? "

"If you like. I daresay we shall be returning to the Castle very soon. "

They sauntered slowly away, in and out among the trees, towards a grassy glade, where there was more open space for walking, and where the afternoon sun shone warmly on the smooth turf.

"I hope you get on very well with Geraldine? " Mr. Fairfax said presently.

It was almost the same phrase Lady Laura had used about her sister.

"I have seen so little of her yet, " Clarissa answered, rather embarrassed by this inquiry. "I should like to know her very much; but she only arrived yesterday, and we have scarcely spoken half-a-dozen words to each other yet. "

"You will hardly like her at first, perhaps, " Mr. Fairfax went on, doubtfully. "People who don't know much of her are apt to fancy her cold and proud; but to those whom she really likes she is all that is charming, and I don't think she can fail to like you. "

"You are very kind to say so. I hope she may like me. Do you know, I have been so much interested in Lady Geraldine from the first, before I saw her even—partly, perhaps, because her sister told me about her engagement. You will think that very romantic and silly, I daresay."

"Not at all; a young lady is bound to be interested in that kind of thing. And I hope your interest in Lady Geraldine was not lessened when you did see her."

"It could scarcely be that. No one could help admiring her."

"Yes, she is very handsome, there is no question about that; she has been an acknowledged beauty ever since she came out. I think I can catch a glimpse of her yonder among the trees; I see a white dress and a scarlet shawl. Geraldine always had a penchant for scarlet draperies."

"Yes, that is Lady Geraldine."

They hastened their steps a little, and came presently to the circle of beeches where they had lunched, and where most of the party were now assembled, preparing for the return journey. Lady Geraldine was sauntering to and fro with Major Mason, listening with a somewhat indifferent air to that gentleman's discourse.

She caught sight of her lover the moment he appeared; and Clarissa saw the statuesque face light up with a faint flush of pleasure that brightened it wonderfully. But however pleased she might be, Lady Geraldine Challoner was the last of women to demonstrate her pleasure in her lover's arrival by any overt act. She received him with the tranquil grace of an empress, who sees only one courtier more approach the steps of her throne. They shook hands placidly, after Mr. Fairfax had shaken hands and talked for two or three minutes with Lady Laura Armstrong, who welcomed him with considerable warmth.

The major dropped quietly away from Lady Geraldine's side, and the plighted lovers strolled under the trees for a little, pending the signal for the return.

"So you know Miss Lovel?" Geraldine said, with an icy air of surprise, as soon as she and George Fairfax were alone.

"I can hardly say that I know her; our acquaintance is the merest accident, " answered Mr. Fairfax; and then proceeded to relate his railway adventure.

"How very odd that she should travel alone! "

"Scarcely so odd, when you remember the fact of her father's poverty. He could not be supposed to find a maid for his daughter. "

"But he might be supposed to take some care of her. He ought not to have allowed her to travel alone—at night too. "

"It was careless and imprudent, no doubt. Happily she came to no harm. She was spared from any encounter with a travelling swell-mobsman, who would have garotted her for the sake of her watch and purse, or an insolent bagman, who would have made himself obnoxiously agreeable on account of her pretty face. "

"I suppose she has been in the habit of going about the world by herself. That accounts for her rather strong-minded air. "

"Do you find her strong-minded? I should have thought her quite gentle and womanly. "

"I really know nothing about her; and I must not say anything against her. She is Laura's last *protégée*; and you know, when my sister takes any one up, it is always a case of rapture. "

After this the lovers began to talk about themselves, or rather George Fairfax talked about himself, giving a detailed account of his proceedings since last they had met.

"I went down to see my uncle, " he said, "the day before yesterday. He is at Lyvedon, and I had a good look at the old house. Really it is the dearest old place in the world, Geraldine, and I should like above all things to live there by-and-by, when the estate is ours. I don't think we are likely to wait very long. The poor old man is awfully shaky. He was very good to me, dear old boy, and asked all manner of kind questions about you. I think I have quite won his heart by my engagement; he regards it as a pledge of my reform. "

"I am glad he is pleased, " replied Lady Geraldine, in a tone that was just a shade more gracious than that in which she had spoken of Clarissa.

The summons to the carriages came almost immediately. Mr. Fairfax conducted his betrothed to her seat in the barouche, and then mounted his horse to ride back to the Castle beside her. He rode by the side of the carriage all the way, indifferent to dust; but there was not much talk between the lovers during that homeward progress, and Clarissa fancied there was a cloud upon Mr. Fairfax's countenance.

* * * * *

CHAPTER VII.

DANGEROUS GROUND.

Life was very pleasant at Hale Castle. About that one point there could be no shadow of doubt. Clarissa wondered at the brightness of her new existence; began to wonder vaguely by-and-by what it was that made it seem brighter every day. There was the usual round of amusements —dinner-parties, amateur concerts, races, flower-shows, excursions to every point of interest within a day's drive, a military ball at the garrison-town twenty miles off, perennial croquet, and gossip, and afternoon tea-drinking in arbours or marquees in the gardens, and unlimited flirtation. It was impossible for the most exacting visitor to be dull. There was always something.

And to Clarissa all these things possessed the charm of freshness. She was puzzled beyond measure by the indifference, real or simulated, of the girls who had seen half-a-dozen London seasons; the frequent declarations that these delights only bored them, that this or that party was a failure. George Fairfax watched her bright face sometimes, interested in spite of himself by her freshness.

"What a delicious thing youth is! " he said to himself. "Even if that girl were less completely lovely than she is, she would still be most charming. If Geraldine were only like that—only fresh and candid and pure, and susceptible to every new emotion! But there is an impassable gulf of ten years between them. Geraldine is quite as handsome—in her own particular style—and she talks much better than Clarissa Lovel, and is more clever, no doubt; and yet there are some men who would be bewitched by that girl before they knew where they were. "

Very often after this Mr. Fairfax fell a-musing upon those apocryphal men who might be subjugated by the charms of Miss Lovel.

When did he awaken to the fatal truth that those charms were exercising a most potent influence upon his own mind? When did he open his eyes for the first time to behold his danger?

Not yet. He was really attached to Geraldine Challoner. Her society had been a kind of habit with him for several years of his life. She had been more admired than any woman he knew, and it was, in some sort, a triumph to have won her. That he never would have won her but for his brother's death he knew very well, and accepted the fact as a matter of course; a mere necessity of the world in which they lived, not as evidence of a mercenary spirit in the lady. He knew that no woman could better discharge the duties of an elevated station, or win him more social renown. To marry Geraldine Challoner was to secure for his house the stamp of fashion, for every detail of his domestic life a warrant of good taste. She had a kind of power over him too, an influence begun long ago, which had never yet been oppressive to him. And he took these things for love. He had been in love with other women during his long alliance with Lady Geraldine, and had shown more ardour in the pursuit of other flames than he had ever evinced in his courtship of her; but these more passionate attachments had come, for the most part, to a sorry end; and now he told himself that Geraldine suited him better than any other woman in the world.

"I have outgrown all foolish notions, " he said to himself, believing that the capacity was dead within him for that blind unreasoning passion which poets of the Byronic school have made of love. "What I want is a wife; a wife of my own rank, or a little above me in rank; a wife who will be true and loyal to me, who knows the world well enough to forgive my antecedents, and to be utterly silent about them, and who will help me to make a position for myself in the future. A man must be something in this world. It is a hard thing that one cannot live one's own life; but it seems inevitable somehow. "

His mother had helped not a little to the bringing about of this engagement. She knew that her son's bachelor life had been at best a wild one; not so bad as it was supposed to be, of course, since nothing in this world ever is so bad as the rest of the world supposes it; and she was very anxious to see him safely moored in the sheltered harbour of matrimony. She was a proud woman, and she was pleased that her son should have an earl's daughter for his wife; and beyond this there was the fact that she liked Lady Geraldine. The girl who had been too proud to let the man she loved divine the depth of her feeling, had not been too proud to exhibit her fondness for his mother. There had grown up a warm friendship between these two women; and Mrs. Fairfax's influence had done much, almost unknown to her son, to bring about this result of his chronic flirtation with Geraldine Challoner.

Just at present he was very well satisfied with the fact of his engagement, believing that he had taken the best possible means for securing his future happiness; an equable, quiet sort of happiness, of course—he was nearly thirty, and had outlived the possibility of anything more than that. It would have bored him to suppose that Geraldine expected more from him than this tranquil kind of worship. Perhaps the lady understood this, and schooled herself to a colder tone than was even natural to her, rather than be supposed for one moment to be the more deeply attached of the two.

Thus it happened that Mr. Fairfax was not severely taxed in his capacity of plighted lover. However exacting Lady Geraldine may have been by nature, she was too proud to demand more exclusive attention than her betrothed spontaneously rendered; indeed, she took pains to let him perceive that he was still in full enjoyment of all his old bachelor liberty. So the days drifted by very pleasantly, and George Fairfax found himself in Clarissa Lovel's society perhaps a little oftener than was well for either of those two.

He was very kind to her; he seemed to understand her better than other people, she thought; and his companionship was more to her than that of any one else—a most delightful relief after Captain Westleigh's incessant frivolity, or Mr. Halkin's solemn small-talk. In comparison with these men, he appeared to such wonderful advantage. Her nature expanded in his society, and she could talk to him as she talked to no one else.

He used to wonder at her eloquence sometimes, as the beautiful face glowed, and the dark hazel eyes brightened; he wondered not a little also at the extent of her reading, which had been wide and varied during that quiet winter and spring-time at Mill Cottage.

"What a learned lady you are! " he said, smiling at her enthusiasm one day, when they had been talking of Italy and Dante; "your close knowledge of the poet puts my poor smattering to shame. Happily, an idler and a worldling like myself is not supposed to know much. I was never patient enough to be a profound reader; and if I cannot tear the heart out of a book, I am apt to throw it aside in disgust. But you must have read a great deal; and yet when we met, less than a year ago, you confessed to being only a schoolgirl fresh from grinding away at Corneille and Racine. "

"I have had the advantage of papa's help since then, " answered Clarissa, "and he is very clever. He does not read many authors, but those he does care for he reads with all his heart. He taught me to appreciate Dante, and to make myself familiar with the history of his age, in order to understand him better. "

"Very wise of him, no doubt. And that kind of studious life with your papa is very pleasant to you, I suppose, Miss Lovel? "

"Yes, " she answered thoughtfully; "I have been quite happy with papa. Some people might fancy the life dull, perhaps, but it has scarcely seemed so to me. Of course it is very different from life here; but I suppose one would get tired of such a perpetual round of pleasure as Lady Laura provides for us. "

"I should imagine so. Life in a country house full of delightful people must be quite intolerable beyond a certain limit. One so soon gets tired of one's best friends. I think that is why people travel so much nowadays. It is the only polite excuse for being alone. "

The time came when Clarissa began to fancy that her visit had lasted long enough, and that, in common decency, she was bound to depart; but on suggesting as much to Lady Laura, that kindly hostess declared she could not possibly do without her dearest Clarissa for ever so long.

"Indeed, I don't know how I shall ever get on without you, my dear, " she said; "we suit each other so admirably, you see. Why, I shall have no one to read Tasso with—no one to help me with my Missal when you are gone. "

Miss Lovel's familiar knowledge of Italian literature, and artistic tastes, had been altogether delightful to Lady Laura; who was always trying to improve herself, as she called it, and travelled from one pursuit to another, with a laudable perseverance, but an unhappy facility for forgetting one accomplishment in the cultivation of another. Thus by a vigorous plunge into Spanish and Calderon this year, she was apt to obliterate the profound impression created by Dante and Tasso last year. Her music suffered by reason of a sudden ardour for illumination; or art went to the wall because a London musical season and an enthusiastic admiration of Hallé had inspired her with a desire to cultivate a more classic style of pianoforte-playing. So in her English reading, each new book blotted out its predecessor. Travels, histories, essays, biographies, flitted across the lady's brain like the coloured shadows of a magic-lantern, leaving only a lingering patch of picture here and there. To be versatile was Lady Laura's greatest pride, and courteous friends had gratified her by treating her as an authority upon all possible subjects. Nothing delighted her so much as to be appealed to with a preliminary, "Now, you who read so much, Lady Laura, will understand this; " or, "Dear Lady Laura, you who know everything, must tell me why, " etc. ; or to be told by a painter, "You who are an artist yourself can of course see this, Lady Laura; " or to be complimented by a musician as a soul above the dull mass of mankind, a sympathetic spirit, to whom the mysteries of harmony are a familiar language.

In that luxurious morning-room of Lady Laura's Clarissa generally spent the first two hours after breakfast. Here the children used to come with French and German governesses, in all the freshness of newly-starched cambric and newly-crimped tresses, to report progress as to their studies and general behaviour to their mother; who was apt to get tired of them in something less than a quarter of an hour, and to dispatch them with kisses and praises to the distant schoolrooms and nurseries where these young exotics were enjoying the last improvements in the forcing system.

Geraldine Challoner would sometimes drop into this room for a few minutes at the time of the children's visit, and would converse not unkindly with her nephews and nieces; but for her sister's accomplishments she displayed a profound indifference, not to say contempt. She was not herself given to the cultivation of these polite arts—nothing could ever induce her to sing or play in public. She read a good deal, but rarely talked about books—it was difficult indeed to say what Lady Geraldine did talk about—yet in the art of conversation, when she chose to please, Geraldine Challoner infinitely surpassed the majority of women in her circle. Perhaps this may have been partly because she was a good listener; and, in some measure, on account of that cynical, mocking spirit in which she regarded most things, and which was apt to pass for wit.

Clarissa had been a month at Hale Castle already; but she stayed on at the urgent desire of her hostess, much too happy in that gay social life to oppose that lady's will.

"If you really, really wish to have me, dear Lady Laura, " she said; "but you have been so kind already, and I have stayed so long, that I begin to feel myself quite an intruder. "

"You silly child! I do really, really wish to have you. I should like to keep you with me always, if I could. You suit me so much better than any of my sisters; they are the most provoking girls in the world, I think, for being uninterested in my pursuits. And your Italian is something wonderful. I have not opened my dictionary since we have been reading together. And beyond all that, I have a very particular reason for wishing you to be here next month. "

"Why next month, Lady Laura? "

"I am not going to tell you that. "

"But you quite mystify me. "

"I mean to mystify you. No, it's not the least use asking questions, Clary; but mind, you must not tease me any more about running away: that is understood. "

In all this time Clarissa had not found herself any nearer to that desired result of getting on well with Geraldine Challoner. That, lady seemed quite as far away from her after a month's acquaintance as she had seemed at the very first. It was not that Lady Geraldine was uncivil. She was polite, after her manner, to Clarissa, but never cordial; and yet she could not fail to see that George Fairfax admired and liked Miss Lovel, and she might have been supposed to wish to think well of any one he liked.

Was she jealous of Clarissa? Well, no, it scarcely seemed possible to associate the fever of jealousy with that serene temperament. She had an air of complete security in all her intercourse with George Fairfax, which was hardly compatible with doubt or the faintest shadow of suspicion.

If ever she did speak of Miss Lovel to her lover, or to any one else, she talked of her as a pretty country girl, and seemed to consider her as far removed, by reason of her youth and obscure position, from herself, as if they had been inhabitants of two separate worlds.

Mr. Lovel had been invited to several dinner-parties at the Castle during his daughter's visit, but was not to be drawn from his seclusion. He had no objection, however, that Clarissa should stay as long as Lady Laura cared to retain her, and wrote very cordially to that effect.

What a pleasant, idle, purposeless life it was, and how rapidly it drifted by for Clarissa! She wondered to find herself so happy; wondered what the charm was which made life so new and sweet, which made her open her eyes on the morning sunshine with such a glad eagerness to greet the beginning of another day, and filled up every hour with such a perfect sense of contentment.

She wondered at this happiness only in a vague dreamy way, not taking much trouble to analyse her feelings. It was scarcely strange that she should be completely happy in a life so different from her dull existence at home. The freshness and beauty of all these pleasant things would be worn off in time, no doubt, and she would become just like those other young women, with their experience of many seasons, and their perpetual complaint of being bored; but just now, while the freshness lasted, everything delighted her.

Clarissa had been more than six weeks at the Castle, while other visitors had come and gone, and the round of country-house gaieties had been unbroken. The Fermors still lingered on, and languidly deprecated the length of their visit, without any hint of actual departure. Captain Westleigh had gone back to his military duties, very much in love with Miss Lovel. He plaintively protested, in his confidences with a few chosen friends, against a Providence which had made them both penniless.

"I don't suppose I shall ever meet such a girl again, " he would declare piteously. "More than once I was on the point of making her an offer; the words were almost out, you know; for I don't go in for making a solemn business of the thing, with a lot of preliminary palaver. If a fellow really likes a girl, he doesn't want to preach a sermon in order to let her know it; and ever so many times, when we've been playing croquet, or when I've been hanging about the piano with her of an evening, I've been on the point of saying, 'Upon my word, Miss Lovel, I think we two are eminently suited to each other, don't you? ' or something plain and straightforward of that kind; and then I've remembered that her father can't give her a sixpence, which, taken in conjunction with my own financial condition, would mean starvation! "

"And do you think she liked you? " a curious friend would perhaps inquire.

"Well, I don't know. She might do worse, you see. As a rule, girls generally do like me. I don't see why there should be any difference in her case. "

Nor did the Captain for a moment imagine that Clarissa would have rejected him, had he been in a position to make an offer of his hand.

Lady Geraldine was a fixture at Hale. She was to stay there till her marriage, with the exception, perhaps, of a brief excursion to London for millinery purposes, Lady Laura told Clarissa. But the date of the marriage had not yet been settled—had been, indeed, only discussed in the vaguest manner, and the event seemed still remote.

"It will be some time this year, I suppose, " Lady Laura said; "but beyond that I can really say nothing. Geraldine is so capricious; and perhaps George Fairfax may not be in a great hurry to give up his bachelor privileges. He is very different from Fred, who worried me into marrying him six weeks after he proposed. And in this case a long engagement seems so absurd, when you consider that they have known each other for ten years. I shall really be very glad when the business is over, for I never feel quite sure of Geraldine. "

* * * * *

CHAPTER VIII.

SMOULDERING FIRES.

With the beginning of August there came a change in the weather. High winds, gloom, and rain succeeded that brilliant cloudless summer-time, which had become, as it were, the normal condition of the universe; and Lady Laura's guests were fain to abandon their picnics and forest excursions, their botanical researches and distant-race meetings—nay, even croquet itself, that perennial source of recreation for the youthful mind, had to be given up, except in the most fitful snatches. In this state of things, amateur concerts and acted charades came into fashion. The billiard-room was crowded from breakfast till dinner time. It was a charmingly composite apartment—having one long wall lined with bookshelves, sacred to the most frivolous ephemeral literature, and a grand piano in an arched recess at one end of the room—and in wet weather was the chosen resort of every socially-disposed guest at Hale. Here Clarissa learned to elevate her pretty little hand into the approved form of bridge, and acquired some acquaintance with the mysteries of cannons and pockets. It was Mr. Fairfax who taught her billiards. Lady Geraldine dropped into the room now and then, and played a game in a dashing off-hand way with her lover, amidst the admiring comments of her friends; but she did not come very often, and Mr. Fairfax had plenty of time for Clarissa's instruction.

Upon one of these wet days he insisted upon looking over her portfolio of drawings; and in going through a heap of careless sketches they came upon something of her brother Austin's. They were sitting in the library, —a very solemn and splendid chamber, with a carved oak roof and deep mullioned windows, —a room that was less used than any other apartment in the Castle. Mr. Fairfax had caught Miss Lovel here, with her portfolio open on the table before her, copying a drawing of Piranesi's; so there could be no better opportunity for inspecting the sketches, which she had hitherto refused to show him.

That sketch of Austin's—a group of Arab horsemen done in pen and ink—set them talking about him at once; and George Fairfax told Clarissa all he could tell about his intercourse with her brother.

"I really liked him so much, " he said gently, seeing how deeply she was moved by the slightest mention of that name. "I cannot say that I ever knew him intimately, that I can claim to have been his friend; but I used at one time to see a good deal of him, and I was very much impressed by his genius. I never met a young man who gave me a stronger notion of undisciplined genius; but, unhappily, there was a recklessness about him which I can easily imagine would lead him into dangerous associations. I was told that he had quarrelled with his family, and meant to sell out, and take to painting as a profession, —and I really believe that he would have made his fortune as a painter; but when I heard of him next, he had gone abroad—to the colonies, some one said. I could never learn anything more precise than that. "

"I would give the world to know where he is, " said Clarissa mournfully; "but I dare not ask papa anything about him, even if he could tell me, which I doubt very much. I did try to speak of him once; but it was no use—papa would not hear his name. "

"That seems very hard; and yet your father must have been proud of him and fond of him once, I should think. "

"I am not sure of that. Papa and Austin never seemed to get on quite well together. There was always something—as if there had been some kind of hidden resentment, some painful feeling in the mind of each. I was too young to be a competent judge, of course; but I know, as a child, I had always a sense that there was a cloud between those two, a shadow that seemed to darken our lives. "

They talked for a long time of this prodigal son; and this kind of conversation seemed to bring them nearer to each other than anything else that had happened within the six weeks of their acquaintance.

"If ever I have any opportunity of finding out your brother's whereabouts, Miss Lovel, you may be sure that I will use every effort to get you some tidings of him. I don't want to say anything that might lead to your being disappointed; but when I go to town again, I will hunt up a man who used to be one of his friends, and try to learn something. Only you must promise me not to be disappointed if I fail. "

"I won't promise that; but I promise to bear my disappointment quietly, and to be grateful to you for your goodness, " Clarissa answered, with a faint smile.

They went on with the inspection of the drawings, in which Mr. Fairfax showed himself deeply interested. His own manipulative powers were of the smallest, but he was an excellent critic.

"I think I may say of you what I said of your brother just now—that you might make a fortune, if you were to cultivate art seriously. "

"I wish I could make a fortune large enough to buy back Arden Court, " Clarissa answered eagerly.

"You think so much of Arden? "

"O yes, I am always thinking of it, always dreaming of it; the dear old rooms haunt me sleeping and waking. I suppose they are all altered now. I think it would almost break my heart to see them different. "

"Do you know, I am scarcely in a position to understand that fervent love for one's birthplace. I may be said to have no birthplace myself. I was born in lodgings, or a furnished house—some temporary ark of that kind—the next thing to being born on board ship, and having Stepney for one's parish. My father was in a hard-working cavalry regiment, and the early days of my mother's married life were spent in perpetual wanderings. They separated, when I was about eight years old, for ever—a sad story, of course—something worse than incompatibility of temper on the husband's side; and from that time I never saw him, though he lived for some years. So, you see, the words 'home' and 'father' are for me very little more than sentimental abstractions. But with my mother I have been quite happy. She has indeed been the most devoted of women. She took a house at Eton when my brother and I were at school there, and superintended our home studies herself; and from that time to this she has watched my career with unchanging care. It is the old story of maternal kindness and filial shortcomings. I have given her a world of trouble; but I am not the less fond of her, or the less grateful to her. " He stopped for a few moments, with something like a sigh, and then went on in a lighter tone: "You can see, however, that having no ancestral home of my own, I am hardly able to understand the depth of your feeling for Arden Court. There is an old place down in Kent, a fine old castellated mansion, built in the days of Edward VI., which is to be mine by-and-by; but I doubt if I shall ever value it as you do your old home. Perhaps I am wanting in the poetic feeling necessary for the appreciation of these things. "

"O no, it is not that, " Clarissa answered eagerly; "but the house you speak of will not have been your home. You won't have that dim, dreamy recollection of childhood spent in the old rooms; another life, the life of another being almost, it seems, as one looks back to it. I have only the faintest memory of my mother; but it is very sweet, and it is all associated with Arden Court. I cannot conjure up her image for a moment without that background. Yes, I do wish for fortune, for that one reason. I would give the world to win back Arden. "

She was very much in earnest. Her cheeks flushed and her eyes brightened with those eager words. Never perhaps had she looked lovelier than at that moment. George Fairfax paused a little before he answered her, admiring the bright animated face; admiring her, he thought, very much as he might have admired some beautiful wayward child. And then he said gravely:

"It is dangerous to wish for anything so intensely. There are wishes the gratification whereof is fatal. There are a dozen old stories in the classics to show that; to say nothing of all those mediaeval legends in which Satan is complaisant to some eager wisher. "

"But there is no chance of my wish being gratified. If I could work my fingers to the bone in the pursuit of art or literature, or any of the professions by which women win money, I should never earn the price of Arden; nor would that hateful Mr. Granger be disposed to sell a place which gives him his position in the county. And I suppose he is fond of it, after a fashion. He has spent a fortune upon improvements. Improvements! " repeated Clarissa contemptuously; "I daresay be has improved away the very spirit of the place. "

"You cherish a strong dislike for this gentleman, it seems, Miss Lovel. "

"I am wicked enough to dislike him for having robbed us of Arden. Of course you will say that any one else might have bought the place. But then I can only reply, that I should have disliked any other purchaser just the same; a little less though, perhaps, if he had been a member of some noble old family—a man with a great name. It would have been some consolation to think that Arden was promoted. "

"I am afraid there is a leaven of good old Tory spirit in your composition, Miss Lovel. "

"I suppose papa is a Tory. I know he has a profound contempt for what he calls new people—very foolish, of course, I quite feel that; but I think he cannot help remembering that he comes of a good old race which has fallen upon evil days. "

"You remember my telling you that I had been to Arden Court. Mr. Granger gave a state dinner once while I was staying here, and I went with Fred and Lady Laura. I found him not by any means a disagreeable person. He is just a little slow and ponderous, and I should scarcely give him credit for a profound or brilliant intellect; but he is certainly sensible, well-informed, and he gave me the idea of being the very essence of truth. "

"I daresay he is very nice, " Clarissa answered with a subdued sigh. "He has always been kind and attentive to papa, sending game and hothouse fruit, and that kind of thing; and he has begged that we would use the park as if it were our own; but I have never crossed the boundary that divides my new home from my old one. I couldn't bear to see the old walks now. "

They talked for a good deal longer, till the clanging of the Castle bell warned Clarissa that it was time to dress for dinner. It is amazing how rapidly time will pass in such serious confidential talk. George Fairfax looked at his watch with an air of disbelief in that supreme authority the Castle bell, which was renowned for its exact observance of Greenwich time. That blusterous rainy August afternoon had slipped away so I quickly.

"It is a repetition of my experience during that night journey to Holborough, " Mr. Fairfax said, smiling. "You have a knack of charming away the hours, Miss Lovel. "

It was the commonest, most conventional form of compliment, no doubt; but Clarissa blushed a little, and bent rather lower over the portfolio, which she was closing, than she had done before. Then she put the portfolio under her arm, murmured something about going to dress, made George Fairfax a gracious curtsey, and left him.

He did not hurry away to make his own toilet, but walked up and down the library for some minutes, thinking.

"What a sweet girl she is! " he said to himself; "and what a pity her position is not a better one! With a father like that, and a brother who has stamped himself as a scapegrace at the beginning of life, what is to become of her? Unless she marries well, I see no hopeful prospect for her future. But of course such a girl as that is sure to make a good marriage. "

Instead of being cheered by this view of the case, Mr. Fairfax's brow grew darker, and his step heavier.

"What does it matter to me whom she chooses for her husband? " he asked himself; "and yet no man would like to see such a girl throw herself away for mercenary reasons. If I had known her a few months ago! If! What is the history of human error but a succession of 'ifs'? Would it have been better for me or for her, that we had learned to know each other while I was free? The happiest thing for *me* would have been never to have met her at all. I felt myself in some kind of danger that night we met in the railway-carriage. Her race is fatal to mine, I begin to think. Any connection in that quarter would have galled my mother to the quick—broken her heart perhaps; and I am bound to consider her in all I do. Nor am I a schoolboy, to fancy that the whole colour of my life is to be governed by such an influence as this. She is only a pretty woman, with a low sweet voice, and gentle winning ways. Most people would call Geraldine the handsomer of the two. Poor child! She ought to seem no more than a child to me. I think she likes me, and trusts me. I wish Geraldine were kinder to her; I wish— —-"

He did not particularise that last wish, even to himself, but went away to dress, having wasted the first quarter of the three-quarters that elapsed between the first and second bell at Hale Castle.

Throughout that evening, which was an unusually quiet and domestic evening for Hale, he did not talk any more to Clarissa. It might even have been thought that he scrupulously, and of a fixed purpose, avoided her. He devoted himself to chess with Lady Geraldine; a game he played indifferently, and for which he cherished a profound aversion. But chess was one of Geraldine Challoner's strong points; and that aristocratic beauty never looked more regal than when she sat before a chess-table, with one thin white hand hovering gently above the carved ivory pieces.

Mr. Fairfax lost four or five games in succession, excusing his own careless play every time by some dexterous compliment to his betrothed. More than once he stifled a yawn—more than once his glances wandered away to the group near the piano, amidst which Clarissa was seated, listening to Lizzy Fermor's brilliant waltzes and mazurkas, with an open music-book on her lap, turning over the leaves now and then, with rather a listless pre-occupied air, Mr. Fairfax thought.

That evening did certainly seem very dreary to Clarissa, in spite of Miss Fermor's dashing music and animated chatter. She missed that other talk, half playful, half earnest, with which George Fairfax had been wont to beguile some part of every evening; finding her out, as if by a subtle instinct, in whatever corner of the room she happened to be, and always devoting one stray half-hour of the evening to her society. To-night all things came to an end: matrons and misses murmured their good-nights and sailed away to the corridor, where there was a regiment of small silver candlesticks, emblazoned with the numerous quarterings of Armstrong and Challoner; and George Fairfax only rose from the chess-table as Lady Laura's guests abandoned the drawing-room. Geraldine bade her lover good-night with her most bewitching smile—a smile in which there was even some faint ray of warmth.

"You have given me some very easy victories, " she said, as they shook hands, "and I won't flatter you by saying you have played well. But it was very good of you to sit so long at a game which I know you detest, only to please me. "

"A very small sacrifice, surely, my dear Geraldine. We'll play chess every night, if you like. I don't care much for the game in the abstract, I admit; but I am never tired of admiring your judicious play, or the exquisite shape of your hands. "

"No, no; I don't want to try you with such severe training. I saw how tired you were more than once to-night, and how your eyes wandered away to those noisy girls by the piano, like an idle boy who is kept at his lessons when his companions are at play. "

Mr. Fairfax's sunburnt countenance reddened a little at this reproof.

"Was I inattentive? " he asked; "I did not know that. I was quite aware of my bad play, and I really believe I was conscientious. "

And so they wished each other good-night and parted. Geraldine Challoner did not go at once to her own room. She had to pass her sister's quarters on her way, and stopped at the door of the dressing-room.

"Are you quite alone, Laura? " she asked, looking in.

"Quite alone. "

A maid was busy unweaving a splendid pyramid of chestnut plaits which had crowned the head of her mistress; but she of course counted for nothing, and could be dismissed at any moment.

"And there will not be half-a-dozen people coming in to gossip? " Lady Geraldine asked in rather a fretful tone, as she flung herself into an arm-chair near the dressing-table.

"Not a soul; I have wished every one good-night. I was rather tired, to tell the truth, and not inclined for talk. But of course I am always glad of a chat with you, Geraldine. —You may go, Parker; I can finish my hair myself. "

The maid retired, as quietly as some attendant spirit.

Lady Laura took up a big ivory brush and began smoothing the long chestnut locks in a meditative way, waiting for her sister to speak. But Lady Geraldine seemed scarcely in the mood for lively conversation; her fingers were twisting themselves in and out upon the arm of her chair in a nervous way, and her face had a thoughtful, not to say moody, expression.

Her sister watched her for some minutes silently.

"What is the matter, Geraldine? " she inquired at last. "I can see there is something wrong. "

"There is very much that is wrong, " the other answered with a kind of suppressed vehemence. "Upon my word, Laura, I believe it is your destiny to stand in my light at every stage of my life, or you would scarcely have happened to have planted that girl here just at this particular time. "

"What girl? " cried Lady Laura, amazed at this sudden accusation.

"Clarissa Lovel. "

"Good gracious me, Geraldine! what has my poor Clarissa done to offend you? "

"Your poor Clarissa has only set her cap at George Fairfax; and as she happens to be several years younger than I am, and I suppose a good deal prettier, she has thoroughly succeeded in distracting his attention—his regard, perhaps—from myself. "

Laura Armstrong dropped the hair-brush, in profound consternation.

"My dear Geraldine, this is the merest jealous folly on your part. Clarissa is the very last girl in the world who would be guilty of such meanness as to try and attract another woman's lover. Besides, I am sure that George's attachment to yourself—"

"Pray, don't preach about that, Laura! " her sister broke in impatiently. "I must be the best judge of his attachment; and you must be the very blindest of women, if you have not seen how your newest pet and *protégée* has contrived to lure George to her side night after night, and to interest him by her pretty looks and juvenile airs and graces. "

"Why, I don't believe George spoke to Miss Lovel once this evening; he was playing chess with you from the moment he came to the drawing-room after dinner. "

"To-night was an exceptional case. Mr. Fairfax was evidently on duty. His manner all the evening was that of a man who has been consciously culpable, and is trying to atone for bad behaviour. And your favourite was wounded by his desertion—I could see that. "

"She did seem a little depressed, certainly, " Lady Laura answered thoughtfully; "I observed that myself. But I know that the girl has a noble nature, and if she has been so foolish as to be just a little attracted by George Fairfax, she will very; quickly awake to a sense of her folly. Pray don't give yourself the faintest uneasiness, Geraldine. I have my plans for Clarissa Lovel, and this hint of yours will make me more anxious to put them into execution. As for George, it is natural to men to flirt; there's no use in being angry with them. I'm sure that wretched Fred of mine has flirted desperately, in his way. "

Lady Geraldine gave her shoulders a contemptuous shrug, expressive of a most profound indifference to the delinquencies of Mr. Armstrong.

"Your husband and George Fairfax are two very different people, " she said.

"But you don't for a moment suppose there is anything serious in this business? " Laura asked anxiously.

"How can I tell? I sometimes think that George has never really cared for me; that he proposed to me because he thought his mother would like the marriage, and because our names had often been linked together, and our marriage was in a manner expected by people, and so on. Yes, Laura, I have sometimes doubted if he ever loved me—I hate to talk of these things, even to you; but there are times when one must confide in some one—and I have been sorely tempted to break off the engagement. "

She rose from her chair, and began to pace up and down the room in a quick impatient way.

"Upon my honour, I believe it would be the happiest thing for both of us, " she said.

Lady Laura looked at her sister with perfect consternation.

"My dearest Geraldine, you would surely never be so mad! " she exclaimed. "You could not be so foolish as to sacrifice the happiness of your future life to a caprice of the moment—a mere outbreak of temper. Pray, let there be an end of such nonsense. I am sure George is sincerely attached to you, and I am very much mistaken in you if you do not like him—love him—better than you can ever hope to love any other man in this world. "

"O yes; I like him well enough, " said Geraldine Challoner impatiently; "too well to endure anything less than perfect sincerity on his part. "

"But, my dearest, I am sure that he is sincere, " Laura answered soothingly. "Now, my own Geraldine, do pray be reasonable, and leave this business to me. As for Clarissa, I have plans for her, the realization of which would set your mind quite at ease; but if I cannot put them into execution immediately, the girl shall go. Of course you are the first consideration. With regard to George, if you would only let me sound him, I am sure I should get at the real state of his feelings and find them all we can wish——"

"Laura! " cried Geraldine indignantly, "if you dare to interfere, in the smallest degree, with this business, I shall never speak to you again. "

"My dear Geraldine! "

"Remember that, Laura, and remember that I mean what I say. I will not permit so much as the faintest hint of anything I have told you. "

"My dearest girl, I pledge myself not to speak one word, " protested Lady Laura, very much, alarmed by her sister's indignation.

Geraldine left her soon after this, vexed with herself for having betrayed so much feeling, even to a sister; left her—not to repose in peaceful, slumbers, but to walk up and down her room till early morning, and look out at daybreak on the Castle gardens and the purple woods beyond, with a haggard face and blank unseeing eyes.

George Fairfax meanwhile had lain himself down to take his rest in tolerable good-humour with himself and the world in general.

"I really think I behaved very well, " he said to himself; "and having made up my mind to stop anything like a flirtation with that perilously fascinating Clarissa, I shall stick to my resolve with the heroism of an ancient Roman; though the Romans were hardly so heroic in that matter, by the way—witness the havoc made by that fatal Egyptian, a little bit of a woman that could be bundled up in a carpet—to say nothing of the general predilection for somebody else's wife which prevailed in those days, and which makes Suetonius read like a modern French novel. I did not think there was so much of the old leaven left in me. My sweet Clarissa! I fancy she likes me—in a sisterly kind of way, of course—and trusts me not a little. And yet I must seem cold to her, and hold myself aloof, and wound the tender untried heart a little perhaps. Hard upon both of us, but I suppose only a common element in the initiatory ordinances of matrimony. "

And so George Fairfax closed hie eyes and fell asleep, with the image of Clarissa before him in that final moment of consciousness, whereby the same image haunted him in his slumbers that night, alternately perplexing or delighting him; while ever and anon the face of his betrothed, pale and statue-like, came between him and that other face; or the perfect hand he had admired at chess that night was stretched out through the darkness to push aside the form of Clarissa Lovel.

That erring dreamer was a man accustomed to take all things lightly; not a man of high principle—a man whose best original impulses had been weakened and deadened not a little by the fellowship he had kept, and the life he had led; a man unhappily destined to exercise an influence over others disproportionate to the weight of his own character.

Lady Laura was much disturbed by her sister's confidence; and being of a temperament to which the solitary endurance of any mental burden is almost impossible, immediately set to work to do the very things which would have been most obnoxious to Geraldine Challoner. In the first place she awakened her husband from comfortable slumbers, haunted by no more awful forms than his last acquisition in horseflesh, or the oxen he was fattening for the next cattle-show; and determinedly kept him awake while she gave him a detailed account of the distressing scene she had just had with "poor Geraldine. "

Mr. Armstrong, whose yawns and vague disjointed replies were piteous to hear, thought there was only one person in question who merited the epithet "poor, " and that person himself; but he made some faint show of being interested nevertheless.

"Silly woman! silly woman! " he mumbled at last. "I've always thought she rides the high horse rather too much with Fairfax. Men don't like that sort of thing, you know. Geraldine's a very fine woman, but she can't twist a man round her fingers as you can, Laura. Why don't you speak to George Fairfax, and hurry on the marriage somehow? The sooner the business is settled the better, with such a restive couple as these two; uncommonly hard to drive in double harness—the mare inclined to jib, and the other with a tendency to shy. You're such a manager, Laura, you'd make matters square in no time. "

If Lady Laura prided herself on one of her attributes more than another—and she did cherish a harmless vanity about many things—it was in the idea that she was a kind of social Talleyrand. So on this particular occasion, encouraged by simple Fred Armstrong, who had a rooted belief that there never had existed upon this earth such a wonderful woman as his wife, my lady resolved to take the affairs of her sister under her protection, and to bring all things to a triumphant issue. She felt very little compunction about breaking her promise to Geraldine.

"All depends upon the manner in which a thing is done, " she said to herself complacently, as she composed herself for slumber; "of course I shall act with the most extreme delicacy. But it would never do for my sister's chances in life to be ruined for want of a little judicious intervention. "

* * * * *

CHAPTER IX.

LADY LAURA DIPLOMATISES.

The weather was fine next day, and the Castle party drove ten miles to a rustic racecourse, where there was a meeting of a very insignificant character, but interesting to Mr. Armstrong, to whom a horse was a source of perennial delight, and a fair excuse for a long gay drive, and a picnic luncheon in carriages and on coach-boxes.

Amongst Lady Laura's accomplishments was the polite art of driving. To-day she elected to drive a high phaeton with a pair of roans, and invited George Fairfax to take the seat beside her. Lady Geraldine had a headache, and had not appeared that morning; but had sent a message to her sister, to request that her indisposition, which was the merest trifle, might not prevent Mr. Fairfax going to the races.

Mr. Fairfax at first seemed much inclined to remain at home, and perform garrison duty.

"Geraldine will come downstairs presently, I daresay, " he said to Lady Laura, "and we can have a quiet stroll in the gardens, while you are all away. I don't care a straw about the Mickleham races. Please leave me at home, Lady Laura. "

"But Geraldine begs that you will go. She'll keep her room all day, I've no doubt; she generally does, when she has one of her headaches. Every one is going, and I have set my heart on driving you. I want to hear what you think of the roans. Come, George, I really must insist upon it. "

She led him off to the phaeton triumphantly; while Frederick Armstrong was fain to find some vent for his admiration of his gifted wife's diplomacy in sundry winks and grins to the address of no one in particular, as he bustled to and fro between the terrace and the hall, arranging the mode and manner of the day's excursion—who was to be driven by whom, and so on.

Clarissa found herself bestowed in a landau full of ladies, Barbara Fermor amongst them; and was very merry with these agreeable companions, who gave her no time to meditate upon that change in

Mr. Fairfax's manner last night, which had troubled her a little in spite of her better sense. He was nothing to her, of course; an accidental acquaintance whom she might never see again after this visit; but he had known her brother, and he had been kind and sympathetic—so much so, that she would have been glad to think that he was really her friend. Perhaps, after all, there was very little cause that she should be perplexed or worried on account of his quiet avoidance of her that one evening; but then Clarissa Lovel was young and inexperienced, and thus apt to be hypersensitive, and easily disturbed about trifles.

Having secured a comfortable *tête-à-tête* with Mr. Fairfax, Lady Laura lost no time in improving the occasion. They were scarcely a mile from the Castle before she began to touch upon the subject of the intended marriage, lightly, and with an airy gaiety of manner which covered her real earnestness.

"When is it to be, George? " she asked. "I really want to know something positive, on account of my own engagement and Fred's, which must all hinge more or less on this important business. There's no use in my talking to Geraldine, for she is really the most impracticable of beings, and I can never get her to say anything definite. "

"My dear Lady Laura, I am almost in the same position. I have more than once tried to induce her to fix the date for her marriage, but she has always put the subject aside somehow or other. I really don't like to bore her, you see; and no doubt things will arrange themselves in due course. "

Lady Laura gave a little sigh of relief. He did not avoid the question—that was something; nor did her interference seem in any manner unpleasant to him. Indeed, nothing could be more perfect than his air of careless good-humour, Lady Laura thought.

But she did not mean the subject to drop here; and after a little graceful manipulation of the reins, a glance backward to see how far behind they had left the rest of the caravan, and some slight slackening of the pace at which they had been going, she went on.

"No doubt things would arrange themselves easily enough, if nothing happened to interfere with our plans. But the fact is, my dear George, I am really most uneasy about the state of poor papa's health. He has been so sadly feeble for the last three or four years, and I feel that we may lose him at any moment. At his age, poor dear soul, it is a calamity for winch we must be prepared, but of course such an event would postpone our marriage for a long time, and I should really like to see my sister happily settled before the blow fell upon her. She has been so much with him, you see, and is so deeply attached to him—it will be worse for her than for any of us. "

"I—I conclude so, " Mr. Fairfax replied rather doubtfully. He could not help wondering a little how his betrothed cared to leave a beloved father in so critical a condition; but he knew that his future sister-in-law was somewhat given to exaggeration, a high colouring of simple facts, as well as to the friendly direction of other people's affairs, he was therefore not surprised, upon reflection, that she should magnify her father's danger and her sister's filial devotion. Nor was he surprised that she should be anxious to hasten his marriage. It was natural to this impulsive matron to be eager for something, some event involving fine dress and invitations, elaborate dinners, and the gathering together of a frivolous crowd to be astonished and delighted by her own cleverness and fascination. To have a handsome sister to marry, and to marry well, was of course a great opportunity for the display of all those powers in which Lady Laura took especial pride.

And then George Fairfax had told himself that this marriage was the best possible thing for him; and being so, it would be well that there should be no unnecessary delay. He had perhaps a vague feeling that he was giving up a good deal in sacrificing his liberty; but on the whole the sacrifice was a wise one, and could not be consummated too quickly.

"I trust you alarm yourself needlessly about your father, my dear Lady Laura, " he said presently; "but, upon my word, you cannot be more anxious to see this affair settled than I am. I want to spend my honeymoon at Lyvedon, the quietest, most picturesque old place you can imagine, but not very enjoyable when the leaves are falling. My good uncle has set his heart on my borrowing his house for this purpose, and I think it would please Geraldine to become acquainted with an estate which must be her own in a few years. "

"Unquestionably, " cried Lady Laura eagerly; "but you know what Geraldine is, or you ought to know—so foolishly proud and sensitive. She has known you so long, and perhaps—she would never forgive me if she knew I had hinted such a thing—had half-unconsciously given you her heart before she had reason to be assured of your regard: and this would make her peculiarly sensitive. Now do, dear George, press the question, and let everything be settled as soon as possible, or I have an apprehension that somehow or other my sister will slip through your fingers. "

Mr. Fairfax looked wonderingly at his charioteer.

"Has she said anything to put this fancy into your head? " he asked, with gravity rather than alarm.

"Said anything! O dear, no. Geraldine is the last person to talk about her own feelings. But I know her so well, " concluded Lady Laura with a solemn air.

After this there came a brief silence. George Fairfax was a little puzzled by my lady's diplomacy, and perhaps just a little disgusted. Again and again he told himself that this union with Geraldine Challoner was the very best thing that could happen to him; it would bring him to anchor, at any rate, and he had been such mere driftwood until now. But he wanted to feel himself quite a free agent, and this pressing-on of the marriage by Lady Laura was in some manner discordant with his sense of the fitness of things. It looked a little like manoeuvring; yet after all she was quite sincere, perhaps, and did really apprehend her father's death intervening to postpone the wedding.

He would not remain long silent, lest she should fancy him displeased, and proceeded presently to pay her some compliments upon the roans, and on her driving; after which they rattled on pleasantly enough till they came to the green slope of a hill, where there was a rude rustic stand and a railed racecourse, with a sprinkling of carriages on one side and gipsy-tents on the other.

Here Mr. Fairfax delivered over Lady Laura to her natural protector; and being free to stroll about at his own pleasure, contrived to spend a very agreeable day, devoting the greater part thereof to attendance upon the landau full of ladies, amongst whom was Clarissa Lovel. And she, being relieved from that harassing notion that she had in some unknown manner offended him, and being so new to all the pleasures of life that even these rustic races were delightful to her, was at her brightest, full of gay girlish talk and merry laughter. He was not to see her thus many times again, in all the freshness of her young beauty, perfectly natural and unrestrained.

Once in the course of that day he left his post by the landau, and went for a solitary ramble; not amongst the tents, where black-eyed Bohemians saluted him as "my pretty gentleman, " or the knock-'em-downs and weighing-machines, or the bucolic babble of the ring, but away across the grassy slope, turning his back upon the racecourse. He wanted to think it out again, in his own phrase, just as he had thought it out the day before in the library at Hale.

"I am afraid I am getting too fond of her, " he said to himself. "It's the old story: just like dram-drinking. I take the pledge, and then go and drink again. I am the weakest of mankind. But it cannot make very much difference. She knows I am engaged—and—Lady Laura is right. The sooner the marriage comes off, the better. I shall never be safe till the knot is tied; and then duty, honour, feeling, and a dozen other motives, will hold me to the right course. "

He strolled back to his party only; a little time before the horses were put in, and on this occasion went straight to the phaeton, and devoted himself to Lady Laura.

"You are going to drive me home, of course? " he said. "I mean to claim my place. "

"I hardly think you have any right to it, after your desertion of me. You have been flirting with those girls in the landau all day. "

"Flirting is one of the melancholy privileges of my condition. An engaged man enjoys an immunity in that matter. When a criminal is condemned to death, they give him whatever he likes to eat, you know. It is almost the same kind of thing. "

He took his place in the phaeton presently, and talked gaily enough all the way home, in that particular strain required to match my lady's agreeable rattle; but he had a vague sense of uneasiness lurking somewhere in his mind, a half-consciousness that he was drifting the wrong way.

All that evening he was especially attentive to Lady Geraldine, whose headache had left her with a pale and pensive look which was not without its charm. The stately beauty had a softer air, the brightness of the blue eyes was not so cold as it was wont to be. They played chess again, and Mr. Fairfax kept aloof from Clarissa. They; walked together in the gardens for a couple of hours next morning; and George Fairfax pressed the question of his marriage with such a show of earnestness and warmth, that Geraldine's rebellious pride was at once solaced and subdued, and she consented to agree to any arrangement he and Lady Laura might make.

"My sister is so much more practical than I am, " she said, "and I would really rather leave everything to her and to you. "

Lightly as she tried to speak of the future, she did on this occasion allow her lover to perceive that he was indeed very dear to her, and that the coldness which had sometimes wounded him was little more than a veil beneath which a proud woman strove to hide her deepest feelings. Mr. Fairfax rather liked this quality of pride in his future wife, even if it were carried so far as to be almost a blemish. It would be the surest safe guard of his home in the time to come. Such women are not prone to petty faults, or given to small quarrels. A man has a kind of security from trivial annoyances in an alliance with such a one.

It was all settled, therefore, in that two hours' stroll in the sunny garden, where the roses still bloomed, in some diminution of their midsummer glory, their sweetness just a little over powered by the spicy odour of innumerable carnations, their delicate colours eclipsed here and there by an impertinent early dahlia. Everything was settled. The very date of the wedding was to be decided at once by Lady Laura and the bridegroom; and when George Fairfax went back to the Castle, he felt, perhaps for the first time in his life, that he really was an engaged man. It was rather a solemn feeling, but not altogether an unpleasant one. He had seen more of Geraldine Challoner's heart this morning than he had ever seen before. It pleased him to discover that she really loved him; that the marriage was to be something more to her than a merely advantageous alliance; that she would in all probability have accepted him had he offered himself to her in his brother's lifetime. Since his thirtieth birthday he had begun to feel himself something of a waif and stray. There had been mistakes in his life, errors he would be very glad to forget in an utterly new existence. It was pleasant to know himself beloved by a proud and virtuous woman, a woman whose love was neither to be easily won nor lightly lost.

He went back to the Castle more at ease with himself than he had felt for some time. His future was settled, and he had done his duty.

* * * * *

CHAPTER X.

LADY LAURA'S PREPARATIONS.

After that interview between Mr. Fairfax and his betrothed, there was no time wasted. Laura Armstrong was enraptured at being made arbiter of the arrangements, and was all haste and eagerness, impetuosity and animation. The wedding was appointed for the second week in September, about five weeks from the period of that garden *tête-à-tête*. Lady Geraldine was to go to town for a week, attended only by her maid, to see her father, and to give the necessary orders for her trousseau. The business of settlements would be arranged between the family lawyers. There were no difficulties. Lord Calderwood was not able to settle anything on his daughter, and Mr. Fairfax was inclined to be very generous. There was no prospect of squabbling or unpleasantness.

George Fairfax was to be away during this brief absence of his betrothed. He had an engagement with an old friend and brother officer who was wont to spend the autumn in a roughly comfortable shooting-box in the north of Scotland, and whom he had promised to visit before his marriage; as a kind of farewell to bachelorhood and bachelor friendship. There could be no other opportunity for the fulfilment of this promise, and it was better that Mr. Fairfax should be away while Lady Geraldine was in London. As the period of his marriage became imminent, he had a vague feeling that he was an object of general attention; that every feminine eye, at any rate, was on him; and that the watch would be all the closer in the absence of his betrothed No, he did not want to dawdle away a week (off duty) at Hale Castle. Never before had he so yearned for the rough freedom of Major Seaman's shooting-quarters, the noisy mirth of those rude Homeric feasts, half dinner, half supper, so welcome after a long day's sport, with a quiet rubber, perhaps, to finish with, and a brew of punch after a recondite recipe of the Major's, which he was facetiously declared to bear tattooed above the region of his heart. Mr. Fairfax had been two months at Hale when Lady Geraldine left on that dutiful visit to her father, and necessary interviewing of milliners and dressmakers; and he was, it is just possible, a little tired of decorous country-house life, with its weekly dinner-parties and perpetual influx of county families to luncheon, and its unfailing croquet. He felt, too, that at such a time it would, be perhaps safer for him to be away from Clarissa Lovel.

Was there any real danger for him in her presence? If he asked himself this question nowadays, he was able to answer boldly in the negative. There might have been a time of peril, just one perilous interval when he was in some danger of stumbling; but he had pulled himself up in time, with an admirable discretion, he thought, and now felt as bold as a lion. After that morning with Lady Geraldine in the garden, he had never wavered. He had not been less kind or polite to Miss Lovel; he had only made a point of avoiding anything like that dangerous confidential friendship which had been so nearly arising between them.

Of course every guest at the Castle knew all about the intended wedding directly things had been finally arranged. Lady Laura was not given to the keeping of secrets, and this important fact she communicated to all her particular friends with a radiant face, and a most triumphant manner. The two Fermor girls and Clarissa she invited to remain at Hale till after the wedding, and to act as bridesmaids.

"My sisters Emily and Louisa will make two more, " she said; "and that pretty little Miss Trellis, Admiral Trellis's daughter, will be the sixth—I shall have only six. We'll have a grand discussion about the dresses to-morrow morning. I should like to strike out something original, if it were possible. We shall see what Madame Albertine proposes. I have written to ask her for her ideas; but a milliner's ideas are so *bornées.* " Lady Laura had obtained permission from her sister to enlist Clarissa in the ranks of the bridesmaids.

"It would look so strange to exclude a pretty girl like that, " she said. Whereupon Geraldine had replied rather coldly that she did not wish to do anything that was strange, and that Miss Lovel was at liberty to be one of her bridesmaids. She had studiously ignored the confession of jealousy made that night in her sister's dressing-room; nor had Laura ever presumed to make the faintest allusion to it. Things had gone so well since, and there seemed nothing easier than to forget that unwonted outbreak of womanly passion.

Clarissa heard the approaching marriage discussed with a strange feeling, a nameless undefinable regret. It seemed to her that George Fairfax was the only person in her small world who really understood her, the only man who could have been her friend and counsellor. It was a foolish fancy, no doubt, and had very little foundation in fact; but, argue with herself as she might against her folly, she could not help feeling that this marriage was in somewise a calamity for her. She was quite sure that Lady Geraldine did not like her, and that, as Lady Geraldine's husband, George Fairfax could not be her friend. She thought of this a great deal in those busy weeks before the wedding, and wondered at the heaviness of her heart in these days. What was it that she had lost? As she had wondered a little while ago at the brightness of her life, she wondered now at its darkness. It seemed as if all the colour had gone out of her existence all at once; as if she had been wandering for a little while in some enchanted region, and found herself now suddenly thrust forth from the gates of that fairy paradise upon the bleak outer world. The memory of her troubles came back to her with a sudden sharpness. She had almost forgotten them of late—her brother's exile and disgrace, her father's coldness, all that made her fate dreary and hopeless. She looked forward to the future with a shudder. What had she to hope for—now?

It was the last week in August when Lady Geraldine went up to London, and George Fairfax hurried northward to his Friend's aerie. The trousseau had been put in hand a day or two after the final settlement of affairs, and the post had carried voluminous letters of instruction from Lady Laura to the milliners, and had brought back little parcels containing snippings of dainty fabrics, scraps of laces, and morsels of delicate silk, in order that colours and materials might be selected by the bride. Everything was in progress, and Lady Geraldine was only wanted for the adjustment of those more important details which required personal supervision.

If Clarissa Lovel could have escaped from all this pleasant bustle and confusion, from the perpetual consultations and discussions which Lady Laura held with all her favourites upon the subject of the coming marriage—if she could by any means have avoided all these, and above all her honourable office of bridesmaid—she would most gladly have done so. A sudden yearning for the perfect peace, the calm eventless days of her old life at Mill Cottage, had taken possession of her. In a moment, as if by some magical change, the glory and delight of that brilliant existence at the Castle seemed to have vanished away. There were the same pleasures, the same people; but the very atmosphere was different, and she began to feel like those other girls whose dulness of soul she had wondered at a little while ago.

"I suppose I enjoyed myself too much when first I came here, " she thought, perplexed by this change in herself. "I gave myself up too entirely to the novelty of this gay life, and have used up my capacity for enjoyment, almost like those girls who have gone through half-a-dozen London seasons. "

When Lady Geraldine and George Fairfax were gone, it seemed to Clarissa that the Castle had a vacant air without them. The play still went on, but the chief actors had vanished from the scene. Miss Lovel had allowed herself to feel an almost morbid interest in Mr. Fairfax's betrothed. She had watched Lady Geraldine from day to day, half unconsciously, almost in spite of herself, wondering whether she really loved her future husband, or whether this alliance were only the dreary simulacrum she had read of in fashionable novels—a marriage of convenience. Lady Laura; certainly declared that her sister was much attached to Mr. Fairfax; but then, in an artificial world, where such a mode of marrying and giving in marriage obtained, it would obviously be the business of the bride's relatives to affect a warm belief in her affection for the chosen victim. In all her watching Clarissa had never surprised one outward sign of Geraldine Challoner's love. It was very difficult for a warm-hearted impulsive girl to believe in the possibility of any depth of feeling beneath that coldly placid manner. Nor did she perceive in Mr. Fairfax himself many of those evidences of affection which she would have expected from a man in his position. It was quite true that as the time of his marriage drew near he devoted himself more and more exclusively to his betrothed; but Clarissa could not help fancying, among her many fancies about these two people, that them was something formal and ceremonial in his devotion; that he had, at the best, something of the air of a man who was doing his duty. Yet it would have seemed absurd to doubt the reality of his attachment to Lady Geraldine, or to fear the result of an engagement that had grown out of a friendship which had lasted for years. The chorus of friends at Hale Castle were never tired of dwelling upon this fact, and declaring what a beautiful and perfect arrangement such a marriage was. It was only Lizzie Fermor who, in moments of confidential converse with Clarissa, was apt to elevate her expressive eyebrows and impertinent little nose, and to make disrespectful comments upon the subject of Lady Geraldine's engagement—remarks which Miss Lovel felt it in some manner her duty to parry, by a warm defence of her friend's sister.

"You are such a partisan, Clarissa, " Miss Fermor would exclaim impatiently; "but take my word for it, that woman only marries George Fairfax because she feels she has come to the end of her chances, and that this is about the last opportunity she may have of making a decent marriage. "

The engaged couple were to be absent only a week—that was a settled point; for on the very day after that arranged for their return there was to be a ball at Hale Castle—the first real ball of the season—an event which would of course lose half its glory if Lady Geraldine and her lover were missing. So Laura Armstrong had been most emphatic in her parting charge to George Fairfax.

"Remember, George, however fascinating your bachelor friends may be—and of course we know that nothing we have to offer you in a civilized way can be so delightful as roughing it in a Highland bothy (bothy is what you call your cottage, isn't it?) with a tribe of wild sportsmen—you are to be back in time for my ball on the twenty-fifth. I shall never forgive you, if you fail me. "

"My dear Lady Laura, I would perish in the struggle to be up to time, rather than be such a caitiff. I would do the journey on foot, like Jeannie Deans, rather than incur the odium of disappointing so fair a hostess. "

And upon this Mr. Fairfax departed, with a gayer aspect than he had worn of late, almost as if it had been a relief to him to get away from Hale Castle.

Lady Laura had a new set of visitors coming, and was full of the business involved in their reception. She was not a person who left every arrangement to servants, numerous and skilful as her staff was. She liked to have a finger in every pie, and it was one of her boasts that no department of the household was without her supervision. She would stop in the middle of a page of Tasso to discuss the day's bill of fare with her cook; and that functionary had enough to do to gratify my lady's eagerness for originality and distinction even in the details of her dinner-table.

"My good Volavent, " she would say, tossing the poor man's list aside, with a despairing shrug of her shoulders, "all these entrees are as old as the hills. I am sure Adam must have had stewed pigeons with green peas, and chicken à la Marengo—they are the very ABC of cookery. Do, pray, strike out something a little newer. Let me see; I copied the menu of a dinner at St. Petersburg from 'Count Cralonzki's Diary of his Own Times, ' the other day, on purpose to show you. There really are some ideas in it. Do look it over, Volavent, and see if it will inspire you. We must try to rise above the level of a West-end hotel. "

In the same manner did my lady supervise the gardens, to the affliction of the chief official and his dozen or so of underlings. To have the first peaches and the last grapes in the county of York, to decorate her table with the latest marvel in pitcher plants and rare butterfly-shaped orchids, was Lady Laura's ambition; to astonish morning visitors with new effects in the garden her unceasing desire. Nor within doors was her influence less actively exercised. Drawing-rooms and boudoirs, morning-rooms and bedchambers, were always undergoing some improving touch, some graceful embellishment, inspired by that changeful fancy. When new visitors were expected at the Castle, Lady Laura flitted about their rooms, inspecting every arrangement, and thinking of the smallest minutiae. She would even look into the rooms prepared for the servants on these occasions, to be sure that nothing was wanting for their comfort. She liked the very maids and valets to go away and declare there was no place so pleasant as Hale Castle. Perhaps when people had been to her two or three times, she was apt to grow a little more careless upon these points. To dazzle and astonish was her chief delight, and of course it is somewhat difficult to dazzle old friends.

In the two days after Geraldine Challoner's departure Lady Laura was in her gayest mood. She had a delightful air of mystery in her converse with Clarissa; would stop suddenly sometimes in the midst of her discourse to kiss the girl, and would contemplate her for a few moments with her sweetest smile.

"My dear Lady Laura, what pleasant subject are you thinking about? " Clarissa asked wonderingly; "I am sure there is something. You have such a mysterious air to-day, and one would suppose by your manner that I must be concerned in this mystery. "

"And suppose you were, Clary—suppose I were plotting for your happiness? But no; there is really nothing; you must not take such silly fancies into your head. You know how much I love you, Clary— as much as if you were a younger sister of my own; and there is nothing I would not do to secure your happiness. "

Clarissa shook her head sadly.

"My dear Lady Laura, good and generous as you are, it is not in your power to do that, " she said, "unless you could make my father love me, or bring my brother happily home. "

"Or give you back Arden Court? " suggested Lady Laura, smiling.

"Ah, that is the wildest dream of all! But I would not even ask Providence for that. I would be content, if my father loved me; if we were only a happy united family. "

"Don't you think your father would be a changed man, if he could get back his old home somehow? The loss of that must have soured him a good deal. "

"I don't know about that. Yes, of course that loss does weigh upon his mind; but even when we were almost children he did not seem to care much for my brother Austin or me. He was not like other fathers. "

"His money troubles may have oppressed him even then. The loss of Arden Court might have been a foreseen calamity. "

"Yes, it may have been so. But there is no use in thinking of that. Even if papa were rich enough to buy it, Mr. Granger would never sell the Court. "

"Sell it! " repeated Lady Laura, meditatively; "well, perhaps not. One could hardly expect him to do that—a place for which he has done so much. But one never knows what may happen; I have really seen such wonderful changes come to pass among friends and acquaintances of mine, that scarcely anything would astonish me— no, Clary, not if I were to see you mistress of Arden Court. "

And then Lady Laura kissed her protégée once more with effusion, and anon dipped her brush in the carmine, and went on with the manipulation of a florid initial in her Missal—a fat gothic M, interlaced with ivy-leaves and holly.

"You haven't asked me who the people are that I am expecting this afternoon, " she said presently, with a careless air.

"My dear Lady Laura, if you were to tell me their names, I don't suppose I should be any wiser than I am now. I know so few people. "

"But you do know these—or at least you know all about them. My arrivals to-day are Mr. and Miss Granger. "

Clarissa gave a faint sigh, and bent a little lower over her work.

"Well, child, are you not surprised? have you nothing to say? " cried Lady Laura, rather impatiently.

"I—I daresay they are very nice people, " Clarissa answered, nervously. "But the truth is—I know you must despise me for such folly—I cannot help associating them with our loss, and I have a kind of involuntary dislike of them. I have never so much as seen them, you know—not even at church; for they go to the gothic chapel which Mr. Granger has built in his model village, and never come to our dear little church at Arden; and it is very childish and absurd of me, no doubt, but I don't think I ever could like them. "

"It is very absurd of you, Clary, " returned my lady; "and if I could be angry with you for anything, it certainly would be for this unjust prejudice against people I want you to like. Think what a nice companion Miss Granger would be for you when you are at home—so near a neighbour, and really a very superior girl. "

"I don't want a companion; I am used to being alone. "

"Well, well, when you come to know her, you will like her very much, I daresay, in spite of yourself; that will be my triumph. I am bent upon bringing about friendly relation, between your father and Mr. Granger. "

"You will never do that, Lady Laura. "

"I don't know. I have a profound faith in my own ideas. "

* * * * *

CHAPTER XI.

DANIEL GRANGER.

After luncheon that day, Clarissa lost sight of Lady Laura. The Castle seemed particularly quiet on this afternoon. Nearly every one was out of doors playing croquet; but Clarissa had begun to find croquet rather a wearisome business of late, and had excused herself on the plea of letters to write. She had not begun her letter-writing yet, however, but was wandering about the house in a purposeless way—now standing still for a quarter of an hour at a time, looking out of a window, without being in the least degree conscious of the landscape she was looking at, and then pacing slowly up and down the long picture gallery with a sense of relief in being alone.

At last she roused herself from this absent dreamy state.

"I am too idle to write this afternoon, " she thought. "I'll go to the library and get a book. "

The Hale library was Clarissa's delight. It was a noble collection gathered by dead-and-gone owners of the Castle, and filled up with all the most famous modern works at the bidding of Mr. Armstrong, who gave his bookseller a standing order to supply everything that was proper, and rarely for his own individual amusement or instruction had recourse to any shelf but one which contained neat editions of the complete works of the Druid and Mr. Apperley, the *Life of Assheton Smith*, and all the volumes of the original *Sporting Magazine* bound in crimson russia. These, with *Ruff's Guide*, the *Racing Calendar*, and a few volumes on farriery, supplied Mr. Armstrong's literary necessities. But to Clarissa, for whom books were at once the pleasure and consolation of life, this library seemed a treasure-house of inexhaustible delights. Her father's collection was of the choicest, but limited. Here she found everything she had ever heard of, and a whole world of literature she had never dreamed of. She was not by any means a pedant or a blue-stocking, and it was naturally amongst the books of a lighter class she found the chief attraction; but she was better read than most girls of her age, and better able to enjoy solid reading.

To-day she was out of spirits, and came to the library for some relief from those vaguely painful thoughts that had oppressed her lately.

The room was so little affected by my lady's butterfly guests that she made sure of having it all to herself this afternoon, when the voices and laughter of the croquet-players, floating in at the open windows, told her that the sport was still at its height.

She went into the room, and stopped suddenly a few paces from the doorway. A gentleman was standing before the wide empty fireplace, where there was a great dog-stove of ironwork and brass which consumed about half a ton of coal a day in winter; a tall, ponderous-looking man, with his hands behind him, glancing downward with cold gray eyes, but not in the least degree inclining his stately head to listen to Lady Laura Armstrong, who was seated on a sofa near him, fanning herself and prattling gaily after her usual vivacious manner.

Clarissa started and drew back at sight of this tall stranger.

"Mr. Granger, " she thought, and tried to make her escape without being seen.

The attempt was a failure. Lady Laura called to her.

"Who is that in a white dress? Miss Lovel, I am sure. —Come here, Clary—what are you running away for? I want to introduce my friend Mr. Granger to you. —Mr. Granger, this is Miss Lovel, the Miss Lovel whose birthplace fortune has given to you. "

Mr. Granger bowed rather stiffly, and with the air of a man to whom a bow was a matter of business.

"I regret, " he said, "to have robbed Miss Lovel of a home to which she was attached. I regret still more that she will not avail herself of my desire to consider the park and grounds entirely at her disposal on all occasions. Nothing would give me greater pleasure than to see her use the place as if it were her own. "

"And nothing could be kinder than such a wish on your part. " exclaimed my lady approvingly.

Clarissa lifted her eyes rather shyly to the rich man's face. He was not a connoisseur in feminine loveliness, but they struck him at once as very fine eyes. He was a connoisseur in pictures, and no mean judge of them, and those brilliant hazel eyes of Clarissa's reminded him of a portrait by Velasquez, of which he was particularly proud.

"You are very kind, " she murmured; "but—but there are some associations too painful to bear. The park would remind me so bitterly of all I have lost since I was a child. "

She was thinking of her brother, and his disgrace—or misfortune; she did not even know which of these two it was that had robbed her of him. Mr. Granger looked at her wonderingly. Her words and manner seemed to betray a deeper feeling than he could have supposed involved in the loss of an estate. He was not a man of sentiment himself, and had gone through life affected only by its sternest realities. There was something rather too Rosa-Matildaish for his taste in this faltered speech of Clarissa's; but he thought her a very pretty girl nevertheless, and was inclined to look somewhat indulgently upon a weakness he would have condemned without compunction in his daughter. Mr. Granger was a man who prided himself upon his strength of mind, and he had a very poor idea of the exclusive recluse whose early extravagances had made him master of Arden Court. He had not seen Mr. Lovel half-a-dozen times in his life, for all business between those two that could be transacted by their respective lawyers had been so transacted; but what he had seen of that pale careworn face, that fragile figure, and somewhat irritable manner, had led the ponderous, strong-minded Daniel Granger to consider Marmaduke Lovel a very poor creature.

He was interested in this predecessor of his nevertheless. A man must be harder than iron who can usurp another man's home, and sit by another man's hearthstone, without giving some thought to the exile he has ousted. Daniel Granger was not so hard as that, and he did profoundly pity the ruined gentleman he had deposed. Perhaps he was still more inclined to pity the ruined gentleman's only daughter, who must needs suffer for the sins and errors of others.

"Now, pray don't run away, Clary, " cried Lady Laura, seeing Clarissa moving towards the door, as if still anxious to escape. "You came to look for some books, I know. —Miss Lovel is a very clever young lady, I assure you, Mr. Granger, and has read immensely. — Sit down, Clary; you shall take away an armful of books by-and-by, if you like. "

Clarissa seated herself near my lady's sofa with a gracious submissive air, which the owner of Arden Court thought a rather pretty kind of thing, in its way. He had a habit of classifying all young women in a general way with his own daughter, as if in possessing that one specimen of the female race he had a key to the whole species. His daughter was obedient—it was one of her chief virtues; but somehow there was not quite such a graceful air in her small concessions as he perceived in this little submission of Miss Lovel's.

Mr. Granger was rather a silent man; but my lady rattled on gaily in her accustomed style, and while that perennial stream of small talk flowed on, Clarissa had leisure to observe the usurper.

He was a tall man, six feet high perhaps, with a powerful and somewhat bulky frame, broad shoulders, a head erect and firmly planted as an obelisk, and altogether an appearance which gave a general idea of strength. He was not a bad-looking man by any means. His features were large and well cut, the mouth firm as iron, and unshadowed by beard or moustache; the eyes gray and clear, but very cold. Such a man could surely be cruel, Clarissa thought, with an inward shudder. He was a man who would have looked grand in a judge's wig; a man whose eyes and eyebrows, lowered upon some trembling delinquent, might have been almost as awful as Lord Thurlow's. Even his own light-brown hair, faintly streaked with grey, which he wore rather long, had something of a leonine air.

He listened to Lady Laura's trivial discourse with a manner which was no doubt meant to be gracious, but with no great show of interest. Once he went so far as to remark that the Castle gardens were looking very fine for so advanced a season, and attended politely to my lady's rather diffuse account of her triumphs in the orchid line.

"I don't pretend to understand much about those things, " he said, in his stately far-off way, as if he lived in some world quite remote from Lady Laura's, and of a superior rank in the catalogue of worlds. "They are pretty and curious, no doubt. My daughter interests herself considerably in that sort of thing. We have a good deal of glass at Arden—more than I care about. My head man tells me that I must have grapes and pines all the year round: and since he insists upon it, I submit. But I imagine that a good many more of his pines and grapes find their way to Covent Garden than to my table. "

Clarissa remembered the old kitchen-gardens at the Court in her father's time, when the whole extent of "glass" was comprised by a couple of dilapidated cucumber-frames, and a queer little greenhouse in a corner, where she and her brother had made some primitive experiments in horticulture, and where there was a particular race of spiders, the biggest specimens of the spidery species it had ever been her horror to encounter.

"I wonder whether the little greenhouse is there still? " she thought. "O, no, no; battered down to the ground, of course, by this pompous man's order. I don't suppose I should know the dear old place, if I were to see it now. "

"You are fond of botany, I suppose, Miss Lovel? " Mr. Granger asked presently, with a palpable effort. He was not an adept in small talk, and though in the course of years of dinner-eating and dinner-giving he had been frequently called upon to address his conversation to young ladies, he never opened his lips to one of the class without a sense of constraint and an obvious difficulty. He had all his life been most at home in men's society, where the talk was of grave things, and was no bad talker when the question in hand was either commercial or political. But as a rich man cannot go through life without being cultivated more or less by the frivolous herd, Mr. Granger had been compelled to conform himself somehow to the requirements of civilised society, and to talk in his stiff bald way of things which he neither understood nor cared for.

"I am fond of flowers, " Clarissa answered, "but I really know nothing of botany. I would always rather paint them than anatomise them. "

"Indeed! Painting is a delightful occupation for a young lady. My daughter sketches a little, but I cannot say that she has any remarkable talent that way. She has been well taught, of course. "

"You will find Miss Lovel quite a first-rate artist, " said Lady Laura, pleased to praise her favourite. "I really know no one of her age with such a marked genius for art. Everybody observes it. " And then, half afraid that this praise might seem to depreciate Miss Granger, the good-natured *châtelaine* went on, "Your daughter illuminates, I daresay? "

"Well, yes, I suppose so, Lady Laura. I know that Sophia does some massy kind of work involving the use of gums and colours. I have seen her engaged in it sometimes. And there are scriptural texts on the walls of our poor-schools which I conclude are her work. A young woman cannot have too many pursuits. I like to see my daughter occupied. "

"Miss Granger reads a good deal, I suppose, like Clarissa, ' Lady Laura hazarded.

"No, I cannot say that she does. My daughter's habits are active and energetic rather than studious. Nor should I encourage her in giving much time to literature, unless the works she read were of a very solid character. I have never found anything great achieved by reading men of my own acquaintance; and directly I hear that, a man is never so happy as in his library, I put him down as a man whose life will be a failure. "

"But the great men of our day have generally been men of wide reading, have they not? "

"I think not, Lady Laura. They have been men who have made a little learning go a long way. Of course there are numerous exceptions amongst the highest class of all—statesmen, and so on. But for success in active life, I take it, a man cannot have his brain too clear of waste rubbish in the way of book-learning. He wants all his intellectual coin in his current account, you see, ready for immediate use, not invested in out-of-the-way corners, where he can't get at it. "

While Mr. Granger and my lady were arguing this question, Clarissa went to the bookshelves and amused herself hunting for some attractive volumes. Daniel Granger followed the slender girlish figure with curious eyes. Nothing could have been more unexpected than this meeting with Marmaduke Lovel's daughter. He had done his best, in the first year or so of his residence at the Court, to cultivate friendly relations with Mr. Lovel, and had most completely failed in that well-meant attempt. Some men in Mr. Granger's position might have been piqued by this coldness. But Daniel Granger was not such a one; he was not given to undervalue the advantage of his friendship or patronage. A career of unbroken prosperity, and a character by nature self-contained and strong-willed, combined to sustain his belief in himself. He could not for a moment conceive that Mr. Lovel declined his acquaintance as a thing not worth having. He therefore concluded that the banished lord of Arden felt his loss too keenly to endure to look upon his successor's happiness, and he pitied him accordingly. It would have been the one last drop of bitterness in Marmaduke Lovel's cup to know that this man did pity him. Having thus failed in cultivating anything approaching intimacy with the father, Mr. Granger was so much the more disposed to feel an interest—half curious, half compassionate—in the daughter. From the characterless ranks of young-ladyhood this particular damsel stood out with unwonted distinctness. He found his mind wandering a little as he tried to talk with Lady Laura. He could not help watching the graceful figure yonder, the slim white-robed figure standing out so sharply against the dark background of carved oaken bookshelves.

Clarissa selected a couple of volumes to carry away with her presently, and then came back to her seat by Lady Laura's sofa. She did not want to appear rude to Mr. Granger, or to disoblige her kind friend, who for some reason or other was evidently anxious she should remain, or she would have been only too glad to run away to her own room.

The talk went on. My lady was confidential after her manner communicating her family affairs to Daniel Granger as freely as she might have done if he had been an uncle or an executor. She told him about her sister's approaching marriage and George Fairfax's expectations.

"They will have to begin life upon an income that I daresay *you* would think barely sufficient for bread and cheese, " she said.

Mr. Granger shook his head, and murmured that his own personal requirements could be satisfied for thirty shillings a week.

"I daresay. It is generally the case with millionaires. They give four hundred a year to a cook, and dine upon a mutton-chop or a boiled chicken. But really Mr. Fairfax and Geraldine will be almost poor at first; only my sister has fortunately no taste for display, and George must have sown all his wild oats by this time. I expect them to be a model couple, they are so thoroughly attached to each other. "

Clarissa opened one of her volumes and bent over it at this juncture. Was this really true? Did Lady Laura believe what she said? Was that problem which she had been perpetually trying to solve lately so very simple, after all, and only a perplexity to her own weak powers of reason? Lady Laura must be the best judge, of course, and she was surely too warm-hearted a woman to take a conventional view of things, or to rejoice in a mere marriage of convenience. No, it must be true. They really did love each other, these two, and that utter absence of all those small signs and tokens of attachment which Clarissa had expected to see was only a characteristic of good taste. What she had taken for coldness was merely a natural reserve, which at once proved their superior breeding and rebuked her own vulgar curiosity.

From the question of the coming marriage, Lady Laura flew to the lighter subject of the ball.

"I hope Miss Granger has brought a ball-dress; I told her all about our ball in my last note. "

"I believe she has provided herself for the occasion, " replied Mr. Granger. "I know there was an extra trunk, to which I objected when my people were packing the luggage. Sophia is not usually extravagant in the matter of dress. She has a fair allowance, of course, and liberty to exceed it on occasion; but I believe she spends more upon her school-children and pensioners in the village than on her toilet. "

"Your ideas on the subject of costume are not quite so wide as Mr. Brummel's, I suppose, " said my lady. "Do you remember his reply, when an anxious mother asked him what she ought to allow her son for dress? "

Mr. Granger did not spoil my lady's delight in telling an anecdote by remembering; and he was a man who would have conscientiously declared his familiarity with the story, had he known it.

"'It might be done on eight hundred a year, madam, ' replied Brummel, 'with the strictest economy. '"

Mr. Granger gave a single-knock kind of laugh.

"Curious fellow, that Brummel, " he said. "I remember seeing him at Caen, when I was travelling as a young man. "

And so the conversation meandered on, my lady persistently lively in her pleasant commonplace way, Mr. Granger still more commonplace, and not at all lively. Clarissa thought that hour and a half in the library the longest she had ever spent in her life. How different from that afternoon in the same room when George Fairfax had looked at his watch and declared the Castle bell must be wrong!

That infallible bell rang at last—a welcome sound to Clarissa, and perhaps not altogether unwelcome to Lady Laura and Mr. Granger, who had more than once sympathised in a smothered yawn.

* * * * *

CHAPTER XII.

MR. GRANGER IS INTERESTED.

When Clarissa went to the great drawing-room dressed for dinner, she found Lizzie Fermor talking to a young lady whom she at once guessed to be Miss Granger. Nor was she allowed to remain in any doubt of the fact; for the lively Lizzie beckoned her to the window by which they were seated, and introduced the two young ladies to each other.

"Miss Granger and I are quite old friends, " she said, "and I mean you to like each other very much. "

Miss Granger bowed stiffly, but pledged herself to nothing. She was a tall young woman of about two-and-twenty, with very little of the tender grace of girlhood about her; a young woman who, by right of a stately carriage and a pair of handsome shoulders, might have been called fine-looking. Her features were not unlike her father's; and those eyes and eyebrows of Daniel Granger's, which would have looked so well under a judicial wig, were reproduced in a modified degree in the countenance of his daughter. She had what would be generally called a fine complexion, fair and florid; and her hair, of which she had an abundant quantity, was of an insipid light brown, and the straightest Clarissa had ever seen. Altogether, she was a young lady who, invested with all the extraneous charms of her father's wealth, would no doubt be described as attractive, and even handsome. She was dressed well, with a costly simplicity, in a dark-blue corded silk, relieved by a berthe of old point lace, and the whiteness of her full firm throat was agreeably set off by a broad band of black velvet, from which there hung a Maltese cross of large rubies.

The two young ladies went on with their talk, which was chiefly of gaieties they had each assisted at since their last meeting, and people they had met.

Clarissa, being quite unable to assist in this conversation, looked on meekly, a little interested in Miss Granger, who was, like herself, an only daughter, and about whose relations with her father she had begun to wonder. Was he very fond of this only child, and in this, as in all else, unlike her own father? He had spoken of her that

116

afternoon several times, and had even praised her, but somewhat coldly, and with a practical matter-of-course air, almost as Mr. Lovel might have spoken of his daughter if constrained to talk of her in society.

Miss Granger said a good deal about the great people she had met that year. They seemed all to be more or less the elect of the earth: but she pulled herself up once or twice to protest that she cared very little for society; she was happier when employed with her schools and poor people—*that* was her real element.

"One feels all the other thing to be so purposeless and hollow, " she said sententiously. "After a round of dinners and dances and operas and concerts in London, I always have a kind of guilty feeling. So much time wasted, and nothing to show for it. And really my poor are improving so wonderfully. If you could see my cottages, Miss Fermor! " (she did not say, "their cottages. ") "I give a prize for the cleanest floors and windows, an illuminated ticket for the neatest garden-beds. I don't suppose you could get a sprig of groundsel for love or money in Arden village. I have actually to cultivate it in a corner of the kitchen-garden for my canaries. I give another prize at Christmas for the most economical household management, accorded to the family which has dined oftenest without meat in the course of the year; and I give a premium of one per cent upon all investments in the Holborough savings-bank—one and a half in the case of widows; a complete suit of clothes to every woman who has attended morning and evening service without missing one Sunday in the year, the consequence of which has been to put a total stop to cooking on the day of rest. I don't believe you could come across so much as a hot potato on a Sunday in one of my cottages. "

"And do the husbands like the cold dinners? " Miss Fermor asked rather flippantly.

"I should hope that spiritual advantage would prevail over temporal luxury, even in their half-awakened minds, " replied Miss Granger. "I have never inquired about their feelings on the subject. I did indeed hear that the village baker, who had driven a profitable trade every Sunday morning before my improvements, made some most insolent comments upon what I had done. But I trust I can rise superior to the impertinence of a village baker. However, you must come to Arden and see my cottages, and judge for yourself; and if you could only know the benighted state in which I found these poor creatures— —"

Lizzie Fermor glanced towards Clarissa, and then gave a little warning look, which had the effect of stopping Miss Granger's disquisition.

"I beg your pardon, Miss Lovel, " she said; "I forgot that I was talking of your own old parish. But you were a mere child, I believe, when you left the Court, and of course could not be capable of effecting much improvement. "

"We were too poor to do much, or to give prizes, " Clarissa answered; "but we gave what we could, and—and I think the people were fond of us. "

Miss Granger looked as if this last fact were very wide from the question.

"I have never studied how to make the people fond of me, " she said. "My constant effort has been to make them improve themselves and their own condition. All my plans are based upon that principle. 'If you want a new gown, cloak, and bonnet at Christmas, ' I tell the women, 'you must earn them by unfailing attendance at church. If you wish to obtain the money-gift I wish to give you, you must first show me something saved by your own economy and self-sacrifice. ' To my children I hold out similar inducements—a prize for the largest amount of plain needlework, every stitch of which I make it my duty to examine through a magnifying glass; a prize for scrupulous neatness in dress; and for scripture knowledge. I have children in my Sunday-schools who can answer any question upon the Old-Testament history from Genesis to Chronicles. "

Clarissa gave a faint sigh, almost appalled by these wonders. She remembered the girls' Sunday-school in her early girlhood, and her own poor little efforts at instruction, in the course of which she had seldom carried her pupils out of the Garden of Eden, or been able to get over the rivers that watered that paradise, as described by the juvenile inhabitants of Arden, without little stifled bursts of laughter on her own part; while, in the very midst of her most earnest endeavours, she was apt to find her brother Austin standing behind her, tempting the juvenile mind by the surreptitious offer of apples or walnuts. The attempts at teaching generally ended in merry laughter and the distribution of nuts and apples, with humble apologies to the professional schoolmistress for so useless an intrusion.

Miss Granger had no time to enlarge farther upon her manifold improvements before dinner, to which she was escorted by one of the officers from Steepleton, the nearest garrison town, who happened to be dining there that day, and was very glad to get an innings with the great heiress. The master of Arden Court had the honour of escorting Lady Laura; but from his post by the head of the long table he looked more than once to that remote spot where Clarissa sat, not far from his daughter. My lady saw those curious glances, and was delighted to see them. They might mean nothing, of course; but to that sanguine spirit they seemed an augury of success for the scheme which had been for a long time hatching in the matron's busy brain.

"What do you think of my pet, Mr. Granger? " she asked presently.

Mr. Granger glanced at the ground near my lady's chair with rather a puzzled look, half expecting to see a Maltese spaniel or a flossy-haired Skye terrier standing on its hind legs.

"What do you think of my pet and *protégée*, Miss Lovel? "

"Miss Lovel! Well, upon my word, Lady Laura, I am so poor a judge of the merits of young ladies in a general way; but she really appears a very amiable young person. "

"And is she not lovely? " asked Lady Laura, contemplating the distant Clarissa in a dreamy way through her double eye-glass. "I think it is the sweetest face I ever saw. "

"She is certainly very pretty, " admitted Mr. Granger. "I was struck by her appearance this afternoon in the library. I suppose there is something really out of the common in her face, for I am generally the most unobservant of men in such matters. "

"Out of the common! " exclaimed Lady Laura. "My dear sir, it is such a face as you do not see twice in a lifetime. Madame Recamier must have been something like that, I should fancy—a woman who could attract the eyes of all the people in the great court of the Luxembourg, and divide public attention with Napoleon. "

Mr. Granger did not seem interested in the rather abstract question of Clarissa's possible likeness to Madame Recamier.

"She is certainly very pretty, " he repeated in a meditative manner; and stared so long and vacantly at a fricandeau which a footman was just offering him, that any less well-trained attendant must have left him in embarrassment.

The next few days were enlivened by a good deal of talk about the ball, in which event Miss Granger did not seem to take a very keen interest.

"I go to balls, of course, " she said; "one is obliged to do so: for it would seem so ungracious to refuse one's friends' invitations; but I really do not care for them. They are all alike, and the rooms are always hot. "

"I don't think you will be able to say that here, " replied Miss Fermor. "Lady Laura's arrangements are always admirable; and there is to be an impromptu conservatory under canvas the whole length of the terrace, in front of the grand saloon where we are to dance, so that the six windows can be open all the evening. "

"Then I daresay it will be a cold night, " said Miss Granger, who was not prone to admire other people's cleverness. "I generally find that it is so, when people take special precautions against heat. "

Clarissa naturally found herself thrown a good deal into Sophia Granger's society; but though they worked, and drove, and walked together, and played croquet, and acted in the same charades, it is doubtful whether there was really much more sympathy between these two than between Clarissa and Lady Geraldine. There was perhaps less; for Clarissa Lovel had been interested in Geraldine Challoner, and she was not in the faintest degree interested in Miss Granger. The cold and shining surface of that young lady's character emitted no galvanic spark. It was impossible to deny that she was wise and accomplished; that she did everything well that she attempted; that, although obviously conscious of her own supreme advantages as the heiress to a great fortune, she was benignly indulgent to the less blessed among her sex, —it was impossible to deny all this; and yet it was not any more easy to get on with Sophia Granger than with Lady Geraldine.

One day, after luncheon, when a bevy of girls were grouped round the piano in the billiard-room, Lizzie Fermor—who indulged in the wildest latitude of discourse—was audacious enough to ask Miss Granger how she would like her father to marry again.

The faultless Sophia elevated her well-marked eyebrows with a look of astonishment that ought to have frozen Miss Fermor. The eyebrows were as hard and as neatly pencilled as the shading in Miss Granger's landscapes.

"Marry again! " she repeated, "papa! —if you knew him better, Miss Fermor, you would never speculate upon such a thing. Papa will never marry again. "

"Has he promised you that? " asked the irrepressible Lizzie.

"I do not require any promise from him. I know him too well to have the slightest doubt upon the subject. Papa might have married brilliantly, again and again, since I was a little thing. " (It was rather difficult to fancy Miss Granger a "little thing" in any stage of her existence.) "But nothing has ever been more remote from his ideas than a second marriage. I have heard people regret it. "

"*You* have not regretted it, of course. "

"I hope I know my duty too well, to wish to stand between papa and his happiness. If it had been for his happiness to marry—a person of a suitable age and position, of course—I should not have considered my own feelings in the matter. "

"Well, I suppose not, " replied Lizzie, rather doubtfully; "still it is nice to have one's father all to oneself—to say nothing of being an heiress. And the worst of the business is, that when a widower of your papa's age does take it into his head to marry, he is apt to fall in love with some chit of a girl. "

Miss Granger stared at the speaker with a gaze as stony as Antigone herself could have turned upon any impious jester who had hinted that Oedipus, in his blindness and banishment, was groping for some frivolous successor to Jocasta.

"My father in love with a girl! " she exclaimed. "What a very false idea you must have formed of his character, Miss Fermor, when you can suggest such an utter absurdity! "

"But, you see, I wasn't speaking of Mr. Granger, only of widowers in general. I have seen several marriages of that kind—men of forty or fifty throwing themselves away, I suppose one ought to say, upon girls scarcely out of their teens. In some cases the marriage seems to turn out well enough; but of course one does sometimes hear of things not going on quite happily. "

Miss Granger was grave and meditative after this—perhaps half disposed to suspect Elizabeth Fermor of some lurking design on her father. She had been seated at the piano during this conversation, and now resumed her playing—executing a sonata of Beethoven's with faultless precision and the highest form of taught expression; so much emphasis upon each note—careful *rallentando* here, a gradual *crescendo* there; nothing careless or slapdash from the first bar to the last. She would play the same piece a hundred times without varying the performance by a hair's-breadth. Nor did she affect anything but classical music. She was one of those young ladies who, when asked for a waltz or a polka, freeze the impudent demander by replying that they play no dance music—nothing more frivolous than Mozart.

The day for the ball came, but there was no George Fairfax. Lady Geraldine had arrived at the Castle on the evening before the festival, bringing an excellent account of her father's health. He had been cheered by her visit, and was altogether so much improved, that his doctors would have given him permission to come down to Yorkshire for his daughter's wedding. It was only his own valetudinarian habits and extreme dread of fatigue which had prevented Lady Geraldine bringing him down in triumph.

Lady Laura was loudly indignant at Mr. Fairfax's non-appearance; and for the first time Clarissa heard Lady Geraldine defend her lover with some natural and womanly air of proprietorship.

"After pledging his word to me as he did! " exclaimed my lady, when it had come to luncheon-time and there were still no signs of the delinquent's return.

"But really, Laura, there is no reason he should not keep his word, " Geraldine answered, with her serene air. "You know men like to do these things in a desperate kind of way—as if they were winning a race. I daresay he has made his plans so as not to leave himself more than half-an-hour's margin, and will reach the Castle just in time to dress. "

"That is all very well; but I don't call that keeping his promise to me, to come rushing into the place just as we are beginning to dance; after travelling all night perhaps, and knocking himself up in all sorts of ways, and with no more animation or vivacity left in him than a man who is walking in his sleep. Besides, he ought to consider our anxiety. "

"Your anxiety, if you please, Laura. I am not anxious. I cannot see that George's appearance at the ball is a matter of such vital importance. "

"But, my deal Geraldine, it would seem so strange for him to be away. People would wonder so. "

"Let them wonder, " Lady Geraldine replied, with a little haughty backward movement of her head, which was natural to her.

Amongst the cases and packages which had been perpetually arriving from London during the last week or so, there was one light deal box which Lady Laura's second maid brought to Clarissa's room one morning with her mistress's love. The box contained the airiest and most girlish of ball-dresses, all cloudlike white tulle, and the most entrancing wreath of wild-roses and hawthorn, such a wreath as never before had crowned Miss Lovel's bright-brown hair. Of course there was the usual amount of thanks and kissing and raptures.

"I am responsible to your father for your looking your best, you see, Clary, " Lady Laura said, laughing; "and I intend you to make quite a sensation to-night. The muslin you meant to wear is very pretty, and will do for some smaller occasion; but to-night is a field-night. Be sure you come to me when you are dressed. I shall be in my own rooms till the people begin to arrive; and I want to see you when Fosset has put her finishing touches to your dress. "

Clarissa promised to present herself before her kind patroness. She was really pleased with her dress, and sincerely grateful to the giver. Lady Laura was a person from whom it was easy to accept benefits. There was something bounteous and expansive in her nature, and her own pleasure in the transaction made it impossible for any but the most churlish recipient to feel otherwise than pleased.

* * * * *

CHAPTER XIII.

OPEN TREASON.

The ball began, and without the assistance of Mr. Fairfax—much to my lady's indignation. She was scarcely consoled by the praises and compliments she received on the subject of her arrangements and decorations; but these laudations were so unanimous and so gratifying, that she did at last forget Mr. Fairfax's defection in the delight of such perfect success.

The Duke—the one sovereign magnate of that district—a tall grand-looking old man with white hair, even deigned to be pleased and surprised by what she had done.

"But then you have such a splendid platform to work upon, " he said; "I don't think we have a place in Yorkshire that can compare with Hale. You had your decorators from London, of course? "

"No, indeed, your grace, " replied my lady, sparkling with delighted pride; "and if there is anything I can boast of, it is that. Fred wanted me to send for London people, and have the thing done in their wholesale manner—put myself entirely into their hands, give them *carte blanche*, and so on; so that, till the whole business was finished, I shouldn't have known what the place was to be like; but that is just the kind of arrangement I detest. So I sent for one of my Holborough men, told him my ideas, gave him a few preliminary sketches, and after a good many consultations and discussions, we arrived at our present notion. Abolish every glimmer of gas, " I said, "and give me plenty of flowers and wax-candles. The rest is mere detail. "

Everything was successful; Miss Granger's prophecy of cold weather was happily unfulfilled. The night was unusually still and sultry, a broad harvest moon steeping terraces and gardens in tender mellow light; not a breath to stir the wealth of blossoms, or to flutter the draperies of the many windows, all wide open to the warm night—a night of summer at the beginning of autumn.

Clarissa found herself in great request for the dances, and danced more than she had done since the days of her schoolgirl waltzes and polkas in the play-room at Belforêt. It was about an hour after the dancing had begun, when Lady Laura brought her no less a partner than Mr. Granger, who had walked a solemn quadrille or two with a stately dowager, and whose request was very surprising to Clarissa. She had one set of quadrilles, however, unappropriated on her card, and expressed herself at Mr. Granger's disposal for that particular dance, and then tripped away, to be whirled round the great room by one of her military partners.

Daniel Granger stood amongst the loungers at one end of the room, watching that aerial revolving figure. Yes, Lady Laura was right; she was very lovely. In all his life he had never before paid much heed to female loveliness, any more than to the grandeurs and splendours of nature, or anything beyond the narrow boundary of his own successful commonplace existence. But in this girl's face there was something that attracted his attention, and dwelt in his memory when he was away from her; perhaps, after all, it was the result of her position rather than her beauty. It was natural that he should be interested in her, poor child. He had robbed her of her home, or it would seem so to her, no doubt; and she had let him see that she set an exaggerated value on that lost home, that she clung to it with a morbid sentimentality.

"I should not wonder if she hates me, " he said to himself. He had never thought as much about her father, but then certainly he had never been brought into such close contact with her father.

He waited quietly for that appointed quadrille, declining a dance in which Lady Laura would have enlisted him, and keeping a close watch upon Clarissa during the interval. What a gay butterfly creature she seemed to-night! He could scarcely fancy this was the same girl who had spoken so mournfully of her lost home in the library that afternoon. He looked from her to his daughter for a moment, comparing the two; Sophia resplendent in pink areophane and pearls, and showing herself not above the pleasures of a polka; eminently a fine young woman, but O, of what a different day from that other one!

Once Miss Fermor, passing the rich man on the arm of her partner, surprised the watchful gray eyes with a new look in them—a look that was neither cold nor stern.

"So, my gentleman, " thought the lively Lizzie, "is it that way your fancies are drifting? It was I whom you suspected of dangerous designs the other day, Miss Granger. Take care your papa doesn't fall into a deeper pitfall. I should like to see him marry again, if it were only to take down that great pink creature's insolence. " Whereby it will be seen that Miss Granger was not quite so popular among her contemporaries as, in the serenity of her self-possessed soul, she was wont to imagine herself.

The quadrille began presently, and Clarissa walked through its serious mazes with the man whom she was apt to consider the enemy of her race. She could not help wondering a little to find herself in this position, and her replies to Mr. Granger's commonplace remarks were somewhat mechanical.

Once he contrived to bring the conversation round to Arden Court.

"It would give me so much pleasure to see you there as my daughter's guest, " he said, in a warmer tone than was usual to him, "and I really think you would be interested in her parish-work. She has done wonders in a small way. "

"I have no doubt. You are very kind, " faltered Clarissa; "but I do not the least understand how to manage people as Miss Granger does, and I could not bear to come to the Court. I was so happy there with my brother, and now that he is gone, and that I am forbidden even to mention his name, the associations of the place would be too painful. "

Mr. Granger grew suddenly grave and silent.

"Yes, there was that business about the brother, " he thought to himself; "a bad business no doubt, or the father would never have turned him out of doors—something very queer perhaps. A strange set these Lovels evidently. The father a spendthrift, the son something worse. "

And then he looked down at Clarissa, and thought again how lovely she was, and pitied her for her beauty and her helplessness—the daughter of such a father, the sister of such a brother.

"But she will marry well, of course, " he said to himself, just as George Fairfax had done; "all these young fellows seem tremendously struck by her. I suppose she is the prettiest girl in the room. She will make a good match, I daresay, and get out of her father's hands. It must be a dreary life for her in that cottage, with, a selfish disappointed man. "

The night waned, and there was no George Fairfax. Lady Geraldine bore herself bravely, and danced a good deal more than she would have done, had there not been appearances to be kept up. She had to answer a great many questions about her lover, and she answered all with supreme frankness. He was away in Scotland with some bachelor friends, enjoying himself no doubt. He promised to be with them to-night, and had broken his promise; that was all—she was not afraid of any accident.

"I daresay he found the grouse-shooting too attractive, " she said coolly.

After supper, while the most determined of the waltzers were still spinning round to a brisk *deux temps* of Charles d'Albert's, Clarissa was fain to tell the last of her partners she could dance no more.

"I am not tired of the ball, " she said; "I like looking on, but I really can't dance another step. Do go and get some one else for this waltz; I know you are dying to dance it. "

This was to the devoted Captain Westleigh, a person with whom Miss Level always felt very much at home.

"With *you*, " he answered tenderly. "But if you mean to sit down, I am at your service. I would not desert you for worlds. And you really are looking a little pale. Shall we find some pleasanter place? That inner room, looks deliciously cool. "

He offered his arm to Clarissa, and they walked slowly away towards a small room at the end of the saloon; a room which Lady Laura had arranged with an artful eye to effect, leaving it almost in shadow. There were only a few wax-candles glimmering here and there among the cool dark foliage of the ferns and pitcher-plants that filled every niche and corner, and the moonlight shone full into the room through a wide window that opened upon a stone balcony a few feet above the terrace.

"If I am left alone with her for five minutes, I am sure I shall propose, " Captain Westleigh thought, on beholding the soft secluded aspect of this apartment, which was untenanted when he and Clarissa entered it.

She sank down upon a sofa near the window, more thoroughly tired than she had confessed. This long night of dancing and excitement was quite a new thing to her. It was nearly over now, and the reaction was coming, bringing with it that vague sense of hopelessness and disappointment which had so grown upon her of late. She had abandoned herself fully to the enchantment of the ball, almost losing the sense of her own identity in that brilliant scene. But self-consciousness came back to her now, and she remembered that she was Clarissa Lovel, for whom life was at best a dreary business.

"Can I get you anything? " asked the Captain, alarmed by her pallor.

"Thanks, you are very kind. If it would not be too much trouble—I know the refreshment-room is a long way off—but I should be glad of a little water. "

"I'll get some directly. But I really am afraid you are ill, " said the Captain, looking at her anxiously, scarcely liking to leave her for fear she should faint before he came back.

"No, indeed, I am not ill—only very tired. If you'll let me lest here a little without talking. "

She half closed her eyes. There was a dizziness in her head very much like the preliminary stage of fainting.

"My dear Miss Lovel, I should be a wretch to bore you. I'll go for the water this moment. "

He hurried away. Clarissa gave a long weary sigh, and that painful dizziness passed off in some degree. All she wanted was air, she thought, if there had been any air to be got that sultry night. She rose from the sofa presently, and went out upon the balcony. Below her was the river; not a ripple upon the water, not a breath stirring the rushes on the banks. Between the balcony and the river there was a broad battlemented walk, and in the embrasures where cannon had once been there were great stone vases of geraniums and dwarf roses, which seemed only masses of dark foliage in the moonlight.

The Captain was some little time gone for that glass of water. Clarissa had forgotten him and his errand as she sat upon a bench in the balcony with her elbow leaning on the broad stone ledge, looking down at the water and thinking of her own life—thinking what it might have been if everything in the world had been different.

A sudden step on the walk below startled her, and a low voice said,

"I would I were a glove upon that hand, that I might kiss that cheek. "

She knew the voice directly, but was not less startled at hearing it just then. The step came near her, and in the next moment a dark figure had swung itself lightly upward from the path below, and George Fairfax was seated on the angle of the massive balustrade.

"Juliet! " he said, in the same low voice, "what put it into your head to play Juliet to-night? As if you were not dangerous enough without that. "

"Mr. Fairfax, how could you startle me so? Lady Laura has been expecting you all the evening. "

"I suppose so. But you don't imagine I've been hiding in the garden all the evening, like the man in Tennyson's *Maud*? I strained heaven and earth to be here in time; but there was a break-down between Edinburgh and Carlisle. Nothing very serious: an engine-driver knocked about a little, and a few passengers shaken and bruised more or less, but I escaped unscathed, and had to cool my impatience for half a dozen hours at a dingy little station where there was no refreshment for body or mind but a brown jug of tepid water and a big Bible. There I stayed till I was picked up by the night-mail, and here I am. I think I shall stand absolved by my lady when she reads the account of my perils in to-morrow's papers. People are just going away, I suppose. It would be useless for me to dress and put in an appearance now. "

"I think Lady Laura would be glad to see you. She has been very anxious, I know. "

"Her sisterly cares shall cease before she goes to sleep to-night. She shall be informed that I am in the house; and I will make my peace to-morrow morning. "

He did not go away however, and Clarissa began to feel that there was something embarrassing in her position. He had stepped lightly across the balustrade, and had seated himself very near her, looking down at her face.

"Clarissa, do you know what has happened to me since I have been away from this place? "

She looked up at him with an alarmed expression. It was the first time he had ever uttered her Christian name, but his tone was so serious as to make that a minor question.

"You cannot guess, I suppose, " he went on, "I've made a discovery—a most perplexing, most calamitous discovery. "

"What is that? "

"I have found out that I love you. "

Her hand was lying on the broad stone ledge. He took it in his firm grasp, and held it as he went on:

"Yes, Clarissa; I had my doubts before I went away, but thought I was master of myself in this, as I have been in other things, and fancied myself strong enough to strangle the serpent. But it would not be strangled, Clarissa; it has wound itself about my heart, and here I sit by your side dishonoured in my own sight, come what may—bound to one woman and loving another with all my soul— yes, with all my soul. What am I to do? "

"Your duty, " Clarissa answered, in a low steady voice.

Her heart was beating so violently that she wondered at her power to utter those two words. What was it that she felt—anger, indignation? Alas, no; Pride, delight, rapture, stirred that undisciplined heart. She knew now what was wanted to make her life bright and happy; she knew now that she had loved George Fairfax almost from the first. And her own duty—the duty she was bound in honour to perform—what was that? Upon that question she had not a moment's doubt. Her duty was to resign him without a murmur; never to let him know that he had touched her heart. Even after having done this, there would be much left to her—the knowledge that he had loved her.

"My duty! what is that? " he asked in a hoarse hard voice. "To keep faith with Geraldine, whatsoever misery it may bring upon both of us? I am not one of those saints who think of everybody's happiness before their own, Clarissa. I am very human, with all humanity's selfishness. I want to be happy. I want a wife for whom I can feel something more than a cold well-bred liking. I did not think that it was in me to feel more than that. I thought I had outlived my capacity for loving, wasted the strength of my heart's youth on worthless fancies, spent all my patrimony of affection; but the light shines on me again, and I thank God that it is so. Yes, Clarissa, come what may, I thank my God that I am not so old a man in heart and feeling as I thought myself. "

Clarissa tried to stem the current of his talk, with her heart still beating stormily, but with semblance of exceeding calmness.

"I must not hear you talk in this wild way, Mr. Fairfax, " she said. "I feel as if I had been guilty of a sin against Lady Geraldine in having listened so long. But I cannot for a moment think you are in earnest. "

"Do not play the Jesuit, Clarissa. You *know* that I am in earnest. "

"Then the railway accident must have turned your brain, and I can only hope that to-morrow morning will restore your reason. "

"Well, I am mad, if you like—madly in love with you. What am I to do? If with some show of decency I can recover my liberty—by an appeal to Lady Geraldine's generosity, for instance—believe me, I shall not break her heart; our mutual regard is the calmest, coolest sentiment possible—if I can get myself free from this engagement, will you be my wife, Clarissa? "

"No; a thousand times no. "

"You don't care for me, then? The madness is all on my side? "

"The madness—if you are really in earnest, and not carrying on some absurd jest—is all on your side. "

"Well, that seems hard. I was vain enough to think otherwise. I thought so strong a feeling on one side could not co-exist with perfect indifference on the other. I fancied there was something like predestination in this, and that my wandering unwedded soul had met its other half—it's an old Greek notion, you know, that men and women were made in pairs—but I was miserably mistaken, I suppose. How many lovers have you rejected since you left school, Miss Lovel? " he asked with a short bitter laugh. "Geraldine herself could not have given me my quietus more coldly. "

He was evidently wounded to the quick, being a creature spoiled by easy conquests, and would have gone on perhaps in the same angry strain, but there was a light step on the floor within, and Lady Laura Armstrong came quickly towards the balcony.

"My dearest Clary, Captain Westleigh tells me that you are quite knocked up—" she began; and then recognizing the belated traveller, cried out, "George Fairfax! Is it possible? "

"George Fairfax, my dear Lady Laura, and not quite so base a delinquent as he seems. I must plead guilty to pushing matters to the last limit; but I made my plans to be here at seven o'clock this evening, and should inevitably have arrived at that hour, but for a smash between Edinburgh and Carlisle. "

"An accident! Were you hurt? "

"Not so much as shaken; but the break-down lost me half a dozen hours. We were stuck for no end of time at a dingy little station whose name I forget, and when I did reach Carlisle, it was too late for any train to bring me on, except the night-mail, which does not stop at Holborough. I had to post from York, and arrived about ten minutes ago—too late for anything except to prove to you that I did make heroic efforts to keep my word. "

"And how, in goodness' name, did you get here, to this room, without my seeing you? "

"From the garden. Finding myself too late to make an appearance in the ball-room, I prowled round the premises, listening to the sounds of revelry within; and then seeing Miss Lovel alone here—playing Juliet without a Romeo—I made so bold as to accost her and charge her with a message for you. "

"You are amazingly considerate; but I really cannot forgive you for having deferred your return to the last moment. You have quite spoilt Geraldine's evening, to say nothing of the odd look your absence must have to our friends. I shall tell her you have arrived, and I suppose that is all I can do. You must want some supper, by the bye: you'll find plenty of people in the dining-room. "

"No, thanks; I had some cold chicken and coffee at Carlisle. I'll ring for a soda-and-brandy when I get to my room, and that's all I shall do to-night. Good-night, Lady Laura; good-night, Miss Lovel. "

He dropped lightly across the balcony and vanished. Lady Laura stood in the window for a few moments in a meditative mood, and then, looking up suddenly, said,

"O, by the bye, Clarissa, I came to fetch you for another dance, the last quadrille, if you feel well enough to dance it. Mr. Granger wants you for a partner. "

"I don't think I can dance any more, Lady Laura. I refused Captain Westleigh the last waltz. "

"Yes, but a quadrille is different. However, if you are really tired, I must tell Mr. Granger so. What was George Fairfax saying to you just now? You both looked prodigiously serious. "

"I really don't know—I forget—it was nothing very particular, " Clarissa answered, conscious that she was blushing, and confused by that consciousness.

Lady Laura looked at her with a sharp scrutinising glance.

"I think it would have been better taste on George's part if he had taken care to relieve my sister's anxiety directly he arrived, instead of acting the balcony scene in *Romeo and Juliet*. I must go back to Mr. Granger with your refusal, Clarissa. O, here comes Captain Westleigh with some water. "

The Captain did appear at this very moment carrying a glass of that beverage, much to Clarissa's relief, for a *tête-à-tête* with Lady Laura was very embarrassing to her just now.

"My dear Miss Lovel, you must think me an utter barbarian, " exclaimed the Captain; "but you really can't conceive the difficulties I've had to overcome. It seemed as if there wasn't a drop of iced water to be had in the Castle. If you'd wanted Strasburg pies or

134

barley-sugar temples, I could have brought you them by cartloads. Moselle and Maraschino are the merest drugs in the market; but not a creature could I persuade to get me this glass of water. Of course the fellows all said, 'Yes, sir; ' and then went off and forgot all about me. And even when I had got my prize, I was waylaid by thirsty dowagers who wanted to rob me of it. It was like searching for the North-west Passage. "

Lady Laura had departed by this time. Clarissa drank some of the water and took the Captain's arm to return to the ball-room, which was beginning to look a little empty. On the threshold of the saloon they met Mr. Granger.

"I am so sorry to hear you are not well, Miss Lovel, " he said.

"Thank you, Mr. Granger, but I am really not ill—only too tired to dance any more. "

"So Lady Laura tells me—very much to my regret. I had hoped for the honour of dancing this quadrille with you. "

"If you knew how rarely Mr. Granger dances, you'd consider yourself rather distinguished, I think, Miss Lovel, " said the Captain, laughing.

"Well, no, I don't often dance, " replied Mr. Granger, with a shade of confusion in his manner; "but really, such a ball as this quite inspires a man—and Lady Laura was good enough to wish me to dance. "

He remained by Clarissa's side as they walked back through the rooms. They were near the door when Miss Granger met them, looking as cold and prim in her pink crape and pearls as if she had that moment emerged from her dressing-room.

"Do you know how late it is, papa? " she asked, contemplating her parent with severe eyes.

"Well, no, one does not think of time upon such an occasion as this. I suppose it is late; but it would not do for us of the household to desert before the rest of the company. "

"I was thinking of saying good-night, " answered Miss Granger. "I don't suppose any one would miss me, or you either, papa, if we slipped away quietly; and I am sure you will have one of your headaches to-morrow morning. "

There is no weapon so useful in the hands of a dutiful child as some chronic complaint of its parent. A certain nervous headache from which Mr. Granger suffered now and then served the fair Sophia as a kind of rod for his correction on occasions.

"I am not tired, my dear. "

"O, papa, I know your constitution better than you do yourself. Poor Lady Laura, how worn out she must be! "

"Lady Laura has been doing wonders all the evening, " said Captain Westleigh. "She has been as ubiquitous as Richmond at Bosworth, and she has the talent of never seeming tired. "

Clarissa took the first opportunity of saying good-night. If so important a person as the heiress of Arden Court could depart and not leave a void in the assembly, there could be assuredly no fear that she would be missed. Mr. Granger shook hands with her for the first time in his life as he wished her good-night, and then stood in the doorway watching her receding figure till it was beyond his ken.

"I like your friend Miss Lovel, Sophia, " he said to his daughter presently.

"Miss Lovel is hardly a friend of mine, papa, " replied that young lady somewhat sharply. "I am not in the habit of making sudden friendships, and I have not known Miss Lovel a week. Besides which, she is not the kind of girl I care for. "

"Why not? " asked her father bluntly.

"One can scarcely explain that kind of thing. She is too frivolous for me to get on very well with her. She takes no real interest in my poor, in spite of her connection with Arden, or in church music. I think she hardly knows one *Te Deum* from another. "

"She is rather a nice girl, though, " said the Captain, who would fain be loyal to Clarissa, yet for whom the good opinion of such an heiress is Miss Granger could not be a matter of indifference—there was always the chance that she might take a fancy to him, as he put it to his brother-officers, and what a lucky hit that would be! "She's a nice girl, " he repeated, "and uncommonly pretty. "

"I was not discussing her looks, Captain Westleigh, " replied Miss Granger with some asperity; "I was talking of her ideas and tastes, which are quite different from mine. I am sorry you let Lady Laura persuade you to dance with a girl like that, papa. You may have offended old friends, who would fancy they had a prior claim on your attention. "

Mr. Granger laughed at this reproof.

"I didn't think a quadrille was such a serious matter, Sophy, " he said. "And then, you see, when a man of my age does make a fool of himself, he likes to have the prettiest girl in the room for his partner. "

Miss Granger made an involuntary wry face, as if she had been eating something nasty. Mr. Granger gave a great yawn, and, as the rooms by this time were almost empty, made his way to Lady Laura in order to offer his congratulations upon her triumph before retiring to rest.

For once in a way, the vivacious châtelaine of Hale Castle was almost cross.

"Do you really think the ball has gone off well? " she asked incredulously. "It seems to me to have been an elaborate failure. " She was thinking of those two whom she had surprised tête-à-tête in the balcony, and wondering what George Fairfax could have been saying to produce Clarissa's confusion. Clarissa was her protégée, and she was responsible to her sister Geraldine for any mischief brought about by her favourite.

* * * * *

CHAPTER XIV.

THE MORNING AFTER.

The day after the ball was a broken straggling kind of day, after the usual manner of the to-morrow that succeeds a festival. Hale Castle was full to overflowing with guests who, having been invited to spend one night, were pressed to stay longer. The men spent their afternoon for the most part in the billiard-room, after a late lingering luncheon, at which there was a good deal of pleasant gossip. The women sat together in groups in the drawing-room, pretending to work, but all desperately idle. It was a fine afternoon, but no one cared for walking or driving. A few youthful enthusiasts did indeed get up a game at croquet, but even this soul-enthralling sport was pursued with a certain listlessness.

Mr. Fairfax and Lady Geraldine walked in the garden. To all appearance, a perfect harmony prevailed between them. Clarissa, sitting alone in an oriel at the end of the drawing-room, watched them with weary eyes and a dull load at her heart, wondering about them perpetually, with a painful wonder.

If she could only have gone home, she thought to herself, what a refuge the dull quiet of her lonely life would have been! She had not slept five minutes since the festival of last night, but had lain tossing wearily from side to side, thinking of what George Fairfax had said to her—thinking of what might have been and could never be, and then praying that she might do her duty; that she might have strength to keep firmly to the right, if he should try to tempt her again.

He would scarcely do that, she thought. That wild desperate talk of last night was perhaps the merest folly—a caprice of the moment, the shallowest rodomontade, which he would be angry with himself for having spoken. She told herself that this was so; but she knew now, as she had not known before last night, that she had given this man her heart.

It would be a hard thing to remain at Hale to perform her part in the grand ceremonial of the marriage, and yet keep her guilty secret hidden from every eye; above all, from his whom it most concerned. But there seemed no possibility of escape from this ordeal, unless she were to be really ill, and excused on that ground. She sat in the oriel that afternoon, wondering whether a painful headache, the natural result of her sleeplessness and hyper-activity of brain, might not be the beginning of some serious illness—a fever perhaps, which would strike her down for a time and make an end to all her difficulties.

She had been sitting in the window for a long time quite alone, looking out at the sunny garden and those two figures passing and repassing upon an elevated terrace, with such an appearance of being absorbed in each other's talk, and all-sufficient for each other's happiness. It seemed to Clarissa that she had never seen them so united before. Had he been laughing at her last night? she asked herself indignantly; was that balcony scene a practical joke? He had been describing it to Lady Geraldine perhaps this afternoon, and the two had been laughing together at her credulity. She was in so bitter a mood just now that she was almost ready to believe this.

She had been sitting thus a long time, tormented by her own thoughts, and hearing the commonplace chatter of those cheerful groups, now loud, now low, without the faintest feeling of interest, when a heavy step sounded on the floor near her, and looking up suddenly, she saw Mr. Granger approaching her solitary retreat. The cushioned seat in the oriel, the ample curtains falling on either side of her, had made a refuge in which she felt herself alone, and she was not a little vexed to find her retreat discovered.

The master of Arden Court drew a chair towards the oriel, and seated himself deliberately, with an evident intention of remaining. Clarissa was obliged to answer his courteous inquiries about her health, to admit her headache as an excuse for the heaviness of her eyes, and then to go on talking about everything he chose to speak of. He did not talk stupidly by any means, but rather stiffly, and with the air of a man to whom friendly converse with a young lady was quite a new thing. He spoke to her a good deal about the Court and its surroundings—which seemed to her an error in taste—and appeared anxious to interest her in all his improvements.

"You really must come and see the place, Miss Lovel, " he said. "I shall be deeply wounded if you refuse. "

"I will come if you wish it, " Clarissa answered meekly; "but you cannot imagine how painful the sight of the dear old house will be to me. "

"A little painful just for the first time, perhaps. But that sort of feeling will soon wear off. You will come, then? That is settled. I want to win your father's friendship if I can, and I look to you to put me in the right way of doing so. "

"You are very good, but papa is so reserved—eccentric, I suppose most people would call him—and he lives shut up in himself, as it were. I have never known him make a new friend. Even my uncle Oliver and he seem scarcely more than acquaintances; and yet I know my uncle would do anything to serve us, and I believe papa knows it too. "

"We must trust to time to break down that reserve, Miss Lovel, " Mr. Granger returned cheerily; "and you will come to see us at the Court—that is understood. I want you to inspect Sophia's schools, and sewing classes, and cooking classes, and goodness knows what. There are plenty of people who remember you, and will be delighted to welcome you amongst them. I have heard them say how kind you were to them before you went abroad. "

"I had so little money, " said Clarissa, "I could do hardly anything. "

"But, after all, money is not everything with that class of people. No doubt they like it better than anything in the present moment; but as soon as it is gone they forget it, and are not apt to be grateful for substantial benefits in the past. But past kindness they do remember. Even in my own experience, I have known men who have been ungrateful for large pecuniary benefits, and yet have cherished the memory of some small kindness; a mere friendly word perhaps, spoken at some peculiar moment in their lives. No, Miss Lovel, you will not find yourself forgotten at Arden. "

He was so very earnest in this assurance, that Clarissa could not help feeling that he meant to do her a kindness. She was ashamed of her unworthy prejudice against him, and roused herself with a great effort from her abstraction, in order to talk and listen to Mr. Granger with all due courtesy. Nor had she any farther opportunity of watching those two figures pacing backward and forward upon the terrace; for Mr. Granger contrived to occupy her attention till the dressing-bell rang, and afforded her the usual excuse for hurrying away.

She was one of the last to return to the drawing-room, and to her surprise found Mr. Granger by her side, offering his arm in his stately way when the procession began to file off to the dining-room, oblivious of the claims which my lady's matronly guests might have upon him.

Throughout that evening Mr. Granger was more or less by Clarissa's side. His daughter, perceiving this with a scarcely concealed astonishment, turned a deaf ear to the designing compliments of Captain Westleigh (who told himself that a fellow might just as well go in for a good thing as not when he had a chance), and came across the room to take part in her parent's conversation. She even tried to lure him away on some pretence or other; but this was vain. He seemed rooted to his chair by Clarissa's side—she listlessly turning over a folio volume of steel plates, he pointing out landscapes and scenes which had been familiar to him in his continental rambles, and remarking upon them in a somewhat disjointed fashion— "Marathon, yes—rather flat, isn't it? But the mountains make a fine background. We went there with guides one day, when I was a young man. The Acropolis—hum! ha! —very fine ruins, but a most inconvenient place to get at. Would you like to see Greece, Miss Lovel? "

Clarissa gave a little sigh—half pain, half rapture. What chance had she of ever treading that illustrious soil, of ever emerging from the bondage of her dull life? She glanced across the room to the distant spot where Lady Geraldine and George Fairfax sat playing chess. *He* had been there. She remembered his pleasant talk of his wanderings, on the night of their railroad journey.

"Who would not like to see Greece? " she said.

"Yes, of course, " Mr. Granger answered in his most prosaic way. "It's a country that ought to be remarkably interesting; but unless one is very well up in its history, one is apt to look at everything in a vague uncertain sort of manner. A mountain here, and a temple there—and then the guides and that kind of people contrive to vulgarise everything somehow; and then there is always an alarm about brigands, to say nothing of the badness of the inns. I really think you would be disappointed in Greece, Miss Lovel. "

"Let me keep my dream, " Clarissa answered rather sadly "I am never likely to see the reality. "

"You cannot be sure of that; at your age all the world is before you. "

"You have read Grote, of course, Miss Lovel? " said Miss Granger, who had read every book which a young lady ought to have read, and who rather prided herself upon the solid nature of her studies.

"Yes, I have read a good deal of Grote, " Clarissa replied meekly.

Miss Granger looked at her as if she rather doubted this assertion, and would like to have come down upon her with some puzzling question about the Archons or the Areopagus, but thought better of it, and asked her father if he had been talking to Mr. Purdew.

Mr. Purdew was a landed gentleman of some standing, whose estate lay near Arden Court, and who had come with his wife and daughters to Lady Laura's ball.

"He in sitting over there, near the piano, " added Sophia; "I expected to find you enjoying a chat with him. "

"I had my chat with Purdew after luncheon, " answered Mr. Granger; and then he went on turning the leaves for Clarissa with a solemn air, and occasionally pointing out to her some noted feature in a landscape or city. His daughter stared at him in supreme astonishment. She had seen him conventionally polite to young ladies before to-night, but this was something more than conventional politeness. He kept his place all the evening, and all that Sophia could do was to remain on guard.

When Clarissa was lighting her candle at a table in the corridor, Mr. Fairfax came up to her for the first time since the previous night.

"I congratulate you on your conquest, Miss Lovel, " he said in a low voice.

She looked up at him with a pale startled face, for she had not known that he was near her till his voice sounded close in her ear. "I don't understand you, " she stammered.

"O, of course not; young ladies never can understand that sort of thing. But I understand it very well, and it throws a pretty clear light upon our interview last night. I wasn't quite prepared for such wise counsel as you gave me then. I can see now whence came the strength of your wisdom. It is a victory worth achieving, Miss Lovel. It means Arden Court. —Yes, that's a very good portrait, isn't it? " he went on in a louder key, looking up at a somewhat dingy picture, as a little cluster of ladies came towards the table; "a genuine Sir Joshua, I believe. "

And then came the usual good-nights, and Clarissa went away to her room with those words in her ears, "It means Arden Court. "

Could he be cruel enough to think so despicably of her as this? Could he suppose that she wanted to attract the attention of a man old enough to be her father, only because he was rich and the master of the home she loved? The fact is that Mr. Fairfax—not too good or high-principled a man at the best of times, and yet accounting himself an honourable gentleman—was angry with himself and the whole world, most especially angry with Clarissa, because she had shown herself strong where he had thought to find her weak. Never before had his vanity been so deeply wounded. He had half resolved to sacrifice himself for this girl—and behold, she cared nothing for him!

* * * * *

CHAPTER XV.

CHIEFLY PATERNAL.

The preparations for the wedding went on. Clarissa's headache did not develop into a fever, and she had no excuse for flying from Hale Castle. Her father, who had written Lady Laura Armstrong several courteous little notes expressing his gratitude for her goodness to his child, surprised Miss Lovel very much by appearing at the Castle one fine afternoon to make a personal acknowledgment of his thankfulness. He consented to remain to dinner, though protesting that he had not dined away from home—except at his brother-in-law's—for a space of years.

"I am a confirmed recluse, my dear Lady Laura, a worn-out old bookworm, with no better idea of enjoyment than a good fire and a favourite author, " he said; "and I really feel myself quite unfitted for civilised society. But you have a knack at commanding, and to hear is to obey; so if you insist upon it, and will pardon my morning-dress, I remain. "

Mr. Lovel's morning-dress was a suit of rather clerical-looking black from a fashionable West-end tailor—a costume that would scarcely outrage the proprieties of a patrician dinner-table.

"Clarissa shall show you the gardens between this and dinner-time, " exclaimed Lady Laura. "It's an age since you've seen them, and I want to know your opinion of my improvements. Besides, you must have so much to say to her. "

Clarissa blushed, remembering how very little her father ever had to say to her of a confidential nature, but declared that she would be very pleased to show him the gardens; so after a little more talk with my lady they set out together.

"Well, Clary, " Mr. Lovel began, with his kindest air, "you are making a long stay of it. "

"Too long, papa. I should be so glad to come home. Pray don't think me ungrateful to Lady Laura, she is all goodness; but I am so tired of this kind of life, and I do so long for the quiet of home. "

"Tired of this kind of life! Did ever any one hear of such a girl! I really think there are some people who would be tired of Paradise. Why, child, it is the making of you to be here! If I were as rich as—as that fellow Granger, for instance; confound Croesus! —I couldn't give you a better chance. You must stay here as long as that good-natured Lady Laura likes to have you; and I hope you'll have booked a rich husband before you come home. I shall be very much disappointed if you haven't. "

"I wish you would not talk in that way, papa; nothing would ever induce me to marry for money. "

"*For* money; no, I suppose not, " replied Mr. Lovel testily; "but you might marry a man *with* money. There's no reason that a rich man should be inferior to the rest of his species. I don't find anything so remarkably agreeable in poor men. "

"I am not likely to marry foolishly, papa, or to offend you in that way, " Clarissa answered with a kind of quiet firmness, which her father inwardly execrated as "infernal obstinacy; " "but no money in the world would be the faintest temptation to me. "

"Humph! Wait till some Yorkshire squire offers you a thousand a year pin-money; you'll change your tone then, I should hope. Have you seen anything of that fellow Granger, by the way? "

"I have seen a good deal of Mr. and Miss Granger, papa. They have been staying here for a fortnight, and are here now. "

"You don't say so! Then I shall be linked into an intimacy with the fellow. Well, it is best to be neighbourly, perhaps. And how do you like Mr. Granger? "

"He is not a particularly unpleasant person, papa; rather stiff and matter-of-fact, but not ungentlemanly; and he has been especially polite to me, as if he pitied me for having lost Arden. "

In a general way Mr. Lovel would have been inclined to protest against being pitied, either in his own person or that of his belongings, by such a man as Daniel Granger. But in his present humour it was not displeasing to him to find that the owner of Arden Court had been especially polite to Clarissa.

"Then he is really a nice fellow, this Granger, eh, Clary? " he said airily.

"I did not say nice, papa. "

"No, but civil and good-natured, and that kind of thing. Do you know, I hear nothing but praises of him about Arden; and he is really doing wonders for the place. Looking at his work with an unjaundiced mind, it is impossible to deny that. And then his wealth! —something enormous, they tell me. How do you like the daughter, by the way? "

This question Mr. Lovel asked with something of a wry face, as if the existence of Daniel Granger's daughter was not a pleasing circumstance in his mind.

"Not particularly, papa. She is very good, I daresay, and seems anxious to do good among the poor; and she is clever and accomplished, but she is not a winning person. I don't think I could ever get on with her very well. "

"That's a pity, since you are such near neighbours. "

"But you have always avoided any acquaintance with the Grangers, papa, " Clarissa said wonderingly.

"Yes, yes, naturally. I have shrunk from knowing people who have turned me out of house and home, as it were. But that sort of thing must come to an end sooner or later. I don't want to appear prejudiced or churlish; and in short, though I may never care to cross that threshold, there is no reason Miss Granger and you should not be friendly. You have no one at Arden of your own age to associate with, and a companion of that kind might be useful. Has the girl much influence with her father, do you think? "

"She is not a girl, papa, she is a young woman. I don't suppose she is more than two or three-and-twenty, but no one would ever think of calling Miss Granger a girl. "

"You haven't answered my question. "

"I scarcely know how to answer it. Mr. Granger seems kind to his daughter, and she talks as if she had a great deal of influence over him; but one does not see much of people's real feelings in a great house like this. It is 'company' all day long. I daresay Mr. and Miss Granger are very fond of one another, but—but—they are not so much to each other as I should like you and me to be, papa, " Clarissa added with a sudden boldness.

Mr. Lovel coughed, as if something had stuck in his throat.

"My dear child, I have every wish to treat you fairly—affectionately, that is to say, " he replied, after that little nervous cough; "but I am not a man given to sentiment, you see, and there are circumstances in my life which go far to excuse a certain coldness. So long as you do not ask too much of me—in the way of sentiment, I mean—we shall get on very well, as we have done since your return from school. I have had every reason to be satisfied. "

This was not much, but Clarissa was grateful even for so little.

"Thank you, papa, " she said in a low voice; "I have been very anxious to please you. "

"Yes, my dear, and I hope—nay, am sure—that your future conduct will give me the same cause for satisfaction; that you will act wisely, and settle the more difficult questions of life like a woman of sense and resolution. There are difficult questions to be solved in life, you know, Clary; and woe betide the woman who lets her heart get the better of her head! "

Clarissa did not quite understand the drift of this remark, but her father dismissed the subject in his lightest manner before she could express her bewilderment.

"That's quite enough serious talk, my dear, " he said; "and now give me the *carte du pays*. Who is here besides these Grangers? and what little social comedies are being enacted? Your letters, though very nice and dutiful, are not quite up to the Horace-Walpole standard, and have not enlightened me much about the state of things. "

Clarissa ran over the names of the Castle guests. There was one which she felt would be difficult to pronounce, but it must needs come at last. She wound up her list with it: "And—and there are Lady Geraldine Challoner, and the gentleman she is going to marry—Mr. Fairfax. "

To her extreme surprise, the name seemed to awaken some unwonted emotion in her father's breast.

"Fairfax! " he exclaimed; "what Fairfax is that? You didn't tell me whom Lady Geraldine was to marry when you told me you were to officiate as bridesmaid. Who is this Mr. Fairfax? "

"He has been in the army, papa, and has sold out. He is the heir to some great estate called Lyvedon, which he is to inherit from an uncle. "

"His son! " muttered Mr. Lovel.

"Do you know Mr. Fairfax, papa? "

"No, I do not know this young man. But I have known others—members of the same family—and have a good reason for hating his name. He comes of a false, unprincipled race. I am sorry for Lady Geraldine. "

"He may not have inherited the faults of his family, papa. "

"May not! " echoed Mr. Lovel contemptuously; "or may. I fancy these vices run in the blood, child, and pass from father to son more surely than a landed estate. To lie and betray came natural to the man I knew. Great Heaven! I can see his false smile at this moment. "

This was said in a low voice; not to Clarissa, but to himself; a half-involuntary exclamation. He turned impatiently presently, and walked hurriedly back towards the Castle.

"Let us go in, " he said. "That name of Fairfax has set my teeth on edge. "

"But you will not be uncivil to Mr. Fairfax, papa? " Clarissa asked anxiously.

"Uncivil to him! No, of course not. The man is Lady Laura's guest, and a stranger to me; why should I be uncivil to him? "

Nor would it have been possible to imagine by-and-by, when Mr. Lovel and George Fairfax were introduced to each other, that the name of the younger man was in any manner unpleasant to the elder. Clarissa's father had evidently made up his mind to be agreeable, and was eminently successful in the attempt. At the dinner-table he was really brilliant, and it was a wonder to every one that a man who led a life of seclusion could shine forth all at once with more than the success of a professed diner-out. But it was to Mr. Granger that Marmaduke Lovel was most particularly gracious. He seemed eager to atone, on this one occasion, for all former coldness towards the purchaser of his estate. Nor was Daniel Granger slow to take advantage of his urbane humour. For some reason or other, that gentleman was keenly desirous of acquiring Mr. Lovel's friendship. It might be the commoner's slavish worship of ancient race, it might be some deeper motive, that influenced him, but about the fact itself there could be no doubt. The master of Arden was eager to place his coverts, his park, his library, his hot-houses, his picture-gallery—everything that he possessed—at the feet of his ruined neighbour. Yet even in his eagerness to confer these benefits there was some show of delicacy, and he was careful not to outrage the fallen man's dignity.

Mr. Lovel listened, and bowed, and smiled; pledged himself to nothing; waived off every offer with an airy grace that was all his own. A prime minister, courted by some wealthy place-hunter, could not have had a loftier air; and yet he contrived to make Mr. Granger feel that this was the inauguration of a friendship between them; that he consented to the throwing down of those barriers which had kept them apart hitherto.

"For myself, I am a hermit by profession, " he said; "but I am anxious that my daughter should have friends, and I do not think she could have a more accomplished or agreeable companion than Miss Granger. "

He glanced towards that young lady with a smile—almost a triumphant smile—as he said this. She had been seated next him at dinner, and he had paid her considerable attention—attention which had not been received by her with quite that air of gratification which Mr. Level's graceful compliments were apt to cause. He was not angry with her, however. He contemplated her with a gentle indulgence, as an interesting study in human nature.

"Well, Mr. Lovel, " said Lady Laura in a confidential tone, when he was wishing her good-night, "what do you think of Mr. Granger now? "

"I think he is a very excellent fellow, my dear Lady Laura; and that I am to blame for having been so prejudiced against him. "

"I am so glad to hear you say that! " cried my lady eagerly. She had drawn him a little way apart from the rest of her visitors, out of earshot of the animated groups of talkers clustered here and there. "And now I want to know if you have made any great discovery? " she added, looking at him triumphantly.

He responded to the look with a most innocent stare.

"A discovery, my dearest Lady Laura—you mystify me. What discovery is there for me to make, except that Hale Castle is the most delightful place to visit? —and that fact I knew beforehand, knowing its mistress. "

"But is it possible that you have seen nothing—guessed nothing? And I should have supposed you such a keen observer—such a profound judge of human nature. "

"One does not enlarge one's knowledge of human nature by being buried amongst books as I have been. But seriously, Lady Laura, what is the answer to the enigma—what ought I to have guessed, or seen? "

"Why, that Daniel Granger is desperately in love with your daughter. "

"With Clarissa! Impossible! Why, the man is old enough to be her father. "

"Now, my dear Mr. Lovel, you know that is *no* reason against it. I tell you the thing is certain—palpable to any one who has had some experience in such matters, as I have. I wanted to bring this about; I had set my heart upon it before Clarissa came here, but I did not think it would be accomplished so easily. There is no doubt about his feelings, my dear Mr. Lovel; I know the man thoroughly, and I never saw him pay any woman attention before. Perhaps the poor fellow is scarcely conscious of his own infatuation yet, but the fact is no less certain. He has betrayed himself to me ever so many times by little speeches he has let fall about our dear Clary. I think even the daughter begins to see it. "

"And what then, my kind friend? " asked Mr. Lovel with an air of supreme indifference. "Suppose this fancy of yours to be correct, do you think Clarissa would marry the man? "

"I do not think she would be so foolish as to refuse him, " Lady Laura answered quickly; "unless there were some previous infatuation on her side. "

"You need have no apprehension of that, " returned Mr. Lovel sharply. "Clarissa has never had the opportunity for so much as a flirtation. "

Lady Laura remembered that scene on the balcony with a doubtful feeling.

"I hope she would have some regard for her own interest, " she said thoughtfully. "And if such an opportunity as this were to present itself—as I feel very sure it will—I hope your influence would be exerted on the right side. "

"My dear Lady Laura, my influence should be exercised in any manner you desired, " replied Mr. Lovel eagerly. "You have been so good to that poor friendless girl, that you have a kind of right to dispose of her fate. Heaven forbid that I should interfere with any plans you may have formed on her behalf, except to promote them. "

"It is so good of you to say that. I really am so fond of my dear Clary, and it would so please me to see her make a great marriage, such as this would be. If Mr. Granger were not a good man, if it were a mere question of money, I would not urge it for a moment; but he really is in every way unexceptionable, and if you will give me your permission to use my influence with Clary— —"

"My dear Lady Laura, as a woman, as a mother, you are the fittest judge of what is best for the girl. I leave her in your hands with entire confidence; and if you bring this marriage about, I shall say Providence has been good to us. Yes, I confess I should like to see my daughter mistress of Arden Court. "

Almost as he spoke, there arose before him a vision of what his own position would be if this thing should come to pass. Was it really worth wishing for at best? Never again could he be master of the home of his forefathers. An honoured visitor perhaps, or a tolerated inmate—that was all. Still, it would be something to have his daughter married to a rich man. He had a growing, almost desperate need of some wealthy friend who should stretch out a saving hand between him and his fast-accumulating difficulties; and who so fitted for this office as a son-in-law? Yes, upon the whole, the thing was worth wishing for.

He bade Lady Laura good-night, declaring that this brief glimpse of the civilised world had been strangely agreeable to him. He even promised to stay at the Castle again before long, and so departed, after kissing his daughter almost affectionately, in a better humour with himself and mankind than had been common to him lately.

"So that is young Fairfax, " he said to himself as he jogged slowly homeward in the Arden fly, the single vehicle of that kind at the disposal of the village gentility; "so that is the son of Temple Fairfax. There is a look of his father in his eyes, but not that look of wicked power in his face that there was in the Colonel's—not that thorough stamp of a bold bad man. It will come, I suppose, in good time. "

* * * * *

CHAPTER XVI.

LORD CALDERWOOD IS THE CAUSE OF INCONVENIENCE.

The preparations for the wedding went on gaily, and whatever inclination to revolt may have lurked in George Fairfax's breast, he made no sign. Since his insolent address that night in the corridor he had scarcely spoken to Clarissa; but he kept a furtive watch upon her notwithstanding, and she knew it, and sickened under it as under an evil influence. He was very angry with her—she was fully conscious of that—unjustifiably, unreasonably angry. More than once, when Mr. Granger was especially attentive, she had encountered a withering glance from those dark gray eyes, and she had been weak enough, wicked enough perhaps, to try and make him perceive that Mr. Granger's attentions were in no way pleasant to her. She could bear anything better than that he should think her capable of courting this man's admiration. She told herself sometimes that it would be an unspeakable relief to her when the marriage was over, and George Fairfax had gone away from Hale Castle, and out of her life for evermore; and then, while she was trying to believe this, the thought would come to her of what her life would be utterly without him, with no hope of ever seeing him again, with the bitter necessity of remembering him only as Lady Geraldine's husband. She loved him, and knew that she loved him. To hear his voice, to be in the same room with him, caused her a bitter kind of joy, a something that was sweeter than common pleasure, keener than common pain. His presence, were he ever so silent or angry, gave colour to her life, and to realise the dull blankness of a life without him seemed impossible.

While this silent struggle was going on, and the date of the marriage growing nearer and nearer, Mr. Granger's attentions became daily more marked. It was impossible even for Clarissa, preoccupied as she was by those other thoughts, to doubt that he admired her with something more than common admiration. Miss Granger's evident uneasiness and anger were in themselves sufficient to give emphasis to this fact. That young lady, mistress of herself as she was upon most occasions, found the present state of things too much for her endurance. For the last ten years of her life, ever since she was a precocious damsel of twelve, brought to a premature state of cultivation by an expensive forcing apparatus of governesses and masters, she had been in the habit of assuring herself and her confidantes that her father would never marry again. She had a very keen sense of the importance of wealth, and from that tender age, of twelve or so upwards, she had been fully aware of the diminution her own position would undergo in the event of a second marriage, and the advent of a son to the house of Granger. Governesses and maidservants had perhaps impressed this upon her at some still earlier stage of her existence; but from this time upwards she had needed nothing to remind her of the fact, and she had watched her father with an unwearying vigilance.

More than once, strong-minded and practical as he was, she had seen him in danger. Attractive widows and dashing spinsters had marked him for their prey, and he had seemed not quite adamant; but the hour of peril had passed, and the widow or the spinster had gone her way, with all her munitions of war expended, and Daniel Granger still unscathed. This time it was very different. Mr. Granger showed an interest in Clarissa which he had never before exhibited in any member of her sex since he wooed and won the first Mrs. Granger; and as his marriage had been by no means a romantic affair, but rather a prudential arrangement made and entered upon by Daniel Granger the elder, cloth manufacturer of Leeds and Bradford, on the one part, and Thomas Talloway, cotton-spinner of Manchester, on the other part, it is doubtful whether Miss Sophy Talloway had ever in her ante-nuptial days engrossed so much of his attention.

Having no one else at Hale to whom she could venture to unbosom herself, Miss Granger was fain to make a confidante of her maid, although she did not, as a general rule, affect familiarity with servants. This maid, who was a mature damsel of five-and-thirty or upwards, and a most estimable Church-of-England person, had been with Miss Granger for a great many years; had curled her hair for her when she wore it in a crop, and even remembered her in her last edition of pinafores. Some degree of familiarity therefore might be excused, and the formal Sophia would now and then expand a little in her intercourse with Warman.

One night, a very little while before Lady Geraldine's wedding-day, the cautious Warman, while brushing Miss Granger's hair, ventured to suggest that her mistress looked out of spirits. Had she said that Sophia looked excessively cross, she would scarcely have been beside the mark.

"Well, Warman, " Miss Granger replied, in rather a shrewish tone, "I *am* out of spirits. I have been very much annoyed this evening by papa's attentions to—by the designing conduct of a young lady here. "

"I think I can guess who the young lady is, miss, " Warman answered shrewdly.

"O, I suppose so, " cried Sophia, giving her head an angry jerk which almost sent the brush out of her abigail's hand; "servants know everything. "

"Well, you see, miss, servants have eyes and ears, and they can't very well help using them. People think we're inquisitive and prying if we venture to see things going on under our very noses; and so hypocrisy gets be almost part of a servant's education, and what people call a good servant is a smooth-faced creature that pretends to see nothing and to understand nothing. But my principles won't allow of my stooping to that sort of thing, Miss Granger, and what I think I say. I know my duty as a servant, and I know the value of my own immortal soul as a human being. "

"How you do preach, Warman! Who wants you to be a hypocrite? " exclaimed Sophia impatiently. "It's always provoking to hear that one's affairs have been talked over by a herd of servants, but I suppose it's inevitable. And pray, what have they been saying about papa? "

"Well, miss, I've heard a good deal of talk of one kind and another. You see, your papa is looked upon as a great gentleman in the county, and people will talk about him. There's Norris, Lady Laura's own footman, who's a good deal in the drawing-room—really a very intelligent-well-brought-up young man, and, I am happy to say, *not* a dissenter. Norris takes a good deal of notice of what's going on, and he has made a good many remarks upon your par's attention to Miss Lovel. Looking at the position of the parties, you see, miss, it would be such a curious thing if it was to be brought round for that young lady to be mistress of Arden Court. "

"Good gracious me, Warman! " cried Sophia aghast, "you don't suppose that papa would marry again? "

"Well, I can't really say, miss. But when a gentleman of your par's age pays so much attention to a lady young enough to be his daughter, it generally do end that way. "

There was evidently no consolation to be obtained from Warman, nor was that astute handmaiden to be betrayed into any expression of opinion against Miss Lovel. It seemed to her more than probable that Clarissa Lovel might come before long to reign over the household at Arden, and this all-powerful Sophia sink to a minor position. Strong language of any kind was therefore likely to be dangerous. Hannah Warman valued her place, which was a good one, and would perhaps be still better under a more impulsive and generous mistress. The safest thing therefore was to close the conversation with one of those pious platitudes which Warman had always at her command.

"Whatever may happen, miss, we are in the hands of Providence, " she said solemnly; "and let us trust that things will be so regulated as to work for the good of our immortal souls. No one can go through life without trials, miss, and perhaps yours may be coming upon you now; but we know that such chastisements are intended for our benefit. "

Sophia Granger had encouraged this kind of talk from the lips of Warman, and other humble disciples, too often too be able to object to it just now; but her temper was by no means improved by this conversation, and she dismissed her maid presently with a very cool good-night.

On the third day before the wedding, George Fairfax's mother arrived at the Castle, in order to assist in this important event in her son's life. Clarissa contemplated this lady with a peculiar interest, and was not a little wounded by the strange coldness with which Mrs. Fairfax greeted her upon her being introduced by Lady Laura to the new arrival. This coldness was all the more striking on account of the perfect urbanity of Mrs. Fairfax's manners in a general way, and a certain winning gentleness which distinguished her on most occasions. It seemed to Clarissa as if she recoiled with something like aversion at the sound of her name.

"Miss Lovel of Arden Court, I believe? " she said, looking at Lady Laura.

"Yes; my dear Clarissa is the only daughter of the gentleman who till lately was owner of Arden Court. It has passed into other hands now. "

"I beg your pardon. I did not know there had been any change. "

And then Mrs. Fairfax continued her previous conversation with Lady Laura, as if anxious to have done with the subject of Miss Lovel.

Nor in the three days before the wedding did she take any farther notice of Clarissa; a neglect the girl felt keenly; all the more so because she was interested in spite of herself in this pale faded lady of fifty, who still bore the traces of great beauty and who carried herself with the grace of a queen. She had that air *du faubourg* which we hear of in the great ladies of a departed era in Parisian society, — a serene and tranquil elegance which never tries to be elegant, a perfect self-possession which never degenerates into insolence.

In a party so large as that now assembled at Hale, this tacit avoidance of one person could scarcely be called a rudeness. It might so easily be accidental. Clarissa felt it nevertheless, and felt somehow that it was not accidental. Though she could never be anything to George Fairfax, though all possibility even of friendship was at an end between them, she would have liked to gain his mother's regard. It was an idle wish perhaps, but scarcely an unnatural one.

She watched Mrs. Fairfax and Lady Geraldine together. The affection between those two was very evident. Never did the younger lady appear to greater advantage than in her intercourse with her future mother-in-law. All pride and coldness vanished in that society, and Geraldine Challoner became genial and womanly.

"She has played her cards well, " Barbara Fermor said maliciously. "It is the mother who has brought about this marriage. "

If Mrs. Fairfax showed herself coldly disposed towards Clarissa, there was plenty of warmth on the parts of Ladies Emily and Louisa Challoner, who arrived at the Castle about the same time, and at once took a fancy to their sister's *protégée.*

"Laura has told us so much about you, Miss Lovel, " said Lady Louisa, "and we mean to be very fond of you, if you will allow us; and, O, please may we call you Clarissa? It is such a *sweet* name! "

Both these ladies had passed that fearful turning-point in woman's life, her thirtieth birthday, and had become only more gushing and enthusiastic with increasing years. They were very much like Lady Laura, had all her easy good-nature and liveliness, and were more or less afraid of the stately Geraldine.

"Do you know, we are quite glad she is going to be married at last, " Lady Emily said in a confidential tone to Clarissa; "for she has kept up a kind of frigid atmosphere at home that I really believe has helped to frighten away all our admirers. Men of the present day don't like that sort of thing. It went out of fashion in England with King Charles I., I think, and in France with Louis XIV. You know how badly the royal household behaved coming home from his funeral, laughing and talking and all that: I believe it arose from their relief at thinking that the king of forms and ceremonies was dead. We always have our nicest little parties—kettle-drums, and suppers after the opera, and that sort of thing—when Geraldine is away; for we can do anything with papa. "

The great day came, and the heavens were propitious. A fine clear September day, with a cool wind and a warm sun; a day upon which the diaphanous costumes of the bridesmaids might be a shade too airy; but not a stern or cruel day, to tinge their young noses with a frosty hue, or blow the crinkles out of their luxuriant hair.

The bridesmaids were the Ladies Emily and Louisa Challoner, the two Miss Fermors, Miss Granger, and Clarissa—six in all; a moderation which Lady Laura was inclined to boast of as a kind of Spartan simplicity. They were all to be dressed alike, in white, with bonnets that seemed composed of waxen looking white heather and tremulous harebells, and with blue sashes to match the harebells. The dresses were Lady Laura's inspiration: they had come to her almost in her sleep, she declared, when she had well-nigh despaired of realising her vague desires; and Clarissa's costume was, like the ball-dress, a present from her benefactress.

The nine-o'clock breakfast—a meal that begun at nine and rarely ended till eleven—was hurried over in the most uncomfortable and desultory manner on this eventful morning. The principals in the great drama did not appear at all, and Clarissa and Miss Granger were the only two bridesmaids who could spare half an hour from the cares of the toilet. The rest breakfasted in the seclusion of their several apartments, with their hair in crimping-pins. Miss Granger was too perfect a being to crinkle her hair, or to waste three hours on dressing, even for a wedding. Lady Laura showed herself among her guests, for a quarter of an hour or so, in a semi-hysterical flutter; so anxious that everything should go off well, so fearful that something might happen, she knew not what, to throw the machinery of her arrangements out of gear.

"I suppose it's only a natural feeling on such an occasion as this, " she said, "but I really do feel as if something were going to happen. Things have gone on so smoothly up to this morning—no disappointments from milliners, no stupid mistakes on the part of those railway people—everything has gone upon velvet; and now it is coming to the crisis I am quite nervous. "

Of course every one declared this was perfectly natural, and recommended his or her favourite specific—a few drops of sal-volatile—a liqueur-glass of dry curaçoa—red lavender—chlorodyne—and so on; and then Lady Laura laughed and called herself absurd, and hurried away to array herself in a pearl-coloured silk, half smothered by puffings of pale pink areophane and Brussels-lace flounces; a dress that was all pearly gray and rose and white, like the sky at early morning.

Mr. Armstrong, Mr. Granger, with some military men and country squires, took their breakfast as calmly as if a wedding were part of the daily business of life. Miss Granger exhibited a polite indifference about the great event; Miss Level was pale and nervous, not able to give much attention to Daniel Granger, who had contrived to sit next her that morning, and talked to her a good deal, with an apparent unconsciousness of the severe gaze of his daughter, seated exactly opposite to him.

Clarissa was glad to make her toilet an excuse for leaving Mr. Granger; but once in the sanctuary of her own room, she sat down in an absent manner, and made no attempt to begin dressing. Fosset, the maid, found her there at a quarter past ten o'clock—the ceremony was to take place at eleven—and gave a cry of horror at seeing the toilet uncommenced.

"Good gracious me, miss! what have you been thinking of? Your hair not begun nor nothing! I've been almost torn to bits with one and another—Miss Fermor's maid bothering for long hair-pins and narrow black ribbon; and Jane Roberts—Lady Emily Challoner's maid—who really never has anything handy, wanting half the things out of my work-box—or I should have been with you ever so long ago. My Lady would be in a fine way if you were late. "

"I think my hair will do very well as it is, Fosset, " Clarissa said listlessly.

"Lor, no, miss; not in that dowdy style. It don't half show it off. "

Clarissa seated herself before the dressing-table with an air of resignation rather than interest, and the expeditious Fosset began her work. It was done very speedily—that wealth of hair was so easy to dress; there was no artful manipulation of long hair-pins and black ribbon needed to unite borrowed tresses with real ones. The dress was put on, and Clarissa was invited to look at herself in the cheval-glass.

"I do wish you had a bit more colour in your cheeks to-day, miss, " Fosset said, with rather a vexed air. "Not that I'd recommend you any of their vinegar rouges, or ineffaceable blooms, or anything of that kind. But I don't think I ever saw you look so pale. One would think *you* were going to be married, instead of Lady Geraldine. *She's* as cool as a cucumber this morning, Sarah Thompson told me just now. You can't put *her* out easily. "

The carriages were driving up to the great door by this time. It was about twenty minutes to eleven, and in ten minutes more the procession would be starting. Hale Church was within five minutes' drive of the Castle.

Clarissa went fluttering down to the drawing-room, where she supposed people would assemble. There was no one there but Mr. Granger, who was stalking up and down the spacious room, dressed in the newest and stiffest of coats and waistcoats, and looking as if he were going to assist at a private hanging. Miss Lovel felt almost inclined to ran away at sight of him. The man seemed to pursue her somehow; and since that night when George Fairfax had offered her his mocking congratulations, Mr. Granger's attentions had been particularly repugnant to her.

She could not draw back, however, without positive rudeness, and it was only a question of five minutes; so she went in and entered upon an interesting little conversation about the weather. It was still fine; there was no appearance of rain; a most auspicious day, really; and so on, —from Mr. Granger; to which novel remarks Clarissa assented meekly.

"There are people who attach a good deal of significance to that kind of thing, " he said presently. "For my own part, *if* I were going to be married to the woman I loved, I should care little how black the sky above us might be. That sounds rather romantic for me, doesn't it? A man of fifty has no right to feel like that. "

This he said with a half-bitter laugh. Clarissa was spared the trouble of answering by the entrance of more bridesmaids—Lady Louisa Challoner and Miss Granger—with three of the military men, who wore hothouse flowers in their buttonholes, and were altogether arrayed like the lilies of the field, but who had rather the air of considering this marriage business a tiresome interruption to partridge-shooting.

"I suppose we are going to start directly, " cried Lady Louisa, who was a fluttering creature of three-and-thirty, always eager to flit from one scene to another. "If we don't, I really think we shall be late— and there is some dreadful law, isn't there, to prevent people being married after eleven o'clock? "

"After twelve, " Mr. Granger answered in his matter of fact way. "Lady Geraldine has ample margin for delay. "

"But why not after twelve? " asked Lady Louisa with a childish air; "why not in the afternoon or evening, if one liked? What can be the use of such a ridiculous law? One might as well live in Russia. "

She fluttered to one of the windows and looked out.

"There are all the carriages. How well the men look! Laura must have spent a fortune in white ribbon and gloves for them—and the horses, dear things! "—a woman of Lady Louisa's stamp is generally enthusiastic about horses, it is such a safe thing—"they look as if they knew it was a wedding. O, good gracious! "

"What is the matter. Lady Louisa? "

"A man from the railway—with a telegram—yes, I am sure it's a telegram! Do you know, I have such a horror of telegrams! I always fancy they mean illness—or death—or something dreadful. Very absurd of me, isn't it? And I daresay this is only a message about some delayed parcel, or some one who was to be here and can't come, or something of that kind. "

The room was full of idle people by this time. Every one went to the open window and stared down at the man who had brought the telegram. He had given his message, and was standing on the broad flight of steps before the Castle door, waiting for the return of the official who had taken it. Whether the electric wires had brought the tidings of some great calamity, or a milliner's apology for a delayed bonnet, was impossible to guess. The messenger stood there stolid and impenetrable, and there was nothing to be divined from his aspect.

But presently, while a vague anxiety possessed almost every one present, there came from the staircase without a sudden cry of woe—a woman's shriek, long and shrill, ominous as the wail of the banshee. There was a rush to the door, and the women crowded, out in a distracted way. Lady Laura was fainting in her husband's arms, and George Fairfax was standing near her reading a telegram.

People had not long to wait for the evil news. Lord Calderwood had been seized with a paralytic stroke—his third attack—at ten o'clock the previous night, and had expired at half-past eight that morning. There could be no wedding that day—nor for many days and weeks to come.

"O, Geraldine, my poor Geraldine, let me go to her! " cried Lady Laura, disengaging herself from her husband's arms and rushing upstairs. Mr. Armstrong hurried after her.

"Laura, my sweet girl, don't agitate yourself; consider yourself, " he cried, and followed, with Lady Louisa sobbing and wailing behind him. Geraldine had not left her room yet. The ill news was to find her on the threshold, calm and lovely in the splendour of her bridal dress.

* * * * *

CHAPTER XVII.

"'TIS DEEPEST WINTER IN LORD TIMOR'S PURSE."

Before nightfall—before the evening which was to have been enlivened by a dinner-party and a carpet-dance, and while bride and bridegroom should have been speeding southwards to that noble Kentish mansion which his uncle had lent George Fairfax—before the rooks flew homeward across the woods beyond Hale—there had been a general flight from the Castle. People were anxious to leave the mourners alone with their grief, and even the most intimate felt more or less in the way, though Mr. Armstrong entreated that there might be no hurry, no inconvenience for any one.

"Poor Laura won't be fit to be seen for a day or two," he said, "and of course I shall have to go up to town for the funeral; but that need make no difference. Hale is large enough for every one, and it will be a comfort to her by-and-by to find her friends round her."

Through all that dreary day Lady Laura wandered about her morning-room, alternately sobbing and talking of her father to those chosen friends with whom she held little interviews.

Her sisters Louisa and Emily were with her for the greater part of the time, echoing her lamentations like a feeble chorus. Geraldine kept her room, and would see no one—not even him who was to have been her bridegroom, and who might have supposed that he had the chiefest right to console her in this sudden affliction.

Clarissa spent more than an hour with Lady Laura, listening with a tender interest to her praises of the departed. It seemed as if no elderly nobleman—more or less impecunious for the last twenty years of his life—had ever supported such a load of virtues as Lord Calderwood had carried with him to the grave. To praise him inordinately was the only consolation his three daughters could find in the first fervour of their grief. Time was when they had been apt to confess to one another that papa was occasionally rather "trying," a vague expression which scarcely involved a lapse of filial duty on the part of the grumbler. But to hear them to-day one would have supposed that they had never been tried; that life with Lord Calderwood in a small house in Chapel-street, Mayfair, had been altogether a halcyon existence.

Clarissa listened reverently, believing implicitly in the merits of the newly lost, and did her best to console her kind friend during the hour Mr. Armstrong allowed her to spend with Lady Laura. At the end of that time he came and solemnly fetched her away, after a pathetic farewell.

"You must come to me again, Clary, and very, very soon, " said my lady, embracing her. "I only wish Fred would let you stay with me now. You would be a great comfort. "

"My dearest Lady Laura, it is better not. You have your sisters. "

"Yes, they are very good; but I wanted you to stay, Clary. I had such plans for you. O, by the bye, the Grangers will be going back to-day, I suppose. Why should they not take you with them in their great travelling carriage? —Frederick, will you arrange for the Grangers to take Clarissa home? " cried Lady Laura to her husband, who was hovering near the door. In the midst of her grief my lady brightened a little; with the idea of managing something, even so small a matter as this.

"Of course, my dear, " replied the affectionate Fred. "Granger shall take Miss Lovel home. And now I must positively hurry her away; all this talk and excitement is so bad for you. "

"I must see the Fermors before they go. You'll let me see the Fermors, Fred? "

"Well, well, I'll bring them just to say good-bye—that's all—Come along, Miss Lovel. "

Clarissa followed him through the corridor.

"O, if you please, Mr. Armstrong, " she said, "I did not like to worry Lady Laura, but I would so much rather go home alone in a fly. "

"Nonsense! the Grangers can take you. You could have Laura's brougham, of course; but if she wants you to go with the Grangers, you must go. Her word is law; and she's sure to ask me about it by-and-by. She's a wonderful woman; thinks of everything. "

They met Mr. and Miss Granger presently, dressed for the journey.

"O, if you please, Granger, I want you to take Miss Lovel home in your carriage. You've plenty of 'room, I know. "

Sophia looked as if she would have liked to say that there was no room, but her father's face quite flushed with pleasure.

"I shall be only too happy, " he said, "if Miss Lovel will trust herself to our care. "

"And perhaps you'll explain toiler father what has happened, and how sorry we are to lose her, and so on. "

"Certainly, my dear Armstrong. I shall make a point of seeing Mr. Lovel in order to do so. "

So Clarissa had a seat in Mr. Granger's luxurious carriage, the proprietor whereof sat opposite to her, admiring the pale patrician face, and wondering a little what that charm was which made it seem to him more beautiful than any other countenance he had ever looked upon. They did not talk much, Mr. Granger only making a few stereotyped remarks about the uncertainties of this life, or occasionally pointing out some feature of the landscape to Clarissa. The horses went at a splendid pace Their owner would have preferred a slower transit.

"Remember, Miss Lovel, " he said, as they approached the village of Arden, "you have promised to come and see us. "

"You are very good; but I go out so little, and papa is always averse to my visiting. "

"But he can't be that any more after allowing you to stay at the Castle, or he will offend commoner folks, like Sophy and me, by his exclusiveness. Besides, he told me he wished Sophy and you to be good friends. I am sure he will let you come to us. When shall it be? Shall we say to-morrow, before luncheon—at twelve or one, say? I will show you what I've done for the house in the morning, and Sophy can take you over her schools and cottages in the afternoon. "

Sophia Granger made no attempt to second this proposition; but her father was so eager and decisive, that it seemed quite impossible for Clarissa to say no.

"If papa will let me come, " she said doubtfully.

"O, I'm quite sure he will not refuse, after what he was good enough to say to me, " replied Mr. Granger; "and if he does not feel equal to going about with us in the morning, I hope we shall be able to persuade him to come to dinner. "

They were at the little rustic gate before Mill Cottage by this time. How small the place looked after Hale Castle! but not without a prettiness of its own. The virginia creeper was reddening on the wall; the casement windows open to the air and sunshine. Ponto ran out directly the gate was opened—first to bark at the carriage, and then to leap joyously about Clarissa, overpowering her with a fond canine welcome.

"You'll come in with us, Sophia? " asked Mr. Granger, when he had alighted, and handed Clarissa out of the carriage.

"I think not, papa. You can't want me; and this dreadful morning has given me a wretched headache. "

"I thought there was something amiss. It would be more respectful to Mr. Lovel for you to come in. I daresay he'll excuse you, however, when he hears you are ill. "

Clarissa held out her hand, which Miss Granger took with an almost obvious reluctance, and the two young ladies said "Good-bye" to each other, without a word from Sophia about the engagement for the next day.

They found Mr. Lovel in his favourite sitting-room; not dreaming over a Greek play or a volume of Bentley, as it was his custom to do, but seriously engaged with a number of open letters and papers scattered on the writing-table before him—papers that looked alarmingly like tradesmens' bills. He was taken by surprise on the entrance of Clarissa and her companion, and swept the papers into an open drawer with rather a nervous hand.

"My dear Clarissa, this is quite unexpected! —How do you do, Mr. Granger? How very good of you to bring my little girl over to see me! Will you take that chair by the window? I was deep in a file of accounts when you came in. A man must examine his affairs sometimes, however small his household may be. —Well, Clary, what news of our kind friends at the Castle? Why, bless my soul, this is the wedding-day, isn't it? I had quite forgotten the date. Has anything happened? "

"Yes, papa; there has been a great misfortune, and the wedding is put off. "

Between them, Mr. Granger and Clarissa explained the state of affairs at the Castle. Mr. Lovel seemed really shocked by the intelligence of the Earl's death.

"Poor Calderwood! He and I were great friends thirty years ago. I suppose it's nearly twenty since I last saw him. He was one of the handsomest men I ever knew—Lady Geraldine takes after him—and when he was in the diplomatic service had really a very brilliant career before him; but he missed it somehow. Had always rather a frivolous mind, I fancy, and a want of perseverance. Poor Calderwood! And so he is gone! How old could he have been? Not much over sixty, I believe. I'll look into Debrett presently. "

As soon as he could decently do so after this, Mr. Granger urged his invitation for the next day.

"O, certainly, by all means. Clary shall come to you as early as you like. It will be a great relief for her from the dulness of this place. And—well—yes, if you insist upon it, I'll join you at dinner. But you see what a perfect recluse I am. There will be no one else, I suppose? "

"You have only to say that you wish it, and there shall be no one else, " Mr. Granger replied courteously.

Never had he been so anxious to propitiate any one. People had courted him more or less all his life; and here he was almost suing for the acquaintance of this broken-down spendthrift—a man whom he had secretly despised until now.

On this assurance Mr. Lovel consented to dine with his neighbour for the first time; and Mr. Granger, having no excuse for farther lingering, took his departure, remembering all at once that he had such a thing as a daughter waiting for him in the carriage outside.

He went, and Clarissa took up the thread of her old life just where she had dropped it. Her father was by no means so gracious or agreeable to-day as he had been during his brief visit to Hale Castle. He took out his tradesmen's letters and bills when Mr. Granger was gone, and went on with his examination of them, groaning aloud now and then, or sometimes stopping to rest his head on his hands with a dreary long-drawn sigh. Clarissa would have been very glad to offer her sympathy, to utter some word of comfort; but there was something in her father's aspect which forbade any injudicious approach. She sat by the open window with a book in her hand, but not reading, waiting patiently in the hope that he would share his troubles with her by-and-by.

He went on with his work for about an hour, and then tied the papers in a bundle with an impatient air.

"Arithmetic is no use in such a case as mine, " he said; "no man can make fifty pounds pay a hundred. I suppose it must end in the bankruptcy court. It will be only our last humiliation, the culminating disgrace. "

"The bankruptcy court! O, papa! " cried Clarissa piteously. She had a very vague idea as to what bankruptcy meant, but felt that it was something unutterably shameful—the next thing to a criminal offence.

"Better men than I have gone through it, " Mr. Lovel went on with a sigh, and without the faintest notice of his daughter's dismay; "but I couldn't stand Arden and Holborough after that degradation. I must go abroad, to some dull old town in the south of France, where I could have my books and decent wine, and where, as regards everything else, I should be in a living grave. "

"But they would never make you bankrupt surely, papa; " Clarissa exclaimed in the same piteous tone.

"*They* would never make me bankrupt! " echoed her father fretfully. "What do you mean by *they*? You talk like a baby, Clarissa. Do you suppose that tradesmen and bankers and bill-discounters would have more mercy upon me than upon other people? They may give me more time than they would give another man, perhaps, because they know I have some pride of race, and would coin my heart's blood rather than adopt expedients that other men make light of; but when they know there is no more to be got out of me, they will do their worst. It is only a question of time. "

"Are you very much in debt, papa? " Clarissa asked timidly, anticipating a rebuff.

"No; that is the most confounded part of the business. My liabilities only amount to a few pitiful hundreds. When I sold Arden—and I did not do that till I was obliged, you may believe—the bulk of the purchase-money went to the mortgagees. With the residue—a paltry sum—I bought myself an annuity; a transaction which I was able to conclude upon better terms than most men of my age, on account of my precarious health, and to which I was most strongly urged by my legal advisers. On this I have existed, or tried to exist, ever since: but the income has not been sufficient even for the maintenance of this narrow household; if I lived in a garret, I must live like a gentleman, and should be always at the mercy of my servants. These are honest enough, I daresay, but I have no power of checking my expenditure. And then I had your schooling to pay for—no small amount, I assure you. "

"Thank heaven that is over, papa! And now, if you would only let me go out as a governess, I might be some help to you instead of a burden. "

"There's time enough to think of that. You are not much of a burden to me at present. I don't suppose you add many pounds a year to the expenses of this house. And if I have to face the inevitable, and see my name in the *Gazette*, we must begin life again upon a smaller scale, and in a cheaper place—some out-of-the-way corner of France or Belgium. The governess notion will keep till I am dead. You can always be of some use to me as a companion, if you choose. "

This was quite a concession. Clarissa came over to her father's chair, and laid her hand caressingly upon his shoulder.

"My dear father, " she said in a low sweet voice, "you make me almost happy, in spite of our troubles. I wish for nothing better than to stay with you always. And by-and-by, if we have to live abroad, where you need not be so particular about our name, I may be able to help you a little—by means of art or music—without leaving home. I think I could be happy anywhere with you, papa, if you would only love me a little. "

That appeal touched a heart not easily moved. Marmaduke Lovel put his hand—such a slender feminine hand—into his daughter's with an affectionate pressure.

"Poor child! " he said sadly. "It would be hard if I couldn't love you a little. But you were born under an evil star, Clarissa; and hitherto perhaps I have tried to shut my heart against you. I won't do that any more. Whatever affection is in me to give shall be yours. God knows I have no reason to withhold it, nor any other creature on this earth on whom to bestow it. God knows it is a new thing for me to have my love sued for. "

There was a melancholy in his tone which touched his daughter deeply. He seemed to have struck the key-note of his life in those few words; a disappointed unsuccessful life; a youth in which there had been some hidden cause for the ungenial temper of his middle age.

It was nearly six o'clock by this time, and Clarissa strolled into the garden with her father while the table was being laid for dinner. There were faint glimpses of russet here and there among the woods around Arden Court, but it still seemed summer time. The late roses were in full bloom in Mr. Lovel's fertile garden, the rosy apples were brightening in the orchard, the plums purpling on a crumbling old red-brick wall that bounded the narrow patch of kitchen-garden. Yes, even after Hale Castle the place seemed pretty; and a pang went through Clarissa's heart, as she thought that this too they might have to leave; even this humble home was not secure to them.

Father and daughter dined together very pleasantly. Clarissa had been almost happy by her father's unwonted tenderness, and Mr. Lovel was in tolerable spirits, in spite of that dreary afternoon's labour, that hopeless task of trying to find out some elastic quality in pounds, shillings, and pence.

* * * * *

CHAPTER XVIII.

SOMETHING FATAL.

AT seven o'clock Mr. Level composed himself for his after-dinner nap, and Clarissa, being free to dispose of herself as she pleased till about nine, at which hour the tea-tray was wont to be brought into the parlour, put on her hat and went out into the village. It would be daylight till nearly eight, and moonlight after that; for the moon rose early, as Miss Lovel remembered. She had a fancy to look at the familiar old plane again—the quiet village street, with its three or four primitive shops, and single inn lying back a little from the road, and with a flock of pigeons and other feathered creatures always on the patch of grass before it; the low white-walled cottages, in which there were only friendly faces for her. That suggestion of a foreign home had made her native village newly dear to her.

She had not held much intercourse with these Arden people since her coming home. The sense of her inability to help them in any substantial way had kept her aloof from them. She had not the gift of preaching, or of laying down the laws of domestic economy, whereby she might have made counsel and admonition serve instead of gold or silver. Being able to give them nothing, she felt herself better out of the way; but there were two or three households upon which she had contrived to bestow some small benefits—a little packet of grocery bought with her scanty pocket-money, a jar of good soup that she had coaxed good-natured Martha to make, and so on—and in which her visits had been very welcome.

All was very quiet this evening. Clarissa went through the village without meeting any one she knew. The gate of the churchyard stood open, and Arden churchyard was a favourite spot with Clarissa. A solemn old place, shadowed by funereal yews and spreading cedars, which must have been trees of some importance before the Hanoverian succession. There was a narrow footpath between two rows of tall quaint old tombstones, with skulls and crossbones out upon the moss-grown stone; a path leading to another gate which opened upon a wide patch of heath skirted by a scanty firwood.

This was the wildest bit of landscape about Arden, and Clarissa loved it with all an artist's love. She had sketched th .t belt of fir-trees under almost every condition—with the evening sun behind them, standing blackly out against the warm crimson light; or later, when the day had left no more than a faint opal glimmer in the western sky; later still, in the fair summer moonlight, or en a blusterous autumn afternoon, tossed by the pitiless wind. There was a poetry in the scene that seemed to inspire her pencil, and yet she could never quite satisfy herself. In short, she was not Turner; and that wood and sky needed the pencil of a Turner to translate them fully. This evening she had brought her pocket sketch-book with her. It was the companion of all her lonely walks.

She sat down upon the low boundary-wall of the churchyard, close by the rustic wooden gate through which she had come, facing the heath and the firwood, and took out her sketch-book. There was always something new; inexhaustible Nature had ever some fresh lesson for her. But this evening she sat idle for a long time, with her pencil in her hand; and when at last she began to draw, it was no feature of heathy ridge or dark firwood, but a man's face, that appeared upon the page.

It was a face that she had drawn very often lately in her idle moods, half unconsciously sometimes—a bold handsome face, that offered none of those difficulties by which some countenances baffle the skill of a painter. It was the face of a man of whom she had told herself it was a sin even to think; but the face haunted her somehow, and it seemed as if her pencil reproduced it in spite of herself.

She was thinking as she drew near of Lady Geraldine's postponed wedding. It would have been better that the marriage should have taken place; better that the story should have ended to-day and that the frail link between herself and George Fairfax should have been broken. That accident of Lord Calderwood's death had made everything more or less uncertain. Would the marriage ever take place? Would George Fairfax, with ample leisure for deliberation, hold himself bound by his promise, and marry a woman to whom he had confessed himself indifferent?

She was brooding over this question when she heard the thud of a horse's hoofs upon the grass, and, looking up, saw a man riding towards her. He was leaning across his horse's head, looking down at her in the next moment—a dark figure shutting out the waving line of fir-trees and the warm light in the western sky. "What are you doing there, Miss Lovel? " asked a voice that went straight to her heart. Who shall say that it was deeper or sweeter than, common voices? but for her it had a thrilling sound.

She started and dropped her book. George Fairfax dismounted, tied his horse's bridle to the churchyard gate, and picked up the little sketch-book.

"My portrait! " he cried, recognizing the carelessly-pencilled bead. "Then you do think of me a little, Clarissa! Do you know that I have been prowling about Arden for the last two hours, waiting and watching for you? I have ridden past your father's cottage twenty times, I think, and was on the point of giving up all hope and galloping back to Hale, when I caught sight of a familiar figure from that road yonder. "

He had taken a knife from his pocket, and was deliberately cutting out the leaf from Miss Lovel's sketch-book.

"I shall keep this, Clarissa, —this one blessed scrap of evidence that you do sometimes think of me. "

"I think of a good many people in the same manner, " she said, smiling, with recovered self-possession. "I have very few acquaintance whose likenesses I have not attempted in some fashion. "

"But you have attempted mine very often, " he answered, looking over the leaves of the book. "Yes, here is my profile amongst bits of foliage, and scroll-work, and all the vagabond thoughts of your artistic brain. You shall not snub me, Clarissa. You do think of me— not as I think of you, perhaps, by day and night, but enough for my encouragement, almost enough for my happiness. Good heavens, how angry I have been with you during the last few weeks! "

"What right had you to be angry with me, Mr. Fairfax? "

"The sublime right of loving you. To my mind that constitutes a kind of moral ownership. And to see you flirting with that fellow Granger, and yet have to hold my peace! But, thank God, all pretences are done with. I recognize the event of to-day as an interposition of Providence. As soon as I can decently do so, I shall tell Lady Geraldine the truth. "

"You will not break your engagement—at such a time—when she has double need of your love? " cried Clarissa indignantly.

She saw the situation from the woman's point of view, and it was of Geraldine Challoner's feelings she thought at this crisis. George Fairfax weighed nothing in the scale against that sorrowing daughter. And yet she loved him.

"My love she never had, and never can have; nor do I believe that honour compels me to make myself miserable for life. Of course I shall not disturb her in the hour of her grief by any talk about our intended marriage; but, so soon as I can do so with kindness, I shall let her know the real state of my feelings. She is too generous to exact any sacrifice from me. "

"And you will make her miserable for life, perhaps? "

"I am not afraid of that. I tell you, Clarissa, it is not in her cold proud nature to care much for any man. We can invent some story to account for the rupture, which will save her womanly pride. The world can be told that it is she who has broken the engagement: all that will be easily settled. Poor Lord Calderwood! Don't imagine that I am not heartily sorry for him; he was always a good friend to me; but his death has been most opportune. It has saved me, Clarissa. But for that I should have been a married man this night, a bound slave for evermore. You can never conceive the gloomy dogged spirit in which I was going to my doom. Thank God, the release came; and here, sitting by your side, a free man, I feel how bitter a bondage I have escaped. "

He put his arm round Clarissa, and tried to draw her towards him; but she released herself from him with a quick proud movement, and rose from her seat on the low wall. He rose at the same moment, and they stood facing each other in the darkening twilight.

"And what then, Mr. Fairfax? " she said, trembling a little, but looking him steadily in the face nevertheless. "When you have behaved like a traitor, and broken your engagement, what then? "

"What then? Is there any possible doubt about what must come then? You will be my wife, Clarissa! "

"You think that I would be an accomplice to such cruelty? You think that I could be so basely ungrateful to Lady Laura, my first friend? Yes, Mr. Fairfax, the first friend I ever had, except my aunt, whose friendship has always seemed a kind of duty. You think that after all her goodness to me I could have any part in breaking her sister's heart? "

"I think there is one person whose feelings you overlook in this business. "

"And who is that? "

"Myself. You seem to forget that I love you, and that my happiness depends upon you. Are you going to stand upon punctilio, Clarissa, and break my heart because Laura Armstrong has been civil to you? "

Clarissa smiled—a very mournful smile.

"I do not believe you are so dreadfully in earnest, " she said. "If I did—"

"If you did, what then, Clarissa? "

"It might be different. I might be foolish enough, wicked enough— But I am sure that this folly of yours is no more than a passing fancy. You will go away and forget all about me. You would be very sorry by-and-by, if I were weak enough to take you at your word; just as sorry as you are now for your engagement to Lady Geraldine. Come, Mr. Fairfax, let us both be sensible, if we can, and let there be an end of this folly for evermore between us. Good-night; I must go home. It is half-past eight o'clock, and at nine papa has his tea. "

"You shall go home in time to pour out Mr. Lovel's tea; but you shall hear me out first, Clarissa, and you shall confess to me. I will not be kept in the dark. "

And then he urged his cause, passionately, eloquently, or with that which seemed eloquence to the girl of nineteen, who heard him with pale cheeks and fast-throbbing heart, and yet tried to seem unmoved. Plead as he might, he could win no admission from her. It was only in her eyes, which could not look denial, on her tremulous lips, which could not simulate coldness, that he read her secret. There he saw enough to make him happy and triumphant.

"Say what you please, my pitiless one, " he cried at last; "in less than three months you shall be my wife! "

The church-clock chimed the three-quarters. He had no excuse for keeping her any longer.

"Come then, Clarissa, " he said, drawing her hand through his arm; "let me see you to your father's door. "

"But your horse—you can't leave him here? "

"Yes, I can. I don't suppose any one will steal him in a quarter of an hour or so; and I daresay we shall meet some village urchin whom I can send to take care of him. "

"There is no occasion. I am quite accustomed to walk about Arden alone. "

"Not at this hour. I have detained you, and am bound to see you safely lodged. "

"But if papa should hear——"

"He shall near nothing. I'll leave you within a few yards of his gate. "

It was no use for her to protest; so they went back to within half a dozen paces of Mill Cottage arm-in-arm; not talking very much, but dangerously happy in each other's company.

"I shall see you again very soon, Clarissa, " George Fairfax said. And then he asked her to tell him her favourite walks; but this she refused to do.

"No matter. I shall find you out in spite of your obstinacy. And remember, child, you owe nothing to Laura Armstrong except the sort of kindness she would show to any pretty girl of good family. You are as necessary to her as the orchids on her dinner-table. I don't deny that she is a warm-hearted little woman, with a great deal that is good in her—just the sort of woman to dispense a large fortune. But I shall make matters all right in that quarter, and at once. "

They were now as near Mill Cottage as Mr. Fairfax considered it prudent to go. He stopped, released Clarissa's hand from his arm, only to lift it to his lips and kiss it—the tremulous little ungloved hand which had been sketching his profile when he surprised her, half an hour before, on the churchyard wall.

There was not a creature on the road before them, as they Stood thus in the moonlight; but in spite of this appearance of security, they were not unobserved. A pair of angry eyes watched them from across a clipped holly hedge in front of the cottage—the eyes of Marmaduke Lovel, who had ventured out in the soft September night to smoke his after-dinner cigar.

"Good-night, Clarissa, " said George Fairfax; "I shall see you again very soon. "

"No, no; I don't wish to see you. No good can come of our seeing each other. "

"You will see me, whether you wish or not. Good-night. There is nine striking. You will be in time to pour out papa's tea. "

He let go the little hand which he had held till now, and went away. When Clarissa came to the gate, she found it open, and her father standing by it. She drew back with a guilty start.

"Pray come in, " said Mr. Lovel, in his most ceremonious tone. "I am very glad that a happy accident has enabled me to become familiar with your new habits. Have you learnt to give clandestine meetings to your lovers at Hale Castle? Have I to thank Lady Laura for this novel development of your character? "

"I don't know what you mean, papa. I was sitting in the churchyard just now, sketching, when Mr. Fairfax rode up to me. He stopped talking a little, and then insisted on seeing me home. That is all. "

"That is all. And so it was George Fairfax—the bridegroom that was to have been—who kissed your hand just now, in that loverlike fashion. Pray come indoors; I think this is a business that requires to be discussed between us quietly. "

"Believe me you have no reason to be angry, papa, " pleaded Clarissa; "nothing could have been farther from my thoughts than the idea of meeting Mr. Fairfax to-night. "

"I have heard that kind of denial before, and know what it is worth, " answered her father coldly. "And pray, if he did not come here to meet you, may I ask what motive brought Mr. Fairfax to Arden to-night? His proper place would have been at Hale Castle, I should have supposed. "

"I don't know, papa. He may have come to Arden for a ride. Everything is in confusion at the Castle, I scarcely think he would be wanted there. "

"You scarcely think! And you encourage him to follow you here— this man who was to have been married to Lady Geraldine Challoner to-day—and you let him kiss your hand, and part from you with the air of a lover. I am ashamed of you, Clarissa. This business is odious enough in itself to provoke the anger of any father, if there were not circumstances in the past to make it trebly hateful to me. "

They had passed in at the open window by this time, and were standing in the lamp-lit parlour, which had a pretty air of home comfort, with its delicate tea-service and quaintly shaped silver urn. Mr. Lovel sank into his arm-chair with a faint groan, and looking at him in the full light of the lamp, Clarissa saw that he was deadly pale.

"Do you know that the father of that man was my deadliest foe? " he exclaimed.

"How should I know that, papa? "

"How should you know it! —no. But that you should choose that man for your secret lover! One would think there was some hereditary curse upon your mother's race, binding her and hers with that hateful name. I tell you, Clarissa, that if there had been no such creature as Temple Fairfax, my life might have been as bright a one as any man need hope for. I owe every misery of my existence to that man. "

"Did he injure you so deeply, papa? "

"He did me the worst wrong that one man can do to another. He came between me and the woman I loved; he stole your mother's heart from me, Clarissa, and embittered both our lives. "

He stopped, and covered his face with his hand. Clarissa could see that the hand trembled. She had never seen her father so moved before. She too was deeply moved. She drew a chair close to him, and sat down by his side, but dared not speak.

"It is just as well that you should hear the story from me, " he said, after a long pause. "You may hear hints and whispers about it from other people by-and-by perhaps, if you go more into society; for it was known to several. It is best you should know the truth. It is a common story enough in the history of the world; but whenever it happens, it is enough to make the misery of one man's life. I was not always what you have known me, Clarissa, —a worn-out machine, dawdling away the remnant of a wasted existence. I once had hopes and passions like the rest of mankind—perhaps more ardent than the most. Your mother was the loveliest and most fascinating woman I ever met, and from the hour of our first meeting I had but one thought—how I should win her for my wife. It was not a prudent marriage. She was my equal by birth; but she was the daughter of a ruined spendthrift, and had learnt extravagance and recklessness in her very nursery. She thought me much richer than I was, and I did not care to undeceive her. Later, when we were married, and I could see that her extravagant habits were hastening my ruin, I was still too much a moral coward to tell her the naked truth. I could not bear to come between her and caprices that seemed a natural accompaniment to her charms. I was weakness itself in all that concerned her. "

"And she loved you, papa? " said Clarissa softly. "I am sure she must have loved you. "

"That is a question that I have never answered with any satisfaction to myself. I thought she loved me. She liked me well enough, I believe, till that man crossed her path, and might have learnt to like me better as she grew older and wiser, and rose above the slavery of frivolous pleasures. But, in the most evil hour of her life, she met Temple Fairfax, and from that hour her heart was turned from me. We were travelling, trying to recover from the expenses of a house perpetually full of my wife's set; and it was at Florence that we first encountered the Colonel. He had just returned from India, had been doing great things there, and was considered rather a distinguished person in Florentine society. I need not stop to describe him. His son is like him. He and I became friends, and met almost daily. It was not till a year afterwards that I knew how pitiful a dupe of this man's treachery I had been from the very first. We were still in Italy when I made my first discovery; it was one that let in the light upon his character, but did not seriously involve my wife. We fought, and I was wounded. When I recovered, I brought my wife home to Arden. Our year's retrenchment had left me poorer than when I left home. Your mother's beauty was a luxury not to be maintained more cheaply at Florence than in Yorkshire. "

There was another pause, and then Marmaduke Lovel went on, in the same bitter tone:

"Within a short time of our return your brother was born. There are things that I can't even hint to you, Clarissa; but there have been times when the shadow of that man has come between me and my children. Passion has made me unjust. I know that in her worst sin against my love—for I went on loving her to the last—your mother remained what the world calls innocent. But years after I had believed there was an end of all communion between those two, I discovered letters, even stolen meetings—rare, I confess, and never without witnesses, but no less a treason against me. Colonel Fairfax had friends at Holborough, by whose aid he contrived to see my wife. That he urged her to leave me, I know, and that she was steadfast in her refusal to do me that last wrong. But I know too that she loved him. I have read the confession of that which she called her 'madness' under her own hand. "

"O, papa, papa, how sad! how dreadful! "

"Within a year or two of your birth she began to fade. From my heart I believe it was this struggle between passion and the last remnant of honour that killed her. I need not tell you the details of my discoveries, some of them made not very long before her death. They led to bitter scenes between us; but I thank God I did believe her protestations of innocence, and that I kept her under my own roof. There were others not so merciful. Colonel Fairfax's wife was told of his devotion to mine at Florence, and the duel which ended our acquaintance. She found out something of his subsequent meetings with your mother, and her jealousy brought about a separation. It was managed quietly enough, but not without scandal; and nothing but my determination to maintain my wife's position could have saved her from utter disgrace. Yes, Clarissa, I loved her to the last, but the misery of that last year was something that no words can tell. She died in my arms, and in her latest hours of consciousness thanked me for what she called my generosity. I went straight from her funeral to London, with a bundle of letters in my pocket, to find Temple Fairfax. What might have happened between us, had we met, I can scarcely guess; but there were no scruples on my side. Fortune favoured him, however; he had sailed for India a few weeks before, in command of his regiment. I had some thoughts of following him even there, but abandoned the notion. My wrongs would keep. I waited for his return, but that never happened. He was killed in Afghanistan, and carried to his Indian grave the reputation of one of the worst men and best soldiers who ever bore the king's commission. "

This was all. To speak of these things had profoundly agitated Marmaduke Lovel; but a sudden impulse had moved this man, who was apt to be so silent about himself and his own feelings, and he had been in a manner constrained to tell this story.

"You can understand now, I suppose, Clarissa, " he said coldly, after another pause, "why this young man, George Fairfax, is hateful to me. "

"Yes, papa. It is only natural that you should be prejudiced against him. Does he know, do you think——" she faltered and stopped, with a bitter sense of shame.

"Does he know what? "

"About the past? "

"Of course he must know. Do you suppose his mother has not told him her grievances? "

Clarissa remembered Mrs. Fairfax's cold manner, and understood the reason of that tacit avoidance which had wounded her so deeply. She too, no doubt, was hateful; as hateful to the injured wife of Colonel Fairfax as his son could be to her father.

"And now, Clarissa, " said Mr. Lovel, "remember that any acquaintance between you and George Fairfax is most repugnant to me. I have told you this story in order that there may be no possibility of any mistake between us. God only knows what it costs a man to open old wounds as I have opened mine to-night. Only this afternoon you affected a considerable regard for me, which I promised to return to the best of my power. All that is a dead letter if you hold any communion with this man. Choose him for your friend, and renounce me for your father. You cannot have both. "

"He is not my friend, papa; he is nothing to me. Even it there were no such thing as this prejudice on your part, I am not so dishonourably as to forget that Mr. Fairfax is engaged to Lady Geraldine. "

"And you promise that there shall be no more meetings, no repetition of the kind of thing I saw to-night? "

"I promise, papa, that of my own free will I will never see him again. Our meeting to-night was entirely accidental. "

"On your part, perhaps; but was it so on his? "

"I cannot tell that, papa. "

Mr. Lovel felt himself obliged to be satisfied with this answer. It seemed to him a hard thing that the son of his enemy should arise thus to torment him—an accident that might have tempted a superstitious man to think that an evil fate brooded over his house; and Marmaduke Lovel's mind, being by no means strongly influenced by belief, was more or less tainted with superstition. Looked at from any point of view, it was too provoking that this man should cross Clarissa's pathway at the very moment when it was all-important to her destiny that her heart should be untouched, her fancy unfettered.

"If nothing comes of this Granger business I shall take her abroad, " Mr. Lovel said to himself; "anything to get her out of the way of a Fairfax. "

He drank his tea in silence, meditating upon that little scene in the moonlight, and stealing a look at his daughter every now and then, as she sat opposite to him pretending to read. He could see that the open book was the merest pretence, and that Clarissa was profoundly agitated. Was it her mother's story that had moved her so deeply, or that other newer story which George Fairfax might have been whispering to her just now in the lonely moonlit road? Mr. Lovel was disturbed by this question, but did not care to seek any farther explanation from his daughter. There are some subjects that will not bear discussion.

* * * * *

CHAPTER XIX.

MR. GRANGER IS PRECIPITATE.

Clarissa had little sleep that night. The image of George Fairfax, and of that dead soldier whom she pictured darkly like him, haunted her all through the slow silent hours. Her mother's story had touched her to the heart; but her sympathies were with her father. Here was a new reason why she should shut her heart against Lady Geraldine's lover, if any reason were wanted to strengthen that sense of honour which reigns supreme in a girl's unsullied soul. In her conviction as to what was right she never wavered. She felt herself very weak where this man was concerned—weak enough to love him in spite of reason and honour; but she did not doubt her power to keep that guilty secret, and to hide her weakness from George Fairfax.

She had almost forgotten her engagement at Arden Court when her father came down to his late breakfast, and found her sketching at a little table near the window, with the affectionate Ponto nestling close at her side.

"I thought you would be dressing for your visit by this time, Clary, " he said very graciously.

"My visit, papa? O, yes, to the Court, " she replied, with a faint sigh of resignation. "I had very nearly forgotten all about it. I was to be there between twelve and one, I think. I shall have plenty of time to give you your breakfast. It's not eleven yet. "

"Be sure you dress yourself becomingly. I don't want you to appear at a disadvantage compared with the heiress. "

"I'll put on my prettiest dress, if you like, papa; but I can't wear such silks and laces as Miss Granger wears. "

"You will have such things some day, I daresay, and set them off better than Miss Granger. She is not a bad-looking young woman— good complexion, fine figure, and so on—but as stiff as a poker. "

"I think she is mentally stiff, papa; she is a sort of person I could never get on with. How I wish you were coming with me this morning! "

"I couldn't manage it, Clarissa. The schools and the model villagers would be more than I could stand. But at your age you ought to be interested in that sort of thing; and you really ought to get on with Miss Granger. "

It was half-past twelve when Miss Lovel opened the gate leading into Arden Park—the first time that she had ever opened it; though she had stood so often leaning on that rustic boundary, and gazing into the well-known woodland, with fond sad looks. There was an actual pain at her heart as she entered that unforgotten domain; and she felt angry with Daniel Granger for having forced this visit upon her.

"I suppose he is determined that we shall pay homage to his wealth, and admire his taste, and drink the bitter cup of humiliation to the very dregs. If he had any real delicacy of feeling, he would understand our reluctance to any intimacy with him. "

While she was thinking of Mr. Granger in this unfriendly spirit, a step sounded on the winding path before her, and looking up, she perceived the subject of her thoughts coming quickly towards her. Was there ever such an intrusive man? She blushed rosy red with vexation.

He came to her, with his hat in his hand, looking very big and stiff and counting-house like among the flickering shadows of forest trees; not an Arcadian figure by any means, but with a certain formal business-like-dignity about him, for all that; not a man to be ridiculed or despised.

"I am glad you have not forgotten your promise to come early, Miss Lovel, " he said, in his strong sonorous voice. "I was just walking over to the cottage to remind you. Sophia is quite ready to do the honours of her schools. But I shall not let her carry you off till after luncheon; I want to show you my improvements. I had set my heart on your seeing the Court for the first time—since its restoration—under my guidance. "

"Pompous, insufferable *parvenu*, " thought Clarissa, to whom this desire on Mr. Granger's part seemed only an odious eagerness to exhibit his wealth. She little knew how much sentiment there was involved in this wish of Daniel Granger's.

They came into the open part of the park presently, and she was fain to confess, that whatever changes had been made—and the alterations here were not many—had been made with a perfect appreciation of the picturesque. Even the supreme neatness with which the grounds were now kept did not mar their beauty. Fairy-like young plantations of rare specimens of the coniferous tribe had arisen at every available point of the landscape, wherever there had been barrenness before. Here and there the old timber had been thinned a little, always judiciously. No cockney freaks of fancy disfigured the scene. There were no sham ruins, no artificial waterfalls poorly supplied with water, no Chinese pagodas, or Swiss cottages, or gothic hermitages. At one point of the shrubbery where the gloom of cypress and fir was deepest, they came suddenly on a Grecian temple, whose slender marble columns might have gleamed amidst the sacred groves of Diana; and this was the only indulgence Mr. Granger had allowed to an architect's fancy, Presently, at the end of a wide avenue, a broad alley of turf between double lines of unrivalled beeches, the first glimpse of the Court burst upon Clarissa's sight—unchanged and beautiful. A man must have been a Goth, indeed, who had altered the outward aspect of the place by a hair's breadth.

The house was surrounded by a moat, and there was a massive stone gateway, of older date than the Court itself—though that was old—dividing a small prim garden from the park; this gatehouse was a noble piece of masonry, of the purest gothic, rich with the mellow tint of age, and almost as perfect as in the days when some wandering companionship of masons gave the last stroke of their chisels to the delicate tracery of window and parapet.

The Court formed three sides of a quadrangle. A dear old place, lovable rather than magnificent, yet with all the grandeur of the middle ages; a place that might have stood a siege perhaps, but had evidently been built for a home. The garden originally belonging to the house was simplicity itself, and covered scarcely an acre. All round the inner border of the moat there ran a broad terrace-walk, divided by a low stone balustrade from a grassy bank that sloped down to the water. The square plot of ground before the house was laid out in quaint old flower-beds, where the roses seemed, to Clarissa at least, to flourish as they flourished nowhere else. The rest of the garden consisted of lawn and flower-beds, with more roses. There were no trees near the house, and the stables and out-offices, which made a massive pile of building, formed a background to the grave old gothic mansion.

Without, at least, Mr. Granger had respected the past. Clarissa felt relieved by this moderation, and was inclined to think him a little less hateful. So far he had said nothing which could seem to betray a boastful spirit. He had watched her face and listened to her few remarks with a kind of deferential eagerness, as if it had been a matter of vital importance to him that she should approve what he had done. A steward, who had been entrusted with the conduct of alterations and renovations during the absence of his master, could scarcely have appeared more anxious as to the result of his operations.

The great iron gates under the gothic archway stood wide open just as they had been wont to do in Mr. Lovel's time, and Clarissa and her companion passed into the quiet garden. How well she remembered the neglected air of the place when last she had seen it—the mossgrown walks, the duckweed in the moat, the straggling rose-bushes, everything out of order, from the broken weathercock on one of the gateway towers, to the scraper by the half-glass door in one corner of the quadrangle, which had been, used instead of the chief entrance! It seems natural to a man of decayed fortune to shut up his hall-door and sneak in and out of his habitation by some obscure portal.

Now all was changed; a kind of antique primness, which had no taint of cockney stiffness, pervaded the scene. One might have expected to see Sir Thomas More or Lord Bacon emerge from the massive gothic porch, and stroll with slow step and meditative aspect towards the stone sun-dial that stood in the centre of that square rose-garden. The whole place had an air of doublet and hose. It seemed older to Clarissa than when she had seen it last—older and yet newer, like the palace of the Sleeping Beauty, restored, after a century of decay, to all its original grandeur.

The door under the porch stood open; but there were a couple of men in a sober livery waiting in the hall—footmen who had never been reared in those Yorkshire wilds—men with powdered hair, and the stamp of Grosvenor-square upon them. Those flew to open inner doors, and Clarissa began with wonder to behold the new glories of the mansion. She followed Mr. Granger in silence through dining and billiard-rooms, saloon and picture-gallery, boudoir and music-room, in all of which the Elizabethan air, the solemn grace of a departed age, had been maintained with a marvellous art. Money can do so much; above all, where a man has no bigoted belief in his own taste or capacity, and will put his trust in the intelligence of professional artists. Daniel Granger had done this. He had said to an accomplished architect, "I give you the house of my choice; make it what it was in its best days. Improve wherever you can, but alter as little as possible; and, above all, no modernising."

Empowered by this *carte blanche*, the architect had given his soul to dreams of mediaeval splendour and had produced a place which, in its way, was faultless. No matter that some of the carved-oak furniture was fresh from the chisel of the carver, while other things were the spoil of old Belgian churches; that the tapestry in one saloon was as old as the days of its designer, Boucher, and that in the adjoining chamber made on purpose for Arden Court at the Gobelins manufactory of his Imperial Majesty Napoleon III. No matter that the gilt-leather hangings in one room had hung there in the reign of Charles I., while those in another were supplied by a West-end upholsterer. Perfect taste had harmonised every detail; there was not so much as a footstool or a curtain that could have been called an anachronism. Clarissa looked at all these things with a strange sense of wandering somewhere in a dream. It was, and yet was not her old home. There was nothing incongruous. The place scarcely seemed new to her, though everything was altered. It was only as it ought to have been always.

She remembered the bare rooms, the scanty shabby furniture of the Georgian era, the patches and glimpses of faded splendour here and there, the Bond-street prettinesses and fripperies in her mother's boudoir, which, even in her early girlhood, had grown tawdry and *rococo*, the old pictures rotting in their tarnished frames; everything with that sordid air of poverty and decay upon it."

"Well, Miss Lovel," Daniel Granger said at last, when they had gone through all the chief rooms almost in silence, "do you approve of what has been done?"

"It is beautiful," Clarissa answered, "most beautiful; but—but it breaks my heart to see it."

The words were wrung from her somehow. In the next moment she was ashamed of them—it seemed like the basest envy.

"O, pray, pray do not think me mean or contemptible, Mr. Granger, " she said; "it is not that I envy you your house, only it was my home so long, and I always felt its neglect so keenly; and to see it now so beautiful, as I could have only pictured it in my dreams—and even in them I could not fancy it so perfect. "

"It may be your home again, Clarissa, if you care to make it so, " said Mr. Granger, coming very close to her, and with a sudden passion in his voice. "I little thought when I planned this place that it would one day seem worthless to me without one lovely mistress. It is all yours, Clarissa, if you will have it—and the heart of its master, who never thought that it was in his nature to feel what he feels for you. "

He tried to take her hand; but she shrank away from him, trembling a little, and with a frightened look in her face.

"Mr. Granger, O, pray, pray don't——"

"For God's sake don't tell me that this seems preposterous or hateful to you—that you cannot value the love of a man old enough to be your father. You do not know what it is for a man of my age and my character to love for the first time. I had gone through life heart-whole, Clarissa, till I saw you. Between my wife and me there was never more than liking. She was a good woman, and I respected her, and we got on very well together. That was all. Clarissa, tell me that there is some hope. I ought not to have spoken so soon; I never meant to be such a fool—but the words came in spite of me. O, my dearest, don't crush me with a point-blank refusal. I know that all this must seem strange to you. Let it pass. Think no more of anything I have said till you know me better—till you find my love is worth having. I believe I fell in love with you that first afternoon in the library at Hale. From that time forth your face haunted me—like some beautiful picture—the loveliest thing I had ever seen, Clarissa. "

"I cannot answer you, Mr. Granger, " she said in a broken voice; "you have shocked and surprised me so much, I——"

"Shocked and surprised you! That seems hard. "

In that very moment it flashed upon her that this was what her father and Lady Laura Armstrong had wished to bring about. She was to win back the lost heritage of Arden Court—win it by the sacrifice of every natural feeling of her heart, by the barter of her very self.

How much more Mr. Granger might have said there is no knowing—for, once having spoken, a man is loth to leave such a subject as this unexhausted—but there came to Clarissa's relief the rustling sound of a stiff silk dress, announcing the advent of Miss Granger, who sailed towards them through a vista of splendid rooms, with a stately uncompromising air that did not argue the warmest possible welcome for her guest.

"I have been hunting for you everywhere, papa, " she said in an aggrieved tone. "Where have you been hiding Miss Lovel? "

And then she held out her hand and shook hands with Clarissa in the coldest manner in which it was possible for a human being to perform that ceremony. She looked at her father with watchful suspicious eyes as he walked away to one of the windows, not caring that his daughter should see his face just at that moment. There was something, evidently, Sophia thought, —something which it concerned her to discover.

* * * * *

CHAPTER XX.

MODEL VILLAGERS.

They went to luncheon in a secondary dining room—a comfortable apartment, which served pleasantly for all small gatherings, and had that social air so impossible in a stately banqueting-chamber—a perfect gem of a room, hung with gilt leather, relieved here and there by a choice picture in a frame of gold and ebony. Here the draperies were of a dark crimson cut velvet, which the sunshine brightened into ruby. The only ornaments in this room were a pair of matchless Venetian girandoles on the mantelpiece, and a monster Palissy dish, almost as elaborate in design as the shield of Achilles, on the oaken buffet.

The luncheon was not a very genial repast; Miss Granger maintained a polite sulkiness; Clarissa had not yet recovered from the agitation which Mr. Granger's most unexpected avowal had occasioned; and even the strong man himself felt his nerves shaken, and knew that he was at a disadvantage, between the daughter who suspected him and the woman who had all but refused his hand. He did his utmost to seem at his ease, and to beguile his daughter into a more cordial bearing; but there was a gloom upon that little party of three which was palpably oppressive. It seemed in vain to struggle against the dismal influence. Mr. Granger felt relieved when, just at the close of the meal, his butler announced that Mr. Tillott was in the drawing-room. Mr. Tillott was a mild inoffensive young man of High-church tendencies, the curate of Arden.

"I asked Tillott to go round the schools with us this afternoon, " Mr. Granger said to his daughter in an explanatory tone. "I know what an interest he takes in the thing, and I thought it would be pleasanter. "

"You are very kind, papa, " Miss Granger replied, with implacable stiffness; "but I really don't see what we want with Mr. Tillott, or with you either. There's not the least reason that we should take you away from your usual occupations; and you are generally so busy of an afternoon. Miss Lovel and I can see everything there is to be seen, without any escort; and I have always heard you complain that my schools bored you. "

"Well, perhaps I may have had rather an overdose of the philanthropic business occasionally, my dear, " answered Mr. Granger, with a good-humoured laugh. "However, I have set my heart upon seeing how all your improvements affect Miss Lovel. She has such a peculiar interest in the place, you see, and is so identified with the people. I thought you'd be pleased to have Tillott. He's really a good fellow, and you and he always seem to have so much to talk about. "

On this they all repaired to the drawing-room, where Mr. Tillott the curate was sitting at a table, turning over the leaves of an illuminated psalter, and looking altogether as if he had just posed himself for a photograph.

To this mild young man Miss Granger was in a manner compelled to relax the austerity of her demeanour. She even smiled in a frosty way as she shook hands with him; but she had no less a sense of the fact that her father had out-manoeuvred her, and that this invitation to Mr. Tillott was a crafty design whereby he intended to have Clarissa all to himself during that afternoon.

"I am sorry you could not come to luncheon with us, Tillott, " said Mr. Granger in his hearty way. "Or are you sure, by the bye, that you have taken luncheon? We can go back to the dining-room and hear the last news of the parish while you wash down some game-pie with a glass or two of the old madeira. "

"Thanks, you are very good; but I never eat meat on Wednesdays or Fridays. I had a hard-boiled egg and some cocoa at half-past seven this morning, and shall take nothing more till sunset. I had duties at Swanwick which detained me till within the last half-hour, or I should have been very happy to have eaten a biscuit with you at your luncheon. "

"Upon my word, Tillott, you are the most indefatigable of men; but I really wish you High-church people had not such a fancy for starving yourselves. So much expenditure of brain-power must involve a waste of the coarser material. Now, Sophy, if you and Miss Lovel are ready, we may as well start. "

They went out into the sunny quadrangle, where the late roses were blooming with all their old luxuriance. How well Clarissa remembered them in those days when they had been the sole glory of the neglected place! In spite of Sophia, who tried her hardest to prevent the arrangement, Mr. Granger contrived that he and Clarissa should walk side by side, and that Mr. Tillott should completely absorb his daughter. This the curate was by no means indisposed to do; for, if the youthful saint had a weakness, it lay in the direction of vanity. He sincerely admired the serious qualities of Miss Granger's mind, and conceived that, blest with such a woman and with the free use of her fortune, he might achieve a rare distinction for his labours in tins fold, to say nothing of placing himself on the high-road to a bishopric. Nor was he inclined to think Miss Granger indifferent to his own merits, or that the conquest would be by any means an impossible one. It was a question of time, he thought; the sympathy between them was too strong not to take some higher development. He thought of St. Francis de Sales and Madame de Chantal, and fancied himself entrusted with the full guidance of Miss Granger's superior mind.

They walked across the park to a small gothic gateway, which had been made since the close of Marmaduke Lovel's reign. Just outside this stood the chapel of Mr. Granger's building, and the new schools, also gothic, and with that bran-new aspect against which architecture can do nothing. They would be picturesque, perhaps, ten years hence. To-day they had the odour of the architect's drawing-board.

Beyond the schools there were some twenty cottages, of the same modern gothic, each habitation more or less borne down and in a manner extinguished by its porch and chimney. If the rooms had been in reasonable proportion to the chimneys, the cottages would have been mansions; but gothic chimneys are pleasing objects, and the general effect was good. These twenty cottages formed the beginning of Mr. Granger's model village—a new Arden, which was to arise on this side of the Court. They were for the most part inhabited by gardeners and labourers more or less dependent on Arden Court, and it had been therefore an easy matter for Miss Granger to obtain a certain deference to her wishes from the tenants.

The inspection of the schools and cottages was rather a tedious business. Sophia would not let her companions off with an iota less than the whole thing. Her model pupils were trotted out and examined in the Scriptures—always in Kings and Chronicles—and evinced a familiarity with the ways of Jezebel and Rehoboam that made Clarissa blush at the thought of her own ignorance. Then there came an exhibition of plain needlework, excruciatingly suggestive of impaired eyesight; then fancy-work, which Miss Granger contemplated with a doubtful air, as having a frivolous tendency; and then the school mistress's parlour and kitchen were shown, and displayed so extreme a neatness that made one wonder where she lived; and then the garden, where the heels of one's boots seemed a profanation; and then, the schools and schoolhouses being exhausted, there came the cottages.

How Clarissa's heart bled for the nice clean motherly women who were put through their paces for Miss Granger's glorification, and were fain to confess that their housekeeping had been all a delusion and a snare till that young lady taught them domestic economy! How she pitied them as the severe Sophia led the way into sacred corners, and lifted the lids of coppers and dustholes, and opened cupboard-doors, and once, with an aspect of horror, detected an actual cobweb lurking in an angle of the whitewashed wall! Clarissa could not admire things too much, in order to do away with some of the bitterness of that microscopic survey. Then there was such cross-examination about church-going, and the shortcomings of the absent husbands were so ruthlessly dragged into the light of day. The poor wives blushed to own that these unregenerate spirits had still a lurking desire for an occasional social evening at the Coach and Horses, in spite of the charms of a gothic chimney, and a porch that was massive enough for the dungeon of a mediaeval fortress. Miss Granger and the curate played into each other's hands, and between the two the model villagers underwent a kind of moral dissection. It was dreary work altogether; and Daniel Granger had been guilty of more than one yawn before it was all over, even though he had the new delight of being near Clarissa all the time. It was finished at last. One woman, who in her benighted state had known Miss Lovel, had shown herself touched by the sight of her.

"You never come anigh me now, miss, " she said tenderly, "though I've knowed you ever since you was a little girl; and it would do my heart good to see your sweet face here once in a way. "

"You've better friends now, you see, Mrs. Rice, " Clarissa answered gently. "I could do so little for you. But I shall be pleased to look in upon you now and then. "

"Do'ee, now, miss; me and my master will be right down glad to see you. However kind new friends may be, " this was said with a conciliatory curtsey to Miss Granger, "we can't forget old friends. We haven't forgot your goodness when my boy Bill was laid up with the fever, miss, and how you sat beside his bed and read to him. "

It was at this juncture that Sophia espied another cobweb, after which the little party left this the last of the cottages, and walked back to the park, Daniel Granger still by Clarissa's side. He did not make the faintest allusion to that desperate avowal of the morning. He was indeed cruelly ashamed of his precipitation, feeling that he had gone the very way to ruin his cause. All that afternoon, while his daughter had been peering into coppers and washing-tubs and dustholes, he had been meditating upon the absurdity of his conduct, and hating himself for his folly. He was not a man who suffered from a mean opinion of his own merits. On the contrary, in all the ordinary commerce of life he fancied himself more than the equal of the best among his fellow-men. He had never wished himself other than what he was, or mistrusted his own judgment, or doubted that he, Daniel Granger, was a very important atom in the scheme of creation. But in this case it was different. He knew himself to be a grave middle-aged man, with none of those attributes that might have qualified him to take a young woman's heart by storm; and as surely as he knew this, he also knew himself to be passionately in love. All the happiness of his future life depended on this girl who walked by his side, with her pale calm face and deep hazel eyes. If she should refuse him, all would be finished. He had dreamed his dream, and life could never any more be what it had been for him. The days were past in which, he himself had been all-sufficient for his own happiness. But, though he repented that hasty betrayal of his feelings, he did not altogether despair. It is not easy to reduce a man of his age and character to the humble level of a despairing lover. He had so much to bestow, and could not separate himself in his own mind from those rich gifts of fortune which went along with him. No, there was every chance of ultimate success, he thought, in spite of his rashness of that morning. He had only to teach himself patience—to bide his time.

* * * * *

CHAPTER XXI.

VERY FAR GONE.

It was a little after six when they came to the gateway of the Court, at which point Mr. Tillott made his adieux. Mr. Granger would have been very glad to ask him to dinner, had he not promised Mr. Lovel that they would be quite alone; so he made up for any apparent inhospitality towards the curate by a hearty invitation for the following Sunday.

There was nearly an hour and a half before dinner; but Sophia carried off her guest to her own rooms at once, for the revision of her toilet, and detained her in those upper regions until just before the ringing of the second bell, very much to the aggravation of Mr. Granger, who paced the long drawing-room in dismal solitude, waiting for Mr. Lovel's arrival.

In her own rooms Miss Granger became a shade more gracious to Clarissa. The exhibition of her *sanctum sanctorum* was always pleasing to her. It was the primmest of apartments, half study, half office; and Sophia, one of whose proudest boasts was of her methodical habits, here displayed herself in full force. It seemed as if she had inherited all the commercial faculties of her father, and having no other outlet for this mercantile genius, was fain to expend her gifts upon the petty details of a woman's life. Never had Clarissa seen such a writing-table, with so many pigeon-holes for the classification of documents, and such ranges of drawers with Brahma locks. Miss Granger might have carried on a small banking business with less paraphernalia than she employed in the conduct of her housekeeping and philanthropy.

"I am my own housekeeper, " she told Clarissa triumphantly, "and know the consumption of this large establishment to an ounce. There is no stint of anything, of course. The diet in the servant's hall is on the most liberal scale, but there is no waste. Every cinder produced in the house is sifted; every candle we burn has been in stock a twelvemonth. I could not pretend to teach my cottagers economy if I did not practise it myself. I rule everything by the doctrine of averages—so much consumed in one month, so much necessarily required in another; and I reduce everything to figures. Figures cannot deceive, as I tell Mrs. Plumptree, my cook, when she shows me a result that I cannot understand or accept. And there are my books. "

Miss Granger waved her hand towards a row of most uncompromising-looking volumes of the ledger or day-book species. The delight which she displayed in these things was something curious to behold. Every small charity Miss Granger performed, every shortcoming of the recipients thereof, was recorded in those inexorable volumes. She had a book for the record of the church-going, a book for the plain needlework, and was wont to freeze the young blood of her school-children by telling them at the end of the year how many inches of cambric frilling they had hemmed, and how many times they had missed afternoon service. To them she appeared a supernatural creature—a kind of prophetess, sent upon earth for their correction and abasement.

On a solid ecclesiastical-looking oak table in one of the windows Miss Granger had a row of brass-bound money-boxes, inscribed, "For the Home Mission, " "For the Extra Curate Society, " and so on—boxes into which Miss Granger's friends and visitors were expected to drop their mite. Clarissa felt that if she had been laden down with shillings, she could not for her very life have approached those formidable boxes to drop one in under Miss Granger's ken; but, of course, this was a morbid fancy. On another table there were little piles of material for plain work; so prim, so square, so geometrically precise, that Clarissa thought the flannel itself looked cold—a hard, fibrous, cruel fabric, that could never be of use to mortal flesh except as an irritant.

Miss Granger's bedroom and dressing-room were like Miss Granger's morning-room. No frivolous mediaevalism here, no dainty upholsterer's work in many-coloured woods, but solid mahogany, relieved by solemn draperies of drab damask, in a style which the wise Sophia called unpretentious. The chief feature in one room was a sewing-machine that looked like a small church organ, and in the other a monster medicine-chest, from the contents of which Miss Granger dealt out doses of her own concoction to her parishioners. Both of these objects she showed to Clarissa with pride, but the medicine-chest was evidently the favourite.

Having improved the time after this manner till twenty minutes past seven, with a very brief interval devoted to the duties of the toilet, the two young ladies went down to the drawing-room, where the lamps were lighted, and Mr. Lovel just arrived.

That gentleman had the honour of taking Miss Granger in to dinner, and did his utmost to render himself agreeable to her in a quiet undemonstrative way, and to take the gauge of her mental powers. She received his attentions graciously enough—indeed it would not have been easy for any one to be ungracious to Marmaduke Lovel when he cared to please—but he could see very clearly that she suspected the state of affairs, and would be, to the last degree, antagonistic to his own and his daughter's interests. He saw how close a watch she kept upon her father all through the dinner, and how her attention was distracted every now and then when he was talking to Clarissa.

"It is only natural that she should set her face against the business, " he said to himself; "no woman in her position could be expected to act otherwise; but it strikes me that Granger is not a man likely to be influenced by domestic opposition. He is the kind of man to take his own way, I fancy, in defiance of an opposing universe—a very difficult man to govern. He seems over head and ears in love, however, and it will be Clarissa's own fault if she doesn't do what she likes with him. Heaven grant she may prove reasonable! Most women would be enchanted with such an opportunity, but with a raw school-girl there is no knowing. And that fellow Fairfax's influence may work against us, in spite of her protestations last night. "

This was the gist of Mr. Level's disjointed musings during the progress of the dinner; but he took care not to neglect Miss Granger even for a moment, and he gave her very little time to listen to her father's conversation with Clarissa.

The dinner ceremonial was performed in a manner which seemed perfection, even to the fastidious taste of Marmaduke Lovel. There was not the faintest indication of ostentation. Daniel Granger's father had been rich before him; he had been born in the commercial purple, as it were, and none of these things were new to him. Before the Arden Court days he had occupied a handsome modern country house southward, near Doncaster. He had only expanded his style of living after the purchase of the Court, that was all. He had good taste too, and a keen sense of the incongruous. He did not affect the orchids and frivolous floral decorations, the fragile fairy-like glass, with which Lady Laura Armstrong brightened her dinner-table; but, on the other hand, his plate, of which he exhibited no vulgar profusion, was in the highest art, the old Indian china dinner-service scarcely less costly than solid silver, and the heavy diamond-cut glass, with gold emblazonment of crest and monogram, worthy to be exhibited behind the glazed doors of a cabinet. There was no such abomination as gas in the state chambers of Arden Court. Innumerable candles, in antique silver candelabra, gave a subdued brightness to the dining-room. More candles, in sconces against the walls, and two pairs of noble moderator-lamps, on bronze and ormolu pedestals six feet high, lighted the drawing-room. In the halls and corridors there was the same soft glow of lamplight. Only in kitchens and out-offices and stables was the gas permitted to blaze merrily for the illumination of cooks and scullions, grooms and helpers.

Miss Granger only lingered long enough to trifle with a cluster of purple grapes before giving the signal for withdrawal Her father started up to open the dining-room door, with a little sudden sigh. He had had Clarissa all to himself throughout the dinner, and had been very happy, talking about things that were commonplace enough in themselves, but finding a perfect contentment in the fact that he was talking to her, that she listened to him and smiled upon him graciously, with a sweet self-possession which put him quite at his ease. She had recovered from that awkward scene of the morning, and had settled in her own mind that the business was rather absurd than serious. She had only to take care that Mr. Granger never had any second opportunity for indulging in such folly.

He held the door open as Clarissa and his daughter went out of the room—held it till that slim girlish figure had vanished at the end of the corridor, and then came back to his seat with another sigh.

"Very far gone, " Mr. Lovel thought, smiling ever so little, as he bent over his claret-glass, pretending to admire the colour of the wine.

It was really wonderful. That vague dream which had grown out of Lady Laura's womanly hints, that pleasant phantom which she had conjured up in Mr. Lovel's mental vision a month or two ago, in the midsummer afternoon, had made itself into a reality so quickly as to astound a man too Horatian in his philosophy to be easily surprised. The fish was such a big one to be caught so easily—without any exercise of those subtle manoeuvres and Machiavellian artifices in which the skilful angler delights—nay, to pounce open-eyed upon the hook, and swallow it bodily!

Mr. Granger filled his glass with such a nervous hand, that half the claret he poured out ran upon the shining oak table. He wiped up the spilt wine clumsily enough, with a muttered denunciation of his own folly, and then made a feeble effort to talk about indifferent things.

It was of no use; with every appearance of courtesy and interest Mr. Lovel contrived *not* to help him. One subject after another fell flat: the state of the Conservative party, the probability of a war—there is always a probability of war somewhere, according to after-dinner politicians—the aspect of the country politically and agriculturally, and so on. No, it was no use; Daniel Granger broke down altogether at last, and thought it best to unbosom himself.

"There is something that I think you have a right to know, Mr. Lovel, " he said, in an awkward hesitating way; "something which I should scarcely like you to learn from your daughter's lips, should she think it worth her while to mention it, before you have heard it from mine. The fact is, in plain English"—he was playing with his dessert-knife as he spoke, and seemed to be debating within himself whereabouts upon the dinning-table he should begin to carve his name—"the fact is, I made an abject fool of myself this morning. I love your daughter—and told her so. "

Mr. Lovel gave a little start, the faintest perceptible movement, expressive of a gentle astonishment.

"I need hardly tell you that you have taken me entirely by surprise, " he said in his quietest tone.

"Of course not. People always are surprised when a man of my age presumes to fall in love with a beautiful girl of eighteen or twenty. If I were to marry some worn-out woman of fashion, some battered widow, steeped to the lips in worldly wisdom, every one would call the match the most suitable thing possible. But if a man of fifty ventures to dream a brighter dream, he is condemned at once for a fool. "

"Pardon me, my dear Granger; I have no idea of looking at things in that light. I only remark that you surprise me, as you no doubt surprised my daughter by any avowal you may have made this morning. "

"Yes; and, I fear, disgusted her still more. I daresay I did my cause all the harm that it was possible to do it. "

"I must own that you were precipitate, " Mr. Lovel answered, with his quiet smile. He felt as if he had been talking to a schoolboy. In his own words the man was so "very far gone. "

"I shall know how to be more careful in future, if not wiser; but I suffered myself to be carried away by impulse this morning. It was altogether unworthy of—of my time of life. " This was said rather bitterly. "Frankly, now, Mr. Lovel: if in the future I were able to gain some hold upon your daughter's affection—without that I would do nothing, no, so help me heaven, however passionately I might love her; if I could—if, in spite of the difference of our ages, I could win her heart—would you be in any way antagonistic to such a marriage? "

"On the contrary, my dear Granger. " Mr. Lovel had already something of the tone of a father-in-law. "Slight as our actual acquaintance has been, I think I know the estimable qualities of your character well enough from other sources to be able to say that such a marriage would be eminently pleasing to me. Nor is this all. I mean to be perfectly candid with you, Granger. My daughter and myself have both an almost romantic attachment to this place, and I freely own that it would be very delightful to me to see her mistress of her old home. But, at the same time, I give you my honour that nothing would induce me to govern her choice by the smallest exercise of parental influence. If you can win her, win her, and my best wishes shall go with your wooing; but I will utter no word to persuade her to be your wife. "

"I respect you for that resolution; I think I should have asked you to be neutral, if you hadn't said as much. I couldn't stand the idea of a wife driven into my arms by fatherly coercion. I suppose such things are done in modern society. No, I must win my treasure myself, or not at all. I have everything against me, no doubt, except a rival. There is no fear of *that*, is there, Lovel? "

"Not the slightest. Clarissa is the merest school-girl. Her visit to Lady Laura Armstrong was her first glimpse of the world. No, Granger, you have the field all before you. And you strike me as a man not likely to be vanquished by small difficulties. "

"I never yet set myself to do a thing which I didn't accomplish in the long run, " answered Mr. Granger; "but then I never set myself to win a woman's heart. My wife and I came together easily enough—in the way of business, as I may say—and liked each other well enough, and I regretted her honestly when she was gone, poor soul! but that was all. I was never 'in love' till I knew your daughter; never understood the meaning of the phrase. Of all the accidents that might have happened to me, this is the most surprising to myself. I can never cease to wonder at my own folly. "

"I do not know why you should call it a folly. You are only in the very middle of a man's life; you have a fortune that exempts you from all care and labour, and of course at the same time leaves you more or less without occupation. Your daughter will marry and leave you in a year or two, no doubt. Without some new tie your future existence must needs be very empty. "

"I have felt that; but only since I have loved your daughter. "

This was all. The men came in with coffee, and put an end to all confidential converse; after which Mr. Granger seemed very glad to go back to the drawing-room, where Clarissa was playing a mazurka; while Sophia sat before a great frame, upon which some splendid achievement in Berlin woolwork, that was to be the glory of an approaching charity bazaar, was rapidly advancing towards completion. The design was a group of dogs, after Landseer, and Miss Granger was putting in the pert black nose of a Skye-terrier as the gentlemen entered. The two ladies were as far apart as they well could be in the spacious room, and had altogether an inharmonious air, Mr. Granger thought; but then he was nervously anxious that these two should become friends.

He went straight to the piano, and seated himself near Clarissa, almost with the air of having a right to take that place.

"Pray go on playing, " he said; "that seems very pretty music. I am no judge, and I don't pretend to care for that classical music which every one talks about nowadays, but I know what pleases me. "

The evening was not an especially gay one; but it seemed pleasant enough to Mr. Granger, and he found himself wondering at its brevity. He showed Clarissa some of his favourite pictures. His collection of modern art was a fine one—not large, but very perfect in its way, and he was delighted to see her appreciation of his treasures. Here at least was a point upon which they might sympathise. He had been a good deal worried by Sophia's obtuseness upon all artistic matters.

Mr. Lovel was not very sorry when the fly from the Arden Inn was announced, and it was time to go home. The pictures were fine, no doubt, and the old house was beautiful in its restored splendour; but the whole business jarred upon Marmaduke Lovel's sensitive nerves just a little, in spite of the sudden realization of that vague dream of his. This place might be his daughter's home, and he return to it: but not as its master. The day of his glory was gone. He was doubtful if he should even care to inhabit that house as his daughter's guest. He had to remind himself of the desperate condition of his own circumstances before he could feel duly grateful to Providence for his daughter's subjugation of Daniel Granger.

He was careful to utter no word about her conquest on the way home, or during the quarter of an hour Clarissa spent with him before going to her room.

"You look pale and tired, my child, " he said, with a sympathetic air, turning over the leaves of a book as he spoke.

"The day was rather fatiguing, papa, " his daughter answered listlessly, "and Miss Granger is a tiring person. She is so strong-minded, that she makes one feel weak and helpless by the mere force of contrast. "

"Yes, she is a tiring person, certainly; but I think I had the worst of her at dinner and in the evening. "

"But there was all the time before dinner, papa. She showed us her cottages—O, how I pitied the poor people! though I daresay she is kind to them, in her way; but imagine any one coming in here and opening all our cupboards, and spying out cobwebs, and giving a little shriek at the discovery of a new loaf in our larder. She found out that one of her model cottagers had been eating new bread. She said it gave her quite a revulsion of feeling. And then when we went home she showed me her account-books and her medicine-chest. It was very tiring. "

"Poor child! and this young woman will have Arden Court some day—unless her father should marry again. "

Clarissa's pale face flamed with sudden crimson.

"Which he is pretty sure to do, sooner or later, " continued Mr. Lovel, with an absent meditative air, as of a man who discusses the most indifferent subject possible. "I hope he may. It would be a pity for such a place to fall into such hands. She would make it a phalanstery, a nest for Dorcas societies and callow curates. "

"But if she does good with her money, papa, what more could one wish? "

"I don't believe that she would do much good. There is a pinched hard look about the lower part of her face which makes me fancy she is mean. I believe she would hoard her money, and make a great talk and fuss about nothing. Yes, I hope Granger will marry again. The house is very fine, isn't it, since its renovation? "

"It is superb, papa. Dearly as I love the place, I did not think it could be made so beautiful. "

"Yes, and everything has been done in good taste, too, " Mr. Lovel went on, in rather a querulous tone. "I did not expect to see that. But of course a man of that kind has only to put himself into the hands of a first-class architect, and if he is lucky enough to select an architect with an artistic mind, the thing is done. All the rest is merely a question of money. Good heavens, what a shabby sordid hole this room looks, after the place we have come from! "

The room was not so bad as to merit that look of angry disgust with which Mr. Lovel surveyed it. Curtains and carpet were something the worse for wear, the old-fashioned furniture was a little sombre; but the rich binding of the books and a rare old bronze here and there redeemed it from commonness—poor jetsam and flotsam from the wreck of the great house, but enough to give some touch of elegance to meaner things.

"O, papa, " Clarissa cried reproachfully, "the room is very nice, and we have been peaceful and happy in it. I don't suppose all the splendour of Arden would have made us much happier. Those external things make so little difference. "

She thought of those evenings at Hale Castle, when George Fairfax had abandoned her to pay duty to his betrothed, and of the desolation of spirit that had come upon her in the midst of those brilliant surroundings.

Her father paced the little room as if it had been a den, and answered her philosophic remonstrance with an exclamation of contempt.

"That's rank nonsense, Clarissa—copybook morality, which nobody in his heart ever believes. External things make all the difference— except when a man is writhing in physical pain perhaps. External things make the difference between a king and a beggar. Do you suppose that man Granger is no happier for the possession of Arden Court—of those pictures of his? Why, every time he looks at a Frith or Millais he feels a little thrill of triumph, as he says to himself, 'And that is mine. ' There is a sensuous delight in beautiful surroundings which will remain to a man whose heart is dead to every other form of pleasure. I suppose that is why the Popes were such patrons of art in days gone by. It was the one legitimate delight left to them. Do you imagine it is no pleasure to dine every night as that man dines? no happiness to feel the sense of security about the future which he feels every morning? Great God, when I think of his position and of mine! "

Never before had he spoken so freely to his daughter; never had he so completely revealed the weakness of his mind.

She was sorry for him, and forbore to utter any of those pious commonplaces by which she might have attempted to bring him to a better frame of mind. She had tact enough to divine that he was best left to himself—left to struggle out of this grovelling state by some effort of his own, rather than to be dragged from the slough of despond by moral violence of hers.

He dismissed her presently with a brief good-night; but lying awake nearly two hours afterwards, she heard him pass her door on the way to his room. He too was wakeful, therefore, and full of care.

* * * * *

CHAPTER XXII.

TAKING THE PLEDGE.

Clarissa had a visitor next day. She was clipping and trimming the late roses in the bright autumnal afternoon, when Lady Laura Armstrong's close carriage drove up to the gate, with my lady inside it, in deep mourning. The visit was unexpected, and startled Clarissa a little, with a sensation that was not all pleasure. She could scarcely be otherwise than glad to see so kind a friend; but there were reasons why the advent of any one from Hale Castle should be somewhat painful to her. That meeting with George Fairfax by the churchyard had never been quite out of her mind since it happened. His looks and his words had haunted her perpetually, and now she was inclined to ascribe Lady Laura's coming to some influence of his. She had a guilty feeling, as if she had indeed tried to steal Lady Geraldine's lover.

Lady Laura greeted her with all the old cordiality. There was a relief in that; and Clarissa's face, which had been very pale when she opened the gate to admit her visitor, brightened a little as my lady kissed her.

"My dear child, I am so glad to see you again! " exclaimed Lady Laura. "I am not supposed to stir outside the Castle in all this dreary week. Poor papa is to be buried to-morrow; but I wanted so much to see you on a most important business; so I ordered the brougham and drove here, with the blinds down all the way; and I'm sure, Clary, you won't think that I feel papa's loss any less because I come to see you just now. But I declare you are looking as pale and wan as any of us at Hale. You have not recovered that dreadful shock yet. "

"It was indeed a dreadful shock, dear Lady Laura, " said Clarissa; and then in a less steady tone she went on: "Lady Geraldine is better, I hope? "

"Geraldine is what she always is, Clary—a marvel of calmness. And yet I know she feels this affliction very deeply. She was papa's favourite, you know, and had a most extraordinary influence over him. He was so proud of her, poor dear! "

"Won't you come into the house, Lady Laura? "

"By and by, just to pay my respects to your papa. But we'll stay in the garden for the present, please, dear. I have something most particular to say to you. "

Clarissa's heart beat a little quicker. This most particular something was about George Fairfax: she felt very sure of that.

"I am going to be quite candid with you, Clary, " Lady Laura began presently, when they were in a narrow walk sheltered by hazel bushes, the most secluded bit of the garden. "I shall treat you just as if you were a younger sister of my own. I think I have almost a right to do that; for I'm sure I love you as much as if you were my sister. "

And here Lady Laura's plump little black-gloved hand squeezed Clarissa's tenderly.

"You have been all goodness to me, " the girl answered; "I can never be too grateful to you. "

"Nonsense, Clary; I will not have that word gratitude spoken between us. I only want you to understand that I am sincerely attached to you, and that I am the last person in the world to hold your happiness lightly. And now, dearest child, tell me the truth— have you seen George Fairfax since you left Hale? "

Clarissa flushed crimson. To be asked for the truth, as if, under any circumstances, she would have spoken anything less than truth about George Fairfax! And yet that unwonted guilty feeling clung to her, and she was not a little ashamed to confess that she had seen him.

"Yes, Lady Laura. "

"I thought so. I was sure of it. He came here on the very day you left—the day which was to have been his wedding-day. "

"It was on that evening that I saw him; but he did not come to this house. I was sitting outside the churchyard sketching when I saw him. "

"He did not come to the house—no; but he came to Arden on purpose to see you, " Lady Laura answered eagerly. "I am sure of that. "

Unhappily Clarissa could not deny the fact. He had told her only too plainly that he had come to Arden determined to see her.

"Now, Clary, let us be perfectly frank. Before my sister Geraldine came to Hale, I told you that the attachment between her and George Fairfax was one of long standing; that I was sure her happiness was involved in the matter, and how rejoiced I was at the turn things had taken. I told you all this, Clary; but I did not tell you that in the years we had known him Mr. Fairfax had been wild and unsteady; that, while always more or less devoted to Geraldine, he had had attachments elsewhere—unacknowledged attachments of no very creditable nature; such affairs as one only hears of by a side wind, as it were. How much Geraldine may have known of this, I cannot tell. I heard the scandals, naturally enough, through Fred; but she may have heard very little. I said nothing of this to you, Clarissa; it was not necessary that I should say anything to depreciate the character of my future brother-in-law, and of a man I really liked. "

"Of course not, " faltered Clarissa.

"Of course not. I was only too happy to find that George had become a reformed person, and that he had declared himself so soon after the change in his fortunes. I was convinced that Geraldine loved him, and that she could only be really happy as his wife. I am convinced of that still; but I know that nothing on earth could induce her to marry him if she had the least doubt of his devotion to herself. "

"I hope that she may never have occasion to doubt that, Lady Laura, " answered Clarissa. It was really all she could find to say under the circumstances.

"I hope not, and I think not, Clary. He has been attached to my sister so long—he proposed to her in such a deliberate manner—that I can scarcely imagine he would prove really inconstant. But I know that he is a slave to a pretty face, and fatally apt to be ruled by the impulse of the moment. It would be very hard now, Clary, if some transient fancy of that kind were to ruin the happiness of two lives—would it not, my dear? "

"It would be very hard. "

"O, Clarissa, do pray be candid. You *must* understand what I mean. That wretched man has been making love to you? "

"You ought not to ask me such a question, Lady Laura, " answered Clarissa, sorely perplexed by this straight attack.

"You must know that I should respect Lady Geraldine's position— that I should be incapable of forgetting her claims upon Mr. Fairfax. Whatever he may have said to me has been, the merest folly. He knows that I consider it in that light, and I have refused ever to see him again if I can possibly help it. "

"That's right, dear! " cried Lady Laura, with a pleased look. "I knew that you would come out of the business well, in spite of everything. Of course you can care nothing for this foolish fellow; but I know Geraldine's sensitive nature so well, and that if she had the faintest suspicion of George's conduct, the whole thing would be off for ever—an attachment of many years' standing, think of that, Clary! Now I want you to promise me that, come what may, you will give Mr. Fairfax no encouragement. Without encouragement this foolish fancy will die out very quickly. Of course, if it were possible you could care for him, I would not come here to ask you such a thing as this. You would have a right to consider your own happiness before my sister's. But as that is out of the question, and the man is almost a stranger to you— —"

"Out of the question—almost a stranger. " Clarissa remembered that night in the railway carriage, and it seemed to her as if she and George Fairfax had never been strangers.

"It is so easy for you to give me this promise. Tell me now, Clary dear, that you will not have anything to say to him, if he should contrive to see you again. "

"I will not, Lady Laura. "

"Is that a promise, now, Clarissa? "

"A most sacred promise. "

Lady Armstrong kissed her young friend in ratification of the compact.

"You are a dear generous-minded girl, " she said, "and I feel as if I had saved my sister's happiness by this bold course. And now tell me what you have been doing since you left us. Have you seen anything more of the Grangers? "

Questioned thus, Clarissa was fain to give her friend some slight account of her day at Arden.

"It must have affected you very much to see the old place. Ah, Clary, it is you who ought to be mistress there, instead of Miss Granger! "

Clarissa blushed, remembering that awkward avowal of Daniel Granger's.

"I am not fit to be mistress of such, a place, " she said. "I could never manage things as Miss Granger does. "

"Not in that petty way, perhaps. I should not care to see you keeping accounts and prying into grocery-lists as she does. You would govern your house on a grander scale. I should like to see you the owner of a great house"

"That is a thing you are never likely to see, Lady Laura. "

"I am not so sure of that. I have an idea that there is a great fortune lying at your feet, if you would only stoop to pick it up. But girls are so foolish; they never know what is really for their happiness; and if by any chance there should happen to be some passing folly, some fancy of the moment, to come between them and good fortune, everything is lost. "

She looked at Clarissa closely as she said this. The girl's face had been changing from red to pale throughout the interview. She was very pale now, but quite self-possessed, and had left off blushing. Had she not given her promise—pledged away her freedom of action with regard to George Fairfax—and thus made an end of everything between them? She felt very calm, but she felt as if she had made a sacrifice. As for Daniel Granger, any reference to him and his admiration for her touched upon the regions of the absurd. Nothing—no friendly manoeuvring of Lady Laura's, no selfish desires of her father's—could ever induce her to listen for a moment to any proposition from that quarter.

She asked her visitor to go into the house presently, in order to put an end to the conversation; and Lady Laura went in to say a few words to Mr. Lovel. They were very melancholy words—all about the dead, and his innumerable virtues—which seemed really at this stage of his history to have been alloyed by no human frailty or shortcoming. Mr. Lovel was sympathetic to the last degree—sighed in unison with his visitor, and brushed some stray drops of moisture from his own eyelids when Lady Laura wept. And then he went out to the carriage with my lady, and saw her drive away, with the blinds discreetly lowered as before.

"What did she come about, Clarissa? " he asked his daughter, while they were going back to the house.

"Only to see me, papa. "

"Only to see you! She must have had something very important to say to you, I should think, or she would scarcely have come at such a time. "

He glanced at his daughter sharply as he said this, but did not question her farther, though he would have liked to do so. He had a shrewd suspicion that this visit of Lady Laura's bore some reference to George Fairfax. Had there been a row at the Castle? he wondered, and had my lady come to scold her protégée?

"I don't suppose they would show her much mercy if she stood in the way of their schemes, " he said to himself. "His brother's death makes this young Fairfax a very decent match. The property must be worth five or six thousand a year—five or six thousand. I wonder what Daniel Granger's income is? Nearer fifty thousand than five, if I may believe what I have been told. "

Mr. Granger and his daughter called at Mill Cottage next day: the fair Sophia with a somewhat unwilling aspect, though she was decently civil to Mr. and Miss Lovel. She had protested against the flagrant breach of etiquette in calling on people who had just dined with her, instead of waiting until those diners had discharged their obligation by calling on her; but in vain. Her father had brought her to look at some of Clarissa's sketches, he told his friends.

"I want her to take more interest in landscape art, Mr. Lovel, " he said, "and I think your daughter's example may inspire her. Miss Lovel seems to me to have a real genius for landscape. I saw some studies of ferns and underwood that she had done at Hale—full of freedom and of feeling. Sophia doesn't draw badly, but she wants feeling. "

The young lady thus coldly commended gave her head rather a supercilious toss as she replied, —

"You must remember that I have higher duties than sketching, papa, " she said; "I cannot devote *all* my existence to ferns and blackberry-bushes. "

"O, yes, of course; you've your schools, and that kind of thing; but you might give more time to art than you do, especially if you left the management of the house more to Mrs. Plumptree. I think you waste time and energy upon details. "

"I hope I know my duty as mistress of a large establishment, papa, and that I shall never feel the responsibility of administering a large income any less than I do at present. It would be a bad thing for you if I became careless of your interests in order to roam about sketching toadstools and blackberry-bushes. "

Mr. Granger looked as if he were rather doubtful upon this point, but it was evidently wisest not to push the discussion too far.

"Will you be so kind as to show us your portfolio, Miss Lovel? " he asked.

"Of course she will, " answered her father promptly; "she will only be too happy to exhibit her humble performances to Miss Granger. Bring your drawing-book, Clary. "

Clarissa would have given the world to refuse. A drawing-book is in some measure a silent confidante—almost a journal. She did not know how far her random sketches—some of them mere vagabondage of the pencil, jotted down half unconsciously—might betray the secrets of her inner life to the cold eyes of Miss Granger.

"I'd better bring down my finished drawings, papa; those that were mounted for you at Belforêt, " she said.

"Nonsense, child; Mr. Granger wants to see your rough sketches, not those stiff schoolgirl things, which I suppose were finished by your drawing-master. Bring that book you are always scribbling in. The girl has a kind of passion for art, " said Mr. Lovel, rather fretfully; "she is seldom without a pencil in her hand. What are you looking for, Clarissa, in that owlish way? There's your book on that table. "

He pointed to the volume—Clarissa's other self and perpetual companion—the very book she had been sketching in when George Fairfax surprised her by the churchyard wall. There was no help for it, no disobeying that imperious finger of her father'~; so she brought the book meekly and laid it open before Sophia Granger.

The father and daughter turned over the leaves together. It was book of "bits: " masses of foliage, bramble, and bird's-nest; here the head of an animal, there the profile of a friend; anon a bit of still life; a vase of flowers, with the arabesqued drapery of a curtain for a background; everywhere the evidence of artistic feeling and a practised hand, everywhere a something much above a schoolgirl's art.

Miss Granger looked through the leaves with an icy air. She was obliged to say, "Very pretty, " or "Very clever, " once in a way; but this cold praise evidently cost her an effort. Not so her father. He was interested in every page, and criticised everything with a real knowledge of what he was talking about, which made Clarissa feel that he was at least no pretender in his love of art; that he was not a man who bought pictures merely because he was rich and picture-buying was the right thing to do.

They came presently to the pages Clarissa had covered at Hale Castle—bits of familiar landscape, glimpses of still life in the Castle rooms, and lightly-touched portraits of the Castle guests. There was one head that appeared very much oftener than others, and Clarissa felt herself blushing a deeper red every time Mr. Granger paused to contemplate this particular likeness.

He lingered longer over each of these sketches, with rather a puzzled air, and though the execution of these heads was very spirited, he forbore to praise.

"There is one face here that I see a good deal of, Miss Lovel, " he said at last. "I think it is Mr. Fairfax, is it not? "

Clarissa looked at a profile of George Fairfax dubiously.

"Yes, I believe I meant that for Mr. Fairfax; his is a very easy face to draw, much easier than Lady Geraldine's, though her features are so regular. All my portraits of her are failures. "

"I have only seen one attempt at Lady Geraldine's portrait in this book, Miss Lovel, " said Sophia.

"I have some more on loose sheets of paper, somewhere; and then I generally destroy my failures, if they are quite hopeless. "

"Mr. Fairfax would be quite flattered if he could see how often you have sketched him, " Sophia continued blandly.

Clarissa thought of the leaf George Fairfax had cut out of her drawing-book; a recollection which did not serve to diminish her embarrassment.

"I daresay Mr. Fairfax is quite vain enough without any flattery of that kind, " said Mr. Lovel. "And now that you have exhibited your rough sketches, you can bring those mounted drawings, if you like, Clarissa. "

This was a signal for the closing of the book, which Clarissa felt was intended for her relief. She put the volume back upon the little side-table from which she had taken it, and ran upstairs to fetch her landscapes. These Miss Granger surveyed in the same cold tolerant manner with which she had surveyed the sketch-book—the manner of a person who could have done much better in that line herself, if she had cared to do anything so frivolous.

After this Mr. Lovel and his daughter called at the Court; and the acquaintance between the two families being thus formally inaugurated by a dinner and a couple of morning calls, Mr. Granger came very often to the Cottage, unaccompanied by the inflexible Sophia, who began to feel that her father's infatuation was not to be lessened by any influence of hers, and that she might just as well let him take his own way. It was an odious unexpected turn which events had taken; but there was no help for it. Her confidential maid, Hannah Warman, reminded her of that solemn truth whenever she ventured to touch upon this critical subject.

"If your pa was a young man, miss, or a man that had admired a great many ladies in his time, it would be quite different, " said the astute Warman; "but never having took notice of any one before, and taking such particular notice of this young lady, makes it clear to any one that's got eyes. Depend upon it, miss, it won't be long before he'll make her an offer; and it isn't likely she'll refuse him—not with a ruined pa to urge her on! "

"I suppose not, " said Sophia disconsolately.

"And after all, miss, he might have made a worse choice. If he were to marry one of those manoeuvring middle-aged widows we've met so often out visiting, you'd have had a regular stepmother, that would have taken every bit of power out of your hands, and treated you like a child. But Miss Lovel seems a very nice young lady, and being so near your own age will be quite a companion for you. "

"I don't want such a companion. There is no sympathy between Miss Lovel and me; you ought to know that, Warman. Her tastes are the very reverse of mine, in every way. It's not possible we can ever get on well together; and if papa marries her, I shall feel that he is quite lost to me. Besides, how could I ever have any feeling but contempt for a girl who would marry for money? and of course Miss Lovel could only marry papa for the sake of his money. "

"It's done so often nowadays. And sometimes those matches turn out very well—better than some of the love-matches, I've heard say. "

"It's no use discussing this hateful business, Warman, " Miss Granger answered haughtily. "Nothing could change my opinion. "

And in this inflexible manner did Daniel Granger's daughter set her face against the woman he had chosen from among all other women for his wife. He felt that it was so, and that there would be a hard battle for him to fight in the future between these two influences; but no silent opposition of his daughter's could weaken his determination to win Clarissa Lovel, if she was to be won by him.

* * * * *

CHAPTER XXIII.

"HE'S SWEETEST FRIEND, OR HARDEST FOE. "

Mr. Granger fell into the habit of strolling across his park, and dropping into the garden of Mill Cottage by that little gate across which Clarissa had so often contemplated the groves and shades of her lost home. He would drop in sometimes in the gloaming, and take a cup of tea in the bright lamplit parlour, where Mr. Lovel dawdled away life over Greek plays, Burton's *Anatomy*, and Sir Thomas Browne—a humble apartment, which seemed pleasanter to Mr. Granger under the dominion of that spell which bound him just now, than the most luxurious of his mediaeval chambers. Here he would talk politics with Mr. Lovel, who took a mild interest in the course of public affairs, and whose languid adherence to the Conservative party served to sustain discussion with Daniel Granger, who was a vigorous Liberal.

After tea the visitor generally asked for music; and Clarissa would play her favourite waltzes and mazourkas, while the two gentlemen went on with their conversation. There were not many points of sympathy between the two, perhaps. It is doubtful whether Daniel Granger had ever read a line of a Greek play since his attainment to manhood and independence, though he had been driven along the usual highway of the Classics by expensive tutors, and had a dim remembrance of early drillings in Caesar and Virgil. Burton he had certainly never looked into, nor any of those other English classics which were the delight of Marmaduke Lovel; so the subject of books was a dead letter between them. But they found enough to talk about somehow, and really seemed to get on very tolerably together. Mr. Granger was bent upon standing well with his poor neighbour; and Mr. Lovel appeared by no means displeased by the rapid growth of this acquaintance, from which he had so obstinately recoiled in the past. He took care, however, not to be demonstrative of his satisfaction, and allowed Mr. Granger to feel that at the best he was admitted to Mill Cottage on sufferance, under protest as it were, and as a concession to his own wishes. Yet Mr. Lovel meant all this time that his daughter should be mistress of Arden Court, and that his debts should be paid, and his future comfort provided for out of the ample purse of Daniel Granger.

"I shall go and live on the Continent, " he thought, "when that is all settled. I could not exist as a hanger-on in the house that was once my own, I might find myself a *pied à terre* in Paris or Vienna, and finish life pleasantly enough among some of the friends I liked when I was young. Six or seven hundred a year would be opulence for a man of my habits. "

Little by little Clarissa came to accept those visits of Mr. Granger's as a common part of her daily life; but she had not the faintest notion that she was drifting into a position from which it would be difficult by-and-by to escape. He paid her no disagreeable attentions; he never alluded to that unfortunate declaration which she remembered with such a sense of its absurdity. It did not seem unreasonable to suppose that he came to Mill Cottage for no keener delight than a quiet chat with Mr. Lovel about the possibility of a coming war, or the chances of a change in the ministry.

Clarissa had been home from Hale nearly six weeks, and she had neither heard nor seen any more of George Fairfax. So far there had been no temptation for the violation of that sacred pledge which she had given to Lady Laura Armstrong. His persistence did not amount to much evidently; his ardour was easily checked; he had sworn that night that she should see him, should listen to him, and six weeks had gone by without his having made the faintest attempt to approach her. It was best, of course, that it should be so—an unqualified blessing for the girl whose determination to be true to herself and her duty was so deeply fixed; and yet she felt a little wounded, a little humiliated, as if she had been tricked by the common phrases of a general wooer—duped into giving something where nothing had been given to her.

"Lady Laura might well talk about his transient folly, " she said to herself. "It has not lasted very long. She need scarcely have taken the trouble to be uneasy about it. "

There had been one brief note for Clarissa from the mistress of Hale Castle, announcing her departure for Baden with Mr. Armstrong, who was going to shoot capercailzies in the Black Forest. Lady Geraldine, who was very much shaken by her father's death, was to go with them. There was not a word about Mr. Fairfax, and Clarissa had no idea as to his whereabouts. He had gone with the Baden party most likely, she told herself.

It was near the close of October. The days were free from rain or blusterous winds, but dull and gray. The leaves were falling silently in the woods about Arden, and the whole scene wore that aspect of subdued mournfulness which is pleasant enough to the light of heart, but very sad to those who mourn. Clarissa Lovel was not light-hearted. She had discovered of late that there was something wanting in her life. The days were longer and drearier than they used to be. Every day she awoke with a faint sense of expectation that was like an undefined hope; something would come to pass, something would happen to her before the day was done, to quicken the sluggish current of her life; and at nightfall, when the uneventful day had passed in its customary blankness, her heart would grow very heavy. Her father watched her somewhat anxiously at this crisis of her life, and was inwardly disturbed on perceiving her depression.

She went out into the garden alone one evening after dinner, as it was her wont to do almost every evening, leaving Mr. Lovel dozing luxuriously in his easy-chair by the fire—she went out alone in the chill gray dusk, and paced the familiar walks, between borders in which there were only pale autumnal flowers, chrysanthemums and china asters of faint yellow and fainter purple. Even the garden looked melancholy in this wan light, Clarissa thought. She made the circuit of the small domain, walked up and down the path by the mill-stream two or three times, and then went into the leafless orchard, where the gnarled old trees cast their misshapen shadows on the close-cropped grass. A week-old moon had just risen, pale in the lessening twilight. The landscape had a cold shadowy beauty of its own; but to-night everything seemed wan and cheerless to Clarissa.

She was near the gate leading into Arden Park, when she heard a crackling of withered leaves, the sound of an approaching footstep. It was Mr. Granger, of course. She gave a sigh of resignation. Another evening of the pattern which had grown so familiar to her, that it seemed almost as if Mr. Granger must have been dropping in of an evening all her life. The usual talk of public matters—the leaders in that day's *Times*, and so on. The usual request for a little music; the usual inquiries about her recent artistic studies. It was as monotonous as the lessons she had learned at Madame Marot's seminary.

"Is my life to go on like that for ever? " she asked herself.

The step came a little nearer. Surely it was lighter and quicker than Daniel Granger's—it had a sharp martial sound; it was like a step she had learned to know very well in the gardens of Hale Castle.

"He is at Baden, " she said to herself.

But the beating of her heart grew faster in spite of that tranquillizing assurance. She heard an unaccustomed hand trying the fastening of the gate, then a bolt withdrawn, the sharp light step upon the turf behind her, and in the next moment George Fairfax was by her side, among the weird shadows of the orchard trees.

He tried to draw her towards him, with the air of an accepted lover.

"My darling! " he said, "I knew I should find you here. I had a fancy that you would be here, waiting for me in the pale moonlight. "

Clarissa laughed—rather an artificial little laugh—but she felt the situation could only be treated lightly. The foolish passionate heart was beating so fast all the time, and the pale face might have told so much, if the light of the new-risen moon had not been dim as yet.

"How long do you suppose I have been waiting at this spot for you, Mr. Fairfax? " she asked lightly. "For six weeks? "

"Six weeks! Yes, it is six weeks since I saw you. It might be six years, if I were to measure the time by my own impatience. I have been at Nice, Clarissa, almost ever since that night we parted. "

"At Nice! with Lady Laura and Lady Geraldine, I suppose, I thought they were going to Baden. "

"They are at Baden; but I have not been with them. I left England with my mother, who had a very bad attack of her chronic asthma earlier than usual this year, and was ordered off to the South of France, where she is obliged to spend all her winters, poor soul. I went with her, and stayed till she was set up again in some measure. I was really uneasy about her; and it was a good excuse for getting away from Hale. "

Clarissa murmured some conventional expression of sympathy, but that was all.

"My darling, " said George Fairfax, taking her cold hand in his—she tried to withdraw it, but it was powerless in that firm grasp—"My darling, you know why I have come here; and you know now why my coming has been so long delayed. I could not write to you. The Fates are against us, Clarissa, and I do not expect much favour from your father. So I feared that a letter might do us mischief, and put off everything till I could come, I said a few words to Laura Armstrong before I left the Castle—not telling her very much, but giving her a strong hint of the truth. I don't think she'll be surprised by anything I may do; and my letters to Geraldine have all been written to prepare the way for our parting. I know she will be generous; and if my position with regard to her is rather a despicable one, I have done all I could to make the best of it. I have not made things worse by deceit or double-dealing. I should have boldly asked for my freedom before this, but I hear such bad accounts of poor Geraldine, who seems to be dreadfully grieved by her father's loss, that I have put off all idea of any direct explanation for the present. I am not the less resolved, however, Clarissa. "

Miss Lovel turned her face towards him for the first time, and looked at him with a proud steady gaze. She had given her promise, and was not afraid that anything, not even his tenderest, most passionate pleading, could ever tempt her to break it; but she knew more and more that she loved him—that it was his absence and silence which, had made her life so blank, that his coming was the event she had waited and watched for day after day.

"Why should you break faith with Lady Geraldine? " she asked calmly.

"Why! Because my bondage has been hateful to me ever since I came to Hale. Because there is only one woman I will have for my wife— and her name is Clarissa Lovel! "

"You had better keep your word, Mr. Fairfax. I was quite in earnest in what I said to you six weeks ago. Nothing in the world would ever induce me to have any part in your breach of faith. Why, even if I loved you—" her voice trembled a little here, and George Fairfax repeated the words after her, "*Even* if you loved me—I could never trust you. How could I hope that, after having been so false to her, you could be true to me? "

"Even if I loved you. Tell me that you do love me—as I have hoped and dreamed—as I dared to believe sometimes at Hale, when my wedding-day was so near, that I seemed like some wretch bound to the wheel, for whom there is no possibility of escape. That is all over now, darling. To all intents and purposes I am free. Confess that you love me. " This was said half tenderly, half imperiously—with the air of a conqueror accustomed to easy triumphs, an air which this man's experience had made natural to him. "Come, Clarissa, think how many miles I have travelled for the sake of this one stolen half hour. Don't be so inexorable. "

He looked down at her with a smile on his face, not very much alarmed by her obduracy. It seemed to him only a new form of feminine eccentricity. Here was a woman who actually could resist him for ten minutes at a stretch—him, George Fairfax!

"I am very sorry you should have come so far. I am very sorry you should have taken so much trouble; it is quite wasted. "

"Then you don't like me, Miss Lovel, " still half playfully—the thing was too impossible to be spoken of in any other tone. "For some reason or other I am obnoxious to you. Look me full in the face, and swear that you don't care a straw for me. "

"I am not going to swear anything so foolish. You are not obnoxious to me. I have no wish to forfeit your friendship; but I will not hear of anything more than friendship from your lips. "

"Why not? "

"For many reasons. In the first place, because there would be treason against Lady Geraldine in my listening to you. "

"Put that delusion out of your mind. There would be no treason; all is over between Lady Geraldine and me. "

"There are other reasons, connected with papa. "

"Oh, your father is against me. Yes, that is only natural. Any more reasons, Clarissa? "

"One more. "

"What is that? "

"I cannot tell you. "

"But I insist upon being told. "

She tried her uttermost to avoid answering his questions; but he was persistent, and she admitted at last that she had promised not to listen to him.

"To whom was the promise given? "

"That is my secret. "

"To your father? "

"That is my secret, Mr. Fairfax. You cannot extort it from me. And now I must go back to papa, if you please, or he will be sending some one to look for me. "

"And I shall be discovered in Mr. Capulet's orchard. Ten minutes more, Clarissa, and I vanish amidst the woods of Arden, through which I came like a poacher in order to steal upon you unawares by that little gate. And now, my darling, since we have wasted almost all our time in fencing with words, let us be reasonable. Promises such as you speak of are pledges given to the winds. They cannot hold an hour against true love. Listen, Clary, listen. "

And then came the pleading of a man only too well accustomed to plead—a man this time very much in earnest: words that seemed to Clarissa full of a strange eloquence, tones that went to her heart of hearts. But she had given her promise, and with her that promise meant something very sacred. She was firm to the last—firm even when those thrilling tones changed from love to auger.

All that he said towards the end she scarcely knew, for there was a dizziness in her brain that confused her, and her chiefest fear was that she should drop fainting at his feet; but the last words of all struck upon her ear with a cruel distinctness, and were never forgotten.

"I am the merest fool and schoolboy to take this matter so deeply to heart, " he said, with a scornful laugh, "when the reason of my rejection is so obvious. What I saw at Hale Castle might have taught me wisdom. Even with my improved prospects I am little better than a pauper compared with Daniel Granger. And I have heard you say that you would give all the world to win back Arden Court. I will stand aside, and make way for a wealthier suitor. Perhaps we may meet again some day, and I may not be so unfortunate as my father. "

He was gone. Clarissa stood like a statue, with her hands clasped before her face. She heard the gate shut by a violent hand. He was gone in supreme anger, with scorn and insult upon his lips, believing her the basest of the base, the meanest of the mean, she told herself. The full significance of his last words she was unable to understand, but it seemed to her that they veiled a threat.

She was going back to the house slowly, tearless, but with something like despair in her heart, when she heard the orchard gate open again. He had come back, perhaps, —returned to forgive and pity her. No, that was not his footstep; it was Mr. Granger, looking unspeakably ponderous and commonplace in the moonlight, as he came across the shadowy grass towards her.

"I thought I saw a white dress amongst the trees, " he said, holding out his hand to her for the usual greeting. "How cold your hand is, Miss Lovel! Is it quite prudent of you to be out so late on such a chilly evening, and in that thin dress? I think I must ask your papa to lecture you. "

"Pray don't, Mr. Granger; I am not in the habit of catching cold, and I am used to being in the gardens at all times and seasons. You are late. "

"Yes; I have been at Holborough all day, and dined an hour later than usual. Your papa is quite well, I hope? "

"He is just the same as ever. He is always more or less of an invalid, you know. "

They came in sight of the broad bay window of the parlour at this moment, and the firelight within revealed Mr. Lovel in a very comfortable aspect, fast asleep, with his pale aristocratic-looking face relieved by the crimson cushions of his capacious easy-chair, and the brown setter's head on his knee. There were some books on the table by his side, but it was evident that his studies since dinner had not been profound.

Clarissa and her companion went in at a half-glass door that opened into a small lobby next the parlour. She knew that to open the window at such an hour in the month of October was an unpardonable crime in her father's eyes. They went into the room very softly; but Mr. Lovel, who was a light sleeper, started up at their entrance, and declared with some show of surprise that he must have been indulging in a nap.

"I was reading a German critic on Aeschylus, " he said. "Those Germans are clever, but too much given to paradoxes. Ring the bell for tea, Clary. I didn't think we should see you to-night, Granger; you said you were going to a dinner at Sir Archer Taverham's. "

"I was engaged to dine with Sir Archer; but I wrote him a note this morning, excusing myself upon the plea of gout. I really had a few twinges last night, and I hate dinner-parties. "

"I am glad you have so much wisdom. I don't think any man under a Talleyrand or an Alvanley can make a masculine dinner worth going to; and as for your mixed herds of men and women, every man past thirty knows that kind of thing to be an abomination. "

The rosy-faced parlour-maid brought in the lamp and the tea-tray, and Clarissa sat quietly down to perform her nightly duties. She took her seat in the full light of the lamp, with no evidence of emotion on her face, and poured out the tea, and listened and replied to Mr. Granger's commonplace remarks, just the same as usual, though the sound of another voice was in her ear—the bitter passionate sound of words that had been almost curses.

* * * * *

CHAPTER XXIV.

"IT MEANS ARDEN COURT."

The time went by, and Daniel Granger pursued his wooing, his tacit undemonstrative courtship, with the quiet persistence of a man who meant to win. He came to Mill Cottage almost every evening throughout the late autumn and early winter months, and Clarissa was fain to endure his presence and to be civil to him. She had no ground for complaint, no opportunity for rebellion. His visits were not made ostensibly on her account, though friends, neighbours, and servants knew very well why he came, and had settled the whole business in their gossiping little coteries. Nor did he take upon himself the airs of a lover. He was biding his time, content to rejoice in the daily presence of the woman he loved; content to wait till custom should have created a tie between them, and till he could claim her for his wife by right of much patience and fidelity. He had an idea that no woman, pure and true as he believed this woman to be, could shut her heart against an honest man's love, if he were only patient and faithful, single-minded and unselfish in his wooing.

George Fairfax kept his word. From the hour of that bitter parting he made no sign of his existence to Clarissa Lovel. The Armstrongs were still in Germany when December came, and people who had any claim upon Lady Laura's hospitality lamented loudly that there were to be no gaieties at the Castle this year. It was the second Christmas that the family had been absent. Mr. Fairfax was with them at Baden most likely, Clarissa thought; and she tried to hope that it was so.

Christmas came, and Miss Lovel had to assist at Miss Granger's triumphs. That young lady was in full force at this time of year, dealing out blankets of the shaggiest and most uncompromising textures—such coverings as might have suited the requirements of a sturdy Highlander or a stalwart bushranger sleeping in the open air, but seemed scarcely the pleasantest gifts for feeble old women or asthmatic old men—and tickets representative of small donations in kind, such as a quart of split-peas, or a packet of prepared groats, with here and there the relief of a couple of ounces of tea. Against plums and currants and candied peel Miss Granger set her face, as verging on frivolity. The poor, who are always given to extravagance, would be sure to buy these for themselves: witness the mountain of currants embellished with little barrows of citron and orange-peel, and the moorland of plums adorned with arabesques of Jamaica ginger in the holly-hung chandler's shop at Arden. Split-peas and groats were real benefits, which would endure when the indigestible delights of plum-pudding were over. Happily for the model villagers, Mr. Granger ordered a bullock and a dozen tons of coal to be distributed amongst them, in a large liberal way that was peculiar to him, without consulting his daughter as to the propriety of the proceeding. She was very busy with the beneficent work of providing her special *protégées* with the ugliest imaginable winter gowns and frocks. Clarissa, who was eager to contribute something to this good work, had wounded her fingers desperately in the manufacture of these implacable fabrics, which set her teeth on edge every time she touched them. Mr. Lovel would not even allow them to be in the room where he sat.

"If you must work at those unspeakably odious garments, Clarissa, " he said, "for pity's sake do it out of my presence. Great Heavens! what cultivator of the Ugly could have invented those loathsome olive-greens, or that revolting mud-colour? evidently a study from the Thames at low water, just above Battersea-bridge. And to think that the poor—to whom nature seems to have given a copyright in warts and wens and boils—should be made still more unattractive by such clothing as that! If you are ever rich, Clarissa, and take to benevolence, think of your landscape before you dress your poor. Give your old women and children scarlet cloaks and gray petticoats, and gratify your men with an orange neckerchief now and then, to make a patch of colour against your russet background. "

There were dinner-parties at Arden Court that winter, to which Mr. Lovel consented to take his daughter, obnoxious as he had declared all such festivities to be to him. He went always as a concession to his host's desires, and took care to let Daniel Granger know that his going was an act of self-sacrifice; but he did go, and he gave his daughter a ten-pound note, as a free-will offering, for the purchase of a couple of new dresses.

Clarissa wondered not a little at the distinction with which her father and herself were treated by every one who met them at Mr. Granger's house. She did not know that a good deal of this attention was given to the future mistress of Arden Court, and that, in the eyes of county people and Holborough gentry alike, she stood in that position. She did not know that her destiny was a settled business in every one's mind except her own: that her aunt Oliver and the Rector, quite as much as her father, looked upon her marriage with Daniel Granger as inevitable. Mr. Lovel had been careful not to alarm his daughter by any hint of his convictions. He was very well satisfied with the progress of affairs. Daniel Granger was too securely caught for there to be any room for fear of change on his part, and Daniel Granger's mode of carrying on the siege seemed to Mr. Lovel an excellent one. Whatever Clarissa's feelings might have been in the beginning, she must needs succumb before such admirable patience, such almost sublime devotion.

Christmas passed, and the new year and all festivities belonging to the season, and a dreary stretch of winter remained, bleak and ungenial, enlivened only by Christmas bills, the chill prelude of another year of struggle. Towards the end of January, Marmarduke Lovel's health broke down all of a sudden. He was really ill, and very fretful in his illness. Those creditors of his became desperately pressing in their demands; almost every morning's post brought him a lawyer's letter; and, however prostrate he might feel, he was obliged to sit up for an hour or so in the day, resting his feverish head upon his hand, while he wrote diplomatic letters for the temporary pacification of impatient attorneys.

Poor Clarissa had a hard time of it in these days. Her father was a difficult patient, and that ever-present terror of insolvency, and all the pains and perils attendant thereupon, tormented her by day and kept her awake at night. Every ring at the cottage gate set her heart beating, and conjured up the vision of some brutal sheriff's officer, such as she had read of in modern romance. She nursed her father with extreme tenderness. He was not confined to his room for any length of time, but was weak and ill throughout the bleak wintry months, with a racking cough and a touch of low fever, lying prostrate for the greater part of the day on a sofa by the fire, and only brightening a little in the evening when Mr. Granger paid his accustomed visit. Clarissa tended him all through these melancholy days, when the rain beat against the windows and the dull gray sky looked as if it would never more be illuminated by a gleam of sunshine; tended him with supreme patience, and made heroic efforts to cheer and sustain his spirits, though her own heart was very heavy. And it came to pass that, in these most trying days, Daniel Granger repeated the avowal of his love, not urging his suit with any hazardous impatience, but offering to wait as long as Clarissa pleased for his sentence. And then, in the midst of the girl's distress at the renewal of this embarrassing declaration, her father spoke to her, and told her plainly that she was, in all honour, bound to become Mr. Granger's wife. She had suffered him to devote himself to her, with a devotion rare in a man of his age and character. She had allowed the outer world to take the business for granted. It would be a cruel wrong done to this man, if she were to draw back now and leave him in the lurch.

"Draw back, papa! " she cried with unmitigated surprise and alarm; "but what have I done to give you or Mr. Granger, or any one else, the slightest justification for supposing I ever thought of him, except as the most commonplace acquaintance? "

"That pretence of unconsciousness is the merest affectation, Clarissa. You must have known why Mr. Granger came here. "

"I thought he came to see you, papa, just like any other acquaintance. "

"Nonsense, child; one man does not dance attendance upon another like that—crying off from important dinner-parties in order to drink tea with his neighbour, and that kind of thing. The case has been clear enough from the beginning, and you must have known how it was—especially as Granger made some declaration to you the first time you went to the Court. He told me what he had done, in a most honourable manner. It is preposterous to pretend, after that, you could mistake his intentions. I have never worried you about the business; it seemed to me wisest and best to let matters take their natural course; and I am the last of men to play the domestic tyrant in order to force a rich husband upon my daughter; but I never for a moment doubted that you understood Mr. Granger's feelings, and were prepared to reward his patience. "

"It can never be, papa, " Clarissa said decisively; "I would not commit such a sin as to marry a man I could not love. I am grateful to Mr. Granger, of course, and very sorry that he should think so much more of me than I deserve, but——"

"For God's sake don't preach! " cried her father fretfully. "You won't have him; that's enough. The only road there was to extrication from my difficulties is shut up. The sheriff's officers can come to-morrow. I'll write no more humbugging letters to those attorneys, trying to stave off the crisis. The sooner the crash comes the better; I can drag out the rest of my existence somehow, in Bruges or Louvain. It is only a question of a year or two, I daresay. "

The dreary sigh with which Mr. Lovel concluded this speech went to Clarissa's heart. It can scarcely be said that she loved him very dearly, but she pitied him very much. To his mind, no doubt, it seemed a hard thing that she should set her face against a change of fortune that would have ensured ease and comfort for his declining years. She knew him weighed down by embarrassments which were very real—which had been known to her before Daniel Granger's appearance as a wooer. There was no pretence about the ruin that menaced them; and it was not strange that her father, who had been loath to move beyond the very outskirts of his lost domain, should shrink with a shuddering dread from exile in a dismal Belgian town.

After that one bitter speech and that one dreary sigh, Mr. Lovel made no overt attempt to influence his daughter's decision. He had a more scientific game to play, and he knew how to play it. Peevish remonstrances might have availed nothing; threats or angry speeches might have provoked a spirit of defiance. Mr. Lovel neither complained nor threatened; he simply collapsed. An air of settled misery fell upon him, an utter hopelessness, that was almost resignation, took possession of him. There was an unwonted gentleness in his manner to his daughter; he endured the miseries of weakness and prostration with unaccustomed patience; meekness pervaded all his words and actions, but it was the meekness of despair. And so—and so—this was how the familiar domestic drama came to be acted once more—the old, old story to be repeated. It was Robin Gray over again. If the cow was not stolen, the sheriff's officers were at the door, and, for lack of a broken arm, Marmaduke Lovel did not want piteous silent arguments. He was weak and ill and despairing, and where threats or jesuitical pleading would have availed little, his silence did much; until at last, after several weary weeks of indecision, during which Mr. Granger had come and gone every evening without making any allusion to his suit, there came one night when Clarissa fell on her knees by her father's sofa, and told him that she could not endure the sight of his misery any longer, and that she was willing to be Daniel Granger's wife. Marmaduke Lovel put his feeble arms round his daughter's neck, and kissed her as he had never kissed her before; and then burst into tears, with his face hidden upon her shoulder.

"It was time, Clarissa, " he said at last. "I could not have kept the brokers out another week. Granger has been offering to lend me money ever since he began to suspect my embarrassments, but I could not put myself under an obligation to him while I was uncertain of your intentions: it will be easy to accept his help now; and he has made most liberal proposals with regard to your marriage settlements. Bear witness, Clary, that I never mentioned that till now. I have urged no sordid consideration upon you to bring about this match; although, God knows, it is the thing I desire most in this world. "

"No, no, papa, I know that, " sobbed Clarissa. And then the image of George Fairfax rose before her, and the memory of those bitter words, "It means Arden Court. "

What would he think of her when he should come to hear that she was to be Daniel Granger's wife? It would seem a full confirmation of his basest suspicions. He would never know of her unavailing struggles to escape this doom—never guess her motives for making this sacrifice. He would think of her, in all the days to come, only as a woman who sold herself for the sake of a goodly heritage.

Once having given her promise, there was no such thing as drawing back for Clarissa, even had she been so minded. Mr. Lovel told the anxious lover that his fate was favourably decided, warning him at the same time that it would be well to refrain from any hazardous haste, and to maintain as far as possible that laudable patience and reserve which had distinguished his conduct up to this point.

"Clarissa is very young, " said her father; "and I do not pretend to tell you that she is able to reciprocate, as fully as I might wish, the ardour of your attachment. One could hardly expect that all at once. "

"No, one could hardly expect that, " Mr. Granger echoed with a faint sigh.

"As a man of the world, you would not, I am sure, my dear Granger, overlook the fact of the very wide difference in your ages, or expect more than is reasonable. Clarissa admires and esteems you, I am sure, and is deeply grateful for a devotion to which she declares herself undeserving. She is not a vain frivolous girl, who thinks a man's best affection only a tribute due to her attractions. And there is a kind of regard which grows up in a girl's heart for a sensible man who loves her, and which I believe with all my soul to be better worth having than the romantic nonsense young people take for the grand passion. I make no profession, you see, my dear Granger, on my daughter's part; but I have no fear but that Clarissa will learn to love you, in good time, as truly as you can desire to be loved. "

"Unless I thought that she had some affection for me, I would never ask her to be my wife, " said Mr. Granger.

"Wouldn't you? " thought Mr. Lovel. "My poor Granger, you are farther gone than you suppose! "

"You can give me your solemn assurance upon one point, eh, Lovel? " said the master of Arden Court anxiously; "there is no one else in the case? Your daughter's heart is quite free? It is only a question as to whether I can win it? "

"Her heart is entirely free, and as pure as a child's. She is full of affection, poor girl, only yearning to find an outlet for it. She ought to make you a good wife, Daniel Granger. There is nothing against her doing so. "

"God grant she may! " replied Mr. Granger solemnly; "God knows how dearly I love her, and what a new thing this love is to me! "

He took heed of his future father-in-law's counsel, and said nothing more about his hopes to Clarissa just yet awhile. It was only by an undefinable change in his manner—a deeper graver tenderness in his tone—that she guessed her father must have told him her decision.

From this day forth all clouds vanished from the domestic sky at Mill Cottage. Mr. Lovel's debts were paid; no more threatening letters made his breakfast-table a terror to him; there were only agreeable-looking stamped documents in receipt of payment, with little apologetic notes, and entreaties for future favours.

Mr. Granger's proposals respecting a settlement were liberal, but, taking into consideration the amount of his wealth, not lavish. He offered to settle a thousand a year upon his wife—five hundred for her own use as pin-money, five hundred as an annuity for her father. He might as easily have given her three thousand, or six thousand, as it was for no lack of generous inclination that he held his hand;

but he did not want to do anything that might seem like buying his wife. Nor did Marmaduke Lovel give the faintest hint of a desire for larger concessions from his future son-in-law: he conducted the business with the lofty air of a man above the consideration of figures. Five hundred a year was not much to get from a man in Granger's position; but, added to his annuity of three hundred, it would make eight—a very decent income for a man who had only himself to provide for; and then of course there would be no possibility of his ever wanting money, with such a son-in-law to fall back upon.

Mr. Granger did not lose any time in making his daughter acquainted with the change that was about to befall her. He was quite prepared to find her adverse to his wishes, and quite prepared to defend his choice; and yet, little subject as he was to any kind of mental weakness, he did feel rather uncomfortable when the time came for addressing Miss Granger.

It was after dinner, and the father and daughter were sitting alone in the small gothic dining-room, sheltered from possible draughts by mediaeval screens of stamped leather and brazen scroll-work, and in a glowing atmosphere of mingled fire and lamp light, making a pretty cabinet-picture of home life, which might have pleased a Flemish painter.

"I think, Sophia, " said Mr. Granger, —"I think, my dear, there is no occasion for me to tell you that there is a certain friend and neighbour of yours who is something more to me than the ordinary young ladies of your acquaintance. "

Miss Granger seemed as if she were trying to swallow some hard substance—a knotty little bit of the pineapple she had just been eating, perhaps—before she replied to this speech of her father's.

"I am sure, papa, I am quite at a loss to comprehend your meaning, " she said at last. "I have no near neighbour whom I can call my friend, unless you mean Mrs. Patterly, the doctor's wife, who has taken such a warm interest in my clothing-club, and who has such a beautiful mind. But you would hardly call her a young lady. "

"Patterly's wife! no, I should think not! " exclaimed Mr. Granger impatiently: "I was speaking of Clarissa Lovel. "

232

Miss Granger drew herself up suddenly, and pinched her lips together as if they were never to unclose again. She did open them nevertheless, after a pause, to say in an icy tone, —

"Miss Lovel is my acquaintance, but not my friend. "

"Why should she not be your friend? She is a very charming girl. "

"Oh, yes, I have no doubt of that, papa, from your point of view; that is to say, she is very pretty, and thinks a great deal of dress, and is quite ready to flirt with any one who likes to flirt with her—I'm sure you must have seen *that* at Hale Castle—and fills her scrap-book with portraits of engaged men; witness all those drawings of Mr. Fairfax. I have no doubt she is just the kind of person gentlemen call charming; but she is no friend of mine, and she never will be. "

"I am sorry to hear that, " said her father sternly; "for she is very likely to be your stepmother. "

It was a death-blow, but one that Sophia Granger had anticipated for a long time.

"You are going to marry Miss Lovel, papa—a girl two years younger than I am? "

"Yes, I am going to marry Miss Lovel, and I am very proud of her youth and beauty; but I do not admit her want of more solid charms than those, Sophia. I have watched her conduct as a daughter, and I have a most perfect faith in the goodness and purity of her heart. "

"Oh, very well, papa. Of course you know what is best for your own happiness. It is not for me to presume to offer an opinion; I trust I have too clear a sense of duty for that. " And here Miss Granger gave a sigh expressive of resignation under circumstances of profound affliction.

"I believe you have, Sophy, " answered her father kindly. "I believe that, however unwelcome this change may be to you at first—and I suppose it is only natural that it should be unwelcome—you will reconcile your mind to it fully when you discover that it is for my happiness. I am not ashamed to confess to you that I love Clarissa very fondly, and that I look forward to a happy future when she is my wife. "

"I hope, papa, that your life has not been unhappy hitherto—that I have not in any manner failed in my duties as a daughter. "

"Oh, dear no, child; of course not. That has nothing to do with the question. "

"Will it—the marriage—be very soon, papa? " asked Miss Granger, with another gulp, as if there were still some obstructive substance in her throat.

"I hope so, Sophy. There is no reason, that I can see, why it should not be very soon. "

"And will Mr. Lovel come to live with us? "

"I don't know; I have never contemplated such a possibility. I think Mr. Lovel is scarcely the kind of person who would care to live in another man's house. "

"But this has been his own house, you see, papa, and will seem to belong to him again when his daughter is the mistress of it. I daresay he will look upon us as interlopers. "

"I don't think so, Sophia. Mr. Lovel is a gentleman, and a sensible man into the bargain. He is not likely to have any absurd ideas of that kind. "

"I suppose he is very much pleased at having secured such a rich husband for his daughter, " Miss Granger hazarded presently, with the air of saying something agreeable.

"Sophia! " exclaimed her father angrily, "I must beg that the question of money may never be mooted in relation to Miss Lovel and myself—by you above all people. I daresay there may be men and women in the world malignant enough to say—mean enough to suppose—that this dear girl can only consent to marry me because I am a rich man. It is my happiness to know her to be much too noble to yield to any sordid consideration of that kind. It is my happiness to know that her father has done nothing to urge this marriage upon her. She gives herself to me of her own free-will, not hurried into a decision by any undue persuasion of mine, and under no pressure from outer circumstances. "

"I am very glad to hear it, papa. I think I should have broken my heart, if I had seen you the dupe of a mercenary woman. "

Mr. Granger got up from his seat with an impatient air, and began to pace the room. His daughter had said very little, but that little had been beyond measure irritating to him. It galled him to think that this marriage should seem to her an astonishing—perhaps even a preposterous—thing. True that the woman he was going to marry was younger, by a year or two, than his own daughter. In his own mind there was so little sense of age, that he could scarcely understand why the union should seem discordant. He was not quite fifty, an age which he had heard men call the very meridian of life; and he felt himself younger now than he had ever been since he first assumed the cares of manhood—first grew grave with the responsibilities involved in the disposal of a great fortune. Was not this newly-born love, this sudden awakening of a heart that had slumbered so long, a renewal of youth? Mr. Granger glanced at his own reflection in a glass over a buffet, as he paced to and fro. The figure that he saw there bore no sign of age. It was a relief to him to discover that—a thing he had never thought of till that moment.

"Why should she not love me? " he asked himself. "Are youth and a handsome face the only high-road to a woman's heart? I can't believe it. Surely constancy and devotion must count for something. Is there another man in the world who would love her as well as I? who could say, at fifty years of age, This is my first love? "

"I am to give up the housekeeping, of course, papa, when you are married, " Miss Granger said presently, with that subdued air of resignation in which she had wrapped herself as in a garment since her father's announcement.

"Give up the housekeeping! " he echoed a little impatiently; "I don't see the necessity for that. Clarissa"—oh, how sweet it was to him to pronounce her name, and with that delicious sense of proprietorship! —"Clarissa is too young to care much for that sort of thing—dealing out groceries, and keeping account-books, as you do. Very meritorious, I am sure, my dear, and no doubt useful. No, I don't suppose you'll be interfered with, Sophy. In all essentials you will still be mistress. If Clarissa is queen, you will be prime minister; and you know it is the minister who really pulls the strings. And I do hope that in time you two will get to love each other. "

"I shall endeavour to do my duty, papa, " Miss Granger answered primly. "We cannot command our feelings. "

It was some feeble relief to her to learn that her grocery-books, her day-books by double-entry, and all those other commercial volumes dear to her heart, were not to be taken away from her; that she was still to retain the petty powers she had held as the sole daughter of Daniel Granger's house and heart. But to resign her place at the head of her father's table, to see Clarissa courted and caressed, to find faltering allegiance perhaps even among her model poor—all these things would be very bitter, and in her heart Sophia Granger was angry with her father for a line of conduct which she considered the last stage of folly. She loved him, after her own precise well-regulated fashion—loved him as well as a creature so self-conscious could be expected to love; but she could not easily forgive him for an act which seemed, in some sort, a fraud upon herself. She had been brought up to believe herself his sole heiress, to look upon his second marriage as an utter impossibility. How often had she heard him ridicule the notion when it was suggested to him by some jocose acquaintance! and it did seem a very hard thing that she should be pushed all at once from this lofty stand-point, and levelled to the very dust. There would be a new family, of course; a brood of sons and daughters to divide her heritage. Hannah Warman had suggested as much when discussing the probability of the marriage, with that friendly candour, and disposition to look at the darker side of the picture, which are apt to distinguish confidantes of her class.

"I am sure, papa, " Miss Granger whimpered by-and-by, not quite able to refrain from some expression of ill-temper, "I have scarcely had a pleasant evening since you have known the Lovels. You are always there, and it is very dull to be alone every night. "

"It has been your own fault in some measure, Sophy. You might have had Clarissa here, if you'd chosen to cultivate her friendship. "

"Our inclinations are beyond our control, papa. Nothing but your express commands, and a sense of duty, would induce me to select Miss Lovel for a companion. There is no sympathy between us. "

"Why should there not be? You cannot think her unamiable, nor question her being highly accomplished. "

"But it is not a question of playing, or singing, or painting, or talking foreign languages, papa. One selects a friend for higher qualities than those. There is Mary Anne Patterly, for instance, who can scarcely play the bass in a set of quadrilles, but whose admirable gifts and Christian character have endeared her to me. Miss Lovel is so frivolous. See how stupid and listless she seemed that day we took her over the schools and cottages. I don't believe she was really interested in anything she saw. And, though she has been at home a year and a half, she has not once offered to take a class in either of the schools. "

"I daresay she sees the schools are well officered, my dear, and doesn't like to interfere with your functions. "

"No, papa, it is not that. She has no vocation for serious things. Her mind is essentially frivolous; you will discover that for yourself by-and-by. I speak in perfect candour, you know, papa. Whatever your feelings about Miss Lovel may be, I am above concealing mine. I believe I know my duty; but I cannot stoop to hypocrisy. "

"I suppose not. But I must say, you might have taken this business in a pleasanter spirit, Sophia. I shall expect, however, to see you take more pains to overcome your prejudice against the young Indy I have chosen for my wife; and I shall be rather slow to believe in your affection for myself unless it shows itself in that manner. "

Miss Granger covered her face with her handkerchief, and burst into a flood of tears.

"Oh, papa, papa, it only needed that! To think that any one's influence can make my father doubt my affection for him, after all these years of duty and obedience! "

Mr. Granger muttered something about "duty, " which was the very reverse of a blessing, and walked out of the room, leaving Sophia to her tears.

* * * * *

CHAPTER XXV.

WEDDING BELLS.

There was no reason why the marriage should not take place very soon. Mr. Granger said so; Mr. Lovel agreed with him, half reluctantly as it were, and with the air of a man who is far from eager to precipitate events. There was no imaginable reason for delay.

Upon this point Mr. and Mrs. Oliver were as strong as Daniel Granger himself. A union in every way so propitious could not be too speedily made secure. Matthew Oliver was full of demonstrative congratulation now when he dined at Mill Cottage.

"Who would have guessed when I brought you home from the station that morning, and we drove through the park, that you were going to be mistress of it so soon, Clary? " he exclaimed triumphantly. "Do you remember crying when you heard the place was sold? I do, poor child; I can see your piteous face at this moment. And now it is going to be yours again. Upon my word, Providence has been very good to you, Clarissa. "

Providence had been very good to her. They all told her the same story. Amongst her few friends there was not one who seemed to suspect that this marriage might be a sacrifice; that in her heart of hearts there might be some image brighter than Daniel Granger's.

She found herself staring at these congratulatory friends in blank amazement sometimes, wondering that they should all look at this engagement of hers from the same point of view, all be so very certain of her happiness.

Had she not reason to be happy, however? There had been a time when she had talked and thought of her lost home almost as Adam and Eve may have done when yet newly expelled from Paradise, with the barren world in all its strangeness before them. Was it not something to win back this beloved dwelling-place—something to obtain comfort for her father's age—to secure an income which might enable her to help her brother in the days to come? Nor was the man she had promised to marry obnoxious to her. He had done much towards winning her regard in the patient progress of his wooing. She believed him to be a good and honourable man, whose affection was something that a woman might be proud of having won—a man whom it would be a bitter thing to offend. She was clear-sighted enough to perceive his superiority to her father—his utter truthfulness and openness of character. She did feel just a little proud of his love. It was something to see this big strong man, vigorous in mind as in body, reduced to so complete a bondage, yet not undignified even in his slavery.

What was it, then, which came between her and the happiness which that congratulatory chorus made so sure of? Only the image of the man she had loved—the man she had rejected for honour's sake one bleak October evening, and whom she had never ceased to think of since that time. She knew that Daniel Granger was, in all likelihood, a better and a nobler man than George Fairfax; but the face that had been with her in the dimly-lighted railway-carriage, the friendly voice that had cheered her on the first night of her womanhood, were with her still.

More than once, since that wintry afternoon when Mr. Granger had claimed her as his own for the first time—taking her to his breast with a grave and solemn tenderness, and telling her that every hope and desire of his mind was centred in her, and that all his life to come would be devoted to securing her happiness—more than once since that day she had been tempted to tell her lover all the truth; but shame kept her silent. She did not know how to begin her confession. On that afternoon she had been strangely passive, like a creature stunned by some great surprise; and yet, after what she had said to her father, she had expected every day that Mr. Granger would speak.

After a good deal of discussion among third parties, and an undeviating urgency on the part of Mr. Granger himself, it was arranged that the wedding should take place at the end of May, and that Clarissa should see Switzerland in its brightest aspect. She had once expressed a longing for Alpine peaks and glaciers in her lover's presence, and he had from that moment, determined that Switzerland should be the scene of his honeymoon. They would go there so early as to avoid the herd of autumnal wanderers. He knew the country, and could map out the fairest roads for their travels, the pleasantest resting-places for their repose. And if Clarissa cared to explore Italy afterwards, and spend October and November in Rome, she could do so. All the world would be bright and new to him with her for his companion. He looked forward with boyish eagerness to revisiting scenes that he had fancied himself weary of until now. Yes; such a love as this was indeed a renewal of youth.

To all arrangements made on her behalf Clarissa was submissive. What could a girl, not a quite twenty, urge against the will of a man like Daniel Granger, supported by such powerful allies as father, and uncle and aunt, and friends? She thanked him more warmly than usual when he proposed the Swiss tour. Yes; she had wished very much to see that country. Her brother had gone there on a walking expedition when he was little more than a boy, and had very narrowly escaped with his life from the perils of the road. She had some of his Alpine sketches, in a small portfolio of particular treasures, to this day.

Mrs. Oliver revelled in the business of the trosseau. Never since the extravagant days of her early youth had she enjoyed such a feast of millinery. To an aunt the provision of a wedding outfit is peculiarly delightful. She has all the pomp and authority of a parent, without a parent's responsibility. She stands *in loco parentis* with regard to everything except the bill. No uneasy twinge disturbs her, as the glistening silk glides through the shopman's hands, and ebbs and flows in billows of brightness on the counter. No demon of calculation comes between her and the genius of taste, when the milliner suggests an extra flounce of Marines, or a pelerine of Honiton.

A trip to London, and a fortnight or so spent in West-end shops, would have been very agreeable to Mrs. Oliver; but on mature reflection she convinced herself that to purchase her niece's trosseau in London would be a foolish waste of power. The glory to be obtained in Wigmore or Regent-street was a small thing compared with the *kudos* that would arise to her from the expenditure of a round sum of money among the simple traders of Holborough. Thus it was that Clarissa's wedding finery was all ordered at Brigson and Holder's, the great linendrapers in Holborough market-place, and all made by Miss Mallow, the chief milliner and dressmaker of Holborough, who was in a flutter of excitement from the moment she received the order, and held little levees amongst her most important customers for the exhibition of Miss Lovel's silks and laces.

Towards the end of April there came a letter of congratulation from Lady Laura Armstrong, who was still in Germany; a very cordial and affectionate letter, telling Clarissa that the tidings of her engagement had just reached Baden; but not telling her how the news had come, and containing not a word of allusion to Lady Geraldine or George Fairfax.

"Now that everything is so happily settled, Clary, " wrote my lady, "without any finesse or diplomacy on my part, I don't mind telling you that I have had this idea in my head from the very first day I saw you. I wanted you to win back Arden Court, the place you love so dearly; and as Mr. Granger, to my mind, is a very charming person, nothing seemed more natural than that my wishes should be realised. But I really did not hope that matters would arrange themselves so easily and so speedily. A thousand good wishes, dear, both for yourself and your papa. We hope to spend the autumn at Hale, and I suppose I shall then have the pleasure of seeing you begin your reign as mistress of Arden Court. You must give a great many parties, and make yourself popular in the neighbourhood at once. *Entre nous*, I think our friend Miss Granger is rather fond of power. It will be wise on your part to take your stand in the beginning of things, and then affairs are pretty sure to go pleasantly. Ever your affectionate

"LAURA ARMSTRONG. "

Not a word about George Fairfax. Clarissa wondered where he was; whether he was still angry with her, or had forgotten her altogether. The latter seemed the more likely state of affairs. She wondered about him and then reminded herself that she had no right even to wonder now. His was an image which must be blotted out of her life. She cut all those careless sketches out of her drawing-book. If it had only been as easy to tear the memory of him out of her mind!

The end of May came very quickly, and with it Clarissa's wedding-day. Before that day Miss Granger made a little formal address to her future stepmother—an address worded with studious humility—promising a strict performance of duty on Miss Granger's part in their new relations.

This awful promise was rather alarming to Clarissa, in whose mind Sophia seemed one of those superior persons whom one is bound to respect and admire, yet against whom some evil spark of the old Adam in our degraded natures is ever ready to revolt.

"Pray don't talk of duty, my dear Sophia, " she answered in a shy tremulous way, clinging a little closer to Mr. Granger's arm. It was at Mill Cottage that this conversation took place, a few days before the wedding. "There can scarcely be a question of duty between people of the same age, like you and me. But I hope we shall get to love each other more and more every day. "

"Of course you will, " cried Daniel Granger heartily. "Why should you not love each other? If your tastes don't happen to be exactly the same just now, habitual intercourse will smooth down all that, and you'll find all manner of things in which you *can* sympathise. I've told Sophy that I don't suppose you'll interfere much with her housekeeping, Clarissa. That's rather a strong point with her, and I don't think it's much in your line. "

Miss Granger tightened her thin lips with a little convulsive movement. This speech seemed to imply that Miss Lovel's was a loftier line than hers.

Clarissa remembered Lady Laura's warning, and felt that she might be doing wrong in surrendering the housekeeping. But then, on the other hand, she felt herself quite unable to cope with Miss Granger's account-books.

"I have never kept a large house, " she said. "I should be very sorry to interfere. "

"I was sure of it, " exclaimed Mr. Granger; "and you will have more time to be my companion, Clarissa, if your brain is not muddled with groceries and butcher's-meat. You see, Sophia has such a peculiarly business-like mind. "

"However humble my gifts may be, I have always endeavoured to employ them for your benefit, papa, " Miss Granger replied with a frosty air.

She had come to dine at Mill Cottage for the first time since she had known of her father's engagement. She had come in deference to her father's express desire, and it was a hard thing for her to offer even this small tribute to Clarissa. It was a little family dinner — the Olivers, Mr. Padget, the rector of Arden, who was to assist cheery Matthew Oliver in tying the fatal knot, and Mr. and Miss Granger — a pleasant little party of seven, for whom Mr. Lovel's cook had prepared quite a model dinner. She had acquired a specialty for about half-a-dozen dishes which her master affected, and in the preparation of these could take her stand against the pampered matron who ruled Mr. Granger's kitchen at a stipend of seventy guineas a year, and whose subordinate and assistant had serious thoughts of launching herself forth upon the world as a professed cook, by advertisement in the *Times* — "clear soups, entrées, ices, &c. "

The wedding was to be a very quiet one. Mr. Lovel had expressed a strong desire that it should be so; and Mr. Granger's wishes in no way clashed with those of his father-in-law.

"I am a man of fallen fortunes, " said Mr. Lovel, "and all Yorkshire knows my history. Anything like pomp or publicity would be out of place in the marriage of my daughter. When she is your wife it will be different. Her position will be a very fine one; for she will have some of the oldest blood in the county, supported by abundance of money. The Lycians used to take their names from their mothers. I think, if you have a son. Granger, you ought to call him Lovel. "

"I should be proud to do so, " answered Mr. Granger. "I am not likely to forget that my wife is my superior in social rank. "

"A superiority that counts for very little when unsustained by hard cash, my dear Granger, " returned Marmaduke Lovel lightly. He was supremely content with the state of affairs, and had no wish to humiliate his son-in-law.

So the wedding was performed as simply as if Miss Lovel had been uniting her fortunes with those of some fledgling of the curate species. There were only two bridesmaids — Miss Granger, who performed the office with an unwilling heart; and Miss Pontifex, a flaxen-haired young lady of high family and no particular means, provided for the occasion by Mrs. Oliver, at whose house she and Clarissa had become acquainted. There was a breakfast, elegant enough in its way — for the Holborough confectioner had been put upon his mettle by Mrs. Oliver — served prettily in the cottage parlour. The sun shone brightly upon Mr. Granger's espousals. The village children lined the churchyard walk, and strewed spring flowers upon the path of bride and bridegroom—tender vernal blossoms which scarcely harmonised with Daniel Granger's stalwart presence and fifty years. Clarissa, very pale and still, with a strange fixed look on her face, came out of the little church upon her husband's arm; and it seemed to her in that hour as if all the life before her was like an unknown country, hidden by a great cloud.

* * * * *

CHAPTER XXVI.

COMING HOME.

The leaves were yellowing in the park and woods round Arden Court, and the long avenue began to wear a somewhat dreary look, before Mr. Granger brought his young wife home. It was October again, and the weather bleaker and colder than one had a right to expect in October. Mr. Lovel was at Spa, recruiting his health in the soft breezes that blow across the pine-clad hills, and leading a pleasant elderly-bachelor existence at one of the best hotels in the bright little inland watering-place. The shutters were closed at Mill Cottage, and the pretty rustic dwelling was left in the care of the honest housekeeper and her handmaiden, the rosy-faced parlour-maid, who dusted master's books and hung linen draperies before master's bookcases with a pious awe.

Miss Granger had spent some part of her father's honeymoon in paying visits to those friends who were eager to have her, and who took this opportunity of showing special attention to the fallen heiress. The sense of her lost prestige was always upon her, however, and she was scarcely as grateful as she might have been for the courtesy she received. People seemed never weary of talking about her father's wife, whose sweetness, and beauty, and other interesting qualities, Miss Granger found herself called upon to discuss continually. She did not bow the knee to the popular idol, however, but confessed with a charming candour that there was no great sympathy between her stepmother and herself.

"Her education has been so different from mine, " she said, "that it is scarcely strange if all our tastes are different. But, of course, I shall do my duty towards her, and I hope and pray that she may make my father happy. "

But Miss Granger did not waste all the summer months in visiting. She was more in her element at the Court. The model children in the new Arden poor-schools had rather a hard time of it during Mr. Granger's honeymoon, and were driven through Kings and Chronicles at a more severe pace than usual. The hardest and driest facts in geography and grammar were pelted like summer hail upon their weak young brains, and a sterner demand was made every day upon their juvenile powers of calculation. This Miss Granger called giving them a solid foundation; but as the edifice destined to be erected upon this educational basis was generally of the humblest—a career of carpentering, or blacksmithing, or housemaiding, or plain-cooking, for the most part—it is doubtful whether that accurate knowledge of the objective case or the longitude of the Sandwich Islands which Miss Granger so resolutely insisted upon, was ever of any great service to the grown-up scholar.

In these philanthropic labours she had always an ardent assistant in the person of Mr. Tillott, whose somewhat sandy head and florid complexion used to appear at the open door of the schoolroom very often when Sophia was teaching. He did really admire her, with all sincerity and singleness of heart; describing her, in long confidential letters to his mother, as a woman possessed of every gift calculated to promote a man's advancement in this world and the next. He knew that her father's second marriage must needs make a considerable change in her position. There would be an heir, in all probability, and Sophia would no longer be the great heiress she had been. But she would be richly dowered doubtless, come what might; and she was brought nearer to the aspirations of a curate by this reduction of her fortune.

Miss Granger accepted the young priest's services, and patronised him with a sublime unconsciousness of his aspirations. She had heard it whispered that his father had been a grocer, and that he had an elder brother who still carried on a prosperous colonial trade in the City. For anything like retail trade Miss Granger had a profound contempt. She had all the pride of a parvenu, and all the narrowness of mind common to a woman who lives in a world of her own creation. So while Mr. Tillott flattered himself that he was making no slight impression upon her heart, Miss Granger regarded him as just a little above the head gardener and the certificated schoolmaster.

October came, and the day appointed for the return of the master of Arden Court; rather a gloomy day, and one in a succession of wet and dismal days, with a dull gray sky that narrowed the prospect, and frequent showers of drizzling rain. Miss Granger had received numerous letters from her father during his travels, letters which were affectionate if brief; and longer epistles from Clarissa, describing their route and adventures. They had done Switzerland thoroughly, and had spent the last month in Rome.

The interior of the old house looked all the brighter, perhaps, because of that dull sky and, and those sodden woods without. Fires were blazing merrily in all the rooms; for, whatever Miss Granger's secret feelings might be, the servants were bent on showing allegiance to the new power, and on giving the house a gala aspect in honour of their master's return. The chief gardener, with a temporary indifference to his own interests, had stripped his hothouses for the decoration of the rooms, and great vases of exotics made the atmosphere odorous, and contrasted pleasantly with the wintry fires.

Miss Granger sat in the principal drawing-room, with her embroidery-frame before her, determined not to be flurried or disturbed by the bride's return. She sat at a respectful distance from the blazing logs, with a screen interposed carefully between her complexion and the fire, the very image of stiffness and propriety; not one of her dull-brown hairs ruffled, not a fold of her dark green-silk dress disarranged.

The carriage was to meet the London express at Holborough station at half-past four, and at a little before five Miss Granger heard the sound of wheels in the avenue. She did not even rise from her embroidery-frame to watch the approach of the carriage, but went on steadily stitch by stitch at the ear of a Blenheim spaniel. In a few minutes more she heard the clang of doors thrown open, then the wheels upon the gravel in the quadrangle, and then her father's voice, sonorous as of old. Even then she did not fly to welcome him, though her heart beat a little faster, and the colour deepened in her cheeks.

"I am nothing to him now, " she thought.

She began to lay aside her wools, however, and rose as the drawing-room door opened, to offer the travellers a stately welcome.

Clarissa was looking her loveliest, in violet silk, with a good deal of fur about her, and with an air of style and fashion which was new to her, Miss Granger thought. The two young women kissed each other in a formal way, and then Mr. Granger embraced his daughter with some show of affection.

"How lovely the dear old place looks! " cried Clarissa, as the one triumph and glory of her marriage came home to her mind: she was mistress of Arden Court. "Everything is so warm and bright and cheerful, such an improvement upon foreign houses. What a feast of fires and flowers you have prepared to welcome us, Sophia! "

She wished to say something cordial to her step-daughter, and she did really believe that the festive aspect of the house was Miss Granger's work.

"I have not interfered with the servants' arrangements, " that young lady replied primly; "I hope you don't find so many exotics oppressive in these hot rooms? *I* do. "

"O dear, no; they are so lovely, " answered Clarissa, bending over a pyramid of stephanotis, "one can scarcely have too many of them. Not if the perfume makes your head ache, however; in that case they had better be sent away at once. "

But Miss Granger protested against this with an air of meek endurance, and the flowers were left undisturbed.

"Well, Sophy, what have you been doing with yourself all this time? " Mr. Granger asked in a cheerful voice; "gadding about finely, according to your letters. "

"I spent a week with the Stapletons, and ten days with the Trevors, and I went to Scarborough with the Chesneys, as you expressed a wish that I should accept their invitation, papa, " Miss Granger replied dutifully; "but I really think I am happier at home. "

"I'm very glad to hear it, my dear, and I hope you'll find your home pleasanter than ever now. —So you like the look of the old place, do you, Clary? " he went on, turning to his wife; "and you don't think we've quite spoilt it by our renovation? "

"O no, indeed. There can be no doubt as to your improvements. And yet, do you know, I was so fond of the place, that I am almost sorry to miss its old shabbiness—the faded, curtains, and the queer Indian furniture which my great-uncle Colonel Radnor, brought home from Bombay. I wonder what became of those curious old cabinets? "

"I daresay they are still extant in some lumber-room in the roof, my dear. Your father took very little of the old furniture away with him, and there was nothing sold. We'll explore the garrets some day, and look for your Indian cabinets. —Will you take Clarissa to her rooms, Sophy, and see what she thinks of our arrangements? "

Miss Granger would gladly have delegated this office to a servant; but her father's word was law; so she led the way to a suite of apartments which Daniel Granger had ordered to be prepared for his young wife, and which Clarissa had not yet been allowed to see. They had been kept as a pleasant surprise for her coming home.

Had she been a princess of the blood royal, she could not have had finer rooms, or a more perfect taste in the arrangement of them. Money can do so much, when the man who dispenses it has the art of intrusting the carrying out of his desires to the best workmen.

Clarissa was delighted with everything, and really grateful for the generous affection which had done so much to gratify her.

"It is all a great deal too handsome, " she said.

"I am glad you like the style in which they have carried out papa's ideas, " replied Miss Granger; "for my own part, I like plainer furniture, and more room for one's work; but it is all a matter of taste. "

They were in the boudoir, a perfect gem of a room, with satin-wood furniture and pale green-silk hangings; its only ornaments a set of priceless Wedgwood vases in cream colour and white, and a few water-coloured sketches by Turner, and Creswick, and Stanfield. The dressing-room opened out of this and was furnished in the same style, with a dressing-table that was a marvel of art and splendour, the looking-glass in a frame of oxydised silver, between two monster jewel-cases of ebony and malachite with oxydised silver mouldings. One entire side of this room was occupied by an inlaid maple wardrobe, with seven doors, and Clarissa's monogram on all of them—a receptacle that might have contained the multifarious costumes of a Princess Metternich.

It would have been difficult for Clarissa not to be pleased with such tribute, ungracious not to have expressed her pleasure; so when Daniel Granger came presently to ask how she liked the rooms, she was not slow to give utterance to her admiration.

"You give me so much more than I deserve, Mr. Granger, " she said, after having admired everything; "I feel almost humiliated by your generosity. "

"Clarissa, " exclaimed her husband, putting his two hands upon her shoulders, and looking gravely down at her, "when will you remember that I have a Christian name? When am I to be something more to you than Mr. Granger? "

"You are all that is good to me, much too good, " she faltered. "I will call you Daniel, if you like. It is only a habit. "

"It has such a cold sound, Clary. I know Daniel isn't a pretty name; but the elder sons of Grangers have been Daniels for the last two centuries. We were stanch Puritans, you know, in the days of old Oliver, and scriptural names became a fashion with us. Well, my dear, I'll leave you to dress for dinner. I'm very glad you like the rooms. Here are the keys of your jewel-cases; we must contrive to fill them by and by. You see I have no family diamonds to reset for you. "

"You have given me more than enough jewelry already, " said Clarissa. And indeed Mr. Granger had showered gifts upon her with a lavish hand during his brief courtship.

"Pshaw, child! only a few trinkets bought at random. I mean to fill those cases with something better. I'll go and change my coat. We dine half an hour earlier than usual to-day, Sophia tells me. "

Mr. Granger retired to his dressing-room on the other side of the spacious bed-chamber, perhaps the very plainest apartment in the house, for he was as simple in his habits as the great Duke of Wellington; a room with a monster bath on one side, and a battered oak office-desk on the other—a desk that had done duty for fifty years or so in an office at Leeds—in one corner a well-filled gunstand, in another a rack of formidable-looking boots—boots that only a strong-minded man could wear.

When she was quite alone, Clarissa sat down in one of the windows of her boudoir, and looked out at the park. How well she remembered the prospect! how often she had looked at it on just such darksome autumnal evenings long ago, when she was little more than a child! This very room had been her mother's dressing-room. She remembered it deserted and tenantless, the faded finery of the furniture growing dimmer and duller year by year. She had come here in an exploring mood sometimes when she was quite a child, but she never remembered the room having been put to any use; and as she had grown older it had come to have a haunted air, and she had touched the inanimate things with a sense of awe, wondering what her mother's life had been like in that room—trying to conjure up the living image of a lovely face, which was familiar to her from more than one picture in her father's possession.

She knew more about her mother's life now; knew that there had been a blight upon it, of which a bad unscrupulous man had been the cause. And that man was the father of George Fairfax.

"Papa had reason to fear the son, having suffered so bitterly from the influence of the father, " she said to herself; and then the face that she had first seen in the railway carriage shone before her once more, and her thoughts drifted away from Arden Court.

She remembered that promise which George Fairfax had made her— the promise that he would try and find out something about her brother Austin.

He had talked of hunting up a man who had been a close friend of the absent wanderer's; but it seemed as if he had made no effort to keep his word. After that angry farewell in the orchard, Clarissa could, of course, expect no favour from him; but he might have done something before that. She longed so ardently to know her brother's fate, to find some means of communication with him, now that she was rich, and able to help him in his exile. He was starving, perhaps, in a strange land, while she was surrounded by all this splendour, and had five hundred a year for pocket-money.

Her maid came in to light the candles, and remind her of the dinner-hour, while she was still looking out at the darkening woods. The maid was an honest country-bred young woman, selected for the office by Mrs. Oliver. She had accompanied her mistress on the honeymoon tour, and had been dazed and not a little terrified by the wonders of Swiss landscape and the grandeurs of fallen Rome.

"I've been listening for your bell ever so long, ma'am, " said the girl; "you'll scarcely have time to dress. "

There was time, however, for Mrs. Granger's toilet, which was not an elaborate one; and she was seated by the drawing-room fire talking to her husband when the second dinner-bell rang.

They were not a very lively party that evening. The old adage about three not being company went near to be verified in this particular case. The presence of any one so thoroughly unsympathetic as Sophia Granger was in itself sufficient to freeze any small circle. But although they did not talk much, Clarissa and her husband seemed to be on excellent terms. Sophia, who watched them closely during that initiatory evening, perceived this, and told herself that her father had not yet discovered the mistake which he had made. That he would make such a discovery sooner or later was her profound conviction. It was only a question of time.

Thus it was that Clarissa's new life began. She knew herself beloved by her husband with a quiet unobtrusive affection, the depth and wide measure whereof had come home to her very often since her marriage with a sense of obligation that was almost a burden. She knew this, and, knew that she could give but little in return for so much—the merest, coldest show of duty and obedience in recompense for all the love of this honest heart. If love had been a lesson to be learnt, she would have learned it, for she was not ungrateful, not unmindful of her obligations, or the vow that she had spoken in Arden Church; but as this flower called love must spring spontaneous in the human breast, and is not commonly responsive to the efforts of the most zealous cultivator, Clarissa was fain to confess to herself after five months of wedded life that her heart was still barren, and that her husband was little more to her than he had been at the very first, when for the redemption Of her father's fortunes she had consented to become his wife.

So the time went on, with much gaiety in the way of feasting and company at Arden Court, and a palpable dulness when there were no visitors. Mr. and Mrs. Granger went out a good deal, sometimes accompanied by Sophia, sometimes without her; and Clarissa was elected by the popular voice the most beautiful woman in that part of the country. The people who knew her talked of her so much, that other people who had not met her were eager to see her, and made quite a favour of being introduced to her. If she knew of this herself, it gave her no concern; but it was a matter of no small pride to Daniel Granger that his young wife should be so much admired.

Was he quite happy, having won for himself the woman he loved, seeing her obedient, submissive, always ready to attend his pleasure, to be his companion when he wanted her company, with no inclination of her own which she was not willing to sacrifice at a moment's notice for his gratification? Was he quite happy in the triumph of his hopes? Well, not quite. He knew that his wife did not love him. It might come some day perhaps, that affection for which he still dared to hope, but it had not come yet. He watched her face sometimes as she sat by his hearth on those quiet evenings when they were alone, and he knew that a light should have shone upon it that was not there. He would sigh sometimes as he read his newspaper by that domestic hearth, and his wife would wonder if he were troubled by any business cares—whether he were disturbed by any abnormal commotion among those stocks or consols or other mysterious elements of the financial world in which all rich men seemed more or less concerned. She did not ever venture to question him as to those occasional sighs; but she would bring the draught-board and place it at his elbow, and sit meekly down to be beaten at a game she hated, but for which Mr. Granger had a peculiar affection.

It will be seen, therefore, that Clarissa was at least a dutiful wife, anxious to give her husband every tribute that gratitude and a deep sense of obligation could suggest. Even Sophia Granger, always on the watch for some sign of weariness or shortcoming, could discover no cause for complaint in her stepmother's conduct.

Mr. Lovel came back to Mill Cottage in December, much improved and renovated by the Belgian waters or the gaieties of the bright little pleasure place. The sense of having made an end of his difficulties, and being moored in a safe harbour for the rest of his life, may have done much towards giving him a new lease of existence. Whatever the cause may have been, he was certainly an altered man, and his daughter rejoiced in the change. To her his manner was at once affectionate and deferential, as if there had been lurking in his breast some consciousness that she had sacrificed herself for his welfare. She felt this, and felt that her marriage had given her something more than Arden Court, if it had won for her her father's love. He spent some time at the Court, in deference to her wishes, during those dark winter months; and they fell hack on their old readings, and the evenings seemed gayer and happier for the introduction of this intellectual element, which was not allowed to prevail to such an extant as to overpower the practical Daniel Granger.

* * * * *

CHAPTER XXVII.

IN THE SEASON.

In the spring Mr. Granger took his wife and daughter to London, where they spent a couple of months in Clarges-street, and saw a good deal of society in what may he called the upper range of middle-class life—rich merchants and successful professional men living in fine houses at the West-end, enlivened with a sprinkling from the ranks of the baronetage and lesser nobility. In this circle Mr. Granger occupied rather a lofty standing, as the owner of one of the finest estates in Yorkshire, and of a fortune which the common love of the marvellous exalted into something fabulous. He found himself more popular than ever since his marriage, as the husband of one of the prettiest women who had appeared that season. So, during the two months of their London life, there was an almost unbroken succession of gaieties, and Mr. Granger found himself yearning for the repose of Arden Court sometimes, as he waited in a crowded ball-room while his wife and daughter danced their last quadrille. It pleased him that Clarissa should taste this particular pleasure-cup— that she should have every delight she had a right to expect as his wife; but it pleased him not the less when she frankly confessed to him one day that this brilliant round of parties and party-giving had very few charms for her, and that she would be glad to go back to Arden.

In London Clarissa met Lady Laura Armstrong; for the first time since that September afternoon in which she had promised that no arts of George Fairfax's should move her to listen to him. Lord Calderwood had been dead a year and a half, and my lady was resplendent once more, and giving weekly receptions in Mr. Armstrong's great house in Portland-place—a corner house, with about a quarter of a mile of drawing-rooms, stretching back into one of the lateral streets. For Mr. and Mrs. Granger she gave a special dinner, with an evening party afterwards; and she took up a good deal of Clarissa's time by friendly morning calls, and affectionate insistance upon Mrs. Granger's company in her afternoon drives, and at her daily kettle-drums—drives and kettle-drums from which Miss Granger felt herself more or less excluded.

It was during one of these airings, when they had left the crowd and splendour of the Park, and were driving to Roehampton, that

Clarissa heard the name of George Fairfax once more. Until this afternoon, by some strange accident as it seemed, Lady Laura had never mentioned her sister's lover.

"I suppose you heard that it was all broken off? " she said, rather abruptly, and apropos to nothing particular.

"Broken off, Lady Laura? "

"I mean Geraldine's engagement. People are so fond of talking about those things; you must have heard, surely, Clary. "

"No, indeed, I have heard nothing.

"That's very curious. It has been broken off ever so long—soon after poor papa's death, in fact. But you know what Geraldine is—so reserved—almost impenetrable, as one may say. I knew nothing of what had happened myself till one day—months after the breach had occurred, it seems—when I made some allusion to Geraldine's marriage, she stopped me, in her cold, proud way, saying, 'It's just as well I should tell you that that affair is all off, Laura. Mr. Fairfax and I have wished each other good-bye for ever. ' That's what I call a crushing blow for a sister, Clarissa. You know how I had set my heart upon that marriage. "

"I am very sorry, " faltered Clarissa. "They had quarrelled, I suppose. "

"Quarrelled! O, dear no; she had not seen him since she left Hale with Frederick and me, and they parted with every appearance of affection. No; there had been some letters between them, that was all. I have never been able to discover the actual cause of their parting. Geraldine refused to answer any questions, in a most arbitrary manner. It is a hard thing, Clarissa; for I know that she loved him. "

"And where is Lady Geraldine now? "

"At Hale, with my children. She has no regular home of her own now, you see, poor girl, and she did not care about another season in London—she has had enough of that kind of thing—so she begged me to let her stay at the Castle, and superintend the governesses, and amuse herself in her own way. Life is full of trouble, Clary! " and here the mistress of Hale Castle, and of some seventy thousand per annum, gave a despondent sigh.

"Have you seen Mr. Fairfax since you came from Germany? " asked Clarissa.

"Yes, I have met him once—some months ago. You may be sure that I was tolerably cool to him. He has been very little in society lately, and has been leading rather a wild life in Paris, I hear. A prudent marriage would have been his redemption; but I daresay it will end in his throwing himself away upon some worthless person. "

It was a relief to Clarissa to hear that George Fairfax was in Paris, though that was very near. But in her ignorance of his whereabouts she had fancied him still nearer, and in all her London festivities had been tormented by a perpetual dread of meeting him. Many times even she had imagined that she saw his face across the crowd, and had been relieved to find it was only a face that bore some faint resemblance to his.

He had kept his word, then, so far as the breaking of his engagement to Geraldine Challoner. He had been more in earnest than Clarissa had believed. She thought that she was sorry for this; but it is doubtful whether the regretful feeling in her heart was really sorrow for Lady Geraldine. She thought of George Fairfax a good deal after this conversation with Lady Laura—alas, when had she ceased to think of him! —and all the splendours and pleasures of her married life seemed to her more than ever worthless. What a hopeless entanglement, what a dismal mistake, her existence was! Had she sold herself for these things—for Arden Court and a town house, and unlimited millinery? No; again and again she told herself she had married Daniel Granger for her father's sake, and perhaps a little from a desire to keep faith with Lady Laura.

This marriage had seemed to her the only perfect fulfilment of her promise that nothing should induce her to marry George Fairfax. But the sacrifice had been useless, since he had broken his engagement to Geraldine Challoner.

Sophia Granger's lynx eyes perceived a change in her step mother about this time. Clarissa had never appeared especially enraptured by the gaieties of fashionable London; but then had come upon her of late a languor and weariness of spirit which she tried in vain to disguise by an assumed air of enjoyment. That simulated gaiety deluded her husband, but it could not deceive Miss Granger.

"She's getting tired of her life already, even here where we have a perpetual round of amusements, " Sophia said to herself. "What will she be when we go back to Yorkshire? "

The time was close at hand for the return to Arden, when the thing which Clarissa had feared came to pass, and the hazard of London life brought her face to face with George Fairfax.

* * * * *

CHAPTER XXVIII.

MR. WOOSTER.

The season was at its height, and the Grangers found every available hour of their existence engaged in visiting and receiving visitors. There were so many people whom Lady Laura insisted upon introducing to her dear Clarissa—there was so much in the way of party-giving that Lady Laura wanted her sweet Mrs. Granger to do. Now it was a morning concert of my lady's planning, at which weird and wonderful-looking denizens of the Norseland—Poles, Hungarians, Danes, and Swedes—with unkempt hair and fierce flashing eyes, performed upon every variety of native instrument, or sang wild national songs in some strange language—concerts to which Lady Laura brought herds of more or less fashionable people, all of whom were languishing to know "that sweet Mrs. Granger. " My lady had taken pains to advertise her share in the manufacturer's marriage. Every one belonging to her set knew that the match was her contriving, and that Clarissa had to thank the mistress of Hale Castle for her millionaire husband. She was really proud of her protégée's success, and was never tired of praising her and "that admirable Granger. "

That admirable Granger endured the accession of party-giving with a very good grace. It pleased him to see his wife admired; it pleased him still more to see her happy; and he was single-minded enough to believe her increased volatility a symptom of increased happiness. Whatever undefined regrets and dim forebodings there might be lurking in his own mind, he had no doubt of his wife's integrity—no fear of hidden perils in this ordeal of fashionable life.

She would come to love him in time, he said to himself, trusting as blindly in the power of time to work this wonder for him as Clarissa herself had trusted when she set herself to win her father's affection. He believed this not so much because the thing was probable or feasible, as because he desired it with an intensity of feeling that blinded him to the force of hard facts. He—the man who had never made a false reckoning in the mathematics of business-life—whose whole career was unmarred by a mistake—whose greatest successes had been the result of unrivalled coolness of brain and unerring foresight—he, the hard-headed, far-seeing man of the world—was simple as a child in this matter, which involved the greater hazard of his heart.

But while Clarissa's husband trusted her with such boundless confidence, Clarissa's stepdaughter watched her with the vigilant eyes of prejudice, not to say hatred. That a young lady so well brought up as Miss Granger—so thoroughly grounded in Kings and Chronicles—should entertain the vulgar passion of hate, seemed quite out of the question; but so far as a ladylike aversion may go, Miss Granger certainly went in relation to her step-mother. In this she was sustained by that model damsel Hannah Warman, who, not having made much progress in Mrs. Granger's liking, had discovered that she could not "take to" that lady, and was always ready to dilate upon her shortcomings, whenever her mistress permitted. Sophia was capricious in this, sometimes listening eagerly, at other times suppressing Miss Warman with a high hand.

So Clarissa had, unawares, an enemy within her gates, and could turn neither to the right nor to the left without her motives for so turning becoming the subject of a close and profound scrutiny. It is hard to say what shape Miss Granger's doubts assumed. If put into the witness-box and subjected to the cross-examination of a popular queen's-counsel, she would have found it very difficult to give a substance or a form to her suspicions. She could only have argued in a general way, that Mrs. Granger was frivolous, and that any kind of wrong-doing might be expected from so light-minded a person.

It was the beginning of June, and West-end London was glorious with the brief brilliancy of the early summer. All the Mayfair balconies were bright with, flowers, and the Mayfair knockers resounded perpetually under the hand of the archetypal Jeames. The weather was unusually warm; the most perfect weather for garden-parties, every one declared, and there were several of these *al fresco* assemblies inscribed in Mrs. Granger's visiting-book: one at Wimbledon; another as far afield as Henley-on-Thames, at a villa whose grounds sloped down to the river.

This Henley party was an affair in which Lady Laura Armstrong was particularly interested. It was given by a bachelor friend of her husband's, a fabulously rich stockbroker; and it was Lady Laura who had brought the proprietor of the villa to Clarges-street, and who had been instrumental in the getting-up of the fête.

"You must really give us some kind of a party at your Henley place this year, Mr. Wooster, " she said. "There is the regatta now; I have positively not seen the Henley regatta for three years. The Putney business is all very well—supremely delightful, in short, while it lasts—but such a mere lightning flash of excitement. I like a long day's racing, such as one gets at Henley. "

"Lady Laura ought to be aware that my house is at her disposal all the year round, and that she has only to signify her pleasure to her most devoted slave. "

"O, that's all very well. " replied my lady. "Of course, I know that if Frederick and I were to come down, you would give us luncheon or dinner, and let us roam about the gardens as long as we liked. But that's not what I want. I want you to give a party on one of the race days, and invite all the nice people in London. "

"Are there any nasty people on this side of Temple-bar, Lady Laura, before the closing of Parliament? I thought, in the season everybody was nice. "

"You know what I mean, sir. I want the really pleasant people. Half-a-dozen painters or so, and some of the nicest literary men—not the men who write the best books, but the men who talk cleverly; and, of course, a heap of musical people—they are always nice, except to one another. You must have marquees on the lawn for the luncheon—your house is too small for anything more than tea and coffee; and for once let there be no such thing as croquet—that alone will give your party an air of originality. I suppose you had better put yourself entirely into Gunter's hands for the commissariat, and be sure you tell him you want novelty—no hackneyed ideas; sparkle and originality in everything, from the eggs to the apples. I should ask you to give us a dance in the evening, with coloured lamps, if that were practicable, but there is the coming back to town; and if we carried the business on to a breakfast next morning, some of the people might begin to be tired, and the women would look faded and limp. So I think we had better confine ourselves to a mere garden-party and luncheon, without any dancing, " Lady Laura concluded with a faint sigh.

"Will you send out the invitations, Lady Laura? "

"O, no; I leave all that to you. You really know everybody—or everybody we need care about. "

In this manner Mr. Wooster's party had been arranged, and to this party the Grangers were bidden. Even the serious Sophia was going; indeed, it is to be observed that this young lady joined in all mundane gaieties, under protest as it were.

"I go out, my dear, but I never enjoy myself, " she would say to a serious friend, as if that were a kind of merit. "Papa wishes me to go, and I have no desire to withdraw myself in any way from Mrs. Granger's amusements, however little sympathy there may be between us. I endeavour to do *my* duty, whatever the result may be. "

Mr. Wooster did know a great many people. His abnormal wealth, and a certain amount of cleverness, had been his sole passports to society. Among Burke's *Landed Gentry* there was no trace of the Wooster family, nor had Mr. Wooster ever been heard to allude to a grandfather. He had begun stockjobbing in the smallest way, but had at a very early stage of his career developed a remarkable genius for this kind of traffic. Those of his own set who had watched his steady ascent declared him to be a very remarkable man; and the denizens of the West-end world, who knew nothing of stockjobbing or stockbroking, were quite ready to receive him when he came to them laden with the gold of Ophir, and with a reputation, of being something distinguished upon 'Change.

Time had begun to thin Mr. Wooster's flowing locks before he landed himself safely upon the shores of fashionable life, and Mr. Wooster's carefully-trained moustache and whiskers had a purplish tinge that looked more like art than nature. He was short and stout, with a florid complexion, sharp black eyes, and a large aquiline nose, and considered himself eminently handsome. He dressed with elaborate splendour—"dressed for two, " as some of his less gorgeous friends were wont to say—and was reputed to spend a small fortune annually in exotics for his buttonhole, and in dress boots.

His chief merits in the estimation of the polite world lay in the possession of a perfectly-appointed town house, the villa at Henley, another villa at Cowes, and a couple of magnificent yachts. He was a perpetual giver of dinners, and spent his existence between the Stock

Exchange and the dinner-table, devoting whatever mental force remained to him after his daily traffic to the study of menus, and the grave consideration of wine-lists.

To dine with Wooster was one of the right things to do once or twice in the course of a season; and Wooster's steam yacht was a pleasant place of rest and haven of safety for any juvenile member of the peerage who had been plunging heavily, and went in fear of the Bankruptcy-court.

So, on a brilliant June morning, the Grangers left the Great Western station by special train, and sped through the summer landscape to Henley. This garden-party at Mr. Wooster's villa was almost their last engagement. They were to return to Arden in two days; and Clarissa was very glad that it was so. That weariness of spirit which had seemed to her so strange in some of the young ladies at Hale Castle had come upon herself. She longed for Arden Court and perfect rest; and then she remembered, with something like a shudder, that there were people invited for the autumn, and that Lady Laura Armstrong had promised to spend a week with her dearest Clarissa.

"I want to put you into the way of managing that great house, Clary, " said my lady, brimming over with good-nature and officiousness. "As to leaving the housekeeping in Miss Granger's hands, that's not to be dreamt of. It might do very well for the first six months—just to let her down gently, as it were—but from henceforth you must hold the reins yourself, Clary, and I'll teach you how to drive. "

"But, dear Lady Laura, I don't want the trouble and responsibility of housekeeping. I would much rather leave all that in Sophy's hands, " protested Clarissa. "You have no idea how clever she is. And I have my own rooms, and my painting. "

"Yes, " exclaimed Lady Laura, "and you will mope yourself to death in your own rooms, with your painting, whenever you have no company in the house. You are not going to become a cipher, surely, Clarissa! What with Miss Granger's schools, and Miss Granger's clothing-club, and Miss Granger's premiums and prizes for this, that, and the other, you stand a fair chance of sinking into the veriest nobody, or you would, if it were not for your pretty face. And then you really must have employment for your mind, Clary. Look at me; see the work I get through. "

"But you are a wonder, dear Lady Laura, and I have neither your energy nor your industry."

Laura Armstrong would not admit this, and held to the idea of putting Clarissa in the right away.

"Wait till I come to you in the autumn, " she said. And in that depression of spirit which had grown upon her of late, Mrs. Granger found it a hard thing to say that she should be rejoiced when that time came.

She wanted to get back to Arden Court, and was proud to think of herself as the mistress of the place she loved so dearly; but it seemed to her that an existence weighed down at once by the wisdom of Sophia Granger and the exuberant gaiety of Lady Laura would be barely endurable. She sighed for Arden Court as she remembered it in her childhood—the dreamy quiet of the dull old house, brightened only by her brother's presence; the perfect freedom of her own life, so different from the life whose every hour was subject to the claims of others.

She had changed very much since that visit to Hale Castle. Then all the pleasures of life were new to her—to-day they seemed all alike flat, stale, and unprofitable. She had been surfeited with splendours and pleasures since her marriage. The wealth which Daniel Granger so freely lavished upon her had rendered these things common all at once. She looked back and wondered whether she had really ever longed for a new dress, and been gladdened by the possession of a five-pound note.

* * * * *

CHAPTER XXIX.

"IF I SHOULD MEET THEE—"

Mr. Wooster's villa was almost perfection in its way; but there was something of that ostentatious simplicity whereby the parvenu endeavours sometimes to escape from the vulgar glitter of his wealth. The chairs and tables were of unpolished oak, and of a rustic fashion. There were no pictures, but the walls of the dining-room were covered with majolica panels of a pale gray ground, whereon sported groups of shepherds and shepherdesses after Boucher, painted on the earthenware with the airiest brush in delicate rose-colour; the drawing-room and breakfast-room were lined with fluted chintz, in which the same delicate grays and rose-colours were the prevailing hues. The floors were of inlaid woods, covered only by a small Persian carpet here and there. There was no buhl or marquetery, not a scrap of gilding or a yard of silk or satin, in the house; but there was an all-pervading coolness, and in every room the perfume of freshly-gathered flowers.

Mr. Wooster told his fashionable acquaintance that in winter the villa was a howling wilderness by reason of damp and rats; but there were those of his Bohemian friends who could have told of jovial parties assembled there in November, and saturnalias celebrated there in January; for Mr. Wooster was a bachelor of very liberal opinions, and had two sets of visitors.

To-day the villa was looking its best and brightest. The hothouses had been almost emptied of their choicest treasures in order to fill jardinières and vases for all the rooms. Mr. Wooster had obeyed Lady Laura, and there was nothing but tea, coffee, and ices to be had in the house; nor were the tea and coffee dispensed in the usual business-like manner, which reduces private hospitality to the level of a counter at a railway station. Instead of this, there were about fifty little tables dotted about the rooms, each provided with a gem of a teapot and egg-shell cups and saucers for three or four, so that Mr. Wooster's feminine visitors might themselves have the delight of dispensing that most feminine of all beverages. This contrivance gave scope for flirtation, and was loudly praised by Mr. Wooster's guests.

The gardens of the villa were large—indeed, the stockbroker had pulled down a fine old family mansion to get a site for his dainty little dwelling. There was a good stretch of river-frontage, from which the crowd could watch the boats flash by; now the striped shirts shooting far ahead to the cry of "Bravo, Brazenose! " anon the glitter of a line of light-blue caps, as the Etonian crew answered to the call of their coxswain, and made a gallant attempt to catch their powerful opponents; while Radley, overmatched and outweighted, though by no means a bad crew, plodded hopelessly but pluckily in the rear. Here Clarissa strolled for some time, leaning on her husband's arm, and taking a very faint interest in the boats. It was a pretty sight, of course; but she had seen so many pretty sights lately, and the brightness of them had lost all power to charm her. She looked on, like a person in a picture-gallery, whose eyes and brain are dazed by looking at too many pictures. Mr. Granger noticed her listlessness, and was quick to take alarm. She was paler than usual, he thought.

"I'm afraid you've been overdoing it with so many parties, Clary, " he said; "you are looking quite tired to-day. "

"I am rather tired. I shall be glad to go back to Arden. "

"And I too, my dear. The fact is, there's nothing in the world I care less for than this sort of thing: but I wanted you to have all the enjoyment to be got out of a London season. It is only right that you should have any pleasure I can give you. "

"You are too good to me, " Clarissa answered with a faint sigh.

Her husband did not notice the sigh; but he did remark the phrase, which was one she had used very often—one that wounded him a little whenever he heard it.

"It is not a question of goodness, my dear, " he said. "I love you, and I want to make you happy. "

Later in the afternoon, when the racing was at its height, and almost all Mr. Wooster's visitors had crowded to the terrace by the river, Clarissa strolled into one of the shrubbery walks, quite alone. It was after luncheon; and the rattle of plates and glasses, and the confusion of tongues that had obtained during the banquet, had increased the nervous headache with which she had begun the day. This grove of shining laurel and arbutus was remote from the river, and as solitary just now as if Mr. Wooster's hundred or so of guests had been miles away. There were rustic benches here and there: and Clarissa seated herself upon one of them, which was agreeably placed in a recess amongst the greenery. She was more than usually depressed to-day, and no longer able to maintain that artificial vivacity by which she had contrived to conceal her depression. Her sin had found her out. The loveless union, entered upon so lightly, was beginning to weigh her down, as if the impalpable tie that bound her to her husband had been the iron chain that links a galley-slave to his companion.

"I have been very wicked, " she said to herself; "and he is so good to me! If I could only teach myself to love him. "

She knew now that the weakness which had made her so plastic a creature in her father's hands had been an injustice to her husband; that it was not herself only she had been bound to consider in this matter. It was one thing to fling away her own chances of happiness; but it was another thing to jeopardise the peace of the man she married.

She was meditating on these things with a hopeless sense of confusion—a sense that her married life was like some dreadful labyrinth, into which she had strayed unawares, and from which there was no hope of escape—when she was startled by an approaching footstep, and, looking up suddenly, saw George Fairfax coming slowly towards her, just as she had seen him in Marley Wood that summer day. How far away from her that day seemed now!

They had not met since that night in the orchard, nearly two years ago. She felt her face changing from pale to burning red, and then growing pale again. But by a great effort she was able to answer him in a steady voice presently when he spoke to her.

"What a happiness to see you again, my dear Mrs. Granger! " he said in his lightest tone, dropping quietly down into the seat by her side. "I was told you were to be here to-day, or I should not have come; I am so heartily sick of all this kind of thing. But I really wanted to see you. "

"You were not at the luncheon, were you? " asked Clarissa, feeling that she must say something, and not knowing what to say.

"No; I have only been here half-an-hour or so. I hunted for you amongst that gaping crowd by the river, and then began a circuit of the grounds. I have been lucky enough to find you without going very far. I have some news for you, Mrs. Granger. "

"News for me? "

"Yes; about your brother—about Mr. Austin Lovel. "

That name banished every other thought. She turned to the speaker eagerly.

"News of him—of my dear Austin? O, thank you a thousand times, Mr. Fairfax! Have you heard where he is, and what he is doing? Pray, pray tell me quickly! " she said, tremulous with excitement.

"I have done more than that: I have seen him. "

"In England—in London? " cried Clarissa, making a little movement as if she would have gone that moment to find him.

"No, not in England. Pray take things quietly, my dear Mrs. Granger. I have a good deal to tell you, if you will only listen calmly. "

"Tell me first that my brother is well—and happy, and then I will listen patiently to everything. "

"I think I may venture to say that he is tolerably well; but his happiness is a fact I cannot vouch for. If he does find himself in a condition so unusual to mankind, he is a very lucky fellow. I never met a man yet who owned to being happy; and my own experience of life has afforded me only some few brief hours of perfect happiness. "

He looked at her with a smile that said as plainly as the plainest words, "And those were when I was with you, Clarissa. "

She noticed neither the look nor the words that went before it. She was thinking of her brother, and of him only.

"But you have seen him, " she said. "If he is not in England, he must be very near—in Paris perhaps. I heard you were in Paris. "

"Yes; it was in Paris that I saw him. "

"So near! O, thank God, I shall see my brother again! Tell me everything about him, Mr. Fairfax—everything. "

"I will. It is best you should have a plain unvarnished account. You remember the promise I made you at Hale? Well, I tried my utmost to keep that promise. I hunted up the man I spoke of—a man who had been an associate of your brother's; but unluckily, there had been no correspondence between them after Mr. Lovel went abroad; in short, he could tell me nothing—not even where your brother went. He had only a vague idea that it was somewhere in Australia. So, you see, I was quite at a standstill here. I made several attempts in other directions, but all with the same result; and at last I gave up all hope of ever being of any use to you in this business. "

"You were very kind to take so much trouble. "

"I felt quite ashamed of my failure; I feel almost as much ashamed of my success; for it was perfectly accidental. I was looking at some water-coloured sketches in a friend's rooms in the Rue du Faubourg St. Honoré—sketches of military life, caricatures full of dash and humour, in a style that was quite out of the common way, and which yet seemed in some manner familiar to me. My friend saw that I admired the things. 'They are my latest acquisitions in the way of art, ' he said; they are done by a poor fellow who lives in a shabby third-floor near the Luxembourg—an Englishman called Austin. If you admire them so much, you might as well order a set of them. It would be almost an act of charity. ' The name struck me at once—your brother's Christian name; and then I remembered that I had been shown some caricature portraits which he had done of his brother-officers—things exactly in the style of the sketches I had been looking at. I asked for this Mr. Austin's address, and drove off at once to find him, with a few lines of introduction from my friend. 'The man is proud, ' he said, 'though he carries his poverty lightly enough. '"

"Poor Austin! " sighed Clarissa.

"I need not weary you with minute details. I found this Mr. Austin, and at once recognized your brother; though he is much altered—very much altered. He did not know me until afterwards, when I told him my name, and recalled our acquaintance. There was every sign of poverty: he looked worn and haggard; his clothes were shabby; his painting-room was the common sitting-room; his wife was seated by the open window patching a child's frock; his two children were playing about the room. "

"He is married, then? I did net even know that. "

"Yes, he is married; and I could see at a glance that an unequal marriage has been one among the causes of his ruin. The woman is well enough—pretty, with a kind of vulgar prettiness, and evidently fond of him. But such a marriage is moral death to any man. I contrived to get a little talk with him alone—told him of my acquaintance with you and of the promise that I had made to you. His manner had been all gaiety and lightness until then; but at the mention of your name he fairly broke down. 'Tell her that I have never ceased to love her, ' he said; 'tell her there are times when I dare not think of her. '"

"He has not forgotten me, then. But pray go on; tell me everything. "

"There is not much more to tell. He gave me a brief sketch of his adventures since he sold out. Fortune had gone against him. He went to Melbourne, soon after his marriage, which he confessed was the chief cause of his quarrel with his father; but in Melbourne, as in every other Australian city to which he pushed his way, he found art at a discount. It was the old story: the employers of labour wanted skilled mechanics or stalwart navigators; there was no field for a gentleman or a genius. Your brother and his wife just escaped starvation in the new world, and just contrived to pay their way back to the old world. There were reasons why he should not show himself in England, so he shipped himself and his family in a French vessel bound for Havre, and came straight on to Paris, where he told me he found it tolerably easy to get employment for his pencil. 'I give a few lessons, ' he said, 'and work for a dealer; and by that means we just contrive to live. We dine every day, and I have a decent coat, though you don't happen to find me in it. I can only afford to wear it when I go to my pupils. It is from-hand-to-mouth work; and if any illness should strike me down, the wife and little ones must starve. '"

"Poor fellow! poor fellow! Did you tell him that I was rich, that I could help him? "

"Yes, " answered Mr. Fairfax, with an unmistakable bitterness in his tone; "I told him that you had married the rich Mr. Granger. "

"How can I best assist him? " asked Clarissa eagerly. "Every penny I have in the world is at his disposal. I can give him three or four hundred a year. I have five hundred quite in my own control, and need not spend more than one. I have been rather extravagant since my marriage, and have not much money by me just now, but I shall economise from henceforward; and I do not mind asking Mr. Granger to help my brother. "

"If you will condescend to take my advice, you will do nothing of that kind. Even my small knowledge of your brother's character is sufficient to make me very certain that an appeal to Mr. Granger is just the very last thing to be attempted in this case. "

"But why so? my husband is one of the most generous men in the world, I think. "

"To you, perhaps, that is very natural. To a man of Mr. Granger's wealth a few thousands more or less are not worth consideration; but where there is a principle or a prejudice at stake, that kind of man is apt to tighten his purse-strings with a merciless hand. You would not like to run the risk of a refusal? "

"I do not think there is any fear of that. "

"Possibly not; but there is your brother to be considered in this matter. Do you think it would be pleasant for him to know that his necessities were exposed to such a—to a brother-in-law whom he had never seen? "

"I do not know, " said Clarissa thoughtfully; "I fancied that he would be glad of any helping hand that would extricate him from his difficulties. I should be so glad to see him restored to his proper position in the world. "

"My dear Mrs. Granger, it is better not to think of that. There is a kind of morass from which no man can be extricated. I believe your brother has sunk into that lower world of Bohemianism from which a man rarely cares to emerge. The denizens of that nethermost circle lose their liking for the upper air, can scarcely breathe it, in fact. No, upon my word, I would not try to rehabilitate him; least of all through the generosity of Mr. Granger. "

"If I could only see him, " said Clarissa despondingly.

"I doubt whether he would come to England, even for the happiness of seeing you. If you were in Paris, now, I daresay it might be managed. We could bring about a meeting. But I feel quite sure that your brother would not care to make himself known to Mr. Granger, or to meet your father. There is a deadly feud between those two; and I should think it likely Mr. Lovel has prejudiced your husband against his son. "

Clarissa was fain to admit that it was so. More than once she had ventured to speak of her brother to Daniel Granger, and on each occasion had quickly perceived that her husband had some fixed opinion about Austin, and was inclined to regard her love for him as an amiable weakness that should be as far as possible discouraged.

"Your father has told me the story of his disagreement with his son, my dear Clarissa, " Daniel Granger had said in his gravest tone, "and after what I have heard, I can but think it would be infinitely wise in you to forget that you had ever had a brother. "

This was hard; and Clarissa felt her husband's want of sympathy in this matter as keenly as she could have felt any overt act of unkindness.

"Will you give me Austin's address" she asked, after a thoughtful pause. "I can write to him, at least, and send him some money, without consulting any one. I have about thirty pounds left of my last quarter's money, and even that may be of use to him. "

"Most decidedly. The poor fellow told me he had been glad to get ten napoleons for half-a-dozen sketches: more than a fortnight's hard work. Would it not be better, by the way, for you to send your letter to me, and allow me to forward it to your brother? and if you would like to send him fifty pounds, or a hundred, I shall be only too proud to be your banker. "

Clarissa blushed crimson, remembering that scene in the orchard, and her baffled lover's menaces. Had he forgiven her altogether, and was this kind interest in her affairs an unconscious heaping of coals of fire on her head? Had he forgiven her so easily? Again she argued with herself, as she had so often argued before, that his love had never been more than a truant fancy, a transient folly, the merest vagabondage of an idle brain.

"You are very good, " she said, with a tinge of hauteur, "but I could not think of borrowing money, even to help my brother. If you will kindly tell me the best method of remitting money to Paris. "

Here, Mr. Fairfax said, there was a difficulty; it ought to be remitted through a banker, and Mrs. Granger might find this troublesome to arrange, unless she had an account of her own. Clarissa said she had no account, but met the objection by suggesting bank notes; and Mr. Fairfax was compelled to own that notes upon the Bank of England could be converted into French coin at any Parisian money-changer's.

He gave Clarissa the address, 13, Rue du Chevalier Bayard, near the Luxembourg.

"I will write to him to-night, " she said, and then rose from the rustic bench among the laurels. "I think I must go and look for my husband now. I left him some time ago on account of a headache. I wanted to get away from the noise and confusion on the river-bank. "

"Is it wise to return to the noise and confusion so soon? " asked Mr. Fairfax, who had no idea of bringing this interview to so sudden a close.

He had been waiting for such a meeting for a long time; waiting with a kind of sullen patience, knowing that it must some sooner or later, without any special effort of his; waiting with a strange mixture of feelings and sentiments—disappointed passion, wounded pride, mortified vanity, an angry sense of wrong that had been done to him by Clarissa's marriage, an eager desire to see her again, which was half a lover's yearning, half an enemy's lust of vengeance.

He was not a good man. Such a life as he had led is a life that no man can lead with impunity. To say that he might still be capable of a generous action or unselfish impulse, would be to say much for him, given the story of his manhood. A great preacher of to-day has declared, that he could never believe the man who said he had never been tempted. For George Fairfax life had been crowded with temptations; and he had not made even the feeblest stand against the tempter. He had been an eminently fortunate man in all the trifles which make up the sum of a frivolous existence; and though his successes had been for the most part small social triumphs, they had not been the less agreeable. He had never felt the sting of failure until he stood in the Yorkshire orchard that chill October evening, and pleaded in vain to Clarissa Lovel. She was little more than a schoolgirl, and she rejected him. It was us if Lauzun, after having played fast-and-loose with that eldest daughter of France who was afterwards his wife, had been flouted by some milliner's apprentice, or made light of by an obscure little soubrette in Molière's troop of comedians. He had neither forgotten nor forgiven this slight; and mingled with that blind unreasoning passion, which he had striven in vain to conquer, there was an ever-present sense of anger and wrong.

When Clarissa rose from the bench, he rose too, and laid his hand lightly on her arm with a detaining gesture.

"If you knew how long; I have been wishing for this meeting, you would not be so anxious to bring it to a close, " he said earnestly.

"It was very good of you to wish to tell me about poor Austin, " she said, pretending to misunderstand him, "and I am really grateful. But I must not stay any longer away from my party. "

"Clarissa—a thousand pardons—Mrs. Granger"—there is no describing the expression he gave to the utterance of that last name—a veiled contempt and aversion that just stopped short of actual insolence, because it seemed involuntary—"why are you so hard upon me? You have confessed that you wanted to escape the noise yonder, and yet to avoid me you would go back to that. Am I so utterly obnoxious to you? "

"You are not at all obnoxious to me; but I am really anxious to rejoin my party. My husband will begin to wonder what has become of me. Ah, there is my stepdaughter coming to look for me. "

Yes, there was Miss Granger, slowing advancing towards them. She had been quite in time to see George Fairfax's entreating gestures, his pleading air. She approached them with a countenance that would have been quite as appropriate to a genteel funeral—where any outward demonstration of grief would be in bad taste—as it was to Mr. Wooster's fête, a countenance expressive of a kind of dismal resignation to the burden of existence in a world that way unworthy of her.

"I was just coming back to the river, Sophia, " Mrs. Granger said, not without some faint indications of embarrassment. "I'm afraid Mr. — I'm afraid Daniel must have been looking for me. "

"Papa *has* been looking for you, " Miss Granger replied, with unrelenting stiffness. —"How do you do, Mr. Fairfax? " shaking hands with him in a frigid manner. —"He quite lost the last race. When I saw that he was growing really anxious, I suggested that he should go one way, and I the other, in search of you. That is what brought me here. "

It was as much as to say, Pray understand that I have no personal interest in your movements.

"And yet I have not been so very long away, " Clarissa said, with a deprecating smile.

"You may not have been conscious of the lapse of time You have been long. You said you would go and rest for a quarter of an hour or so; and you have been resting more than an hour. "

"I don't remember saying that; but you are always so correct, Sophia. "

"I make a point of being exact in small things. We had better go round the garden to look for papa. —Good-afternoon, Mr. Fairfax. "

"Good-afternoon, Miss Granger. "

George Fairfax shook hands with Clarissa.

"Good-bye, Mrs. Granger. "

That was all, but the words were accompanied by a look and a pressure of the hand that brought the warm blood into Clarissa's cheeks. She had made for herself that worst enemy a woman can have—a disappointed lover.

While they were shaking hands, Mr. Granger came in sight at the other end of the walk; so it was only natural that Mr. Fairfax, who had been tolerably intimate with him at Hale Castle, should advance to meet him. There were the usual salutations between the two men, exchanged with that stereotyped air of heartiness which seems common to Englishmen.

"I think we had better get home by the next train, Clarissa, " said Mr. Granger; "5.50. I told them to have the brougham ready for us at Paddington from half-past six. "

"I am quite ready to go, " Clarissa said.

"Your headache is better, I hope. "

"Yes; I had almost forgotten it. "

Miss Granger gave an audible sniff, which did not escape George Fairfax.

"What! suspicious already? " he said to himself.

"You may as well come and dine with us, Mr. Fairfax, if you have nothing better to do, " said Mr. Granger, with his lofty air, as much as to say, "I suppose I ought to be civil to this young man. "

"It is quite impossible that I could have anything better to do, " replied Mr. Fairfax.

"In that case, if you will kindly give your arm to my daughter, we'll move off at once. I have wished Mr. Wooster good-afternoon on your part, Clary. I suppose we may as well walk to the station. "

"If you please. "

And in this manner they departed, Miss Granger just touching George Fairfax's coat-sleeve with the tips of her carefully-gloved fingers; Clarissa and her husband walking before them, arm in arm. Mr. Fairfax did his utmost to make himself agreeable during that short walk to the station; so much so that Sophia unbent considerably, and was good enough to inform him of her distaste for these frivolous pleasures, and of her wonder that other people could go on from year to year with an appearance of enjoyment.

"I really don't see what else one can do with one's life, Miss Granger, " her companion answered lightly. "Of course, if a man had the genius of a Beethoven, or a Goethe, or a Michael Angelo—or if he were 'a heaven-born general, ' like Clive, it would be different; he would have some purpose and motive in his existence. But for the ruck of humanity, what can they do but enjoy life, after their lights? "

If all the most noxious opinions of Voltaire, and the rest of the Encyclopedists, had been expressed in one sentence, Miss Granger could not have looked more horrified than she did on hearing this careless remark of Mr. Fairfax's.

She gave a little involuntary shudder, and wished that George Fairfax had been one of the model children, so that she might have set him to learn the first five chapters in the first book of Chronicles, and thus poured the light of what she called Biblical knowledge upon his benighted mind.

"I do not consider the destiny of a Michael Angelo or a Goethe to be envied, " she said solemnly. "Our lives are given us for something better than painting pictures or writing poems. "

"Perhaps; and yet I have read somewhere that St. Luke was a painter, " returned George Fairfax.

"Read somewhere, " was too vague a phrase for Miss Granger's approval.

"I am not one of those who set much value on tradition, " she said with increased severity. "It has been the favourite armour of our adversaries. "

"Our adversaries? "

"Yes, Mr. Fairfax. Of ROME! "

Happily for George Fairfax, they were by this time very near the station. Mr. and Mrs. Granger had walked before them, and Mr. Fairfax had been watching the tall slender figure by the manufacturer's side, not ill-pleased to perceive that those two found very little to say to each other during the walk. In the railway-carriage, presently, he had the seat opposite Clarissa, and was able to talk to her as much as he liked; for Mr. Granger, tired with staring after swift-flashing boats in the open sunshine, leaned his head back against the cushions and calmly slumbered. The situation reminded Mr. Fairfax of his first meeting with Clarissa. But she was altered since then: that charming air of girlish candour, which he had found so fascinating, had now given place to a womanly self-possession that puzzled him not a little. He could make no headway against that calm reserve, which was yet not ungracious. He felt that from first to last in this business he had been a fool. He had shown his cards in his anger, and Clarissa had taken alarm.

He was something less than a deliberate villain: but he loved her; he loved her, and until now fate had always given him the thing that he cared for. Honest Daniel Granger, sleeping the sleep of innocence, seemed to him nothing more than a gigantic stumbling-block in his way. He was utterly reckless of consequences—of harm done to others, above all—just as his father had been before him. Clarissa's rejection had aroused the worst attributes of his nature—an obstinate will, a boundless contempt for any human creature not exactly of his own stamp—for that prosperous trader, Daniel Granger, for instance—and a pride that verged upon the diabolic.

So, during that brief express journey, he sat talking gaily enough to Clarissa about the Parisian opera-houses, the last new plays at the Gymnase and the Odéon, the May races at Chantilly, and so on; yet hatching his grand scheme all the while. It had taken no definite shape as yet, but it filled his mind none the less. "

"Strange that this fellow Granger should have been civil, " he said to himself. "But that kind of man generally contrives to aid and abet his own destruction. "

And then he glanced at this fellow Granger, sleeping peacefully with his head in an angle of the carriage, and made a contemptuous comparison between himself and the millionaire. Mr. Granger had been all very well in the abstract, before he became an obstacle in the path of George Fairfax. But things were altered now, and Mr. Fairfax scrutinized him with the eyes of an enemy.

The dinner in Clarges-street was a very quiet affair. George Fairfax was the only visitor, and the Grangers were "due" at an evening party. He learned with considerable annoyance that they were to leave London at the end of that week, whereby he could have little opportunity of seeing Clarissa. He might have followed her down to

Yorkshire, certainly; but such a course would have been open to remark, nor would it be good taste for him to show himself in the neighbourhood of Hale Castle while Geraldine Challoner was there. He had an opportunity of talking confidentially to Clarissa once after dinner, when Mr. Granger, who had not fairly finished his nap in the railway-carriage, had retired to a dusky corner of the drawing-room and sunk anew into slumber, and when Miss Granger seemed closely occupied in the manufacture of an embroidered pincushion for a fancy fair. Absorbing as the manipulation of chenille and beads might be, however, her work did not prevent her keeping a tolerably sharp watch upon those two figures by the open piano: Clarissa with one hand wandering idly over the keys, playing some random passage, *pianissimo*, now and then; George Fairfax standing by the angle of the piano, bending down to talk to her with an extreme earnestness.

He had his opportunity, and he knew how to improve it. He was talking of her brother. That subject made a link between them that nothing else could have made. She forgot her distrust of George Fairfax when he spoke with friendly interest of Austin.

"Is the wife *very* vulgar? " Clarissa asked, when they had been talking some time.

"Not so especially vulgar. That sort of thing would be naturally toned down by her association with your brother. But she has an unmistakable air of Bohemianism; looks like a third-rate actress, or dancer, in short; or perhaps an artist's model. I should not wonder if that were her position, by the way, when your brother fell in love with her. She is handsome still, though a little faded and worn by her troubles, poor soul and seems fond of him. "

"I am glad of that. How I should like to see him, and the poor wife, and the children—my brother's children! I have never had any children fond of me. "

She thought of Austin in his natural position, as the heir of Arden Court, with his children playing in the old rooms—not as they were now, in the restored splendour of the Middle Ages, but as they had been in her childhood, sombre and faded, with here and there a remnant of former grandeur.

Mr. Granger woke presently, and George Fairfax wished him good-night.

"I hope we shall see you at the Court some day, " Clarissa's husband said, with a kind of stately cordiality. "We cannot offer you the numerous attractions of Hale Castle, but we have good shooting, and we generally have a houseful in September and October. "

"I shall be most happy to make one of the houseful, " Mr. Fairfax said, with a smile—that winning smile which had helped him to make so many friends, and which meant so little. He went away in a thoughtful spirit.

"Is she happy? " he asked himself. "She does not seem unhappy; but then women have such a marvellous power of repression, or dissimulation, one can never be sure of anything about them. At Hale I could have sworn that she loved me. Could a girl of that age be absolutely mercenary, and be caught at once by the prospect of bringing down such big game as Daniel Granger? Has she sold herself for a fine house and a great fortune, and is she satisfied with the price? Surely no. She is not the sort of woman to be made happy by splendid furniture and fine dresses; no, nor by the common round of fashionable pleasures. There was sadness in her face when I came upon her unawares to-day. Yes, I am sure of that. But she has schooled herself to hide her feelings. "

"I wonder you asked Mr. Fairfax to Arden, papa, " said Miss Granger, when the visitor had departed.

"Why, my dear? He is a very pleasant young man; and I know he likes our part of the country. Besides, I suppose he will be a good deal at Hale this year, and that his marriage will come off before long. Lord Calderwood must have been dead year. "

"Lord Calderwood has been dead nearly two years, " replied Miss Granger. "I fancy that engagement between Mr. Fairfax and Lady Geraldine must have been broken off. If it were not so, they would surely have been married before now. And I observed that Mr. Fairfax was not with Lady Laura to-day. I do not know how long he may have been in the gardens, " Miss Granger added, with a suspicious glance at her stepmother, "but he certainly was not with Lady Laura during any part of the time. "

Clarissa blushed when Lady Geraldine's engagement was spoken of. She felt as if she had been in some manner guilty in not having communicated the intelligence Lady Laura had given her. It seemed awkward to have to speak of it now.

"Yes, " she said, with a very poor attempt at carelessness, "the engagement is broken off. Lady Laura told me so some time ago. "

"Indeed! " exclaimed Sophia. "How odd that you should not mention it! "

Daniel Granger looked first at his daughter, and then at his wife. There was something in this talk, a sort of semi-significance, that displeased him. What was George Fairfax, that either his wife or his daughter should be interested in him?

"Clarissa may not have thought the fact worth mentioning, my dear, " he said stiffly. "It is quite unimportant to us. "

He waived the subject away, as he might have done if it had been some small operation in commerce altogether unworthy of his notice; but in his secret heart he kept the memory of his wife's embarrassed manner. He had not forgotten the portfolio of drawings among which the likeness of George Fairfax figured go prominently. It had seemed a small thing at the time—the merest accident; one head was as good to draw as another, and so on—he had told himself; but he knew now that his wife did not love him, and he wanted to know if she had ever loved any one else.

* * * * *

CHAPTER XXX.

THE HEIR OF ARDEN.

Clarissa wrote to her brother—a long letter full of warmth and tenderness, with loving messages for his children, and even for the wife who was so much beneath him. She enclosed three ten-pound notes, all that remained to her of a quarter's pin-money; and O, how bitterly she regretted the frivolous extravagances that had reduced her exchequer to so low a condition! Toward the close of her letter she came to a standstill. She had begged Austin to write to her, to tell her all he could about himself, his hopes, his plans for the future; but when it came to the question of receiving a letter from him she was puzzled. From the first day of her married life she had made a point of showing all her letters to her husband, as a duty, just as she had shown them to her father; who had very rarely taken the trouble to read them, by the way. But Daniel Granger did read his wife's letters, and expected that they should be submitted to him. It would be impossible to reserve from him any correspondence that came to her in the common way. So Clarissa, though not given to secrecy, was on this occasion fain to be secret. After considerable deliberation, she told her brother to write to her under cover to her maid, Jane Target, at Arden Court. The girl seemed a good honest girl, and Mrs. Granger believed that she could trust her.

They went back to Arden a day or two afterwards; and Miss Granger returned with rapture to her duties as commander-in-chief of the model villagers. No martinet ever struck more terror into the breasts of rank and file than did this young lady cause in the simple minds of her prize cottagers, conscience-stricken by the knowledge that stray cobwebs had flourished and dust-bins run to seed during her absence. There was not much room for complaint, however, when she did arrive. The note of warning had been sounded by the servants of the Court, and there had been a general scrubbing and cleansing in the habitations of New Arden—that particular Arden which Mr. Granger had built for himself, and the very bricks whereof ought to have been stamped with his name and titles, as in the case of Nebuchadnezzar, son of Nabopolassar, king of Babylon. For a week before Miss Granger's coming there had been heard the splashing of innumerable pails of water, and the scrubbing of perpetual scrubbing-brushes; windows had been polished to the highest degree of transparency; tin tea-kettles had been sandpapered until they became as silver; there had been quite a run upon the village chandler for mottled soap and hearthstone.

So, after a rigorous inspection, Miss Granger was obliged to express her approval—not an unqualified approval, by any means. Too much praise would have demoralized the Ardenites, and lowered the standard of perfection.

"I like to be able to say that my papa's village is the cleanest village in England, " she said; "not one of the cleanest, but *the* cleanest. Why have you turned the back of that tea-kettle to the wall, Mrs. Binks? I'm afraid it's smoky. Now there never need be a smoky kettle. Your place looks very nice, Mrs. Binks; but from the strong smell of soap, I fancy it must have been cleaned *very lately*. I hope you have not been neglecting things while I've been away. That sort of thing would militate against your obtaining my prize for domestic cleanliness next Christmas. "

Mrs. Binks did not know what "militate" meant, unless it might be something in connection with the church militant, of which she had heard a great deal; but she was not a mild-tempered woman, and she grew very red in the face at this reproof. "

"Well, miss, if to toil and scrub early and late, with a husband and five children to do for, and to keep the place pretty much as you see it now, though I don't say as it ain't a little extry perhaps, in honour of your coming back—if that ain't hard work and cleanliness, and don't deserve a prize of two pound at the year's end, I don't know what do. It's hard-earned money, Miss Granger, when all's said and done. "

Sophia turned the eyes of reproof upon Mrs. Binks.

"I did not think it was the money you cared for, " she said; "I thought it was the honour you valued most. "

She pointed to a card framed and glazed over the mantelpiece—a card upon which, with many nourishes and fat initial letters in red ink, the model schoolmaster had recorded the fact, that Mrs. Binks, at the preceding Christmas distributions, had obtained Miss Granger's annual reward for domestic cleanliness.

"Well, of course, miss, I set store by the card. It's nice to see one's name wrote out like that, and any strangers as chance to come in the summer time, they takes notice; but to a hard-working man's wife two pound is a consideration. I'm sure I beg your parding humbly, miss, if I spoke a bit short just now; but it is trying, when one has worked hard, to have one's work found fault with. "

"I am not aware that I found fault with your work, Mrs. Sinks, " Sophia replied with supreme dignity; "I merely remarked that it appeared to have been done hastily. I don't approve of spasmodic industry. "

And with this last crushing remark, Miss Granger sailed out of the cottage, leaving the luckless Mrs. Binks to repent her presumption at leisure, and to feel that she had hazarded her hopes of Christmas bounties, and enhanced the chances of her detested rival of three doors off, Mrs. Trotter, a sanctimonious widow, with three superhuman children, who never had so much as a spot on their pinafores, and were far in advance of the young Binkses in Kings and Chronicles; indeed the youngest Trotter had been familiar with all the works of Hezekiah before the eldest Binks had grasped the abstract idea of Saul.

For Clarissa the change to Arden Court was a pleasant one. That incessant succession of London gaieties had wearied her beyond measure. Here, for a little time before her visitors began to arrive, she lived her own life, dreaming away a morning over a sketch-book, or reading some newly-published volume in a favourite thicket in the park. There was a good deal of time, of course, that she was obliged to devote to her husband, walking or driving or riding with him, in rather a ceremonial manner, almost as she might have done had she belonged to that charmed circle whose smallest walk or drive is recorded by obsequious chroniclers in every journal in the united kingdom. Then came six brilliant weeks in August and September, when Arden Court was filled with visitors, and Clarissa began to feel how onerous are the duties of a châtelaine. She had not Lady Laura Armstrong's delight in managing a great house. She was sincerely anxious that her guests might be pleased, but somewhat over-burdened by the responsibility of pleasing them. It was only after some experience that she found there was very little to be done, after all. With a skilful combination of elements, the result was sure to be agreeable. Morning after morning the cheerful faces gathered round the breakfast-table; and morning after morning vast supplies of dried salmon, fresh trout, grilled fowl, and raised pie—to say nothing of lighter provender, in the way of omelets, new-laid eggs, hot buttered cakes of various descriptions, huge wedges of honeycomb, and jars of that Scotch marmalade, so dear to the hearts of boating-men—vanished like smoke before a whirlwind. Whatever troubles these nomads may have had were hidden in their hearts for the time being. A wise custom prevailed in Mr. Granger's establishment with regard to the morning letters, which were dealt out to each guest with his or her early cup of tea, and not kept back for public distribution, to the confusion of some luckless recipient, who feels it difficult to maintain an agreeable smirk upon his countenance while he reads, that unless such or such an account is settled immediately, proceedings will be taken without delay.

Lady Laura came, as she had promised, and gave her dearest Clarissa lessons in the art of presiding over a large establishment, and did her utmost to oust Miss Granger from her position of authority in the giving out of stores and the ordering of grocery. This, however, was impossible. Sophia clung to her grocer's book as some unpopular monarch tottering on his insecure throne might cling to his sceptre. If she could not sit in the post of honour at her father's dinner-table, as she had sat so long, it was something to reign supreme in the store-room; if she found herself a secondary person in the drawing-room, and that unpunctilious callers were apt to forget the particular card due to her, she could at least hold on by the keys of those closets in which the superfine china services for Mr. Granger's great dinners were stored away, with chamois leather between all the plates and dishes. She had still the whip-hand of the housekeeper, and could ordain how many French plums and how many muscatel raisins were to be consumed in a given period. She could bring her powers of arithmetic to bear upon wax-candles, and torment the souls of hapless underlings by the precision of her calculations. She had an eye to the preserves; and if awakened suddenly in the dead of the night could have told, to a jar, how many pots of strawberry, and raspberry, and currant, and greengage were ranged on the capacious shelves of that stronghold of her power, the store-room.

Even Lady Laura's diplomacy failed here. The genius of a Talleyrand would not have dislodged Miss Granger.

"I like to feel that I am of *some* use to papa, " she remarked very often, with the air of a household Antigone. "He has new outlets for his money now, and it is more than ever my duty as a daughter to protect him from the wastefulness of servants. With all my care, there are some things in Mrs. Plumptree's management which I do not understand. I'm sure what becomes of all the preserved-ginger and crystallized apricots that I give out, is a mystery that no one could fathom. Who ever eats preserved-ginger? I have taken particular notice, and could never see any one doing it. The things are not eaten; *they disappear.* "

Lady Laura suggested that, with such a fortune as Mr. Granger's, a little waste more or less was hardly worth thinking of.

"I cannot admit that, " Miss Granger replied solemnly. "It is the abstract sinfulness of waste which I think of. An under-butler who begins by wasting preserved-ginger may end by stealing his master's plate. "

The summer went by. Picnics and boating parties, archery meetings and flower-shows, and all the familiar round of country pleasures repeated themselves just as they had done at Hale Castle two years ago; and Clarissa wondered at the difference in her own mind which made these things so different. It was not that all capacity for enjoyment was dead in her. Youth is too bright a thing to be killed so easily. She could still delight in a lovely landscape, in exquisite flowers, in that art which she had loved from her childhood—she could still enjoy good music and pleasant society; but that keen sense of happiness which she had felt at Hale, that ardent appreciation of small pleasures, that eager looking forward to the future—these were gone. She lived in the present. To look back to the past was to recall the image of George Fairfax, who seemed somehow interwoven with her girlhood; to look forward to the future was to set her face towards a land hidden in clouds and darkness. She had positively nothing to hope for.

Mr. Granger took life very calmly. He knew that his wife did not love him; and he was too proud a man to lay himself out to win her love, even if he had known how to set about a task so incongruous with the experience of his life. He was angry with himself for having ever been weak enough to think that this girlish creature—between whom and himself there stretched a gulf of thirty years—could by any possibility be beguiled into loving him. Of course, she had married him for his money. There was not one among his guests who would not have thought him a fool for supposing that it could be otherwise, or for expecting more from her than a graceful fulfilment of the duties of her position.

He had little ground for complaint. She was gentle and obedient, deferential in her manner to him before society, amiable always; he only knew that she did not love him—that was all. But Daniel Granger was a proud man, and this knowledge was a bitter thing to him. There were hours in his life when he sat alone in his own room—that plainly-furnished chamber which was half study, half dressing-room—withdrawing himself from his guests under pretence of having business-letters to write to his people at Bradford and Leeds; sat with his open desk before him, and made no attempt to write; sat brooding over thoughts of his young wife, and regretting the folly of his marriage.

Was it true that she had never cared for any one else? He had her father's word for that; but he know that Marmaduke Lovel was a selfish man, who would be likely enough to say anything that would conduce to his own advantage. Had her heart been really true and pure when he won her for his wife? He remembered those sketches of George Fairfax in the portfolio, and one day when he was waiting for Clarissa in her morning-room he took the trouble to look over her drawings. There were many that he recollected having seen that day at Mill Cottage, but the portraits of Mr. Fairfax were all gone. He looked through the portfolio very carefully, but found none of those careless yet life-like sketches which had attracted the attention of Sophia Granger.

"She has destroyed them, I suppose, " he said to himself; and the notion of her having done so annoyed him a little. He did not care to question her about them. There would have been an absurdity in that, he thought: as if it could matter to him whose face she chose for her unstudied sketches—mere vagabondage of the pencil.

Upon rare occasions Marmaduke Lovel consented to take a languid share in the festivities at Arden. But although he was very well pleased that his daughter should be mistress of the house that he had lost, he did not relish a secondary position in the halls of his forefathers; nor had the gaieties of the place any charm for him. He was glad to slip away quietly at the beginning of September, and to go back to Spa, where the waters agreed with his rheumatism—that convenient rheumatism which was an excuse for anything he might choose to do.

As for his daughter, he washed his hands of all responsibility in connection with her. He felt as if he had provided for her in a most meritorious manner by the diplomacy which had brought about her marriage. Whether she was happy in her new life, was a question which he had never asked himself; but if any one else had propounded such a question, he would have replied unhesitatingly in the affirmative. Of course Clarissa was happy. Had she not secured for herself all the things that women most value? could she not run riot in the pleasures for which women will imperil their souls? He remembered his own wife's extravagance, and he argued with himself, that if she could have had a perennial supply of fine dresses, and a perpetual round of amusement, she would speedily have forgotten Colonel Fairfax. It was the dulness of her life, and the dismal atmosphere of poverty, that had made her false.

So he went back to Spa, secure in the thought that he could make his home at Arden whenever he pleased. Perhaps at some remote period of old age, when his senses were growing dim, he might like to inhabit the familiar rooms, and feel no sting in the thought that he was a guest, and not the master. It would be rather pleasant to be carried to his grave from Arden Court, if anything about a man's burial could be pleasant. He went back to Spa and led his own life, and in a considerable measure forgot that he had ever had a son and a daughter.

With September and October there came guests for the shooting, but George Fairfax was not among them. Mr. Granger had not renewed that careless invitation of his in Clarges-street. After supervising Clarissa's existence for two or three weeks, Lady Laura had returned to Hale, there to reign in all her glory. Mr. and Mrs. Granger dined at the castle twice in the course of the autumn, and Clarissa saw Lady Geraldine for the first time since that fatal wedding-day.

There was very little alteration in the fair placid face. Geraldine Challoner was not a woman to wear the willow in any obvious manner. She was still coldly brilliant, with just a shade more bitterness, perhaps, in those little flashes of irony and cynicism which passed for wit. She talked rather more than of old, Clarissa thought; she was dressed more elaborately than in the days of her engagement to George Fairfax, and had altogether the air of a woman who means to shine in society. To Mrs. Granger she was polite, but as cold as was consistent with civility.

After a fortnight's slaughter of the pheasants, there was a lull in the dissipations of Arden Court. Visitors departed, leaving Mr. Granger's gamekeepers with a plethora of sovereigns and half-sovereigns in their corduroy pockets, and serious thoughts of the Holborough Savings Bank, and Mr. Granger's chief butler with views that soared as high as Consols. All the twitter and cheerful confusion of many voices in the rooms and corridors of the grand old house dwindled and died away, until Mr. Granger was left alone with his wife and daughter. He was not sorry to see his visitors depart, though he was a man who, after his own fashion, was fond of society. But before the winter was over, an event was to happen at Arden which rendered quiet indispensable.

Late in December, while the villagers were eating Mr. Granger's beef, and warming themselves before Mr. Granger's coals, and reaping the fruit of laborious days in the shape of Miss Granger's various premiums for humble virtue—while the park and woodland were wrapped in snow, and the Christmas bells were still ringing in the clear crisp air, God gave Clarissa a son—the first thing she had ever held in her arms which she could and might love with all her heart.

It was like some strange dream to her, this holy mystery of motherhood. She had not looked forward to the child's coming with any supreme pleasure, or supposed that her life would be altered by his advent. But from the moment she held him in her arms, a helpless morsel of humanity, hardly visible to the uninitiated amidst his voluminous draperies, she felt herself on the threshold of a new existence. With him was born her future—it was a most complete realization of those sweet wise words of the poet, —

"a child, more than all other gifts
That earth can offer to declining man,
Brings hope with it, and forward-looking thoughts. "

Mr. Granger was enraptured. For him, too, even more than for his wife, this baby represented the future. Often and often, after some brilliant stroke of business which swelled the figures upon the left side of his bank-book to an abnormal amount, he had felt a dismal sense of the extinction that must befall his glory by-and-by. There was no one but Sophia. She would inherit a fortune thrice as large as any woman need desire, and would in all likelihood marry, and give her wealth to fill the coffers of a stranger, whose name should wipe out the name of Granger—or preserve it in a half-and-half way in some inane compound, such, as Granger-Smith, or Jones-Granger, extended afterwards into Jones-Granger-Jones, or Granger-Smith-Granger.

Perhaps those wintry days that began the new year were the purest, happiest of Daniel Granger's life. He forgot that his wife did not love him. She seemed so much more his wife, seated opposite to him beside that quiet hearth, with her baby in her arms. She made such a lovely picture, bending over the child in her unconscious beauty. To sit and watch the two was an all-sufficient delight for him—sometimes withdrawing his mind from the present, to weave the web of his boy's future.

"I shall send him to Westminster, Clary, " he said—it was a long time, by the way, since he had called his wife Clary, though she herself was hardly aware of the fact. "I shall certainly send him to Westminster. A provincial public school is all very well—my father sent me to one—but it's not *quite* up to the mark. I should like him to be a good classical scholar, which I never was, though I was a decent mathematician. I used to do my Virgil with a crib—a translation, you know—and I never could get on with Greek. I managed to struggle through the New Testament, but stuck in the first book of Thucydides. What dreary work it was! I was glad when it was all over, and my father let me come into his office. But with this fellow it will be different. He will have no occasion to soil his hands with trade. He will be a country gentleman, and may distinguish himself in the House of Commons. Yes, Clary, there may be the material for a great man in him, " Mr. Granger concluded, with an almost triumphant air, as he touched the soft little cheek, and peered curiously into the bright blue eyes. They were something like his own eyes, he thought; Clarissa's were hazel.

The mother drew the soft mass of muslin a little nearer to her heart. She did not care to think of her baby as a man, addressing a noisy constituency in Holborough market-place, nor even, as a Westminster boy, intent upon Virgil and cricket, Euclid and football. She liked to think of him as he was now, and as he would be for the next few years—something soft and warm and loving, that she could hold in her arms; beside whose bed she could watch and pray at night. Her future was bounded by the years of her son's childhood. She thought already, with a vague pang, of the time when he should go out into the world, and she be no longer necessary to him.

The day came when she looked back to that interval of perfect quiet—the dimly-lighted rooms, the low wood fire, and her husband's figure seated by the hearth—with a bitter sense of regret. Daniel Granger was so good to her in those days—so entirely devoted, in a quiet unobtrusive way—and she was so selfishly absorbed by the baby as to be almost unconscious of his goodness at the time. She was inclined to forget that the child belonged to any one but herself; indeed, had the question been brought home to her, she would have hardly liked to admit his father's claim upon him. He was her own—her treasure beyond all price—given to her by heaven for her comfort and consolation.

Not the least among the tranquil pleasures of that period of retirement—which Clarissa spun out until the spring flowers were blooming in the meadows about Arden—was a comparative immunity from the society of Miss Granger. That young lady made a dutiful call upon her stepmother every morning, and offered a chilling forefinger—rather a strong-minded forefinger, with a considerable development of bone—to the infant. On the child not receiving this advance with rapture, Miss Granger was wont to observe that he was not so forward in taking notice as some of her model children; at which the young mother flamed up in defence of her darling, declaring that he did take notice, and that it was a shame to compare him to "nasty village children. "

"The 'nasty village children' have immortal souls, " Sophia replied severely.

"So they may; but they don't take notice sooner than my baby. I would never believe that. He knows me, the precious darling; " and the little soft warm thing in voluminous muslin was kissed and squeezed about to extinction.

Miss Granger was great upon the management of infancy, and was never tired of expounding her ideas to Clarissa. They were of a Spartan character, not calculated to make the period of babyhood a pleasant time to experience or to look back upon. Cold water and nauseous medicines formed a conspicuous part of the system, and where an ordinary nurse would have approached infancy with a sponge, Miss Granger suggested a flesh-brush. The hardest, most impracticable biscuits, the huskiest rusks, constituted Miss Granger's notion of infant food. She would have excluded milk, as bilious, and would have forbidden sugar, as a creator of acidity; and then, when the little victim was about one and a half, she would have seated it before the most dry-as-dust edition of the alphabet, and driven it triumphantly upon the first stage on the high-road to Kings and Chronicles.

Among the model villagers Miss Granger had ample opportunity of offering advice of this kind, and fondly believed that her counsel was acted upon. Obsequious matrons, with an eye to Christmas benefactions, pretended to profit by her wisdom; but it is doubtful whether the model infants were allowed to suffer from a practical exposition of her Spartan theories.

Clarissa had her own ideas about the heir of the Grangers. Not a crumpled rose-leaf—had rose-leaves been flying about just then— must roughen her darling's bed. The softest lawn, the downiest, most delicate woollens, were hardly good enough to wrap her treasure. She had solemn interviews with a regiment of nurses before she could discover a woman who seemed worthy to be guardian of this infant demigod. And Mr. Granger showed himself scarcely less weak. It almost seemed as if this boy was his first child. He had been a busy man when Sophia was born—too entirely occupied by the grave considerations of commerce to enter into the details of the nursery—and the sex of the child had been something of a disappointment to him. He was rich enough even then to desire an heir to his wealth. During the few remaining years of his first wife's life, he had hoped for the coming of a son; but no son had been given to him. It was now, in his sober middle age, that the thing he had longed for was granted to him, and it seemed all the more precious because of the delay. So Daniel Granger was wont to sit and stare at the infant as if it had been something above the common clay of which infancy is made. He would gaze at it for an hour together, in a dumb rapture, fully believing it to be the most perfect object in creation; and about this child there sprung up between his wife and himself a sympathy that had never been before. Only deep in Clarissa's heart there was a vague jealousy. She would have liked her baby to be hers alone. The thought of his father's claim frightened her. In the time to come her child might grow to love his father better than her.

Finding her counsel rejected, Miss Granger would ask in a meek voice if she might be permitted to kiss the baby, and having chilled his young blood by the cool and healthy condition of her complexion, would depart with an air of long-suffering; and this morning visit being over, Clarissa was free of her for the rest of the day. Miss Granger had her "duties." She devoted her mornings to the regulation of the household, her afternoons to the drilling of the model villagers. In the evening she presided at her father's dinner, which seemed rather a chilling repast to Mr. Granger, in the absence of that one beloved face. He would have liked to dine off a boiled fowl in his wife's room, or to have gone dinnerless and shared Clarissa's tea-and-toast, and heard the latest wonders performed by the baby, but he was ashamed to betray so much weakness.

So he dined in state with Sophia, and found it hard work to keep up a little commonplace conversation with her during the solemn meal—his heart being elsewhere all the time.

That phase of gloom and despondency, through which, his mind had passed during the summer that was gone, had given place to brighter thoughts. A new dawn of hope had come for him with the birth of his child.

He told himself again, as he had so often told himself in the past, that his wife would grow to love him—that time would bring him the fruition of his desires. In the meanwhile he was almost entirely happy in the possession of this new blessing. All his life was coloured by the existence of this infant. He had a new zest in the driest details of his position as the master of a great estate. He had bought some two thousand acres of neighbouring land at different times since his purchase of Arden Court; and the estate, swollen by these large additions, was fast becoming one of the finest in the county.

There was not a tree he planted in the beginning of this new year which he did not consider with reference to his boy; and he made extensive plantations on purpose that he might be able to point to them by-and-by and say, "These trees were planted the year my son was born." When he went round his stables, he made a special survey of one particularly commodious loose-box, which would do for his boy's pony. He fancied the little fellow trotting by his side across farms and moorlands, or deep into the woods to see the newly-felled timber, or to plan a fresh clearing.

It was a pleasant day dream.

* * * * *

CHAPTER XXXI.

THE NEAREST WAY TO CARLSRUHE.

A great event befell George Fairfax in the spring of the new year. He received a summons to Lyvedon, and arrived there only in time to attend his uncle's death bed. The old man died, and was buried in the tomb of his forefathers—a spacious vaulted chamber beneath Lyvedon church—and George Fairfax reigned in his stead. Since his brother's death he had known that this was to be, and had accepted the fact as a matter of course. His succession caused him very little elation. He was glad to have unlimited ready-money, but, in the altered aspect of his life, Le did not care much for the estate. With Geraldine Challoner for his wife, the possession of such a place as Lyvedon would have been very agreeable to him. He could have almost resigned himself to the ordinary country gentleman's life: to be a magnate in the county; to attend at petty sessions, and keep himself well posted in parochial questions; to make himself a terror to the soul of poachers, and to feel that his youth was over. But now it was different. He had no wife, nor any prospect of a wife. He had no definite plans for his future. For a long time he had been going altogether the wrong way; leading a roving, desultory kind of existence; living amongst men whose habits and principles were worse than his own.

He sent for his mother, and installed her as mistress of Lyvedon. The place and the position suited her to admiration. He spent a month in dawdling about the neighbourhood, taking stock of his new possessions, now and then suggesting some alteration or improvement, but always too lazy to carry it out; strolling in the park with a couple of dogs and a cigar, or going fly-fishing along the bank of a little winding river; driving in an open carriage with his mother; yawning over a book or a newspaper all the evening, and then sitting up till late into the night, writing letters which might just as easily have been written in the day. His manner made his mother anxious. Once, with a sigh, she ventured to say how much she regretted the breaking-off his engagement to Lady Geraldine.

"You were so admirably adapted for each other, " she said.

"Yes, mother, admirably adapted, no doubt; but you see we did not love each other. " He felt a little pang of remorse as he said this, for it misgave him that Geraldine *had* loved him. "It would have been like those chestnut ponies you drive; they go very well together, and look superb, but they are always snapping at each other's heads. I don't mean to say that Geraldine and I would have quarrelled—one might as well try to quarrel with a rock—but we shouldn't have got on. In short, I have a prejudice in favour of marrying a woman I could love."

"And yet I thought you were so much attached to her."

"I was—in the way of friendship. Her society had become a kind of habit with me. I do really like her, and shall always consider her one of the handsomest and cleverest women I know; but it was a mistake to ask her to marry me, and might have been a fatal one. You will say, of course, that a man ought not to make that kind of mistake. I quite agree with you there; but I made it, and I think it infinitely better to pull up even at an awkward point than to make two lives miserable."

Mrs. Fairfax sighed, and shook her head doubtfully.

"O, George, George, I'm afraid there was some newer fancy—some secret reason for your conduct to poor Geraldine," she said in a reproachful tone.

"My dear mother, I have a dozen fancies in a month, and rarely know my own mind for a week at a stretch; but I do know that I never really loved Geraldine Challoner, and that it is better for me to be free from an ill-advised engagement."

Mrs. Fairfax did not venture to press the question any farther. She had her suspicions, and her suspicions pointed to Clarissa. But Clarissa now being married and fairly out of the way, she had some faint hope that her son would return to his old allegiance, and that she might even yet have Geraldine Challoner for her daughter. In the meantime she was fain to be patient, and to refrain from any irritating persistence upon a subject that was very near to her heart.

So far as her own interests were concerned, it would have been a pleasant thing for Mrs. Fairfax that her son should remain a bachelor. The sovereignty of Lyvedon was a pure and perfect delight to her. The place was the home of her childhood; and there was not a thicket in the park, or a flower-bed in the garden, that was not familiar and dear to her. Every corner of the sombre old rooms—in which the furniture had been unchanged for a century—had its tender associations. All the hopes and dreams of her long-vanished youth came back to her, faint and pale, like faded flowers shut in the leaves of a book. And in the event of her son's marriage, she must of course resign all this—must make a new home for herself outside the walls of Lyvedon; for she was not a woman to accept a secondary place in any household. Considering the question merely from a selfish point of view, she had every reason to be satisfied with the existing state of things; but it was not of herself she thought. She saw her son restless and unsettled, and had a secret conviction that he was unhappy. There had been much in the history of his past life that had troubled her; and for his future her chief hope had been in the security of a judicious marriage. She was a woman of strong religious feeling, and had shed many bitter tears and prayed many prayers on account of this beloved son.

The beloved son in the meanwhile dawdled away life in a very unsatisfactory manner. He found the roads and lanes about Lyvedon remarkable for nothing but their dust. There were wild flowers, of course—possibly nightingales and that sort of thing; but he preferred such imported bouquets, grown on the flowery slopes of the Mediterranean, as he could procure to order at Covent Garden; and the song of nightingales in the dusky after dinner-time made him melancholy. The place was a fine old place and it was undoubtedly a good thing to possess it; but George Fairfax had lived too wild a life to find happiness in the simple pleasures of a Kentish squire. So, after enduring the placid monotony of Lyvedon for a couple of months, he grew insufferably weary all at once, and told his mother that he was going to the Black Forest.

"It's too early to shoot capercailzies, " he said; "but I daresay I shall find something to do. I am nothing but a bore to you here, mother; and you can amuse yourself, while I'm gone, in carrying out any of the improvements we've discussed. "

Mrs. Fairfax assured her son that his presence was always a delight to her, but that, of course, there was nothing in the world she desired so much as his happiness, and that it had been a pain to her to see him otherwise than happy.

"I had hoped that the possession of this place would have given you so much occupation, " she said, "that you would have gone into parliament and made a position for yourself. "

"My dear mother, I never had any affection for politics; and unless a man could be a modern Pitt, I don't see the use of that kind of thing. Every young Englishman turns his face towards the House of Commons, as the sunflower turns to the sun-god; and see what a charming level of mediocrity we enjoy in consequence thereof. "

"Anything that would occupy your mind, George, " remonstrated Mrs. Fairfax.

"The question is, whether I have any mind to be occupied, mother, " replied the young man with a laugh. "I think the average modern intellect, when it knows its own capacity, rarely soars above billiards. That is a science; and what can a man be more than scientific? "

"It is so easy to laugh the subject down in that way, George, " returned the mother with a sigh. "But a man has duties to perform. "

"Surely not a man with an estate like this, mother! I can never understand that talk about the duties of a rich man, except to pay his income-tax properly. A fellow with a wife and children, and no income to speak of, has duties, of course—imprimis, the duty of working for his belongings; but what are the privileges of wealth, if one may not take life as one pleases? "

"Oh, George, George, I used to hope such great things of you! "

"The fond delusion common to maternity, my dearest mother. A brat learns his A B C a shade quicker than other children, or construes *Qui fit Maecenas* with tolerable correctness; and straightway the doting mother thinks her lad is an embryo Canning. You should never have hoped anything of me, except that I would love you dearly all my life. You have made that very easy to me. "

Mr. Fairfax took his portmanteau and departed, leaving his servant to carry the rest of his luggage straight to Paris, and await his master's arrival at one of the hotels in the Rue de Rivoli. The master himself took a somewhat circuitous route, and began his journey to the Black Forest by going down to Holborough.

"I can take a steamer from Hull to Hamburg, " he said to himself, "and push on from there to Carlsruhe. "

He wanted to see Clarissa again. He knew that she was at Arden Court, and that Lady Laura Armstrong was not at Hale Castle. He wanted to see her; his ulterior views were of the vaguest; but that passionate yearning to see her, to hear the sweet winning voice, to look into the soft hazel eyes, was strong upon him. It was a year since the day he dined in Clarges-street; and in all that year he had done his uttermost to forget her, had hated himself for the weakness which made her still dearer to him than any other woman; and then, alike angry with her and with himself, had cried, with Wilmot Earl of Rochester, —

> "Such charms by nature you possess,
> 'Twere madness not to love you. "

He went up to London early one morning, and straight from London to Holborough, where he arrived late in the evening. He slept at the chief inn of the place; and in the golden summer noontide set out for Arden Court—not to make a formal visit, but rather to look about him in a somewhat furtive way. He did not care to make his advent known to Daniel Granger just yet; perhaps, indeed, he might find it expedient to avoid any revelation of himself to that gentleman. He wanted to find out all he could of Clarissa's habits, so that he might contrive an interview with her. He had seen the announcement of the baby's birth, and oh, what a bitter pang the commonplace paragraph had given him! Never before had the fact that she was another man's wife come home to him so keenly. He tried to put the subject out of his thoughts, to forget that there had been a son born to the house of Granger; but often in the dreary spring twilight, walking among the oaks of Lyvedon, he had said to himself, "*Her* child ought to have been heir to this place. "

He went in at the lodge gate, and strolled idly into the park, not being at all clear as to how he was to bring about what he wanted. The weather was lovely—weather in which few people, untrammelled by necessity, would have cared to remain indoors. There was just the chance that Mrs. Granger might be strolling in the park herself, and the still more remote contingency that she might be alone. He was quite prepared for the possibility of meeting her accompanied by the lynx-eyed Miss Granger; and was not a man to be thrown off his guard, or taken at a disadvantage, come what might.

The place wore its fairest aspect: avenues of elms, that had begun to grow when England was young; gigantic oaks dotted here and there upon the undulating open ground, reputed a thousand years old; bright young plantations of rare fir and pine, that had a pert crisp newness about them, like the air of a modern dandy; everywhere the appearance of that perfect care and culture which is the most conclusive evidence of unlimited wealth.

George Fairfax looked round him with a sigh. The scene he looked upon was very fair. It was not difficult to understand how dear association might have made so beautiful a spot to such a girl as Clarissa. She had told him she would give the world to win back her lost home; and she had given—something less than the world—only herself. "Paris is worth a mass, " said the great Henry; and Clarissa's perjury was only one more of the many lies which men and women have told to compass their desires.

He kept away from the carriage-roads, loitering in the remoter regions of the park, and considering what he should do. He did not want to present himself at the Court as a formal visitor. In the first place, it would have been rather difficult to give any adequate reason for his presence in Holborough; and in the second, he had an unspeakable repugnance to any social intercourse with Clarissa's husband.

How he was ever to see her in the future without that hideous hypocrisy of friendliness towards Daniel Granger, he knew not; but he knew that it would cost him dearly to take the hand of the man who had supplanted him.

He wandered on till he came to a dell where the ground was broken a good deal, and where the fern seemed to grow more luxuriantly than in any other part of the park. There was a glimpse of blue water at the bottom of the slope—a narrow strip of a streamlet running between swampy banks, where the forget-me-nots and pale water-plants ran riot. This verdant valley was sheltered by some of the oldest hawthorns George Fairfax had ever seen—very Methuselahs of trees, whose grim old trunks and crooked branches time had twisted into the queerest shapes, and whose massive boles and strange excrescences of limb were covered with the moss of past generations. It was such a valley as Gustave Doré would love to draw; a glimpse of wilderness in the midst of cultivation.

There were not wanted figures to brighten the landscape. A woman dressed in white sat under one of the hawthorns, with a baby on her lap; and a nursemaid, in gayer raiment, stood by, looking down at the child.

How well George Fairfax remembered the slight girlish figure, and the day when he had come upon it unawares in Marley Wood! He stood a few paces off, and listened to the soft sweet voice.

Clarissa was talking to her baby in the unintelligible mother-language inspired by the occasion. A baby just able to smile at her, and coo and crow and chuckle in that peculiarly unctious manner common to babies of amiable character; a fair blue-eyed baby, big and bonny, with soft rings of flaxen hair upon his pink young head, and tender little arms that seemed meant for nothing so much as to be kissed.

After a good deal of that sweet baby-talk, there was a little discussion between the mistress and maid; and then the child was wrapped up as carefully as if destruction were in the breath of the softest June zephyr. Mr. Fairfax was afraid the mother was going away with the child, and that his chance would be lost; but it was not so. The maid tripped off with the infant, after it had been brought back two or three times to be half smothered with kisses—kisses which it seemed to relish in its own peculiar way, opening its mouth to receive them, as if they had been something edible. The baby was carried away at last, and Clarissa took up a book and began to read.

George Fairfax waited till the maid had been gone about ten minutes, and then came slowly down the hollow to the spot where Clarissa was seated. The rustle of the fern startled her; she looked up, and saw him standing by her side. It was just a year since he had surprised her in Mr. Wooster's garden at Henley. She had thought of him very much in that time, but less since the birth of her boy. She turned very pale at sight of him; and when she tried to speak, the words would not come: her lips only moved tremulously.

"I hope I did not alarm you very much, " he said, "by the suddenness of my appearance. I thought I heard your voice just now, speaking to some one"—he had not the heart to mention her baby—"and came down here to look for you. What a charming spot it is! "

She had recovered her self-possession by this time, and was able to answer him quite calmly. "Yes, it is very pretty. It was a favourite spot of Austin's. I have at least a dozen sketches of it done by him. But I did not know you were in Yorkshire, Mr. Fairfax. "

She wondered whether he was staying at Hale; and then it flashed upon her that there had been a reconciliation between him and Lady Geraldine.

"I have not been long in Yorkshire. I am merely here *en passant*, in short. My only excuse for approaching you lies in the fact that I have come to talk to you about your brother. "

"About Austin! " exclaimed Clarissa, with a look of alarm. "There is nothing wrong—he is well, I hope? "

"Pray don't alarm yourself. Yes, he is tolerably well, I believe; and there is nothing wrong—nothing that need cause you any immediate concern at least. I am going to Paris, and I thought you might be glad to send some message. "

"You are very kind to think of that; yes, I shall be glad to send to him. He is not a good correspondent, and I get very anxious about him sometimes. What you said just now seemed to imply that there was something wrong. Pray be candid with me, Mr. Fairfax. "

He did not answer her immediately; in fact, for the moment he scarcely was conscious of her words. He was looking at the beautiful face—looking at it with a repressed passion that was deeper and more real than any he had ever felt in his life. His thoughts wandered away from Austin Level. He was thinking what he would have given, what peril he would have dared, to call this woman his own. All this lower world seemed nothing to him when weighed against her; and in such a moment a man of his stamp rarely remembers any other world.

"There is something wrong, " repeated Clarissa with increasing anxiety. "I entreat you to tell me the truth! "

"Yes, there is something wrong, " he answered vaguely; and then, wrenching his mind away from those wild speculations as to what he would or would not do to win Daniel Granger's wife, he went on in another tone: "The truth is, my dear Mrs. Granger, I was in Paris last winter, and saw something of your brother's mode of life; and I cannot say that I consider it a satisfactory one. You have sent him a good deal of money since I saw you last, I daresay? Pray understand that there is nothing intrusive or impertinent in my question. I only wish to be some use to you, if I can. "

"I am sure of that. Yes; I have sent him what I could—about four hundred pounds—since last June; and he has been very grateful, poor fellow! He ought to know that he is welcome to every shilling I have. I could send him much more, of course, if I cared to ask my husband for money. "

"It is wiser to trust to your own resources. And I doubt if the command of much money would be a positive benefit to your brother. You have asked me to be candid; and I shall obey you, even at the hazard of giving you pain. There is a kind of constitutional weakness in your brother's nature. He is a man open to every influence, and not always governed by the best influences. I saw a good deal of him when I was last in Paris, and I saw him most in the fastest society, amongst people who petted him for the sake of his genius and vivacity, but who would turn their backs upon him to-morrow if he were no longer able to amuse them; the set into which an artist is so apt to fall when his home influences are not strong enough to keep him steady, and when he has that lurking disposition to Bohemianism which has been the bane of your brother's life. I speak entirely without reserve, you see. "

"I am grateful to you for doing so. Poor Austin! if he had only chosen more wisely! But his wife is fond of him, you say? "

"Too fond of him, perhaps; for she is very much given to torment him with jealous outbreaks; and he is not a man to take that sort of thing pleasantly. She does not go into society with him: indeed, I doubt if half-a-dozen out of the people whom he lives amongst know that he has a wife. I found his social position considerably improved; thanks to your remittances, no doubt. He was still in the Rue du Chevalier Bayard—as, of course, you know—but had moved a stage lower down, and had furnished a painting-room in the stereotyped style—Flemish carved buffets, dingy tapestry from a passage behind the Rue Richelieu, and a sprinkling of bric-a-brac from the Quai Voltaire. The poor little woman and her children were banished; and he had a room full of visitors chattering round him while he painted. You know his wonderful facility. The atmosphere was cloudy with tobacco-smoke; and the men were drinking that abominable concoction of worm-wood with which young France cultivates madness and early doom. "

"It is not a pleasant picture, " said Clarissa with a profound sigh.

"No, my dear Mrs. Granger; but it is a faithful one. Mr. Lovel had won a certain reputation for his airy style of art, and was beginning to get better prices for his pictures; but I fancy he has a capacity for spending money, and an inability to save it, which would bring him always to the same level of comparative insolvency. I have known so many men like that; and a man who begins in that way so rarely ends in any other way. "

"What am I to do! " exclaimed Clarissa piteously; "what can I do to help him? "

"I am almost at a loss to suggest anything. Perhaps if you were on the spot, your influence might do something. I know he loves you, and is more moved by the mention of your name than by any sermon one could preach to him. But I suppose there is no chance of your being in Paris. "

"I don't know. Mr. Granger talked some time ago of spending the autumn abroad, and asked me if I should like to see a New-Year's day in Paris. I think, if I were to express a wish about it, he would take me there; and it would be such happiness to me to see Austin! " And then Mrs. Granger thought of her baby, and wondered whether the atmosphere of Paris would be favourable to that rare and beauteous blossom; whether the tops-and-bottoms of the French capital would agree with his tender digestive machinery, and if the cowkeepers of the Faubourg St. Honoré were an honest and unadulterating race. The very notion of taking the treasure away from his own nurseries, his own cow, his own goat-chaise, was enough to make her shudder.

"It would be the best chance for his redemption. A little womanly kindness and counsel from you to the wife might bring about a happier state of things in his home; and a man who can be happy at home is in a measure saved. It is hardly possible for your brother to mix much with the people amongst whom I saw him without injury to himself. They are people to whom dissipation is the very salt of life; people who breakfast at the Moulin Rouge at three o'clock in the afternoon, and eat ices at midnight to the music of the cascade in the Bois; people to be seen at every race-meeting; men who borrow money at seventy-five per cent to pay for opera-boxes and dinners at the Café Riche, and who manage the rest of their existence on credit. "

"But what could my influence do against such friends as these? " asked Clarissa in a hopeless tone.

"Who can say? It might do wonders. I know your brother has a heart, and that you have power to touch it. Take my advice, Mrs. Granger, and try to be in Paris as soon as you can. "

"I will, " she answered fervently. "I would do anything to save him. " She looked at her watch, and rose from the seat under the hawthorn. "It is nearly two o'clock, " she said, "and I must go back to the house. You will come to luncheon, of course? "

"Thanks—no. I have an engagement that will take me back to the town immediately. "

"But Mr. Granger will be surprised to hear that you have been here without calling upon him. "

"Need Mr. Granger hear of my coming? " George Fairfax asked in a low tone.

Clarissa flushed scarlet.

"I have no secrets from my husband, Mr. Fairfax, " she said, "even about trifles. "

"Ten thousand pardons! I scarcely want to make my presence here a secret; but, in short, I came solely to speak to you about a subject in which I knew you were deeply interested, and I had not contemplated calling upon Mr. Granger. "

They were walking slowly up the grassy slope as they talked; and after this there came a silence, during which Clarissa quickened her pace a little, George Fairfax keeping still by her side. Her heart beat faster than its wont; and she had a vague sense of danger in this man's presence—a sense of a net being woven round her, a lurking suspicion that this apparent interest in her brother veiled some deeper feeling.

They came out of the hollow, side by side, into a short arcade of flowering limes, at the end of which there was a broad sweep of open grass. A man on a deep-chested strong-limbed gray horse was riding slowly towards them across the grass—Daniel Granger.

That picture of his wife walking in the little avenue of limes, with George Fairfax by her side, haunted Mr. Granger with a strange distinctness in days to come, —the slight white-robed figure against the background of sunlit greenery; the young man's handsome head, uncovered, and stooping a little as he spoke to his companion.

The master of Arden Court dismounted, and led his horse by the bridle as he came forward to meet Mr. Fairfax. The two men shook hands; but not very warmly. The encounter mystified Daniel Granger a little. It was strange to find a man he had supposed to be at the other end of England strolling in the park with his wife, and that man the one about whom he had had many a dreary half-hour of brooding. He waited for an explanation, however, without any outward show of surprise. The business was simple and natural enough, no doubt, he told himself.

"Have you been to the house? " he asked; "I have been out all the morning. "

"No; I was on my way there, when I came upon Mrs. Granger in the most romantic spot yonder. I felt that I was rather early for a morning-call even in the depths of the country, and had strolled out of the beaten path to get rid of an hour or so. "

"I did not know you were in Yorkshire, " said Mr. Granger, not in the most cordial tone. "You are staying at Hale, I suppose? "

"No; Lady Laura is away, you know. "

"Ah—to be sure; I had forgotten. "

"I am spending a few days with a bachelor friend in Holborough. I am off to Germany before the week is out. "

Mr. Granger was not sorry to hear this. He was not jealous of George Fairfax. If anybody had suggested the possibility of his entertaining such a sentiment, that person would have experienced the full force of Daniel Granger's resentment; but this was just the one man whom he fancied his wife might have cared for a little before her marriage. He was not a man given to petty jealousies; and of late, since the birth of his son, there had been growing up in his mind a sense of security in his wife's fidelity—her affection even. The union between them had seemed very perfect after the advent of the child; and the master of Arden Court felt almost as if there were nothing upon this earth left for him to desire. But he was a little puzzled by the presence of George Fairfax, nevertheless.

Holborough was a small place; and he began to speculate immediately upon the identity of this bachelor friend of Mr. Fairfax's. It was not a garrison town. The young men of the place were for the most part small professional men—half-a-dozen lawyers and doctors, two or three curates, a couple of bankers' sons, an auctioneer or two, ranking vaguely between the trading and professional classes, and the sons of tradesmen. Among them all Mr. Granger could remember no one likely to be a friend of George Fairfax. It might possibly be one of the curates; but it seemed scarcely probable that Mr. Fairfax would come two hundred and fifty miles to abide three days with a curate. Nor was it the season of partridges. There was no shooting to attract Mr. Fairfax to the neighbourhood of Holborough. There was trout, certainly, to be found in abundance in brooks, and a river within a walk of the town; and Mr. Fairfax might be passionately fond of fly-fishing.

"You will come in and have some luncheon, of course, " Mr. Granger said, when they came to the gateway, where George Fairfax pulled up, and began to wish them good-bye. Not to ask the man to eat and drink would have seemed to him the most unnatural thing in the world.

"Thanks. I think I had better deny myself that pleasure, " Mr. Fairfax said doubtfully. "The day is getting on, and—and I have an engagement for the afternoon. " ("Trout, no doubt, " thought Mr. Granger.) "I have seen you, that is the grand point. I could not leave Yorkshire without paying my respects to you and Mrs. Granger. "

"Do you leave so soon? "

"To-morrow, I think. "

"A hurried journey for trout, " thought Mr. Granger.

He insisted upon the visitor coming in to luncheon. George Fairfax was not very obdurate. It was so sweet to be near the woman he loved, and he had not the habit of refusing himself the things that were sweet to him. They went into the small dining-room. The luncheon bell had rung a quarter of an hour ago, and Miss Granger was waiting for her parents, with an air of placid self-abnegation, by an open window.

There was a good deal of talk during luncheon, but the chief talker was George Fairfax. Clarissa was grave and somewhat absent. She was thinking of her brother Austin, and the gloomy account of him which she had just heard. It was hardly a surprise to her. His letters had been few and far between, and they had not been hopeful, or, at the best, brightened by only a flash of hopefulness, which was more like bravado, now and then. His necessity for money, too, had seemed without limit. She was planning her campaign. Come what might, she must contrive some means of being in Paris before long. Mr. Fairfax was going on to Carlsruhe, that was an advantage; for something in his manner to-day had told her that he must always be more or less than her friend. She had a vague sense that his eagerness to establish a confidence between her and himself was a menace of danger to her.

"If I can only go to Austin myself, " she thought, "there need be no intermediary. "

Luncheon was over, and still Mr. Fairfax lingered—strangely indifferent to the waning of an afternoon which seemed peculiarly advantageous for fly-fishing, Mr. Granger thought. They went into the drawing-room, and Mr. Fairfax dawdled an hour away talking of Lyvedon, and giving a serio-comic description of himself in the novel character of a country gentleman. It was not till Mr. Granger had looked at his watch once or twice in a surreptitious manner, thinking of an engagement to meet his architect for the inspection of some dilapidated cottages on the newest part of his estate, that the visitor rose to depart. Daniel Granger had quite warmed to him by this time. His manner was so natural in its pleasant airiness: it was not easy to think there could be any lurking evil beneath such a show of candour.

"Can't you stay and dine with us? " asked Mr. Granger; "or will you go back to Holborough and fetch your friend? We shall be very glad to know him, if we don't know him already. "

If a blush had been possible to George Fairfax, this friendly speech would have raised it; but the capacity had departed from him before he left Eton. He did feel ashamed of himself, nevertheless.

"You are more than good, " he said, "but my friend seldom goes anywhere. Good-bye. "

He made his adieux with an agreeable abruptness, not caring to prolong the dinner question. Such men as he tell lies without stint upon occasion; but the men are few to whom it is actually congenial to lie. He was glad to get away even from the woman he loved, and the sense of shame was strong upon him as he departed.

If his mother, who was anxiously awaiting a letter from Paris or Carlsruhe, could have known of his presence here in this place, to which his father had come years ago to betray her! If she who loved him so fondly, and was so full of prayers and hopes for his future, could have seen him so utterly on the wrong road, what bitter shame and lamenting there would have been in the halls of Lyvedon that day—those deserted halls in which the lady sat alone among the sombre old-world grandeurs of oak and tapestry, and sighed for her absent son!

* * * * *

Instead of going straight back to the Holborough high-road, Mr. Fairfax struck across the woods by that path which led to the mill-stream and the orchard, where he had parted from Clarissa on that cheerless October night nearly three years ago. He knew that Mr. Lovel was away, and the cottage only tenanted by servants, and he had a fancy for looking at the place where he had been so angry and so miserable—the scene of that one rejection which had stung him to the very quick, the single humiliation of his successful career. It was only the morbid fancy of an idle man, who had an afternoon to dispose of somehow.

Half-way between the Court and the cottage, he heard the jingling of bells, and presently, flashing and gleaming among the trees, he saw a gaily-painted carriage drawn by a pair of goats, with plated harness that shone in the sun. Mixed with the joyous jingle of the bells, there came the sound of an infant's laughter. It was the baby taking his after-dinner airing, attended by a couple of nurses. A turn in the path brought George Fairfax and the heir of Arden face to face.

A sudden impulse seized him—a sudden impulse of tenderness for *her* child. He took the little bundle of rosy babyhood and lace and muslin in his arms, and kissed the soft little face as gently as a woman, and looked into the innocent blue eyes, dilated to an almost impossible extent in a wondering stare, with unspeakable love and melancholy in his own. Great Heaven! if Clarissa had been his wife, this child his son, what a happy man he might have been, what a new charm there would have been in the possession of a fine estate, what a new zest in life, the savour of which seemed to have departed altogether of late!

He put the little one back into his cushioned seat in the goat-chaise with supreme care and gentleness, not ruffling so much as a plume in his dainty white satin hat.

"A fine boy, Mrs. Nurse, " he said, feeling in his waistcoat-pocket for bacsheesh; to which proposition the portly head-nurse, who had stared at him, aghast with horror, while had handled the infant, assented with enthusiasm.

"I never nursed a finer, sir; and I was head-nurse to Lady Fitz-Lubin, which my lady had five boys, and not a girl between them; and Mrs. Granger does dote on him so. I never see a ma that rapt up in her child. "

Mr. Fairfax gave her half-a-sovereign, stooped down to kiss the baby again—it is doubtful if he had ever kissed a baby before—and then walked on, wondering at the new sensation. Such a little soft thing, that opened its mouth to be kissed, like a petted bird! And yet he could contemplate a future in which he should come between Clarissa and this child; he could dream of a possibility which should make its mother's name a shame to this little one.

* * * * *

Mr. Granger kept his appointment with the architect, and came to the natural conclusion of a rich roan upon the subject of dilapidated buildings. After inspecting the lop-sided old cottages, with their deep roomy chimneys, in which the farm labourer loved to sit of a night, roasting his ponderous boots, and smoking the pipe of meditation, and their impossible staircases, which seemed to have been designed with a deliberate view to the breaking of legs and endangerment of spines, Mr. Granger made a wry face, and ordered that rubbish to be swept away.

"You can build me half-a-dozen upon the new Arden design, " he said; "red brick, with stone dressings; and be sure you put a tablet with the date in front of each. "

He was thinking of his son, anxious that there should be some notable improvement, some new building every year, to mark the progress of his boy's existence.

The farm-labourers and their wives did not look so delighted as they might have been by this edict. These benighted souls liked the old cottages, lop-sided as they were—liked the crooked staircase squeezed into a corner of the living room below, the stuffy little dens above, with casement windows which only opened on one side, letting in the smallest modicum of air, and were not often opened at all. Cottages on the Now Arden model meant stone floors below and open rafters above, thorough draughts everywhere, and, worst of all, they meant weekly inspection by Miss Granger. The free sons and daughters of Hickly-on-the-Hill—this little cluster of houses which formed a part of Mr. Granger's new estate—had rejoiced that they were not as the Ardenites; that they could revel in warmth and dirt, and eat liver-and-bacon for supper on a Saturday night, without any fear of being lectured for their extravagance by the omniscient Sophia on the following Monday, convicted of their guilt by the evidence of the grease in an unwashed frying-pan; that their children could sport on the hillside in garments that were guiltless of strings; that, in short, they were outside the circle of Miss Granger's sympathies and could live their own lives. But that sweet liberty was all over now: with the red brick and stone dressings would come the Draconian laws of New Arden; no more corners for the comfortable accumulation of dirt, no more delicious little cupboards for the stowing away of rubbish. Everything was to be square and solid and stony. They heard Mr. Granger giving orders that the chimney was to be flush with the wall, and so on; the stove, an "Oxford front, " warranted to hold not more than a pound and a half of coal; no recesses in which old age could sit and croon, no cosy nook for the cradle of infancy.

After this interview with the architect, Mr. Granger rode home through Holborough. His way took him past that very hotel where

George Fairfax was staying—the chief inn of the town, a fine old red-brick building that filled nearly one side of the market-place.

It happened that just as Mr. Granger rode along the High-street, where there were some half-a-dozen stragglers visible upon a wide expanse of pavement, and one carriage waiting at the draper's, Mr. Fairfax walked up the broad steps of the hotel and entered—entered with the air of a man who lived there, Daniel Granger thought. And he had said that he was staying with a bachelor friend. Mr. Granger rode slowly past the principal part of the hotel to an archway at the end—an archway leading to livery stables, where the ostler was lounging. He stopped opposite this archway, and beckoned the man over to him.

"There was a gentleman went into the hotel just now, " he said; "did you see him? "

"Yes, sir, I seed him. Mr. Fairfax; him as was to have married Lady Laura Armstrong's sister. "

"Is he staying in the house, do you know? "

"Yes, sir; came last night, down from London. Shall I take him your card, sir? "

"No, thank you, Giles; I won't call upon him this afternoon, I only wanted to be sure. Good-day. "

He rode on. What was the meaning of this lie which George Fairfax had told him? Had it any meaning which it behoved him to fathom? It was strange, at the least—strange enough to make Mr. Granger very uncomfortable as he rode slowly back to the Court.

* * * * *

CHAPTER XXXII.

AUSTIN.

Late in the autumn of that year, Mr. Granger and his household took up their abode in Paris. Clarissa had expressed a wish to winter in that brilliant city, and Daniel Granger had no greater desire than to please her. But, in making any concession of this kind, he did it in such a quiet unobtrusive way, that his wife was scarcely aware how entirely her wishes had been studied. He was too proud a man to parade his affection for her; he kept a check upon himself rather, and in a manner regulated his own conduct by the standard of hers. There was never any show of devotion on his part. The world might have taken them for a couple brought together by convenience, and making the best of their loveless union.

So, with regard to the gratification of her wishes, it seemed always that the thing which Clarissa desired, happened to suit his own humour, rather than that he sacrificed all personal feeling for her pleasure. In this Parisian arrangement it had been so, and his wife had no idea that it was entirely on her account that Daniel Granger set up his tent in the Faubourg St. Honoré.

The fair Sophia had, however, a very shrewd suspicion of the fact, and for some weeks prior to the departure from Arden, existed in a state of suppressed indignation, which was not good for the model villagers; her powers of observation were, if possible, sharpened in the matter of cobwebs; her sense of smell intensified in relation to cabbage-water. Nor did she refrain from making herself eminently disagreeable to her stepmother.

"I should not have supposed you would so soon be tired of Arden Court, " she remarked pleasantly, during that dreary quarter of an hour after dinner which Mr. Granger and his wife and daughter were wont to pass in the contemplation of crystallized apricots and hothouse grapes, and the exchange of the baldest commonplaces in the way of conversation; Perhaps if Clarissa and her husband had been alone on such occasions that air of ceremony might have vanished. The young wife might have drawn her chair a little nearer her husband's, and there might have been some pleasant talk about that inexhaustible source of wonder and delight, the baby. But with Miss Granger always at hand, the dessert was as ceremonious as if there had been a party of eighteen, and infinitely more dreary, lacking the cheery clatter and buzz of company. She ate five hothouse grapes, and sipped half a glass of claret, with as solemn an air as if she had been making a libation to the gods.

Mr. Granger looked up from his plate when his daughter made this remark about Arden, and glanced inquiringly at his wife, with a shadow of displeasure in his face. Yielding and indulgent as he had been to her, there was in his composition something of the stuff that makes a tyrant. His wife must love the things that he loved. It would have been intolerable to him to suppose that Mrs. Granger could grow weary of the house that he had beautified.

"I am not tired of the Court, " Clarissa answered with a sad smile. "There are too many recollections to make it dear to me. "

Daniel Granger's face flushed ever so slightly at this speech.

It was the past, then, and not the present, that rendered the place dear to her.

"I could never grow tired of Arden, " she went on; "but I think it will be very nice to spend a winter in Paris. "

"Lady Laura Armstrong has put that notion into your head, no doubt, " said Miss Granger, with the faintest suspicion of a sneer. She was not very warmly attached to the lady of Hale Castle nowadays, regarding her as the chief promoter of Mr. Granger's marriage.

"Lady Laura has said that they enjoyed themselves very much in Paris the winter before last, " Clarissa answered frankly; "and has promised me plenty of introductions. She even promises that she and Mrs. Armstrong will come over for a week or two, while we are there. "

"And poor Lady Geraldine Challoner? "

Miss Granger always exhibited a profound pity for Lady Geraldine, and never lost any opportunity of dwelling upon Mr. Fairfax's bad conduct.

"No; I don't suppose Lady Geraldine would go with them, " Clarissa answered, colouring a little. The name of Geraldine Challoner was always painful to her. "She doesn't care about going anywhere. "

"Perhaps she would not care to run the risk of meeting Mr. Fairfax, " suggested Sophia.

Mr. Granger looked up again, with that shadow of displeasure upon his countenance.

"She would not be more likely to meet him in Paris than at Hale, " replied Clarissa. "He has gone to Germany. "

"Yes, for the autumn, he said. Depend upon it, he will spend the winter in Paris. I have always observed that those dissipated kind of men prefer Paris to London. "

"I don't think you have any right to call Mr. Fairfax dissipated, Sophia, " said her father, with an offended air; "and I don't think that his movements can be of the smallest consequence to you, nor those of the Hale Castle people either? Clarissa and I have determined to spend two or three months in Paris, and we are not in the slightest degree dependent upon our English friends for our enjoyment there. If you are disinclined to accompany us, and would rather remain at Arden— —"

"O, papa, papa! " cried Sophia, with an injured look, "don't say that; don't allow me to think I have grown quite indifferent to you. "

"You have not grown indifferent to me; but I don't want to take you away from home against your wish. "

"My wish is to be anywhere with you, papa; *anywhere*—even though you may feel me an incumbrance. I could endure the humiliation of feeling that, so long as I was allowed to remain with you. "

Mr. Granger gave a sigh that was almost a groan, and, for perhaps the first time in his life, it occurred to him that it would be a pleasant thing if his only daughter were to fall in love with some fortunate youth, and desire to marry him. A curate even. There was Tillott. Why shouldn't she marry Tillott? He, Daniel Granger, would give his child a handsome portion, and they could go through life inspecting model cottages, and teaching village children the works and ways of all those wicked kings of Israel, who made groves and set up the idols of their heathen neighbours; a pure and virtuous and useful life, without question, if tempered with come consideration for the feelings of the model cottagers, and some mercy for the brains of the humble scholars.

In the interval between this little after-dinner scene and the departure from Arden, Mr. Granger invited Mr. Tillott to dinner two or three times, and watched him with the eyes of anxiety as he conversed with Sophia. But although the curate was evidently eager to find favour in the sight of the damsel, the damsel herself showed no sign of weakness. Mr. Granger sighed, and told himself that the lamp of hope burned dimly in this quarter.

"She really ought to marry, " he said to himself. "A girl of her energetic indefatigable nature would be a treasure to some man, and she is only wasting herself here. Perhaps in Paris we shall meet some one; " and then there arose before Mr. Granger the vision of some foreign adventurer, seeking to entangle the wealthy English "meess" in his meshes. Paris might be a dangerous place; but with such, a girl as Sophia, there could be no fear; she was a young woman who might be trusted to walk with unfaltering steps through the most tortuous pathways of this life, always directing herself aright, and coming in at the finish just at that very point at which a well brought-up young person should arrive.

Mr. Granger made his Parisian arrangements on the large scale which became him as a landed gentleman of unlimited wealth. A first floor of some ten spacious rooms was selected in one of the bran-new stone mansions in a bran-new street in the fashionable Faubourg; a house that seemed to have been built for the habitation of giants; a house made splendid by external decoration in carved stonework, garlands of stone-fruit and flowers, projecting lion-heads, caryatides, and so on: no gloomy *porte-cochère*, but a street-door, through which a loaded drag might have been driven without damage to the hats of the outside passengers. A house glorified within by egg-and-dart mouldings, white enamelled woodwork and much gilding; but a house in which the winter wind howled as in a primeval forest, and which required to be supplied with supplementary padded crimson-velvet doors before the spacious chambers could be made comfortable. Here Mr. Granger took up his abode, with ten of his Arden Court servants quartered on a floor above. The baby had a nursery loosing into the broad bare street, where some newly-planted sticks of the sycamore species shivered in the north-east wind; and the baby took his matutinal airings in the Tuileries Gardens, and his afternoon drives in the Bois, while every movement of his infant existence was watched or directed by the tenderest of mothers. The chief nurse, who had lived with more fashionable mistresses, for whom the duties of the nursery were subordinate to the business of society, pronounced Mrs. Granger "fidgety"; a very sweet lady, but too fond of interfering about trifles, and not reposing boundless confidence in the experience of her nurse.

There were a good many English people in Paris this year whom the Grangers knew, and Lady Laura had insisted upon giving Clarissa introductions to some of her dearest friends among the old French nobility—people who had known Lord Calderwood in their days of exile—and more than one dearest friend among the newer lights of the Napoleonic firmament. Then there were a Russian princess and a Polish countess or so, whom Lady Laura had brought to Mrs. Granger's receptions in Clarges-street: so that Clarissa and her husband found themselves at once in the centre of a circle, from the elegant dissipations whereof there was no escape. The pretty Mrs. Granger and the rich Mr. Granger were in request everywhere; nor was the stately Sophia neglected, although she took her share in all festivities with the familiar Sunday-school primness, and seemed to vivacious Gaul the very archetype of that representative young English lady who is always exclaiming "Shocking! " Even after her arrival in Paris, when she felt herself so very near him, after so many years of severance, Clarissa did not find it the easiest thing in the world to see her brother. Mr. and Mrs. Granger had only spent a couple of days in Paris during their honeymoon, and Daniel Granger planned a round of sight-seeing, in the way of churches, picture-galleries, and cemeteries, which fully occupied the first four or five days after their arrival. Clarissa was obliged to be deeply interested in all the details of Gothic architecture—to appreciate Ingres, to give her mind to Gérome—when her heart was yearning for that meeting which he had waited so long to compass. Mr. Granger, as an idle man, with no estate to manage—no new barns being built within his morning's ride—no dilapidated cottages to be swept away—was not easily to be got rid of. He devoted his days to showing his wife the glories of the splendid city, which he knew by heart himself, and admired sufficiently in a sober business-like way. The evenings were mortgaged to society. Clarissa had been more than a week in Paris before she had a morning to herself; and even then there was Miss

Granger to be disposed of, and Miss Granger's curiosity to be satisfied.

Mr. Granger had gone to breakfast at the Maison Dorée with a mercantile magnate from his own country—a solemn commercial breakfast, whereat all the airy trifles and dainty compositions of fish, flesh, and fowl with which the butterfly youth of France are nourished, were to be set before unappreciative Britons. At ten o'clock Clarissa ordered her carriage. It was best to go in her own carriage, she thought, even at the risk of exciting the curiosity of servants. To send for a hired vehicle would have caused greater wonder; to walk alone was impossible; to walk with her nurse and child might have been considered eccentric.

She could not even take an airing, however, without some discussion with Miss Granger. That young lady was established in the drawing-room—the vast foreign chamber, which never looked like a home—illuminating a new set of Gothic texts for the adornment of her school. She sorely missed the occupation and importance afforded her by the model village. In Paris there was no one afraid of her; no humble matrons to quail as her severe eyes surveyed wall and ceiling, floor and surbase. And being of a temperament which required perpetual employment, she was fain to fall back upon illumination, Berlin-wool work, and early morning practice of pianoforte music of the most strictly mathematical character. It was her boast that she had been thoroughly "grounded" in the science of harmony; but although she could have given a reason for every interval in a sonata, her playing never sparkled into brilliancy or melted into tenderness, and never had her prim cold fingers found their way to a human soul.

"Are you going out so early? " this wise damsel asked wonderingly, as Clarissa came into the drawing-room in her bonnet and shawl.

"Yes, it is such a fine morning, and I think baby will enjoy it. I have not had a drive with him since we have been here. "

"No, " replied Sophia, "you have only had papa. I shouldn't think he would be very much flattered if he heard you preferred baby. "

"I did not say that I preferred baby, Sophia. What a habit you have of misrepresenting me! "

The nurse appeared at this moment, carrying the heir of the Grangers, gloriously arrayed in blue velvet, and looking fully conscious of his magnificence.

"But I do like to have a drive with my pet-lamb, don't I, darling? " said the mother, stooping to kiss the plump rosy cheek. And then there followed some low confidential talk, in the fond baby language peculiar to young mothers.

"I should have thought you would have been glad to get a morning alone, for once in a way, " remarked Sophia, coming over to the baby, and giving him a stately kiss. She liked him tolerably well in her own way, and was not angry with him for having come into the world to oust her from her proud position as sole heiress to her father's wealth. The position had been very pleasant to her, and she had not seen it slip away from her without many a pang; but, however she might dislike Clarissa, she was not base enough to hate her father's child. If she could have had the sole care and management of him, physicked and dieted him after her own method, and developed the budding powers of his infant mind by her favourite forcing system—made a model villager of him, in short—she might have grown even to love him. But these privileges being forbidden to her—her wisdom being set at naught, and her counsel rejected—she could not help regarding Lovel Granger as more or less an injury.

"I should have thought you would have been glad of a morning at home, Clarissa, " she repeated.

"Not such a fine morning as this, Sophy. It would be such a pity for baby to lose the sunshine; and I have really nothing to do. "

"If I had known a little sooner that you were going, I would have gone with you, " said Miss Granger.

Clarissa's countenance fell. She could not help that little troubled look, which told Miss Granger that her society would not have been welcome.

"You would have had no objection to my coming with you, I suppose? " the fair Sophia said sharply. "Baby is not quite a monopoly. "

"Of course not. If you'll put on your things now, Sophia, I'll wait for you. "

It was a hard thing for Clarissa to make the offer, when she had been waiting so anxiously for this opportunity of seeing her brother. To be in the same city with him, and not see him, was more painful than to be divided from him by half the earth, as she had been. It was harder still to have to plot and plan and stoop to falsehood in order to compass a meeting. But she remembered the stern cold look in her husband's face when she had spoken of Austin, and she could not bring herself to degrade her brother by entreating Daniel Granger's indulgence for his past misdeeds, or Daniel Granger's interest in his future fortunes.

Happily Sophia had made elaborate preparations for the Gothic texts, and was not inclined to waste so much trouble.

"I have got my colours all ready, " she said, "and have put everything out, you see. No, I don't think I'll go to-day. But another time, if you'll be so kind as to let me know *beforehand*, I shall be pleased to go with my brother. I suppose you know there's an east wind to-day, by-the-bye. "

The quarter whence the wind came, was a subject about which Clarissa had never concerned herself. The sun was shining, and the sky was blue.

"We have plenty of wraps, " she said, "and we can have the carriage closed if we are cold. "

"It is not a day upon which *I* should take an infant out, " Miss Granger murmured, dipping her brush in some Prussian-blue; "but of course you know best. "

"O, we shall take care of baby, depend upon it. Good-bye, Sophy. "

And Clarissa departed, anxious to avoid farther remonstrance on the part of her step-daughter. She told the coachman to drive to the Luxembourg Gardens, intending to leave the nurse and baby to promenade that favourite resort, while she made her way on foot to the Rue du Chevalier Bayard. She remembered that George Fairfax had described her brother's lodging as near the Luxembourg.

They drove through the gay Parisian streets, past the pillar in the Place Vend'me, and along the Rue de la Paix, all shining with jewellers' ware, and the Rue de Rivoli, where the chestnut-trees in the gardens of the Tuileries were shedding their last leaves upon the pavement, past the airy tower of St. Jacques, and across the bridge into that unknown world on the other side of the Seine. The nurse, who had seen very little of that quarter of the town, wondered what obscure region she was traversing, and wondered still more when they alighted at the somewhat shabby-looking gardens.

"These are the Luxembourg Gardens, " said Clarissa. "As you have been to the Tuileries every day, I thought it would be a change for you to come here. "

"Thank you, ma'am, " replied Mrs. Brobson, the chief nurse; "but I don't think as these gardings is anyways equal to the Tooleries—nor to Regent's Park even. When I were in Paris with Lady Fitz-Lubin we took the children to the Tooleries or the Bore de Boulong every day—but, law me! the Bore de Boulong were a poor place in those days to what it is now. "

Clarissa took a couple of turns along one of the walks with Mrs. Brobson, and then, as they were going back towards the gate, she said, as carelessly as she could manage to say: "There is a person living somewhere near here whom I want to see, Mrs. Brobson. I'll leave you and baby in the gardens for half an hour or so, while I go and pay my visit. "

Mrs. Brobson stared. It was not an hour in the day when any lady she had ever served was wont to pay visits; and that Mrs. Granger of Arden Court should traverse a neighbourhood of narrow streets and tall houses, on foot and alone, to call upon her acquaintance at eleven o'clock in the morning, seemed to her altogether inexplicable.

"You'll take the carriage, won't you, ma'am? " she said, with undisguised astonishment.

"No, I shall not want the carriage; it's very near. Be sure you keep baby warm, Mrs. Brobson. "

Clarissa hurried out into the street. The landau, with its pair of Yorkshire-bred horses, was moving slowly up and down, to the admiration of juvenile Paris, which looked upon Mr. Granger's deep-chested, strong-limbed bays almost as a new order in the animal creation. Mrs. Granger felt that the eyes of coachman and footman were upon her as she turned the first corner, thinking of nothing for the moment, but how to escape the watchfulness of her own servants. She walked a little way down the street, and then asked a sleepy-looking waiter, who was sweeping the threshold of a very dingy restaurant, to direct her to the Rue du Chevalier Bayard. It was *tous près*, the man said; only a turn to the right, at that corner yonder, and the next turning was the street she wanted. She thanked him, and hurried on, with her heart beating faster at every step. Austin might be out, she thought, and her trouble wasted; and there was no knowing when she might have another opportunity. Even if he were at home, their interview must needs be brief: there was the nurse waiting and wondering; the baby exposed to possible peril from east winds.

The Rue du Chevalier Bayard was a street of tall gaunt houses that had seen better days—houses with *porte-cochères*, exaggerated iron knockers, and queer old lamps; dreary balconies on the first floor, with here and there a plaster vase containing some withered member of the palm tribe, or a faded orange-tree; everywhere and in everything an air of dilapidation and decay; faded curtains, that had once been fine, flapping in the open windows; Venetian shutters going to ruin; and the only glimpse of brightness or domestic comfort confined to the humble parlour of the portress, who kept watch and ward over one of the dismal mansions, and who had a birdcage hanging in her window, an Angora cat sunning itself on the stone sill, and a row of scarlet geraniums in the little iron balcony.

But this model portress did not preside over the house inhabited by Austin Lovel. There Clarissa found only a little deaf old man, who grinned and shook his head helplessly when she questioned him, and shrugged his shoulders and pointed to the staircase—a cavernous stone staircase, with an odour as of newly opened graves. She went up to the first-floor, past the *entresol*, where the earthy odour was subjugated by a powerful smell of cooking, in which garlic was the prevailing feature. One tall door on the first-floor was painted a pale pink, and had still some dingy indications of former gilding upon its mouldings. On this pink door was inscribed the name of Mr. Austin, Painter.

Clarissa rang a bell, and a tawdry-looking French servant, with big earrings and a dirty muslin cap, came to answer her summons. Mr.

Austin was at home; would madame please to enter. Madame, having replied in the affirmative, was shown into a small sitting-room, furnished with a heterogeneous collection of cabinets, tables, and sofas, every one of which bore the stamp of the broker's shop—things which had been graceful and pretty in their day, but from which the ormolu-moulding had been knocked off here, and the inlaid-wood chipped away there, and the tortoiseshell cracked in another place, until they seemed the very emblems of decay. It was as if they had been set up as perpetual monitors—monuments of man's fragility. "This is what life comes to, " they said in their silent fashion. This faded rubbish in buhl and marqueterie was useful enough to Mr. Lovel, however; and on his canvas the faded furniture glowed and sparkled with all its original brightness, fresh as the still-life of Meissonier. There were a child's toys scattered on the floor; and Clarissa heard a woman's voice talking to a child in an adjoining room, on the other side of a pair of tall pink folding-doors. Then she heard her brother's voice saying something to the servant; and at the sound she felt as if she must have fallen to the ground. Then one of the doors was opened, and a woman came in; a pretty, faded-looking woman, dressed in a light-blue morning wrapper that might very well have been cleaner; a woman with a great deal of dyed hair in an untidy mass at the back of her head; a woman whom Clarissa felt it must be a difficult thing to like.

This was her brother's wife, of course. There was a boy of four or five years old clinging to his mother's gown, and Clarissa's heart yearned to the child. He had Austin's face. It would be easy to love *him*, she thought.

"Mr. Austin is in his paintin'-room, madame, " said the wife, putting on a kind of company manner. "Did you wish to see him about a picture? Je parle très poo de Français, mais si— —"

"I am English, " Clarissa answered, smiling; "if you will kindly tell Mr. Austin a lady from England wishes to see him. What a, dear little boy! May I shake hands with him? "

"Give the lady your hand, Henery, " said the mother. "Not that one, " as the boy, after the invariable custom of childhood, offered his left—"the right hand. "

Clarissa took the sticky little paw tenderly in her pearl-gray glove. To think that her brother Austin Lovel should have married a woman who could call her son "Henery, " and who had such an unmistakable air of commonness!

The wife went back to the painting-room; and returned the next minute to beg the visitor to "step this way, if you please, ma'am. " She opened one of the folding-doors wide as she spoke, and Clarissa went into a large room, at the other end of which there stood a tall slim young man, in a short velvet coat, before a small easel.

It was her brother Austin; pale and a trifle haggard, too old in looks for his years, but very handsome—a masculine edition of Clarissa herself, in fact: the same delicate clearly-cut features, the same dark hazel eyes, shaded by long brown lashes tinged with gold. This was what Mrs. Granger saw in the broad noonday sunshine; while the painter, looking up from his easel, beheld a radiant creature approaching him, a woman in pale-gray silk, that it would have been rapture to paint; a woman with one of the loveliest faces he had ever seen, crowned with a broad plait of dark-brown hair, and some delicate structure of point-lace and pink roses, called by courtesy a bonnet.

He laid down his mahl-stick, and came to meet her, with a puzzled look on his face. Her beauty seemed familiar to him somehow, and yet he had no recollection of ever having seen her before. He saw the faded counterpart of that bright face every morning in his looking-glass.

She held out both her hands.

"Austin, don't you know me? "

He gave a cry of pleased surprise, and caught her in his arms.

"Clarissa! " he exclaimed; "why, my darling, how lovely you have grown! My dear little Clary! How well I remember the sweet young face, and the tears, and kisses, and the slender little figure in its childish dress, that day your father carried you off to school! My own little Clary, what a happiness to see you! But you never told me you were coming to Paris. "

"No, dear, I kept that for a surprise. And are you really glad to see me, Austin? "

"Really glad! Is there any one in the world could make me gladder? "

"I am so happy to hear that. I was almost afraid you had half forgotten me. Your letters were so few, and so short. "

"Letters! " cried Austin Lovel, with a laugh; "I never was much of a hand at letter-writing; and then I hadn't anything particularly pleasant to write about. You mustn't gauge my affection by the length of my letters, Clary. And then I have to work deucedly hard when I am at home, and have very little time for scribbling. "

Clarissa glanced round the room while he was speaking. Every detail in her brother's surroundings had an interest for her. Here, as in the drawing-room, there was an untidy air about everything—a want of harmony in all the arrangements. There were Flemish carved-oak cabinets, and big Japan vases; a mantelpiece draped with dusty crimson velvet, a broken Venetian glass above it, and a group of rusty-looking arms on each side; long limp amber curtains to the three tall windows, with festooned valances in an advanced state of disarrangement and dilapidation. There were some logs burning on the hearth, a pot of chocolate simmering among the ashes, and breakfast laid for one person upon a little table by the fire—the remnant of a perigord pie, flanked by a stone bottle of curaçoa.

She looked at her brother with anxious scrutinising eyes. No, George Fairfax had not deceived her. He had the look of a man who was going the wrong way. There were premature lines across the forehead, and about the dark brilliant eyes; a nervous expression in the contracted lips. It was the face of a man who burns the candle of life at both ends. Late hours, anxiety, dissipation of all kinds, had set their fatal seal upon his countenance.

"Dear Austin, you are as handsome as ever; but I don't think you are looking well, " she said tenderly.

"Don't look so alarmed, my dear girl, " he answered lightly; "I am well enough; that is to say, I am never ill, never knock under, or strike work. There are men who go through life like that—never ill, and never exactly well. I rarely get up in the morning without a headache; but I generally brighten considerably as the sun goes down. We move with a contrary motion, Helios and I. "

"I am afraid you work too hard, and sit up too late. "

"As to working hard, my dear, that is a necessity; and going out every night is another necessity. I get my commissions in society. "

"But you must have a reputation by this time, Austin; and commissions would come to you, I should think, without your courting them. "

"No, child; I have only a reputation *de salon*, I am only known in a certain set. And a man must live, you see. To a man himself that is the primary necessity. Your *generosity* set me on my legs last year, and tempted me to take this floor, and make a slight advance movement altogether. I thought better rooms would bring me better work—sitters for a new style of cabinet-portraits, and so on. But so far the rooms have been comparatively a useless extravagance. However, I go out a good deal, and meet a great many influential people; so I can scarcely miss a success in the end. "

"But if you sacrifice your health in the meantime, Austin. "

"Sacrifice my health! That's just like a woman. If a man looks a trifle pale, and dark under the eyes, she begins to fancy he's dying. My poor little wife takes just the same notions into her head, and would like me to stop at home every evening to watch her darn the children's stockings. "

"I think your wife is quite right to be anxious, Austin; and it would be much better for you to stay at home, even to see stockings darned. It must be very dull for her too when you are out, poor soul. "

Mr. Lovel shrugged his shoulders with a deprecating air.

"*C'est son metier,* " he said. "I suppose she does find it rather dismal at times; but there are the children, you see—it is a woman's duty to find all-sufficient society in her children. And now, Clary, tell me about yourself. You have made a brilliant match, and are mistress of Arden Court. A strange stroke of fortune that. And you are happy, I hope, my dear? "

"I ought to be very happy, " Clarissa answered, with a faint sigh, thinking perhaps that, bright as her life might be, it was not quite the fulfilment of her vague girlish dreams—not quite the life she had fancied lying before her when the future was all unknown; "I ought to be very happy and very grateful to Providence; and, O Austin, my boy is the sweetest darling is the world! "

Austin Lovel looked doubtful for a moment, half inclined to think "my boy" might stand for Daniel Granger.

"You must see him, Austin, " continued his sister; "he is nearly ten months old now, and such a beauty! "

"O, the baby! " said Austin, rather coolly. "I daresay he's a nice little chap, and I should like to see him very much, if it were practicable. But how about Granger himself? He is a good sort of fellow, I hope. "

"He is all goodness to me, " Clarissa answered gravely, casting down her eyes as she spoke; and Austin Lovel knew that the marriage which had given his sister Arden Court had been no love-match.

They talked for some time; talked of the old days when they had been together at Arden; but of the years that made the story of his life, Austin Lovel spoke very little.

"I have always been an unlucky beggar, " he said, in his careless way. "There's very little use in going over old ground. Some men never get fairly on the high-road of life. They spend their existence wading across swamps, and scrambling through bushes, and never reach any particular point at the end. My career has been that sort of thing. "

"But you are so young, Austin, " pleaded Clarissa, "and may do so much yet. "

He shook his head with an air of hopelessness that was half indifference.

"My dear child, I am neither a Raffaelle nor a Dore, " he said, "and I need be one or the other to redeem my past But so long as I can pick up enough to keep the little woman yonder and the bairns, and get a decent cigar and an honest bottle of Bordeaux, I'm content. Ambition departed from me ten years ago. "

"O Austin, I can't bear to hear you say that! With your genius you ought to do so much. I wish you would be friends with my husband, and that he could be of use to you. "

"My dear Clarissa, put that idea out of your mind at once and for ever. There can be no such thing as friendship between Mr. Granger and me. Do you remember what Samuel Johnson said about some one's distaste for clean linen—'And I, sir, have no passion for it! ' I confess to having no passion for respectable people. I am very glad to hear Mr. Granger is a good husband; but he's much too respectable a citizen for my acquaintance. "

Clarissa sighed; there was a prejudice here, even if Daniel Granger could have been induced to think kindly of his brother-in-law.

"Depend upon it, the Prodigal Son had a hard time of it after the fatted calf had been eaten, Clary, and wished himself back among the swine. Do you think, however lenient his father might be, that his brother and the friends of the family spared him? His past was thrown in his face, you may be sure. I daresay he went back to his evil ways after a year or so. Good people maintain their monopoly of virtue by making the repentant sinner's life a burden to him. "

Clarissa spoke of his wife presently.

"You must introduce me to her, Austin. She took me for a stranger just now, and I did not undeceive her. "

"Yes I'll introduce you. There's not much in common between you; but she'll be very proud of your acquaintance. She looks upon my relations as an exalted race of beings, and myself as a kind of fallen angel. You mustn't be too hard upon her, Clary, if she seems not quite the sort of woman you would have chosen for your sister-in-law. She has been a good wife to me, and she was a good daughter to her drunken old father—one of the greatest scamps in London, who used to get his bread—or rather his gin—by standing for Count Ugolino and Cardinal Wolsey, or anything grim and gray and aquiline-nosed in the way of patriarchs. The girl Bessie was a model too in her time; and it was in Jack Redgrave's painting-room—the pre-Raphaelite fellow who paints fearfully and wonderfully made women with red hair and angular arms—I first met her. Jack and I were great chums at that time—it was just after I sold out—and I used to paint at his rooms. I was going in for painting just then with a great spurt, having nothing but my brush to live upon. You can guess the rest. As Bessie was a very pretty girl, and neither she nor I had a sixpence wherewith to bless ourselves, of course we fell in love with each other. Poor little thing, how pretty she used to look in those days, standing on Jack's movable platform, with her hair falling loose about her face, and a heap of primroses held up in her petticoat! —such a patient plaintive look in the sweet little mouth, as much as to say, 'I'm very tired of standing here; but I'm only a model, to be hired for eighteenpence an hour; go on smoking your cigars, and talking your slangy talk about the turf and the theatres, gentlemen. I count for nothing. ' Poor little patient soul! she was so helpless and so friendless, Clary. I think my love for her was something like the compassion one feels for some young feeble bird that has fallen out of its nest. So we were married one morning; and for some time lived in lodgings at Putney, where I used to suffer considerable affliction from Count Ugolino and two bony boys, Bessie's brothers, who looked as if the Count had been acting up to his character with too great a fidelity. Ugolino himself would come prowling out of a Saturday afternoon to borrow the wherewithal to pay his week's lodging, lest he should be cast out into the streets at nightfall; and it was a common thing for one of the bony boys to appear at breakfast-time with a duplicate of his father's coat, pledged over-night for drink, and without the means of redeeming which he could not pursue his honourable vocation. In short, I think it was as much the affliction of the Ugolino family as my own entanglements that drove me to seek my fortunes on the other side of the world. "

Austin Lovel opened one of the doors, and called his wife "Come here, Bessie; I've a pleasant surprise for you. "

Mrs. Lovel appeared quickly in answer to this summons. She had changed her morning dress for a purple silk, which was smartly trimmed, but by no means fresh, and she had dressed her hair, and refreshed her complexion by a liberal application of violet powder. She had a look which can only be described as "flashy" —a look that struck Clarissa unpleasantly, in spite of herself.

Her expressions of surprise did not sound quite so natural as they might have done—for she had been listening at the folding-doors during a considerable part of the interview; but she seemed really delighted by Mrs. Granger's condescension, and she kissed that lady with much affection.

"I'm sure I do feel proud to know any relation of Austin's, " she said, "and you most of all, who have been so kind to him. Heaven knows what would have become of us last winter, if it hadn't been for your generosity. "

Clarissa laid her hand upon Bessie Lovel's lips.

"You mustn't talk of generosity between my brother and me, " she said; "all I have in the world is at his service. And now let me see my nephews, please; and then I must run away. "

The nephews were produced; the boy Clarissa had seen, and another of smaller growth—pale-faced, bright-eyed little fellows; They too had been subjected to the infliction of soap-and-water and hair-brushes, clean pinafores, and so on, since Mrs. Granger's arrival.

She knelt down and kissed them both, with real motherly tenderness, thinking of her own darling, and the difference between his fortunes and theirs; and then, after a warm caress, she slipped a napoleon into each little warm hand, "to buy toys, " and rose to depart.

"I must hurry away now, Austin, " she said; "but I shall come again very soon, if I may. Good-bye, dear, and God bless you. "

The embrace that followed was a very fervent one. It had been sweet to meet again after so many years, and it was hard to leave him so soon—to leave him with the conviction that his life was a wreck. But Clarissa had no time to linger. The thought of the baby in the Luxembourg Gardens had been distracting her for ever so long. These stolen meetings must needs be short.

She looked at her watch when she got back to the street, and found, to her horror, that she had been very nearly an hour away from the nurse and her charge. The carriage was waiting at the gate, and she had to encounter the full fire of her servants' gaze as she crossed the road and went into the gardens. Yes, there was the baby's blue-velvet pelisse resplendent at the end of an avenue, Clarissa walked quickly to meet him.

"My darling! " she cried. "Has he been waiting for his mamma? I hope he has not been tired of the gardens, nurse? "

"Yes, ma'am, he have been tired, " replied Mrs. Brobson, with an outraged air. "There ain't much in these gardens to keep a baby of his age amused for an hour at a stretch; and in a east wind too! It's right down cutting at that corner. "

"Why didn't you take him home in the carriage, nurse? It would have been better than running any risk of his catching cold. "

"What, and leave you without a conveyance, ma'am? I couldn't have done that! "

"I was detained longer than I expected to stay. O, by the bye, you need not mention to Miss Granger that I have been making a call. The people I have been to see are—are in humble circumstances; and I don't want her to know anything about it. "

"I hope I know my duty, ma'am, " replied Mrs. Brobson stiffly. That hour's parading in the gardens, without any relief from her subordinate, had soured her temper, and inclined her to look with unfavourable eyes upon the conduct of her mistress. Clarissa felt that she had excited the suspicion of her servant, and that all her future meetings with her brother would involve as much plotting and planning as would serve for the ripening of a political conspiracy.

* * * * *

CHAPTER XXXIII.

ONLY A PORTRAIT-PAINTER.

While Clarissa was pondering on that perplexing question, how she was to see her brother frequently without Mr. Granger's knowledge, fortune had favoured her in a manner she had never anticipated. After what Mr. Fairfax had said to her about Austin Lovel's "set, " the last thing she expected was to meet her brother in society—that fast Bohemian world in which she supposed him to exist, seemed utterly remote from the faultless circle of Daniel Granger's acquaintance. It happened, however, that one of the dearest friends to whom Lady Laura Armstrong had introduced her sweet Clarissa was a lady of the Leo-Hunter genus—a certain Madame Caballero, *née* Bondichori, a little elderly Frenchwoman, with sparkling black eyes and inexhaustible vivacity; the widow of a Portuguese wine-merchant; a lady whose fortune enabled her to occupy a first floor in one of the freestone palaces of the Champs Elysées, to wear black velvet and diamonds in perpetuity, and to receive a herd of small lions and a flock of admiring nobodies twice a-week. The little widow prided herself on her worship of genius. All members of the lion tribe came alike to her: painters, sculptors, singers; actors, and performers upon every variety of known and unknown musical instruments; budding barristers, who had won forensic laurels by the eloquent defence of some notorious criminal; homoeopathic doctors, lady doctresses, or lawyeresses, or deaconesses, from America; and pretty women who had won a kind of renown by something special in the way of eyebrows, or arms, or shoulders.

To these crowded saloons Mr. Granger brought his wife and daughter one evening. They found a great many people assembled in three lofty rooms, hung with amber satin, in the remotest and smallest of which apartments Madame Caballero made tea *à l'anglaise*, for her intimates; while, in the largest, some fearful and wonderful instrumental music was going on, with the very smallest possible amount of attention from the audience. There was a perpetual buzz of conversation; and there was a considerable sprinkling of curious-looking people; weird men with long unkempt hair, strong-minded women, who counterbalanced these in a manner by wearing their hair preternaturally short. Altogether, the assembly was an usual one; but Madame Caballero's guests seemed to enjoy themselves very much. Their good spirits may have been partly due

330

to the fact that they had the pleasing anticipation of an excellent supper, furnished with all the choicest dainties that Chevet can provide; for Madame Caballero's receptions were of a substantial order, and she owed a good deal of her popularity to the profusion that distinguished the commissariat department.

Mr. and Mrs. Granger made their way to the inner room by and by. It was the prettiest room of the three, with a great semi-circular window overlooking nothing particular in the daytime, but making a handsome amber-hung recess at night. Here there was a sea-coal fire *à l'anglaise*, and only a subdued glimmering of wax candles, instead of the broad glare in the larger saloons. Here, too were to be found the choicest of Madame Caballero's guests; a cabinet minister, an ambassador, a poet of some standing, and one of the most distinguished soprano's of the season, a fair-haired German girl, with great pathetic blue eyes.

Even in this society Madame Caballero was rejoiced to see her sweet Mrs. Granger and her charming Miss Granger, who was looking unutterably stiff, in mauve silk and white lace. The lady and her friends had been talking of some one as the Grangers entered, talking rapturously.

"*J'en raffole!* " exclaimed Madame; "such a charming young man, gifted with talents of the most original order. "

The ambassador was looking at a portrait — the likeness of Madame Caballero herself — a mere sketch in oils, with a mark of the brush upon it, but remarkable for the *chic* and daring of the painter's style, and for that idealised resemblance which is always so agreeable to the subject.

Clarissa's heart gave a little throb. The picture was like one she had seen on the easel in the Rue du Chevalier Bayard.

"*Mais c'est charmant!* " exclaimed the ambassador; and the adjective was echoed in every key by the rest of the little coterie.

"I expect him here this evening, " said Madame; "and I shall be very much gratified if you will permit me to present him to your excellency. "

The ambassador bowed. "Any *protégée* of Madame's, " he said, and so on.

Mr. Granger, who was really a judge of art, fastened on to the picture immediately.

"There's something fresh in the style, Clary, " he said. "I should like this man to paint your portrait. What's the signature? Austin! That's hardly a French name, I should think—eh, Madame Caballero? "

"No, " replied Madame; "Mr. Austin is an Englishman. I shall be charmed if you will allow him to paint Mrs. Granger; and I'm sure he will be delighted to have such a subject. "

There was a good deal of talk about Mr. Austin's painting, and art in general. There were some half dozen pictures of the modern French school in this inner room, which helped to sustain the conversation. Mr. Granger talked very fair French, of a soundly grammatical order; and Clarissa's tongue ran almost as gaily as in her schoolgirl days at Belforêt. She was going to see her brother—to see him shining in good society, and not in the pernicious "set" of which George Fairfax had spoken. The thought was rapture to her. They might have a few minutes' talk to themselves, perhaps, before the evening was over. That interview in the Rue du Chevalier Bayard had been so sadly brief, and her heart too full for many words.

Austin Lovel came in presently, looking his handsomest, in his careful evening-dress, with a brilliant light in his eyes, and that appearance of false brightness which is apt to distinguish the man who is burning the candle of life at both ends. Only by just the faintest elevation of his eyebrows did he betray his surprise as he looked at his sister; and his air, on being presented to her a few moments afterwards, was perfect in its serene unconsciousness.

Mr. Granger talked to him of his picture pleasantly enough, but very much as he would have talked to his architect, or to one of his clerks in the great Bradford establishment. There was a marked difference between the tone of the rich English trader and the German ambassador, when he expressed himself on the subject of Mr. Austin's talent; but then the Englishman intended to give the painter a commission, and the German did not.

"I should like you to paint my wife—and—and—my daughter, " said Mr. Granger, throwing in Sophia as an after-thought. It would be only civil to have his daughter's portrait painted, he thought.

Mr. Austin bowed. "I shall be most happy, " he said. Clarissa's eyes sparkled with delight. Sophia Granger saw the pleased look, and thought, "O, the vanity of these children of perdition! " But she did not offer any objection to the painting of her own likeness.

"When shall we begin? " asked Mr. Granger.

"My time is entirely at your disposal. "

"In that case, the sooner the thing is done the better. My wife cannot come to your studio—she has so many claims upon her time—but that would make no difficulty, I suppose? "

"Not at all. I can paint Mrs. Granger in her own rooms as well as in mine, if the light will serve. "

"One of our drawing-rooms faces the north, " answered Mr. Granger, "and the windows are large—larger than I like. Any loss of time which you may suffer in accommodating Mrs. Granger must, of course, be considered in the price of your pictures. "

"I have only one price for my pictures, " replied Mr. Austin, with a loftiness that astonished his patron. "I charge fifty guineas for a portrait of that kind—whether it is painted for a duke or a grocer in the Rue St. Honoré. "

"I will give you a hundred guineas for each of the pictures, if they are successes, " said Mr. Granger. "If they are failures, I will give you your own price, and make you a present of the canvasses. "

"I am not a stoic, and have no objection to accept a premium of a hundred guineas from so distinguished a capitalist as Mr. Granger, " returned Austin Lovel, smiling. "I don't think Mrs. Granger's portrait will be a failure, " he added confidently, with a little look at Clarissa.

Sophia Granger saw the look, and resented it. The painter had said nothing of her portrait. It was of Clarissa's only that he thought. It was a very small thing; but when her father's wife was concerned, small things were great in the eyes of Miss Granger.

There was no opportunity for confidential talk between Austin Lovel and his sister that evening; but Clarissa went home happy in the expectation of seeing her brother very often in the simplest, easiest way. The portraits would take some time to paint, of course; indeed Austin might make the business last almost as long as he liked.

It was rather hard, however, to have to discuss her brother's merits with Mr. and Miss Granger as if he had been a stranger; and Clarissa had to do this going home in the carriage that night, and at breakfast next morning. The young man was handsome, Mr. Granger remarked, but had rather a worn look—a dissipated look, in point of fact. That sort of people generally were dissipated.

Mrs. Granger ventured to say that she did not think Mr. Austin looked dissipated—a little worn, perhaps, but nothing more; and that might be the effect of hard work.

"My dear Clary, what can you know of the physiology of dissipation? I tell you that young man is dissipated. I saw him playing *écarté* with a Frenchman just before we left Madame Caballero's; and, unless I am profoundly mistaken, the man is a gambler. "

Clarissa shuddered. She could not forget what George Fairfax had said to her about her brother's ways, nor the fact that her remittances had seemed of so little use to him. He seemed in good repute too, and talked of fifty guineas for a picture with the utmost coolness. He must have earned a good deal of money, and the money must have gone somewhere. In all the details of his home there was evidence of extravagance in the past and poverty in the present.

He came at eleven o'clock on the second morning after Madame Caballero's reception; came in a hired carriage, with his easel and all the paraphernalia of his art. Mr. Granger had made a point of being present at this first sitting, much to the discomfiture of Clarissa, who was yearning for a long uninterrupted talk with her brother. Even when Mr. Granger was absent, there would be Miss Granger, most likely, she thought, with vexation; and, after all, these meetings with Austin would be only half meetings. It would be pleasant only to see him, to hear his voice; but she was longing to talk freely of the past, to give him counsel for the future.

The drawing-room looking north was rather a dreary apartment, if any apartment furnished with blue-satin damask and unlimited gilding can be called dreary. There was splendour, of course, but it was a chilling kind of splendour. The room was large and square, with two tall wide windows commanding a view of one of the dullest streets in new Paris—a street at the end of which workmen were still busy cutting away a hill, the removal whereof was necessary for the realisation of the Augustan idea of that archetypal city, which was to be left all marble. Mr. Granger's apartments were in a corner house, and he had the advantage of this side view. There was very little of what Mr. Wemmick called "portable property" in this northern drawing-room. There were blue-satin divans running along the walls, a couple of blue-satin easy-chairs, an ormolu stand with a monster Sèvres dish for cards, and that was all—a room in which one might, "receive," but could scarcely live.

The light was capital, Mr. Austin said. He set up his easel, settled the position of his sister, after a little discussion with Mr. Granger, and began work. Clarissa's was to be the first portrait. This being arranged, Mr. Granger departed to write letters, leaving Sophia established, with her Berlin-wool work, at one of the windows. Clarissa would not, of course, like to be left tête-à-tête for two or three hours with a strange painter, Miss Granger opened.

Yes, it was very pleasant to have him there, even though their talk was restrained by the presence of a third person, and they could only speak of indifferent things. Perhaps to Austin Lovel himself it was pleasanter to have Miss Granger there than to be quite alone with his sister. He was very fond of Clarissa, but there was much in his past life—some things in his present life even—that would not bear talking of, and he shrank a little from his sister's tender questioning. Protected by Miss Granger and her Berlin-wool spaniels, he was quite at his ease, and ran gaily on about all manner of things as he sketched his outline and set his palette. He gave the two ladies a lively picture of existing French art, with little satirical touches here and there. Even Sophia was amused, and blushed to find herself comparing the social graces of Mr. Austin the painter with those of Mr. Tillott the curate, very much to the advantage of the former— blushed to find herself so much interested in any conversation that was not strictly utilitarian or evangelical in its drift. Once or twice

Austin spoke of his travels, his Australian experiences; and at each mention, Clarissa looked up eagerly, anxious to hear more. The history of her brother's past was a blank to her, and she was keenly interested by the slightest allusion that cast a ray of light upon it. Mr. Austin did not care, however, to dwell much upon his own affairs. It was chiefly of other people that he talked. Throughout that first sitting Miss Granger maintained a dignified formality, tempered by maidenly graciousness. The young man was amusing, certainly, and it was not often Miss Granger permitted herself to be amused. She thought Clarissa was too familiar with him, treated him too much with an air of perfect equality. A man who painted portraits for hire should be received, Miss Granger thought, as one would receive a superior kind of bootmaker.

More than once, in fact, in the course of that agreeable morning, Clarissa had for a moment forgotten that she was talking to Mr. Austin the painter, and not to her brother Austin Lovel. More than once an unconscious warmth or softness in her tone had made Miss Granger look up from her embroidery-frame with the eyes of wonder.

Mr. Granger came back to the drawing-room, having finished his letter-writing just as the sitting concluded, and, luncheon being announced at the same time, asked Mr. Austin to stay for that meal. Austin had no objection to linger in his sister's society. He wanted to know what kind of man this Daniel Granger was; and perhaps wanted to see what probability there was of Daniel Granger's wife being able to supply him with money in the future. Austin Lovel had, from his earliest boyhood, possessed a fatal capacity for getting rid of money, and for getting into debt; not common plain-sailing debt, which would lead at the worst to the Bankruptcy Court, but liability of a more disreputable and perilous character, involving the terror of disgrace, and entanglements that would have to be unravelled by a police-magistrate.

Racing debts, gambling debts, and bill-discounting transactions, had been the agreeable variety of difficulties which had beset Austin Level's military career; and at the end there had been something— something fully known to a few only—which had made the immediate sale of his commission a necessity. He was *allowed* to sell it; and that was much, his friends said. If his commanding officer had not been an easy-going kind of man, he would scarcely have got off so cheaply.

"I wonder how this fellow Granger would treat me, if he knew who I was? " he thought to himself. "He'd inaugurate our acquaintance by kicking me out of his house most likely, instead of asking me to luncheon. " Notwithstanding which opinion Mr. Austin sat down to share the sacred bread and salt with his brother-in-law, and ate a cutlet *a la Maintenon*, and drank half a bottle of claret, with a perfect enjoyment of the situation. He liked the idea of being patronised by the man who would not have tolerated his society for a moment, had he been aware of his identity.

He talked of Parisian life during luncheon, keeping carefully clear of all subjects which the "young person, " as represented by Miss Granger, might blush to hear; and Mr. Granger, who had only an Englishman's knowledge of the city, was amused by the pleasant gossip. The meal lasted longer than usual, and lost all its wonted formality; and the fair Sophia found herself more and more interested in this fascinating painter, with his brilliant dark eyes, and sarcastic mouth, and generally agreeable manner. She sat next him at luncheon, and, when there came a little pause in the conversation, began to question him about the state of the Parisian poor. It was very bad, was it not?

Mr. Austin shrugged his shoulders.

"I don't know, " he said, "but I don't think it would be possible for a man to starve to death in Paris under the Imperial regime; and it seems very easy for an Englishman to do it in Spitalfields or Mile-end New Town. You don't hear of men and women found dead in their garrets from sheer hunger. But of course there is a good deal of poverty and squalor to be found in the city. "

And then Mr. Austin launched into a graphic description of some interesting phases of life among the lower classes, borrowed from a novel that had been recently delighting the reading public of France, but appropriated with such an air of reality, that Miss Granger fancied this delightful painter must spend some considerable part of his existence as a district visitor or city missionary.

"What a pity that Mr. Tillott has not his persuasive powers! " she thought; Mr. Tillott's eloquence being, in fact, of a very limited order, chiefly exhibiting itself in little jerky questions about the spiritual and temporal welfare of his humble parishioners—

questions which, in the vernacular language of agricultural labourers, "put a chap's back up, somehow. "

"I should like to show Mr. Austin the baby, Daniel, " Clarissa said to her husband shyly, while Miss Granger was keeping Austin hard and fast to the amelioration of the working classes; "he would make such a lovely picture. "

Mr. Granger smiled, a quiet well-satisfied smile. He, the strong man, the millowner and millionaire, was as weak as the weakest woman in all things concerning the child of his mature age.

"Yes, " he said, with some affectation of indifference; "Lovel would make a nice picture enough. We'll have him painted if you like, Clary, some day. Send for him, my dear. "

She had her hand upon the bell directly.

"Yes, " she cried, "he would make the sweetest picture in the world, and Austin shall paint him. "

The familiar mention of the name Austin, *tout court*, scared Mr. Granger almost as much as a cannon fired close at his elbow might have done. He stared at his wife with grave displeasure.

"*Mr.* Austin can paint him some day, if you wish it, Clarissa, " he said.

Mrs. Granger blushed crimson; again she remembered that this brother she loved so dearly was only a strange painter of portraits, whom it behoved her to treat with only the most formal courtesy. She hated the deception; and having a strong faith in her husband's generosity, was sorely tempted to put an end to this acted lie on the spot, and to tell him who his guest was; but fear of her brother's anger stopped her. She had no right to betray him; she must wait his permission to tell the secret.

"Even Sophia seems to like him, " she thought; "and I don't think Daniel could help being pleased with him, in spite of anything papa may have said to his prejudice. "

The baby was brought, and, being in a benignant humour, was graciously pleased to look his brightest and prettiest, and in nurse's phraseology, to "take to" his unknown uncle. The unknown uncle kissed him affectionately, and said some civil things about the colour of his eyes, and the plumpness of his limbs — "quite a Rubens baby, " and so on, but did not consider a boy-baby an especially wonderful creature, having had two boy-babies of his own, and not having particularly wanted them. He looked upon them rather as chronic perplexities, like accommodation bills that had matured unawares.

"And this is the heir of Arden, " he said to himself, as he looked down at the fat blue-eyed thing struggling in Clarissa's arms, with that desperate desire to get nowhere in particular, common to infancy. "So this little lump of humanity is the future lord of the home that should have been mine. I don't know that I envy him. Country life and Arden would hardly have suited me. I think I'd rather have an *entresol* in the Champs Elysees, and the run of the boulevards, than the gray old Court and a respectable position. Unless a man's tastes are 'horsey' or agricultural, country life must be a bore. "

Mr. Austin patted the plump young cheeks without any feeling of enmity.

"Poor little beggar! What ghosts will haunt him in the old rooms by-and-by, I wonder? " he said to himself, smiling down at the child.

* * * * *

CHAPTER XXXIV.

AUSTIN'S PROSPECTS.

The picture made rapid progress. For his very life—though the finishing of his work had been the signal of his doom, and the executioner waiting to make a sudden end of him when the last touch was laid upon the canvas, Austin Lovel could not have painted slowly. The dashing offhand brush was like a young thoroughbred, that could not be pulled, let the jockey saw at his mouth as he might. And yet the painter would have liked much to prolong this easy intercourse with his sister. But after Clarissa's portrait was finished, there was Miss Granger to be painted; and then they would want a picture of that unapproachable baby, no doubt; and after that, perhaps, Mr. Granger might consent to have his massive features perpetuated. Austin considered that the millionaire should be good for three hundred guineas or so; he had promised two hundred, and the painter was spending the money by anticipation as fast as he could.

He came every other morning to the Rue de Morny, and generally stayed to luncheon; and those mornings spent in his company were very pleasant to Clarissa—as pleasant as anything could be which involved deception; there was always the sting of that fact. Miss Granger was rarely absent for ten minutes together on these occasions; it was only some lucky chance which took her from the room to fetch some Berlin wool, or a forgotten skein of floss silk for the perennial spaniels, and afforded the brother and sister an opportunity for a few hurried words. The model villagers almost faded out of Miss Granger's mind in this agreeable society. She found herself listening to talk about things which were of the earth earthy, and was fain to confess herself interested in the conversation. She dressed as carefully to receive the painter as if he had been, to use her particular phraseology, "a person in her own sphere; " and Mr. Tillott would have thought his chances of success at a very low point, if he could have seen her in Austin Lovel's presence.

That gentleman himself was not slow to perceive the impression he had made.

"It's rather a pity I'm married, isn't it, Clary? " he said to his sister one day, when Sophia, whose habits had not been quite so methodical of late, had gone in search of some white beads for the spaniels, some of which were of a beady nature. "It would have been a great chance for me, wouldn't it? "

What do you mean, Austin? "

"Miss Granger, " answered the painter, without looking up from his work, "I think she rather likes me, do you know; and I suppose her father will give her fifty thousand or so when she marries, in spite of young Lovel. He seems to have no end of money. It would have been an uncommonly good thing, wouldn't it? "

"I don't think it's any use talking of it, Austin, however good it might have been; and I don't think Sophia would have suited you as a wife. "

"Not suited me—bosh! Any woman with fifty thousand pounds would have suited me. However, you're right—there's no good in talking of *that*. I'm booked. Poor little woman, she's a good wife to me; but it's rather a pity. You don't know how many chances I might have had but for that entanglement. "

"I wish, Austin, for your poor wife's sake, you'd let me tell my husband who you are. This concealment seems so hard upon her, as well as a kind of wrong to Daniel. I can do so little to serve her, and I might do so much, if I could own her as my sister-in-law. I don't think Daniel could help liking you, if he knew everything. "

"Drop that, if you please, Clarissa, " said Austin, with a darkening countenance. "I have told you that your husband and I can never be friends, and I mean it. I don't want to be degraded by any intercession of yours. *That's* a little too much even for me. It suits my purpose well enough to accept Mr. Granger's commissions; and of course it's very agreeable to see you; but the matter must end there. "

Miss Granger returned at this moment; but had she stayed away for an hour, Clarissa could scarcely have pressed the question farther. In the old days when they had been boy and girl together, Austin seven years her senior, Clarissa had always been just a little afraid of her brother; and she was afraid of him now.

The very fact of his somewhat dependent position made her more fearful of offending him. She was anxious about his future anxious too about his present mode of life; but she dared not question closely upon either subject. Once, when she had ventured to ask him about his plan of life, he answered in his careless off-hand way, —

"My dearest Clary, I have no plans. I like Paris; and if I am not particularly successful here, I don't suppose I should be more successful anywhere else. I mean to stay here as long as I can hold out. I know a good many people, and sometimes get a stroke of luck. "

"But you are ruining your health. Austin, I fear, with—late hours, and—and—parties. "

"Who told you I keep late hours? The Parisians, as a rule, don't go to bed at curfew. I don't suppose I'm worse than my neighbours. If I didn't go out, Clary, and keep myself in the minds of my patrons, I might rot in a garret. You don't know how soon a man is forgotten— even a man who has made his mark more positively than I have; and then you see, my dear, I like society, and have no taste for the domestic hearth, except for variety, once in a way, like dining on a bouillon after a week's high feeding. Yes, come what may, I shall stay in Paris—as long as I can. "

There was something in the tone of the last words that alarmed Clarissa.

"You—you—are not in debt, are you, Austin? " she asked timidly.

"No—no—I'm not in debt; but I owe a good deal of money. "

Clarissa looked puzzled.

"That is to say, I have no vulgar debts—butcher and baker, and so on; but there are two or three things, involving some hundreds, which I shall have to settle some of these days or else— —"

"Or else what, Austin? "

"Cut Paris, Clary, that's all. "

Clarissa turned pale. Austin began to whistle a popular *café-chantant* air, as he bent over his palette, squeezing little dabs of Naples yellow out of a leaden tube. Some hundreds! —that was a vague phrase, which might mean a great deal of money; it was a phrase which alarmed Clarissa; but she was much more alarmed by the recklessness of her brother's tone.

"But if you owe money, you must pay it, Austin, " she said; "you can't leave a place owing money. "

The painter shrugged his shoulders.

"It's not an agreeable thing to do, " he said, "but it has been done. Of the two, it's pleasanter than staying in a place where you owe money. "

"Of course I shall do all I can to help you, dear, " said his sister. "There will be a hundred and twenty-five pounds due to me at Christmas, and I'll give you the hundred. "

"You're a first-rate girl, Clary, but I think that fellow Granger might give you more pin-money. Five hundred a year is a beggarly pittance for a man of his means. "

"It is more than I fancied I could ever want; and Daniel allows papa five hundred a year, you know Austin. "

"Humph! that makes a thousand—no great things for a millionaire. A pretty girl, married to a man of that stamp, ought to have unlimited command of money, " replied her brother. "It's the only compensation, " he said to himself afterwards.

"I don't like to hear you say these things, Austin. My husband is very kind to me. I'm afraid I'm not half as grateful as I ought to be. "

"Gratitude be——! " He did not finish the ejaculation.

"Gratitude from a Lovel of twenty to a Granger of fifty! My dear Clary, that's too good a joke! The man is well enough—better than I expected to find him: but such a girl as you is a prize for which such a man could not pay too highly. "

It was rarely they had the opportunity for so long a conversation as this; and Austin was by no means sorry that it was so. He had very pressing need of all the money his sister could give him; but he did not care to enter into explanations about the state of his affairs.

* * * * *

CHAPTER XXXV.

SISTERS-IN-LAW.

Clarissa did not forget the existence of the poor little wife in the Rue du Chevalier Bayard; and on the very first afternoon which she had to herself, Mr. Granger having gone to see some great cattle-fair a few miles from Paris, and Miss Granger being afflicted with a headache, she took courage to order her coachman to drive straight to the house where her brother lived.

"It is much better than making a mystery of it, " she thought.

"The man will think that I have come to see a milliner or some one of that kind. "

The footman would fain have escorted Mrs. Granger the way she should go, and held himself in readiness to accompany her into the house; but she waved him aside on the threshold of the darksome *porte-cochère*, out of which no coach ever came nowadays.

"I shan't want you, Trotter, " she said. "Tell Jarvis to walk the horses gently up and down. I shall not be very long. "

The man bowed and obeyed, wondering what business his mistress could have in such a dingy street, "on the Surrey side of the water, too, " as he said to his comrade.

Austin was out, but Mrs. Lovel was at home, and it was Mrs. Lovel whom Clarissa had come chiefly to see. The same tawdrily-dressed maid admitted her to the same untidy sitting-room, a shade more untidy to-day, where Bessie Lovel was dozing in an easy-chair by the fire, while the two boys played and squabbled in one of the windows.

Mrs. Granger, entering suddenly, radiant in golden-brown moiré and sables, seemed almost to dazzle the eyes of Austin's wife, who had not seen much of the brighter side of existence Her life before her marriage had been altogether sordid and shabby, brightness or luxury of any kind for her class being synonymous with vice; and Bessie Stanford the painter's model had never been vicious. Her life since her marriage had been a life of trouble and difficulty, with only occasional glimpses of spurious kind of brilliancy. She lived outside her husband's existence, as it were, and felt somehow that she was only attached to him by external links, as a dog might have been. He had a certain kind of affection for her, was conscious of her fidelity, and grateful for her attachment; and there an end. Sympathy between them there was none; nor had he ever troubled himself to cultivate her tastes, or attempted in the smallest degree to bring her nearer to him. To Bessie Lovel, therefore, this sister of her husband's, in all the glory of her fresh young beauty and sumptuous apparel, seemed a creature of another sphere, something to be gazed upon almost in fear and trembling.

"I beg your parding! " she faltered, rubbing her eyes. She was apt, when agitated, to fall back upon the pronunciation of her girlhood, before Austin Lovel had winced and ejaculated at her various mutilations of the language. "I was just taking forty winks after my bit of dinner. "

"I am so sorry I disturbed you, " said Clarissa, in her gracious way. "You were tired, I daresay. "

"O, pray don't mention it! I'm sure I feel it a great compliment your comin'. It must seem a poor place to you after your beautiful house in the Roo de Morny. Austin told me where you lived; and I took the liberty of walking that way one evening with a lady friend. I'm sure the houses are perfect palaces. "

"I wish you could come to my house as my sister-in-law ought, " replied Clarissa. "I wanted to confide in my husband, to bring about a friendship between him and my brother, if I could; but Austin tells me that is impossible. I suppose he knows best. So, you see, I am obliged to act in this underhand way, and to come to see you by stealth, as it were. "

"It's very good of you to come at all, " answered the wife with a sigh. "It isn't many of Austin's friends take any notice of me. I'm sure most of 'em treat me as if I was a cipher. Not that I mind that, provided he could get on; but it's dinners there, and suppers here, and never no orders for pictures, as you may say. He had next to nothing to do all the autumn; Paris being so dull, you know, with all the high people away at the sea. He painted Madame Caballero for nothing, just to get himself talked of among her set; and if it wasn't for Mr. Granger's orders, I don't know where we should be. —Come and speak to your aunt, Henery and Arthur, like good boys. "

This to the olive-branches in the window, struggling for the possession of a battered tin railway-engine with a crooked chimney.

"She ain't my aunt, " cried the eldest hope. "I haven't got no aunt. "

"Yes, this is your aunt Clarissa. You've heard papa talk of her. "

"Yes, I remember, " said the boy sharply. "I remember one night when he talked of Arden Court and Clarissa, and thumped his forehead on the mantelpiece like that; " and the boy pantomimed the action of despair.

"He has fits of that kind sometimes, " said Bessie Lovel, "and goes on about having wasted his life, and thrown away his chances, and all that. He used to go on dreadful when we were in Australia, till he made me that nervous I didn't know what to do, thinking he'd go and destroy himself some day. But he's been better since we've been in Paris. The gaiety suits him. He says he can't live without society. "

Clarissa sighed. Little as she knew of her brother's life, she knew enough to be very sure that love of society had been among the chief causes of his ruin. She took one of her nephews on her lap, and talked to him, and let him play with the trinkets on her chain. Both the children were bright and intelligent enough, but had that air of premature sharpness which comes from constant intercourse with grown-up people, and an early initiation in the difficulties of existence.

She could only stay half an hour with her sister-in-law; but she could see that her visit of duty had gratified the poor little neglected wife. She had not come empty-handed, but had brought an offering for Bessie Lovel which made the tired eyes brighten with something of their old light—a large oval locket of massive dead gold, with a maltese cross of small diamonds upon it; one of the simplest ornaments which Daniel Granger had given her, and which she fancied herself justified in parting with. She had taken it to a jeweller in the Palais Royal, who had arranged a lock of her dark-brown hair, with a true-lover's knot of brilliants, inside the locket, and had engraved the words "From Clarissa" on the back.

Mrs. Lovel clasped her hands in rapture as Clarissa opened the morocco case and showed her this jewel.

"For me! " she cried. "I never had anything half as beautiful in my life. And your 'air, too! " She said "'air" in her excitement. "How good of you to give it to me! I don't know how to thank you. "

And the poor little woman made a rapid mental review of her wardrobe, wondering if she had any gown good enough to wear with that splendid jewel. Her purple silk—the one silk dress she possessed—was a little shiny and shabby by daylight, but looked very well by candle-light still, she thought. She was really delighted with the locket. In all her life she had had so few presents; and this one gift was worth three times the sum of them. But Clarissa spoke of it in the lightest, most careless way.

"I wanted to bring you some little souvenir, " she said, "and I thought you might like this. And now I must say good-bye, Bessie. I may call you Bessie, mayn't I? And remember, you must call me Clarissa. I am sorry I am obliged to hurry away like this; but I expect Mr. Granger back rather early, and I want to be at home when he returns. Good-bye, dear! "

She kissed her brother's wife, who clung to her affectionately, touched by her kindness; kissed the two little nephews also, one of whom caught hold of her dress and said, —

"You gave me that money for toys the other day, didn't you, aunt Clarissa? "

"Yes, darling. "

"But I didn't have it to spend, though. Pa said he'd lay it out for me; and he brought me home a cart from the Boulevard; but it didn't cost two napoleons. It was a trumpery cart, that went smash the first time Arthur and I stood in it. "

"You shouldn't stand in a toy-cart, dear. I'll bring you some toys the next time I come to see mamma. "

They were out on the landing by this time. Clarissa disengaged herself from the little fellow, and went quickly down the darksome staircase.

"Will that be soon? " the boy called over the banisters.

"I do hope I shall be able to keep it, " said Bessie Lovel presently, as she stood in the window gloating over her locket; whereby it will be seen that Austin's wife did not feel so secure as she might have done in the possession of her treasure.

* * * * *

CHAPTER XXXVI.

"AND THROUGH THY LIFE HAVE I NOT WRIT MY NAME? "

Mid-Winter had come, and the pleasures and splendours of Paris were at their apogee. The city was at its gayest—that beautiful city, which we can never see again as we have seen it; which we lament, as some fair and radiant creature that has come to an untimely death. Paris the beautiful, Paris the beloved, imperial Paris, with her air of classic splendour, like the mistress of a Caesar, was in these days overshadowed by no threatening thundercloud, forerunner of the tempest and earthquake to come. The winter season had begun; and all those wanderers who had been basking through the autumn under the blue skies that roof the Pyrenees, or dawdling away existence in German gambling-saloons, or climbing Alpine peaks, or paddling down the Danube, flocked back to the central city of civilization in time to assist at Patti's reappearance in the Rue Lepelletier, or to applaud a new play of Sardou's at the Gymnase.

Amongst this flock of returning pilgrims came George Fairfax, very much the worse for two or three months spent in restless meanderings between Baden and Hombourg, with the consciousness of a large income at his disposal, and a certain reckless indifference as to which way his life drifted, that had grown upon him of late years.

He met Mr. and Mrs. Granger within twenty-four hours of his arrival in Paris, at a ball at the British embassy—the inaugural fête of the season, as it were, to which the master of Arden Court, by right of his wealth and weight in the North Riding, had been bidden. The ambassadorial card had ignored Miss Granger, much to the damsel's dissatisfaction.

Clarissa came upon Mr. Fairfax unawares in the glazed colonnade upon which the ball-room opened, where he was standing alone, staring moodily at a tall arum lily shooting up from a bed of ferns, when she approached on her partner's arm, taking the regulation promenade after a waltz. The well-remembered profile, which had grown sharper and sterner since she had seen it for the first time, struck her with a sudden thrill, half pleasure, half terror. Yes; she was pleased to see him; she, the wife of Daniel Granger, felt her heart beating faster, felt a sense of joy strangely mingled with fear. In all the occupations of her life, even amidst the all-absorbing delight of her child's society, she had not been able quite to forget this man. The one voice that had touched her heart, the one face that had haunted her girlish dream, came back to her again and again in spite of herself. In the dead of the night she had started up from her pillow with the sound of George Fairfax's familiar tones in her ears; in too many a dream she had acted over again the meeting in the orchard, and heard his voice upbraiding her, and had seen his face dark and angry in the dim light. She had done her duty to Daniel Granger; but she had not forgotten the man she had loved, and who had loved her after his fashion; and often in her prayers she had entreated that she might never see him again.

Her prayers had not been granted—perhaps they did not come so entirely from the heart, as prayers should, that would fain bring a blessing. He was here; here to remind her how much she had loved him in the days gone by—to bewilder her brain with conflicting thoughts. He turned suddenly from that gloomy contemplation of the arum lily, and met her face to face.

That evening-dress of ours, which has been so liberally abused for its ugliness, is not without a certain charm when worn by a handsome man. A tall man looks taller in the perfect black. The broad expanse of shirt-front, with its delicate embroidery, not obtrusively splendid, but minutely elaborate rather, involving the largest expenditure of needlework to produce the smallest and vaguest effect—a suspicion of richness, as it were, nothing more; the snowy cambric contrasts with the bronzed visage of the soldier, or blends harmoniously with the fair complexion of the fopling, who has never exposed his countenance to the rough winds of heaven; the expanse of linen proclaims the breadth of chest, and gives a factitious slimness to the waist. Such a costume, relieved perhaps by the flash of some single jewel, not large, but priceless, is scarcely unbecoming, and possibly more aesthetic in its simplicity than the gem-besprinkled brocades and velvets of a Buckingham, in the days when men wore jewelled cloaks on their shoulders, and point d'Alençon flounces round their knees.

George Fairfax, in this evening dress, looked supremely handsome. It is a poor thing, of course, in man or woman, this beauty; but it has its charm nevertheless, and in the being who is loved for other and far higher qualities, the charm is tenfold. Few women perhaps have ever fallen in love with a man on account of his good looks; they leave such weak worship for the stronger sex; but having loved him for some other indefinable reason, are not indifferent to the attraction of splendid eyes or a faultless profile.

Clarissa trembled a little as she held out her hand to be clasped in George Fairfax's strong fingers, the quiet pressure whereof seemed to say, "You *know* that you and I are something more to each other than the world supposes. "

She could not meet him without betraying, by some faint sign, that there was neither forgetfulness nor indifference in her mind as to the things that concerned him.

Her late partner—a youthful secretary of legation, with straw-coloured hair and an incipient moustache—murmured something civil, and slid away, leaving those two alone beside the arum lily, or as much alone as they could be in a place, where the guests were circulating freely, and about half-a-dozen flirtations ripening amidst the shining foliage of orange-trees and camellias.

"I thought I should meet you here to-night, " he said. "I came here in the hope of meeting you. "

She was not an experienced woman of the world, skilled in the art of warding off such a speech as this. She had never flirted in her life, and sorely felt the want of that facility which comes from long practice.

"Have you seen my husband? " she asked, awkwardly enough, in her distress.

"I did not come to see Mr. Granger. It was the hope of seeing you that brought me here. I am as great a fool as I was at Hale Castle, you see, Clarissa. There are some follies of which a man cannot cure himself. "

"Mr. Fairfax! "

She looked up at him gravely, reproachfully, with as much anger as she could bring herself to feel against him; but as their eyes met, something in his—a look that told too plainly of passion and daring—made her eyelids fall, and she stood before him trembling like a frightened child. And this moment was perhaps the turning-point in Clarissa's life—the moment in which she took the first step on the wrong road that was to lead her so far away from the sacred paths of innocence and peace.

George Fairfax drew her hand through his arm—she had neither strength nor resolution to oppose him—and led her away to the quietest corner of the colonnade—a recess sheltered by orange-trees, and provided with a rustic bench.

There is no need to record every word that was spoken there; it was the old story of a man's selfish guilty love, and a woman's sinful weakness. He spoke, and Clarissa heard him, not willingly, but with faint efforts of resistance that ended in nothing. She heard him. Never again could she meet Daniel Granger's honest gaze as she had done—never, it seemed to her, could she lose the sense of her sin.

He told her how she had ruined his life. That was his chief reproach, and a reproach that a woman can rarely hear unmoved. He painted in the briefest words the picture of what he might have been, and what he was. If his life were wrecked utterly—and from his own account of himself it must needs be so, —the wreck was her fault. He had been ready to sacrifice everything for her. She had basely cheated him. His upbraiding stung her too keenly; she could keep her secret no longer.

"I had promised Laura Armstrong, " she said—"I had promised her that no power on earth should tempt me to marry you—if you should ask me. "

"You had promised! " he cried contemptuously. "Promised that shallow trickster! I might have known she had a hand in my misery. And you thought a promise to her more sacred than good faith to me? That was hard, Clarissa. "

"It was hard, " she answered, in a heart-broken voice.

"My God! " he cried, looking at her with those passionate eyes, "and yet you loved me all the time? "

"With all my heart, " she faltered, and then hid her face in her hands.

It seemed as if the confession had been wrung from her somehow. In the next moment she hated herself for having said the words, and calming herself with a great effort, said to him quietly.

"And now that you know how weak I was, when I seemed indifferent to you, have pity upon me, Mr. Fairfax. "

"Pity! " he exclaimed. "It is not a question of pity; it is a question of two lives that have been blighted through your foolish submission to that plotting woman. But there must be some recompense to be found in the future for all the tortures of the past. I have broken every tie for your sake, Clarissa; you must make some sacrifice for me. "

Clarissa looked at him wonderingly. Was he so mad as to suppose that she was of the stuff that makes runaway wives?

"Your father tempted my mother, Mr. Fairfax, " she said, "but I thank Heaven she escaped him. The role of seducer seems hereditary in your family. You could not make me break my word when I was free to marry you; do you believe that you can make me false to my husband? "

"Yes, Clarissa. I swore as much that night in the orchard—swore that I would win you, in spite of the world. "

"And my son, " she said, with the tone she might have used if he had been one-and-twenty, "is he to blush for his mother by and by? "

"I have never found that sons have a faculty for blushing on account of that kind of thing, " Mr. Fairfax answered lightly. —"Egad, there'd be a great deal of blushing going on at some of the crack clubs if they had! " he said to himself afterwards.

Clarissa rose from the seat amongst the orange-trees, and George Fairfax did not attempt to detain her.

He offered her his arm to conduct her back to the ball-room; they had been quite long enough away. He did not want to attract attention; and he had said as much as he cared to say.

He felt very sure of his ground now. She loved him—that was the all-important point. His wounded self-esteem was solaced by this knowledge. His old sense of power came back to him. He had felt himself all at sea, as it were, when he believed it possible that any woman he cared to win could be indifferent to him.

From the other side of the ball-room Mr. Granger saw his wife re-enter arm-in-arm with George Fairfax. The sight gave him a little shock. He had hoped that young man was far enough away, ruining himself in a fashionable manner somehow; and here he was in attendance upon Clarissa. He remembered how his daughter had said that George Fairfax was sure to meet them in Paris, and his own anger at the suggestion. He would be obliged to be civil to the young man, of course. There was no reason indeed that he should be otherwise than civil—only that lurking terror in his mind, that this was the man his wife had loved. *Had* loved? is there any past tense to that verb?

Mrs. Granger dropped Mr. Fairfax's arm directly they came to a vacant seat.

"I am rather tired, " she said, in her coldest voice. "I think I'll rest a little, if you please. I needn't detain you. I daresay you are engaged for the next dance. "

"No. I seldom dance. "

He stood by her side. One rapid glance across the room had shown him Daniel Granger making his way towards them, looking unspeakably ponderous and British amidst that butterfly crowd. He did not mean to leave her just yet, in spite of her proprietor's approach. She belonged to him, he told himself, by right of that confession just now in the conservatory. It was only a question when he should take her to himself. He felt like some bold rover of the seas, who has just captured a gallant craft, and carries her proudly over the ocean chained to his gloomy hull.

She was his, he told himself; but before he could carry her away from her present surroundings he must play the base part which he had once thought he never could play. He must be civil to Daniel Granger, mask his batteries, win his footing in the household, so that he might have easy access to the woman he loved, until one day the thunderbolt would descend, and an honest man be left desolate, "with his household gods shattered. " It was just one of those sins that will not bear contemplation. George Fairfax was fain to shut his eyes upon the horror and vileness of it, and only to say to himself doggedly, "I have sworn to win her. "

Mr. Granger greeted him civilly enough presently, and with the stereotyped cordiality which may mean anything or nothing. Was Mr. Fairfax going to remain long in Paris? Yes, he meant to winter there, if nothing better turned up.

"After all, you see, " he said, "there is no place like Paris. One gets tired of it, of course, in time; but I find that in other places one is always tired. "

"A very pleasant ball, " remarked Mr. Granger, with the air of saying something original. "You have been dancing, I suppose? "

"No, " replied Mr. Fairfax, smiling; "I have come into my property. I don't dance. 'I range myself, ' as our friends here say. "

He thought, as he spoke, of sundry breakneck gallops and mahlstrom waltzes danced in gardens and saloons, the very existence whereof was ignored by or unknown to respectability; and then thought, "If I were safely planted on the other side of the world with *her* for my wife, it would cost me no more to cut all that kind of thing than it would to throw away a handful of withered flowers. "

* * * * *

CHAPTER XXXVII.

STOLEN HOURS.

Miss Granger's portrait was finished; and the baby picture—a chubby blue-eyed cherub, at play on a bank of primroses, with a yellowhammer perched on a blossoming blackthorn above his head, and just a glimpse of blue April sky beyond; a dainty little study of colour in which the painter had surpassed himself—was making rapid progress, to the young mother's intense delight. Very soon Mr. Austin would have no longer the privilege of coming every other day to the Rue da Morny. Daniel Granger had declined sitting for his portrait.

"I did it once, " he said. "The Bradford people insisted upon making me a present of my own likeness, life-size, with my brown cob, Peter Pindar, standing beside me. I was obliged to hang the picture in the hall at Arden—those good fellows would have been wounded if I hadn't given it a prominent position; but that great shining brown cob plays the mischief with my finest Velasquez, a portrait of Don Carlos Baltazar, in white satin slashed with crimson. No; I like your easy, dashing style very much, Mr. Austin; but one portrait in a lifetime is quite enough for me. "

As the Granger family became more acclimatised, as it were, Clarissa found herself with more time at her disposal. Sophia had attached herself to a little clique of English ladies, and had her own engagements and her separate interests. Clarissa's friends were for the most part Frenchwomen, whom she had known in London, or to whom she had been introduced by Lady Laura. Mr. Granger had his own set, and spent his afternoons agreeably enough, drinking soda water, reading *Galignani,* and talking commerce or politics with his compeers at the most respectable cafe on the Boulevards. Being free therefore to dispose of her afternoons, Clarissa, when Lovel's picture was finished, went naturally to the Rue du Chevalier Bayard. Having once taken her servants there, she had no farther scruples. "They will think I come to see a dressmaker, " she said to herself. But in this she did not give those domestic officers credit for the sharpness of their class. Before she had been three times to her brother's lodgings, John Thomas, the footman, had contrived— despite his utter ignorance of the French tongue—to discover who were the occupants of No. 7, and had ascertained that Mr. Austin, the painter, was one of them.

"Who'd have thought of her coming to see that chap Hostin? " said John Thomas to the coachman. "That's a rum start, ain't it? "

"Life is made up of rum starts, John Thomas, " replied the coachman sententiously. "Is there a Mrs. Hostin, do you know? "

"Yes, he's got a wife. I found that out from the porter, though the blessed old buffer can't speak anything but his French gibberish. 'Madame? ' I said, bawling into his stupid old ear. 'Mossoo and Madame Hostin? comprenny? ' and he says, 'Ya-ase, ' and then bursts out laughing, and looks as proud as a hen that's just laid a hegg—' Ya-ase, Mossoo et Madame. "

George Fairfax and Clarissa met very frequently after that ball at the Embassy. It happened that they knew the same people; Mr. Fairfax, indeed, knew every one worth knowing in Paris; and he seemed to have grown suddenly fond of respectable society, going everywhere in the hope of meeting Mrs. Granger, and rarely staying long anywhere, if he did not meet her. There were those who observed this peculiarity in his movements, and shrugged their shoulders significantly. It was to be expected, of course, said this butterfly section of humanity: a beautiful young woman, married to a man old enough to be her father, would naturally have some one interested in her.

Sometimes Clarissa met George Fairfax in her brother's painting-room; so often, indeed, that she scarcely cared to keep an account of these meetings. Austin knew a good many clever agreeable Americans and Frenchmen, and his room was a pleasant lounge for idle young men, with some interest in art, and plenty to say upon every subject in the universe. If there were strangers in the painting-room when Mrs. Granger came to the Rue du Chevalier Bayard, she remained in the little salon, talking to her sister-in-law and the two precocious nephews; but it happened generally that George Fairfax, by some mysterious means, became aware of her presence, and one of the folding-doors would open presently, and the tall figure appear.

"Those fellows have fairly smoked me out, Mrs. Austin, " he would say. —"Ah, how do you do, Mrs. Granger? I hope you'll excuse any odour of Victorias and Patagas I may bring with me. Your brother's Yankee friends smoke like so many peripatetic furnaces. "

And then he would plant himself against a corner of the mantelpiece, and remain a fixture till Clarissa departed. It was half-an-hour's talk that was almost a tête-à-tête. Bessie Lovel counted for so little between those two. Half-an-hour of dangerous happiness, which made all the rest of Mrs. Granger's life seem dull and colourless; the thought of which even came between her and her child.

Sometimes she resolved that she would go no more to that shabby street on the "Surrey side"; but the resolve was always broken. Either Austin had asked her to come for some special reason, or the poor little wife had begged some favour of her, which required personal attention; there was always something.

Those were pleasant afternoons, when the painting-room was empty of strangers, and Clarissa sat in a low chair by the fire, while George Fairfax and her brother talked. Austin was never so brilliant as in George's company; the two men suited each other, had lived in the same world, and loved the same things. They talked of all things in heaven and earth, touching lightly upon all, and with a careless kind of eloquence that had an especial fascination for the listener. It seemed as if she had scarcely lived in the dull interval between those charmed days at Hale Castle and these hours of perilous delight; as if she had been half-stifled by the atmosphere of common-sense which had pervaded her existence—crushed and borne down by the weight of Daniel Granger's sober companionship. *This* was fairyland—a region of enchantment, fall of bright thoughts and pleasant fancies; *that* a dismal level drill-ground, upon which all the world marched in solid squares, to the monotonous cry of a serjeant-major's word of command. One may ride through a world of weariness in a barouche-and-pair. Clarissa had not found her husband's wealth by any means a perennial source of happiness, nor even the possession of Arden an unfailing consolation.

It was strange how this untidy painting-room of Austin's, with its tawdry dilapidated furniture—all of which had struck her with a sense of shabbiness and dreariness at first—had grown to possess a charm for her. In the winter gloaming, when the low wood fire glowed redly on the hearth, and made a flickering light upon the walls, the room had a certain picturesque aspect. The bulky Flemish cabinets, with their coarse florid carving, stood boldly out from the background, with red gleams from the fire reflected on chubby cherub heads and mediaeval monsters. The faded curtains lost their look of poverty, and had only the sombre air of age; an old brass chandelier of the Louis Quatorze period, which Austin had hung in in the centre of his room, flashed and glittered in the uncertain, light; and those two figures—one leaning against the mantelpiece, the other prowling restlessly to and fro as he talked, carrying a mahl-stick, which he waved ever and anon like the rod of a magician—completed the picture. It was a glimpse of the behind-the-scenes in the great world of art, a peep into Bohemia; and O, how much brighter a region it seemed to Clarissa than that well-regulated world in which she dined every day at the same hour, with four solemn men watching the banquet, and wound up always with the game dismal quarter of an hour's sitting in state at dessert!

Those stolen hours in Austin's painting-room had too keen a fascination for her. Again and again she told herself that she would come no more, and yet she came. She was so secure of her own integrity, so fenced and defended by womanly pride, that she argued with herself there could be neither sin nor danger in these happy respites from the commonplace dreariness of her life. And yet, so inconsistent is human nature, there were times when this woman flung herself upon the ground beside her baby's crib, and prayed God to pardon her iniquities.

Austin was much too careless to be conscious of his sister's danger. George Fairfax had made an afternoon lounge of his rooms in the previous winter; it was no new thing for him to come there three or four times a week; and Austin did not for a moment suspect that Clarissa's occasional presence had anything to do with these visits.

When the three portraits were finished, Mr. Granger expressed himself highly content with them, and gave Austin Lovel a cheque for three hundred pounds; a sum which, in the painter's own words, ought to have set him upon his legs. Unhappily, Austin's legs, from a financial point of view, afforded only the most insecure basis—were always slipping away from him, in fact. Three hundred pounds in solid cash did not suffice for even his most pressing needs. He saw nothing before him but the necessity of an ignominious flight from Paris. It was only a question of when and where he should fly; there was no question as to the fact.

He did not care to tell Clarissa this, however. It would be time enough when the thing was done, or just about to be done. All his life he had been in the habit of shirking unpleasant subjects, and he meant to shirk this as long as he could. He might have borrowed money of George Fairfax, no doubt; but unfortunately he was already in that gentleman's debt, for money borrowed during the previous winter; so he scarcely cared to make any new appeal in that quarter.

So the unsubstantial Bohemian existence went on; and to Clarissa, for whom this Bohemia was an utterly new world, it seemed the only life worth living. Her brother had been pleased to discover the ripening of her artistic powers, and had given her some rough-and-ready lessons in the art she loved so well. Sometimes, on a bright wintry morning, when Mr. Granger was engaged out of doors, she brought her portfolio to the Rue du Chevalier Bayard, and painted there for an hour or so. At first this had been a secure hour for unreserved talk with her brother; but after she had been there two or three mornings in this way, Mr. Fairfax seemed mysteriously aware of her movements, and happened to drop in while she was taking her lesson.

It is not to be supposed that Clarissa could be so much away from home without attracting the attention of Miss Granger. Whether that young lady was at home or abroad, she contrived to keep herself always well informed as to the movements of her stepmother. She speculated, and wondered, and puzzled herself a good deal about these frequent outings; and finding Clarissa singularly reticent upon the subject, grew daily more curious and suspicious; until at last she could endure the burden of this perplexity no longer, without some relief in words, and was fain to take the judicious Warman into her confidence.

"Has Mrs. Granger been out again this afternoon, Warman? " she asked one evening, when the handmaiden was dressing her hair for dinner.

"Yes, miss. The carriage came home just now. I heard it Mrs. Granger went out almost directly after you did. "

"I wonder she can care to waste so much time in calls, " said Sophia.

"Yes, miss, it is odd; and almost always the same place too, as you may say. But I suppose Mrs. Granger was intimate with Mr. and Mrs. Austin before her marriage. "

"Mr. and Mrs. Austin! What do you mean, Warman? "

"Lor', miss, I thought you would know where she went, as a matter of course. It seems only natural you should. I've heard Jarvis mention it at supper. Jarvis has his meals at *our* table, you know, miss. 'We've been to the Rue du Cavalier Barnard again to-day, ' he says, 'which I suppose is French for Barnard's-inn. Missus and them Austins must be very thick. ' Jarvis has no manners, you know, miss; and that's just his uncultivated way of speaking. But from what I've heard him remark, I'm sure Mrs. Granger goes to call upon the Austins as much as three times a week, and seldom stops less than an hour. "

A deadly coldness had crept over Sophia Granger—a cold, blank feeling, which had never come upon her until that moment. He had a wife, then, that dashing young painter with the brilliant brown eyes—the only man who had ever aroused the faintest interest in her well-regulated soul. He was married, and any vague day-dream with which she had interwoven his image was the merest delusion and phantasmagoria. She was unspeakably angry with herself for this unworthy weakness. A painter—a person paid by her father— something less than a curate—if it was possible for any creature to seem less than Mr. Tillott in Sophia's estimation. He was a married man—a base impostor, who had sailed under false colours—a very pirate. All those graceful airy compliments, those delicate attentions, which had exercised such a subtle influence over her narrow mind— had, indeed, awakened in her something that was almost sentiment—were worse than meaningless, were the wiles of an adventurer trading on her folly.

"He wanted to paint papa's picture, " she thought, "and I suppose he fancied my influence might help him. "

But what of Clarissa's visits to the painter's lodgings? what possible reason could she have for going there? Miss Granger's suspicions were shapeless and intangible as yet, but she did suspect. More than once—many times, in fact—during the painting of the portrait, she had seen, or had imagined she could see, signs and tokens of a closer intimacy between the painter and her father's wife than was warranted by their ostensible acquaintance. The circumstances were slight enough in themselves, but these fragile links welded together made a chain which would have been good enough evidence in a criminal court, skilfully handled by an Old Bailey lawyer. Sophia Granger racked her brain to account for this suspected intimacy. When and where had these two been friends, lovers perhaps? Mr. Austin had been away from England for many years, if his own statement were to be believed. It must have been abroad, therefore, that Clarissa had known him—in her school-days. He had been drawing-master, perhaps, in the seminary at Belforêt. What more likely?

Miss Granger cherished the peculiar British idea of all foreign schools, that they were more or less sinks of iniquity. A flirtation between drawing-master and pupil would be a small thing in such a pernicious atmosphere. Even amidst the Arcadian innocence of native academies such weeds have flourished This flirtation, springing up in foreign soil, would be of course ten times more desperate, secret, jesuitical in fact, than any purely English product.

Yes, Miss Granger decided at the end of every silent debate in which she argued this question with herself—yes, that was the word of the enigma. These two had been lovers in the days that were gone; and meeting again, both married, they were more than half lovers still.

Clarissa made some excuse to see her old admirer frequently. She was taking lessons in painting, perhaps. Miss Granger observed that she painted more than usual lately—merely for the sake of seeing him.

And how about George Fairfax? Well, that flirtation, of course, was of later date and a less serious affair. Jealousy—a new kind of jealousy, more bitter even than that which she had felt when Clarissa came between her and her father—sharpened Miss Granger's suspicions in this case. She was jealous even of that supposed flirtation at Belforêt, four or five years ago. She was angry with Clarissa for having once possessed this man's heart; ready to suspect her of any baseness in the past, any treason in the present.

The Grangers were at Madame Caballero's two or three evenings after this revelation of Warman's, and Sophia had an opportunity of gleaning some scraps of information from the good-natured little lion-huntress. Madame had been asking her if Mr. Austin's portraits had been a success.

"Yes; papa thinks they are excellent, and talks about having them exhibited in the salon. Mr. Austin is really very clever. Do you know, I was not aware that he was married, till the other day? " Sophia added, with a careless air.

"Indeed! Yes, there is a wife, I understand; but she never goes into society; no one hears of her. For my part I think him charming. "

"Has he been long in Paris? "

Madame Caballero shrugged her shoulders. "I don't know, " she said. "I have only known of his existence since he became famous — in a small way — a very small way, of course. He exhibited some military sketches, which attracted the attention of a friend of mine, who talked to me about him. I said at once, 'Bring him here. I can appreciate every order of genius, from Ary Scheffer to Gavarni. ' The young man came, and I was delighted with him. I admitted him among my intimates; and he insisted on painting the picture which your papa was good enough to admire. "

"Do you know how he lived before he came into notice — if he has ever been a drawing-master, for instance? "

"I know that he has given lessons. I have heard him complain of the drudgery of teaching. "

This sustained Miss Granger's theory. It seemed so likely. No other hypothesis presented itself to her mind.

Day by day she watched and waited and speculated, hearing of all Clarissa's movements from the obsequious Warman, who took care to question Mrs. Granger's coachman in the course of conversation, in a pleasant casual manner, as to the places to which he had taken his mistress. She waited and made no sign. There was treason going on. The climax and explosion would come in good time.

In the meanwhile, Clarissa seemed almost entirely free. Mr. Granger, after living for nearly fifty years of his life utterly unaffected by feminine influence, was not a man to hang upon his wife's footsteps or to hold her bound to his side. If she had returned his affection with equal measure, if that sympathy for which he sighed in secret could have arisen between them, he might have been as devoted a slave as love could make an honest man. As it was, his married life at its best was a disappointment. Only in the fond hopes and airy visions which his son had inspired, did he find the happiness he had dreamt of when he first tried to win Clarissa for his wife. Here alone, in his love for his child, was there a pure and perfect joy. All other dreams ended in bitter waking. His wife had never loved him, never would love him. She was grateful for his affection, obedient, submissive; her grace and beauty gave him a reflected lustre in society. She was a creature to be proud of, and he was proud of her; but she did not love him. And with this thought there came always a sudden agony of jealousy. If not him, what other had she loved? Whose image reigned in the heart so closely shut against him? Who was that man, the mere memory of whom was more to her than the whole sum of her husband's devotion?

* * * * *

CHAPTER XXXVIII.

"FROM CLARISSA. "

That jewel which Clarissa had given to Bessie Lovel was a treasure of price, the very possession whereof was almost an oppressive joy to the poor little woman, whose chief knowledge of life came from the experience of its debts and difficulties. That the massive gold locket with the diamond cross would be required of her sooner or later, to be handed into the ruthless paw of a clerk at the *mont de piété*, she had little doubt. Everything that she or her husband had ever possessed worth possessing had so vanished—had been not an absolute property, but a brief fleeting joy, a kind of supernal visitant, vanishing anon into nothingness, or only a pawnbroker's duplicate. The time would come. She showed the trinket to her husband with a melancholy foreboding, and read his thoughts as he weighed it in his palm, by mere force of habit, speculating what it would fetch, if in his desperate needs this waif might serve him.

She was not surprised, therefore—only a little distressed—when Austin broached the subject one day at his late breakfast—that breakfast at which it needed nearly a bottle of claret to wash down three or four mouthfuls of savoury pie, or half a tiny cutlet. She had possessed the bauble more than a month, holding it in fear and trembling, and only astonished that it had not been demanded of her.

"O, by the way, Bess, " Austin Lovel said carelessly, "I was abominably unlucky last night, at Madame Caballero's. I'm generally lugged in for a game or two at *écarté there*, you know. One can't refuse in a house of that kind. And I had been doing wonders. They were betting on my game, and I stood to win something handsome, when the luck changed all in a moment. The fellow I was playing against marked the king three times running; and, in short, I rose a considerable loser—considerable for me, that is to say. I told my antagonist I should send him the money to-day. He's a kind of man I can't afford to trifle with; and you know the Caballero connection is of too much use to be jeopardised. So I've been thinking, Bess, that if you'd let me have that gimcrack locket my sister gave you, I could raise a tenner on it. Clary can afford to give you plenty of such things, even if it were lost, which it need not be. "

Of course not. Mrs. Lovel had been told as much about the little Geneva watch which her husband had given her a few days after her marriage, and had taken away from her six weeks later. But the watch had never come back to her. She gave a faint sigh of resignation. It was not within the compass of her mind to oppose him.

"We shall never get on while you play cards, Austin, " she said sadly.

"My dear Bessie, a man may win as well as lose. You see when I go into society there are certain things expected of me; and my only chance of getting on is by making myself agreeable to the people whose influence is worth having. "

"But I can't see that card-playing leads to your getting commissions for pictures, Austin, no more than horseracing nor billiards. It all seems to end the same—in your losing money. "

The painter pushed away his plate with an impatient gesture. He was taking his breakfast in his painting-room, hours after the family meal, Bessie waiting upon him, and cobbling some juvenile garment during the intervals of her attendance. He pushed his plate aside, and got up to pace the room in the restless way that was common to him on such occasions.

"My dear child, if you don't want to give me the locket, say so, " he said, "but don't treat me to a sermon. You can keep it if you like, though I can't conceive what use the thing can be to you. It's not a thing you can wear. "

"Not at home, dear, certainly; and I never go out, " the wife answered, with the faintest touch of reproachfulness. "I am very fond of it, though, for your sister's sake. It was so kind of her to bring it to me, and such a new thing for me to have a present. But you are welcome to it, Austin, if you really want it. "

"If I really want it! Do you suppose I should be mean enough to ask you for it if I didn't? I shouldn't so much care about it, you see, only I am to meet the man to-morrow evening at dinner, and I can't face him without the money. So if you'll look the thing out some time to-day, Bess, I'll take it down to the Quai between this and to-morrow afternoon, and get the business over. "

Thus it was that George Fairfax, strolling into Mrs. Lovel's sitting-room that afternoon while Austin was out, happened to find her seated in a pensive attitude, with an open work-box before her and Clarissa's locket in her hand. It was a shabby battered old box, but had been for years the repository of all Bessie's treasures.

She had kept the locket there, looking at it very often, and wondering if she would ever be able to wear it—if Austin would take her to a theatre, for instance, or give a little dinner at home instead of abroad, for once in a way, to some of the men whose society absorbed so much of his time.

There was no hope of this now. Once gone from her hand; the treasure would return no more. She knew that very well and was indulging her grief by a farewell contemplation of the trinket, when Mr. Fairfax came into the room.

The flash of the diamonds caught his quick eye.

"What a pretty locket you've got there, Mrs. Austin! " he said, as he shook hands with her. "A new-year's gift from Austin, I suppose. "

"No, it was my sister-in-law, Mrs. Granger, who gave it me, " Bessie answered, with a sigh.

He was interested in it immediately, but was careful not to betray his interest. Mrs. Lovel put it into his hands. She was proud of it even in this last hour of possession. "Perhaps you'd like to look at it, " she said. "It's got her 'air inside. "

Yes, there was a circlet of the dark brown hair he knew so well, and the two works, "From Clarissa. "

"Upon my word, it's very handsome, " he said, looking at the diamond cross outside, but thinking of the love-lock within. "I never saw a locket I liked better. You are very fond of it, I daresay? " he added interrogatively.

"O, yes, I like it very much! I can't bear to part with it. "

And here Bessie Lovel, not being gifted with the power of concealing her emotions, fairly broke down and cried like a child.

"My dear Mrs. Austin, " exclaimed George Fairfax, "pray don't distress yourself like that. Part with it? Why should you part with your locket? "

"O, Mr. Fairfax, I oughtn't to have told you—Austin would be so angry if he knew—but he has been losing money at that horrid ecarty, and he says he must have ten pounds to-morrow; so my beautiful locket must go to the pawnbroker's. "

George Fairfax paused. His first impulse was to lend the poor little woman the money—the veriest trifle, of course, to the lord of Lyvedon. But the next moment another idea presented itself to him. He had the locket lying in the open palm of his hand. It would be so sweet to possess that lock of hair—to wear so dear a token of his mistress. Even those two words, "From Clarissa, " had a kind of magic for him. It was a foolish weakness, of course; but then love is made up of such follies.

"If you really mean to part with this, " he said, "I should be very glad to have it. I would give you more than any pawnbroker—say, twenty instead of ten pounds, for instance—and a new locket for yourself into the bargain. I shouldn't like to deprive you of an ornament you valued without some kind of compensation. I have taken a fancy to the design of the thing, and should really like to have it. What do you say now, Mrs. Austin—shall that be a transaction between you and me, without any reference to your husband, who might be angry with you for having let me into domestic secrets? You can tell him you got the money from the *mont de piété*. Look here, now; let's settle the business at once. "

He opened his purse, and tumbled the contents out upon the table. Bessie Lovel thought what a blessed state of existence that must be in which people walked this world with all that ready money about them.

"There are just four-and-twenty pounds here, " he said cheerily; "so we'll say four-and-twenty. "

He saw that she was yielding.

"And would you really give me a locket for myself, " she said, almost incredulously, "as well as this money? "

"Unquestionably. As good a one as I can find in the Rue de la Paix. This has diamonds, and that shall have diamonds. It's the design, you see, " he added persuasively, "that has taken my fancy. "

"I'm sure you are very generous, " Bessie murmured, still hesitating.

"Generous! Pshaw, not at all. It's a caprice; and I shall consider myself under an obligation to you if you gratify it. "

The temptation was irresistible. To obtain the money that was required—more than double the sum her husband had wanted—and to have another locket as well! Never, surely, had there been such a bargain since the famous magician offered new lamps for old ones. Of course, it was only Mr. Fairfax's delicate way of doing them a kindness; his fancy for the locket was merely a benevolent pretence. What could he care for that particular trinket; he who might, so to speak, walk knee-deep in diamonds, if he pleased?

She took the twenty-four pounds—an English ten-pound note, and the rest in new glittering napoleons—and then began to speculate upon the possibility of giving Austin twenty pounds, and appropriating the balance to her own uses. The children wanted so many things—that perpetual want of the juvenile population above all, shoe-leather; and might she not even screw some cheap dress for herself out of the sum? while if it were all given to Austin, it would vanish, like smoke before the wind, leaving no trace behind.

So George Fairfax put the bauble in his waistcoat-pocket, and whatever sentimental pleasure might be derived from such a talisman was his. There are those among our disciples of modern magic who believe there is a subtle animal magnetism in such things; that the mere possession of such a token constitutes a kind of spiritual link between two beings. Mr. Fairfax had no such fancy; but it pleased him to have obtained that which no prayers of his could have won from Clarissa herself. Not at present, that is to say. It would all come in good time. She loved him; secure of that one fact, he believed all the rest a mere question of patience and constancy.

"And she is worth the winning, " he said to himself. "A man might serve for a longer slavery than Jacob's, and yet be rewarded by such a conquest. I think, by the way, that Rachel must have been just a trifle faded when the patriarch was out of his time. "

He dawdled away an hour or so in Bessie's salon—telling the poor little woman the news of the day, and playing with the two boys, who regarded him as a beneficent being, from whose hands flowed perpetual toys and sweetmeats. He waited as long as he could without making his motive obvious; waited, in the hope that Clarissa would come; and then, as there was no sign of her coming, and Austin was still out, he wished Bessie good-bye.

"I shan't forget the locket, " he said, as he departed.

Austin came in five minutes afterwards. The boys had been scuttled off to take their evening meal in the kitchen—a darksome cupboard about eight feet square—where the tawdry servant was perpetually stewing savoury messes upon a small charcoal stove.

Bessie handed her husband the ten-pound note, and twelve bright napoleons.

"Why, what's this? " he asked.

"The—the money for the locket, Austin. I thought you might be late home; so I ran round to the Quai with it myself. And I asked for twenty pounds, and the man gave it to me. "

"Why, that's a brave girl! " cried Austin, kissing the pleading face uplifted to his. "I don't believe they'd have given me as much. An English tenner, though; that's odd! " he added carelessly, and then slipped the cash loose into his pocket, with the air of a man for whom money is at best a temporary possession.

* * * * *

CHAPTER XXXIX.

THAT IS WHAT LOVE MEANS.

The Grangers and Mr. Fairfax went on meeting in society; and Daniel Granger, with whom it was a kind of habit to ask men to dinner, could hardly avoid inviting George Fairfax. It might have seemed invidious to do so; and for what reason should he make such a distinction? Even to himself Mr. Granger would not be willing to confess that he was jealous of this man. So Mr. Fairfax came with others of his species to the gorgeous caravanserai in the Rue de Morny, where the rooms never by any chance looked as if people lived in them, but rather as if they were waiting-rooms at some railway station got up with temporary splendour for the reception of royalty.

He came; and though Clarissa sometimes made feeble efforts to avoid him, it happened almost always, that before the evening was out he found some few minutes for unreserved talk with her. There is little need to record such brief stolen interviews—a few hurried words by the piano, a sentence or two in a lowered voice at parting. There was not much in the words perhaps—only very common words, that have done duty between thousands of men and women—a kind of signal code, as it were; and yet they had power to poison Clarissa's life, to take the sweetness out of every joy, even a mother's innocent idolatry of her child.

The words were spoken; but so carefully did George Fairfax play his part, that not even Sophia's sharp eyes could perceive more than was correct in the conduct of her stepmother. No, she told herself, that other flirtation was the desperate one. Clarissa might have had some preference for George Fairfax; there had been occasional indications of such a feeling in her manner at Hale Castle; but the dark spot of her life, the secret of her girlhood, was a love affair with Mr. Austin.

By way of experiment, one day she asked her father's wife a question about the painter.

"You seemed to admire Mr. Austin very much, Clarissa, " she said, "and I admit that he is remarkably clever; but he appears such a waif and stray. In all his conversation with us he never threw much light upon his own history. Do you know anything of his antecedents? "

Clarissa blushed in spite of herself. The deception she had sustained so long was unspeakably distasteful her. Again and again she had been tempted to hazard everything, and acknowledge Austin as her brother, whether he liked or not that she should do so. It was only his peremptory tone that had kept her silent.

"What should I know of his antecedents more than you, Sophy? " she said, avoiding a more direct reply. "It is quite enough for me to know that he has undeniable genius. "

The blush, and a certain warmth in her tone, seemed to Sophia conclusive evidence of her hidden regard for this man. Miss Granger's heart beat a good deal faster than usual, and little jealous sparkles shone in her cold gray eyes. She had never admired any man so much as she had admired this brilliant young painter. Many men had paid her compliments; as the rich Mr. Granger's sole daughter and heiress, she had been gratified with no meagre share of mankind's worship; but no words ever spoken had sounded so sweet in her ears as those few civil speeches that Mr. Austin had found time to address to her during his visits to the Rue de Morny. And after having taken so much pleasure in his converse, and thought so much more about him than she would have considered it proper for any model villager to think about an individual of the opposite sex, it was a hard thing to find—first, that the base impostor had a wife; and secondly, that whatever illegitimate worship he might have to render, was to be offered at the shrine of Clarissa.

"Indeed! " she exclaimed, with an air of extreme surprise. "You seemed on such very friendly terms with him, that I fancied you must really have known each other before, and that you had some motive for concealing the fact from papa. "

Clarissa blushed a deeper crimson at this homethrust, and bent a little lower over her drawing-board. It seemed a fortunate thing that she happened to be painting when Miss Granger opened her guns upon her in this manner.

"He gives lessons, I believe; does he not? " asked Sophia.

"Yes—I—I believe—I have heard so. "

"Do you know, I took it into my head that he might have been your drawing-master at Belforêt. "

Clarissa laughed aloud at this suggestion. Miss Granger's persistent curiosity amused her a little, dangerous as the ground was.

"Oh dear no, he was not our master at Belforêt, " she said. "We had a little old Swiss—such an ancient, ancient man—who took snuff continually, and was always talking about his *pays natal* and Jean Jacques Rousseau. I think he had known Rousseau; and I am sure he was old enough to remember the night they locked him out of Geneva. "

Sophia was fairly posed; she had been on a false scent evidently, and yet she was sure there was something. That is how she shaped her doubts in her own mind—there was *something*. Warman thought so, she knew; and Warman was gifted with no ordinary amount of penetration.

So Mrs. Granger went her way, with suspicion around and about her, and danger ahead. Whatever peace had been hers in the brief period of her married life—and the quiet spring-time and summer that came after her baby's birth had been very peaceful—had vanished now. A cloud of fear encompassed her; a constant melancholy possessed her; a pleading voice, which she ought never to have heard, was always in her ears—a voice that charged her with the burden of a broken life—a voice that told her it was only by some sacrifice of her own she could atone for the sacrifice that had been made for her—a too persuasive voice, with a perilous charm in its every accent.

She loved him. That she could ever be weak enough, or vile enough, to sink into that dread abyss, whereto some women have gone down for the love of man, was not within the compass of her thought. But she knew that no day in her life was sinless now; that no pure and innocent joys were left to her; that her every thought of George Fairfax was a sin against her husband.

And yet she went on loving him. Sometimes, when the dense of her guilt was strongest, she would fain have asked her husband to take her back to Arden; which must needs be a kind of sanctuary, as it were, she thought. Nay, hardly so; for even in that tranquil retreat Temple Fairfax had contrived to pursue her mother, with the poison of his influence and his presence. Very often she felt inclined to ask her husband this favour; but she could not do so without running some risk of betraying herself—Heaven knows how much she might betray—unawares. Again, their sojourn in the Rue de Morny was not to endure for ever. Already Mr. Granger had expressed himself somewhat tired of Paris; indeed, what denizen of that brilliant city does not become a little weary of its brightness, sooner or later, and fall sick of the Boulevard-fever—a harassing sense of all-pervading glare and confusion, a sensation of Paris on the brain?

There was some talk of returning to Arden at the end of a month. They were now at the close of January; by the first of March Mr. Granger hoped to be at the Court. His architect and his head-bailiff were alike eager for his return; there were more pullings down and reconstructions required on the new estate; there were all manner of recondite experiments to be tried in scientific farming: there were new leases to be granted, and expiring leases, the covenants whereof must be exacted.

Since they were likely to leave Paris so soon, it would be foolish to excite wonder by asking to leave sooner, Mrs. Granger thought. It mattered so little, after all, she told herself sometimes. It mattered this much only—that day by day her feet were straying farther from the right road.

O those happy winter afternoons in the Rue du Chevalier Bayard! Such innocent happiness, too, in all seeming—only a little animated rambling talk upon all manner of subjects, from the loftiest problems in philosophy to the frothiest gossip of the Faubourg St. Honoré; only the presence of two people who loved each other to distraction. A dim firelit room; a little commonplace woman coming in and out; two young men disputing in the dusk; and Clarissa in her low chair by the fire, listening to the magical voice that was now the only music of her dreams. If it could have gone on for ever thus—a sweet sentimental friendship like that which linked Madame Roland and Brissot, Madame Recamier and Chateaubriand—there would surely have been no harm, Clarissa sometimes argued with herself. She was married to a man whom she could respect for many qualities of his heart and mind, against whom she could never seriously offend. Was it so great a sin if the friendship of George Fairfax was dear to her? if the few happy hours of her life were those she spent in his company? But such special pleading as this was the poorest sophistry; at heart she was conscious that it was so. A woman has a double conscience, as it were—a holy of holies within the temple of her mind, to which falsehood cannot enter. She may refuse to lift the screen, and meet the truth face to face; but it is there—not to be extinguished—eternal, immutable; the divine lamp given for her guidance, if only she will not withdraw herself from its light.

Just a little less than a month before his intended departure, Mr. Granger had a letter from that exacting bailiff, entreating his return. Something in the scientific farming had gone wrong, some great sewage question was at issue, and none but the lord of the soil himself could settle the matter. Very dear to Daniel Granger were those lands of Arden, that Arden-Court estate which he had made to spread itself so far over the face of the county. Sweet are ancestral domains, no doubt; dear by association, made holy by the pride of the race; but perhaps sweeter to the soul of man are those acres he has won by the work of his own strong hand, or his own steadfast brain. Next to his wife and children, in Mr. Granger's regard, were the lands of Arden: the farms and homesteads, in valleys and on hill-tops; the cottages and school-houses, which he had built for the improvement of his species; the bran-new slack-baked gothic church in an outlying village, where the church had never been before his coming.

He was very sorry to leave his wife; but the question at stake was an important one. If he could have carried his household away with him at an hour's notice, he would gladly have done so; but to move Clarissa and the nurse, and the baby, and Miss Granger, would be rather a formidable business—in fact, not to be done without elaborate preparation. He had the apartments in the Rue du Morny on his hands, too, until the beginning of March; and even a millionaire seldom cares to waste such a rental as Parisian proprietors exact for houseroom in a fashionable quarter. So he decided upon going to Arden at once—which was essential—and returning directly he had adjusted matters with his bailiff, and done a morning's work with his architect.

He told Clarissa of his intention one evening when they had returned from a dinner-party, and she was seated before her dressing-table, taking off her jewels in a slow, absent way. She looked up with a start as her husband came into the room, and planted himself on the white sheepskin rug, with his back against the mantelpiece.

"I am obliged to go back to Yorkshire, Clary, " he said.

She thought he meant they were all going back—that it was an interposition of Providence, and she was to be taken away from sin and danger. But O, how hard it seemed to go—never again to look forward to those stolen twilights in her brother's painting-room!

"I am glad! " she exclaimed. "I shall be very glad to go back to Arden. "

"You, my dear! " said her husband; "it is only I who am going. There is some hitch in our experiments on the home farm, and Forley knows how anxious I am about making a success this year. So he wants me to run over and see to things; he won't accept the responsibility of carrying on any longer without me. I needn't be away above two or three days, or a week at most. You can get on very well without me. "

Clarissa was silent, looking down at a bracelet which she was turning idly round her arm. Get on without him! Alas, what part had Daniel Granger played in her life of late beyond that of some supernumerary king in a stage-play? —a person of importance by rank and title in the play-bill, but of scarcely any significance to the story. Her guilty heart told her how little he had ever been to her; how, day by day, he had been growing less and less. And while he was away, she might go to the Rue du Chevalier Bayard every day. There would be nothing to prevent her so doing if she pleased. The carriage was nominally and actually hers. There was a brougham at Miss Granger's disposal; but the landau was essentially Clarissa's carriage.

"You can get on very well without me, " repeated Mr. Granger. "I do not think my presence or absence makes very much difference to you, Clarissa, " he added, in a grave displeased tone.

It was almost his first hint of a reproach. To his wife's guilty heart it struck sharply home, like an unexpected blow. She looked up at him with a pale conscience-stricken face, in which he might have read much more than he did read there. He only thought that he had spoken a shade too severely—that he had wounded her.

"I—I don't know what you mean by that, " she faltered helplessly, "I always try to please you. "

"Try to please me! " he repeated passionately. "Yes, Clary, as a child tries to please a schoolmaster. Do you know, that when I married you I was mad enough to hope the day would come when you would love me—that you loved me a little even then? Do you know how I have waited for that day, and have learned to understand, little by little, that it never can dawn for me upon this earth? You are my wife, and the mother of my child; and yet, God knows, you are no nearer to me than the day I first saw you at Hale Castle—a slim, girlish figure in a white dress, coming in at the door of the library. Not a whit nearer, " he went on, to himself rather than to Clarissa; "but so much more dear. "

There was a passion in his words which touched his wife. If it had only been possible for her to love him! If gratitude and respect, joined together, could have made up the sum of love; but they could not. She knew that George Fairfax was in all moral qualities this man's inferior; yet, for some indefinable charm, some trick of tone or manner, some curious magic in a smile or a glance, she loved him.

She was silent. Perhaps the sense of her guilt came more fully home to her in this moment than it had ever done before. What words could she speak to bring comfort to her husband's soul—she whose whole life was a lie?

Daniel Granger wandered up and down the room for some minutes in a vague restless way, and then came to his wife's chair, and looked down at her very tenderly.

"My dear, I do wrong to worry you with reproaches, " he said. "The mistake has been mine. From first to last, I have been to blame. I suppose in the wisest life there must always be some folly. Mine has been the hope that I could win your love. It has gone now, Clarissa; it is quite gone. Not even my child has given me a place in your heart. "

She looked up at him again, with that look which expressed such a depth of remorse.

"I am very wicked, " she said, "I am utterly unworthy of all you have done for me. It would have been better for you never to have seen my face. "

"Wicked! no, Clary. Your only sin has been to have disappointed a foolish fancy. What right had I to suppose you loved me? Better never to have seen your face? —yes, perhaps that might have been better. But, once having seen you, I would rather be wretched with you than happy with any other woman in the world. That is what love means, Clary. "

He stooped down to kiss her.

"Say no more, dear, " he said, "I never meant to speak as I have spoken to-night. I love you for ever. "

The day came when she remembered those words, "I love you for ever. "

If she could have thrown herself upon his breast and acknowledged all her weakness, beseeching him to shield her from herself in obedience to the impulse of that moment, what a world of anguish might have been spared to these two! But she let the impulse pass, and kept silence.

* * * * *

CHAPTER XL.

LYING IN WAIT.

Mr. Granger went back to Yorkshire; and Clarissa's days were at her own disposal. They were to leave Paris at the beginning of March. She knew it was only for a very short time that she would be able to see her brother. It was scarcely natural, therefore, that she should neglect such an opportunity as this. There was so much in Austin's life that caused her uneasiness; he seemed in such sore need of wiser counsel than his poor empty-headed little wife could give him; and Clarissa believed that she had some influence with him: that if he would be governed by the advice of any creature upon earth, that counsellor was herself.

So she spent her mornings in baby-worship, and went every afternoon to the Rue du Chevalier Bayard, where it happened curiously that Mr. Fairfax came even oftener than usual just at this time. In the evening she stayed at home—not caring to keep her engagements in society without her husband's escort—and resigned herself to the edifying companionship of Miss Granger, who was eloquent upon the benighted condition of the Parisian poor as compared with her model villagers. She described them sententiously as a people who put garlic in everything they ate, and never read their Bibles.

"One woman showed me a book with little pictures of saints printed upon paper with lace edges, " said Sophia, "as if there were any edification to be derived from lace edges; and such a heathen book too—Latin on one side and French on the other. And there the poor forsaken creatures sit in their churches, looking at stray pictures and hearing a service in an unknown tongue. "

Daniel Granger had been away nearly a week; and as yet there was no announcement of his return; only brief business-like letters, telling Clarissa that the drainage question was a complicated one, and he should remain upon the spot till he and Forley could see their way out of the difficulty. He had been away nearly a week, when George Fairfax went to the Rue du Chevalier Bayard at the usual hour, expecting to find Austin Lovel standing before his easel with a cigar in his mouth, and Clarissa sitting in the low chair by the fire, in the attitude he knew so well, with the red glow of the embers lighting up gleams of colour in her dark velvet dress, and shining on the soft brown hair crowned with a coquettish little seal-skin hat—a *toque*, as they called it on that side of the Channel.

What was his astonishment to find a pile of trunks and portmanteaus on the landing, Austin's easel roughly packed for removal, and a heap of that miscellaneous lumber without which even poverty cannot shift its dwelling! The door was open; and Mr. Fairfax walked straight into the sitting-room, where the two boys were eating some extemporised meal at a side-table under their mother's supervision; while Austin lounged with his back against the chimney-piece, smoking. He was a man who would have smoked during the culminating convulsions of an earthquake.

"Why, Austin, what the—I beg your pardon, Mrs. Austin—what *does* this mean? "

"It means Brussels by the three-fifteen train, my dear Fairfax, that's all. "

"Brussels? With those children and that luggage? What, in Heaven's name, induces you to carry your family off like this, at an hour's notice? "

"It is not an hour's notice; they've had an hour and three-quarters. As to my reasons for this abrupt hegira—well, that involves rather a long story; and I haven't time to tell it to-day. One thing is pretty clear—I can't live in Paris. Perhaps I may be able to live in Brussels. I can't very well do worse than I've done here—that's *one* comfort. "

At this Bessie Lovel began to cry—in a suppressed kind of way, like a woman who is accustomed to cry and not to be taken much notice of. George Fairfax flung himself into a chair with an impatient gesture. He was at once sorry for this man and angry with him; vexed to see any man go to ruin with such an utter recklessness, with such a deliberate casting away of every chance that might have redeemed him.

"You have got into some scrape, I suppose, " he said presently.

"Got into a scrape! " cried Austin with a laugh, tossing away the end of one cigar and preparing to light another. "My normal condition is that of being in a scrape. Egad! I fancy I must have been born so. —

For God's sake don't whimper, Bessie, if you want to catch the three-fifteen train! *I* go by that, remember, whoever stays behind. — There's no occasion to enter into explanations, Fairfax. If you could help me I'd ask you to do it, in spite of former obligations; but you can't. I have got into a difficulty—pecuniary, of course; and as the law of liability in this city happens to be a trifle more stringent than our amiable British code, I have no alternative but to bid good-bye to the towers of Notre Dame. I love the dear, disreputable city, with her lights and laughter, and music and mirth; but she loves not me. — When those boys have done gorging themselves, Bessie, you had better put on your bonnet. "

"His wife cast an appealing glance at George Fairfax, as if she felt she had a friend in him who would sustain her in any argument with her husband. Her face was very sad, and bore the traces of many tears.

"If you would only tell me why we are going, Austin, " she pleaded, "I could bear it so much better. "

"Nonsense, child! Would anything I could tell you alter the fact that we are going? Pshaw, Bessie! why make a fuss about trifles? The packing is over: that was the grand difficulty, I thought. I told you we could manage that. "

"It seems so hard—running away like criminals. "

Austin Lovel's countenance darkened a little.

"I can go alone, " he said.

"No, no, " cried the wife piteously: "I'll go with you. I don't want to vex you, Austin. Haven't I shared everything with you—everything? I would go with you if it was to prison—if it was to death. You know that. "

"I know that we shall lose the three-fifteen train if you don't put on your bonnet. "

"Very well, Austin; I'm going. And Clarissa—what will she think of us? I'm so sorry to leave her. "

"O, by the way, George, " said Austin, "you might manage that business for me. My sister was to be here at five o'clock this afternoon. I've written her a letter telling her of the change in my plans. She was in some measure prepared for my leaving Paris; but not quite so suddenly as this. I was going to send the letter by a commissionnaire; but if you don't mind taking it to the Rue de Morny, I'd rather trust it to you. I don't want Clary to come here and find empty rooms. "

He took a sealed letter from the mantelpiece and handed it to George Fairfax, who received it with somewhat of a dreamy air, as of a man who does not quite understand the mission that is intrusted to him. It was a simple business enough, too—only the delivery of a letter.

Mrs. Lovel came out of the adjoining room dressed for the journey, and carrying a collection of wraps for the children. It was wonderful to behold what comforters, and scarves, and gaiters, and muffetees those juvenile individuals required for their equipment.

"Such a long cold journey! " the anxious mother exclaimed, and went on winding up the two children in woollen stuffs, as if they had been royal mummies. She pushes little papers of sandwiches into their pockets—sandwiches that would hardly be improved by the squeezing and sitting upon they must need undergo in the transit.

When this was done, and the children ready, she looked into the painting-room with a melancholy air.

"Think of all the furniture, Austin, " she exclaimed; "the cabinets and things! "

"Yes; there's a considerable amount of money wasted there Bess; for I don't suppose we shall ever see the things again, but there's a good many of them not paid for. There's comfort in that reflection. "

"You take everything go lightly, " she said with a hopeless sigh.

"There's nothing between that and the Morgue, my dear. You'd scarcely like to see me framed and glazed *there*, I think. "

"O, Austin! "

"Precisely. So let me take things lightly, while I can. Now, Bess, the time is up. Good-bye, George. "

"I'll come downstairs with you, " said Mr. Fairfax, still in a somewhat dreamy state. He had put Austin's letter into his pocket, and was standing at a window looking down into the street, which had about as much life or traffic for a man to stare at as some of the lateral streets in the Bloomsbury district—Caroline-place, for instance, or Keppel-street.

There was a great struggling and bumping of porters and coachman on the stairs, with a good deal more exclamation than would have proceeded from stalwart Englishmen under the same circumstances; and then Austin went down to the coach with his wife and children, followed by George Fairfax. The painter happened not to be in debt to his landlord—a gentleman who gave his tenants small grace at any time; so there was no difficulty about the departure.

"I'll write to Monsieur Meriste about my furniture, " he said to the guardian of the big dreary mansion. "You may as well come to the station with us, George, " he added, looking at Mr. Fairfax, who stood irresolute on the pavement, while Bessie and the boys were being packed into the vehicle, the roof of which was laden with portmanteaus and the painter's "plant. "

"Well—no; I think not. There's this letter to be delivered, you see. I had better do that at once. "

"True; Clarissa might come. She said five o'clock, though; but it doesn't matter. Good-bye, old fellow. I hope some of these days I may be able to make things square with you. Good-bye, Tell Clary I shall write to her from Brussels, under cover to the maid as usual. "

He called out to the coachman to go on; and the carriage drove off, staggering under its load. George Fairfax stood watching it till it was out of sight, and then turned to the porter.

"Those rooms up-stairs will be to let, I suppose? " he said.

"But certainly, monsieur. "

"I have some thoughts of taking them for—for a friend. I'll just take another look round them now they're empty. And perhaps you wouldn't mind my writing a letter up-stairs—eh? "

He slipped a napoleon into the man's hand—by no means the first that he had given him. New-Year's day was not far past; and the porter remembered that Mr. Fairfax had tipped him more liberally than some of the lodgers in the house. If monsieur had a legion of letters to write, he was at liberty to write them. The rooms up yonder were entirely at his disposal; the porter laid them at his feet, as it were. He might have occupied them rent-free for the remainder of his existence, it would have been supposed from the man's manner.

"If madame, the sister of Monsieur Austin, should come by-and-by, you will permit her to ascend, " said Mr. Fairfax. "I have a message for her from her brother. "

"Assuredly, monsieur. "

The porter retired into his den to meditate upon his good fortune. It was a rendezvous, of course, cunningly arranged on the day of the painter's departure. It seemed to him like a leaf out of one of those flabby novels on large paper, with a muddy wood-cut on every sixteenth page, which he thumbed and pored over now and then of an evening.

George Fairfax went up-stairs. How supremely dismal the rooms looked in their emptiness, with the litter of packing lying about! — old boots and shoes in one corner; a broken parasol in another; battered fragments of toys everywhere; empty colour-tubes; old newspapers and magazines; a regiment of empty oil-flasks and wine-bottles in the den of a kitchen—into which Mr. Fairfax peered curiously, out of very weariness. It was only half-past three; and there was little hope of Clarissa's arrival until five. He meant to meet her there. In the moment that Austin put the letter in his hand some such notion flashed into his mind. He had never intended to deliver the letter. How long he had waited for this chance—to see her alone, free from all fear of interruption, and to be able to tell his story and plead his cause, as he felt that he could plead!

He walked up and down the empty painting-room, thinking of her coming, meditating what he should say, acting the scene over in his brain. He had little fear as to the issue. Secure as she seemed in the panoply of her woman's pride, he knew his power, and fancied that it needed only time and opportunity to win her. This was not the first time he had counted his chances and arranged his plan of action. In the hour he first heard of her marriage he had resolved to win her. Outraged love transformed itself into a passion that was something akin to revenge. He scarcely cared how low he might bring her, so long as he won her for his own. He did not stop to consider whether hers was a mind which could endure dishonour. He knew that she loved him, and that her married life had been made unhappy because of this fatal love.

"I will open the doors of her prison-house, " he said to himself, "poor fettered soul! She shall leave that dreary conventional life, with its forms and ceremonies of pleasure; and we will wander all over the earth together, only to linger wherever this world is brightest. What can she lose by the exchange? Not wealth. For the command of all that makes life delightful, I am as rich a man as Daniel Granger, and anything beyond that is a barren surplus. Not position; for what position has she as Mrs. Granger? I will take her away from all the people who ever knew her, and guard her jealously from the hazard of shame. There will only be a couple of years in her life which she will have to blot out—only a leaf torn out of her history. "

And the child? the blue-eyed boy that George Fairfax had stopped to kiss in Arden Park that day? It is one thing to contemplate stealing a wife from her husband—with George Fairfax's class there is a natural antipathy to husbands, which makes that seem a fair warfare, like fox-hunting—but it is another to rob a child of its mother. Mr. Fairfax's meditations came to a standstill at this point—the boy blocked the line.

There was only one thing to be done; put on the steam, and run down the obstacle, as Isambard Brunel did in the Box-tunnel, when he saw a stray luggage-truck between him and the light.

"Let her bring the boy with her, and he shall be my son, " he thought.

Daniel Granger would go in for a divorce, of course. Mr. Fairfax thought of everything in that hour and a half of solitary reflection. He would try for a divorce, and there would be no end of scandal—leading articles in some of the papers, no doubt, upon the immorality of the upper middle classes; a full-flavoured essay in the Saturday, proving that Englishwomen were in the habit of running away from their husbands. But she should be far away from the bruit of that scandal. He would make it the business of his life to shield her from the lightest breath of insult. It could be done. There were new worlds, in which men and women could begin a fresh existence, under new names; and if by chance any denizen of the old world should cross their path untimely—well, such unwelcome wanderers are generally open to negotiation. There is a good deal of charity for such offenders among the travelled classes, especially when the chief sinner is lord of such an estate as Lyvedon.

Yet, varnish the picture how one will, dress up the story with what flowers of fancy one may, it is at best but a patched and broken business. The varnish brings out dark spots in the picture; the flowers have a faded meretricious look, not the bloom and dew of the garden; no sophistry can overcome the inherent ugliness of the thing—an honest man's name dishonoured; two culprits planning a future life, to be spent in hiding from the more respectable portion of their species; two outcasts, trying to make believe that the wildernesses beyond Eden are fairer than that paradise itself.

His mother—what would she feel when she came to know what he had done with his life? It would be a disappointment to her, of course; a grief, no doubt; but she would have Lyvedon. He had gone too far to be influenced by any consideration of that kind; he had gone so far that life without Clarissa seemed to him unendurable. He paced the room, contemplating this crisis of his existence from every point of view, till the gray winter sky grew darker, and the time of Clarissa's coming drew very near. There had been some logs smouldering on the hearth when he came, and these he had replenished from time to time. The glow of the fire was the only thing that relieved the dreariness of the room.

Nothing could be more fortunate, he fancied, than the accident which had brought about this meeting. Daniel Granger was away. The flight, which was to be the preface of Clarissa's new existence, could not take place too soon; no time need be wasted on preparations, which could only serve to betray. Her consent once gained, he had only to put her into a hackney-coach and drive to the Marseilles station. Why should they not start that very night? There was a train that left Paris at seven, he knew; in three days they might be on the shores of the Adriatic.

* * * * *

CHAPTER XLI.

MR. GRANGER'S WELCOME HOME.

Clarissa left the Rue de Morny at three o'clock that day. She had a round of calls to make, and for that reason had postponed her visit to her brother's painting-room to a later hour than usual. The solemn dinner, which she shared with Miss Granger in stately solitude, took place at half-past seven, until which hour she considered her time at her own disposal.

Sophia spent that particular afternoon at home, illuminating the new gothic texts for her schoolrooms at Arden. She had been seated at her work about an hour after Clarissa's departure, when the door opened behind her, and her father walked into the room.

There had been no word of his return in his latest letter; he had only said generally in a previous epistle, that he should come back directly the business that had called him to Yorkshire was settled.

"Good gracious me, papa, how you startled me! " cried Miss Granger, dabbing at a spot of ultramarine which had fallen upon her work. It was not a very warm welcome; but when she had made the best she could of that unlucky blue spot, she laid down her brush and came over to her father, to whom she offered a rather chilly kiss. "You must be very tired, papa, " she remarked, with striking originality.

"Well, no; not exactly tired. We had a very fair passage; but the journey from Calais is tedious. It seems as if Calais oughtn't to be any farther from Paris than Dover is from London. There's something lop-sided in it. I read the papers all the way. Where's Clarry? "

"Clarissa has gone to pay some visits. "

"Why didn't you go with her? "

"I rarely do go with her, papa. Our sets are quite different; and I have other duties. "

"Duties, pshaw! Messing with those paint-brushes; you don't call that duty, I hope? You had much better have gone out with your stepmother. "

"I was not wanted, papa. Mrs. Granger has engagements which do not in the least concern me. I should only be in the way. "

"What do you mean by that, Sophia? " asked her father sternly. "And what do you mean by calling my wife Mrs. Granger? "

"There are some people so uncongenial to each other, papa, that any pretence of friendship can be only the vilest hypocrisy, " replied Sophia, turning very pale, and looking her father full in the face, like a person prepared to do battle.

"I am very sorry to hear this, Sophia, " said Mr. Granger. "for if this is really the case, it will be necessary for you to seek some other home. I will have no one in my house who cannot value my wife. "

"You would turn me out of doors, papa? "

"I should certainly endeavour to provide you with a more congenial—congenial, that was the word you used, I think—more congenial home. "

"Indeed! " exclaimed Sophia. "Then I suppose you quite approve of all my stepmother's conduct—of her frequent, almost daily visits to such a person as Mr. Austin? "

"Clarissa's visits to Austin! What, in heaven's name, do you mean? "

"What, papa! is it possible you are ignorant of the fact? I thought that, though my stepmother never talked to *me* of her visits to the Rue du Chevalier Bayard, you of course knew all about them. Though I hardly supposed you would encourage such an intimacy. "

"Encourage such an intimacy! You must be dreaming, girl. My wife visit a portrait-painter—a single man? "

"He is not a single man, papa. There is a wife, I understand; though he never mentioned her to us. And Clarissa visits them almost every day. "

388

"I don't believe it. What motive could she have for cultivating such people? "

"I can't imagine—except that she is fond of that kind of society, and of painting. She may have gone to take lessons of Mr. Austin. He teaches, I know. "

Daniel Granger was silent. It was not impossible; and it would have been no crime on his wife's part, of course. But the idea that Clarissa could have done such a thing without his knowledge and approval, offended him beyond measure. He could hardly realize the possibility of such an act.

"There is some misapprehension on your part, Sophia, I am convinced, " he said. "If Clarissa had wished to take drawing lessons from Austin, she would have told me so. "

"There is no possibility of a mistake on my part, papa. I am not in the habit of making statements which I cannot support. "

"Who told you of these visits? Clarissa herself? "

"O dear, no; Clarissa is not in the habit of telling me her affairs. I heard it from Warman; not in reply to any questioning of mine, I can assure you. But the thing has been so frequent, that the servants have begun to talk about it. Of course, I always make a point of discouraging any speculations upon my stepmother's conduct. "

The servants had begun to talk; his wife's intimacy with people of whom he knew scarcely anything had been going on so long as to provoke the gossip of the household; and he had heard nothing of it until this moment! The thought stung him to the quick. That domestic slander should have been busy with her name already; that she should have lived her own life so entirely without reference to him! Both thoughts were alike bitter. Yet it was no new thing for him to know that she did not love him.

He looked at his watch meditatively.

"Has she gone there this afternoon, do you think? " he asked.

"I think it is excessively probable. Warman tells me she has been there every afternoon during your absence. "

"She must have taken a strange fancy to these people. Austin's wife is some old schoolfellow of Clary's perhaps. "

Miss Granger shook her head doubtfully.

"I should hardly think that, " she said.

"There must be some reason—something that we cannot understand. She may have some delicacy about talking to me of these people; there may be something in their circumstances to—"

"Yes, " said Miss Granger, "there is *something*, no doubt. I have been assured of that from the first. "

"What did you say the address was? "

"The Rue du Chevalier Bayard, Number 7. "

Mr. Granger left the room without another word. He was not a man to remain long in doubt upon any question that could be solved by prompt investigation. He went out into the hall, where a footman sat reading *Galignani* in the lamplight.

"Has Mrs. Granger's carriage come back, Saunders? " he asked.

"Yes, sir; the carriage has been back a quarter of an hour. I were out with my mistress. "

"Where is Mrs. Granger? In her own rooms? "

"No, sir; Mrs. Granger didn't come home in the carriage. We drove her to the Shangs Elysy first, sir, and afterwards to the Rue du Cavalier Baynard; and Mr. Fairfax, he came down and told me my mistress wouldn't want the carriage to take her home. "

"Mr. Fairfax—in the Rue du Chevalier Bayard! "

"Yes, sir; he's an intimate friend of Mr. Hostin's, I believe. Leastways, we've seen him there very often. "

George Fairfax! George Fairfax a frequent guest of those people whom she visited! That slumbering demon, which had been sheltered in Daniel Granger's breast so long, arose rampant at the sound of this name. George Fairfax, the man he suspected in the past; the man whom he had done his best to keep out of his wife's pathway in the present, but who, by some fatality, was not be avoided. Had Clarissa cultivated an intimacy with this Bohemian painter and his wife only for the sake of meeting George Fairfax without her husband's knowledge? To suppose this was to imagine a depth of depravity in the heart of the woman he loved. And he had believed her so pure, so noble a creature. The blow was heavy. He stood looking at his servant for a moment or so, paralysed; but except that one blank gaze, he gave no sign of his emotion. He only took up his hat, and went quietly out. "His looks was orful! " the man said afterwards in the servants' hall.

Sophia came out of the drawing-room to look for her father, just a little disturbed by the thought of what she had done. She had gone too far, perhaps. There had been something in her father's look when he asked her for that address that had alarmed her. He was gone; gone *there*, no doubt, to discover his wife's motives for those strange visits. Miss Granger's heart was not often fluttered as it was this evening. She could not "settle to anything, " as she said herself, but wandered up into the nursery, and stood by the dainty little cot, staring absently at her baby brother as he slept.

"If anything should happen, " she thought—and that event which she vaguely foreshadowed was one that would leave the child motherless—"I should make it *my* duty to superintend his rearing. No one should have power to say that I was jealous of the brother who has robbed me of my heritage. "

* * * * *

CHAPTER XLII.

CAUGHT IN A TRAP.

It was dusk when Clarissa's carriage drove into the Rue du Chevalier Bayard—the dull gray gloaming of February—and the great bell of Notre Dame was booming five. She had been paying visits of duty, talking banalities in fashionable drawing-rooms, and she was weary. She seemed to breathe a new life as she approached her brother's dwelling. Here there would be the free reckless utterance of minds that harmonised, of souls that sympathised: — instead of stereotyped little scraps of gossip about the great world, or arid discussion of new plays and famous opera-singers.

She did not stop to ask any questions of the complacent porter. It was not her habit to do so. She had never yet failed to find Austin, or Austin's wife, at home at this hour. She went swiftly up the darksome staircase, where never a lamp was lighted to illumine the stranger, only an occasional candle thrust out of a doorway by some friendly hand. In the dusk of this particular evening there was not so much as a glimmer.

The outer door was ajar—not such an uncommon thing as to occasion any surprise to Clarissa. She pushed it open and went in, across a dingy lobby some four feet square, on which abutted the kitchen, and into the salon. This was dark and empty; but one of the folding-doors leading into the painting-room was open, and she saw the warm glow of the fire shining on the old Flemish cabinets and the brazen chandelier. That glow of firelight had a comfortable look after the desolation and darkness of the salon.

She went into the painting-room. There was a tall figure standing by one of the windows, looming gigantic through the dusk—a figure she knew very well, but not Austin's. She looked quickly round the room, expecting to see her brother lounging by the chimney-piece, or wandering about somewhere in his desultory way; but there was no one else, only that tall figure by the window.

The silence and emptiness of the place, and *his* presence, startled her a little.

"Good-evening, Mr. Fairfax, " she said. "Isn't Austin here? "

"Not at this moment. How do you do, Mrs. Granger? " and they shook hands. So commonplace a meeting might almost have disappointed the sentimental porter.

"And Bessie? " Clarissa asked.

"She too is out of the way for the moment, " replied George Fairfax, glancing out of the window. "You came in your carriage, I suppose, Mrs. Granger? If you'll excuse me for a moment, I'll just ran and see if—if Austin has come in again. "

He went quickly out of the room and downstairs, not to look for Austin Lovel, who was on his way to Brussels by this time, but to tell Mrs. Granger's coachman she had no farther use for the carriage, and would not be home to dinner. The man looked a little surprised at this order, but Mr. Fairfax's tone was too peremptory to be unauthorised; so he drove homeward without hesitation.

Clarissa was seated in her favourite easy-chair, looking pensively at the wood-fire, when George Fairfax came back. She heard his returning footsteps, and the sharp click of a key turning in the outer door. This sound set her wondering. What door was that being locked, and by whom?

Mr. Fairfax came into the painting-room. It was the crisis of his life, he told himself. If he failed to obtain some promise from her to-night—some definite pledge of his future happiness—he could never hope to succeed.

"Time and I against any two, " he had said to himself sometimes in relation to this business. He had been content to bide his time; but the golden opportunity had come at last. If he failed to-night, he failed forever.

"Is he coming? " Clarissa asked, rather anxiously. There was something ominous in the stillness of the place, and the absence of any sign of life except George Fairfax's presence.

"Not immediately. Don't alarm yourself, " he said hurriedly, as Clarissa rose with a frightened look. "There is nothing really wrong, only there are circumstances that I felt it better to break to you gently. Yet I fear I am an awkward hand at doing that, at the best. The fact is, your brother has left Paris. "

"Left Paris! "

"Yes, only a couple of hours ago. " And then Mr. Fairfax went on to tell the story of Austin's departure, making as light of it as he could, and with no word of that letter which had been given him to deliver.

The news was a shock to Clarissa. Very well did she remember what her brother had told her about the probability of his being compelled to "cut Paris. " It had come, then, some new disgrace, and banished him from the city he loved—the city in which his talents had won for him a budding reputation, that might have blossomed into fame, if he had only been a wiser and a better man. She heard George Fairfax in silence, her head bowed with shame. This man was her brother, and she loved him so dearly.

"Do you know where they have gone? " she asked at last.

"To Brussels. He may do very well there, no doubt, if he will only keep himself steady—turn his back upon the rackety society he is so fond of—and work honestly at his art. It is a place where they can live more cheaply, too, than they could here. "

"I am so sorry they are gone without a word of parting. It must have been very sudden. "

"Yes. I believe the necessity for the journey arose quite suddenly; or it may have been hanging over your brother for a long time, and he may have shut his eyes to the fact until the last moment. He is such a fellow for taking things easily. However, he did not enter into explanations with me. "

"Poor Austin! What a wretched life! "

Clarissa rose and moved slowly towards the folding-doors. George Fairfax stopped her at the threshold, and quietly closed the door.

"Don't go yet, Clarissa. I want to speak to you. "

His tone told her what was coming—the scene in the conservatory was to be acted over again. This was the first time they had been actually alone since that too-well-remembered night.

She drew herself up haughtily. A woman's weakness makes her desperate in such a case as this.

"I have no time to talk now, Mr. Fairfax. I am going home. "

"Not yet, Clarissa. I have waited a long time for this chance. I am determined to say my say. "

"You will not compel me to listen to you? "

"Compel is a very hard word. I beseech you to hear me. My future life depends on what I have to say, and on your answer. "

"I cannot hear a word! I will not remain a moment! "

"The door yonder is locked, Clarissa, and the key in my pocket. Brutal, you will say. The circumstances of our lives have left me no option. I have watched and waited for such an opportunity as this; and now, Clarissa, you shall hear me. Do you remember that night in the orchard, when you drove me away by your coldness and obstinacy? And yet you loved me! You have owned it since. Ah, my darling, how I have hated myself for my dulness that night! —hated myself for not having seized you in my arms, if need were, and carried you off to the end of the world to make you my wife. What a fool and craven I must have been to be put off so easily! "

"Nothing can be more foolish than to discuss the past, Mr. Fairfax, " replied Clarissa, in a low voice that trembled a little. "You have made me do wrong more than once in my life. There must be an end of this. What would my husband think, if he could hear you? what would he think of me for listening to you? Let me pass, if you please; and God grant that we may never meet again after to-night! "

"God grant that we may never part, Clarissa! O, my love, my love, for pity's sake be reasonable! We are not children to play fast and loose with our lives. You love me, Clary. No sweet-spoken pretences, no stereotyped denials, will convince me. You love me, my darling, and the world is all before us. I have mapped-out our future; no sorrow or discredit shall ever come nigh you—trust a lover's foresight for that. Whatever difficulties may lie in our pathway are difficulties that I will face and conquer—alone. You have only to forget that you have ever been Daniel Granger's wife, and leave Paris with me to-night. "

"Mr. Fairfax! are you mad? "

"Never more reasonable—never so much in earnest. Come with me, Clarissa. It is not a sacrifice that I ask from you: I offer you a release. Do you think there is any virtue or beauty in your present life, or any merit in continuing it? From first to last, your existence is a lie. Do you think a wedding-ring redeems the honour of a woman who sells herself for money? There is no slavery more degrading than the bondage of such an alliance. "

"Open the door, Mr. Fairfax, and let me go! "

His reproaches stung her to the quick; they were so bitterly true.

"Not till you have heard me, my darling—not till you have heard me out. "

His tone changed all at once, softening into ineffable tenderness. He told her of his love with words of deeper passion than he had ever spoken yet—words that went home to the heart that loved him. For a moment, listening to that impassioned pleading, it seemed to Clarissa that this verily was life indeed—that to be so loved was in itself alone the perfect joy and fulness of existence, leaving nothing more to be desired, making shame as nothing in the balance. In that one moment the guilty heart was well-nigh yielding; the bewildered brain could scarcely maintain the conflict of thought and feeling. Then suddenly this mental agony changed to a strange dulness, a mist rose between Clarissa and the eager face of her lover. She was nearer fainting than she had ever been in her life before.

George Fairfax saw her face whiten, and the slender figure totter ever so slightly. In a moment a strong arm was round her. The weary head sank on his shoulder.

"My darling, " he whispered, "why not leave Paris to-night? It cannot be too soon. Your husband is away. We shall have a start of two or three days, and avoid all risk of pursuit. "

"Not quite, " said a voice close behind him; and looking round, George Fairfax saw one of the folding-doors open, and Daniel Granger standing on the threshold. The locked outer door had availed the traitor nothing. Mr. Granger had come upstairs with the porter, who carried a bunch of duplicate keys in his pocket.

Clarissa gave a sudden cry, which rose in the next instant to a shrill scream. Two men were struggling in the doorway, grappling each other savagely for one dreadful minute of confusion and agony. Then one fell heavily, his head crashing against the angle of the doorway, and lay at full length, with his white face looking up to the ceiling.

This was George Fairfax.

Clarissa threw herself upon her knees beside the prostrate figure.

"George! George! " she cried piteously.

It was the first time she had ever uttered his Christian name, except in her dreams; and yet it came to her lips as naturally in that moment of supreme agony as if it had been their every-day utterance.

"George! George! " she cried again, bending down to gaze at the white blank face dimly visible in the firelight; and then, with a still sharper anguish, "He is dead! "

The sight of that kneeling figure, the sound of that piteous imploring voice, was well-nigh maddening to Daniel Granger. He caught his wife by the arm, and dragged her up from her knees with no tender hand.

"You have killed him, " she said.

"I hope I have. "

Whatever latent passion there was in this man's nature was at white heat now. An awful fury possessed him. He seemed transformed by the intensity of his anger. His bulky figure rose taller; his full gray eyes shone with a pitiless light under the straight stern brows.

"Yes, " he said, "I hope I have killed your lover. "

"My lover! "

"Your lover—the man with whom you were to have left Paris to-night. Your lover—the man you have met in this convenient rendezvous, day after day for the last two months. Your lover—the man you loved before you did me the honour to accept the use of my fortune, and whom you have loved ever since. "

"Yes, " cried Clarissa, with a wild hysterical laugh, "my lover! You are right. I am the most miserable woman upon earth, for I love him. "

"I am glad you do not deny it. Stand out of the way, if you please, and let me see if I have killed him. "

There were a pair of half-burned wax candles on the mantelpiece. Mr. Granger lighted one of them, and then knelt down beside the prostrate figure with the candle in his hand. George Fairfax had given no sign of life as yet. There had not been so much as a groan.

He opened his enemy's waistcoat, and laid his hand above the region of the heart. Yes, there was life still—a dull beating. The wretch was not dead.

While he knelt thus, with his hand upon George Fairfax's heart, a massive chain, loosened from its moorings, fell across his wrist. Attached to the chain there was a locket—a large gold locket with a diamond cross—one of the ornaments that Daniel Granger had given to his wife.

He remembered it well. It was a very trifle among the gifts be had showered upon her; but he remembered it well. If this had been the one solitary gem he had given to his wife, he could not have been quicker to recognise it, or more certain of its identity.

He took it in the palm of his hand and touched the spring, holding the candle still in the other hand. The locket flew open, and he saw the ring of silky brown hair and the inscription, "From Clarissa. "

He looked up at his wife with a smile—such a smile! "You might have afforded your lover something better than a secondhand *souvenir*, " he said.

Clarissa's eyes wandered from the still white face, with its awful closed eyes, only to rest for a moment on the unlucky locket.

"I gave that to my sister-in-law, " she said indifferently. "Heaven only knows how he came by it. " And then, in a different tone, she asked, "Why don't you do something for him? Why don't you fetch some one? Do you want him to die? "

"Yes. Do you think anything less than his death would satisfy me? Don't alarm yourself; I am not going to kill him. I was quite ready to do it just now in hot blood. But he is safe enough now. What good would there be in making an end of him? There are two of you in it. "

"You can kill me, if you like, " said Clarissa "Except for my child's sake, I have little wish to live. "

"For your child's sake! " echoed her husband scornfully. "Do you think there is anything in common between my son and you, after to-night. "

He dropped the locket on George Fairfax's breast with a contemptuous gesture, as if he had been throwing away a handful of dirt. *That* folly had cost dearly enough.

"I'll go and fetch some one, " he said. "Don't let your distraction make you forget that the man wants all the air he can get. You had better stand away from him. "

Clarissa obeyed mechanically. She stood a little way off, staring at that lifeless figure, while Daniel Granger went to fetch the porter. The house was large, and at this time in the evening for the most part untenanted, and Austin's painting-room was over the arched carriage-way. Thus it happened that no one had heard that fall of George Fairfax's.

Mr. Granger explained briefly that the gentleman had had a fall, and was stunned—would the porter fetch the nearest doctor? The man looked a him rather suspiciously. The lovely lady's arrival in the gloaming; a locked door; this middle-aged Englishman's eagerness to get into the rooms; and now a fall and the young Englishman is disabled. The leaf out of a romance began to assume a darker aspect. There had been murder done, perhaps, up yonder. The porter's comprehensive vision surveyed the things that might be—the house fallen into evil repute by reason of this crime, and bereft of lodgers. The porter was an elderly man, and did not care to shift his household gods.

"What have they come to do up there? " he asked. "I think I had better fetch the *sergent de ville.* "

"You are quite at liberty to do that, provided you bring a doctor along with him, " replied Daniel Granger coolly, and then turned on his heel and walked upstairs again.

He roamed through the empty rooms with a candle in his hand until he found a bottle of water, some portion of which he dashed into his enemy's face, kneeling by his side to do it, but with a cool off-hand air, as if he were reviving a dog, and that a dog upon, which he set no value.

George Fairfax opened his eyes, very slowly, and groaned aloud.

"O God, my head! " he said. "What a blow! "

He had a sensation of lying at the bottom of a steep hill—on a sharp inclined plane, as it were, with his feet uppermost—a sense of suffocation, too, as if his throat had been full of blood. There seemed to him to be blood in his eyes also; and he could only see things in a dim cloudy way—a room—what room he could not remember—one candle flaring on the mantelpiece, and the light of an expiring fire.

Of the things that had happened to him immediately before that struggle and that fall, he had, for the time being, no memory. But by slow degrees it dawned upon him that this was Austin Lovel's painting-room.

"Where the devil are you, Austin? " he asked impatiently.

"Can't you pick a fellow up? "

A grasp stronger than ever Austin Lovel's had been, dragged him to his feet, and half led, half pushed him into the nearest chair. He sat there, staring blankly before him. Clarissa had moved away from him, and stood amid the deep shadows at the other end of the studio, waiting for her doom. It seemed to her to matter very little what that doom should be. Perfect ruin had come upon her. The porter came in presently with a doctor—a little old grey-headed man, who wore spectacles, and had an ancient doddering manner not calculated to inspire beholders with any great belief in his capacity.

He bowed to Mr. Granger in on old-fashioned ceremonious way, and went over to the patient.

"A fall, I believe you say, monsieur! " he said.

"Yes, a fall. He struck his head against the angle of that doorway. "

Mr. Granger omitted to state that it was a blow between the eyes from his clenched fist which had felled George Fairfax—a blow sent straight out from the powerful shoulder.

"There was no seizure—no fit of any kind, I hope? "

"No. "

The patient had recovered himself considerably by this time, and twitched his wrist rather impatiently from the little doctor's timid grasp.

"I am well enough now, " he said in a thick voice. "There was no occasion to send for a medical man. I stumbled at the doorway yonder, and knocked my head in falling—that's all. "

The Frenchman was manipulating Mr. Fairfax's cranium with cautious fingers.

"There is a considerable swelling at the back of the skull, " he said. "But there appears to have been another blow on the forehead. There is a puffiness, and a slight abrasion of the skin. "

Mr. Fairfax extricated his head from this investigation by standing up suddenly out of reach of the small doctor. He staggered a little as he rose to his feet, but recovered himself after a moment or so, and stood firmly enough, with his hand resting on the back of the chair.

"If you will be good enough to accept this by way of fee, " he said, slipping a napoleon into the doctor's hand, "I need give you no farther trouble. "

The old man looked rather suspiciously from Mr. Fairfax to Mr. Granger and then back again. There was something queer in the business evidently, but a napoleon was a napoleon, and his fees were neither large nor numerous. He coughed feebly behind his hand, hesitated a little, and then with a sliding bow slipped from the room.

The porter lingered, determined to see the end of the romance, at any rate.

It was not long.

"Are you ready to come away? " Daniel Granger asked his wife, in a cold stern voice. And then, turning to George Fairfax, he said, "You know where to find me, sir, when you wish to settle the score between us. "

"I shall call upon you to-morrow morning, Mr. Granger. "

Clarissa looked at George Fairfax piteously for a moment, wondering if he had been much hurt—if there were any danger to be feared from the effects or that crushing fall. Never for an instant of her life had she meant to be false to her husband; but she loved this man; and her secret being discovered now, she deemed that the bond between her and Daniel Granger was broken. She looked at George Fairfax with that brief yearning look, just long enough to see that he was deadly pale; and then left the room with her husband, obeying him mechanically They went down the darksome staircase, which had grown so familiar to Clarissa, out into the empty street. There was a hackney carriage waiting near the archway—the carriage that had brought Mr. Granger. He put his wife into it without a word, and took his seat opposite to her; and so they drove home in profound silence.

Clarissa went straight to her room—the dressing-room in which Daniel Granger had talked to her the night before ha went to England. How well she remembered his words, and her own inclination to tell him everything! If she had only obeyed that impulse—if she had only confessed the truth—the shame and ignominy of to-night would have been avoided. There would have been no chance of that fatal meeting with George Fairfax; her husband would have sheltered her from danger and temptation— would have saved her from herself.

Vain regrets. The horror of that scene was still present with her— must remain so present with her till the end of her life, she thought. Those two men grappling each other, and then the fall—the tall figure crashing down with the force of a descending giant, as it had seemed to that terror-stricken spectator. For a long time she sat thinking of that awful moment—thinking of it with a concentration which left no capacity for any other thought in her mind. Her maid had come to her, and removed her out-of-door garments, and stirred the fire, and had set out a dainty little tea-tray on a table close at hand, hovering about her mistress with a sympathetic air, conscious that there was something amiss. But Clarissa had been hardly aware of the girl's presence. She was living over again the agony of that moment in which she thought George Fairfax was dead.

This could not last for ever. She awoke by and by to the thought of her child, with her husband's bitter words ringing in her ears, —

"Do you think there is anything in common between my son and you, after to-night? "

"Perhaps they will shut me out of my nursery, " she thought.

The rooms sacred to Lovel Granger were on the same floor as her own—she had stipulated that it should be so. She went out into the corridor from which all the rooms opened. All was silent. The boy had gone to bed, of course, by this time; very seldom had she been absent at the hour of his retirement. It had been her habit to spend a stolen half-hour in the nursery just before dressing for dinner, or to have her boy brought to her dressing-room—one of the happiest half-hours in her day. No one barred her entrance to the nursery. Mrs. Brobson was sitting by the fire, making-believe to be busy at needlework, with the under-nurse in attendance—a buxom damsel, whose elbows rested on the table as she conversed with her superior. Both looked up in some slight confusion at Clarissa's entrance. They had been talking about her, she thought, but with a supreme indifference. No petty household slander could trouble her in her great sorrow. She went on towards the inner room, where her darling slept, the head-nurse following obsequiously with a candle. In the night-nursery there was only the subdued light of a shaded lamp.

"Thank you, Mrs. Brobson, but I don't want any more light, " Clarissa said quietly. "I am going to sit with baby for a little while. Take the candle away, please; it may wake him. "

It was the first time she had spoken since she had left the Rue du Chevalier Bayard. Her own voice sounded strange to her; and yet its tone could scarcely have betrayed less agitation.

"The second dinner-bell has rung, ma'am, " Mrs. Brobson said, with a timorously-suggestive air; "I don't know whether you are aware. "

"Yes, I know, but I am not going down to dinner; I have a wretched headache. You can tell Target to say so, if they send for me. "

"Yes, ma'am; but you'll have something sent up, won't you? "

"Not yet; by and by, perhaps, I'll take a cup of tea in my dressing-room. Go and tell Target, please, Mrs. Brobson; Mr. Granger may be waiting dinner. "

She was so anxious to get rid of the woman, to be alone with her baby. She sat down by the cot. O, inestimable treasure! had she held him so lightly as to give any other a place in her heart? To harbour any guilty thought was to have sinned against this white-souled innocent. If those clear eyes, which looked up from her breast sometimes with such angelic tenderness, could have read the secrets of her sinful heart, how could she have dared to meet their steadfast gaze? To-night that sleeping baby seemed something more to her than her child; he was her judge.

"O, my love, my love, I am not good enough to have you for my son! " she murmured, sobbing, as she knelt by his side, resting her tired head upon his pillow, thinking idly how sweet it would be to die thus, and make an end of all this evil.

She stayed with her child for more than an hour undisturbed, wondering whether there would be any attempt to take him away from her—whether there was any serious meaning in those pitiless words of Daniel Granger's. Could he think for a moment that she would surrender him? Could he suppose that she would lose this very life of her life, and live?

At a little after nine o'clock, she heard the door of the outer nursery open, and a masculine step in the room—her husband's. The door between the two nurseries was half open. She could hear every word that was spoken; she could see Daniel Granger's figure, straight and tall and ponderous, as he stood by the table talking to Mrs. Brobson.

"I am going back to Arden the day after to-morrow, Brobson, " he said; "you will have everything ready, if you please. "

"O, certainly, sir; we can be ready. And I'm sure I shall rejoice to see our own house again, after all the ill-conveniences of this place. " And Mrs. Brobson looked round the handsomely-furnished apartment as if it had been a hovel. "Frenchified ways don't suit me, " she remarked. "If, when they was furnishing their houses, they laid out more money upon water-jugs and wash-hand basins, and less upon clocks and candelabras, it would do them more credit; and if there was a chair to be had not covered with red velvet, it would be a comfort. Luxury is luxury; but you may overdo it. "

This complaint, murmured in a confidential tone, passed unnoticed by Daniel Granger.

"Thursday morning, then, Mrs. Brobson, remember; the train leaves at seven. You'll have to be very early. "

"It can't be too early for me. "

"I'm glad to hear that; I'll go in and take a look at the child—asleep, I suppose? "

"Yes, sir; fast asleep. "

He went into the dimly-lighted chamber, not expecting to see that kneeling figure by the cot. He gave a little start at seeing it, and stood aloof, as if there had been infection that way. Whatever he might feel or think, he could scarcely order his wife away from her son's bedside. Her son! Yes, there was the sting. However he might put her away from himself, he could not utterly sever *that* bond. He would do his best; but in the days to come his boy might revolt against him, and elect to follow that guilty mother.

He had loved her so fondly, he had trusted her so completely; and his anger against her was so much the stronger because of this. He could not forgive her for having made him so weak a dupe. Her own ignominy—and he deemed her the most shameful of women—was not so deep as his disgrace.

He stood aloof, looking at his sleeping boy, looking across the kneeling figure as if not seeing it, but with a smouldering anger in his eyes that betrayed his consciousness of his wife's presence. She raised her haggard eyes to his face. The time would come when she would have to tell him her story—to make some attempt to justify herself—to plead for his pardon; but not yet. There was time enough for that. She felt that the severance between them was utter. He might believe, he might forgive her; but he would never give her his heart again. She felt that this was so, and submitted to the justice of the forfeiture. Nor had she loved him well enough to feel this loss acutely. Her one absorbing agony was the fear of losing her child.

Daniel Granger stood for a little while watching his son's placid slumber, and then left the room without a word. What could he say to his wife? His anger was much too great for words; but there was something more than anger: there was a revulsion of feeling, that made the woman he had loved seem hateful to him—hateful in her fatal beauty, as a snake is hateful in its lithe grace and silvery sheen. She had deceived him so completely; there was something to his mind beyond measure dastardly in her stolen meetings with George Fairfax; and he set down all her visits to the Rue du Chevalier Bayard to that account. She had smiled in his face, and had gone every other day to meet her lover.

Clarissa stayed with her child all that night. The servants would wonder and speculate, no doubt. She knew that; but she could not bring herself to leave him. She had all manner of fantastic fears about him. They would steal him from her in the night, perhaps. That order of Daniel Granger's about Thursday morning might be only a ruse. She laid herself down upon a sofa near the cot, and pretended to sleep, until the nurse had gone to bed, after endless fussings and rustlings and movings to and fro, that were torture to Mrs. Granger's nerves; and then listened and watched all the night through.

No one came. The wintry morning dawned, and found her child still slumbering sweetly, the rosy lips ever so slightly parted, golden-tinted lashes lying on the round pink cheeks. She smiled at her own folly, as she sat watching him in that welcome daylight. What had she expected? Daniel Granger was not an ogre. He could not take her child from her.

Her child! The thought that the boy was *his* child very rarely presented itself to her. Yet it had been suggested rather forcibly by those bitter words of her husband's: "Do you think there is anything in common between my son and you, after to-night? "

For Daniel Granger and herself there might be parting, an eternal severance; but there could be no creature so cruel as to rob her of her child.

She stayed with him during his morning ablutions; saw him splash and kick in the water with the infantine exuberance that mothers love to behold, fondly deeming that no baby ever so splashed or so kicked before; saw him arrayed in his pretty blue-braided frock, and dainty lace-bedizened cambric pinafore. What a wealth of finery and prettiness had been lavished upon the little mortal, who would have been infinitely happier dressed in rags and making mud-pies in a gutter, than in his splendid raiment and well-furnished nursery; an uninteresting nursery, where there were no cupboards full of broken wagons and head-less horses, flat-nosed dolls and armless grenadiers, the cast-off playthings of a flock of brothers and sisters— a very chaos of rapture for the fingers of infancy! Only a few expensive toys from a fashionable purveyor—things that went by machinery, darting forward a little way with convulsive jerks and unearthly choking noises, and then tumbling ignominiously on one side.

Clarissa stayed with the heir of Arden until the clock in the day-nursery struck nine, and then went to her dressing-room, looking very pale and haggard after her sleepless night. In the corridor she met her husband. He bent his head gravely at sight of her, as he might have saluted a stranger whom he encountered in his own house.

"I shall be glad to speak to you for a quarter of an hour, by and by, " he said. "What time would suit you best? " "Whenever you please. I shall be in my dressing-room, " she answered quietly; and then, growing desperate in her desire to know her fate, she exclaimed, "But O, Daniel, are we really to go back to Arden to-morrow? "

"We are not, " he said, with a repelling look. "My children are going back to-morrow. I contemplate other arrangements for you. "

"You mean to separate my baby and me? " she cried incredulously.

"This is neither the place nor the time for any discussion about that. I will come to your dressing-room by and by. "

"I will not be parted from my child! "

"That is a question which I have to settle. "

"Do not make any mistake, Mr. Granger, " Clarissa said firmly, facing him with a dauntless look that surprised him a little—yet what cannot a woman dare, if she can betray the man who has loved and trusted her? "You may do what you please with me; but I will not submit to have my child taken from me. "

"I do not like talking in passages, " said her husband; "if you insist upon discussing this matter now, we had better go into your room. "

They were close to the dressing-room door. He opened it, and they went in. The fire was burning brightly, and the small round table neatly laid for breakfast. Clarissa had been in the habit of using this apartment as her morning-room. There were books and drawing-materials, a table with a drawing-board upon it, and a half-finished sketch.

She sank down into a chair near the fire, too weak to stand. Her husband stood opposite to her. She noticed idly that he was dressed with his usual business-like neatness, and that there was no sign of mental anguish in his aspect. He seemed very cold and hard and cruel as he stood before her, strong in his position as an injured man.

"I am not going to talk about last night any more than I am positively obliged, " he said; "nothing that I or you could say would alter the facts of the case, or my estimation of them. I have made my plans for the future. Sophia and Lovel will go back to Yorkshire to-morrow. You will go with me to Spa, where I shall place you under your father's protection. Your future life will be free from the burden of my society. "

"I am quite willing to go back to my father, " replied Clarissa, in a voice that trembled a little. She had expected him to be very angry, but not so hard and cold as this—not able to deal with her wrong-doing in such a business-like manner, to dismiss her and her sin as coolly as if he had been parting with a servant who had offended him.

"I am ready to go to my father, " she repeated, steadying her voice with an effort; "but I will go nowhere without my child. "

"We will see about that, " said Mr. Granger, "and how the law will treat your claims; if you care to advance them—which I should suppose unlikely. I have no compunction about the justice of my decision. You will go nowhere without your child, you say? Did you think of that last night when your lover was persuading you to leave Paris? "

"What! " cried Clarissa aghast. "Do you imagine that I had any thought of going with him, or that I heard him with my free will? "

"I do not speculate upon that point; but to my mind the fact of his asking you to run away with him argues a foregone conclusion. A man rarely comes to that until he has established a right to make the request. All I know is, that I saw you on your knees by your lover, and that you were candid enough to acknowledge your affection for him. This knowledge is quite sufficient to influence my decision as to my son's future—it must not be spent with Mr. Fairfax's mistress. "

Clarissa rose at the word, with a shrill indignant cry. For a few moments she stood looking at her accuser, magnificent in her anger and surprise.

"You dare to call me *that*! " she exclaimed.

"I dare to call you what I believe you to be. What! I find you in an obscure house, with locked doors; you go to meet your lover alone; and I am to think nothing! "

"Never alone until last night, and then not with my consent, I went to see Mr. and Mrs. Austin—I did not know they had left Paris. "

"But their departure was very convenient, was it not? It enabled your lover to plead his cause, to make arrangements for your flight. You were to have three days' start of me. Pshaw! why should we bandy words about the shameful business? You have told me that you love him—that is enough. "

"Yes, " she said, with the anger and defiance gone out of her face and manner, "I have been weak and guilty, but not as guilty as you suppose. I have done nothing to forfeit my right to my son. You shall not part us! "

"You had better tell your maid you are going on a journey to-morrow. She will have to pack your things—your jewels, and all you care to take. "

"I shall tell her nothing. Remember what I have said—I will not be separated from Lovel! "

"In that case, I must give the necessary orders myself, " said Mr. Granger coolly, and saying this he left the room to look for his wife's maid.

Jane Target, the maid, came in presently. She was the young woman chosen for Clarissa's service by Mrs. Oliver; a girl whose childhood had been spent at Arden, and to whose childish imagination the Levels of Arden Court had always seemed the greatest people in the world. The girl poured out her mistress's tea, and persuaded her to take something. She perceived that there was something amiss, some serious misunderstanding between Clarissa and her husband. Had not the business been fully discussed in the Areopagus downstairs, all those unaccountable visits to the street near the Luxembourg, and Mr. Fairfax's order to the coachman?

"Nor it ain't the first time I've seen him there neither, " Jarvis had remarked; "me and Saunders have noticed him ever so many times, dropping in promiscuous like while Mrs. G. was there, Fishy, to say the least of it! "

Jane Target was very fond of her mistress, and would as soon have doubted that the sun was fire as suspected any flaw in Clarissa's integrity. She had spoken her mind more than once upon this subject in the servants' hall, and had put the bulky Jarvis to shame.

"Do, ma'am, eat something! " she pleaded, when she had poured out the tea. "You had no dinner yesterday, and no tea, unless you had it in the nursery. You'll be fit for nothing, if you go on like this. "

Fit for nothing! The phrase roused Clarissa from her apathy. Too weak to do battle for her right to the custody of her child, she thought; and influenced by this idea, she struggled through a tolerable breakfast, eating delicate *petite pains* which tasted like ashes, and drinking strong tea with a feverish eagerness.

The tea fortified her nerves; she got up and paced her room, thinking what she ought to do.

Daniel Granger was going to take her child from her—that was certain—unless by some desperate means she secured her darling to herself. Nothing could be harder or more pitiless than his manner that morning. The doors of Arden Court were to be shut against her.

"And I sold myself for Arden! " she thought bitterly. She fancied how the record of her life would stand by-and-by, like a verse in those Chronicles which Sophia was so fond of: "And Clarissa reigned a year and a half, and did that which was evil"—and so on. Very brief had been her glory; very deep was her disgrace.

What was she to do? Carry her child away before they could take him from her—secure him to herself somehow. If it were to be done at all, it must be done quickly; and who had she to help her in this hour of desperate need.

She looked at Jane Target, who was standing by the dressing-table dusting the gold-topped scent-bottles and innumerable prettinesses scattered there—the costly trifles with which women who are not really happy strive to create for themselves a factitious kind of happiness. The girl was lingering over her work, loth to leave her mistress unless actually dismissed.

Jane Target, Clarissa remembered her a flaxen-haired cottage girl, with an honest freckled face and a calico-bonnet; a girl who was always swinging on five-barred gates, or overturning a baby brother out of a primitive wooden cart—surely this girl was faithful, and would help her in her extremity. In all the world, there was no other creature to whom she could appeal.

"Jane, " she said at last, stopping before the girl and looking at her with earnest questioning eyes, "I think I can trust you. " "Indeed you can, ma'am, " answered Jane, throwing down her feather dusting-brush to clasp her hands impetuously. "There's nothing in this world I would not do to prove myself true to you. "

"I am in great trouble, Jane. "

"I know that, ma'am, " the girl answered frankly.

"I daresay you know something of the cause. My husband is angry about—about an accidental meeting which arose between a gentleman and me. It was entirely accidental on my part; but he does not choose to believe this, and——" The thought of Daniel Granger's accusation flashed upon her in this moment in all its horror, and she broke down, sobbing hysterically.

The girl brought her mistress a chair, and was on her knees beside her in a moment, comforting her and imploring her to be calm.

"The trouble will pass away, ma'am, " said the maid, soothingly. "Mr. Granger will come to see his mistake. He can't be angry with you long, I'm sure; he loves you so. "

"Yes, yes, he has been very good to me—better than I have ever deserved; but that is all over now. He won't believe me—he will hardly listen to me. He is going to take away my boy, Jane. "

"Going to take away Master Lovel? "

"Yes; my darling is to go back to Arden, and I am to go to papa. "

"What! " cried Jane Target, all the woman taking fire in her honest heart. "Part mother and child! He couldn't do that; or if he could, he *shouldn't*, while I had the power to hinder him. "

"How are we to prevent him, Jane—you and I? "

"Let's take the darling away, ma'am, before he can stop us. "

"You dear good soul! " cried Clarissa. "It's the very thing I've been thinking of. Heaven knows how it is to be done; but it must be done somehow. And you will come with me, Jane? and you will brave all for me, you good generous girl? "

"Lor, ma'am, what do you think I'm frightened of? Not that stuck-up Mrs. Brobson, with her grand airs, and as lazy as the voice of the sluggard into the bargain. Just you make up your mind, mum, where you'd like to go, and when you'd like to start, and I shall walk into the nursery as bold as brass, and say I want Master Lovel to come and amuse his mar for half an hour; and once we've got him safe in this room, the rest is easy. Part mother and child indeed! I should like to see him do it! I warrant we'll soon bring Mr. Granger to his senses. "

Where to go? yes, there was the rub. What a friendless creature Clarissa Granger felt, as she pondered on this serious question! To her brother? Yes, he was the only friend she would care to trust in this emergency. But how was she to find him? Brussels was a large place, and she had no clue to his whereabouts there. Could she feel even sure that he had really gone to Brussels?

Somewhither she must go, however—that was certain. It could matter very little where she found a refuge, if only she had her darling with her. So the two women consulted together, and plotted and planned in Clarissa's sanctum; while Daniel Granger paced up and down the great dreary drawing-room, waiting for that promised visit from George Fairfax.

* * * * *

CHAPTER XLIII.

CLARISSA'S ELOPEMENT.

Mr. Fairfax came a little after noon—came with a calm grave aspect, as of a man who had serious work before him. With all his heart he wished that the days of duelling had not been over; that he could have sent his best friend to Daniel Granger, and made an end of the quarrel in a gentlemanlike way, in some obscure alley at Vincennes, or amidst the shadowy aisles of St. Germains. But a duel nowadays is too complete an anachronism for an Englishman to propose in cold blood. Mr. Fairfax came to his enemy's house for one special purpose. The woman he loved was in Daniel Granger's power; it was his duty to explain that fatal meeting in Austin's rooms, to justify Clarissa's conduct in the eyes of her husband. It was not that he meant to surrender his hope of their future union—indeed, he hoped that the scene of the previous evening would bring about a speedy separation between husband and wife. But he had placed her in a false position; she was innocent, and he was bound to assert her innocence.

He found Daniel Granger like a man of iron, fully justifying that phrase of Lady Laura's—"*Carré par la base.*" The ignominy of his own position came fully home to him at the first moment of their meeting. He remembered the day when he had liked and respected this man: he could not despise him now.

He was conscious that he carried the mark of last night's skirmish in an unpleasantly conspicuous manner. That straight-out blow of Daniel Granger's had left a discoloration of the skin—what in a meaner man might have been called a black eye. He, too, had hit hard in that brief tussle; but no stroke of his had told like that blow of the Yorkshireman's. Mr. Granger bore no trace of the encounter.

The two men met with as serene an air as if they had never grappled each other savagely in the twilight.

"I considered it due to Mrs. Granger that I should call upon you, " George Fairfax began, "in order to explain her part in the affair of last night. "

"Go on, sir. The old story, of course—Mrs. Granger is spotless; it is only appearances that are against her. "

"So far as she is concerned, our meeting yesterday afternoon was an accident. She came there to see another person. "

"Indeed I Mr. Austin the painter, I suppose? —a man who painted her portrait, and who had no farther acquaintance with her than that. A very convenient person, it seems, since she was in the habit of going to his rooms nearly every afternoon; and I suppose the same kind of accident as that of yesterday generally brought you there at the same time. "

"Mrs. Granger went to see her brother. "

"Her brother? "

"Yes, Austin Lovel; otherwise Mr. Austin the painter. I have been pledged to him to keep his identity a secret; but I feel myself at liberty to break my promise now—in his sister's justification. "

"You mean, that the man who came to this house as a stranger is my wife's brother? "

"I do. "

"What duplicity! And this is the woman I trusted! "

"There was no voluntary duplicity on your wife's part. I know that she was most anxious you should be told the truth. "

"*You* know! Yes, of course; *you* are in my wife's confidence—an honour I have never enjoyed. "

"It was Austin who objected to make himself known to you. "

"I scarcely wonder at that, considering his antecedents. The whole thing has been very cleverly done, Mr. Fairfax, and I acknowledge myself completely duped. I don't think there is any occasion for us to discuss the subject farther. Nothing that you could say would alter my estimation of the events of last night. I regret that I suffered myself to be betrayed into any violence—that kind of thing is behind the times. We have wiser remedies for our wrongs nowadays. "

415

"You do not mean that you would degrade your wife in a law court! " cried Mr. Fairfax. "Any legal investigation must infallibly establish her innocence; but no woman's name can escape untainted from such an ordeal. "

"No, I am not likely to do that. I have a son, Mr. Fairfax. As for my wife, my plans are formed. It is not in the power of any one living to alter them. "

"Then it is useless for me to say more. On the honour of a gentleman, I have told you nothing but the truth. Your wife is innocent. "

"She is not guiltless of having listened to you. That is quite enough for me. "

"I have done, sir, " said George Fairfax gravely, and, with a bow and a somewhat cynical smile, departed.

He had done what he felt himself bound to do. He had no ardent wish to patch up the broken union between Clarissa and her husband. From the first hour in which he heard of her marriage, he had held it in jealous abhorrence. He had very little compunction about what had happened. It must bring matters to a crisis, he thought. In the meantime, he would have given a great deal to be able to communicate with Clarissa, and began accordingly to deliberate how that might best be done.

He did not deliberate long; for while he was meditating all manner of roundabout modes of approach, he suddenly remembered how Austin Lovel had told him he always wrote to his sister under cover to her maid. All he had to do, therefore, was to find out the maid's name.

That would be easy enough, Mr. Fairfax imagined, if his servant was good for anything. The days of Leporello are over; but a well-bred valet may still have some little talent for diplomacy.

"My fellow has only to waylay one of Granger's grooms, " Mr. Fairfax said to himself, "and he can get the information I want readily enough. "

There was not much time to be lost, he thought. Mr. Granger had spoken of his plans with a certain air of decision. Those plans involved some change of residence, no doubt. He would take his wife away from Paris; punish her by swift banishment from that brilliant city; bury her alive at Arden Court, and watch her with the eyes of a lynx for the rest of his life.

"Let him watch you never so closely, or shut you in what prison he may, I will find a door of escape for you, my darling, " he said to himself.

The mistress and maid were busy meanwhile, making arrangements for a sudden flight. There was very little packing to be done; for they could take nothing, or scarcely anything, with them. The great difficulty would be, to get the child out of the house. After a good deal of deliberation they had decided the manner in which their attempt was to be made. It was dusk between five and six; and at dusk Jane was to go to the nursery, and in the most innocent manner possible, carry off the boy for half-an-hour's play in his mother's dressing-room. It was, fortunately, a usual thing for Clarissa to have him with her at this time, when she happened to be at home so early. There was a dingy servants' staircase leading from the corridor to the ground-floor; and down this they were to make their escape unobserved, the child bundled up in a shawl, Jane Target having slipped out beforehand and hired a carriage, which was to wait for them a little way off in a side-street. There was a train leaving Paris at seven, which would take them to Amiens, where they could sleep that night, and go on to Brussels in the morning. Once in Brussels, they must contrive somehow to find Austin Lovel.

Of her plans for the future—how she was to live separated from her husband, and defying him—Clarissa thought nothing. Her mind was wholly occupied by that one consideration about her child. To secure him to herself was the end and aim of her existence.

It was only at Jane's suggestion that she set herself to calculate ways and means. She had scarcely any ready money—one five-pound note and a handful of silver comprised all her wealth. She had given her brother every sixpence she could spare. There were her jewels, it is true; jewels worth three or four thousand pounds. But she shrank from the idea of touching these.

While she sat with her purse in her hand, idly counting the silver, and not at all able to realise the difficulties of her position, the faithful Jane came to her relief.

"I've got five-and-twenty pounds with me, ma'am; saved out of my wages since I've been in your service; and I'm sure you're welcome to the money. "

Jane had brought her little hoard with her, intending to invest some part of it in presents for her kindred—a shawl for her mother, and so on; but had been disappointed, by finding that the Parisian shops, brilliant as they were, contained very much the same things she had seen in London, and at higher prices. She had entertained a hazy notion that cashmere shawls were in some manner a product of the soil of France, and could be bought for a mere trifle; whereby she had been considerably taken aback when the proprietor of a plate-glass edifice on the Boulevard des Italiens asked her a thousand francs for a black cashmere, which she had set her mind upon as a suitable covering for the shoulders of Mrs. Target.

"You dear good girl! " said Clarissa, touched by this new proof of fidelity; "but if I should never be able to pay you the money! "

"Stuff and nonsense, ma'am! no fear of that; and if you weren't, I shouldn't care. Father and mother are comfortably off; and I'm not going to work for a pack of brothers and sisters. I gave the girls new bonnets last Easter, and sent them a ribbon apiece at Christmas; and that's enough for *them*. If you don't take the money, ma'am, I shall throw it in the fire. "

Clarissa consented to accept the use of the money. She would be able to repay it, of course. She had a vague idea that she could earn money as a teacher of drawing in some remote continental city, where they might live very cheaply. How sweet it would be to work for her child! much sweeter than to be a millionaire's wife and dress him in purple and fine linen that cost her nothing.

She spent some hours in looking over and arranging her jewels. From all of these she selected only two half-hoop diamond rings, as a reserve against the hour of need. These and these only of Daniel Granger's gifts would she take with her. She made a list of her trinkets, with a *nota bene* stating her appropriation of the two rings, and laid it at the top of her principal jewel-case. After this, she wrote a letter to her husband—a few lines only, telling him how she had determined to take her child away with her, and how she should resist to the last gasp any attempt to rob her of him.

"If I were the guilty wretch you think me, " she wrote, "I would willingly surrender my darling, rather than degrade him by any association with such a fallen creature. But whatever wrong I have committed against you—and that wrong was done by my marriage—I have not forfeited the right to my child's affection. "

This letter written, there was nothing more to be done. Jane packed a travelling-bag with a few necessary items, and that was all the luggage they could venture to carry away with them.

The afternoon post brought a letter from Brussels, addressed to Miss Jane Target, which the girl brought in triumph to her mistress.

"There'll be no bother about finding Mr. Austin, ma'am, " she cried. "Here's a letter! "

The letter was in Austin's usual brief careless style, entering into no explanations; but it told the quarter in which he had found a lodging; so Clarissa was at least sure of this friendly shelter. It would be a poor one, no doubt; nor was Austin Lovel by any means a strong rock upon which to lean in the hour of trouble. But she loved him, and she knew that he would not turn his back upon her.

The rest of the day seemed long and dreary. Clarissa wandered into the nursery two or three times in order to assure herself, by the evidence of her own eyes, of her boy's safety. She found the nursemaid busy packing, under Mrs. Brobson's direction.

The day waned. Clarissa had not seen her husband since that meeting in the corridor; nor had she gone into any of the rooms where Miss Granger might be encountered.

That young lady, painfully in the dark as to what had happened, sat at her table in the window, diligently illuminating, and wondering when her father would take her into his confidence. She had been told of the intended journey on the next day, and that she and her brother were to go back to Arden Court, under the protection of the servants, while Mr. Granger and his wife went elsewhere, and was not a little puzzled by the peculiarity of the arrangement. Warman was packing, complaining the while at having to do so much in so short a time, and knew nothing of what had occurred in the Rue du Chevalier Bayard, after the dismissal of the carriage by Mr. Fairfax.

"There must have been something, miss, " she said, "or your pa would never have taken, this freak into his head—racing back as if it was for a wager; and me not having seen half I wanted to see, nor bought so much as a pincushion to take home to my friends. I had a clear month before me, I thought, so where was the use of hurrying; and then to be scampered and harum-scarumed off like this! It's really too bad. "

"I have no doubt papa has good reasons for what he is doing, Warman, " answered Miss Granger, with dignity.

"O, of course, miss; gentlefolks has always good reasons for *their* goings-on! " Warman remarked snappishly, and then "took it out" of one of Miss Granger's bonnets during the process of packing.

Twilight came at last, the longed-for dusk, in which the attempt was to be made. Clarissa had put on one of her darkest plainest dresses, and borrowed a little black-straw bonnet of her maid's. This bonnet and her sealskin jacket she deferred putting on until the last; for there was always the fear that Mr. Granger might come in at some awkward moment. At half-past five Jane Target went to the nursery and fetched the year-old heir of Arden Court.

He was always glad to go to his mother; and he came to-night crowing and laughing, and kicking his little blue shoes in boisterous rapture. Jane kept guard at the door while Clarissa put on her bonnet and jacket, and wrapped up the baby—first in a warm fur-lined opera-jacket, and then in a thick tartan shawl. They had no hat for him, but tied up his pretty flaxen head in a large silk handkerchief, and put the shawl over that. The little fellow submitted to the operation, which he evidently regarded in the light of an excellent joke.

Everything was now ready. Clarissa carried her baby, Jane went before with the bag, leading the way down the darksome servants' staircase, where at any moment they might meet one of Mr. Granger's retainers. Luckily, they met no one; the descent only occupied about two minutes; and at the bottom of the stairs, Clarissa found herself in a small square stone lobby, lighted by a melancholy jet of gas, and pervaded by the smell of cooking. In the next moment Jane—who had made herself mistress of all minor details—opened a door, and they were out in the dull quiet street—the side-street, at the end of which workmen were scalping away a hill.

A few doors off they found the carriage, which Jane had secured half an hour before, and a very civil driver. Clarissa told the driver where to go, and then got in, with her precious burden safe in her arms.

The precious burden set up a wail at this juncture, not understanding or approving these strange proceedings, and it was as much as his mother could do to soothe him. A few yards round the corner they passed a man, who looked curiously at the vehicle. This was George Fairfax, who was pacing the street in the gloaming in order to reconnoitre the dwelling of the woman he loved, and who let her pass him unaware. His own man was busy at the same time entertaining one of Mr. Granger's footmen in a neighbouring wine-shop, in the hope of extracting the information his master required about Mrs. Granger's maid. They reached the station just five minutes before the train left for Amiens; and once seated in the railway-carriage, Clarissa almost felt as if her victory was certain, so easily had the first stage been got over. She kissed and blessed Jane Target, whom she called her guardian angel; and smothered her baby with kisses, apostrophising him with all manner of fond foolishness.

Everything favoured her. The flight was not discovered until nearly three-quarters of an hour after Clarissa had eloped with her baby down that darksome stair. Mrs. Brobson, luxuriating in tea, toast, and gossip before the nursery fire, and relieved not a little by the absence of her one-year-old charge, had been unconscious of the progress of time. It was only when the little clock upon the chimney-piece chimed the half-hour after six, that she began to wonder about the baby.

"His mar's had him longer than ever, " she said; "you'd better go and fetch him, Liza. She'll be wanting to dress for dinner, I dessay. I suppose she's going down to dinner to-night, though there is something up. "

"She didn't go down to breakfast, nor yet to lunch, " said Eliza, who had her information fresh and fresh from one of the footmen; "and Mr. Granger's been a-walking up and down the droring-room as if he was a-doing of it for a wager, William Baker says. Mr. Fairfax come this morning, and didn't stop above a quarter of an hour; but William was outside the droring-room door all the time, and there was no loud talking, nor quarrelling, nor nothink. "

"That Fairfax is a villain, " replied Mrs. Brobson. "I don't forget the day he kissed baby in Arden Park. I never see any good come of a single gentleman kissing a lady's baby, voluntary. It isn't their nature to do it, unless they've a hankering after the mar. "

"Lor, Brobson, how horful! " cried Eliza. And in this pleasant converse, the nurse and her subordinate wasted another five minutes.

The nursemaid frittered away a few more minutes in tapping gingerly at the dressing-room door, until at last, emboldened by the silence, she opened it, and, peering in, beheld nothing but emptiness. Mrs. Granger had gone to the drawing-room perhaps; but where was baby? and where was Jane Target? The girl went in search of her favourite, William Baker. Were Mrs. Granger and baby in the drawing-room? No; Mr. Baker had been in attendance all the afternoon. Mrs. Granger had not left her own apartments.

"But she's not there, " cried Eliza, aghast; "nor Target either. I've been looking for baby. "

She ran back to the dressing-room; it was still empty, and the bedroom adjoining. Mr. Granger's dressing-room was beyond that, and he was there writing letters. At this door—this sacred door, the threshold whereof she had never crossed—Eliza the nursemaid tapped nervously.

"O, if you please, sir, have you got Master Lovel? "

"No, " cried Daniel Granger, starting up from his desk. "What made you think him likely to be here? "

"I can't find him, please, sir. I've been looking in Mrs. Granger's dressing-room, and everywhere almost. Jane Target fetched him for his ma close upon a hour ago; and Mrs. Brobson sent me for him, and I fancied as you might have got him with you, sir. "

Mr. Granger came out of his room with the lamp in his hand, and came through the bedroom to his wife's dressing-room, looking with that stern searching gaze of his into every shadowy corner, as if he thought Clarissa and her baby might be playing hide-and-seek there. But there was no one—the cheval-glass and the great glass door of the wardrobe reflected only his own figure, and the scared nursemaid peering from behind his elbow. He went on to the nursery, opening the doors of all the rooms as he passed, and looking in. There are some convictions that come in a minute. Before that search was finished, Daniel Granger felt very sure that his wife had left him, and had taken her child away with her.

In what manner and to what doom had she gone? Was her flight a shameful one, with George Fairfax for her companion? He knew now, for the first time, that in the depths of his mind there had been some lurking belief in her innocence, it was so supreme an agony to him to imagine that she had taken a step which must make her guilt a certainty. He did not waste much time in questioning the verbose Brobson. The child was missing—that was quite clear—and his wife, and his wife's maid. It was some small relief to him to know that she had taken the honest Yorkshire girl. If she had been going to ignominy, she would scarcely have taken any one who knew her past history, above all, one whom she had known in her childhood.

What was he to do? To follow her, of course, if by any means he could discover whither she had gone. To set the telegraph wires going, also, with a view to discovering her destination. He drove off at once to the chief telegraph office, and wrote a couple of messages, one to Mr. Lovel, at Spa—the other to Mr. Oliver, at Holborough Rectory; with a brief stern request to be informed immediately if his wife should arrive at either place. There was Lady Laura Armstrong, her most intimate friend, with whom she might possibly seek a refuge in the hour of her trouble; but he did not care to make any application in that quarter, unless driven to do so. He did not want to make his wrongs public.

From the telegraph office he drove to the Northern Railway Station, and made minute inquiries about the trains. There was a train by which she might have gone to Calais half an hour before he arrived there. He enlisted the services of an official, and promenaded the waiting-rooms and platforms, the dreary chambers in which travellers wait for their luggage, to and fro between the barriers that torment the soul of the impatient. He asked this man, and several other men, if a lady, with her baby and maid, had been observed to take their departure by any train within the last hour. But the men shrugged their shoulders hopelessly. Ladies and maids and babies came and went in flocks, and no one noticed them. There were always babies. Yes; one of the men did remember a stout lady in a red shawl, with a baby and a birdcage and a crowd of boxes, who had gone by the second-class. Is it that that was the lady monsieur was looking for, *par hasard*?

"She will go to her father, " Mr. Granger said to himself again and again; and this for the moment seemed to him such a certainty, that he had half made up his mind to start for Spa by the next train that would carry him in that direction. But the thought of George Fairfax—the possibility that his wife might have had a companion in her flight—arrested him in the next moment. "Better that I should stop to make sure of *his* whereabouts, " he thought; and drove straight to the Champs Elysées, where Mr. Fairfax had his bachelor quarters.

Here he saw the valet, who had not long returned from that diplomatic expedition to the neighbourhood of the Rue de Morny; but who appeared the very image of unconsciousness and innocence notwithstanding. Mr. Fairfax was dining at home with some friends. Would Mr. Granger walk in? The dinner was not served yet. Mr. Fairfax would be delighted to see him.

Mr. Granger refused to go in; but told the man he should be glad to see Mr. Fairfax there, in the ante-room, for a moment. He wanted to be quite sure that the valet was not lying.

Mr. Fairfax came out, surprised at the visit.

"I had a special reason for wishing to know if you were at home this evening, " said Daniel Granger. "I am sorry to have disturbed you, and will not detain you from your friends. "

And then the question flashed upon him—*Was she there?* No; that would be too daring. Any other refuge she might seek; but surely not this.

George Fairfax had flung the door wide open in coming out. Mr. Granger saw the dainty bachelor room, with its bright pictures shining in the lamp-light, and two young men in evening-dress lolling against the mantelpiece. The odours of an elaborate dinner were also perceptible. The valet had told the truth. Daniel Granger murmured some vague excuse, and departed.

"Queer! " muttered Mr. Fairfax as he went back to his friends.

"I'm afraid the man is going off his head; and yet he seemed cool enough to-day. "

From the Champs Elysees Mr. Granger drove to the Rue du Chevalier Bayard. There was another possibility to be considered: if Austin the painter were indeed Austin Lovel, as George Fairfax had asserted, it was possible that Clarissa had gone to him; and the next thing to be done was to ascertain his whereabouts. The ancient porter, whom Mr. Granger had left the night before in a doubtful and bewildered state of mind, was eating some savoury mess for his supper comfortably enough this evening, but started up in surprise, with his spectacles on his forehead, at Mr. Granger's reappearance.

"I want to know where your lodger Mr. Austin went when he left here? " Mr. Granger demanded briefly.

The porter shrugged his shoulders.

"Alas, monsieur, that is an impossibility. I know nothing of Mr. Austin's destination; only that he went away yesterday, at three o'clock, in a hackney-coach, which was to take him to the Northern Railway. "

"Is there no one who can tell me what I want to know? " asked Mr. Granger.

"I doubt it, monsieur. Monsieur Austin was in debt to almost every one except his landlord. He promised to write about his furniture, — some of the movables in those rooms upstairs are his—cabinets, carved chairs, tapestries, and so on; but he said nothing as to where he was going. "

"He promised to write, " repeated Mr. Granger. "That's an indefinite kind of promise. You could let me know, I suppose, if you heard anything? "

"But certainly, " replied the porter, who saw Mr. Granger's fingers in his waistcoat pocket, and scented a fee, "monsieur should know immediately. "

Mr. Granger wrote his address upon a card, and gave it to the porter, with a napoleon.

"You shall have another when you bring me any information. Good-night. "

At home, Daniel Granger had to face his daughter, who had heard by this time of her stepmother's departure and the abstraction of the baby.

"O, papa, " she exclaimed, "I do so feel for you! " and made as if she would have embraced her parent; but he stood like a rock, not inviting any affectionate demonstration.

"Thank you, my dear, " he said gravely; "but I can do very well without pity. It's a kind of thing I'm not accustomed to. I am annoyed that Clarissa should have acted in—in this ill-advised manner; but I have no doubt matters will come right in a little time. "

"Lovel—my brother is safe, papa? " inquired Sophia, clasping her hands.

"I have every reason to believe so. He is with his mother. "

Miss Granger sighed profoundly, as much as to say, "He could not be in worse hands. "

"And I think, my dear, " continued her father, "that the less you trouble yourself about this business the bettor. Any interference on your part will only annoy me, and may occasion unpleasantness between us. You will go back to Arden, to-morrow, as I intended, with Warman, and one of the men to take care of your luggage. The rest of the establishment will follow in a day or so. "

"And you, papa? "

"My plans are uncertain. I shall return to Arden as soon as I can. "

"Dear old Arden! " exclaimed Sophia; "how I wish we had never left it! How happy I was for the first four years of my life there! "

This apostrophe Mr. Granger perfectly understood—it meant that, with the advent of Clarissa, happiness had fled away from Sophia's dwelling-place. He did not trouble himself to notice the speech; but it made him angry nevertheless.

"There is a letter for you, papa, " said Miss Granger, pointing to a side-table; "a letter which Warman found upstairs. "

The lynx-eyed Warman, prying and peering about, had spied out Clarissa's letter to her husband, half hidden among the frivolities on the dressing-table. Mr. Granger pounced upon it eagerly, full of hope. It might tell him all he wanted to know.

It told him nothing. The words were not consistent with guilt, unless Clarissa were the very falsest of women. But had she not been the falsest? Had she not deceived him grossly, unpardonably? Alas, he was already trying to make excuses for her—trying to believe her innocent, innocent of what society calls sin—yes, she might be that. But had he not seen her kneeling beside her lover? Had she not owned that she loved him? She had; and the memory of her words were poison to Daniel Granger.

* * * * *

CHAPTER XLIV.

UNDER THE SHADOW OF ST. GUDULE.

It was about half an hour before noon on the following day when Clarissa arrived at Brussels, and drove straight to her brother's lodging, which was in an obscure street under the shadow of St. Gudule. Austin was at work in a room opening straight from the staircase—a bare, shabby-looking chamber—and looked up from his easel with profound astonishment on beholding Mrs. Granger with her maid and baby.

"Why, Clary, what in the name of all that's wonderful, brings you to Brussels? " he exclaimed.

"I have come to live with you for a little while, Austin, if you will let me, " she answered quietly. "I have no other home now. "

Austin Lovel laid down his palette, and came across the room to receive her.

"What does it all mean, Clary? —Look here, young woman, " he said to Jane Target; "you'll find my wife in the next room; and she'll help you to make that youngster comfortable. —Now, Clary, " he went on, as the girl curtseyed and vanished through the door that divided the two rooms, "what does it all mean? "

Clarissa told him her story—told it, that is to say, as well as she could tell a story which reflected so much discredit upon herself.

"I went to the Rue du Chevalier Bayard at 5 on Tuesday—as I promised, you know, Austin—and found Mr. Fairfax there. You may imagine how surprised I was when I heard you were gone. He did not tell me immediately; and he detained me there—talking to me. "

The sudden crimson which mounted to her very temples at this juncture betrayed her secret.

"Talking to you! " cried Austin; "you mean making love to you! The infernal scoundrel! "

"It was—very dishonourable! "

428

"That's a mild way of putting it. What! he hung about my rooms when I had gone, to get you into a trap, as it were, at the risk of compromising you in a most serious manner! You never gave him any encouragement, did you, Clarissa? "

"I never meant to do so. "

"You never meant! But a woman must know what she is doing. You used to meet him at my rooms very often. If I had dreamt there was any flirtation between you, I should have taken care to put a stop to *that*. Well, go on. You found Fairfax there, and you let him detain you, and then— —? "

"My husband came, and there was a dreadful scene, and he knocked Mr. Fairfax down. "

"Naturally. I respect him for doing it. "

"And for a few minutes I thought he was dead, " said Clarissa with a shudder; and then she went on with her story, telling her brother how Daniel Granger had threatened to separate her from her child.

"That was hard lines, " said Austin; "but I think you would have done better to remain passive. It's natural that he should take this business rather seriously at first: but that would wear off in a short time. What you have done will only widen the breach. "

"I have got my child, " said Clarissa.

"Yes; but in any case you must have had him. That threat of Granger's was only blank cartridge. He could not deprive you of the custody of your son. "

"He will try to get a divorce, perhaps. He thinks me the vilest creature in the world. "

"A divorce—bosh! Divorces are not obtained so easily. What a child you are, Clarissa! "

"At any rate, he was going to take me back to papa in disgrace. I could not have endured that. My father would think me guilty, perhaps. "

Again the tell-tale crimson flushed Clarissa's face. The memory of that September evening at Mill Cottage flashed across her mind, and her father's denunciation of George Fairfax and his race.

"Your father would be wise enough to defend his child, I imagine, " replied Austin, "although he is not a person whose conduct I would pretend to answer for. But this quarrel between you and your husband must be patched up, Clary. "

"That will never be. "

"It must be—for your son's sake, if not for yours. You pretend to love that boy, and are yet so blind to his interests? He is not the heir to an entailed estate, remember. Granger is a self-made man, and if you offend him, may leave Arden Court to his daughter's children. "

She had robbed her son of his birthright, perhaps. For what? Because she had not had the strength to shut her heart against a guilty love; because, in the face of every good resolution she had ever made, she had been weak enough to listen when George Fairfax chose to speak.

"It seems very hard, " she said helplessly.

"It would be uncommonly hard upon that child, if this breach were not healed. But it must be healed. "

"You do not know half the bitter things Mr. Granger said. Nothing would induce me to humiliate myself to him. "

"Not the consideration of your son's interests? "

"God will protect my son; he will not be punished for any sin of his mother's. "

"Come now, Clary, be reasonable. Let me write to Granger in my own proper character, telling him that you are here. "

"If you do that, I will never forgive you. It would be most dishonourable, most unkind. You will not do that, Austin? "

"Of course I will not, if you insist upon it. But I consider that you are acting very foolishly. There must have been a settlement, by the way, when you married. Do you remember anything about it? "

"Very little. There was five hundred a year settled on me for pin money; and five hundred a year for papa, settled somehow. The reversion to come to me, I think they said. And—yes, I remember—If I had any children, the eldest son was to inherit Arden Court. "

"That's lucky! I thought your father would never be such a fool as to let you marry without some arrangement of that sort. "

"Then my darling is safe, is he not? "

"Well, yes, I suppose so. "

"And you will not betray me, Austin? " said Clarissa imploringly.

"Betray you! If you put it in that way, of course not. But I should be acting more in your interests if I wrote to Granger. No good can come of the step you have taken. However, we must trust to the chapter of accidents, " added Austin, with a resumption of his habitual carelessness. "I needn't tell you that you are heartily welcome to my hospitality, such as it is. Our quarters are rough enough, but Bessie will do what she can to make you comfortable; and I'll put on a spurt and work hard to keep things together. I have found a dealer in the Montagne de la Cour, who is willing to take my sketches at a decent price. Look here, Clary, how do you like this little bit of *genre?* 'Forbidden Fruit'—a chubby six-year-old girl, on tiptoe, trying to filch a peach growing high on the wall; flimsy child, and pre-Raphaelite wall. Peach, carnation velvet; child's cheek to match the peach. Rather a nice thing, isn't it? " asked Austin lightly.

Clarissa made some faint attempt to appear interested in the picture, which she only saw in a dim far-off way.

"I shall be very glad to see where you are going to put baby, " she said anxiously.

The bleak and barren aspect of the painting-room did not promise much for the accommodation or comfort of Mr. Lovel's domicile.

"Where I am going to put baby! Ah, to be sure, you will want a room to sleep in, " said Austin, as if this necessity had only just struck him. "We'll soon manage that; the house is roomy enough, —a perfect barrack, in fact. There was a lace-factory carried on in it once, I believe. I daresay there's a room on this floor that we can have. I'll go and see about that, while you make yourself comfortable with Bessie. We have only two rooms—this and the next, which is our bedroom; but we shall do something better by and by, if I find my pictures sell pretty fast. "

He went off whistling an opera air, and by no means oppressed by the idea that he had a sister in difficulties cast upon his hands.

There was a room—a darksome chamber at the back of the house—looking into a narrow alley, where domestic operations of some kind seemed to be going on in every window and doorway, but sufficiently spacious, and with two beds. It was altogether homely, but looked tolerably clean; and Clarissa was satisfied with it, although it was the poorest room that had ever sheltered her. She had her baby—that was the grand point; and he rolled upon the beds, and crowed and chattered, in his half inarticulate way, with as much delight as if the shabby chamber had been an apartment in a palace.

"If he is happy, I am more than content! " exclaimed Mrs. Granger.

A fire was lighted in the stove, and Bessie brought them a second breakfast of coffee and rolls, and a great basin of bread and milk for young Lovel. The little man ate ravenously, and did not cry for Brobson—seemed indeed rather relieved to have escaped from the jurisdiction of that respectable matron. He was fond of Jane Target, who was just one of those plump apple-cheeked young women whom children love instinctively, and who had a genius for singing ballads of a narrative character, every verse embellished with a curious old-fashioned quavering turn.

After this refreshment—the first that Clarissa had taken with any approach to appetite since that luckless scene in her brother's painting-room—Jane persuaded her mistress to lie down and rest, which she did, falling asleep peacefully, with her boy's bright young head nestling beside her on the pillow. It was nearly dark when she awoke; and after dinner she went out for a walk with Austin, in the bright gas-lit streets, and along a wide boulevard, where the tall bare trees looked grim in the darkness. The freedom of this new life seemed strange to her, after the forms and ceremonies of her position as Daniel Granger's wife, and Sophia Granger's stepmother—strange, and not at all unpleasant.

"I think I could be very happy with you and Bessie always, Austin, " she said, "if they would only leave me in peace. "

"Could you, Clary? I'm sure I should be very glad to have you; but it would be rather hard upon Granger. "

"He was going to take me back to papa; he wanted to get rid of me. "

"He was in a passion when he talked about that, rely upon it. "

"He was as cold as ice, Austin. I don't believe he was ever in a passion in his life. "

* * * * *

CHAPTER XLV.

TEMPTATION.

It was Sunday; and Clarissa had been nearly a week in Brussels—a very quiet week, in which she had had nothing to do but worship her baby, and tremblingly await any attempt that might be made to wrest him from her. She lived in hourly fear of discovery, and was startled by every step on the staircase and fluttered by every sudden opening of a door, expecting to see Daniel Granger on the threshold.

She went to church alone on this first Sunday morning. Austin was seldom visible before noon, dawdling away the bleaker morning hours smoking and reading in bed. Bessie had a world of domestic business on her hands, and the two boys to torment her while she attempted to get through it. So Clarissa went alone to St. Gudule. There were Protestant temples, no doubt, in the Belgian city wherein she might have worshipped; but that solemn pile drew her to itself with a magnetic attraction. She went in among the gay-looking crowd—the old women in wondrous caps, the sprinkling of soldiers, the prosperous citizens and citizenesses in their Sunday splendour—and made her way to a quiet corner remote from the great carved-oak pulpit and the high altar—a shadowy corner behind a massive cluster of columns, and near a little wooden door in one of the great portals, that opened and shut with a clanging noise now and then, and beside which a dilapidated-looking old man kept watch over a shell-shaped marble basin of holy water, and offered a brush dipped in the sacred fluid to devout passers-by. Here she could kneel unobserved, and in her ignorant fashion, join in the solemn service, lifting up her heart with the elevation of the host, and acknowledging her guiltiness in utter humility of spirit.

Yet not always throughout that service could she keep her thoughts from wandering. Her mind had been too much troubled of late for perfect peace or abstraction of thought to be possible to her. The consideration of her own folly was very constantly with her. What a wreck and ruin she had made of her life—a life which from first to last had been governed by impulse only!

"If I had been an honourable woman, I should never have married Daniel Granger, " she said to herself. "What right had I to take so much and give so little—to marry a man I could not even hope to love for the sake of winning independence for my father, or for the sake of my old home? "

Arden Court—was not that the price which had made her sacrifice tolerable to her? And she had lost it; the gates of the dwelling she loved were closed upon her once again—and this time for ever. How the memory of the place came back to her this chill March morning! —the tall elms rocking in the wind, the rooks' nests tossing in the topmost branches, and the hoarse cawing of discontented birds bewailing the tardiness of spring.

"It will be my darling's home in the days to come, " she said to herself; but even this thought brought no consolation. She dared not face her son's future. Would it not involve severance from her? Now, while he was an infant, she might hold him; but by-and-by the father's stern claim would be heard. They would take the boy away from her—teach him to despise and forget her. She fancied herself wandering and watching in Arden Park, a trespasser, waiting for a stolen glimpse of her child's face.

"I shall die before that time comes, " she thought gloomily.

Some such fancy as this held her absorbed when the high mass concluded, and the congregation began to disperse. The great organ was pealing out one of Mozart's Hallelujahs. There was some secondary service going on at either end of the church. Clarissa still knelt, with her face hidden in her hands, not praying, only conjuring up dreadful pictures of the future. Little by little the crowd melted away; there were only a few worshippers murmuring responses in the distance; the last chords of the Hallelujah crashed and resounded under the vaulted roof; and at last Clarissa looked up and found herself almost alone.

She went out, but shrank from returning immediately to her child. Those agitating thoughts had affected her too deeply. She walked away from the church up towards the park, hoping to find some quiet place where she might walk down the disturbance in her mind, so as to return with a calm smiling face to her darling. It was not a tempting day for any purposeless pedestrian. The sky had darkened at noon, and there was a drizzling rain coming down from the dull gray heavens. The streets cleared quickly now the services were over; but Clarissa went on, scarcely conscious of the rain, and utterly indifferent to any inconvenience it might cause her.

She was in the wide open place near the park, when she heard footsteps following her, rapidly, and with a purpose, as it seemed. Some women have a kind of instinct about these things. She knew in a moment, as if by some subtle magnetism, that the man following her was George Fairfax.

"Clarissa, " said a voice close in her ear; and turning quickly, she found herself face to face with him.

"I was in the church, " he said, "and have followed you all the way here. I waited till we were clear of the narrow streets and the crowd. O, my darling, thank God I have found you! I only knew yesterday that you had left Paris; and some happy instinct brought me here. I felt sure you would come to Austin. I arrived late last night, and was loafing about the streets this morning, wondering how I should discover your whereabouts, when I turned a corner and saw you going into St. Gudule. I followed, but would not disturb your orisons, fair saint. I was not very far off, Clarissa—only on the other side of the pillar. "

"Was it kind of you to follow me here, Mr. Fairfax? " Clarissa asked gravely. "Have you not brought enough trouble upon me as it is? "

"Brought trouble upon you! Yes, that seems hard; but I suppose it was my fate to do that, and to make amends for it afterwards, dearest, in a life that shall know no trouble. "

"I am here with my son, Mr. Fairfax. It was the fear of being separated from him that drove me away from Paris. If you have one spark of generous feeling, you will not pursue me or annoy me here. If my husband were to see us together, or were to hear of our being seen together, he would have just grounds for taking my child away from me. "

"Clarissa, " exclaimed George Fairfax, with intensity, "let us make an end of all folly and beating about the bush at once and for ever. I do not say that I am not sorry for what happened the other night—so far as it caused annoyance to you—but I am heartily glad that matters have been brought to a crisis. The end must have come sooner or later, Clary—so much the better if it has come quickly. There is only one way to deal with the wretched mistake of your marriage, and that is to treat it as a thing that has never been. There are places enough in the world, Clary, in which you and I are nameless and unknown, and we can be married in one of those places. I will run all risks of a criminal prosecution and seven, years at Portland. You shall be my wife, Clarissa, by as tight a knot as Church and State can tie. "

She looked at him with a half scornful smile.

"Do you think you are talking to a child? " she said.

They had been standing in the chill drizzling rain all this time, unconscious, and would have so stood, perhaps, if a shower of fire and brimstone had been descending upon Brussels. But at this juncture Mr. Fairfax suddenly discovered that it was raining, and that Clarissa's shawl was growing rapidly damper.

"Good heavens! " he exclaimed, "what a brute I am. I must find you some kind of shelter. "

There was a café near at hand, the café attached to the Théâtre du Pare, with rustic out-of-door constructions for the accommodation of its customers. Mr. Fairfax conducted Clarissa to one of these wooden arbours, where they might remain till the rain was over, or till he chose to bring her a carriage. He did not care to do that very soon. He had a great deal to say to her. This time he was resolved not to accept defeat.

A solitary waiter espied them promptly, having so little to do in this doleful weather, and came for orders. Mr. Fairfax asked for some coffee, and waited in silence while the man brought a little tray with cups and saucers and a great copper coffee-pot, out of which he poured the black infusion with infinite flourish.

"Bring some cognac, " said Mr. Fairfax; and when the spirit had been brought, he poured half a wine-glassful into a cup of coffee, and entreated Clarissa to drink it as an antidote to cold.

"You were walking ever so long in the rain, " he said.

She declined the nauseous dose.

"I am not afraid of catching cold, " she said; "but I shall be very glad if you will let that man fetch me a fly. I ought to have been at home half an hour ago. "

"At home! Is it permissible to ask where you live? "

"I would rather not tell you my address. I hope, if my being here had anything to with your coming to Brussels, that you will go back to Paris at once. "

"I shall never go back to Paris unless I enter its gates with you some day. I am going to the East, Clary; to Constantinople, and Athens, and all the world of fable and story, and you are going with me— you and young Lovel. Do you know there is one particular spot in the island of Corfu which I have pitched upon for the site of a villa, just such a fairy place as you can sketch for me—your own architecture—neither gothic nor composite, neither classic nor rustic, only *le style Clarisse*; not for our permanent dwelling—to my mind, nothing but poverty should ever chain a man to one habitation—but as a nest to which we might fly now and then, when we were weary of roaming. "

He was talking lightly, after his nature, which was of the lightest, but for a purpose, also, trying to beguile Clarissa from serious considerations, to bring a smile to the pale sad face, if he could. In vain; the hazel eyes looked straight forward with an unwonted fixedness, the lips were firmly set, the hands clasped rigidly.

After this, his tone grew more earnest; again he pleaded, very much as he had pleaded before, but with a stronger determination, with a deeper passion, painting the life that might be for those two in the warmest, brightest colours that his fancy could lend it. What had she to care for? he argued. Absolutely nothing. She had broken with her husband, whom George Fairfax knew by his own experience to be implacable in his resentment. And oh, how much to gain! A life of happiness; all her future spent with the man who loved her; spent wherever and however she pleased. What was he but her slave, to obey her?

She was not unmoved by his pleading. Unmoved? These were words and tones that went home to her heart of hearts. Yes, she could imagine the life he painted so well. Yes, she knew what the future would seem to her, if it were to be spent with him. She loved him dearly—had so loved him ever since that night in the railway-carriage, she thought. When had his image really been absent from her since that time?

He insisted that she should hear him to the end, and she submitted, not unwillingly, perhaps. She had no thought of yielding; but it was sweet to her to hear his voice—for the last time, she told herself; this must be the last time. Even while he pleaded and argued and demonstrated that the wisest thing in the world she could do was to run away with him, she was meditating her plan of escape. Not again must they meet thus. She had a certain amount of strength of mind, but it was not inexhaustible, and she felt her weakness.

"You forget that I have a son, " she said at last, when he urged her to speak.

"He shall be my son. Do you think I do not love that rosy yearling? He shall inherit Lyvedon, if you like; there is no entail; I can do what I please with it. Yes, though I had sons of my own he should be first, by right of any wrong we may do him now. In the picture I have made of our future life, I never omitted that figure, Clarissa. Forget your son! No, Clary; when I am less than a father to him, tell me that I never loved you. "

This was the man's way of looking at the question; the boy's future should be provided for, he should have a fine estate left him by way of solatium. The mother thought of what her son would think of *her*, when he grew old enough to consider her conduct.

"I must ask you to get me a fly somehow, Mr. Fairfax, " she said quietly. "It is still raining, and I am really anxious to get home to Lovel. I am sorry you should have taken so much trouble about me; it is quite useless, believe me. I know that I have been very weak— guilty even—in many ways since I have known you; but that is all over now. I have paid the penalty in the loss of my husband's esteem. I have nothing now to live for but my child. "

"And is that to be the end of everything, Mrs. Granger? " asked George Fairfax, with an angry look in his eyes. "Are we to part upon that? It is such an easy thing to lure a man on to a certain point, and then turn upon him and protest you never meant to go beyond that point. You have paid the penalty! Do you think I have paid no penalty? Was it a pleasant thing to me, do you suppose, to jilt Geraldine Challoner? I trampled honour in the dust for your sake, Clarissa. Do you know that there is a coolness between my mother and me at this moment, because of my absence from England and that broken-off marriage? Do you know that I have turned my back for ever upon a place that any man might be proud to call his home, for the sake of being near you? I have cast every consideration to the winds; and now that you have actually broken loose from your bondage, now that there is nothing to come between us and a happy future, you set up your son as an obstacle, and" —he concluded with a bitter laugh—"ask me to fetch you a fly! "

"I am sorry to wound you; but—but—I cannot bring dishonour upon my son. "

"Your son! " cried George Fairfax savagely. "An east wind may blow your son off the face of the earth to-morrow. Is a one-year-old baby to stand between a man and his destiny? Come, Clary, I have served my apprenticeship; I have been very patient; but my patience is exhausted. You must leave this place with me to-night. "

"Mr. Fairfax, will you get me a fly, or must I walk home? "

He looked at her fixedly for a few moments, intent upon finding out if she were really in earnest, if this cold persistence were unconquerable even by him. Her face was very pale, the eyes downcast, the mouth firm as marble.

"Clarissa, " he cried, "I have been fooled from first to last—you have never loved me! "

Those words took her off her guard; she lifted her eyes to meet his, eyes full of love and despair, and again he told himself success was only a question of time. His apprenticeship was not finished yet; he must be content to serve a little longer. When she had tasted the bitterness of her new life, its helplessness, its desolation, with only such a broken reed as Austin Lovel to lean upon, she would turn to him naturally for comfort and succour, as the fledgling flies back to its nest.

But if in the meantime Daniel Granger should relent and pursue her, and take her back to his heart with pardon and love? There was the possibility of that event; yet to press matters too persistently would be foolish, perilous even. Better to let her have her own way for a little, since he knew that she loved him.

He went to look for the depressed waiter, whom he dispatched in quest of a vehicle, and then returned to the rustic shelter, where

Clarissa sat like a statue, watching the rain pouring down monotonously in a perpetual drizzle. They heard t e wheels of the carriage almost immediately. Mr. Fairfax offered his arm to Clarissa, and led her out of the garden; the obsequious waiter on the other side holding an umbrella over her head.

"Where shall I tell the man to drive? " he asked.

"To St. Gudule. "

"But you don't live in the cathedral, like Hugo's Esmeralda. Am I not to know your address? "

"It is better not. Austin knows that you were the cause of my leaving Paris. If you came, there might be some misunderstanding. "

"I am not afraid of facing Austin. "

"But I am afraid of any meeting between you. I cannot tell you where I am living, Mr. Fairfax. "

"That seems rather hard upon me. But you will let me see you again, won't you, Clary? Meet me here to-morrow at dusk—say at six o'clock. Promise to do that, and I will let you off. "

She hesitated, looking nervously to the right and left, like a hunted animal.

"Promise, Clary; it is not very much to ask. "

"Very well, then, I promise. Only please let the man drive off to St. Gudule, and pray don't follow me. "

Mr. Fairfax grasped her hand. "Remember, you have promised, " he said, and then gave the coachman his orders. And directly the fly containing Clarissa had rattled off, he ran to the nearest stand and chartered another.

"Drive to St. Gudule, " he said to the man, "and when you see a carriage going that way, keep behind it, but not too near. "

It happened, however, that the first driver had the best horse, and, being eager to earn his fare quickly, had deposited Clarissa in the

Place Gudule before George Fairfax's charioteer could overtake him. She had her money ready to slip into the man's hand, and she ran across the square and into the narrow street where Austin lived, and vanished, before Mr. Fairfax turned the corner of the square.

He met the empty vehicle, and dismissed his own driver thereupon in a rage. "Your horse ought to be suppressed by the legal authorities, " he said, as he gave the man his fare.

She must live very near the cathedral, he concluded, and he spent a dreary hour patrolling the narrow streets round about in the wet. In which of those dull-looking houses has she her dwelling? He could not tell. He walked up and down, staring up at all the windows with a faint hope of seeing her, but in vain; and at last went home to his hotel crestfallen and disappointed.

"She escapes me at every turn, " he said to himself. "There is a kind of fatality. Am I to grow old and gray in pursuing her, I wonder? I feel ten years older already, since that night when she and I travelled together. "

* * * * *

CHAPTER XLVI.

ON THE WING.

Clarissa hung over her baby with all manner of fond endearments.

"My darling! my darling! " she sobbed; "is it a hard thing to resist temptation for your sake? "

She had shed many bitter tears since that interview with George Fairfax, alone in the dreary room, while Level slept the after-dinner sleep of infancy, and while Mrs. Level and Jane Target gossipped sociably in the general sitting-room. Austin was out playing dominoes at the café of a Thousand Columns, with some Bohemianishly-disposed Bruxellois.

She had wept for the life that might have been, but which never could be. On that point she was decided. Not under the shadow of dishonour could she spend her days. She had her son. If she had been alone, utterly desolate, standing on some isolated rock, with nothing but the barren sea around her, she might perhaps have listened to that voice which was so very sweet to her, and yielded. But to take this dreadful leap which she was asked to take, alone, was one thing; to take it with her child in her arms, another. Her fancy, which was very vivid, made pictures of what her boy's future might be, if she were to do this thing. She thought of him stung by the mention of his mother's name, as if it were the foulest insult. She thought of his agony when he heard other men talk of their mothers, and remembered the blackness of darkness that shrouded his. She thought of the boyish intellect opening little by little, first with vague wonder, then fearful curiosity, to receive this fatal knowledge; and then the shame for that young innocent soul!

"O, not for worlds! " she cried, "O, not for worlds! God keep me from any more temptation! "

Not with mere idle prayers did she content herself. She knew her danger; that man was resolute, unscrupulous, revengeful even: and she loved him. She determined to leave Brussels. She would go and lose herself in the wide world of London; and then, after a little while, when all possibility of her movements being traced was over, she would take her child to some secluded country place, where there were woods and meadows, and where the little dimpled hands could gather bright spring flowers. She announced her intention to her brother that evening, when he came home at a latish hour from the Thousand Columns, elated by having won three francs and a half at dominoes—an amount which he had expended on cognac and syphons for himself and his antagonist.

He was surprised, vexed even, by Clarissa's decision. Why had she come to him, if she meant to run away directly? What supreme folly to make such a journey for nothing! Why did she not go from Paris to London at once?

"I did not think of that, Austin; I was almost out of my senses that day, I think, after Daniel told me he was going to separate me from my boy; and it seemed natural to me to fly to you for protection. "

"Then why run away from me? Heaven knows, you are welcome to such a home as I can give. The quarters are rough, I know; but we shall improve that, by-and-by. "

"No, no, Austin, it is not that. I should be quite happy with you, only—only—I have a particular reason for going to London. "

"Clarissa! " cried her brother sternly, "has that man anything to do with this? Has he tried to lure you away from here, to your destruction? "

"No, no, no! you ought to know me better than that. Do you think I would bring dishonour upon my boy? "

Her face told him that she was speaking the truth.

"Very well, Clary, " he said with a sigh of resignation; "you must do as you please. I suppose your reason is a good one, though you don't choose to trust me. "

So, by an early train next morning, Clarissa, with her nurse and child, left Brussels for Ostend—a somewhat dreary place wherein to arrive in early spring-time, with March winds blowing bleak across the sandy dunes.

They had to spend a night here, at a second-rate hotel on the Quay.

"We must go to humble-looking places, you know, Jane, to make our money last, " Clarissa said on the journey. They had travelled second-class; but she had given a five-pound note to her brother, by way of recompense for the brief accommodation he had given her, not telling him how low her stock was. Faithful Jane's five-and-twenty pounds were vanishing. Clarissa looked at the two glittering circlets on her wedding finger.

"We cannot starve while we have these, " she thought; and once in London, she could sell her drawings. Natural belief of the school-girl mind, that water-coloured sketches are a marketable commodity!

Again in the dismal early morning—that sunrise of which poets write so sweetly, but which to the unromantic traveller is wont to seem a dreary thing—mother and nurse and child went their way in a great black steamer, redolent of oil and boiled mutton; and at nine o'clock at night—a starless March night—Clarissa and her belongings were deposited on St. Katharine's Wharf, amidst a clamour and bustle that almost confused her senses.

She had meditated and debated and puzzled herself all through the day's voyage, sitting alone on the windy deck, brooding over her troubles, while Jane kept young Lovel amused and happy below. Inexperienced in the ways of every-day life as a child—knowing no more now than she had known in her school-girl days at Belforêt— she had made her poor little plan, such as it was.

Two or three times during her London season she had driven through Soho—those weird dreary streets between Soho Square and Regent Street—and had contemplated the gloomy old houses, with a bill of lodgings to let here and there in a parlour-window; anon a working jeweller's humble shop breaking out of a private house; here a cheap restaurant, there a French laundress; everywhere the air of a life which is rather a struggle to live than actual living. In this neighbourhood, which was the only humble quarter of the great city whereof she had any knowledge, Clarissa fancied they might find a temporary lodging—only a temporary shelter, for all her hopes and dreams pointed to some fair rustic retreat, where she might live happily with her treasure. Once lodged safely and obscurely, where it would be impossible for either her husband or George Fairfax to track her, she would spend a few shillings in drawing-materials, and set to work to produce a set of attractive sketches, which she might sell to a dealer. She knew her brother's plan of action, and fancied she could easily carry it out upon a small scale.

"So little would enable us to live happily, Jane, " she said, when she revealed her ideas to her faithful follower.

"But O, mum, to think of you living like that, with such a rich husband as Mr. Granger, and him worshipping the ground you walk upon, as he did up to the very last; and as to his anger, I'm sure it was only tempory, and he's sorry enough he drove you away by this time, I'll lay. "

"He wanted to take away my child, Jane. "

They took a cab, and drove from Thames-street to Soho. Clarissa had never been through the City at night before, and she thought the streets would never end. They came at last into that quieter and dingier region; but it was past ten o'clock, and hard work to find a respectable lodging at such an hour. Happily the cabman was a kindly and compassionate spirit, and did his uttermost to help them, moving heaven and earth, in the way of policemen and small shopkeepers, until, by dint of much inquiry, he found a decent-looking house in a *cul-de-sac* out of Dean-street—a little out-of-the-way quadrangle, where the houses were large and stately, and had been habitations of sweetness and light in the days when Soho was young, and Monmouth the young man of the period.

To one of these houses the cabman had been directed by a good-natured cheesemonger, at a corner not far off; and here Clarissa found a second-floor—a gaunt-looking sitting-room, with three windows and oaken window-seats, sparsely furnished, but inexorably clean; a bedroom adjoining—at a rent which seemed moderate to this inexperienced wayfarer. The landlady was a widow—is it not the normal state of landladies? —cleanly and conciliating, somewhat surprised to see travellers with so little luggage, but reassured by that air of distinction which was inseparable from Mrs. Granger, and by the presence of the maid.

The cabman was dismissed, with many thanks and a princely payment; and so Clarissa began life alone in London.

* * * * *

446

CHAPTER XLVII.

IN TIME OF NEED.

It was a dreary habitation, that London lodging, after the gardens and woods of Arden, the luxurious surroundings and innumerable prettinesses which Mr. Granger's wealth had provided for the wife of his love; dreary after the holiday brightness of Paris; dreary beyond expression to Clarissa in the long quiet evenings when she sat alone, trying to face the future—the necessity for immediate action being over, and the world all before her.

She had her darling. That was the one fact which she repeated to herself over and over again, as if the words had been a charm—an amulet to drive away guilty thoughts of the life that might have been, if she had listened to George Fairfax's prayer.

It was not easy for her to shut *that* image out of her heart, even with her dearest upon earth beside her. The tender pleading words, the earnest face, came back to her very often. She thought of him wandering about those hilly streets in Brussels, disappointed and angry: thought of his reproaches, and the sacrifices he had made for her.

And then from such weak fancies she was brought suddenly back by the necessities of every-day life Her money was very nearly gone; the journeys had cost so much, and she had been obliged to buy clothing for Jane and Lovel and herself at Brussels. She had spent a sovereign on colours and brushes and drawing-paper at Winsor and Newton's—her little stock-in-trade. She looked at her diamond rings meditatively as she sat brooding in the March twilight, with as vague an idea of their value as a child might have had. The time was very near when she would be obliged to turn them into money.

Fortunately the woman of the house was friendly, and the rooms were clean. But the airs of Soho are not as those breezes which come blowing over Yorkshire wolds and woods, with the breath of the German Ocean; nor had they the gay Tuileries garden and the Bois for Master Lovel's airings. Jane Target was sorely puzzled where to take the child. It was a weary long way to St. James's Park on foot; and the young mother had a horror of omnibuses—in which she supposed smallpox and fever to be continually raging. Sometimes

447

they had a cab, and took the boy down to feed the ducks and stare at the soldiers. But in the Park Clarissa had an ever-present terror of being seen by some one she knew. Purposeless prowlings with baby in the streets generally led unawares into Newport-market, from which busy mart Mrs. Granger fled aghast, lest her darling should die of the odour of red herrings and stale vegetables. In all the wider streets Clarissa was afflicted by that perpetual fear of being recognised; and during the airings which Lovel enjoyed with Jane alone the poor mother endured unspeakable torments. At any moment Mr. Granger, or some one employed by Mr. Granger, might encounter the child, and her darling be torn from her; or some accident might befall him. Clarissa's inexperience exaggerated the perils of the London streets, until every paving-stone seemed to bristle with dangers. She longed for the peace and beauty of the country; but not until she had found some opening for the disposal of her sketches could she hope to leave London. She worked on bravely for a fortnight, painting half a dozen hours a day, and wasting the rest of her day in baby worship, or in profound plottings and plannings about the future with Jane Target. The girl was thoroughly devoted, ready to accept any scheme of existence which her mistress might propose. The two women made their little picture of the life they were to lead when Clarissa had found a kindly dealer to give her constant employment: a tiny cottage, somewhere in Kent or Surrey, among green fields and wooded hills, furnished ever so humbly, but with a garden where Lovel might play. Clarissa sketched the ideal cottage one evening—a bower of roses and honeysuckle, with a thatched roof and steep gables. Alas, when she had finished her fortnight's work, and carried half a dozen sketches to a dealer in Rathbone-place, it was only to meet with a crushing disappointment. The man admitted her power, but had no use for anything of that kind. Chromolithographs were cheap and popular—people would rather buy a lithograph of some popular artist's picture than a nameless water-colour. If she liked to leave a couple of her sketches, he would try to dispose of them, but he could not buy them—and giving her permanent employment was quite out of the question.

"Do you know anything about engraving? " he asked.

Clarissa shook her head sadly.

"Can you draw on the wood? "

"I have never tried, but I daresay I could do that. "

"I recommend you to turn your attention that way. There's a larger field for that sort of thing. You might exhibit some of your sketches at the next Water-Colour Exhibition. They would stand a chance of selling there. "

"Thanks. You are very good, but I want remunerative employment immediately. "

She wandered on—from dealer to dealer, hoping against hope always with the same result—from Rathbone-place to Regent-street, and on to Bond-street, and homewards along Oxford-street, and then back to her baby, broken-hearted.

"It is no use, Jane, " she sobbed. "I can understand my brother's life now. Art is a broken reed. We must get away from this dreadful London—how pale my Lovel is looking! —and go into some quiet country-place, where we can live very cheaply. I almost wish I had stayed in Belgium—in one of the small out-of-the-way towns, where we might have been safely hidden. We must go down to the country, Jane, and I must take in plain needle-work. "

"I'm a good un at that, you know, mum, " Jane cried with a delighted grin.

And then they began to consider where they should go. That was rather a difficult question. Neither of them knew any world except the region surrounding Arden Court. At last Clarissa remembered Beckenham. She had driven through Beckenham once on her way to a garden-party. Why should they not go to Beckenham? —the place was so near London, could be reached with so little expense, and yet was rustic.

"We must get rid of one of the rings, Jane, " Clarissa said, looking at it doubtfully.

"I'll manage that, mum—don't you fidget yourself about that. There's a pawnbroker's in the next street. I'll take it round there in the evening, if you like, mum. "

449

Clarissa shuddered. Commerce with a pawnbroker seemed to her inexperience a kind of crime—something like taking stolen property to be melted down.

But Jane Target was a brave damsel, and carried the ring to the pawnbroker with so serene a front, and gave her address with so honest an air, that the man, though at first inclined to be doubtful, believed her story; namely, that the ring belonged to her mistress, a young married lady who had suffered a reverse of fortune.

She went home rejoicing, having raised fifteen pounds upon a ring that was worth ninety. The pawnbroker had a notice that it would never be redeemed—young married ladies who suffer reverse of fortune rarely recover their footing, but generally slide down, down, down to the uttermost deeps of poverty.

They were getting ready for that journey to Beckenham, happy in the idea of escaping from the monotonous unfriendly streets, and the grime and mire and general dinginess of London life, when an unlooked-for calamity befell them, and the prospect of release had, for the time at least, to be given up. Young Lovel fell ill. He was "about his teeth, " the woman of the house said, and tried to make light of the evil. These innocents are subject to much suffering in this way. He had a severe cold, with a tiresome hacking cough which rent Clarissa's heart. She sent for a doctor immediately—a neighbouring practitioner recommended by the landlady—and he came and saw the child lying in his mother's lap, and the mother young and beautiful and unhappy, and was melted accordingly, and did all he could to treat the matter lightly. Yet he was fain, after a few visits, and no progress for the better, to confess that these little lives hang by a slender thread.

"The little fellow has a noble frame and an excellent constitution, " he said; "I hope we shall save him. "

Save him! An icy thrill went through Clarissa's veins. Save him! Was there any fear of losing him? O God, what would her life be without that child? She looked at the doctor, white to the lips and speechless with horror.

"I don't wish to alarm you, " he said gently, "but I am compelled to admit that there is danger. If the little one's father is away, " he added doubtfully, "and you would like to summon him, I think it would be as well to do so. "

"O, my flower, my angel, my life! " she cried, flinging herself down beside the child's bed; "I cannot lose you! "

"I trust in God you will not, " said the surgeon. "We will make every effort to save him. " And then he turned to Jane Target, and murmured his directions.

"Is there any one else, " said Clarissa in a hoarse voice, looking up at the medical man—"anyone I can send for besides yourself—any one who can cure my baby? "

"I doubt whether it would be of any use. The case is such a simple one. I have fifty such in a year. But if you would like a physician to see the little fellow, there is Dr. Ormond, who has peculiar experience in children's cases. You might call him in, if you liked. "

"I will send for him this minute. —Jane, dear, will you go? "

"I don't think it would be any use, just now. He will be out upon his rounds. There is no immediate danger. If you were to send to him this evening—a note would do—asking him to call to-morrow—that would be the best way. Remember, I don't for a moment say the case is hopeless. Only, if you have any anxiety about the little one's father, and if he is within a day's journey, I would really advise you to send for him. "

Clarissa did not answer. She was hanging over the bed, watching every difficult breath with unutterable agony. The child had only begun to droop a week ago, had been positively ill only four days.

All the rest of that day Clarissa was in a kind of stupor. She watched the child, and watched Jane administering her remedies, and the landlady coming in now and then to look at the boy, or to ask about him with a friendly anxiety. She tried to help Jane sometimes, in a useless tremulous way, sometimes sat statue-like, and could only gaze. She could not even pray—only now and then, she whispered with her dry lips, "Surely God will not take away my child! "

At dusk the doctor came again, but said very little. He was leaving the room, when Clarissa stopped him with a passionate despairing cry. Until that moment she had seemed marble.

"Tell me the truth, " she cried. "Will he be taken away from me? He is all the world to me—the only thing on earth I have to love. Surely God will not be so pitiless! What difference can one angel more make in heaven? and he is all the world to me. "

"My dear lady, these things are ordered by a Wisdom beyond our comprehension, " the doctor answered gently. That picture of a disconsolate mother was very common to him—only Clarissa was so much lovelier than most of the mothers, and her grief had a more romantic aspect and touched him a little more than usual. "Believe me, I shall make every effort to pull the little fellow through, " he added with the professional air of hopefulness. "Have you written to Dr. Ormond? "

"Yes, my letter was posted an hour after you called. "

"Then we shall hear what he says to-morrow. You can have no higher opinion. And now pray, my dear Mrs. Graham"—Clarissa had called herself Graham in these Soho lodgings—"pray keep up your spirits; remember your own health will suffer if you give way— and I really do not think you are strong. "

He looked at her curiously as he spoke. She was deadly pale, and had a haggard look which aged her by ten years: beauty less perfect in its outline would have been obscured by that mental anguish— hers shone through all, ineffaceable.

"Do not forget what I said about the little one's father, " urged the doctor, lingering for a minute on the threshold. "There is really too great a responsibility in keeping him ignorant of the case, if he is anywhere within reach. "

Clarissa smiled for the first time since her boy's illness—a strange wan smile. She was thinking how Daniel Granger had threatened her with separation from her child; and now Death had come between them to snatch him from both.

"My son! " She remembered the proud serenity, the supreme sense of possession, with which she had pronounced those words.

And the child would die perhaps, and Daniel Granger never look upon his face again. A great terror came into her mind at that thought. What would her husband say to her if he came to claim his boy, and found him dead? For the first time since she had left him— triumphant in the thought of having secured this treasure—the fact that the boy belonged to him, as well as to herself, came fully home to her. From the day of the baby's birth she had been in the habit of thinking of him as her own—hers by a right divine almost—of putting his father out of the question, as it were—only just tolerating to behold that doating father's fond looks and caresses—watching all communion between those two with a lurking jealousy.

Now all at once she began to feel what a sacred bond there was between the father and son, and how awful a thing it would be, if Daniel Granger should find his darling dead. Might he not denounce her as the chief cause of his boy's death? Those hurried journeys by land and sea—that rough shifting to and fro of the pampered son and heir, whose little life until that time had been surrounded with such luxurious indulgences, so guarded from the faintest waft of discomfort—who should say that these things had not jeopardised the precious creature? And out of her sin had this arisen. In that dread hour by her darling's sick-bed, what unutterably odious colours did her flirtation with George Fairfax assume—her dalliance with temptation, her weak hankering after that forbidden society! She saw, as women do see in that clear after-light which comes with remorse, all the guilt and all the hatefulness of her sin.

"God gave me my child for my redemption, " she said to herself, "and I went on sinning. "

What was it the doctor had said? Again and again those parting words came back to her. The father should be summoned. But to summon him, to reveal her hiding-place, and then have her darling taken from her, saved from the grasp of death only to be torn from her by his pitiless unforgiving father! No thought of what Daniel Granger had been to her in all the days of her married life arose to comfort or reassure her. She only thought of him as he had been after that fatal meeting in her brother's painting-room; and she hoped for no mercy from him.

"And even if I were willing to send for him, I don't know where he is, " she said at last helplessly.

Jane Target urged her to summon him.

"If you was to send a telegraft to the Court, mum, Miss Granger is pretty sure to be there, and she'd send to her pa, wherever he was. "

Clarissa shivered. Send to Miss Granger! suffer those cold eyes to see the depth of her humiliation! That would be hard to endure. Yet what did anything in the world matter to her when her boy was in jeopardy?

"We shall save him, Jane, " she said with a desperate hopefulness, clasping her hands and bending down to kiss the troubled little one, who had brief snatches of sleep now and then in weary hours of restlessness. "We shall save him. The doctor said so. "

"God grant we may, mum! But the doctor didn't say for certain—he only said he *hoped*; and it would be so much better to send for master. It seems a kind of crime not to let him know; and if the poor dear should grow worse—"

"He will not grow worse! " cried Clarissa hysterically. "What, Jane! are you against me? Do you want me to be robbed of him, as his father would rob me without mercy? No, I will keep him, I will keep him! Nothing but death shall take him from me. "

Later in the evening, restless with the restlessness of a soul tormented by fear, Clarissa began to grow uneasy about her letter to Dr. Ormond. It might miscarry in going through the postoffice. She was not quite sure that it had been properly directed, her mind had been so bewildered when she wrote it. Or Dr. Ormond might have engagements next morning, and might not be able to come. She was seized with a nervous anxiety about this. "

"If there were any one I could send with another note, " she said.

Jane shook her head despondently. In that house there was no messenger to be procured. The landlady was elderly, and kept no servant—employing only a mysterious female of the charwoman species, who came at daybreak, dyed herself to the elbows with blacking or blacklead before breakfast, and so remained till the afternoon, when she departed to "do for" a husband and children— the husband and children passing all the earlier part of the day in a desolate and un-"done-for" condition.

"There's no one to take a letter, mum, " said Jane, looking wistfully at her mistress, who had been watching without rest or slumber for three days and three nights. "But why shouldn't you go yourself, mum? Cavendish Square isn't so very far. Don't you remember our going there one morning with baby? It's a fine evening, and a little fresh air would do you good. "

Clarissa was quite willing to go on the errand herself. It would be doing something at least. She might see the physician, and obtain his promise to come to her early next day; and beside that sick-bed she was of so little use. She could only hold her darling in her lap, when he grew weary of his bed, or carry him up and down the room sometimes. Jane, whose nerves were as steady as a rock, did all the rest.

She looked at the bed. It was hard to leave that tender little sufferer even for half an hour.

"If he should grow worse while I am away? " she said doubtfully.

"No fear of that, " replied Jane. "He's sleeping better now than he has slept for ever so long. God grant he's upon the turn! "

"God grant it! And you won't forget the medicine at half-past eight? "

"Lor', mum, as if I should forget! "

"Then I'll go, " said Clarissa.

She put on her bonnet and shawl, startled a little by the white face that looked at her from the glass. The things she had worn when she left Paris were the darkest and plainest in her wardrobe. They had grown shabby by this time, and had a very sombre look. Even in these garments the tall slim figure had a certain elegance; but it was not a figure to be remarked at nightfall, in the London streets. The mistress of Arden Court might have been easily mistaken for a sempstress going home from her work.

Just at first the air made her giddy, and she tottered a little on the broad pavement of the quiet *cul-de-sac*. It seemed as if she had not been out of doors for a month. But by degrees she grew more accustomed to the keen March atmosphere and the noise of Oxford-street, towards which she was hastening, and so hurried on, thinking only of her errand. She made her way somehow to Cavendish-square. How well she remembered driving through it in the summer gloaming, during the brief glory of her one season, on her way to a commercial magnate's Tusculum in the Regent's-park! It had seemed remote and out of the world after Mayfair—a locality which one might be driven by reverse of fortune to inhabit, not otherwise. But to-night the grave old square had an alarming stateliness of aspect after slipshod Soho.

She found Dr. Ormond's house, and saw his butler, a solemn bald-headed personage, who looked wise enough to prescribe for the most recondite diseases of humanity. The doctor himself was dining out, but the butler pledged himself for his master's appearance at Clarissa's lodgings between eleven and two to-morrow.

"He never disappints; and he draws no distinctions, " said the official, with an evident reference to the humility of the applicant's social status. "There's not many like him in the medical perfession. "

"And you think he is sure to come? " urged Clarissa anxiously.

"Don't you be afraid, mum. I shall make a particular pint of it myself. You may be quite easy about his comin'. "

Clarissa thanked the man, and surprised him with half-a-crown gently slipped into his fat palm. She had not many half-crowns now; but the butler seemed to pity her, and might influence his master to come to her a little sooner than he would come in the ordinary way.

Her errand being done, she turned away from the house with a strange sinking at the heart. An ever-present fear of his illness coming to a fatal end, and a guilty sense of the wrong she was doing to Daniel Granger, oppressed her. She walked in a purposeless way, took the wrong turning after coming out of the square, and so wandered into Portland-place. She came to a full stop suddenly in that wide thoroughfare, and looking about her like an awakened sleep-walker, perceived that she had gone astray—recognised the place she was in, and saw that she was within a few doors of Lady Laura Armstrong's house.

Although the London season had begun, there was an air of stillness and solitude in this grave habitation of splendours that have for the most part vanished. At one door there was a carriage waiting; here and there lighted windows shone out upon the night; but the general aspect was desolation. If there were gaiety and carousing anywhere, closed shutters hid the festival from the outer world. The underground world of Egypt could scarcely have seemed more silent than Portland-place.

Clarissa went on to the familiar corner house, which was made conspicuous to the stranger by encaustic tiled balconies, or glass fern and flower cases at every available window, and by a certain colour and glitter which seemed almost a family likeness to Lady Laura herself. There were lights burning dimly in the two last windows on the drawing-room floor looking into the side street. Clarissa remembered the room very well—it was Lady Laura's own especial sanctum, the last and smallest of four drawing-rooms—a nest lined with crimson silk, and crowded with everything foolish in the way of ebony and ormolu, Venetian glass and Sèvres china, and with nothing sensible in it except three or four delicious easy-chairs of the *pouff* species, immortalised by Sardou. Alas for that age of pouff which he satirised with such a caustic pen! To what dismal end has it come! End of powder and petroleum, and instead of beauty, burning!

The lonely wanderer, so sorely oppressed with cares and perplexities, looked wistfully up at those familiar windows. How often she had loitered away the twilight with Lady Laura, talking idly in that flower-laden balcony! As she looked at it to-night, there came into her mind a foolish wonder that life could have had any interest for her in those days, before the birth of her son.

"If I were to lose him now, I should be no poorer than I was then, " she thought; and then, after a moment's reflection, "O yes, yes, a thousand times poorer, once having had him. "

She walked a little way down the street, and then came back again and lingered under those two-windows, with an unspeakable yearning to cast herself upon her friend in this hour of shipwreck. She had such bitter need of sympathy from some one nearer her own level than the poor honest faithful Yorkshire girl.

"She was once my friend, " she said to herself, still hovering there irresolute, "and seemed very fond of me. She could advise me, knowing the world so well as she does; and I do not think she would betray me. She owes me something, too. But for my promise to her, I might have been George Fairfax's wife, and all this trouble might have been avoided. "

George Fairfax's wife! What a strange dreamlike fancy it seemed! And yet it might have been; it had needed only one little word from herself to make the dream a fact.

"I tried to do my duty, " she thought, "and yet ruin and sorrow have come upon me. " And then the small still voice whispered, "Tried to do your duty, but not always; sometimes you left off trying, and dared to be happy in your own way. Between the two roads of vice and virtue, you tried to make a devious pathway of your own, not wholly on one side or the other. "

Once having seen that light, feeling somehow that there was sympathy and comfort near, she could not go away without making some attempt to see her friend. She thought with a remorseful pang of times and seasons during her wedded life when Laura Armstrong's too solicitous friendship had seemed to her something of a bore. How different was it with her now!

She summoned up resolution at last, and in a half desperate mood, went round to the front door and knocked—a tremulous conscience-stricken knock, as of some milliner's apprentice bringing home a delayed bonnet. The man who opened the door; looked involuntarily for her basket.

"What is it? " he asked dubiously, scenting a begging-letter writer in the tall slim figure and closely-veiled face, and being on principle averse from gentility that did not ride in its carriage. "What is it, young woman? "

"Can I see Lady Laura Armstrong? I want to see her very particularly. "

"Have you got an appointment? "

"No; but I wish to see her. "

"You're from Madame Lecondre's, I suppose. You can see my lady's maid; but it's quite out of the question for you to see my lady herself, at this time of night. "

"Will you take a message to her, on a slip of paper? I am almost sure she will see me. " And again Clarissa opened her slender purse, and slipped a florin into the man's hand, by way of bribe.

He was somewhat melted by this, but yet had an eye to the portable property in the hall.

"You can come in, " he said, pointing with a lofty air to a table whereon were pens and paper, "and write your message. " And then rang an electric bell, which summons brought a second powdered footman, who was, as it were, a Corsican Brother or Siamese Twin, without the ligature, to the first.

Clarissa scrawled a few hasty lines on a sheet of paper, and folded it.

"Be so kind as to take that to your mistress, " she said. "I am sure she will see me. "

The second footman was that superior young man, Norris, whom Hannah Warman had praised. He stared aghast, recognising Mrs. Granger's voice and bearing, in spite of the thick veil folded over her face, in spite of her shabby garments.

"My lady shall have your note immediately, ma'am, " he said with profound respect, and sped off as if to carry the message of a cabinet minister, much to the bewilderment of his brother officer, who did not know Mrs. Granger.

He reappeared in about two minutes, and ushered Clarissa duly up the broad staircase—dimly lighted to-night, the family being in Portland-place, in a kind of semi-state, only newly arrived, and without so much as a hall-porter—through the corridor, where there were velvet-cushioned divans against the walls, whereon many among Lady Laura's guests considered it a privilege to sit on her great reception nights, content to have penetrated so far, and with no thought of struggling farther, and on to the white-and-gold door at the farther end, which admitted the elect into my lady's boudoir.

Laura Armstrong was sitting at an ebony writing-table, with innumerable little drawers pulled out to their utmost extent, and all running over with papers, a chaotic mass of open letters before her, and a sheet of foolscap scrawled over with names. She had been planning her campaign for the season—so many dinners, so many dances, alternate Thursdays in May and June; and a juvenile fancy ball, at which a Pompadour of seven years of age could lead off the Lancers with a Charles the Twelfth of ten, with an eight-year-old Mephistopheles and a six-year-old Anna Boleyn for their *vis-à-vis.*

As the footman opened the door, and ushered in Mrs. Granger, there was a faint rustling of silk behind the *portière* dividing Lady Laura's room from the next apartment; but Clarissa was too agitated to notice this.

Laura Armstrong received her with effusion.

"My dearest girl, " she exclaimed, rising, and grasping both Clarissa's hands, as the man closed the door, "how glad I am to see you! Do you know, something told me you would come to me? Yes, dear; I said to myself ever so many times, 'That poor misguided child will come to me. ' O, Clary, Clary, what have you been doing! Your husband is like a rock. He was at Arden for a few days, about a fortnight ago, and I drove over to see him, and entreated him to confide in me; but he would tell nothing. My poor, poor child! how pale, how changed! "

She had thrown back Clarissa's veil, and was scrutinising the haggard face with very womanly tenderness.

"Sit down, dear, and tell me everything. You know that you can trust me. If you had gone ever so wrong—and I don't believe it is in you to do that—I would still be your friend. "

Clarissa made a faint effort to speak, and then burst into tears. This loving welcome was quite too much to bear.

"He told me he was going to take my boy away from me, " she sobbed, "so I ran away from him, with my darling—and now my angel is dying! "

And then, with many tears, and much questioning and ejaculation from Lady Laura, she told her pitiful story—concealing nothing, not even her weak yielding to temptation, not even her love for George Fairfax.

"I loved him always, " she said; "yes—always, always, always— from that first night when we travelled together! I used to dream of him sometimes, never hoping to see him again, till that summer day when he came suddenly upon me in Marley Wood. But I kept my promise; I was true to you, Lady Laura; I kept my promise. "

"My poor Clary, how I wish I had never exacted that promise! It did no good; it did not save Geraldine, and it seems to have made you miserable. Good gracious me, " cried Lady Laura with sudden impetuosity, "I have no patience with the man! What is one man more than another, that there should be so much fuss about him? "

"I must go home to Lovel, " Clarissa said anxiously. "I don't know how long I have been away from him. I lost my head, almost; and I felt that I *must* come to you. "

"Thank God you did come, you poor wandering creature! Wait a few minutes, Clary, while I send for a cab, and put on my bonnet. I am coming with you. "

"You, Lady Laura? "

"Yes, and I too, " said a calm voice, that Clarissa remembered very well; and looking up at the door of communication between the two rooms, she saw the *portière* pushed aside, and Geraldine Challoner on the threshold.

"Let me come and nurse your baby, Mrs. Granger, " she said gently; "I have had a good deal of experience of that sort of thing. "

"You do not know what an angel she is to the poor round Hale, " said Lady Laura; "especially to the children. And she nursed three of mine, Maud, Ethel, and Alick—no; Stephen, wasn't it? " she asked, looking at her sister for correction—"through the scarlatina. Nothing but her devotion could have pulled them through, my doctor assured me. Let her come with us, Clary. "

"O, yes, yes! God bless you, Lady Geraldine, for wanting to help my darling! "

"Norris, tell Fosset to bring me my bonnet and shawl, and fetch a cab immediately; I can't wait for the carriage. "

Five minutes afterwards, the three women were seated in the cab, and on their way to Soho.

"You have sent for Mr. Granger, of course, " said Lady Laura.

"No, not yet. I trust in God there may be no necessity; my darling will get well; I know he will! Dr. Ormond is to see him to-morrow. "

"What, Clarissa! you have not sent for your husband, although you say that his boy is in danger? "

"If I let Mr. Granger know where I am, he will come and take my son away from me. "

"Nonsense, Clary; he can't do that. It is very shameful of you to keep him in ignorance of the child's state. " And as well as she could, amidst the rattling of the cab, Lady Laura tried to awaken Clarissa to a sense of the wrong she was doing. Jane Target stared in amazement on seeing her mistress return with these two ladies.

"O, ma'am, I've been, so frightened! " she exclaimed. "I couldn't think what was come of you. "

Clarissa ran to the bed.

"He has been no worse? " she asked eagerly.

"No, ma'am. I do think, if there's any change, it is for the better. "

"O thank God, thank God! " cried Clarissa hysterically, falling on her knees by the bed. "Death shall not rob me of him! Nobody shall take him from me! " And then, turning to Laura Armstrong, she said, "I need not send for my husband, you see; my darling will recover. "

* * * * *

462

CHAPTER XLVIII.

"STRANGERS YET. "

Lady Laura went back to Portland-place in an hour; but Geraldine Challoner stayed all night with the sick child. God was very merciful to Clarissa; the angel of death passed by. In the night the fever abated, if only ever so little; and Dr. Ormond's report next day was a cheering one. He did not say the little one was out of danger; but he did say there was hope.

Lady Geraldine proved herself an accomplished nurse. The sick child seemed more tranquil in her arms than even in his mother's. The poor mother felt a little pang of jealousy as she saw that it was so; but bore the trial meekly, and waited upon Geraldine with humble submission.

"How good you are! " she murmured once, as she watched the slim white hands that had played chess with George Fairfax adjusting poultices—"how good you are! "

"Don't say that, my dear Mrs. Granger. I would do as much for any cottager's child within twenty miles of Hale; it would be hard if I couldn't do it for my sister's friend. "

"Have you always been fond of the poor? " Clarissa asked wonderingly.

"Yes, " Geraldine answered, with a faint blush; "I was always fond of them. I can get on with poor people better than with my equals sometimes, I think; but I have visited more amongst them lately, since I have gone less into society—since papa's death, in fact. And I am particularly fond of children; the little things always take to me. "

"My baby does, at any rate. "

"Have you written or telegraphed to Mr. Granger? " Lady Geraldine asked gravely.

"No, no, no; there can be no necessity now. Dr. Ormond says there is hope. "

"Hope, yes; but these little lives are so fragile. I implore you to send to him. It is only right. "

"I will think about it, by and by, perhaps, if he should grow any worse; but I know he is getting better. O, Lady Geraldine, have some pity upon me! If my husband finds out where I am, he will rob me of my child. "

The words were hardly spoken, when there was a loud double-knock at the door below, a delay of some two minutes, and then a rapid step on the stair—a step that set Clarissa's heart beating tumultuously. She sat down by the bed, clinging to it like an animal at bay, guarding her cub from the hunter.

The door was opened quickly, and Daniel Granger came into the room. He went straight to the bed, and bent down to look at his child.

The boy had been light-headed in the night, but his brain was clear enough now. He recognised his father, and smiled—a little wan smile, that went to the strong man's heart.

"My God, how changed he is! " exclaimed Mr. Granger. "How long has he been ill? "

"Very little more than a week, sir, " Jane Target faltered from the background.

"More than a week! and I am only told of his illness to-day, by a telegram from Lady Laura Armstrong! I beg your pardon, Lady Geraldine; I did not see you till this moment. I owe it to your sister's consideration that I am here in time to see my boy before he dies. "

"We have every hope of saving him, " said Geraldine.

"And what a place I find him in! He has had some kind of doctor attending him, I suppose? "

"He has had a surgeon from the neighbourhood, who seems both kind and clever, and Dr. Ormond. "

Mr. Granger seated himself at the foot of the bed, a very little way from Clarissa, taking possession of his child, as it were.

"Do you know, Mrs. Granger, that I have scarcely rested night or day since you left Paris, hunting for my son? " he said. And this was the first time he acknowledged his wife's presence by word or look.

Clarissa was silent. She had been betrayed, she thought—betrayed by her own familiar friend; and Daniel Granger had come to rob her of her child. Come what might, she would not part with him without a struggle.

After this, there came a weary time of anxious care and watching. The little life trembled in the balance; there were harassing fluctuations, a fortnight of unremitting care, before a favourable issue could be safely calculated upon. And during all that time Daniel Granger watched his boy with only the briefest intervals for rest or refreshment. Clarissa watched too; nor did her husband dispute her right to a place in the sick-room, though he rarely spoke to her, and then only with the coldest courtesy.

Throughout this period of uncertainty, Geraldine Challoner was faithful to the duty she had undertaken; spending the greatest part of her life at Clarissa's lodgings, and never wearying of the labours of the sick-room. The boy grew daily fonder of her; but, with a womanly instinct, she contrived that it should be Clarissa who carried him up and down the room when he was restless—Clarissa's neck round which the wasted little arm twined itself.

Daniel Granger watched the mother and child sometimes with haggard eyes, speculating on the future. If the boy lived, who was to have him? The mother, whose guilt or innocence was an open question—who had owned to being at heart false to her husband—or the father, who had done nothing to forfeit the right to his keeping? And yet to part them was like plucking asunder blossom and bud, that had grown side by side upon one common stem. In many a gloomy reverie the master of Arden Court debated this point.

He could never receive his wife again—upon that question there seemed to him no room for doubt. To take back to his home and his heart the woman who had confessed her affection for another man, was hardly in Daniel Granger's nature. Had he not loved her too much already—degraded himself almost by so entire a devotion to a woman who had given him nothing, who had kept her heart shut against him?

"She married Arden Court, not me, " he said to himself; "and then she tried to have Arden Court and her old lover into the bargain. Would she have run away with him, I wonder, if he had had time to persuade her that day? *Can* any woman be pure, when a man dares ask her to leave her husband? "

And then the locket that man wore—"From Clarissa"—was not that damning evidence?

He thought of these things again and again, with a weary iteration—thought of them as he watched the mother walking slowly to and fro with her baby in her arms. *That* picture would surely live in his mind for ever, he thought. Never again, never any more, in all the days to come, could he take his wife back to his heart; but, O God, how dearly he had loved her, and how desolate his home would be without her! Those two years of their married life seemed to be all his existence; looking back beyond that time, his history seemed, like Viola's, "A blank, my lord. " And he was to live the rest of his life without her. But for that ever-present anxiety about the child, which was in some wise a distraction, the thought of these things might have driven him mad.

At last, after those two weeks of uncertainty, there came a day when Dr. Ormond pronounced the boy out of danger—on the very high-road to recovery, in fact.

"I would say nothing decided till I could speak with perfect certainty, " he said. "You may make yourselves quite happy now. "

Clarissa knelt down and kissed the good old doctor's hand, raining tears upon it in a passion of gratitude. He seemed to her in that moment something divine, a supernal creature who, by the exercise of his power, had saved her child Dr. Ormond lifted her up, smiling at her emotion.

"Come, come, my dear soul, this is hysterical, " he said, in his soothing paternal way, patting her shoulder gently as he spoke; "I always meant to save the little fellow; though it has been a very severe bout, I admit, and we have had a tussle for it. And now I expect to see your roses come back again. It has been a hard time for you as well as for baby. "

When Mr. Granger went out of the room with the physician presently, Dr. Ormond said gravely, —

"The little fellow is quite safe, Mr. Granger; but you must look to your wife now. "

"What do you mean? "

"She has a nasty little hacking cough—a chest cough—which I don't like; and there's a good deal of incipient fever about her. "

"If there is anything wrong, for God's sake see to her at once! " cried Daniel Granger. "Why didn't you speak of this before? "

"There was no appearance of fever until to-day. I didn't wish to worry her with medicines while she was anxious about the child; indeed, I thought the best cure for her would be the knowledge of his safety. But the cough is worse to-day; and I should certainly like to prescribe for her, if you will ask her to come in here and speak to me for a few minutes. "

So Clarissa went into the dingy lodging-house sitting-room to see the doctor, wondering much that any one could be interested in such an insignificant matter as *her* health, now that her treasure was safe. She went reluctantly, murmuring that she was well enough—quite well now; and had hardly tottered into the room, when she sank down upon the sofa in a dead faint.

Daniel Granger looked on aghast while they revived her.

"What can have caused this? " he asked.

"My dear sir, you are surely not surprised, " said Dr. Ormond. "Your wife has been sitting up with her child every night for nearly a month—the strain upon her, bodily and mental, has been enormous, and the reaction is of course trying. She will want a good deal of care, that is all. Come now, " he went on cheerfully, as Clarissa opened her eyes, to find her head lying on Jane Target's shoulder, and her husband standing aloof regarding her with affrighted looks—"come now, my dear Mrs. Granger, cheer up; your little darling is safely over his troubles. "

She burst into a flood of tears.

"They will take him away from me! " she sobbed.

"Take him away from you—nonsense! What are you dreaming of? "

"Death has been merciful; but you will be more cruel, " she cried, looking at her husband. "You will take him away. "

"Come, come, my dear lady, this is a delusion; you really must not give way to this kind of thing, " murmured the doctor, rather complacently. He had a son-in-law who kept a private madhouse at Wimbledon, and began to think Mrs. Granger was drifting that way. It was sad, of course, a sweet young woman like that; but patients are patients, and Daniel Granger's wife would be peculiarly eligible.

He looked at Mr. Granger, and touched his forehead significantly. "The brain has been sorely taxed, " he murmured, confidentially; "but we shall set all that right by-and-by. " This with as confident an air as if the brain had been a clock.

Daniel Granger went over to his wife, and took her hand—it was the first time those two hands had met since the scene in Austin's painting-room—looking down at her gravely.

"Clarissa, " he said, "on my word of honour, I will not attempt to separate you from your son. "

She gave a great cry—a shriek, that rang through the room—and cast herself upon her husband's breast.

"O, God bless you for that! " she sobbed; "God bless—" and stopped, strangled by her sobs.

Mr. Granger put her gently back into her faithful hand-maiden's arms. *That* was different. He might respect her rights as a mother; he could never again accept her as his wife.

But a time came now in which all thought of the future was swept away by a very present danger. Before the next night, Clarissa was raving in brain-fever; and for more than a month life was a blank to her—or not a blank, an age of confused agony rather, to be looked back upon with horror by-and-by.

They dared not move her from the cheerless rooms in Soho. Lovel was sent down to Ventnor with Lady Geraldine and a new nurse. It could do no harm to take him away from his mother for a little while, since she was past the consciousness of his presence. Jane Target and Daniel Granger nursed her, with a nursing sister to relieve guard occasionally, and Dr. Ormond in constant attendance.

The first thing she saw, when sense came back to her, was her husband's figure, sitting a little way from-the bed, his face turned towards her, gravely watchful. Her first reasonable words—faintly murmured in a wondering tone—moved him deeply; but he was strong enough to hide all emotion.

"When she has quite recovered, I shall go back to Arden, " he said to himself; "and leave her to plan her future life with the help of Lady Geraldine's counsel. That woman is a noble creature, and the best friend my wife can have. And then we must make some fair arrangement about the boy—what time he is to spend with me, and what with his mother. I cannot altogether surrender my son. In any case he is sure to love her best. "

When Clarissa was at last well enough to be moved, her husband took her down to Ventnor, where the sight of her boy, bright and blooming, and the sound of his first syllables—little broken scraps of language, that are so sweet to mothers' ears—had a better influence than all Dr. Ormond's medicines. Here, too, came her father, from Nice, where he had been wintering, having devoted his days to the pleasing duty of taking care of himself. He would have come sooner, immediately on hearing of Clarissa's illness, he informed Mr. Granger; but he was a poor frail creature, and to have exposed himself to the north-cast winds of this most uncertain climate early in April would have been to run into the teeth of danger. It was the middle of May now, and May this year had come without her accustomed inclemency.

"I knew that my daughter was in good hands, " he said. Daniel Granger signed, and answered nothing.

Mr. Lovel's observant eyes soon perceived that there was something amiss; and one evening, when he and Mr. Granger were strolling on the sands between Ventnor and Shanklin, he plainly taxed his son-in-law with the fact.

"There is some quarrel between Clary and you, " he said; "I can see that at a glance. Why, I used to consider you a model couple — perfectly Arcadian in your devotion — and now you scarcely speak to each other. "

"There is a quarrel that must last our lives, " Daniel Granger answered moodily, and then told his story, without reservation.

"Good heavens! " cried Mr. Lovel, at the end, "there is a curse upon that man and his race. "

And then he told his own story, in a very few words, and testified to his undying hatred of all the house of Fairfax.

After this there came a long silence, during which Clarissa's father was meditative.

"You cannot, of course, for a moment suppose that I can doubt my daughter's innocence throughout this unfortunate business, " he said at last. "I know the diabolical persistency of that race too well. It was like a Fairfax to entangle my poor girl in his net — to compromise her reputation, in the hope of profiting by his treachery. I do not attempt to deny, however, that Clarissa was imprudent. We have to consider her youth, and that natural love of admiration which tempts women to jeopardise their happiness and character even for the sake of an idle flirtation. I do not pretend that my daughter is faultless; but I would stake my life upon her purity. At the same time I quite agree with you, Granger, that under existing circumstances, a separation — a perfectly amicable separation, my daughter of course retaining the society of her child — would be the wiser course for both parties. "

Mr. Granger had a sensation as of a volume of cold water dashed suddenly in his face. This friendly concurrence of his father-in-law's took him utterly by surprise. He had expected that Mr. Lovel would insist upon a reconciliation, would thrust his daughter upon her husband at the point of the sword, as it were. He bowed acquiescence, but for some moments could find no words to speak.

"There is no other course open to me, " he said at last. "I cannot tell you how I have loved your daughter — God alone knows that — and how my every scheme of life has been built up from that one foundation. But that is all over now. I know, with a most bitter certainty, from her own lips, that I have never possessed her heart. "

"I can scarcely imagine that to be the case, " said Mr. Lovel, "even though Clarissa may have been betrayed into some passionate admission to that effect. Women will say anything when they are angry. "

"This was not said in anger. "

"But at the worst, supposing her heart not to have been yours hitherto, it might not be too late to win it even now. Men have won their wives after marriage. "

"I am too old to try my hand at that, " replied Mr. Granger, with a bitter smile. He was mentally comparing himself with George Fairfax, the handsome soldier, with that indescribable charm of youth and brightness about him.

"If you were a younger man, I would hardly recommend such a separation, " Mr. Lovel went on coolly; "but at your age—well, existence is quite tolerable without a wife; indeed there is a halcyon calm which descends upon a man when a woman's influence is taken out of his life, that is, perhaps, better than happiness. You have a son and heir, and that, I should imagine, for a man of your position, is the chief end and aim of marriage. My daughter can come abroad with me, and we can lead a pleasant drowsy life together, dawdling about from one famous city or salubrious watering-place to another. I shall, as a matter of course, surrender the income you have been good enough to allow me; but, *en revanche*, you will no doubt make Clarissa an allowance suitable to her position as your wife. "

Mr. Granger laughed aloud.

"Do you think there can ever be any question of money between us? " he asked. "Do you think that if, by the surrender of every shilling I possess, I could win back my faith in my wife, I should hold the loss a heavy one? "

Mr. Lovel smiled, a quiet, self-satisfied smile, in the gloaming.

"He will make her income a handsome one, " he said to himself, "and I shall have my daughter—who is really an acquisition, for I was beginning to find life solitary—and plenty of ready money. Or he will come after her in three months' time. That is the result I anticipate. "

They walked till a late moon had risen from the deep blue waters, and when they went back to the house everything was settled. Mr. Lovel answered for his daughter as freely as if he had been answering for himself. He was to take her abroad, with his grandson and namesake Lovel, attended by Jane Target and the new nurse, vice Mrs. Brobson, dismissed for neglect of her charge immediately after Clarissa's flight. If the world asked any questions, the world must be told that Mr. and Mrs. Granger had parted by mutual consent, or that Mrs. Granger's doctor had ordered continental travel. Daniel Granger could settle that point according to his own pleasure; or could refuse to give the world any answer at all, if he pleased.

Mr. Lovel told his daughter the arrangement that he had made for her next morning.

"I am to have my son? " she asked eagerly.

"Yes, don't I tell you so? You and Lovel are to come with me. You can live anywhere you please; you will have a fair income, a liberal one, I daresay. You are very well off, upon my word, Clarissa, taking into consideration the fact of your supreme imprudence—only you have lost your husband. "

"And I have lost Arden Court. Does not there seem a kind of retribution in that? I made a false vow for the love of Arden Court—and—and for your sake, papa. "

"False fiddlestick! " exclaimed Mr. Lovel, impatiently; "any reasonable woman might have been happy in your position, and with such a man as Granger; a man who positively worshipped you. However, you have lost all that. I am not going to lecture you—the penalty you pay is heavy enough, without any sermonising on my part. You are a very lucky woman to retain custody of your child, and escape any public exposure; and I consider that your husband has shown himself most generous. "

Daniel Granger and his wife parted soon after this; parted without any sign of compunction—there was a dead wall of pride between them. Clarissa felt the burden of her guilt, but could not bring herself

472

to make any avowal of her repentance to the husband who had put her away from him, —so easily, as it seemed to her. *That* touched her pride a little.

On that last morning, when the carriage was waiting to convey the travellers to Ryde, Mr. Granger's fortitude did almost abandon him at parting with his boy. Clarissa was out of the room when he took the child up in his arms, and put the little arms about his neck. He had made arrangements that the boy was to spend so many weeks in every year with him—was to be brought to him at his bidding, in fact; he was not going to surrender his treasure entirely.

And yet that parting seemed almost as bitter as if it had been for ever. It was such an outrage upon nature; the child who should have been so strong a link to bind those two hearts, to be taken from him like this, and for no sin of his. Resentment against his wife was strong in his mind at all times, but strongest when he thought of this loss which she had brought upon him. And do what he would, the child would grow up with a divided allegiance, loving his mother best.

One great sob shook him as he held the boy in that last embrace, and then he set him down quietly, as the door opened, and Clarissa appeared in her travelling-dress, pale as death, but very calm.

Just at the last she gave her hand to her husband, and said gently, — "I am very grateful to you for letting me take Lovel. I shall hold him always at your disposal. "

Mr. Granger took the thin cold hand, and pressed it gently.

"I am sorry there is any necessity for a divided household, " he said gravely. "But fate has been stronger than I. Good-bye. "

And so they parted; Mr. Granger leaving Ventnor later in the day, purposeless and uncertain, to moon away an evening at Ryde, trying to arrive at some decision as to what he should do with himself.

He could not go back to Arden yet awhile, that was out of the question. Farming operations, building projects, everything else, must go on without him, or come to a standstill. Indeed, it seemed to him doubtful whether he should ever go back to the house he had beautified, and the estate he had expanded: to live there alone—as he had lived before his marriage, that is to say, in solitary state with his daughter—must surely be intolerable His life had been suddenly shorn of its delight and ornament He knew now, even though their union had seemed at its best so imperfect, how much his wife had been to him.

And now he had to face the future without her. Good heavens! what a blank dismal prospect it seemed! He went to London, and took up his abode at Claridge's, where his life was unspeakably wearisome to him. He did not care to see people he knew, knowing that he would have to answer friendly inquiries about his wife. He had nothing to do, no interest in life; letters from architect and builder, farm-bailiff and steward, were only a bore to him; he was too listless even to answer them promptly, but let them lie unattended to for a week at a time. He went to the strangers' gallery when there was any debate of importance, and tried to give his mind to politics, with a faint idea of putting himself up for Holborough at the next election. But, as Phèdre says, "Quand ma bouche implorait le nom de la déesse, j'adorais Hippolyte; " so Mr. Granger, when he tried to think of the Irish-Church question, or the Alabama claims, found himself thinking of Clarissa. He gave lip the idea at last, convinced that public life was, for the most part, a snare and a delusion; and that there were plenty of men in the world better able to man the great ship than he. Two years ago he had been more interested in a vestry meeting than he was now in the most stirring question of the day.

Finally, he determined to travel; wrote a brief letter to Sophia, announcing his intention; and departed unattended, to roam the world; undecided whether he should go straight to Marseilles, and then to Africa, or whether he should turn his face northwards, and explore Norway and Sweden. It ended by his doing neither. He went to Spa to see his boy, from whom he had been separated something over two months.

* * * * *

CHAPTER XLIX.

BEGINNING AGAIN.

Mr. Lovel had taken his daughter to Spa, finding that she was quite
indifferent whither she went, so long as her boy went with her. It
was a pleasant sleepy place out of the season, and he liked it; having
a fancy that the mineral waters had done wonders for him. He had a
villa on the skirts of the pine-wood, a little way beyond the town; a
villa in which there was ample room for young Lovel and his
attendants, and from which five minutes' walk took them into
shadowy deeps of pine, where the boy might roll upon the soft short
grass.

By and by, Mr. Lovel told Clarissa they could go farther afield, travel
wherever she pleased, in fact; but, for the present, perfect rest and
quiet would be her best medicine. She was not quite out of the
doctor's hands yet; that fever had tried her sorely, and the remnant
of her cough still clung to her. At first she had a great terror of
George Fairfax discovering her retreat. He had found her at Brussels;
why should he not find her at Spa? For the first month of her
residence in the quiet inland watering-place she hardly stirred out of
doors without her father, and sat at home reading or painting day
after day, when she was longing to be out in the wood with her baby
and nurse.

But when the first four weeks had gone by, and left her unmolested,
Mrs. Granger grew bolder, and wandered out every day with her
child, and saw the young face brighten daily with a richer bloom, as
the boy gained strength, and was almost happy. The pine-wood was
very pretty; but those slender trees, shooting heavenwards, lacked
the grandeur of the oaks and beeches of Arden, and very often
Clarissa thought of her old home with a sigh. After all, it was lost to
her; twice lost, by a strange fatality, as it seemed.

In these days she thought but seldom of George Fairfax. In very truth
she was well-nigh cured of her guilty love for him. Her folly had cost
her too dear; "almost the loss of my child, " she said to herself
sometimes.

There are passions that wear themselves out, that are by their very
nature self-destroying—a lighted candle that will burn for a given

time, and then die out with ignominious smoke and sputtering, not the supernal lamp that shines on, star-like, for ever. Solitude and reflection brought this fact home to Clarissa, that her love, fatal as it had been, was not eternal. A woman's heart is scarcely wide enough to hold two great affections; and now baby reigned supreme in the heart of Clarissa. She had plenty of money now at her disposal; Mr. Granger having fixed her allowance at three thousand a year, with extensive powers should that sum prove insufficient; so the Bohemian household under the shadow of St. Gudule profited by her independence. She sent her brother a good deal of money, and received very cheery letters in acknowledgment of her generosity, with sometimes a little ill-spelt scrawl from Bessie, telling her that Austin was much steadier in Brussels than he had been in Paris, and was working hard for the dealers, with whom he was in great favour. English and American travellers, strolling down the Montagne de la Cour, were caught by those bright "taking" bits, which Austin Lovel knew so well how to paint. An elderly Russian princess had bought his Peach picture, and given him a commission for portraits of a brood of Muscovian bantlings. In one way and another he was picking up a good deal of money; and, with the help of Clarissa's remittances, had contrived to arrange some of those awkward affairs in Paris.

"Indeed, there is very little in this world that money won't settle, " he wrote to his sister; "and I anticipate that enlightened stage of our criminal code when wilful murder will be a question of pounds, shillings, and pence. I fancy it in a police report: 'The fine was immediately paid, and Mr. Greenacre left the court with his friends. ' I have some invitation to go back to my old quarters in the only city I love; there is a Flemish buffet in the Rue du Chevalier Bayard that was a fortune to me in my backgrounds; but the little woman pleads so earnestly against our return, that I give way. Certainly, Paris is a dangerous place for a man of my temperament, who has not yet mastered the supreme art of saying no at the right moment. I am very glad to hear you are happy with your father and the little one. I wish I had him here for a model; my own boys are nothing but angles. Yet I would rather hear of you in your right position with your husband. That fellow Fairfax is a scoundrel; I despise myself for ever having asked him to put his name to a bill; and, still more, for being blind to his motives when he was hanging about my painting-room last winter. You have had a great escape, Clary; and God grant you wisdom to avoid all such perilous paths in time to come. Preachment of any kind comes with an ill grace from me, I know; but

I daresay you remember what Portia says: 'If to do were as easy as to know what were good to do, chapels had been churches, and poor men's cottages princes' palaces;' and every man, however fallen, has a kind of temple in his breast, wherein is enshrined the image of his nearest and dearest. Let my garments be never so besmirched and bedraggled, my sister's robes must be spotless."

There was comfort in these good tidings of her brother—comfort for which Clarissa was very grateful to Providence. She would have been glad to go to Brussels to see him, but had that ever-present terror of coming athwart the pathway of George Fairfax; nor could she go on such an errand without some kind of explanation with her father. She was content to abide, therefore, among the quiet pine-woods and umbrageous avenues, which the holiday world had not yet invaded, and where she was almost as free to wander with her boy as amidst the beloved woods of Arden Court.

Life thus spent was very peaceful—peaceful, and just a little monotonous. Mr. Lovel sipped his chocolate, and trifled with his maintenon cutlet, at 11 A. M., with an open volume of Burton or Bentley beside his cup, just as in the old days of Clarissa's girlhood. It was just like the life at Mill Cottage, with that one ever fresh and delicious element—young Lovel. That baby voice lent a perpetual music to Clarissa's existence; the sweet companionship of that restless clambering infant seemed to her the perfection of happiness.

And yet—and yet—there were times when she felt that her life was a failure, and lamented somewhat that she had so wrecked it. She was not hard of heart; and sometimes she thought of Daniel Granger with a remorseful pang, that cams upon her sharply in the midst of her maternal joys; thought of all that he had done for love of her— the sublime patience wherewith he had endured her coldness, the generous eagerness he had shown in the indulgence of her caprices; in a word, the wealth of wasted love he had lavished on an ungrateful woman.

"It is all over now," she said to herself sadly. "It is not every woman who in all her lifetime can win so great a love as I have lost."

The tranquil sensuous life went on. There were hours in it which her child could not fill—long hours, in which that marvellous blossom folded its petals, slumbering sweetly through the summer noontide, and was no better company than a rose-bud. Clarissa tried to interest herself in her old studies; took up her Italian, and read Dante with her father, who was a good deal more painstaking in his explanations of obscure idioms and irregular verbs for the benefit of Mrs. Granger with a jointure of three thousand per annum, than he had been wont to show himself for the behoof of Miss Lovel without a sixpence. She drew a great deal; but somehow these favourite pursuits had lost something of their charm. They could not fill her life; it seemed blank and empty in spite of them.

She had her child—the one blessing for which she had prayed—about which she had raved with such piteous bewailings in her delirium; but there was no sense of security in the possession. She was full of doubts and fears about the future. How long would Daniel Granger suffer her to keep her treasure? Must not the day come when he would put forth his stronger claim, and she would be left bereaved and desolate?

Scarcely could she dare to think of the future; indeed, she did her uttermost to put away all thought of it, so fraught was it with terror and perplexity; but her dreams were made hideous by scenes of parting—weird and unnatural situations, such as occur in dreams; and her health suffered from these shadowy fears. Death, too, had been very near her boy; and she watched him with a morbid apprehension, fearful of every summer breeze that ruffled his flaxen hair.

She was tired of Spa, and secretly anxious to cross the frontier, and wander through Germany, away to the further-most shores of the Danube; but was fain to wait patiently till her father's medical adviser—an English physician, settled at Spa—should pronounce him strong enough to travel.

"That hurried journey to the Isle of Wight sent me back prodigiously, " Mr. Lovel told his daughter. "It will take me a month or two to recover the effects of those abominable steamers. The Rhine and the Danube will keep, my dear Clary. The castled crag of Drachenfels can be only a little mouldier for the delay, and I believe the mouldiness of these things is their principal charm. "

So Clarissa waited. She had not the courage to tell her father of those shapeless terrors that haunted her by day, and those agonising dreams that visited her by night, which she fancied might be driven away by movement and change of scene; she waited, and went on suffering, until at last that supreme egotist, Marmaduke Lovel, was awakened to the fact, that his daughter was looking no better than when he first brought her to Belgium—worse rather, incontestably worse. He took alarm immediately. The discovery moved him more than he could have supposed anything outside himself could have affected him.

"What? " he asked himself. "Is my daughter going to languish and fade, as my wife faded? Is she too to die of a Fairfax? "

The English physician was consulted; hummed and ha'd a little, prescribed a new tonic; and finding, after a week or two, that this produced no result, and that the pulse was weaker and more fitful, recommended change of air and scene, —a remedy which common-sense might have suggested in the first instance.

"We will start for Cologne to-morrow morning. Tell Target to pack, Clary. You shall sleep under the shadow of the great cathedral to-morrow night. "

Clarissa thanked her father warmly, and then burst into tears.

"Hysteria, " murmured the physician.

"I shall get away from that dreadful room, " she sobbed, "where I have such hideous dreams; " and then went away to set Jane Target to work.

"I don't quite like the look of that, " the doctor said gravely, when she was gone. "Those distressing dreams are a bad sign. But Mrs. Granger is yet very young, and has an excellent constitution, I believe. Change of scene, and the amusement of travelling, may do all we want. "

He left Mr. Lovel very thoughtful.

"If she doesn't improve very speedily, I shall telegraph to Granger, " he said to himself.

He had no occasion to do this. Daniel Granger, after going half way to Marseilles, with a notion of exploring Algiers and Morocco, had stopped short, and made his way by road and rail—through sirocco, clouds of dust, and much inconvenience—to Liége, where he had lingered to recover and calm himself down a little before going to see his child.

Going to see his child—that was the sole purpose of his journey; not for a moment would he have admitted that it mattered anything to him that he was also going to see his wife.

It was between seven and eight o'clock, on a bright June evening—a flush of rosy light behind the wooded hills—and Clarissa was sitting on some felled timber, with her boy asleep in her arms. He had dropped off to sleep in the midst of his play; and she had lingered, unwilling to disturb him. If he went on sleeping, she would be able to carry him home presently, and put him to bed without awaking him. The villa was not a quarter of a mile away.

She was quite alone with her darling, the nurse being engaged in the grand business of packing. They were all to start the next morning after a very early breakfast. She was looking down at the young sleeper, singing to him softly—a commonplace picture perhaps, but a very fair one—a *Madonna aux champs*.

So thought Daniel Granger, who had arrived at Spa half an hour ago, made his inquiries at the villa, and wandered into the wood in quest of his only son. The mother's face, with its soft smile of ineffable love, lips half parted, breathing that fragment of a tender song, reminded him of a picture by Raffaelle. She was nothing to him now; but he could not the less appreciate her beauty, spiritualised by sorrow, and radiant with the glory of the evening sunlight.

He came towards the little group silently, his footfall making no sound upon the moss-grown earth. He did not approach quite near, however, in silence, afraid of startling her, but stopped a little way off, and said gently, —

"They told me I should most likely find you somewhere about here, with Lovel. "

His wife gave a little cry, and looked up aghast.

"Have you come to take him away from me? " she asked, thinking that her dreams had been prophetic.

"No, no, I am not going to do that; though you told me he was to be at my disposal, remember, and I mean to claim him sometimes. I can't allow him to grow up a stranger to me. —God bless him, how well he is looking! Pray don't look so frightened, " he went on, in an assuring voice, alarmed by the dead whiteness of Clarissa's face; "I have only come to see my boy before——. The fact is, I have some thoughts of travelling for a year or two. There is a rage for going to Africa nowadays, and I am not without interest in that sort of thing. "

Clarissa looked at him wonderingly. This sudden passion for foreign wanderings seemed to her very strange in him. She had been accustomed to suppose his mind entirely absorbed by new systems of irrigation, and model-village building, and the extension of his estate. His very dreams, she had fancied, were of the hedgerows that bounded his lands—boundaries that vanished day by day, as the lands widened, with now a whole farm added, and now a single field. Could he leave Arden, and the kingdom that he had created for himself, to roam in sandy deserts, and hob-and-nob with Kaffir chiefs under the tropic stars?

Mr. Granger seated himself upon the timber by his wife's side, and bent down to look at his son, and to kiss him gently without waking him. After that fond lingering kiss upon the little one's smooth cheek, he sat for some minutes in silence, looking at his wife.

It was only her profile he could see; but he saw that she was looking ill, worse than she had looked when they parted at Ventnor. The sight of the pale face, with a troubled look about the mouth, touched him keenly. Just in that moment he forgot that there was such a being as George Fairfax upon this earth; forgot the sin that his wife had sinned against him; longed to clasp her to his breast; was only deterred by a kind of awkward shyness—to which such strong men as he are sometimes liable—from so doing.

"I am sorry to see that you are not looking very well, " he said at last, with supreme stiffness, and with that peculiarly unconciliating air which an Englishman is apt to put on, when he is languishing to hold out the olive-branch.

"I have not been very well; but I daresay I shall soon be better, now we are going to travel. "

"Going to travel! "

"Yes, papa has made up his mind to move at last. We go to Cologne to-morrow. I thought they would have told you that at the house. "

"No; I only waited to ask where you—where the boy was to be found. I did not even stop to see your father. "

After this there came a dead silence—a silence that lasted for about five minutes, during which they heard the faint rustle of the pine branches stirred ever so lightly by the evening wind. The boy slept on, unconscious and serene; the mother watching him, and Daniel Granger contemplating both from under the shadow of his eyebrows.

The silence grew almost oppressive at last, and Mr. Granger was the first to break it.

"You do not ask me for any news of Arden, " he said.

Clarissa blushed, and glanced at him with a little wounded look. It was hard to be reminded of the paradise from which she had been exiled.

"I—I beg your pardon. I hope everything is going on as you wish; the home farm, and all that kind of thing. Miss Granger—Sophia—is well, I hope? "

"Sophia is quite well, I believe. I have not seen her since I left Ventnor. "

"She has been away from Arden, then? "

"No; it is I who have not been there. Indeed, I doubt if I shall ever go there again—without you, Clarissa. The place is hateful to me. "

Again and again, with infinite iteration, Daniel Granger had told himself that reconciliation with his wife was impossible. Throughout his journey by road and rail—and above all things is a long journey conductive to profound meditation—he had been firmly resolved to see his boy, and then go on his way at once, with neither delay nor wavering. But the sight of that pale pensive face to-night had well-nigh unmanned him. Was this the girl whose brightness and beauty had been the delight of his life? Alas, poor child, what sorrow his foolish love had brought upon her! He began all at once to pity her, to think of her as a sacrifice to her father's selfishness, his own obstinacy.

"I ought to have taken my answer that day at the Court, when I first told her my secret, " he said to himself. "That look of pained surprise, which came into her face when I spoke, might surely have been enough for me. Yet I persisted, and was not man enough to face the question boldly—whether she had any heart to give me. "

Clarissa rose, with the child still in her arms.

"I am afraid the dew is beginning to fall, " she said; "I had better take Lovel home. "

"Let me carry him, " exclaimed Mr. Granger; and in the next moment the boy was in his father's strong arms, the flaxen head nestling in the paternal waistcoat.

"And so you are going to begin your travels to-morrow morning, " he said, as they walked slowly homeward side by side.

"Yes, the train leaves at seven. But you would like to see more of Lovel, perhaps, having come so far to see him. We can defer our journey for a day or two. "

"You are very good. Yes, I should like you to do that. "

"And with regard to what you were saying just now, " Clarissa said, in a low voice, that was not quite steady, "I trust you will not let the memory of any pain I may have given you influence your future life, or disgust you with a place to which you were so much attached as I know you were to Arden. Pray put me out of your thoughts. I am not worthy to be regretted by you. Our marriage was a sad mistake on your part—a sin upon mine. I know now that it was so. "

"A mistake—a sin! O, Clary, Clary, I could have been so happy, if you had only loved me a little—if you had only been true to me.

"I never was deliberately false to you. I was very wicked; yes, I acknowledge that. I did trifle with temptation. I ought to have avoided the remotest chance of any meeting with George Fairfax. I ought to have told you the truth, told you all my weakness; but—but

I had not the courage to do that. I went to the Rue du Chevalier Bayard to see my brother. "

"Was that honest, Clarissa, to allow me to be introduced to your brother as a stranger? "

"That was Austin's wish, not mine. He would not let me tell you who he was; and I was so glad for you to be kind to him, poor fellow! so glad to be able to see him almost daily; and when the picture was finished, and Austin had no excuse for coming to us any more, I went to see him very often, and sometimes met Mr. Fairfax in his painting-room; but I never went with any deliberate intention of meeting him. "

"No, " interjected Mr. Granger bitterly; "you only went, knowing that he was likely to be there! "

"And on that unhappy day when you found me there, " Clarissa went on, "I had gone to see my brother, having no idea that he had left Paris. I wanted to come away at once; but Mr. Fairfax detained me. I was very angry with him. "

"Yes, it appeared so, when he was asking you to run away with him. It is a hard thing for a man to believe in his wife's honour, when things have come to such a pass as that, Clarissa. "

"I have told you the truth, " she answered gravely; "I cannot say any more. "

"And the locket—the locket I gave you, which I found on that man's breast? "

"I gave that locket to my sister-in-law, Bessie Lovel. I wished to give her something, poor soul; and I had given Austin all my money. I had so many gifts of yours, Daniel"—that sudden sound of his Christian name sent a thrill through Mr. Granger's veins—"parting with one of them seemed not to matter very much. "

There was a pause. They were very near the villa by this time. Mr. Granger felt as if he might never have an opportunity for speaking to his wife again, if he lost his chance now.

"Clarissa, " he said earnestly, "if I could forget all that happened in Paris, and put it out of my mind as if it had never been, could you forget it too? "

"With all my heart, " she answered.

"Then, my darling, we will begin the world again—we will begin life over again, Clarissa! "

So they went home together reconciled. And Mr. Lovel, looking up from Aimé Martin's edition of Molière, saw that what he had anticipated had come to pass. His policy had proved as successful as it had been judicious. In less than three months Daniel Granger had surrendered. This was what came of Mr. Granger's flying visit to his boy.

* * * * *

CHAPTER L.

HOW SUCH THINGS END.

After that reconciliation, which brought a wonderful relief and comfort to Clarissa's mind—and who shall say how profoundly happy it made her husband? —Mr. and Mrs. Granger spent nearly a year in foreign travel. For his own part, Daniel Granger would have been glad to go back to Arden, now that the dreary burden was lifted off his mind, and his broken life pieced together again; but he did not want county society to see his wife till the bloom and brightness had come back to her face, nor to penetrate the mystery of their brief severance. To remain away for some considerable time was the surest way of letting the scandal, if any had ever arisen, die out.

He wrote to his daughter, telling her briefly that he and his wife had arranged all their little differences—little differences! Sophia gave a shrill scream of indignation as she went over this sentence in her father's letter, scarcely able to believe her eyes at first—and they were going through Germany together with the intention of wintering at Borne. As Clarissa was still somewhat of an invalid, it would be best for them to be alone, he thought; but he was ready to further any plans for his daughter's happiness during his absence.

Miss Granger replied curtly, that she was tolerably happy at Arden, with her "duties, " and that she had no desire to go roaming about the world in quest of that contented mind which idle and frivolous persons rarely found, go where they might. She congratulated her father upon the termination of a quarrel which she had supposed too serious to be healed so easily, and trusted that he would never have occasion to regret his clemency. Mr. Granger crushed the letter in his hand, and threw it over the side of the Rhine steamer, on which he had opened his budget of English correspondence, on that particular morning.

They had a very pleasant time of it in Germany, moving in a leisurely way from town to town, seeing everything thoroughly without hurry or restlessness. Young Lovel throve apace the new nurse adored him; and faithful Jane Target was a happy as the day was long, amidst all the foreign wonders that surrounded her pathway. Daniel Granger was contented and hopeful; happy in the contemplation of his wife's fair young face, which brightened daily; in the society of his boy, who, with increasing intelligence, developed an ever-increasing appreciation of his father—the strong arms, that tossed him aloft and caught him so skilfully; the sonorous voice, that rang so cheerily upon his ear; the capacious pockets, in which there was wont to lurk some toy for his delectation.

Towards the middle of November they took up their winter quarters in Rome—not the November of fogs and drizzle, known to the denizens of London, but serene skies and balmy air, golden sunsets, and late-lingering flowers, that seemed loath to fade and vanish from a scene so beautiful. Clarissa loved this city of cities, and felt a thrill of delight at returning to it. She drove about with her two-year-old son, showing him the wonders and glories of the place as fondly as if its classic associations had been within the compass of his budding mind. She went on with her art-studies with renewed vigour, as if there had been a Raffaelle fever in the very air of the place, and made plans for copying half the pictures in the Vatican. There was plenty of agreeable society in the city, English and foreign; and Clarissa found herself almost as much in request as she had been in Paris. There were art-circles in which she was happiest, and where Daniel Granger held his own very fairly as a critic and connoisseur. And thus the first two winter months slipped away very pleasantly, till they came to January, in which month they were to return to Arden.

They were to return there to assist at a great event—an event the contemplation whereof was a source of unmitigated satisfaction to Mr. Granger, and which was more than pleasing to Clarissa. Miss Granger was going to be married, blest with her papa's consent and approval, of course, and in a manner becoming a damsel whose first consideration was duty. After refusing several very fair offers, during the progress of her girlhood, she had at last suffered herself to be subjugated by the constancy and devotion of Mr. Tillott, the curate of New Arden.

It was not in any sense a good match. Mr. Tillott's professional income was seventy-five pounds a year; his sole private means an allowance of fifty from his brother, who, Mr. Tillott admitted, with a blush, was in trade. He was neither handsome nor accomplished. The most his best friends could say of him was, that he was "a very worthy young man. " He was not an orator: he had an atrocious delivery, and rarely got through the briefest epistle, or collect even, without blundering over a preposition. His demeanour in pulpit and reading-desk was that of a prisoner at the bar, without hope of acquittal, and yet he had won Miss Granger—that prize in the matrimonial market, which many a stout Yorkshireman had been eager to win.

He had flattered her; with a slavish idolatry he followed her footsteps, and ministered to her caprices, admiring, applauding, and imitating all her works and ways, holding her up for ever as the pattern and perfection of womankind. Five times had Miss Granger rejected him; on some occasions with contumely even, letting him know that there was a very wide gulf between their social positions, and that although she might be spiritually his sister, she stood, in a worldly sense, on a very remote platform from that which it was his mission to occupy. Mr. Tillott swallowed every humiliation with a lowly spirit, that had in it some leaven of calculation, and bore up against every repulse; until at last the fair Sophia, angry with her father, persistently opposed to her stepmother, and out of sorts with the world in general, consented to accept the homage of this persevering suitor. He, at least, was true to her; he, at least, believed in her perfection. The stout country squires, who could have given her houses and lands, had never stooped to flatter her foibles; had shown themselves heartlessly indifferent to her dragooning of the model villagers; had even hinted their pity for the villagers under that martial rule. Tillott alone could sympathise with her, trudging patiently from cottage to cottage in bleak Christmas weather, carrying parcels of that uncomfortable clothing with which Miss Granger delighted to supply her pensioners.

Nor was the position which this marriage would give her, humble as it might appear, altogether without its charm. As Mr. Tillott's wife, she would be a very great lady amongst small people; and Mr. Tillott himself would be invested with a reflected glory from having married an heiress. The curate stage would, of course, soon be past. The living of Arden was in Mr. Granger's gift; and no doubt the present rector could be bought out somehow, after a year or so, and Mr. Tillott installed in his place. So, after due deliberation, and after the meek Tillott had been subjected to a trial of his faith which might have shaken the strongest, but which left him firm as a rock, Miss Granger surrendered, and acknowledged that she thought her sphere of usefulness would be enlarged by her union with Thomas Tillott.

"It is not my own feelings which, I consider, " remarked the maiden, in a tone which was scarcely flattering to her lover; "I have always held duty above those. I believe that New Arden is my proper field, and that it is a Providence that leads me to accept a tie which binds me more closely to the place. I could never have remained in *this* house after Mrs. Granger's return. "

Upon this, the enraptured Tillott wrote a humble and explanatory letter to Mr. Granger, stating the blessing which had descended upon him in the shape of Sophia's esteem, and entreating that gentleman's approval of his suit.

It came by return of post, in a few hearty words.

> "MY DEAR TILLOTT, —Yes; with all my heart! I have always thought you a good fellow; and I hope and believe you will make my daughter a good husband. Mrs. Granger and I will be home in three weeks, in time to make all arrangements for the wedding. —Yours, &c.
>
> "DANIEL GRANGER. "

"Ah, " said Miss Granger, when this epistle was shown her by her triumphant swain, "I expected as much. I have never been anything to papa since his marriage, and he is glad to get rid of me. "

The Roman season was at its height, when there arose a good deal of talk about a lady who did not belong to that world in which Mrs. Granger lived, but who yet excited considerable curiosity and interest therein.

She was a Spanish dancer, known as Donna Rita, and had been creating a *furore* in St. Petersburg, Paris, Vienna, all over the civilised world, in fact, except in London, where she was announced as likely to appear during the approaching season. She had taken the world by storm by her beauty, which was exceptional, and by her dancing, which made up in *chic* for anything it may have lacked in genius. She was not a Taglioni; she was only a splendid dark-haired woman, with eyes that reminded one of Cleopatra, a figure that was simply perfection, the free grace of some wild creature of the forest, and the art of selecting rare and startling combinations of colour and fabric for her dress.

She had hired a villa, and sent a small army of servants on before her to take possession of it—men and women of divers nations, who contrived to make their mistress notorious by their vagaries before she arrived to astonish the city by her own eccentricities. One day brought two pair of carriage horses, and a pair of Arabs for riding; the next, a train of carriages; a week after came the lady herself; and all Rome—English and American Rome most especially—was eager to see her. There was an Englishman in her train, people said. Of course, there was always some one—*elle en mange cinq comme ça tous les ans*, remarked a Frenchman.

Clarissa had no curiosity about this person. The idle talk went by her like the wind, and made no impression; but one sunny afternoon, when she was driving with her boy, Daniel Granger having an engagement to look at a new picture which kept him away from her, she met the Senora face to face—Donna Rita, wrapped in sables to the throat, with a coquettish little turban-shaped sable hat, a couple of Pomeranian dogs on her lap—half reclining in her barouche—a marvel of beauty and insolence. She was not alone. A gentleman— the Englishman, of course—sat opposite to her, and leant across the white bear-skin carriage-rug to talk to her. They were both laughing at something he had just said, which the Senora characterised as *"pas si bête. "*

He looked up as the two carriages passed each other; for just one brief moment looked Clarissa Granger in the face; then, pale as death, bent down to caress one of the dogs.

It was George Fairfax.

It was a bitter ending; but such stories are apt to end so; and a man with unlimited means, and nothing particular to do with himself, must find amusement somehow. Clarissa remained in Rome a fortnight after this, and encountered the Senora several times—never unattended, but never again with George Fairfax.

She heard the story afterwards from Lady Laura. He had been infatuated, and had spent thousands upon "that creature. " His poor mother had been half broken-hearted about it.

"The Lyvedon estate spoiled him, my dear, " Lady Laura said conclusively. "He was a very good fellow till he came into his property. "

Mr. Fairfax reformed, however, a couple of years later, and married a fashionable widow with a large fortune; who kept him in a whirl of society, and spent their combined incomes royally. He and Clarissa meet sometimes in society—meet, touch hands even, and know that every link between them is broken.

And is Clarissa happy? Yes, if happiness can be found in children's voices and a good man's unchanging affection. She has Arden Court, and her children; her father's regard, growing warmer year by year, as with increasing age he feels increasing need of some one to love him; her brother's society now and then—for Mr. Granger has been lavish in his generosity, and all the peccadilloes of Austin's youth have been extinguished from the memories of money-lenders and their like by means of Mr. Granger's cheque-book.

The painter can come to England now, and roam his native woods unburdened by care; but though this is very sweet to him once in a way, he prefers a Continental city, with its *café* life, and singing and dancing gardens, where he may smoke his in the gloaming. He grows steadier as he grows older, paints better, and makes friends worth making; much to the joy of poor Bessie, who asks no greater privilege than to stand humbly by, gazing fondly while he puts on his white cravat, and sallies forth radiant, with a hot-house flower in his button-hole, to dine in the great world.

But this is only a glance into the future. The story ends in the orthodox manner, to the sound of wedding bells—Miss Granger's—who swears to love, honour, and obey Thomas Tillott, with a fixed intention to keep the upper baud over the said Thomas in all things. Yet these men who are so slavish as wooers are apt to prove of sterner mould as husbands, and life is all before Mrs. Tillott, as she journeys in chariot and posters to Scarborough for her unpretentious honeymoon, to return in a fortnight to a bran-new gothic villa on the skirts of Arden, where one tall tree is struggling vainly to look at home in a barren waste of new-made garden. And in the servants' hall and housekeeper's room at Arden Court there is rejoicing, as when the elder Miss Pecksniff went away from the little village near Salisbury.

For some there are no marriage bells—for Lady Geraldine, for instance, who is content to devote herself unostentatiously to the care of her sister's neglected children—neglected in spite of French and German governesses, Italian singing masters, Parisian waiting-maids, and half an acre or so of nursery and schoolroom—and to wider charities: not all unhappy, and thankful for having escaped that far deeper misery—the fate of an unloved wife.

THE END

CPSIA information can be obtained at www.ICGtesting.com
Printed in the USA
LVOW08s2007210515

439405LV00001B/141/P